★ "This is distinguished by the
dreamy California setting and poetic images
that will draw readers into Lennie's world."
—*PUBLISHERS WEEKLY*, STARRED REVIEW

★ "It's romantic without being gooey
and tear-jerking without being campy—
what more could a reader want?"
—*BCCB*, STARRED REVIEW

★ "This is a passionate, vulnerable,
wonderfully complete and irresistible book."
—*VOYA*, STARRED REVIEW

"Brimming with humor and life, full of
music and the poems Lennie drops all over town,
The Sky Is Everywhere explores betrayal and
forgiveness through a vibrant cast of characters."
—*SLJ*

"A story of love, loss, and healing that will resonate
with readers long after they've finished reading."
—*BOOKLIST*

"A finely drawn portrait of grief and first love."
—*THE DAILY BEAST*

"A story about love and loss . . . both heartfelt and literary."
—*KIRKUS REVIEWS*

"WOW. I sobbed my eyes out and then laughed through the tears. I have not fallen in love with a story and its characters like this in a long time. Stunning, heartbreaking, hilarious. A story that shakes the earth."
— AN NA, NATIONAL BOOK AWARD FINALIST AND PRINTZ AWARD–WINNING AUTHOR OF *A STEP FROM HEAVEN*

"Okay, I admit it. I have a huge crush on this book—it's beautiful, brilliant, passionate, funny, sexy, and deep. Come to think of it, I might even want to *marry* this book."
—SONYA SONES, AUTHOR OF *WHAT MY MOTHER DOESN'T KNOW*

"Full of heart, quirky charm, and beautiful writing, *The Sky Is Everywhere* simply shines."
—DEB CALETTI, NATIONAL BOOK AWARD FINALIST AND PRINTZ HONOR–WINNING AUTHOR OF *A HEART IN A BODY IN THE WORLD*

"Jandy Nelson's story of grief somehow manages to be an enchantment, a celebration, a romance— without forsaking the rock-hard truths of loss."
—SARA ZARR, NATIONAL BOOK AWARD FINALIST AND AUTHOR OF *STORY OF A GIRL* AND *SWEETHEARTS*

What kind of girl?

I roll onto my back and before long I'm holding my pillow in my arms and kissing the air with an embarrassing amount of passion. Not again, I think. What's wrong with me? What kind of girl wants to kiss every boy at a funeral, wants to maul a guy in a tree after making out with her [dead] sister's boyfriend the previous night? *Speaking of which, what kind of girl makes out with her sister's boyfriend, period?*

OTHER BOOKS YOU MAY ENJOY

The sky is everywhere

JANDY NELSON

DIAL BOOKS

DIAL BOOKS
An imprint of Penguin Random House LLC, New York

First published in the United States of America by Dial Books, 2010
First paperback edition published by Speak, 2011
This edition published by Dial Books, 2022
Copyright © 2010 by Jandy Nelson

Dial & colophon are registered trademarks of Penguin Random House LLC.

Penguin Books & colophon are registered trademarks of Penguin Books Limited.

Visit us online at penguinrandomhouse.com.

THE LIBRARY OF CONGRESS HAS CATALOGED THE HARDCOVER EDITION AS FOLLOWS:
Nelson, Jandy.
The sky is everywhere / by Jandy Nelson.
p. cm.
Summary: In the months after her sister dies, seventeen-year-old Lennie falls into a love triangle
and discovers the strength to follow her dream of becoming a musician.
ISBN: 978-0-8037-3495-1 (hc)
[1. Grief—Fiction. 2. Death—Fiction. 3. Sisters—Fiction. 4. Musicians—Fiction.] I. Title.
PZ7.N433835Sk 2010
[Fic]—dc22 2009022809
Printed in the United States of America

ISBN 9780593616017

1 3 5 7 9 10 8 6 4 2

LSCH

Design by Jennifer Kelly

For my mother

part
one

chapter 1

GRAM IS WORRIED about me. It's not just because my sister Bailey died four weeks ago, or because my mother hasn't contacted me in sixteen years, or even because suddenly all I think about is sex. She is worried about me because one of her houseplants has spots.

Gram has believed for most of my seventeen years that this particular houseplant, which is of the nondescript variety, reflects my emotional, spiritual, and physical well-being. I've grown to believe it too.

Across the room from where I sit, Gram—all six feet and floral frock of her, looms over the black-spotted leaves.

"What do you mean it might not get better this time?" She's asking this of Uncle Big: arborist, resident pothead, and mad scientist to boot. He knows something about everything, but he knows everything about plants.

To anyone else it might seem strange, even off the wall, that Gram, as she asks this, is staring at me, but it doesn't to Uncle Big, because he's staring at me as well.

"This time it has a very serious condition." Big's voice trumpets as if from stage or pulpit; his words carry weight, even *pass the salt* comes out of his mouth in a thou-shalt-Ten-Commandments kind of way.

Gram raises her hands to her face in distress, and I go back to scribbling a poem in the margin of *Wuthering Heights*. I'm huddled into a corner of the couch. I've no use for talking, would just as soon store paper clips in my mouth.

"But the plant's always recovered before, Big, like when Lennie broke her arm, for instance."

"That time the leaves had white spots."

"Or just last fall when she auditioned for lead clarinet but had to be second chair again."

"Brown spots."

"Or when—"

"This time it's different."

I glance up. They're still peering at me, a tall duet of sorrow and concern.

Gram is Clover's Garden Guru. She has the most extraordinary flower garden in Northern California. Her roses burst with more color than a year of sunsets, and their fragrance is so intoxicating that town lore claims breathing in their scent can cause you to fall in love on the spot. But despite her nurturing and renowned green thumb, this plant seems to follow the trajectory of my life, independent of her efforts or its own vegetal sensibility.

I put my book and pen down on the table. Gram leans in close to the plant, whispers to it about the importance of *joie de vivre*, then lumbers over to the couch, sitting down next to me.

Then Big joins us, plopping his enormous frame down beside Gram. We three, each with the same unruly hair that sits on our heads like a bustle of shiny black crows, stay like this, staring at nothing, for the rest of the afternoon.

This is us since my sister Bailey collapsed one month ago from a fatal arrhythmia while in rehearsal for a local production of *Romeo & Juliet*. It's as if someone vacuumed up the horizon while we were looking the other way.

chapter 2

The morning of the day Bailey died,
she woke me up
by putting her finger in my ear.
I hated when she did this.
She then started trying on shirts, asking me:
Which do you like better, the green or the blue?
The blue.
You didn't even look up, Lennie.
Okay, the green. Really, I don't care what shirt you wear . . .
Then I rolled over in bed and fell back asleep.
I found out later
she wore the blue
and those were the last words I ever spoke to her.

(Found written on a lollipop wrapper on the trail to the Rain River)

My FIRST DAY back to school is just as I expect, the hall does a Red Sea part when I come in, conversations hush, eyes swim with nervous sympathy, and everyone stares as if I'm holding Bailey's dead body in my arms, which I guess I am. Her death is all over me, I can feel it and everyone can see it, plain as a big black coat wrapped around me on a beautiful spring day. But what I don't expect is the unprecedented hubbub over some new boy, Joe Fontaine, who arrived in my month-long absence. Everywhere I go it's the same:

"Have you seen him yet?"

"He looks like a Gypsy."

"Like a rock star."

"A pirate."

"I hear he's in a band called Dive."

"That he's a musical genius."

"Someone told me he used to live in Paris."

"That he played music on the streets."

"Have you seen him yet?"

I have seen him, because when I return to my band seat, the one I've occupied for the last year, he's in it. Even in the stun of grief, my eyes roam from the black boots, up the miles of legs covered in denim, over the endless torso, and finally settle on a face so animated I wonder if I've interrupted a conversation between him and my music stand.

"Hi," he says, and jumps up. He's treetop tall. "You must be Lennon." He points to my name on the chair. "I heard about— I'm sorry." I notice the way he holds his clarinet, not precious with it, tight fist around the neck, like a sword.

"Thank you," I say, and every available inch of his face busts into a smile—whoa. Has he blown into our school on a gust of wind from another world? The guy looks unabashedly jack-o'-lantern happy, which couldn't be more foreign to the sullen demeanor most of us strove to perfect. He has scores of messy brown curls that flop every which way and eyelashes so spider-leg long and thick that when he blinks he looks like he's batting his bright green eyes right at you. His face is more open than an open book, like a wall of graffiti really. I realize I'm writing *wow* on my thigh with my finger, decide I better open my mouth and snap us out of this impromptu staring contest.

"Everyone calls me Lennie," I say. Not very original, but better than *guh,* which was the alternative, and it does the trick. He looks down at his feet for a second and I take a breath and regroup for Round Two.

"Been wondering about that actually, Lennon after John?" he asks, again holding my gaze—it's entirely possible I'm going to faint. Or burst into flames.

I nod. "Mom was a hippie." This is *northern* Northern California after all—the final frontier of freakerdom. Just in the eleventh grade we have a girl named Electricity, a guy named Magic Bus, and countless flowers: Tulip, Begonia, and Poppy— all parent-given-on-the-birth-certificate names. Tulip is a two-ton bruiser of a guy who would be the star of our football team if we were the kind of school that had a football team. We're not. We're the kind of school that has optional morning medi-tation in the gym.

"Yeah," Joe says. "My mom too, and Dad, as well as aunts, uncles, brothers, cousins . . . welcome to Commune Fontaine."

I laugh out loud. "Got the picture."

But whoa again—should I be laughing so easily like this? And should it feel this good? Like slipping into cool river water.

I turn around, wondering if anyone is watching us, and see that Sarah has just walked—rather, exploded—into the music room. I've hardly seen her since the funeral, feel a pang of guilt.

"Lennieeeee!" She careens toward us in prime goth-gone-cowgirl form: vintage slinky black dress, shit-kicker cowboy boots, blond hair dyed so black it looks blue, all topped off with a honking Stetson. I note the breakneck pace of her approach, wonder for an instant if she's going to actually jump into my arms right before she tries to, sending us both skidding into Joe, who somehow retains his balance, and ours, so we all don't fly through the window.

This is Sarah, subdued.

"Nice," I whisper in her ear as she hugs me like a bear even though she's built like a bird. "Way to bowl down the gorgeous new boy." She cracks up, and it feels both amazing and disconcerting to have someone in my arms shaking from laughter rather than heartbreak.

Sarah is the most enthusiastic cynical person on the planet. She'd be the perfect cheerleader if she weren't so disgusted by the notion of school spirit. She's a literature fanatic like me, but reads darker, read Sartre in tenth grade—*Nausea*—which is when she started wearing black (even at the beach), smoking cigarettes (even though she looks like the healthiest girl you've ever seen), and obsessing about her existential crisis (even as she partied to all hours of the night).

"Lennie, welcome back, dear," another voice says. Mr. James—also known in my mind as Yoda for both outward appearance and inward musical mojo—has stood up at the piano and is looking over at me with the same expression of bottomless sadness I've gotten so used to seeing from adults. "We're all so very sorry."

"Thank you," I say, for the hundredth time that day. Sarah and Joe are both looking at me too, Sarah with concern and Joe with a grin the size of the continental United States. Does he look at everyone like this, I wonder. Is he a wingnut? Well, whatever he is, or has, it's catching. Before I know it, I've matched his continental U.S. and raised him Puerto Rico and Hawaii. I must look like The Merry Mourner. Sheesh. And that's not all, because now I'm thinking what it might be like to kiss him, to *really* kiss him—uh-oh. This is a problem, an entirely new un-Lennie-like problem that began (*WTF-edly?!*) at the funeral: I was drowning in darkness and suddenly all these boys in the room were glowing. Guy friends of Bailey's from work or college, most of whom I didn't know, kept coming up to me saying how sorry they were, and I don't know if it's because they thought I looked like Bailey, or because they felt bad for me, but later on, I'd catch some of them staring at me in this charged, urgent way, and I'd find myself staring back at them, like I was someone else, thinking things I hardly ever had before, things I'm mortified to have been thinking in a church, let alone at my sister's funeral.

This boy beaming before me, however, seems to glow in a class all his own. He must be from a very friendly part of the Milky Way, I'm thinking as I try to tone down this nutso smile on my face, but instead almost blurt out to Sarah, "He looks like Heathcliff," because I just realized he does, well, except for the happy smiling part—but then all of a sudden the breath is kicked out of me and I'm shoved onto the cold hard concrete floor of my life now, because I remember I can't run home after school and tell Bails about a new boy in band.

My sister dies over and over again, all day long.

"Len?" Sarah touches my shoulder. "You okay?"

I nod, willing away the runaway train of grief barreling straight for me.

Someone behind us starts playing "Approaching Shark," aka the *Jaws* theme song. I turn to see Rachel Brazile gliding toward us, hear her mutter, "Very funny," to Luke Jacobus, the saxophonist responsible for the accompaniment. He's just one of many band-kill Rachel's left in her wake, guys duped by the fact that all that haughty horror is stuffed into a spectacular body, and then further deceived by big brown fawn eyes and Rapunzel hair. Sarah and I are convinced God was in an ironic mood when he made her.

"See you've met The Maestro," she says to me, casually touching Joe's back as she slips into her chair—first chair clarinet—where I should be sitting.

She opens her case, starts putting together her instrument. "Joe studied at a conservatory in *Fronce*. Did he tell you?" Of course she doesn't say *France* so it rhymes with *dance* like a normal English-speaking human being. I can feel Sarah bristling beside me. She has zero tolerance for Rachel ever since she got first chair over me, but Sarah doesn't know what really happened—no one does.

Rachel's tightening the ligature on her mouthpiece like she's trying to asphyxiate her clarinet. "Joe was a *fabulous* second in your absence," she says, drawing out the word *fabulous* from here to the Eiffel Tower.

I don't fire-breathe at her: "Glad everything worked out for you, Rachel." I don't say a word, just wish I could curl into a ball and roll away. Sarah, on the other hand, looks like she wishes there were a battle-ax handy.

The room has become a clamor of random notes and scales. "Finish up tuning, I want to start at the bell today," Mr. James calls from the piano. "And take out your pencils, I've made some changes to the arrangement."

"I better go beat on something," Sarah says, throwing Rachel a disgusted look, then huffs off to beat on her timpani.

Rachel shrugs, smiles at Joe—no not smiles: twinkles—oh brother. "Well, it's true," she says to him. "You were—I mean, are—*fabulous*."

"Not so." He bends down to pack up his clarinet. "I'm a hack, was just keeping the seat warm. Now I can go back to where I belong." He points his clarinet at the horn section.

"You're just being modest," Rachel says, tossing fairy-tale locks over the back of her chair. "You have *so* many colors on your tonal palette."

I look at Joe expecting to see some evidence of an inward groan at these imbecilic words, but see evidence of something else instead. He smiles at Rachel on a geographical scale too. I feel my neck go hot.

"You know I'll miss you," she says, pouting.

"We'll meet again," Joe replies, adding an eye-bat to his repertoire. "Like next period, in history."

I've disappeared, which is good really, because suddenly I

don't have a clue what to do with my face or body or smashed-up heart. I take my seat, noting that this grinning, eye-batting fool from Fronce looks nothing like Heathcliff. I was mistaken.

I open my clarinet case, put my reed in my mouth to moisten it and instead bite it in two.

At 4:48 p.m. on a Friday in April,
my sister was rehearsing the role of Juliet
and less than one minute later
she was dead.
To my astonishment, time didn't stop

with her heart.
People went to school, to work, to restaurants;
they crushed crackers into their clam chowder,
fretted over exams,
sang in their cars with the windows up.
For days and days, the rain beat its fists
on the roof of our house—
evidence of the terrible mistake

God had made.
Each morning, when I woke
I listened for the tireless pounding,
looked at the drear through the window

and was relieved
that at least the sun had the decency
to stay the hell away from us.

(Found on a piece of staff paper, spiked on a low branch, Flying Man's Gulch)

chapter 3

THE REST OF the day blurs by and before the final bell, I sneak out and duck into the woods. I don't want to take the roads home, don't want to risk seeing anyone from school, especially Sarah, who informed me that while I've been in hiding, she's been reading up on loss and according to all the experts, it's time for me to talk about what I'm going through—but she, and the experts, and Gram, for that matter, don't get it. I can't. I'd need a new alphabet, one made of falling, of tectonic plates shifting, of the deep devouring dark.

As I walk through the redwood trees, my sneakers sopping up days of rain, I wonder why bereaved people even bother with mourning clothes when grief itself provides such an unmistakable wardrobe. The only one who didn't seem to spot it on me today—besides Rachel, who doesn't count—was the new boy. He will only ever know this new sisterless me.

I see a scrap of paper on the ground dry enough to write on, so I sit on a rock, take out the pen that I always keep in my back pocket now, and scribble a conversation I remember having with Bailey on it, then fold it up and bury it in the moist earth.

When I break out of the forest onto the road to our house, I'm flooded with relief. I want to be at home, where Bailey is most alive, where I can still see her leaning out the window, her wild black hair blowing around her face as she says, "C'mon, Len, let's get to the river pronto."

"Hey you." Toby's voice startles me. Bailey's boyfriend of two years, he's part cowboy, part skate rat, all love slave to my sister, and totally MIA lately despite Gram's many invitations. "We really need to reach out to him now," she keeps saying.

He's lying on his back in her garden with the neighbor's two red dogs, Lucy and Ethel, sprawled out asleep beside him. This is a common sight in the springtime. When the angel's trumpets and lilacs bloom, her garden is positively soporific. A few moments among the blossoms and even the most energetic find themselves on their backs counting clouds.

"I was, uh, doing some weeding for Gram," he says, obviously embarrassed about his kick-back position.

"Yeah, it happens to the best of us." With his surfer flop of hair and wide face sun-spattered in freckles, Toby is the closest a human can come to lion without jumping species. When Bailey first saw him, she and I were out road-reading (we all road-read; the few people who live on our street know this about our family and inch their way home in their cars just in case one of us is out strolling and particularly rapt). I was reading *Wuthering Heights*, as usual, and she was reading *Like Water for Chocolate*, her favorite, when a magnificent chestnut brown horse trotted past us on the way to the trailhead. *Nice horse*, I thought, and went back to Cathy and Heathcliff, only looking up a few seconds later when I heard the thump of Bailey's book as it hit the ground.

She was no longer by my side but had stopped a few paces back.

"What's wrong with you?" I asked, taking in my suddenly lobotomized sister.

"Did you see that guy, Len?"

"What guy?"

"God, what's wrong with *you,* that gorgeous guy on that horse, it's like he popped out of my novel or something. I can't believe you didn't see him, Lennie." Her exasperation at my disinterest in boys was as perpetual as my exasperation at her preoccupation with them. "He turned around when he passed us and smiled right at me—he was *so* good-looking . . . just like the Revolutionary in this book." She reached down to pick it up, brushing the dirt off the cover. "You know, the one who whisks Gertrudis onto his horse and steals her away in a fit of passion—"

"Whatever, Bailey." I turned back around, resumed reading, and made my way to the front porch, where I sunk into a chair and promptly got lost in the stampeding passion of the two on the English moors. I liked love safe between the covers of my novel, not in my sister's heart, where it made her ignore me for months on end. Every so often though, I'd look up at her, posing on a rock by the trailhead across the road, so obviously feigning reading her book that I couldn't believe she was an actress. She stayed out there for hours waiting for her Revolutionary to come back, which he finally did, but from the other direction, having traded in his horse some-where for a skateboard. Turns out he didn't pop out of her novel after all, but out of Clover High like the rest of us, only he hung out with the ranch kids and skaters, and because she was exclusively a drama diva, their paths never crossed until that day. But by that point it didn't matter where he came from or what he rode in on because that image of him gallop-ing by had burned into Bailey's psyche and stolen from her the capacity for rational thought.

I've never really been a member of the Toby Shaw fan club. Neither his cowboy bit nor the fact that he could do a 180 Ollie into a Fakie Feeble Grind on his skateboard made up for the fact that he had turned Bailey into a permanent love zombie.

That, and he's always seemed to find me as noteworthy as a baked potato.

"You okay, Len?" he asks from his prone position, bringing me back to the moment.

For some reason, I tell the truth. I shake my head, back and forth, back and forth, from disbelief to despair, and back again.

He sits up. "I know," he says, and I see in his marooned expression that it's true. I want to thank him for not making me say a word, and getting it all the same, but I just remain silent as the sun pours heat and light, as if from a pitcher, all over our bewildered heads.

He pats the grass with his hand for me to join him. I sort of want to but feel hesitant. We've never really hung out before without Bailey.

I motion toward the house. "I need to go upstairs."

This is true. I want to be back in The Sanctum, full name: The Inner Pumpkin Sanctum, newly christened by me, when Bailey, a few months ago, persuaded me the walls of our bedroom just had to be orange, a blaringly unapologetic orange that had since made our room sunglasses optional. Before I'd left for school this morning, I'd shut the door, purposefully, wishing I could barricade it from Gram and her cardboard boxes. I want The Sanctum the way it is, which means exactly the way it was. Gram seems to think this means: *I'm out of my tree and running loose through the park,* Gramese for *mental.*

"Sweet pea." She's come out onto the porch in a bright purple frock covered in daisies. In her hand is a paintbrush, the first time I've seen her with one since Bailey died. "How was your first day back?"

I walk over to her, breathe in her familiar scent: patchouli, paint, garden dirt.

"It was fine," I say.

She examines my face closely like she does when she's preparing to sketch it. Silence tick-tocks between us, as it does lately. I can feel her frustration, how she wishes she could shake me like she might a book, hoping all the words will just fall out.

"There's a new boy in honor band," I offer.

"Oh yeah? What's he play?"

"Everything, it seems." Before I escaped into the woods at lunch, I saw him walking across the quad with Rachel, a guitar swinging from his hand.

"Lennie, I've been thinking . . . it might be good for you now, a real comfort . . ." Uh-oh. I know where this is going. "I mean, when you were studying with Marguerite, I couldn't rip that instrument out of your hands—"

"Things change," I say, interrupting her. I can't have this conversation. Not again. I try to step around her to go inside. I just want to be in Bailey's closet, pressed into her dresses, into the lingering scents of riverside bonfires, coconut suntan lotion, rose perfume—her.

"Listen," she says quietly, reaching her free hand out to straighten my collar. "I invited Toby for dinner. He's quite out of his tree. Go keep him company, help him weed or something."

It occurs to me she probably said something similar to him about me to get him to finally come over. Ugh.

And then without further ado, she dabs my nose with her paintbrush.

"Gram!" I cry out, but to her back as she heads into the house. I try to wipe off the green with my hand. Bails and I spent much of our lives like this, ambushed by Gram's swash-buckling green-tipped paintbrush. Only green, mind you. Gram's paintings line the walls of the house, floor to ceiling, stack behind couches, chairs, under tables, in closets, and each and every one of them is a testament to her undying devotion to the color green. She has every hue from lime to forest and uses them to paint primarily one thing: willowy women who look half mermaid, half Martian. "They're my ladies," she'd tell Bails and me. "Halfway between here and there."

Per her orders, I drop my clarinet case and bag, then plant myself in the warm grass beside a supine Toby and the sleeping dogs to help him "weed."

"Tribal marking," I say, pointing to my nose.

He nods disinterestedly in his flower coma. I'm a green-nosed baked potato. Great.

I turtle up, tucking my knees to my chest and resting my head in the crevice between them. My eyes move from the wisteria cascading down the trellis to the several parties of daffodils gossiping in the breeze to the indisputable fact that springtime has shoved off its raincoat today and is just prancing around—it makes me queasy, like the world has already forgotten what's happened to us.

"I'm not going to pack up her things in cardboard boxes," I say without thinking. "Ever."

Toby rolls on his side, shields his face with his hand trying to block the sun so he can see me, and to my surprise says, "Of course not."

I nod and he nods back, then I flop down on the grass, cross my arms over my head so he can't see that I'm secretly smiling a little into them.

The next thing I know the sun has moved behind a mountain and that mountain is Uncle Big towering over us. Toby and I must have both crashed out.

"I feel like Glinda the Good Witch," Big says, "looking down on Dorothy, Scarecrow, and two Totos in the poppy field outside of Oz." A few narcotic springtime blooms are no match for Big's bugle of a voice. "I guess if you don't wake up, I'm going to have to make it snow on you." I grin groggily up at him with his enormous handlebar mustache poised over his lip like a grand Declaration of Weird. He's carrying a red cooler as if it were a briefcase.

"How's the distribution effort going?" I ask, tapping the

cooler with my foot. We are in a ham predicament. After the funeral, there seemed to be a prime directive in Clover that everyone had to stop by our house with a ham. Hams were everywhere; they filled the fridge, the freezer, lined the counters, the stove, sat in the sink, the cold oven. Uncle Big attended to the door as people stopped by to pay their respects. Gram and I could hear his booming voice again and again, "Oh a ham, how thoughtful, thank you, come in." As the days went on Big's reaction to the hams got more dramatic for our benefit. Each time he exclaimed "A ham!" Gram and I found each other's eyes and had to suppress a rush of inappropriate giggles. Now Big is on a mission to make sure everyone in a twenty-mile radius has a ham sandwich a day.

He rests the cooler on the ground and reaches his hand down to help me up. "It's possible we'll be a hamless house in just a few days."

Once I'm standing, Big kisses my head, then reaches down for Toby. When he's on his feet, Big pulls him into his arms, and I watch Toby, who is a big guy himself, disappear in the mountainous embrace. "How you holding up, cowboy?"

"Not too good," he admits.

Big releases him, keeping one hand on his shoulder, and puts the other one on mine. He looks from Toby to me. "No way out of this but through . . . for any of us." He says it like Moses, so we both nod as if we've been bestowed with a great wisdom. "And let's get you some turpentine." He winks at me. Big's an ace winker—five marriages to his name to prove it. After his beloved fifth wife left him, Gram insisted he move in with us, saying, "Your poor uncle will starve himself if he stays in this lovelorn condition much longer. A sorrowing heart poisons recipes."

This has proven to be true, but for Gram. Everything she cooks now tastes like ashes.

Toby and I follow Big into the house, where he stops before the painting of his sister, my missing mother: Paige Walker. Before she left sixteen years ago, Gram had been painting a portrait of her, which she never got to finish but put up anyway. It hovers over the mantel in the living room, half a mother, with long green hair pooling like water around an incomplete face.

Gram had always told us that our mother would return. "She'll be back," she'd say like Mom had gone to the store for some eggs, or a swim at the river. Gram said it so often and with such certainty that for a long while, before we learned more, we didn't question it, just spent a whole lot of time waiting for the phone to ring, the doorbell to sound, the mail to arrive.

I tap my hand softly against Big, who's staring up at The Half Mom like he's lost in a silent mournful conversation. He sighs, puts an arm around me and one around Toby, and we all plod into the kitchen like a three-headed, six-legged, ten-ton sack of sad.

Dinner, unsurprisingly, is a ham and ash casserole that we hardly touch.

After, Toby and I camp out on the living room floor, listening to Bailey's music, poring over countless photo albums, basically blowing our hearts to smithereens.

I keep sneaking looks at him from across the room. I can almost see Bails flouncing around him, coming up from behind and dropping her arms around his neck the way she always did.

She'd say sickeningly embarrassing things in his ear, and he'd tease her back, both of them acting like I wasn't there.

"I feel Bailey," I say finally, the sense of her overwhelming me. "In this room, with us."

He looks up from the album on his lap, surprised. "Me too. I've been thinking it this whole time."

"It's *so* nice," I say, relief spilling out of me with the words.

He smiles and it makes his eyes squint like the sun is in his face. "It is, Len." I remember Bailey telling me once that Toby doesn't talk all that much to humans but is able to gentle startled horses at the ranch with just a few words. Like St. Francis, I'd said to her, and I believe it—the low slow lull of his voice is soothing, like waves lapping the shore at night.

I return to the photos of Bailey as Wendy in the Clover Elementary production of *Peter Pan*. Neither of us mentions it again, but the comfort of feeling Bailey so close stays with me for the rest of the evening.

Later, Toby and I stand by the garden, saying good-bye. The dizzy, drunk fragrance of the roses engulfs us.

"It was great hanging out with you, Lennie, made me feel better."

"Me too," I say, plucking a lavender petal. "Much better, really." I say this quietly and to the rosebush, not sure I even want him to hear, but when I peek back up at his face, it's kind, his leonine features less lion, more cub.

"Yeah," he says, looking at me, his dark eyes both shiny and sad. He lifts his arm, and for a second I think he's going to touch my face with his hand, but he just runs his fingers through the tumble of sunshine that is his hair.

We walk the few remaining steps to the road in slow motion. Once there, Lucy and Ethel emerge out of nowhere and start climbing all over Toby, who has dropped to his knees to say good-bye to them. He holds his skateboard in one hand, ruffling and petting the dogs with the other as he whispers unintelligible words into their fur.

"You really are St. Francis, huh?" I have a thing for the saints—the miracles, not the mortifications.

"It's been said." A soft smile meanders across the broad planes of his face, landing in his eyes. "Mostly by your sister." For a split second, I want to tell him it was me who thought that, not Bailey.

He finishes his farewell, stands back up, then drops his skateboard to the ground, steadying it with his foot. He doesn't get on. A few years pass.

"I should go," he says, not going.

"Yeah," I say. A few more.

Before he finally hops on his board, he hugs me good-bye and we hold on to each other so tightly under the sad, starless sky that for a moment I feel as if our heartbreak were one instead of two.

But then all of a sudden, I feel a hardness against my hip, him, *that. Holy fucking shit!* I pull back quickly, say good-bye, and run back into the house.

I don't know if he knows that I felt him.

I don't know anything.

Someone from Bailey's drama class
yelled *bravo* at the end of the service
and everyone jumped to their feet
and started clapping
I remember thinking the roof would blow
from the thunder in our hands
that grief was a room filled
with hungry desperate light
We clapped for nineteen years
of a world with Bailey in it
did not stop clapping
when the sun set, moon rose
when all the people streamed into our house
with food and frantic sorrow
did not stop clapping
until dawn
when we closed the door
on Toby
who had to make his sad way home
I know we must have moved from that spot
must have washed and slept and ate
but in my mind, Gram, Uncle Big and I
stayed like that for weeks
just staring at the closed door
with nothing between our hands
but air

(Found on a piece of notebook paper blowing down Main Street)

chapter 4

THIS IS WHAT happens when Joe Fontaine has his debut trumpet solo in band practice: I'm the first to go, swooning into Rachel, who topples into Cassidy Rosenthal, who tumbles onto Zachary Quittner, who collapses onto Sarah, who reels into Luke Jacobus—until every kid in band is on the floor in a bedazzled heap. Then the roof flies off, the walls collapse, and when I look outside I see that the nearby stand of redwoods has uprooted and is making its way up the quad to our classroom, a gang of giant wooden men clapping their branches together. Lastly, the Rain River overflows its banks and detours left and right until it finds its way to the Clover High music room, where it sweeps us all away—he is *that* good.

When the rest of us lesser musical mortals have recovered enough to finish the piece, we do, but as we put our instruments away at the end of practice, the room is as quiet and still as an empty church.

Finally, Mr. James, who's been staring at Joe like he's an ostrich, regains the power of speech and says, "Well, well. As you all say, that sure sucked." Everyone laughs. I turn around to see what Sarah thought. I can just about make out an eye under a giant Rasta hat. She mouths *unfreakingbelievable*. I look over at Joe. He's wiping his trumpet, blushing from the response or flushed from playing, I'm not sure which. He looks up, catches my eye, then raises his eyebrows expectantly at me, almost like the storm that has just come out of his horn has been for me. But why would that be? And why is it I keep catching him watching me play? It's not interest, I mean, *that* kind of interest, I can tell. He watches me clinically, intently, the way Marguerite used to during a lesson when she was trying to figure out what in the world I was doing wrong.

"Don't even think about it," Rachel says as I turn back around. "That trumpet player's accounted for. Anyway, he's like so out of your league, Lennie. I mean, when's the last time you had a boyfriend? Oh yeah, never."

I think about lighting her hair on fire.

I think about medieval torture devices: The Rack, in particular.

I think about telling her what really happened at chair auditions last fall.

Instead I ignore her like I have all year, swab my clarinet, and wish I were indeed preoccupied by Joe Fontaine rather than by what happened with Toby—each time I recall the sensation of him pressing into me, shivers race all through my body—definitely not the appropriate reaction to your sister's boyfriend's hard-on! And what's worse is that in the privacy of my mind, I don't pull away like I actually did but stay wrapped in his arms under the still sky, and that makes me flush with shame.

I shut my clarinet case wishing I could do the same on these thoughts of Toby. I scan the room—the other horn players have gathered around Joe, as if the magic were contagious. Not a word between him and me since my first day back. Hardly a word between me and anyone at school really. Even Sarah.

Mr. James claps to get the attention of the class. In his excited, crackly voice, he begins talking about summer band practice because school's out in less than a week. "For those who are around, we will be practicing, starting in July. Who shows up will determine what we play. I'm thinking jazz"—he snaps his fingers like a flamenco dancer—"maybe some hot Spanish jazz, but I'm open to suggestions."

He raises his arms like a priest before a congregation. "Find the beat and keep it, my friends." The way he ends every class. But then after a moment he claps again. "Almost forgot, let me see a show of hands of those who plan on auditioning for All-State next year." Oh no. I drop my pencil and bend over to avoid any possible eye collision with Mr. James. When I emerge from my careful inspection of the floor, my phone vibrates in my pocket. I turn to Sarah, whose visible eye is popping out of her head. I sneak out my phone and read her text.

> *Y didn't u raise ur hand???*
> *Solo made me think of u—that day!*
> *Come over 2nite???*

I turn around, mouth: *Can't.*

She picks up one of her sticks and dramatically feigns stabbing it into her stomach with both hands. I know behind the hari-kari is a hurt that's growing, but I don't know what to do about it. For the first time in our lives, I'm somewhere she can't find, and I don't have the map to give her that leads to me.

I gather my things quickly to avoid her, which is going to be easy because Luke Jacobus has cornered her, and as I do, the day she mentioned comes racing back. It was the beginning of freshman year and we had both made honor band. Mr. James, particularly frustrated with everyone, had jumped on a chair and shouted, "What's wrong with you people? You think you're musicians? You have to stick your asses in the wind!" Then he said, "C'mon, follow me. Those of you who can, bring your instruments."

We filed out of the room, down the path into the forest where the river rushed and roared. We all stood on the banks, while he climbed up onto a rock to address us.

"Now, listen, learn, and then play, just *play*. Make *noise*. Make *something*. Make *muuuuuuuuusic*." Then he began conducting the river, the wind, the birds in the trees like a total loon. After we got over our hysterics and piped down, one by one, those of us who had our instruments started to play. Unbelievably, I was one of the first to go, and after a while, the river and wind and birds and clarinets and flutes and oboes mixed all together in a glorious cacophonous mess and Mr. James turned his attention from the forest back to us, his body swaying, his arms flailing left and right, saying, "That's it, that's it. *That's it!*"

And it was.

When we got back to the classroom, Mr. James came over to me and handed me Marguerite St. Denis's card. "Call her," he said. "Right away."

I think about Joe's virtuoso performance today, can feel it in my fingers. I ball them into fists. Whatever it was, whatever that thing is Mr. James took us in the woods that day to find, whether it's abandon, or passion, whether it's innovation, or simply courage, Joe has it.

His ass is in the wind. Mine is in second chair.

chapter 5

Lennie?

Yeah?

You awake?

Yeah.

We did it.

Did what?

Toby and I did it, had sex last night.

I thought you already had, like 10,000 times.

Nope.

Well . . .

It was incredible.

Congratulations then.

Sheesh, why can't you ever be happy for me about Toby?

I don't know.

What is it, are you jealous?

I don't know . . . sorry.

It's okay. Forget it, go to sleep.

Talk about it if you want to.

I don't want to anymore.

Fine.

Fine.

*(Found on a to-go
cup along the banks
of the Rain River)*

I KNOW IT's him, and wish I didn't. I wish my first thought was of anyone in the world but Toby when I hear the ping of a pebble on the window. I'm sitting in Bailey's closet, writing a poem on the wall, trying to curb the panic that hurls around inside my body like a trapped comet.

I take off the shirt of Bailey's I'd put on over mine, grab the doorknob, and hoist myself back into The Sanctum. Crossing to the window, my bare feet press into the three flattened blue rugs that scatter the room, pieces of bright sky that Bailey and I pounded down with years of cut-throat dance competitions to out-goofball the other without cracking up. I always lost because Bailey had in her arsenal The Ferret Face, which when combined with her masterful Monkey Moves, was certifiably deadly; if she pulled the combo (which took more unself-consciousness than I could ever muster), I was a goner, reduced to a helpless heap of hysterics, every time.

I lean over the sill, see Toby, as I knew I would, under a near full moon. I've had no luck squelching the mutiny inside me. I take a deep breath, then go downstairs and open the door.

"Hey, what's up?" I say. "Everyone's sleeping." My voice sounds creaky, unused, like bats might fly out of my mouth. I take a good look at him under the porch light. His face is wild with sorrow. It's like looking in a mirror.

"I thought maybe we could hang out," he says. This is what I hear in my mind: *boner, boner, erection, hard-on, woody, boner, boner, boner*—"I have something to tell you, Len, don't know who else to tell." The need in his voice sends a shudder right through me. Over his head, the red warning light could not be flashing brighter, but still I can't seem to say no, don't want to. "C'mon in, sir."

He touches my arm in a friendly, brotherly way as he passes, which sets me at ease, maybe guys get hard-ons all the time, for no reason—I have zero knowledge of boner basics. I've only ever kissed three guys, so I'm totally inexperienced with real-life boys, though quite an expert at the kind in books, especially Heathcliff, who doesn't get erections—wait, now that I'm thinking about it, he must get them *all the time* with Cathy on the moors. Heathcliff must be a total freaking boner boy.

I close the door behind him and motion for him to be quiet as he follows me up the steps to The Sanctum, which is sound-proofed so as to protect the rest of the house against years of barky bleating clarinet notes. Gram would have a coronary that he's here visiting me at almost two a.m. on a school night. *On any night, Lennie.* This is most definitely not what she had in mind by reaching out to him.

Once the door of The Sanctum is closed, I put on some of the indie-kill-yourself music I've been listening to lately, and sit down next to Toby on the floor, our backs to the wall, legs outstretched. We sit in silence like two stone slabs. Several centuries pass.

When I can't handle it anymore, I joke, "It's possible you've taken this whole strong silent type thing to an extreme."

"Oh, sorry." He shakes his head, embarrassed. "Don't even realize I'm doing it."

"Doing it?"

"Not talking . . . "

"Really? What is it you think you're doing?"

He tilts his head, smiling squintily, adorably. "I was going for the oak tree in the yard."

I laugh. "Very good then, you do a perfect oak impersonation."

"Thank you . . . think it drove Bails mad, my silent streak."

"Nah, she liked it, she told me, less chance of disagreements . . . plus more stage time for her."

"True." He's quiet for a minute, then in a voice ragged with emotion, says, "We were so different."

"Yeah," I say softly. Quintessential opposites, Toby always serene and still (when not on horse or board) while Bailey did everything: walk, talk, think, laugh, party, at the speed of light, and with its gleam.

"*You* remind me of her . . ." he says.

I want to blurt out: *What!? You've always acted like I was a baked potato!* but instead I say, "No way, don't have the wattage."

"You have plenty . . . it's me that has the serious shortage," he says, sounding surprisingly like a spud.

"Not to her," I say. His eyes warm at that—it kills me. What are we going to do with all this love?

He shakes his head in disbelief. "I got lucky. That chocolate book . . ."

The image assaults me: Bailey leaping off the rock the day they met when Toby returned on his board. "I knew you'd come back," she'd exclaimed, throwing the book in the air. "Just like in this story. I knew it!"

I have a feeling the same day is playing out in Toby's mind, because our polite levity has screeched to a halt—all the past tense in our words suddenly stacking up as if to crush us.

I can see the despair inching across his face as it must be across mine.

I look around our bedroom, at the singing orange paint we'd slathered over the dozy blue we'd had for years. Bailey had said, "If this doesn't change our lives, I don't know what will—this, Lennie, is *the color of extraordinary*." I remember thinking I didn't want our lives to change and didn't understand why she did. I remember thinking I'd always liked the blue.

I sigh. "I'm really glad you showed up, Toby. I'd been hiding in Bailey's closet freaking out for hours."

"Good. That you're glad, I mean, didn't know if I should bug you, but couldn't sleep either . . . did some stupid-ass skating that could've killed me, then ended up here, sat under the plum tree for an hour trying to decide . . ."

The rich timbre of Toby's voice suddenly makes me aware of the other voice in the room, the singer blaring from the speakers who sounds like he's being strangled at best. I get up to put on something more melodic, then when I sit back down, I confide, "No one gets it at school, not really, not even Sarah."

He tips his head back against the wall. "Don't know if it's possible to get it until you're in it like we are. I had no idea . . ."

"Me neither," I say, and suddenly, I want to hug Toby because I'm just so relieved to not have to be in it by myself anymore tonight.

He's looking down at his hands, his brow furrowed, like he's struggling with how to say something. I wait.

And wait.

Still waiting here. How did Bailey brave the radio silence?

When he looks up, his face is all compassion, all cub. The words spill out of him, one on top of the next. "I've never known sisters so close. I feel so bad for you, Lennie, I'm just so sorry. I keep thinking about you without her."

"Thanks," I whisper, meaning it, and all of a sudden wanting to touch him, to run my hand over his, which rests on his thigh just inches from mine.

I glance at him sitting there so close to me that I can smell his shampoo, and I am stuck with a startling, horrifying thought: He is really good-looking, alarmingly so. How is it I never noticed before?

I'll answer that: He's Bailey's boyfriend, Lennie. What's wrong with you?

Dear Mind, I write on my jeans with my finger, *Behave*.

I'm sorry, I whisper to Bailey inside my head, I don't mean to think about Toby this way. I assure her it won't happen again.

It's just that he's the only one who understands, I add. *Oh brother*.

After a wordless while, he pulls a pint of tequila out of his jacket pocket, uncaps it.

"Want some?" he asks. Great, that'll help.

"Sure." I hardly ever drink, but maybe it will help, maybe it'll knock this madness out of me. I reach for the pint and our fingers graze a moment too long as I take it—I decide I imagined it, put the bottle to my lips, take a healthy sip, and then very daintily spit it out all over us. "Yuck, that's disgusting." I wipe my mouth with my sleeve. "Whoa."

He laughs, holds out his arms to show what a mess I've made of him. "It takes time to get used to it."

"Sorry," I say. "Had no idea it was so nasty."

He cheers the bottle to the air in response and takes a swig. I'm determined to try again and not projectile spew. I reach for the bottle, bring it to my lips, and let the liquid burn down my throat, then take another sip, bigger.

"Easy," Toby says, taking the pint from me. "I need to tell you something, Len."

"Okay." I'm enjoying the warmth that has settled over me.

"I asked Bailey to marry me . . ." He says it so quickly it doesn't register at first. He's looking at me, trying to gauge my reaction. It's stark, raving WTF!

"Marry you? Are you kidding?" Not the response he wants, I'm sure, but I'm totally blindsided; he could have just as easily told me she'd been secretly planning a career in fire-eating. Both of them were just nineteen, and Bailey a marriage-o-phobe to boot.

"What'd she say?" I'm afraid to hear the answer.

"She said yes." He says it with as much hope as hopelessness, the promise of it still alive in him. *She said yes.* I take the tequila, swig, don't even taste it or feel the burn. I'm stunned that Bailey wanted this, hurt that she wanted it, really hurt that she never told me. I have to know what she'd been thinking. I can't believe I can't ask her. Ever. I look at Toby, see the earnestness in his eyes; it's like a soft, small animal.

"I'm sorry, Toby," I say, trying to bottle my incredulity and hurt feelings, but then I can't help myself. "I don't know why she didn't tell me."

"We were going to tell you guys that very next week. I'd just asked . . ." His use of *we* jars me; the big *we* has always been

Bailey and me, not Bailey and Toby. I suddenly feel left out of a future that isn't even going to happen.

"But what about her acting?" I say instead of: *What about me*?

"She was acting . . ."

"Yeah, but . . ." I look at him. "You know what I mean." And then I see by his expression that he doesn't know what I mean at all. Sure some girls dream of weddings, but Bailey dreamt of Juilliard: the Juilliard School in New York City. I once looked up their mission statement on the Web: *To provide the highest caliber of artistic education for gifted musicians, dancers, and actors from around the world, so that they may achieve their fullest potential as artists, leaders, and global citizens.* It's true after the rejection she enrolled last fall at Clover State, the only other college she applied to, but I'd been certain she'd reapply. I mean, how could she not? It was her dream.

We don't talk about it anymore. The wind's picked up and has begun rattling its way into the house. I feel a chill run through me, grab a throw blanket off the rocker, pull it over my legs. The tequila makes me feel like I'm melting into nothing, I want to, want to disappear. I have an impulse to write all over the orange walls—I need an alphabet of endings ripped out of books, of hands pulled off of clocks, of cold stones, of shoes filled with nothing but wind. I drop my head on Toby's shoulder. "We're the saddest people in the world."

"Yup," he says, squeezing my knee for a moment. I ignore the shivers his touch sends through me. *They were getting married.*

"How will we do this?" I say under my breath. "Day after day after day without her . . ."

"Oh, Len." He turns to me, smoothes the hair around my face with his hand.

I keep waiting for him to move his hand away, to turn back around, but he doesn't. He doesn't take his hand or gaze off of me. Time slows. Something shifts in the room, between us. I look into his sorrowful eyes and he into mine, and I think, *He misses her as much as I do*, and that's when he kisses me—his mouth: soft, hot, so alive, it makes me moan. I wish I could say I pull away, but I don't. I kiss him back and don't want to stop because in that moment I feel like Toby and I together have, somehow, in some way, reached across time, and pulled Bailey back.

He breaks away, springs to his feet. "I don't understand this." He's in an instant-just-add-water panic, pacing the room.

"God, I should go, I *really* should go."

But he doesn't go. He sits down on Bailey's bed, looks over at me and then sighs as if giving in to some invisible force. He says my name and his voice is so hoarse and hypnotic it pulls me up onto my feet, pulls me across miles of shame and guilt. I don't want to go to him, but I do want to too. I have no idea what to do, but still I walk across the room, wavering a bit from the tequila, to his side. He takes my hand and tugs on it gently.

"I just want to be near you," he whispers. "It's the only time I don't die missing her."

"Me too." I run my finger along the sprinkle of freckles on his cheek. He starts to well up, then I do too. I sit down next to him and then we lie down on Bailey's bed, spooning. My last thought before falling asleep in his strong, safe arms is that I hope we are not replacing our scents with the last remnants of Bailey's own that still infuse the bedding.

When I wake again, I'm facing him, our bodies pressed together, breath intermingling. He's looking at me.

"You're beautiful, Len."

"No," I say. Then choke out one word. "Bailey."

"I know," he says. But he kisses me anyway. "I can't help it." He whispers it right into my mouth.

I can't help it either.

I
wish
my
shadow
would
get
up
and
walk
beside
me

(Found on the back of a French quiz in a planter, Clover High)

chapter 6

There were once two sisters who shared the same room,
the same clothes,
the same thoughts at the same moment.
These two sisters did not have a mother
but they had each other.
The older sister walked ahead of the younger
so the younger one always knew where to go.
The older one took the younger to the river
where they floated on their backs
like dead men.
The older girl would say:
Dunk your head under a few inches,
then open your eyes and look up at the sun
The younger girl:
I'll get water up my nose
The older:
C'mon, do it
and so the younger girl did it
and her whole world filled with light.

(Found on a piece of notebook paper caught in a fence up on the ridge)

JUDAS, BRUTUS, BENEDICT Arnold, and me.

And the worst part is every time I close my eyes I see Toby's lion face again, his lips a breath away from mine, and it makes me shudder head to toe, not with guilt, like it should, but with desire—and then, just as soon as I allow myself the image of us kissing, I see Bailey's face twisting in shock and betrayal as she watches us from above: her boyfriend, her *fiancé* kissing her traitorous little sister *on her own bed*. Ugh. Shame watches me like a dog.

I'm in self-imposed exile, cradled between split branches, in my favorite tree in the woods behind school. I've been coming here every day at lunch, hiding out until the bell rings, whittling words into the branches with my pen, allowing my heart to break in private. I can't hide a thing—everyone in school sees clear to my bones.

I'm reaching into the brown bag Gram packed for me, when I hear twigs crack underneath me. Uh-oh. I look down and see Joe Fontaine. I freeze. I don't want him to see me: Lennie Walker: Mental Patient Eating Lunch in a Tree (it being decidedly out of your tree to hide out in one!). He walks in confused circles under me like he's looking for someone. I'm hardly breathing but he isn't moving on, has settled just to the right of my tree. Then I inadvertently crinkle the bag and he looks up, sees me.

"Hi," I say, like it's the most normal place to be eating lunch.

"Hey, there you are—" He stops, tries to cover. "I was wondering what was back here . . ." He looks around. "Perfect spot for a gingerbread house or maybe an opium den."

"You already gave yourself away," I say, surprised at my own boldness.

"Okay, guilty as charged. I followed you." He smiles at me—
that same smile—wow, no wonder I'd thought—

He continues, "And I'm guessing you want to be alone. Probably don't come all the way out here and then climb a tree because
you're starving for conversation." He gives me a hopeful look.
He's charming me, even in my pitiful emotional state, my Toby
turmoil, even though he's accounted for by Cruella de Vil.

"Want to come up?" I present him a branch and he bounds
up the tree in about three seconds, finds a suitable seat right
next to me, then bats his eyelashes at me. I'd forgotten about
the eyelash endowment. Wow squared.

"What's to eat?" He points to the brown bag.

"You kidding? First you crash my solitude, now you want to
scavenge. Where were you raised?"

"Paris," he says. "So I'm a scavenger *raffiné*."

Oh so glad *j'étudie le français*. And jeez, no wonder the
school's abuzz about him, no wonder I'd wanted to kiss him. I
even momentarily forgive Rachel the idiotic baguette she had
sticking out of her backpack today. He goes on, "But I was
born in California, lived in San Francisco until I was nine. We
moved back there about a year ago and now we're here. Still
want to know what's in the bag though."

"You'll never guess," I tell him. "I won't either, actually. My
grandmother thinks it's really funny to put all sorts of things
in our—my lunch. I never know what'll be inside: e. e. cum-
mings, flower petals, a handful of buttons. She seems to have
lost sight of the original purpose of the brown bag."

"Or maybe she thinks other forms of nourishment are more
important."

"That's exactly what she thinks," I say, surprised. "Okay, you want to do the honors?" I hold up the bag.

"I'm suddenly afraid, is there ever anything alive in it?" Bat. Bat. Bat. Okay, it might take me a little time to build immunity to the eyelash bat.

"Never know . . ." I say, trying not to sound as swoony as I feel. And I'm going to just pretend that sitting-in-a-tree k-i-s-s-i-n-g rhyme did not just pop into my head.

He takes the bag, then reaches in with a grand gesture, and pulls out—an apple.

"An apple? How anti-climactic!" He throws it at me. "Everyone gets apples."

I urge him to continue. He reaches in, pulls out a copy of *Wuthering Heights.*

"That's my favorite book," I say. "It's like a pacifier. I've read it twenty-three times. She's always putting it in."

"*Wuthering Heights*—twenty-three times! Saddest book ever, how do you even function?"

"Do I have to remind you? I'm sitting in a tree at lunch."

"True." He reaches in again, pulls out a stemless purple peony. Its rich scent overtakes us immediately. "Wow," he says, breathing it in. "Makes me feel like I might levitate." He holds it under my nose. I close my eyes, imagine the fragrance lifting me off my feet too. I can't. But something occurs to me.

"My favorite saint of all time is a Joe," I tell him. "Joseph of Cupertino, he levitated. Whenever he thought of God, he would float into the air in a fit of ecstasy."

He tilts his head, looks at me skeptically, eyebrows raised. "Don't buy it."

I nod. "Tons of witnesses. Happened all the time. Right during Mass."

"Okay, I'm totally jealous. Guess I'm just a wannabe levitator."

"Too bad," I say. "I'd like to see you drifting over Clover playing your horn."

"Hell yeah," he exclaims. "You could come with, grab my foot or something."

We exchange a quick searching glance, both of us wondering about the other, surprised at the easy rapport—it's just a moment, barely perceptible, like a lady bug landing on your arm.

He rests the flower on my leg and I feel the brush of his fingers through my jeans. The brown bag is empty now. He hands it to me, and then we're quiet, just listening to the wind rustle around us and watching the sun filter through the redwoods in impossibly thick foggy rays just like in children's drawings.

Who is this guy? I've talked more to him in this tree than I have to anyone at school since I've been back. But how could he have read *Wuthering Heights* and still fall for Rachel Bitch-zilla? Maybe it's because she's been to Fronce. Or because she pretends to like music that no one else has heard of, like the wildly popular Throat Singers of Tuva.

"I saw you the other day," he says, picking up the apple. He tosses it with one hand, catches it with the other. "By The Great Meadow. I was playing my guitar in the field. You were across the way. It looked like you were writing a note or something against a car, but then you just dropped the piece of paper—"

"Are you stalking me?" I ask, trying to keep my sudden delight at that notion out of my voice.

"Maybe a little." He stops tossing the apple. "And maybe I'm curious about something."

"Curious?" I ask. "About what?"

He doesn't answer, starts picking at moss on a branch. I notice his hands, his long fingers full of calluses from guitar strings.

"What?" I say again, dying to know what made him curious enough to follow me up a tree.

"It's the way you play the clarinet . . ."

The delight drains out of me. "Yeah?"

"Or the way you don't play it, actually."

"What do you mean?" I ask, knowing exactly what he means.

"I mean you've got loads of technique. Your fingering's quick, your tonguing fast, your range of tones, man . . . but it's like it all stops there. I don't get it." He laughs, seemingly unaware of the bomb he just detonated. "It's like you're sleep-playing or something."

Blood rushes to my cheeks. Sleep-playing! I feel caught, a fish in a net. I wish I'd quit band altogether like I'd wanted to. I look off at the redwoods, each one rising to the sky surrounded only by its loneliness. He's staring at me, I can feel it, waiting for a response, but one is not forthcoming—this is a no trespassing zone.

"Look," he says cautiously, finally getting a clue that his charms have worn off. "I followed you out here because I wanted to see if we could play together."

"Why?" My voice is louder and more upset than I want it to be. A slow familiar panic is taking over my body.

"I want to hear John Lennon play for real, I mean, who wouldn't, right?"

His joke crashes and burns between us.

"I don't think so," I say as the bell rings.

"Look—" he starts, but I don't let him finish.

"I don't want to play with you, okay?"

"Fine." He hurls the apple into the air. Before it hits the ground and before he jumps out of the tree, he says, "It wasn't my idea anyway."

chapter 7

I WAKE TO Ennui, Sarah's Jeep, honking down the road—it's an ambush. I roll over, look out the window, see her jump out in her favorite black vintage gown and platform combat boots, back-to-blond hair tweaked into a nest, cigarette hanging from bloodred lips in a pancake of ghoulish white. I look at the clock: 7:05 a.m. She looks up at me in the window, waves like a windmill in a hurricane.

I pull the covers over my head, wait for the inevitable.

"I've come to suck your blood," she says a few moments later.

I peek out of the covers. "You really do make a stunning vampire."

"I know." She leans into the mirror over my dresser, wiping some lipstick off her teeth with her black-nail-polished finger. "It's a good look for me . . . Heidi goes goth." Without the accoutrements, Sarah could play Goldilocks. She's a sun-kissed beach girl who goes gothgrungepunkhippierockeremocoremetal-freakfashionistabraingeekboycrazyhiphoprastagirl to keep it under wraps. She crosses the room, stands over me, then pulls a corner of the covers down and hops into bed with me, boots and all.

"I miss you, Len." Her enormous blue eyes are shining down on me, so sincere and incongruous with her getup. "Let's go to breakfast before school. Last day of junior year and all. It's tradition."

"Okay," I say, then add, "I'm sorry I've been so awful."

"Don't say that, I just don't know what to do for you. I can't imagine . . ." She doesn't finish, looks around The Sanctum. I see the dread overtake her. "It's so unbearable . . ." She stares at Bailey's bed. "Everything is just as she left it. God, Len."

"Yeah." My life catches in my throat. "I'll get dressed."

She bites her bottom lip, trying not to cry. "I'll wait downstairs. I promised Gram I'd talk with her." She gets out of bed and walks to the door, the leap in her from moments before now a shuffle. I pull the covers back over my head. I know the bedroom is a mausoleum. I know it upsets everyone (except Toby, who didn't even seem to notice), but I want it like this. It makes me feel like Bailey's still here or like she might come back.

On the way to town, Sarah tells me about her latest scheme to bag a babe who can talk to her about her favorite existentialist, Jean-Paul Sartre. The problem is her insane attraction to lumphead surfers who (not to be prejudicial) are not customarily the most well-versed in French literature and philosophy, and therefore must constantly be exempted from Sarah's Must-Know-Who-Sartre-Is-or-at-Least-Have-Read-Some-of-D.H.-Lawrence-or-at-the-Minimum-One-of-the-Brontës-Preferably-Emily criteria of going out with her.

"There's an afternoon symposium this summer at State in French Feminism," she tells me. "I'm going to go. Want to come?"

I laugh. "That sounds like the perfect place to meet guys."

"You'll see," she says. "The coolest guys aren't afraid to be feminists, Lennie."

I look over at her. She's trying to blow smoke rings, but blowing smoke blobs instead.

I'm dreading telling her about Toby, but I have to, don't I? Except I'm too chicken, so I go with less damning news.

"I hung out with Joe Fontaine the other day at lunch."

"You didn't!"

"I did."

"No way."

"Yes way."

"Nah-uh."

"Uh-huh."

"Not possible.

"So possible."

We have an incredibly high tolerance for yes-no.

"You duck! You flying yellow duck! And you took this long to tell me?!" When Sarah gets excited, random animals pop into her speech like she has an Old MacDonald Had a Farm kind of Tourette syndrome. "Well, what's he like?"

"He's okay," I say distractedly, looking out the window. I can't figure out whose idea it could've been that we play together. Mr. James, maybe? But why? And argh, how freaking mortifying.

"Earth to Lennie. Did you just say Joe Fontaine is *okay*? The guy's holy horses *unfreakingbelievable*! And I heard he has two older brothers: holy horses to the third power, don't you think?"

"Holy horses, Batgirl," I say, which makes Sarah giggle, a sound that doesn't seem quite right coming out of her Batgoth face. She takes a last drag off her cigarette and drops it into a can of soda. I add, "He likes Rachel. What does that say about him?"

"That he has one of those Y chromosomes," Sarah says, shoving a piece of gum into her orally fixated mouth. "But really, I don't see it. I heard all he cares about is music and she plays like a screeching cat. Maybe it's those stupid Throat Singers she's always going on about and he thinks she's in the musical know or something." Great minds . . . Then suddenly Sarah's jumping in her seat like she's on a pogo stick. "Oh Lennie, do it! Challenge her for first chair. Today! C'mon. It'll be so exciting—probably never happened in the history of honor band, a chair challenged on the last day of school!"

I shake my head. "Not going to happen."

"But why?"

I don't answer her, don't know how to.

An afternoon from last summer pops into my head. I'd just quit my lessons with Marguerite and was hanging out with Bailey and Toby at Flying Man's. He was telling us that Thoroughbred racing horses have these companion ponies that always stay by their sides, and I remember thinking, *That's me*. I'm a companion pony, and companion ponies don't solo. They don't play first chair or audition for All-State or compete nationally or seriously consider a certain performing arts conservatory in New York City like Marguerite had begun insisting.

They just don't.

Sarah sighs as she swerves into a parking spot. "Oh well, guess I'll have to entertain myself another way on the last day of school."

"Guess so."

We jump out of Ennui, head into Cecilia's, and order up an obscene amount of pastries that Cecilia gives us for free with that same sorrowful look that follows me everywhere I go now. I think she would give me every last pastry in the store if I asked.

We land on our bench of choice by Maria's Italian Deli, where I've been chief lasagna maker every summer since I was fourteen. I start up again tomorrow. The sun has burst into millions of pieces, which have landed all over Main Street. It's a gorgeous day. Everything shines except my guilty heart.

"Sarah, I have to tell you something."

A worried look comes over her. "Sure."

"Something happened with Toby the other night." Her worry has turned into something else, which is what I was afraid of. Sarah has an ironclad girlfriend code of conduct regarding guys. The policy is sisterhood before all else.

"Something like something? Or something like *something*?" Her eyebrow has landed on Mars.

My stomach churns. "Like *something* . . . we kissed." Her eyes go wide and her face twists in disbelief, or perhaps it's horror. This is the face of my shame, I think, looking at her. *How could I have kissed Toby?* I ask myself for the thousandth time.

"Wow," she says, the word falling like a rock to the ground. She's making no attempt to hold back her disdain. I bury my head in my hands, assume the crash position—I shouldn't have told her.

"It felt right in the moment, we both miss Bails so much, he just gets it, gets me, he's like the only one who does. . . and I was drunk." I say all this to my jeans.

"Drunk?" She can't contain her surprise. I hardly ever even have a beer at the parties she drags me to. Then in a softer voice, I hear, "Toby's the only one who gets you?"

Uh-oh.

"I didn't mean that," I say, lifting my head to meet her eyes, but it's not true, I did mean it, and I can tell from her expression she knows it. "Sarah."

She swallows, looks away from me, then quickly changes the topic back to my disgrace. "I guess it does happen. Grief sex is kind of a thing. It was in one of those books I read." I still hear the judgment in her voice, and something more now too.

"We didn't have sex," I say. "I'm still the last virgin standing."

She sighs, then puts her arm around me, awkwardly, as if she has to. I feel like I'm in a headlock. Neither of us has a clue how to deal with what's not being said, or what is.

"It's okay, Len. Bailey would understand." She sounds totally unconvincing. "And it's not like it's ever going to happen again, right?"

"Of course not," I say, and hope I'm not lying.

And hope I am.

Everyone has always said I look like Bailey,
but I don't.
I have gray eyes to her green,
an oval face to her heart-shaped one,
I'm shorter, scrawnier, paler,
flatter, plainer, tamer.
All we shared is a madhouse of curls
that I imprison in a ponytail
while she let hers rave
like madness
around her head.
I don't sing in my sleep
or eat the petals off flowers
or run into the rain instead of out of it.
I'm the unplugged-in one,
the side-kick sister,
tucked into a corner of her shadow.
Boys followed her everywhere;
they filled the booths at the restaurant
where she waitressed,
herded around her at the river.
One day, I saw a boy come up behind her
and pull a strand of her long hair.
I understood this—
I felt the same way.
In photographs of us together,
she is always looking at the camera,
and I am always looking at her.

(Found on a folded-up piece of paper half buried in pine
needles on the trail to the Rain River)

chapter 8

I AM SITTING at Bailey's desk with St. Anthony: Patron of Lost Things.

He doesn't belong here. He belongs on the mantel in front of The Half Mom where I've always kept him, but Bailey must've moved him, and I don't know why. I found him tucked behind the computer in front of an old drawing of hers that's tacked to the wall—the one she made the day Gram told us our mother was an explorer (of the Christopher Columbus variety).

I've drawn the curtains, and though I want to, I won't let myself peek out the window to see if Toby is under the plum tree. I won't let myself imagine his lips lost and half wild on mine either. No. I let myself imagine igloos, nice frigid arctic igloos. I've promised Bailey nothing like what happened that night will ever happen again.

It's the first day of summer vacation and everyone from school is at the river. I just got a drunken call from Sarah informing me that not one, not two, but three unfreakingbelievable Fontaines are supposed to be arriving momentarily at Flying Man's, that they are going to play outside, that she just found out the two older Fontaines are in a seriously awesome band in L.A., where they go to college, and I better get my butt down there to witness the glory. I told her I was staying in and to revel in their Fontainely glory for me, which resurrected the bristle from yesterday: "You're not with Toby, are you, Lennie?"

Ugh.

I look over at my clarinet abandoned in its case on my playing chair. It's in a coffin, I think, then immediately try to unthink it. I walk over to it, unlatch the lid. There never was a question what instrument I'd play. When all the other girls ran to the flutes in fifth-grade music class, I beelined for a clarinet. It reminded me of me.

I reach in the pocket where I keep my cloth and reeds and feel around for the folded piece of paper. I don't know why I've kept it (for over a year!), why I fished it out of the garbage later that afternoon, after Bailey had tossed it with a cavalier "Oh well, guess you guys are stuck with me," before throwing herself into Toby's arms like it meant nothing to her. But I knew it did. How could it not? It was Juilliard.

Without reading it a final time, I crumple Bailey's rejection letter into a ball, toss it into the garbage can, and sit back down at her desk.

I'm in the exact spot where I was that night when the phone blasted through the house, through the whole unsuspecting world. I'd been doing chemistry, hating every minute of it like I always do. The thick oregano scent of Gram's chicken fricassee was wafting into our room and all I wanted was Bailey to hurry home already so we could eat because I was starving and hated isotopes. How can that be? How could I have been thinking about fricassee and carbon molecules when across town my sister had just taken her very last breath? What kind of world is this? And what do you do about it? What do you do when the worst thing that can happen actually happens? When you get *that* phone call? When you miss your sister's roller coaster of a voice so much that you want to take apart the whole house with your fingernails?

This is what I do: I take out my phone and punch in her number. In a blind fog of a moment the other day I called to see when she'd be home and discovered her account hadn't yet been canceled.

Hey, this is Bailey, Juliet for the month, so dudes, what say'st thou? Hast thou not a word of joy? Some comfort . . .

I hang up at the tone, then call back, again and again, and again, and again, wanting to just pull her out of the phone. Then one time I don't hang up.

"Why didn't you tell me you were getting married?" I whisper, before snapping the phone shut and laying it on her desk. Because I don't understand. Didn't we tell each other everything? *If this doesn't change our lives, Len, I don't know what will,* she'd said when we painted the walls. Is that the change she'd wanted then? I pick up the cheesy plastic St. Anthony. And what about him? Why bring him up here? I look more closely at the drawing he was leaning against. It's been up so long that the paper has yellowed and the edges have curled, so long that I haven't taken notice of it for years. Bailey drew it when she was around eleven, the time she started questioning Gram about Mom with an unrelenting ferocity.

She'd been at it for weeks.

"How do you know she'll be back?" Bailey asked for the millionth time. We were in Gram's art room, Bailey and I lay sprawled out on the floor drawing with pastels while Gram painted one of her ladies at a canvas in the corner, her back to us. She'd been skirting Bailey's questions all day, artfully changing the subject, but it wasn't working this time. I watched Gram's arm drop to her side, the brush sending droplets of a hopeful green onto the bespattered floor. She sighed, a big lonely sigh, then turned around to face us.

"I guess you're old enough, girls," she said. We perked up, immediately put down our pastels, and gave her our undivided attention. "Your mother is . . . well . . . I guess the best way to describe it . . . hmmm . . . let me think . . ." Bailey looked at me in shock—we'd never known Gram to be at a loss for words.

"What, Gram?" Bailey asked. "What is she?"

"Hmmm . . ." Gram bit her lip, then finally, hesitantly, she said, "I guess the best way to say it is . . . you know how some people have natural tendencies, how I paint and garden, how Big's an arborist, how you, Bailey, want to grow up and be an actress—"

"I'm going to go to Juilliard," she told us.

Gram smiled. "Yes, we know, Miss Hollywood. Or Miss Broadway, I should say."

"Our mom?" I reminded them before we ended up talking some more about that dumb school. All I'd hoped was that it was in walking distance if Bailey was going there. Or at least close enough so I could ride my bike to see her every day. I'd been too scared to ask.

Gram pursed her lips for a moment. "Okay, well, your mother, she's a little different, she's more like a . . . well, like an explorer."

"Like Columbus, you mean?" Bailey asked.

"Yes, like that, except without the *Niña, Pinta,* and *Santa Maria.* Just a woman, a map, and the world. A solo artist." Then she left the room, her favorite and most effective way of ending a conversation.

Bailey and I stared at each other. In all our persistent musings on where Mom was and why she left, we never ever imagined anything remotely this good. I followed after Gram to try and find out more, but Bailey stayed on the floor and drew this picture.

In it, there's a woman at the top of a mountain looking off into the distance, her back to us. Gram, Big, and I—with our names beneath our feet—are waving up at the lone figure from the base of the mountain. Under the whole drawing, it says in green *Explorer.* For some reason, Bailey did not put herself in the picture.

I bring St. Anthony to my chest, hold him tight. I need him now, but why did Bailey? What had she lost?

What was it she needed to find?

I put on her clothes.
I button one of her frilly shirts
over my own T-shirt.
Or I wrap one, sometimes two,
sometimes all of her diva scarves around my neck.
Or I strip and slip one of her slinkier dresses over my head,
letting the fabric
fall over my skin like water.
I always feel better then,
like she's holding me.
Then I touch all the things
that haven't moved since she died:
crumpled-up dollars
dredged from a sweaty pocket,
the three bottles of perfume
always with the same amount of liquid in them now,
the Sam Shepherd play
Fool For Love
where her bookmark will never move forward.
I've read it for her twice now,
always putting the bookmark back
where it was when I finish—
it kills me
she will never find out
what happens
in the end.

(Found on the inside cover of
Wuthering Heights, *Clover High library)*

chapter 9

Gram spends the night
in front of The Half Mom.
I hear her weeping—
sad
endless
rain.
I sit at the top of the stairs,
know she's touching

Mom's cold flat cheek
as she says: I'm sorry
I'm so sorry.
I think a terrible thing.
I think: You should be.
I think: How could you have   let this happen?
How could you have let both   of them leave me?

(Found written on the wall of the bathroom at Cecilia's Bakery)

SCHOOL'S BEEN OUT for two weeks. Gram, Big, and I are certifiably out of our trees and running loose through the park—all in opposite directions.

Exhibit A: Gram's following me around the house with a teapot. The pot is full. I can see the steam coming out the spout. She has two mugs in her other hand. Tea is what Gram and I used to do together, before. We'd sit around the kitchen table in the late afternoons and drink tea and talk before the others came home. But I don't want to have tea with Gram anymore because I don't feel like talking, which she knows but still hasn't accepted. So she's followed me up the stairs and is now standing in the doorway of The Sanctum, pot in hand.

I flop onto the bed, pick up my book, pretend to read.

"I don't want any tea, Gram," I say, looking up from *Wuthering Heights,* which I note is upside down and hope she doesn't.

Her face falls. Epically.

"Fine." She puts a mug on the ground, fills the other one in her hand for herself, takes a sip. I can tell it's burned her tongue, but she pretends it hasn't. "Fine, fine, fine," she chants, taking another sip.

She's been following me around like this since school got out. Normally, summer is her busiest time as Garden Guru, but she's told all her clients she is on hiatus until the fall. So instead of guruing, she happens into Maria's while I'm at the deli, or into the library when I'm on my break, or she tails me to Flying Man's and paces on the path while I float on my back and let my tears spill into the water.

But teatime is the worst.

"Sweet pea, it's not healthy . . ." Her voice has melted into a familiar river of worry. I think she's talking about my remoteness, but when I glance over at her I realize it's the other thing. She's staring at Bailey's dresser, the gum wrappers strewn about, the hairbrush with a web of her black hair woven through the teeth. I watch her gaze drifting around the room to Bailey's dresses thrown over the back of her desk chair, the towel flung over her bedpost, Bailey's laundry basket still piled over with her dirty clothes . . . "Let's just pack up a few things."

"I told you, I'll do it," I whisper so I don't scream at the top of my lungs. "I'll do it, Gram, if you stop stalking me and leave me alone."

"Okay, Lennie," she says. I don't have to look up to know I've hurt her.

When I do look up, she's gone. Instantly, I want to run after her, take the teapot from her, pour myself a mug and join her, just spill every thought and feeling I'm having.

But I don't.

I hear the shower turn on. Gram spends an inordinate amount of time in the shower now and I know this is because she thinks she can cry under the spray without Big and me hearing. We hear.

Exhibit B: I roll onto my back and before long I'm holding my pillow in my arms and kissing the air with an embarrassing amount of passion. Not again, I think. What's wrong with me? What kind of girl wants to kiss every boy at a funeral, wants to maul a guy in a tree after making out with her sister's boyfriend the previous night? *Speaking of which, what kind of girl makes out with her sister's boyfriend, period?*

Let me just unsubscribe to my own mind already, because

I don't get any of it. I hardly ever thought about sex before, much less did anything about it. Three boys at three parties in four years: Casey Miller, who tasted like hot dogs; Dance Rosencrantz, who dug around in my shirt like he was reaching into a box of popcorn at the movies. And Jasper Stolz in eighth grade because Sarah dragged me into a game of spin the bottle. Total blobfish feeling inside each time. Nothing like Heathcliff and Cathy, like Lady Chatterley and Oliver Mellors, like Mr. Darcy and Elizabeth Bennet! Sure, I've always been into the Big Bang theory of passion, but as something theoretical, something that happens in books that you can close and put back on a shelf, something that I might secretly want bad but can't imagine ever happening to me. Something that happens to the heroines like Bailey, to the commotion girls in the leading roles. But now I've gone mental, kissing everything I can get my lips on: my pillow, arm chairs, doorframes, mirrors, always imagining the one person I should not be imagining, the person I promised my sister I will never ever kiss again. The one person who makes me feel just a little less afraid.

The front door slams shut, jarring me out of Toby's forbidden arms.

It's Big. Exhibit C: I hear him stomp straight into the dining room, where only two days ago, he unveiled his pyramids. This is always a bad sign. He built them years ago, based on some hidden mathematics in the geometry of the Egyptian pyramids. (Who knows? The guy also talks to trees.) According to Big, his pyramids, like the ones in the Middle East, have extraordinary properties. He's always believed his replicas would be able to prolong the life of cut flowers and fruit, even revive bugs, all of which he would place under them for ongoing study. During his pyramid spells, Big, Bails, and I would spend hours searching the house for dead spiders or flies, and then each morning we'd run to the pyramids hoping to witness a resurrection. We never did. But whenever Big's really upset, the necromancer in him comes out, and with it, the pyramids. This time, he's at it with a fervor, sure it will work, certain that he only failed before because he forgot a key element: an electrically charged coil, which he's now placed under each pyramid.

A little while later, a stoned Big drifts past my open door. He's been smoking so much weed that when he's home he seems to hover above Gram and me like an enormous balloon—every time I come upon him, I want to tie him to a chair.

He backtracks, lingers in my doorway for a moment.

"I'm going to add a few dead moths tomorrow," he says, as if picking up on a conversation we'd been having.

I nod. "Good idea."

He nods back, then floats off to his room, and most likely, right out the window.

This is us. Two months and counting. Booby Hatch Central.

THE NEXT MORNING, a showered and betoweled Gram is fixing breakfast ashes, Big is sweeping the rafters for dead moths to put under the pyramids, and I am trying not to make out with my spoon, when there's a knock at the door. We freeze, all of us suddenly panicked that someone might witness the silent sideshow of our grief. I walk to the front door on tiptoe, so as not to let on that we are indeed home, and peek through the peephole. It's Joe Fontaine, looking as animated as ever, like the front door is telling him jokes. He has a guitar in his hand.

"Everybody hide," I whisper. I prefer all boys safe in the recesses of my sex-crazed mind, not standing outside the front door of our capsizing house. Especially this minstrel. I haven't even taken my clarinet out of its case since school ended. I have no intention of going to summer band practice.

"Nonsense," Gram says, making her way to the front of the house in her bright purple towel muumuu and pink towel turban ensemble. "Who is it?" she asks me in a whisper hundreds of decibels louder than her normal speaking voice.

"It's that new kid from band, Gram, I can't deal." I swing my arms back and forth trying to shoo her into the kitchen.

I've forgotten how to do anything with my lips but kiss furniture. I have no conversation in me. I haven't seen anyone from school, don't want to, haven't called back Sarah, who's taken to writing me long e-mails (essays) about how she's not judging me at all about what happened with Toby, which just lets me know how much she's judging me about what happened with Toby. I duck into the kitchen, back into a corner, pray for invisibility.

"Well, well, a troubadour," Gram says, opening the door. She has obviously noticed the mesmery that is Joe's face and has already begun flirting. "Here I thought we were in the twenty-first century . . ." She is starting to purr. I have to save him.

I reluctantly come out of hiding and join swami seductress Gram. I get a good look at him. I've forgotten quite how luminous he is, like another species of human that doesn't have blood but light running through their veins. He's spinning his guitar case like a top while he talks to Gram. He doesn't look like he needs saving, he looks amused.

"Hi, John Lennon." He's beaming at me like our tree-spat never happened.

What are you doing here? I think so loudly my head might explode.

"Haven't seen you around," he says. Shyness overtakes his face for a quick moment—it makes my stomach flutter. Uh, I think I need to get a restraining order for all boys until I can get a handle on this newfound body buzz.

"Do come in," Gram says, as if talking to a knight. "I was just preparing breakfast." He looks at me, asking if it's okay with his eyes. Gram's still talking as she walks back into the kitchen. "You can play us a song, cheer us up a bit." I smile at him, it's impossible not to, and motion a welcome with my arm. As we enter the kitchen, I hear Gram whisper to Big, still in knight parlance, "I daresay, the young gentleman batted his extraordinarily long eyelashes at me."

We haven't had a real visitor since the weeks following the funeral and so don't know how to behave. Uncle Big has seemingly floated to the floor and is leaning on the broom he had been using to sweep up the dead. Gram stands, spatula in hand, in the middle of the kitchen with an enormous smile on her face. I'm certain she's forgotten what she's wearing. And I sit upright in my chair at the table. No one says anything and all of us stare at Joe like he's a television we're hoping will just turn itself on.

It does.

"That garden is wild, never seen flowers like that, thought some of those roses might chop off *my* head and put me in a vase." He shakes his head in amazement and his hair falls too adorably into his eyes. "It's like Eden or something."

"Better be careful in Eden, all that temptation." The thunder of Big's God voice surprises me—he's been my partner in muteness lately, much to Gram's displeasure. "Smelling Gram's flowers has been known to cause all sorts of maladies of the heart."

"Really?" Joe says. "Like what?"

"Many things. For instance, the scent of her roses causes a mad love to flourish." At that, Joe's gaze ever so subtly shifts to me—whoa, or did I imagine it? Because now his eyes are back on Big, who's still talking. "I believe this to be the case from personal experience and five marriages." He grins at Joe. "Name's Big, by the way, I'm Lennie's uncle. Guess you're new around here or you'd already know all this."

What he would know is that Big is the town lothario. Rumors have it that at lunchtime women from all over pack a picnic and set out to find which tree that arborist is in, hoping for an invitation to lunch with him in his barrel high in the canopy. The stories go that shortly after they dine, their clothes flutter down like leaves.

I watch Joe taking in my uncle's gigantism, his wacked-out mustache. He must like what he sees, because his smile immediately brightens the room a few shades.

"Yup, we moved here just a couple months ago from the city, before that we were in Paris—" Hmm. He must not have read the warning on the door about saying the word *Paris* within a mile radius of Gram. It's too late. She's already off on a Franco-philiac rhapsody, but Joe seems to share her fanaticism.

He laments, "Man, *if only* we still lived—"

"Now, now," she interrupts, wagging her finger like she's scolding him. Oh no. Her hands have found her hips. Here it comes: She singsongs, "*If only* I had wheels on my ass, I'd be a trolley cart." A Gram standard to forestall wallowing. I'm appalled, but Joe cracks up.

Gram's in love. I don't blame her. She's taken him by the hand and is now escorting him on a docent walk through the house, showing off her willowy women, with whom he seems duly and truly impressed, from the exclamations he's making, in French, I might add. This leaves Big to resume his scavenging for bugs and me to replace fantasies of my spoon with Joe Fontaine's mouth. I can hear them in the living room, know they are standing in front of The Half Mom because everyone who comes in the house has the same reaction to it.

"It's so haunting," Joe says.

"Hmm, yes . . . that's my daughter, Paige. Lennie and Bailey's mom, she's been away for a long, long time . . ." I'm shocked. Gram hardly ever talks about Mom voluntarily. "One day I'll finish this painting, it's not done . . ." Gram has always said she'll finish it when Mom comes back and can pose for her.

"Come now, let's eat." I can hear the heartache in Gram's voice through three walls. Mom's absence has grown way more pronounced for her since Bailey's death. I keep catching her and Big staring at The Half Mom with a fresh, almost desperate kind of longing. It's become more pronounced for me too.

Mom was what Bails and I did together before bed when we'd imagine where she was and what she was doing. I don't know how to think about Mom without her.

I'm jotting down a poem on the sole of my shoe when they come back in.

"Run out of paper?" Joe asks.

I put my foot down. Ugh. What's your major, Lennie? Oh yeah: Dorkology.

Joe sits down at the table, all limbs and graceful motion, an octopus.

We are staring at him again, still not certain what to make of the stranger in our midst. The stranger, however, appears quite comfortable with us.

"What's up with the plant?" He points to the despairing Lennie houseplant in the middle of the table. It looks like it has leprosy. We all go silent, because what do we say about my doppelganger houseplant?

"It's Lennie, it's dying, and frankly, we don't know what to do about it," Big booms with finality. It's as if the room itself takes a long awkward breath, and then at the same moment Gram, Big, and I lose it—Big slapping the table and barking laughter like a drunk seal, Gram leaning back against the counter wheezing and gasping for breath, and me doubled over trying to breathe in between my own uncontrolled gasping and snorting, all of us lost in a fit of hysterics the likes of which we haven't had in months.

"Aunt Gooch! Aunt Gooch!" Gram is shrieking in between peals of laughter. Aunt Gooch is the name Bailey and I gave to Gram's laugh because it would arrive without notice like a crazy relative who shows up at the door with pink hair, a suitcase full of balloons, and no intention of leaving.

Gram gasps, "Oh my, oh my, I thought she was gone for good."

Joe seems to be taking the outburst quite well. He's leaned back in his chair, is balancing on its two back legs; he looks entertained, like he's watching, well, like he's watching three heartbroken people lose their marbles. I finally settle enough to explain to Joe, amidst tears and residual giggles, the story of the plant. If he hadn't already thought he'd gained entry to the local loony bin, he was sure to now. To my amazement, he doesn't make an excuse and fly out the door, but takes the predicament quite seriously, like he actually cares about the fate of the plain, sickly plant that will not revive.

After breakfast, Joe and I go onto the porch, which is still eerily cloaked in morning fog. The moment the screen door closes behind us, he says, "One song," as if no time has elapsed since we were in the tree.

I walk over to the railing, lean against it, and cross my arms in front of my chest. "You play. I'll listen."

"I don't get it," he says. "What's the deal?"

"The deal is I don't want to."

"But why? Your pick, I don't care what."

"I told you, I don't—"

He starts to laugh. "God, I feel like I'm pressuring you to have sex or something." Every ounce of blood in a ten-mile radius rushes to my cheeks. "C'mon. I know you want to . . ." he jokes, raising his eyebrows like a total dork. What I want is to hide under the porch, but his giant loopy grin makes me laugh. "Bet you like Mozart," he says, squatting to open his case. "All clarinetists do. Or maybe you're a Bach's Sacred Music devotee?" He squints up at me. "Nah, don't seem like one of those." He takes the guitar out, then sits on the edge of the coffee table, swinging it over his knee. "I've got it. No clarinet player with blood in her veins can resist Gypsy jazz." He plays a few sizzling chords. "Am I right? Or I know!" He starts beating a rhythm on his guitar with his hand, his foot pounding the floor. "Dixieland!"

The guy's life-drunk, I think, makes Candide look like a sourpuss. Does he even know that death exists?

"So, whose idea was it?" I ask him.

He stops finger-drumming. "What idea?"

"That we play together. You said—"

"Oh, that. Marguerite St. Denis is an old friend of the family—the one I blame actually for my exile up here. She might've mentioned something about how Lennie Walker *joue de la clarinette comme un reve.*" He twirls his hand in the air like Marguerite. *"Elle joue a ravir, de merveille."*

I feel a rush of something, everything, panic, pride, guilt, nausea—it's so strong I have to hold on to the railing. I wonder what else she told him.

"Quel catastrophe," he continues. "You see, I thought *I* was her only student who played like a dream." I must look confused, because he explains, "In France. She taught at the conservatory, most summers."

As I take in the fact that my Marguerite is also Joe's Marguerite, I see Big barreling past the window, back at it, broom overhead, looking for creatures to resurrect. Joe doesn't seem to notice, probably a good thing. He adds, "I'm joking, about me, clarinet's never been my thing."

"Not what I heard," I say. "Heard you were *fabulous*."

"Rachel doesn't have much of an ear," he replies matter-of-factly, without insult. Her name falls too easily from his lips, like he says it all the time, probably right before he kisses her. I feel my face flush again. I look down, start examining my shoes. What's with me? I mean really. He just wants to play music together like normal musicians do.

Then I hear, "I thought about you . . ."

I don't dare look up for fear I imagined the words, the sweet tentative tone. But if I did, I'm imagining more of them. "I thought about how crazy sad you are, and . . ."

He's stopped talking. *And what?* I lift my head to see that he's examining my shoes too. "Okay," he says, meeting my gaze. "I had this image of us holding hands, like up at The Great Meadow or somewhere, and then taking off into the air."

Whoa—I wasn't expecting that, but I like it. "A la St. Joseph?"

He nods. "Got into the idea."

"What kind of launch?" I ask. "Like rockets?"

"No way, an effortless takeoff, Superman-style." He raises one arm up and crosses his guitar with the other to demonstrate. "You know."

I do know. I know I'm smiling just to look at him. I know that what he just said is making something unfurl inside. I know that all around the porch, a thick curtain of fog hides us from the world.

I want to tell him.

"It's not that I don't want to play with you," I say quickly so I don't lose my nerve. "It's that, I don't know, it's different, playing is." I force out the rest. "I didn't want to be first chair, didn't want to do the solos, didn't want to do any of it. I blew it, the chair audition . . . on purpose." It's the first time I've said it aloud, to anyone, and the relief is the size of a planet. I go on. "I hate soloing, not that you'd understand that. It's just so . . ." I'm waving my arm around, unable to find the words. But then I point my hand in the direction of Flying Man's. "So like jumping from rock to rock in the river, but in this kind of thick fog, and you're all alone, and every single step is . . ."

"Is what?"

I suddenly realize how ridiculous I must sound. I have no clue what I'm talking about, no clue. "It doesn't matter," I say.

He shrugs. "Tons of musicians are afraid to face-plant."

I can hear the steady whoosh of the river as if the fog's parted to let the sound through.

It's not just performance anxiety though. That's what Marguerite thought too. It's why she thought I quit—*You must work on the nerves, Lennie, the nerves*—but it's more than that, way more. When I play, it's like I'm all shoved and crammed and scared inside myself, like a jack-in-the-box, except one without a spring. And it's been like that for over a year now.

Joe bends down and starts flipping through the sheet music in his case; lots of it is handwritten. He says, "Let's just try. Guitar and clarinet's a cool duet, untapped."

He's certainly not taking my big admission too seriously. It's like finally going to confession only to find out the priest has earplugs in.

I tell him, "Maybe sometime," so he'll drop it.

"Wow." He grins. "Encouraging."

And then it's as if I've vanished. He's bent over the strings, tuning his guitar with such passionate attention I almost feel like I should look away, but I can't. In fact, I'm full-on gawking, wondering what it would be like to be cool and casual and fearless and passionate and so freaking alive, just like he is—and for a split second, I want to play with him. I want to disturb the birds.

Later, as he plays and plays, as all the fog burns away, I think, he's right. That's exactly it—I am crazy sad, and somewhere deep inside, all I want is to fly.

chapter 10

Grief is a house
where the chairs
have forgotten how to hold us
the mirrors how to reflect us
the walls how to contain us
Grief is a house that disappears
each time someone knocks at the door
or rings the bell
a house that blows into the air
at the slightest gust
that buries itself deep in the ground
while everyone is sleeping
Grief is a house where no one can protect you
where the younger sister
will grow older than the older one
where the doors
no longer let you in
or out

(Found under a stone in Gram's garden)

As USUAL I can't sleep and am sitting at Bailey's desk, holding St. Anthony, in a state of dread about packing up her things. Today, when I got home from lasagna detail at the deli, there were cardboard boxes open by her desk. I've yet to crack a drawer. I can't. Each time I touch the wooden knobs, I think about her never thumbing through her desk for a notebook, an address, a pen, and all the breath races out of my body with one thought: *Bailey's in that airless box—*

No. I shove the image into a closet in my mind, kick the door shut. I close my eyes, take one, two, three breaths, and when I open them, I find myself staring again at the picture of Explorer Mom. I touch the brittle paper, feel the wax of the crayon as I glide my finger across the fading figure. Does her human counterpart have any idea one of her daughters has died at nineteen years old? Did she feel a cold wind or a hot flash or was she just eating breakfast or tying her shoe like it was any other ordinary moment in her extraordinary itinerant life?

Gram told us our mom was an explorer because she didn't know how else to explain to us that Mom had what generations of Walkers call the "restless gene." According to Gram, this restlessness has always plagued our family, mostly the women. Those afflicted keep moving, they go from town to town, continent to continent, love to love—this is why Gram explained Mom had no idea who either of our fathers were, and so neither did we—until they wear themselves out and return home. Gram told us her aunt Sylvie and a distant cousin Virginia also had the affliction, and after many years adventuring across the globe, they, like all the others before them, found their way back. It's their destiny to leave, she told us, and their destiny to return, as well.

"Don't boys get it?" I asked Gram when I was ten years old and "the condition" was becoming more understandable to me. We were walking to the river for a swim.

"Of course they do, sweet pea." But then she stopped in her tracks, took my hands in hers, and spoke in a rare solemn tone. "I don't know if at your mature age you can understand this, Len, but this is the way it is: When men have it, no one seems to notice, they become astronauts or pilots or cartographers or criminals or poets. They don't stay around long enough to know if they've fathered children or not. When women get it, well, it's complicated, it's just different."

"How?" I asked. "How is it different?"

"Well, for instance, it's not customary for a mother to not see her own girls for this many years, is it?"

She had a point there.

"Your mom was born like this, practically flew out of my womb and into the world. From day one, she was running, running, running."

"Running away?"

"Nope, sweet pea, never *away*, know that." She squeezed my hand. "She was always running toward."

Toward what? I think, getting up from Bailey's desk. What was my mother running toward then? What is she running toward now? What was Bailey? What am I?

I walk over to the window, open the curtain a crack and see Toby, sitting under the plum tree, under the bright stars, on the green grass, in the world. Lucy and Ethel are draped over his legs—it's amazing how those dogs only come around when he does.

I know I should turn off the light, get into bed, and moon about Joe Fontaine, but that is not what I do.

I meet Toby under the tree and we duck into the woods to the river, wordlessly, as if we've had a plan to do this for days. Lucy and Ethel follow on our heels a few paces, then turn back around and go home after Toby has an indecipherable talk with them.

I'm leading a double life: Lennie Walker by day, Hester Prynne by night.

I tell myself, I will not kiss him, no matter what.

It's a warm, windless night and the forest is still and lonely. We walk side by side in the quiet, listening to the fluted song of the thrush. Even in the moonlit stillness, Toby looks sun-drenched and windswept, like he's on a sailboat.

"I know I shouldn't have come, Len."

"Probably not."

"Was worried about you," he says quietly.

"Thanks," I say, and the cloak of being fine that I wear with everyone else slips right off my shoulders.

Sadness pulses out of us as we walk. I almost expect the trees to lower their branches when we pass, the stars to hand down some light. I breathe in the horsy scent of eucalyptus, the thick sugary pine, aware of each breath I take, how each one keeps me in the world a few seconds longer. I taste the sweetness of the summer air on my tongue and want to just gulp and gulp and gulp it into my body—this living, breathing, heart-beating body of mine.

"Toby?"

"Hmm?"

"Do you feel more alive since . . ." I'm afraid to ask this, like I'm revealing something shameful, but I want to know if he feels it too.

He doesn't hesitate. "I feel more *everything* since."

Yeah, I think, more everything. Like someone flipped on the switch of the world and everything is just on now, including me, and everything in me, bad and good, all cranking up to the max.

He grabs a twig off a branch, snaps it between his fingers. "I keep doing this stupid stuff at night on my board," he says, "gnarly-ass tricks only show-off dip-shits do, and I've been doing it alone . . . and a couple times totally wasted."

Toby is one of a handful of skaters in town who regularly and spectacularly defy gravity. If he thinks he's putting himself in danger he's going full-on kamikaze.

"She wouldn't want that, Toby." I can't keep the pleading out of my voice.

He sighs, frustrated. "I know that, I know." He picks up his pace as if to leave behind what he just told me.

"She'd kill me." He says it so definitively and passionately that I wonder if he's really talking about skating or what happened between us.

"I won't do it anymore," he insists.

"Good," I say, still not totally sure what he's referring to, but if it's us, he doesn't have to worry, right? I've kept the curtains drawn. I've promised Bailey nothing will ever happen again.

Though even as I think this, I find my eyes drinking him in, his broad chest and strong arms, his freckles. I remember his mouth hungrily on mine, his big hands in my hair, the heat coursing through me, how it made me feel—

"It's just so reckless . . ." he says.

"Yeah." It comes out a little too breathy.

"Len?"

I need smelling salts.

He looks at me funny, but then I think he reads in my eyes what has been going on in my head, because his eyes kind of widen and spark, before he quickly looks away.

GET A GRIP, LENNIE.

We walk in silence then through the woods and it snaps me back into my senses. The stars and moon are mostly hidden over the thick tree cover, and I feel like I'm swimming through darkness, my body breaking the air as if it were water. I can hear the rush of the river getting louder with every step I take, and it reminds me of Bailey, day after day, year after year, the two of us on this path, lost in talk, the plunge into the pool, and then the endless splaying on the rocks in the sun—

I whisper, "I'm left behind."

"Me too . . ." His voice catches. He doesn't say anything else, doesn't look at me; he just takes my hand and holds it and doesn't let it go as the cover above us gets thicker and we push together farther into the deepening dark.

I say softly, "I feel so guilty," almost hoping the night will suck my words away before Toby hears.

"I do too," he whispers back.

"But about something else too, Toby . . ."

"What?"

With all the darkness around me, with my hand in Toby's, I feel like I can say it. "I feel guilty that I'm still here . . ."

"Don't. Please, Len."

"But she was always so much . . . more—"

"No." He doesn't let me finish. "She'd hate for you to feel that way."

"I know."

And then I blurt out what I've forbidden myself to think, let alone say: "She's in a coffin, Toby." I say it so loud, practically shriek it—the words make me dizzy, claustrophobic, like I need to leap out of my body.

I hear him suck in air. When he speaks, his voice is so weak I barely hear it over our footsteps. "No, she isn't."

I know this too. I know both things at once.

Toby tightens his grip around my hand.

Once at Flying Man's, the sky floods through the opening in the canopy. We sit on a flat rock and the full moon shines so brightly on the river, the water looks like pure rushing light.

"How can the world continue to shimmer like this?" I say as I lie down under a sky drunk with stars.

Toby doesn't answer, just shakes his head and lies down next to me, close enough for him to put his arm around me, close enough for me to put my head on his chest if he did so. But he doesn't, and I don't.

He starts talking then, his soft words dissipating into the night like smoke. He talks about how Bailey wanted to have the wedding ceremony here at Flying Man's so they could jump into the pool after saying their vows. I lean up on my elbows and can see it as clearly in the moonlight as if I were watching a movie, can see Bailey in a drenched bright orange wedding dress laughing and leading the party down the path back to the house, her careless beauty so huge it had to walk a few paces ahead of her, announcing itself. I see in the movie of Toby's words how happy she would have been, and suddenly, I just don't know where all that happiness, her happiness, and ours, will go now, and I start to cry, and then Toby's face is above mine and his tears are falling onto my cheeks until I don't know whose are whose, just know that all that happiness is gone, and that we are kissing again.

When I'm with him,
there is someone with me
in my house of grief,
someone who knows
its architecture as I do,
who can walk with me,
from room to sorrowful room,
making the whole rambling structure
of wind and emptiness
not quite as scary as lonely
as it was before.

(Found on a branch of a tree outside Clover High)

chapter 11

Joe Fontaine's knocking. I'm lying awake in bed, thinking about moving to Antarctica to get away from this mess with Toby. I prop myself up on an elbow to look out the window at the early, bony light.

Joe's our rooster. Each morning since his first visit, a week and a half ago, he arrives at dawn with his guitar, a bag of chocolate croissants from the bakery, and a few dead bugs for Big. If we aren't up, he lets himself in, makes a pot of coffee thick as tar, and sits at the kitchen table strumming melancholy chords on his guitar. Every so often he asks me if I feel like playing, to which I reply *no,* to which he replies *fine.* A polite standoff. He hasn't mentioned Rachel again, which is okay by me.

The strangest part about all this is that it's not strange at all, for any of us. Even Big, who is not a morning person, pads down the stairs in his slippers, greets Joe with a boisterous back slap, and after checking the pyramids (which Joe has already checked), he jumps right back into their conversation from the previous morning about his obsession du jour: exploding cakes.

Big heard that a woman in Idaho was making a birthday cake for her husband when the flour ignited. They were having a dry spell, so there was lots of static electricity in the air. A cloud of flour dust surrounded her and due to a spark from a static charge in her hand, it exploded: an inadvertent flour bomb. Now Big is trying to enlist Joe to reenact the event with him for the sake of science. Gram and I have been adamantly opposed to this for obvious reasons. "We've had enough catastrophe, Big," Gram said yesterday, putting her foot down. I think the amount of pot Big's been smoking has made the idea of the exploding cake much funnier and more fascinating than it really is, but somehow Joe is equally enthralled with the concept.

It's Sunday and I have to be at the deli in a few hours. The kitchen's bustling when I stumble in.

"Morning, John Lennon," Joe says, looking up from his guitar strings and throwing me a jaw-dropping grin—what am I doing making out with Toby, *Bailey's* Toby, I think as I smile back at the holy horses unfreakingbelievable Joe Fontaine, who has seemingly moved into our kitchen. Things are so mixed up—the boy who should kiss me acts like a brother and the boy who should act like a brother keeps kissing me. Sheesh.

"Hey, John Lennon," Gram echoes.

Unbelievable. This can't be catching on. "Only Joe's allowed to call me that," I grumble at her.

"John Lennon!" Big whisks into the kitchen and me into his arms, dancing me around the room. "How's my girl today?"

"Why's everyone in such a good mood?" I feel like Scrooge.

"I'm not in a good mood," Gram says, beaming ear to ear, looking akin to Joe. I notice her hair is dry too. No grief-shower this morning. A first. "I just got an idea last night. It's a surprise." Joe and Big glance at me and shrug. Gram's ideas often rival Big's on the bizarre scale, but I doubt this one involves explosions or necromancy.

"We don't know what it is either, honey," Big bellows in a baritone unfit for eight a.m. "In other breaking news, Joe had an epiphany this morning: He put the Lennie houseplant under one of the pyramids—I can't believe I never thought of that." Big can't contain his excitement, he's smiling down on Joe like a proud father. I wonder how Joe slipped in like this, wonder if it's somehow because he never knew her, doesn't have one single memory of her, he's like the world without our heartbreak—

My cell phone goes off. I glance at the screen. It's Toby. I let it go to voicemail, feeling like the worst person in the world because just seeing his name recalls last night, and my stomach flies into a sequence of contortions. How could I have let this happen?

I look up, all eyes are on me, wondering why I didn't pick up the phone. I have to get out of the kitchen.

"Want to play, Joe?" I say, heading upstairs for my clarinet.

"Holy shit," I hear, then apologies to Gram and Big.

Back on the porch, I say, "You start, I'll follow."

He nods and starts playing some sweet soft chords in G minor. But I feel too unnerved for sweet, too unnerved for soft. I can't shake off Toby's call, his kisses. I can't shake off cardboard boxes, perfume that never gets used, bookmarks that don't move, St. Anthony statues that do. I can't shake off the fact that Bailey at eleven years old did not put herself in the drawing of our family, and suddenly, I am so upset I forget I'm playing music, forget Joe's even there beside me.

I start to think about all the things I haven't said since Bailey died, all the words stowed deep in my heart, in our orange bedroom, all the words in the whole world that aren't said after someone dies because they are too sad, too enraged, too devastated, too guilty, to come out—all of them begin to course inside me like a lunatic river. I suck in all the air I can, until there's probably no air left in Clover for anyone else, and then I blast it all out my clarinet in one mad bleating typhoon of a note. I don't know if a clarinet has ever made such a terrible sound, but I can't stop, all the years come tumbling out now—Bailey and me in the river, the ocean, tucked so snug into our room, the backseat of cars, bathtubs, running through the trees, through days and nights and months and years without Mom—I am breaking windows, busting through walls, burning up the past, pushing Toby off me, taking the dumb-ass Lennie houseplant and hurling it into the sea—

I open my eyes. Joe's staring at me, astonished. The dogs next door are barking.

"Wow, I think I'll follow next time," he says.

I'd been making decisions for days.
I picked out the dress Bailey would wear forever—
a black slinky one—inappropriate—that she loved.
I chose a sweater to go over it, earrings, bracelet, necklace,
her most beloved strappy sandals.
I collected her makeup to give to the funeral director with a recent photo—
I thought it would be me that would dress her;
I didn't think a strange man should see her naked
touch her body
shave her legs
apply her lipstick
but that's what happened all the same.
I helped Gram pick out the casket,
the plot at the cemetery.
I changed a few lines
in the obituary that Big composed.
I wrote on a piece of paper what I thought
should go on the headstone.
I did all this without uttering a word.
Not one word, for days,
until I saw Bailey before the funeral
and lost my mind.
I hadn't realized that when people say so-and-so
snapped
that's what actually happens—
I started shaking her—
I thought I could wake her up
and get her the hell out of that box.
When she didn't wake,
I screamed: *Talk to me.*
Big swooped me up into his arms,
carried me out of the room, the church,
into the slamming rain,
and down to the creek
where we sobbed together
under the black coat he held over our heads
to protect us from the weather.

(Found on a piece of staff paper crumpled up by the trailhead)

chapter 12

I WISH I had my clarinet, I think as I walk home from the deli. If I did, I'd head straight into the woods where no one could hear me and face-plant like I did on the porch this morning. *Play the music, not the instrument*, Marguerite always said. And Mr. James: *Let the instrument play you.* I never got either instruction until today. I always imagined music trapped inside my clarinet, not trapped inside of me. But what if music is what escapes when a heart breaks?

I turn onto our street and see Uncle Big road-reading, tripping over his massive feet, greeting his favorite trees as he passes them. Nothing too unusual, but for the flying fruit. There are a few weeks every year when if circumstances permit, like the winds are just so and the plums particularly heavy, the plum trees around our house become hostile to humans and begin using us for target practice.

Big waves his arm east to west in enthusiastic greeting, narrowly escaping a plum to the head.

I salute him, then when he's close enough, I give a hello

twirl to his mustache, which is waxed and styled to the hilt, the fanciest (i.e., freakiest) I've seen it in some time.

"Your friend is over," he says, winking at me. Then he puts his nose back into his book and resumes his promenade. I know he means Joe, but I think of Sarah and my stomach twists a little. She sent me a text today: *Sending out a search party for our friendship.* I haven't responded. I don't know where it is either.

A moment later, I hear Big say, "Oh, Len, Toby called for you, wants you to ring him right away."

He called me on my cell again too while I was at work. I didn't listen to the voicemail. I reiterate the oath I've been swearing all day that I will never see Toby Shaw again, then I beg my sister for a sign of forgiveness—*no need for subtlety either, Bails, an earthquake will do.*

As I get closer, I see that the house is inside out—in the front yard are stacks of books, furniture, masks, pots and pans, boxes, antiques, paintings, dishes, knickknacks—then I see Joe and someone who looks just like him but broader and even taller coming out of the house with our sofa.

"Where do you want this, Gram?" Joe says, like it's the most natural thing in the world to be moving the couch outside. This must be Gram's surprise. We're moving into the yard. Great.

"Anywhere's fine, boys," Gram says, then sees me. "Lennie." She glides over. "I'm going to figure out what's causing the terrible luck," she says. "This is what came to me in the middle of the night. We'll move anything suspicious out of the house, do a ritual, burn sage, then make sure not to put anything unlucky back inside. Joe was nice enough to go get his brother to help."

"Hmmm," I say, not knowing what else to say, wishing I could've seen Joe's face as Gram very sanely explained this INSANE idea to him. When I break away from her, Joe practically gallops over. He's such a downer.

"Just another day at the psych ward, huh?" I say.

"What's quite perplexing . . ." he says, pointing a finger professorially at his brow, "is just how Gram is making the lucky or unlucky determination. I've yet to crack the code." I'm impressed at how quickly he's caught on that there is nothing to do but grab a wing when Gram's aflight with fancy.

His brother comes up then, rests his hand carelessly on Joe's shoulder, and it instantly transforms Joe into a little brother— the slice into my heart is sharp and sudden—*I'm no longer a little sister*. No longer a sister, period.

Joe can barely mask his adulation and it topples me. I was just the same—when I introduced Bailey I felt like I was presenting the world's most badass work of art.

"Marcus is here for the summer, goes to UCLA. He and my oldest brother are in a band down there." Brothers and brothers and brothers.

"Hi," I say to another beaming guy. Definitely no need for lightbulbs Chez Fontaine.

"I heard you play a mean clarinet," Marcus says. This makes me blush, which makes Joe blush, which makes Marcus laugh and punch his brother's arm. I hear him whisper, "Oh Joe, you've got it so bad." Then Joe blushes even more, if that's possible, and heads into the house for a lamp.

I wonder why though if Joe's got it so bad he doesn't make a move, even a suggestion of one. I know, I know, I'm a feminist, I could make a move, but a) I've never made a move on anyone in my life and therefore have no moves to make, b) I've been a wee bit preoccupied with the bat in my belfry who doesn't belong there, and c) Rachel—I mean, I know he spends mornings at our house, but how do I know he doesn't spend evenings at hers.

Gram's taken a shine to the Fontaine boys. She's flitting around the yard, telling them over and over again how handsome they are, asking if their parents ever thought about selling them. "Bet they'd make a bundle on you boys. Shame to give boys eyelashes like yours. Don't you think so, Lennie? Wouldn't you kill for eyelashes like that?" God, I'm embarrassed, though she's right about the eyelashes. Marcus doesn't blink either, they both bat.

She sends Joe and Marcus home to get their third brother, convinced that all Fontaine brothers have to be here for the ritual. It's clear both Marcus and Joe have fallen under her spell. She probably could get them to rob a bank for her.

"Bring your instruments," she yells after them. "You too, Lennie."

I do as I'm told and get my clarinet from the tree it's resting in with an assortment of my worldly possessions. Then Gram and I take some of the pots and pans she has redeemed lucky back into the kitchen to cook dinner. She prepares the chickens while I quarter the potatoes and spice them with garlic and rosemary. When everything is roasting in the oven, we go outside to gather some strewn plums to make a tart. She is rolling out the dough for the crust while I slice tomatoes and avocados for the salad. Every time she passes me, she pats my head or squeezes my arm.

"This is nice, cooking together again, isn't it, sweet pea?"

I smile at her. "It is, Gram." Well, it was, because now she's looking at me in her talk-to-me-Lennie way. The Gramouncements are about to begin.

"Lennie, I'm worried about you." Here goes.

"I'm all right."

"It's really time. At the least, tidy up, do her laundry, or allow me to. I can do it while you're at work."

"I'll do it," I say, like always. And I will, I just don't know when.

She slumps her shoulders dramatically. "I was thinking you and I could go to the city for the day next week, go to lunch—"

"That's okay."

I drop my eyes back to my task. I don't want to see her disappointment.

She sighs in her big loud lonely way and goes back to the crust. Telepathically, I tell her I'm sorry. I tell her I just can't confide in her right now, tell her the three feet between us feels like three light-years to me and I don't know how to bridge it.

Telepathically, she tells me back that I'm breaking her broken heart.

When the boys come back they introduce the oldest Fontaine, who is also in town for the summer from L.A.

"This is Doug," Marcus says just as Joe says, "This is Fred."

"Parents couldn't make up their mind," the newest Fontaine offers. This one looks positively deranged with glee. Gram's right, we should sell them.

"He's lying," Marcus pipes in. "In high school, Fred wanted to be sophisticated so he could hook up with lots of French girls. He thought Fred was way too uncivilized and Flintstone-ish so decided to use his middle name, Doug. But Joe and I couldn't get used to it."

"So now everyone calls him DougFred on two continents." Joe hand-butts his brother's chest, which provokes a counter-attack of several jabs to the ribs. The Fontaine boys are like a litter of enormous puppies, rushing and swiping at each other, stumbling all around, a whirl of perpetual motion and violent affection.

I know it's ungenerous, but watching them, their camaraderie, makes me feel lonely as the moon. I think about Toby and me holding hands in the dark last night, kissing by the river, how with him, I'd felt like my sadness had a place to be.

We eat sprawled out on what is now our lawn furniture. The wind has died down a bit, so we can sit without being pelted by fruit. The chicken tastes like chicken, the plum tart like plum tart. It's too soon for there not to be one bite of ash.

Dusk splatters pink and orange across the sky, beginning its languorous summer stroll. I hear the river through the trees sounding like possibility—

She will never know the Fontaines.

She will never hear about this dinner on a walk to the river.

She will not come back in the morning or Tuesday or in three months.

She will not come back ever.

She's gone and the world is ambling on without her—

I can't breathe or think or sit for another minute.

I try to say "I'll be right back," but nothing comes out, so I just turn my back on the yard full of concerned faces and hurry toward the tree line. When I get to the path, I take off, trying to outrun the heartache that is chasing me down.

I'm certain Gram or Big will follow me, but they don't, Joe does. I'm out of breath and writing on a piece of paper I found on the path when he comes up to me. I ditch the note behind a rock, try to brush away my tears.

This is the first time I've seen him without a smile hidden somewhere on his face.

"You okay?" he asks.

"You didn't even know her." It's out of my mouth, sharp and accusatory, before I can stop it. I see the surprise cross his face.

"No."

He doesn't say anything more, but I can't seem to shut my insane self up. "And you have all these brothers." As if it were a crime, I say this.

"I do."

"I just don't know why you're hanging out with us all the time." I feel my face get hot as embarrassment snakes its way through my body—the real question is why I am persisting like a full-fledged maniac.

"You don't?" His eyes rove my face, then the corners of his mouth begin to curl upward. "I like you, Lennie, duh." He looks at me incredulously. "I think you're amazing . . ." Why would he think this? Bailey is amazing and Gram and Big, and of course Mom, but not me, I am the two-dimensional one in a 3-D family.

He's grinning now. "Also I think you're really pretty and I'm incredibly shallow."

I have a horrible thought: *He only thinks I'm pretty, only thinks I'm amazing, because he never met Bailey,* followed by a really terrible, horrible thought: *I'm glad he never met her.* I shake my head, try to erase my mind, like an Etch A Sketch.

"What?" He reaches his hand to my face, brushes his thumb slowly across my cheek. His touch is so tender, it startles me. No one has ever touched me like this before, looked at me the way he's looking at me right now, deep into me. I want to hide from him and kiss him all at the same time.

And then: Bat. Bat. Bat.

I'm sunk.

I think his acting-like-a-brother stint is over.

"Can I?" he says, reaching for the rubber band on my ponytail.

I nod. Very slowly, he slides it off, the whole time holding my eyes in his. I'm hypnotized. It's like he's unbuttoning my shirt. When he's done, I shake my head a little and my hair springs into its habitual frenzy.

"Wow," he says softly. "I've wanted to do that . . ."

I can hear our breathing. I think they can hear it in New York.

"What about Rachel?" I say.

"What about her?"

"You and her?"

"You," he answers. Me!

I say, "I'm sorry I said all that, before . . ."

He shakes his head like it doesn't matter, and then to my surprise he doesn't kiss me but wraps his arms around me instead. For a moment, in his arms, with my mind so close to his heart, I listen to the wind pick up and think it just might lift us off our feet and take us with it.

chapter 13

THE DRY TRUNKS of the old growth redwoods creak and squeak eerily over our heads.

"Whoa. What is *that*?" Joe asks, all of a sudden pulling away as he glances up, then over his shoulder.

"What?" I ask, embarrassed how much I still want his arms around me. I try to joke it off. "Sheesh, how to ruin a moment. Don't you remember? I'm having a crisis?"

"I think you've had enough freak-outs for one day," he says, smiling now, and twirling his finger by his ear to signify what a wack-job I am. This makes me laugh out loud. He's looking all around again in a mild panic. "Seriously, what was that?"

"Are you scared of the deep, dark forest, city boy?"

"Of course I am, like most sane people, remember lions and tigers and bears, oh my?" He curls his finger around my belt loop, starts veering me back to the house, then stops suddenly. "That, right then. That creepy horror movie noise that happens right before the ax murderer jumps out and gets us."

"It's the old growths creaking. When it's really windy, it

sounds like hundreds of doors squeaking open and shut back here, all at the same time, it's beyond spooky. Don't think you could handle it."

He puts his arm around me. "A dare? Next windy day then." He points to himself—"Hansel"—then at me—"Gretel."

Right before we break from the trees, I say, "Thanks, for following me, and . . ." I want to thank him for spending all day moving furniture for Gram, for coming every morning with dead bugs for Big, for somehow being there for them when I can't be. Instead, I say, "I really love the way you play." Also true.

"Likewise."

"C'mon," I say. "That wasn't playing. It was honking. Total face-plant."

He laughs. "No way. Worth the wait. Testament to why if given the choice I'd rather lose the ability to talk than play. By far the superior communication."

This I agree with, face-plant or not. Playing today was like finding an alphabet—it was like being sprung. He pulls me even closer to him and something starts to swell inside, something that feels quite a bit like joy.

I try to ignore the insistent voice inside: *How dare you, Lennie? How dare you feel joy this soon?*

When we emerge from the woods, I see Toby's truck parked in front of the house and it has an immediate bone-liquefying effect on my body. I slow my pace, disengage from Joe, who looks quizzically over at me. Gram must have invited Toby to be part of her ritual. I consider staging another freak-out and running back into the woods so I don't have to be in a room with Toby and Joe, but I am not the actress and know I couldn't pull it off. My stomach churns as we walk up the steps, past Lucy and Ethel, who are, of course, sprawled out on the porch awaiting Toby's exit, and who, of course, don't move a muscle as we pass. We push through the door and then cross the hall into the living room. The room is aglow with candles, the air thick with the sweet scent of sage.

DougFred and Marcus sit on two of the remaining chairs in the center of the room playing flamenco guitar. The Half Mom hovers above them as if she's listening to the coarse, fiery chords that are overtaking the house. Uncle Big towers over the mantel clapping his hand on his thigh to the feverish beat. And Toby stands on the other side of the room, apart from everyone, looking as lonely as I felt earlier—my heart immediately lurches toward him. He leans against the window, his golden hair and skin gleaming in the flickery light. He watches us enter the room with an inappropriate hawkish intensity that is not lost on Joe and sends shivers through me. I can feel Joe's bewilderment without even looking to my side.

Meanwhile, I am now imagining roots growing out of my feet so I don't fly across the room into Toby's arms, because I have a big problem: Even in this house, on this night, with all these people, with Joe Fabulous Fontaine, who is no longer acting like my brother, right beside me, I still feel this invisible rope pulling me across the room toward Toby and there doesn't seem to be anything I can do about it.

I turn to Joe, who looks like I've never seen him: unhappy, his body stiff with confusion, his gaze shifting from Toby to me and back again. It's as if all the moments between Toby and me that never should have happened are spilling out of us in front of Joe.

"Who's that guy?" Joe asks, with none of his usual equanimity.

"Toby." It comes out oddly robotic.

Joe looks at me like: *Well, who's Toby, you imbecile?*

"I'll introduce you," I say, because I have no choice and cannot just keep standing here like I've had a stroke.

There's no other way to put it: THIS BLOWS.

And on top of everything, the flamenco has begun to crescendo all around us, whipping fire and sex and passion every which way. Perfect. Couldn't they have chosen some sleepy sonata? Waltzes are lovely too, boys. With me on his heels, Joe crosses the room toward Toby: the sun on a collision course with the moon.

The dusky sky pours through the window, framing Toby. Joe and I stop a few paces in front of him, all of us now caught in the uncertainty between day and night. The music continues its fiery revolution all around us and there is a girl inside of me that wants to give in to the fanatical beat—she wants to dance wild and free all around the thumping room, but unfortunately, that girl's in me, not me. Me would like an invisibility cloak to get the hell out of this mess.

I look over at Joe and am relieved to see that the fevered chords have momentarily hijacked his attention. His one hand plays his thigh, his foot drums the ground, and his head bobs around, which flops his hair into his eyes. He can't stop smiling at his brothers, who are pounding their guitars into notes so ferocious they probably could overthrow the government. I realize I'm smiling like a Fontaine as I watch the music riot through Joe. I can feel how intensely he wants his guitar, just as, all of a sudden, I can feel how intensely Toby wants me. I steal a glance at him, and as I suspected, he's watching me watch Joe, his eyes clamped on me. How did we get ourselves into this? It doesn't feel like solace in this moment at all, but something else. I look down, write *help* on my jeans with my finger, and when I look back up I see that Toby's and Joe's eyes have locked. Something passes silently between them that has everything to do with me, because as if on cue they look from each other to me, both saying with their eyes: *What's going on, Lennie?*

Every organ in my body switches places.

Joe puts his hand gently on my arm as if it will remind me to open my mouth and form words. At the contact, Toby's eyes flare. What's going on with him tonight? He's acting like my boyfriend, not my sister's, not someone I made out with twice under very extenuating circumstances. And what about me and this inexplicable and seemingly inescapable pull to him despite everything?

I say, "Joe just moved to town." Toby nods civilly and I sound human, a good start. I'm about to say "Toby was Bailey's boyfriend," which I loathe saying for the *was* and for how it will make me feel like the traitorous person that I am.

But then Toby looks right at me and says, "Your hair, it's down." Hello? This is not the right thing to say. The right thing to say is "Oh, where'd you move from, dude?" or "Clover's pretty cool." Or "Do you skate?" Or basically anything but "Your hair, it's down."

Joe seems unperturbed by the comment. He's smiling at me like he's proud that he was the one that let my hair out of its bondage.

Just then, I notice Gram in the doorway, looking at us. She blows over, holding her burning stick of sage like a magic wand. She gives me a quick once-over, seems to decide I've recovered, then points her wand at Toby and says, "Let me introduce you boys. Joe Fontaine, this is Toby Shaw, Bailey's boyfriend."

Whoosh—I see it: a waterfall of relief pours over Joe. I see the case close in his mind, as he probably thinks there couldn't be anything going on—because what kind of sister would ever cross that kind of line?

"Hey, I'm so sorry," he tells Toby.

"Thanks." Toby tries to smile, but it comes out all wrong and homicidal. Joe, however, so unburdened by Gram's revelation, doesn't even notice, just turns around buoyant as ever, and goes to join his brothers, followed by Gram.

"I'm going to go, Lennie." Toby's voice is barely audible over the music. I turn around, see that Joe is now bent over his guitar, oblivious to everything but the sound his fingers are making.

"I'll walk you out," I say.

Toby says good-bye to Gram, Big, and the Fontaines, all of whom are surprised he's leaving so soon, especially Gram, who I can tell is adding some things up.

I follow him to his truck—Lucy, Ethel, and I, all yapping at his feet. He opens the door, doesn't get in, leans against the cab. We are facing each other and there's not a trace of the calm or gentleness I've become so accustomed to seeing in his expression, but something fierce and unhinged in its place. He's in total tough-skater-dude mode, and though I don't want to, I'm finding it arresting. I feel a current coursing between us, feel it begin to rip out of control inside of me. *What is it?* I think as he looks into my eyes, then at my mouth, then sweeps his gaze slowly, proprietarily over my body. *Why can't we stop this?* I feel so reckless—like I'm reeling with him into the air on his board with no regard for safety or consequence, with no regard for anything but speed and daring and being hungrily, greedily alive—but I tell him, "No. Not now."

"When?"

"Tomorrow. After work," I say, against my better judgment, against any judgment.

What do you girls want for dinner?
What do you girls think about my new painting?
What do the girls want to do this weekend?
Did the girls leave for school yet?
I haven't seen the girls yet today.
I told those girls to hurry up!
Where are those girls?
Girls, don't forget your lunches.
Girls, be home by 11 p.m.
Girls, don't even think of swimming—it's freezing out.
Are the Walker Girls coming to the party?
The Walker Girls were at the river last night.
Let's see if the Walker Girls are home.

(Found written on the wall of Bailey's closet)

chapter 14

I FIND GRAM, who is twirling around the living room with her sage wand like an overgrown fairy. I tell her that I'm sorry, but I don't feel well and need to go upstairs.

She stops mid-whirl. I know she senses trouble, but she says, "Okay, sweet pea." I apologize to everyone and say good night as nonchalantly as possible.

Joe follows me out of the room, and I decide it might be time to join a convent, just cloister up with the Sisters for a while.

He touches my shoulder and I turn around to face him. "I hope what I said in the woods didn't freak you out or something . . . hope that's not why you're crashing . . ."

"No, no." His eyes are wide with worry. I add, "It made me pretty happy, actually." Which of course is true except for the slight problem that immediately after hearing his declaration, I made a date with my dead sister's boyfriend to do *God knows what!*

"Good." He brushes his thumb on my cheek, and again his tenderness startles me. "Because I'm going crazy, Lennie." Bat.

Bat. Bat. And just like that, I'm going crazy too because I'm thinking Joe Fontaine is about to kiss me. Finally.

Forget the convent.

Let's get this out of the way: My previously nonexistent floozy-factor is blowing right off the charts.

"I didn't know you knew my name," I say.

"So much you don't know about me, *Lennie*." He smiles and takes his index finger and presses it to my lips, leaves it there until my heart lands on Jupiter: three seconds, then removes it, turns around, and heads back into the living room. Whoa— well, that was either the dorkiest or sexiest moment of my life, and I'm voting for sexy on account of my standing here dumbstruck and giddy, wondering if he did kiss me after all.

I am totally out of control.

I do not think this is how normal people mourn.

When I can move my legs one in front of the other, I make my way up to The Sanctum. Thankfully, it has been deemed fairly lucky by Gram so is mostly untouched, especially Bailey's things, which she mercifully didn't touch at all. I go straight over to her desk and start talking to the explorer picture like we sometimes talk to The Half Mom.

Tonight, the woman on the mountaintop will have to be Bailey.

I sit down and tell her how sorry I am, that I don't know what's wrong with me and that I'll call Toby and cancel the date first thing in the morning. I also tell her I didn't mean to think what I thought in the woods and I would do anything for her to be able to meet Joe Fontaine. Anything. And then I ask her again to please give me a sign that she forgives me before the list of unpardonable things I think and do gets too long and I become a lost cause.

I look over at the boxes. I know I'm going to have to start eventually. I take a deep breath, banish all morbid thoughts from my mind, and put my hands on the wooden knobs of the top desk drawer. Only to immediately think about Bailey and my anti-snooping pact. I never broke it, not once, despite a natural propensity for nosing around. At people's houses, I open medicine cabinets, peek behind shower curtains, open drawers and closet doors whenever possible. But with Bailey, I adhered to the pact—

Pacts. So many between us, breaking now. And what about the unspoken ones, those entered into without words, without pinky swears, without even realizing it? A squall of emotion lands in my chest. Forget talking to the picture, I take out my phone, punch in Bailey's number, listen impatiently to her as Juliet, heat filling my head, then over the tone, I hear myself say, "What happens to a stupid companion pony when the racehorse dies?" There's both anger and despair in my voice and immediately and illogically I wish I could erase the message so she won't hear it.

I slowly open the desk drawer, afraid of what I might find, afraid of what else she might not have told me, afraid of this rollicking bananas pact-breaking me. But there are just things, inconsequential things of hers, some pens, a few playbills from shows at Clover Repertory, concert tickets, an address book, an old cell phone, a couple of business cards, one from our dentist reminding her of her next appointment, and one from Paul Booth, Private Investigator with a San Francisco address.

WTF?

I pick it up. On the back in Bailey's writing it says *4/25 4 p.m., Suite 2B.* The only reason I can think of that she would go see a private investigator would be to find Mom. But why would she do that? We both knew that Big already tried, just a few years ago in fact, and that the PI had said it would be impossible to find her.

The day Big told us about the detective, Bailey had been furious, torpedoing around the kitchen while Gram and I snapped peas from the garden for dinner.

Bailey said, "I know you know where she is, Gram."

"How could I know, Bails?" Gram replied.

"Yeah, how could she know, Bails?" I repeated. I hated when Gram and Bailey fought, and sensed things were about to blow.

Bailey said, "I could go after her. I could find her. I could bring her back." She grabbed a pod, putting the whole thing, shell and all, into her mouth.

"You couldn't find her, and you couldn't bring her back either." Big stood in the doorway, his words filled the room like gospel. I had no idea how long he'd been listening.

Bailey went to him. "How do you know that?"

"Because I've tried, Bailey."

Gram and I stopped snapping and looked up at Big. He hulked over to the table and sat in a kitchen chair, looking like a giant in a kindergarten classroom. "I hired a detective a few years back, a good one, figured I would tell you all if he came up with something, but he didn't. He said it's the easiest thing to be lost if you don't want to be found. He thinks Paige changed her name and probably changes her social security number if she moves . . ." Big strummed his fingers on the table—it sounded like little claps of thunder.

"How do we even know she's alive?" Big said under his breath, but we all heard it as if he hollered it from the mountaintop. Strangely, this had never occurred to me and I don't think it had ever occurred to Bailey either. We were always told she would be back and we believed it, deeply.

"She's alive, she's most certainly alive," Gram said to Big. "And she will be back."

I saw suspicion dawn again on Bailey's face.

"How do you know, Gram? You must know something if you're so sure."

"A mother knows, okay? She just does." With that, Gram left the room.

I put the card back in the desk drawer, take St. Anthony with me, and get into bed. I put him on the nightstand. Why was she keeping so many secrets from me? And how in the world can I possibly be mad at her about it now? About anything. Even for a moment.

Bailey and I didn't talk too much
about Gram's spells,
what she called her Private Times,
days spent in the art room
without break.
It was just a part of things,
like green summer leaves,
burning up in fall.
I'd peek through the crack in the door,
see her surrounded by easels
of green women, half formed—
the paint still wet and hungry.
She'd work on them all at once,
and soon, she'd begin
to look like one of them too,
all that green spattered on her clothes,
her hands, her face.
Bails and I would pack
our own brown bags those days,
would pull out our sandwiches at noon,
hating the disappointment of a world
where polka-dotted scarves,
sheets of music, blue feathers,
didn't surprise us at lunch.

After school, we'd bring her tea
or a sliced apple with cheese,
but it'd just sit on the table, untouched.
Big would tell us to ride it out—
that everyone needs a break
from the routine now and then.
So we did—
it was like Gram would go
on vacation with her ladies
and like them
would get caught somewhere
between here and there.

(Found on a brown paper bag in Lennie's clarinet case)

Len, you awake?

Yeah.

Let's do Mom.

Okay, I'll start. She's in Rome—

She's always in Rome lately—

Well, now she's a famous Roman pizza chef and it's late at night, the restaurant just closed and she's drinking a glass of wine with—

With Luigi, the drop-dead gorgeous waiter, they just grabbed the bottle of wine and are walking through the moonlit streets, it's hot, and when they come to a fountain she takes off her shoes and jumps in . . .

Luigi doesn't even take off his shoes, just jumps in and splashes her, they're laughing. . .

But standing in the fountain under the big, bright moon makes her think of Flying Man's, how she used to swim at night with Big . . .

You really think so, Bails? You really think she's in a fountain in Rome on a hot summer night with gorgeous Luigi and thinking about us? About Big?

Sure.

No way.

We're thinking about her.

That's different.

Why?

Because we're not in a fountain in Rome on a hot summer night with gorgeous Luigi.

True.

Night, Bails.

(Found on a piece of notebook paper balled up in a shoe in Lennie's closet)

chapter 15

THE DAY EVERYTHING happens begins like all others lately with Joe's soft knock. I roll over, peek out the window, and see only the lawn through the morning fog. Everything must have been moved back into the house after I'd gone to sleep.

I go downstairs, find Gram sitting at her seat at the kitchen table, her hair wrapped in a towel. She has her hands around a mug of coffee and is staring at Bailey's chair. I sit down next to her. "I'm really sorry about last night," I say. "I know how much you wanted to do a ritual for Bailey, for us."

"It's okay, Len, we'll do one. We have plenty of time." She takes my hand with one of hers, rubs it absentmindedly with the other. "And anyway, I think I figured out what was causing the bad luck."

"Yeah?" I say. "What?"

"You know that mask Big brought back from South America when he was studying those trees. I think that it might have a curse on it."

I've always hated that mask. It has fake hair all over it, eyebrows that arch in astonishment, and a mouth baring shiny, wolfish teeth. "It always gave me the creeps," I tell her. "Bailey too."

Gram nods but she seems distracted. I don't think she's really listening to me, which couldn't be more unlike her lately.

"Lennie," she says tentatively. "Is everything okay between you and Toby?"

My stomach clenches. "Of course," I say, swallowing hard, trying to make my voice sound casual. "Why?" She owl-eyes me.

"Don't know, you both seemed funny last night around each other." Ugh. Ugh. Ugh.

"And I keep wondering why Sarah isn't coming around. Did you get in a fight?" she says to further send me into a guilt spiral.

Just then, Big and Joe come in, saving me. Big says, "We thought we saw life in spider number six today."

Joe says, "I swear I saw a flutter."

"Almost had a heart attack, Joe here, practically launched through the roof, but it must have been a breeze, little guy's still dead as a doornail. The Lennie plant's still languishing too. I might have to rethink things, maybe add a UV light."

"Hey," Joe says, coming behind me, dropping a hand to my shoulder. I look up at the warmth in his face and smile at him. I think he could make me smile even while I was hanging at the gallows, which I'm quite certain I'm headed for. I put my hand over his for a second, see Gram notice this as she gets up to make us breakfast.

I feel somehow responsible for the scrambled ashes that we are all shoveling into our mouths, as if I've somehow derailed the path to healing that our household was on yesterday morning. Joe and Big banter on about resurrecting bugs and exploding cakes—the conversation that would not die—while I actively avoid Gram's suspicious gaze.

"I need to get to work early today, we're catering the Dwyers' party tonight." I say this to my plate but can see Gram nodding in my periphery. She knows because she's been asked to help with the flower arrangements. She's asked all the time to oversee flower arrangements for parties and weddings but rarely says yes because she hates cut flowers. We all knew not to prune her bushes or cut her blooms under penalty of death. She probably said yes this time just to get out of the house for an afternoon. Sometimes I imagine the poor gardeners all over town this summer without Gram, standing in their yards, scratching their heads at their listless wisteria, their forlorn fuchsias.

Joe says, "I'll walk you to work. I need to go to the music store anyway." All the Fontaine boys are supposedly working for their parents this summer, who've converted a barn into a workshop where his dad makes specialty guitars, but I get the impression they spend all day working on new songs for their band Dive.

We embark on the seven-block walk to town, which looks like it's going to take two hours because Joe comes to a standstill every time he has something to say, which is every three seconds.

"You can't walk and talk at the same time, can you?" I ask.

He stops in his tracks, says "Nope." Then continues on for a minute in silence until he can't take it anymore and stops, turns to me, takes my arm, forcing me to stop, while he tells me how I have to go to Paris, how we'll play music in the metro, make tons of money, eat only chocolate croissants, drink red wine, and stay up all night every night because no one ever sleeps in Paris. I can hear his heart beating the whole time and I'm thinking, *Why not?* I could step out of this sad life like it's an old sorry dress, and go to Paris with Joe—we could get on a plane and fly over the ocean and land in *France*. We could do it today even. I have money saved. I have a beret. A hot black bra. I know how to say *Je t'aime*. I love coffee and chocolate and Baudelaire. And I've watched Bailey enough to know how to wrap a scarf. We could really do it, and the possibility makes me feel so giddy I think I might catapult into the air. I tell him so. He takes my hand and puts his other arm up Superman-style.

"You see, I was right," he says with a smile that could power the state of California.

"God, you're gorgeous," I blurt out and want to die because I can't believe I said it aloud and neither can he—his smile, so huge now, he can't even get any words past it.

He stops again. I think he's going to go on about Paris some more—but he doesn't. I look up at him. His face is serious like it was last night in the woods.

"Lennie," he whispers.

I look into his sorrowless eyes and a door in my heart blows open.

And when we kiss, I see that on the other side of that door is sky.

chapter 16

I can't shove the dark out of my head

(*Found written*
on the bench outside of Maria's Italian Deli)

I MAKE A million lasagnas in the window at the deli, listening to Maria gossip with customer after customer, then come home to find Toby lying on my bed. The house is still as stone with Gram at the Dwyers' and Big at work. I punched Toby's number into my phone ten times today, but stopped each time before pressing send. I was going to tell him I couldn't see him. Not after promising Bailey. Not after kissing Joe. Not after Gram's inquisition. Not after reaching into myself and finding some semblance of conscience. I was going to tell him that we had to stop this, had to think how it would make Bailey feel, how bad it makes us feel. I was going to tell him all these things, but didn't because each time I was about to complete the call, I got transported back to the moment by his truck last night and that same inexplicable recklessness and hunger would overtake me until the phone was closed and lying silent on the counter before me.

"Hi, you." His voice is deep and dark and unglues me instantly.

I'm moving toward him, unable not to, the pull, unavoidable, tidal. He gets up quickly, meets me halfway across the room. For one split second we face each other; it's like diving into a mirror. And then I feel his mouth crushing into mine, teeth and tongue and lips and all his raging sorrow crashing right into mine, all our raging sorrow together now crashing into the world that did this to us. I'm frantic as my fingers unbutton his shirt, slip it off his shoulders, then my hands are on his chest, his back, his neck, and I think he must have eight hands because one is taking off my shirt, another two are holding my face while he kisses me, one is running through my hair, another two are on my breasts, a few are pulling my hips to his and then the last undoes the button on my jeans, unzips the fly and we are on the bed, his hand edging its way between my legs, and that is when I hear the front door slam shut—

We freeze and our eyes meet—a midair collision of shame: All the wreckage explodes inside me. I can't bear it. I cover my face with my hands, hear myself groan. What am I doing? What did we almost do? I want to press the rewind button. Press it and press it and press it. But I can't think about that now, can only think about not getting caught in this bed with Toby.

"Hurry," I say, and it unfreezes and de-panics both of us.

He springs to his feet and I scramble across the floor like a crazed crab, put on my shirt, throw Toby his. We're both dressing at warp speed—

"No more," I say, fumbling with the buttons on my shirt, feeling criminal and wrong, full of ick and shame. "Please."

He's straightening the bedding, frenetically puffing pillows, his face flushed and wild, blond hair flying in every direction. "I'm sorry, Len—"

"It doesn't make me miss her less, not anymore." I sound half resolute, half frantic. "It makes it worse."

He stops what he's doing, nods, his face a wrestling match of competing emotions, but it looks like hurt is winning out. God, I don't want to hurt him, but I don't want to do this anymore either. I can't. And what is *this* anyway? Being with him just now didn't feel like the safe harbor it did before—it was different, desperate, like two people struggling for breath.

"John Lennon," I hear from downstairs. "You home?"

This can't be happening, it can't. Nothing used to happen to me, nothing at all for seventeen years and now everything at once. Joe is practically singing my name, he sounds so elated, probably still riding high from that kiss, that sublime kiss that could make stars fall into your open hands, a kiss like Cathy and Heathcliff must have had on the moors with the sun beating on their backs and the world streaming with wind and possibility. A kiss so unlike the fearsome tornado that moments before ripped through Toby and me.

Toby is dressed and sitting on my bed, his shirt hanging over his lap. I wonder why he doesn't tuck it in, then realize he's trying to cover a freaking hard-on—oh God, who am I? How could I have let this get so out of hand? And why doesn't my family do anything normal like carry house keys and lock front doors?

I make sure I'm buttoned and zipped. I smooth my hair and wipe my lips before I swing open the bedroom door and stick my head out just as Joe is barreling down the hallway. He smiles wildly, looks like love itself stuffed into a pair of jeans, black T-shirt, and backward baseball cap.

"Come over tonight. They're all going to the city for some jazz show." He's out of breath—I bet he ran all the way here. "Couldn't wait . . ." He reaches for my hand, takes it in his, then sees Toby sitting on the bed behind me. First he drops my hand, and then the impossible happens: Joe Fontaine's face shuts like a door.

"Hey," he says to Toby, but his voice is pinched and wary.

"Toby and I were just going through some of Bailey's things," I blurt out. I can't believe I'm using Bailey to lie to Joe to cover up fooling around with her boyfriend. A new low even for the immoral girl I've become. I'm a Gila monster of a girl. Loch Ness Lennie. No convent would even take me.

Joe nods, mollified by that, but he's still looking at me and Toby and back again with suspicion. It's as if someone hit the dimmer switch and turned down his whole being.

Toby stands up. "I need to get home." He crosses the room, his carriage slumped, his gait awkward, uncertain. "Good seeing you again," he mumbles at Joe. "I'll see you soon, Len." He slips past us, sad as rain, and I feel terrible. My heart follows after him a few paces, but then it ricochets back to Joe, who stands before me without a trace of death anywhere on him.

"Lennie, is there—"

I have a pretty good idea what Joe is about to ask and so I do the only thing I can think of to stop the question from coming out of his mouth: I kiss him. I mean *really* kiss him, like I've wanted to do since that very first day in band. No sweet soft peck about it. With the same lips that just kissed someone else, I kiss away his question, his suspicion, and after a while, I kiss away the someone else too, the something else that almost just happened, until it is only the two of us, Joe and me, in the room, in the world, in my crazy swelling heart.

Holy horses.

I put aside for a moment the fact that I've turned into a total strumpet-harlot-trollop-wench-jezebel-tart-harridan-chippy-nymphet because I've just realized something incredible. *This is it*—what all the hoopla is about, what *Wuthering Heights* is about—it all boils down to this feeling rushing through me in this moment with Joe as our mouths refuse to part. Who knew all this time I was one kiss away from being Cathy and Juliet and Elizabeth Bennet and Lady Chatterley!?

Years ago, I was crashed in Gram's garden and Big asked me what I was doing. I told him I was looking up at the sky. He said, "That's a misconception, Lennie, the sky is everywhere, it begins at your feet."

Kissing Joe, I believe this, for the first time in my life.

I feel delirious, Joelirious, I think as I pull away for a moment, and open my eyes to see that the Joe Fontaine dimmer switch has been cranked back up again and that he is Joelirious too.

"That was—" I can hardly form words.

"Incredible," he interrupts. "Fucking *incroyable*."

We're staring at each other, stunned.

"Sure," I say, suddenly remembering he invited me over tonight.

"Sure what?" He looks at me like I'm speaking Swahili, then smiles and puts his arms around me, says, "Ready?" He lifts me off my feet and spins me around and I am suddenly in the dorkiest movie ever, laughing and feeling a happiness so huge I am ashamed to be feeling it in a world without my sister.

"Sure, I'll come over tonight," I say as everything stops spinning and I land back on my own two feet.

chapter 17

What's wrong, Lennie?
Nothing.
Tell me.
No.
C'mon, spill it.
Okay. It's just that you're different now.
How?
Like Zombieville.
I'm in love, Len—I've never felt like this before.
Like what?
Like forever.
Forever?
Yeah, this is it. He's it.
How do you know?
My toes told me. The toes knows.

(Found on a napkin stuffed in a mug, Cecilia's Bakery)

"I'M GOING OVER to Joe's," I say to Gram and Big, who are both home now, camped out in the kitchen, listening to a baseball game on the radio, circa 1930.

"That sounds like a plan," Gram says. She's taken the still despairing Lennie houseplant out from under the pyramid and is sitting beside it at the table, singing to it softly, something about greener pastures. "I'll just freshen up and get my bag, sweet pea."

She can't be serious.

"I'll go too," says Big, who is hunched over a crossword puzzle. He's the fastest puzzler in all Christendom. I look over and note, however, that this time he's putting numbers in the boxes instead of letters. "As soon as I finish this, we can all head up to the Fontaines'."

"Uh, I don't think so," I say.

They both look up at me, incredulous.

Big says, "What do you mean, Len, he's here every single morning, it's only fair that—"

And then he can't keep it up anymore and bursts out laughing, as does Gram. I'm relieved. I had actually started to imagine trucking up the hill with Gram and Big in tow: the Munsters follow Marilyn on a date.

"Why, Big, she's all dressed up. And her hair's down. Look at her." This is a problem. I was going for the short flowery dress and heels and lipstick and wild hair look that no one would notice is any different from the jeans, ponytail, and no makeup look I've mastered every other day of my life. I know I'm blushing, also know I better get out of the house before I run back upstairs and challenge Bailey's Guinness-Book-of-

Changing-Clothes-Before-a-Date record of thirty-seven out-fits. This was only my eighteenth, but clothes-changing is an exponential activity, the frenzy only builds, it's a law of nature. Even St. Anthony peering at me from the nightstand, remind-ing me of what I'd found in the drawer last night, couldn't snap me out of it. I'd remembered something about him though. He was like Bailey, charismatic as all get out. He had to give his sermons in marketplaces because he overflowed even the largest of churches. When he died all the church bells in Padua rang of their own accord. Everyone thought angels had come to earth.

"Good-bye, you guys," I say to Gram and Big, and head for the door.

"Have fun, Len . . . and not too late, okay?"

I nod, and am off on the first real date of my life. The other nights I've had with boys don't count, not the ones with Toby I'm actively trying not to think about, and definitely not the parties, after which I'd spent the next day, week, month, year thinking of ways to get my kisses back. Nothing has been like this, nothing has made me feel like I do right now walking up the hill to Joe's, like I have a window in my chest where sun-light is pouring in.

When
Joe
plays
his
horn
I
fall

out
of
my
chair
and
onto
my

knees
When
he
plays
all
the
flowers

swap
colors
and
years
and
decades
and

centuries
of
rain
pour
back
into
the
sky

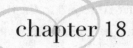

chapter 18

THE FEELING I had earlier today with Joe in The Sanctum overwhelms me the moment I see him sitting on the stoop of the big white house playing his guitar. He's bent over it, singing softly, and the wind is carrying his words through the air like fluttering leaves.

"Hey, John Lennon," he says, putting aside his guitar, standing up and jumping off the front step. "Uh-oh. You look *vachement* amazing. Too good to be alone with me all night long." He's practically leaping over. His delight quotient mesmerizes me. At the human factory, someone must have messed up and just slipped him more than the rest of us. "I've been thinking about a duet we could do. I just need to rearrange—"

I'm not listening anymore. I hope he just keeps talking up a storm, because I can't

(Found on the bathroom wall, music room, Clover High)

utter a word. I know the expression *love bloomed* is metaphorical, but in my heart in this moment, there is one badass flower, captured in time-lapse photography, going from bud to wild radiant blossom in ten seconds flat.

"You okay?" he asks. His hands are on either side of my arms and he's peering into my face.

"Yes." I'm wondering how people breathe in these situations. "I'm fine."

"You are *fine*," he says, looking me over like a major dork, which immediately snaps me out of my love spell.

"Ugh, *quel dork*," I say, pushing him away.

He laughs and slips his arm around my shoulders. "C'mon, you enter Maison Fontaine at your own risk."

The first thing I notice about Maison Fontaine is that the phone is ringing and Joe doesn't seem to notice. I hear a girl's voice on an answering machine far away in another room and think for a minute it sounds like Rachel before deciding it doesn't. The second thing I notice is how opposite this house is to Maison Walker. Our house looks like Hobbits live there. The ceilings are low, the wood is dark and gnarly, colorful rag rugs line the floors, paintings, the walls, whereas Joe's house floats high in the sky with the clouds. There are windows everywhere that reveal sunburned fields swimming in the wind, dark green woods that cloister the river, and the river itself as it wends from town to town in the distance. There are no tables piled with weeks of mail, shoes kicked around under furniture, books open on every surface. Joe lives in a museum. Hanging all over the walls are gorgeous guitars of every color, shape, and size. They look so animate, like they could make music all by themselves.

"Pretty cool, huh? My dad makes amazing instruments. Not just guitars either. Mandolins, lutes, dulcimers," he says as I ogle one and then the next.

And now for something completely different: Joe's room. The physical manifestation of chaos theory. It's overflowing with instruments I've never seen before and can't even imagine what kind of sound they'd make, CDs, music magazines, library books in French and English, concert posters of French bands I've never heard of, comic books, notebooks with tiny boxlike weirdo boy writing in them, sheets of music, stereo equipment unplugged and plugged, broken-open amps and other sound equipment I don't recognize, odd rubber animals, bowls of blue marbles, decks of cards, piles of clothes as high as my knee, not to mention the dishes, bottles, glasses . . . and over his desk a small poster of John Lennon.

"Hmm," I say, pointing to the poster. I look around, taking it all in. "I think your room is giving me new insight into Joe Fontaine aka freaking madman."

"Yeah, thought it best to wait to show you the bombroom until . . ."

"Until what?"

"I don't know, until you realized . . ."

"Realized what?"

"I don't know, Lennie." I can see he's embarrassed. Somehow things have turned uncomfortable.

"Tell me," I say. "Wait until I realized what?"

"Nothing, it's stupid." He looks down at his feet, then back up at me. Bat. Bat. Bat.

"I want to know," I say.

"Okay, I'll say it: Wait until you realized that maybe you liked me too."

The flower is blooming again in my chest, this time three seconds from bud to showstopper.

"I do," I say, and then without thinking, add, "A lot." What's gotten into me? Now I really can't breathe. A situation made worse by the lips that are suddenly pressing into mine.

Our tongues have fallen madly in love and gotten married and moved to Paris.

After I'm sure I've made up for all my former years of kiss-lessness, I say, "I think if we don't stop kissing, the world is going to explode."

"Seems like it," he whispers. He's staring dreamily into my eyes. Heathcliff and Cathy have nothing on us. "We can do something else for a while," he says. "If you want . . ." He smiles. And then: Bat. Bat. Bat. I wonder if I am going to survive the night.

"Want to play?" he asks.

"I do," I tell him, "but I didn't bring my instrument."

"I'll get one." He leaves the room, which gives me a chance to recover, and unfortunately, to think about what happened with Toby earlier. How scary and out of control it was today, like we were trying to break each other apart. But why? To find Bailey? To wrench her from the other's heart? The other's body? Or was it something worse? Were we trying to forget her, to wipe out her memory for one passionate moment? But no, it's not that, it can't be, can it? When we're together, Bailey's all around us like air we can breathe; that's been the comfort until today, until it got so out of hand. I don't know. The only thing I do know is that it's all about her, because even now if I imagine Toby alone with his heartache while I am here with Joe obliterating my own, I feel guilty, like I've abandoned him, and with him, my grief, and with my grief, my sister.

The phone rings again and it mercifully ejects me from these thoughts, and crash-lands me back into the bombroom—this room where Joe sleeps in this unmade bed and reads these books strewn everywhere and drinks out of these five hundred half-full glasses seemingly at once. I feel giddy with the intimacy of being where he thinks and dreams, where he changes his clothes and flings them absolutely all over the place, where he's naked. *Joe, naked*. The thought of it, him, all of him— *guh*. I've never even seen a real live guy totally naked, ever. Only some Internet porn Sarah and I devoured for a while. That's it. I've always been scared of seeing all, seeing *it*. The first time Sarah saw one hard, she said more animal names came flying out of her mouth in that one moment than all other moments in her life combined. Not animals you'd think either. No pythons and eels. According to her it was a full-on menagerie: hippos, elephants, orangutans, tapirs, gazelles, etc.

All of a sudden I'm walloped with missing her. How could I be in Joe Fontaine's freaking bedroom without her knowing? How could I have blown her off like this? I take out my phone, text: *Call back the search party. Please. Forgive.*

I look around again, curbing all impulses to go through drawers, peek under the bed, read the notebook lying open at my feet. Okay, I curb two out of three of those impulses. It's been a bad day for morality. And it's not really reading someone's journal if it's open and you can glance down and make out your name, well, your name to him, in a sentence that says . . .

I bend my knees, and without touching the notebook in any way, read just the bit around the initials JL.

I'VE NEVER MET ANYONE AS HEARTBROKEN AS JL, I WANT TO MAKE HER FEEL BETTER, WANT TO BE AROUND HER ALL THE TIME, IT'S CRAZY, IT'S LIKE SHE'S ON FULL BLAST, AND EVERYONE ELSE IS JUST ON MUTE, AND SHE'S HONEST, SO HONEST, NOTHING LIKE GENEVIEVE, NOTHING AT ALL LIKE GENEVIEVE . . .

I hear his steps in the hall, stand up. The phone is ringing yet again.

He comes back with two clarinets, a B flat and a bass, holds them up. I go for the soprano like I'm used to.

"What's the deal with the phone?" I say, instead of saying *Who's Genevieve?* Instead of falling to my knees and confessing that I'm anything but honest, that I'm probably just exactly like Genevieve, whoever she is, but without the exotic French part.

He shrugs. "We get a lot of calls," he says, then begins his tuning ritual that makes everything in the world but him and a handful of chords disappear.

The untapped duet of guitar and clarinet is awkward at first. We stumble around in sound, fall over each other, look up embarrassed, try again. But after a while, we begin to click and when we don't know where the other is going, we lock eyes and listen so intently that for fleeting moments it's like our souls are talking. One time after I improvise alone for a while, he exclaims, "Your tone is awesome, so so lonely, like, I don't know, a day without birds or something," but I don't feel lonely at all. I feel like Bailey is listening.

"WELL, YOU'RE NO different late at night, exactly the same John Lennon." We're sitting on the grass, drinking some wine Joe swiped from his father. The front door is open and a French chanteuse is blasting out of it into the warm night. We're swigging out of the bottle and eating cheese and a baguette. I'm finally in France with Joe, I think, and it makes me smile.

"What?" he asks.

"I don't know. This is nice. I've never drunk wine before."

"I have my whole life. My dad mixed it with water for us when we were little."

"Really? Drunken little Fontaine boys running into walls?"

He laughs. "Yup, exactly. That's my theory of why French children are so well behaved. They're drunk off their *petits mignons* asses most of the time." He tips the bottle and takes a sip, passes it to me.

"Are both your parents French?"

"Dad is, born and raised in Paris. My mom's from around here originally. But Dad makes up for it, he's Central Casting French." There's a bitterness in his voice, but I don't pursue it. I've only just recovered from the consequences of my snooping, have almost forgotten about Genevieve and the importance of honesty to Joe, when he says, "Ever been in love?" He's lying on his back, looking up at a sky reeling with stars.

I don't holler, *Yes, right now, with you, stupid,* like I suddenly want to, but say, "No. I've never been anything."

He gets up on one elbow, looks over at me. "What do you mean?"

I sit, hugging my knees, looking out at the spattering of lights down in the valley.

"It's like I was sleeping or something, happy, but sleeping, for seventeen years, and then Bailey died . . ." The wine has made it easier to talk but I don't know if I'm making any sense. I look over at Joe. He's listening to me so carefully, like he wants to catch my words in his hands as they fall from my lips.

"And now?"

"Well, now I don't know. I feel so different." I pick up a pebble and toss it into the darkness. I think how things used to be: predictable, sensible. How I used to be the same. I think how there is no inevitability, how there never was, I just didn't know it then. "I'm awake, I guess, and maybe that's good, but it's more complicated than that because now I'm someone who knows the worst thing can happen at any time."

Joe's nodding like I'm making sense, which is good, because I have no idea what I just said. I know what I meant though. I meant that I know now how close death is. How it lurks. And who wants to know that? Who wants to know we are just one carefree breath away from the end? Who wants to know that the person you love and need the most can just vanish forever?

He says, "But if you're someone who knows the worst thing can happen at any time, aren't you also someone who knows the best thing can happen at any time too?"

I think about this and instantly feel elated. "Yeah, that's right," I say. "Like right now with you, actually . . ." It's out of my mouth before I can stop it, and I see the delight wash across his face.

"Are we drunk?" I ask.

He takes another swig. "Quite possibly."

"Anyway, have you ever . . ."

"I've never experienced anything like what you're going through."

"No, I mean, have you ever been in love?" My stomach clenches. I want him to say no so badly, but I know he won't, and he doesn't.

"Yeah, I was. I guess." He shakes his head. "I think so anyway."

"What happened?"

A siren sounds in the distance. Joe sits up. "During the summers, I boarded at school. I walked in on her and my roommate, killed me. I mean really killed me. I never talked to her again, or him, threw myself into music in kind of an insane way, swore off girls, well, until now, I guess . . ." He smiles, but not like usual. There's a vulnerability in it, a hesitancy; it's all over his face, swimming around in his beautiful green eyes too. I shut my eyes to not have to see it, because all I can think about is how he almost walked in on Toby and me today.

Joe grabs the bottle of wine and drinks. "Moral of the story: Violinists are insane. I think it's that crazy-ass bow." Genevieve, the gorgeous French violinist. Ugh.

"Yeah? What about clarinetists?"

He smiles. "The most soulful." He trails his finger across my face, forehead to cheek to chin, then down my neck. "And so beautiful." Oh my, I totally get why King Edward VIII of

England abdicated his throne for love. If I had a throne, I'd abdicate it just to relive the last three seconds.

"And horn players?" I ask, intertwining my fingers with his.

He shakes his head. "Crazy hellions, steer clear. All-or-nothing types, no middle ground for the blowhards." Uh-oh. "Never want to cross a horn player," he adds flippantly, but I don't hear it flippantly. I can't believe I lied to him today. I have to stay away from Toby. Far away.

A pair of coyotes howl in the distance, sending a shiver up my spine. Nice timing, dogs.

"Didn't know you horn guys were so scary," I say, letting go of his hand and taking a swig off the bottle. "And guitarists?"

"You tell me."

"Hmm, let me think . . ." I trail my finger over his face this time. "Homely and boring, and of course, talentless—" He cracks up. "I'm not done. But they make up for all that because they are so, so passionate—"

"Oh, God," he whispers, reaching his hand behind my neck and bringing my lips to his. "Let's let the whole fucking world explode this time."

And we do.

chapter 19

I'M LYING IN bed, hearing voices.

"What do you think is wrong with her?"

"Not sure. Could be the orange walls getting to her." A pause, then I hear: "Let's think about it logically. Symptoms: still in bed at noon on a sunny Saturday, goofy grin on her face, stains on her lips likely from red wine, a beverage she's not allowed to drink, which we will address later, and the giveaway, still in her clothes, a dress I might add, with flowers on it."

"Well, my expert opinion, which I draw from vast experience and five glorious, albeit flawed marriages, is that Lennie Walker aka John Lennon is out of her mind in love."

Big and Gram are smiling down at me. I feel like Dorothy waking in her bed, surrounded by her Kansans after having been over the rainbow.

"Do you think you're ever going to get up again?" Gram is sitting on the bed now, patting my hand, which is in hers.

"I don't know." I roll over to face her. "I just want to lie here forever and think about him." I haven't decided which is better: experiencing last night, or the blissed-out replay in my mind where I can hit pause and turn ecstatic seconds into whole hours, where I can loop certain moments until the sweet grassy taste of Joe is again in my mouth, the clove scent of his skin is in the air, until I can feel his hands running through my hair, all over my dress, just one thin, thin layer between us, until the moment when he slipped his hands under the fabric and I felt his fingers on my skin like music—all of it sending me again and again right off the cliff that is my heart.

This morning, for the first time, Bailey wasn't my first thought on waking and it had made me feel guilty. But the guilt didn't have much of a chance against the dawning realization that I was falling in love. I had stared out the window at the early-morning fog, wondering for a moment if she had sent Joe to me so I would know that in the same world where she could die, this could happen.

Big says, "Would you look at her. We've got to cut down those damn rosebushes." His hair is particularly coiled and springy today, and his mustache is unwaxed, so it looks like a squirrel is running across his face. In any fairy tale, Big plays the king.

Gram chides him, "Hush now, you don't even believe in that." She doesn't like anyone to perpetuate the rumor about the aphrodisiacal nature of her roses, because there was a time when desperate lovers would come and steal them to try to change the hearts of their beloveds. It made her crazy. There is not much Gram takes more seriously than proper pruning.

Big won't let it go though. "I follow the proof-is-in-the-pudding scientific method: Please examine the empirical evidence in this bed. She's worse than me."

"No one is worse than you, you're the town swain." Gram rolls her eyes.

"You say swain, but imply swine," Big retorts, twisting his squirrel for effect.

I sit up in bed, lean my back against the sill to better enjoy their verbal tennis match. I can feel the summery day through the window, deliciously warming my back. But when I look over at Bailey's bed, I'm leveled. How can something this momentous be happening to me without her? And what about all the momentous things to come? How will I go through each and every one of them without her? I don't care that she was keeping things from me—I want to tell her absolutely everything about last night, about everything that will ever happen to me! I'm crying before I even realize it, but I don't want us all to tailspin, so I swallow and swallow it all down, and try to focus on last night, on falling in love. I spot my clarinet across the room, half covered with the paisley scarf of Bailey's I recently started wearing.

"Joe didn't come by this morning?" I ask, wanting to play again, wanting to blow all this everything I'm feeling out my clarinet.

Big replies, "No, bet a million dollars he's exactly where you are, though he probably has his guitar with him. Have you asked him if he sleeps with it yet?"

"He's a musical genius," I say, feeling my earlier giddiness returning. Without a doubt, I've gone bipolar.

"Oh, jeez. C'mon Gram, she's a lost cause." Big winks at me, then heads for the door.

Gram stays seated next to me, ruffling my hair like I'm a

little kid. She's looking at me closely and a little too long. Oh no. I've been in such a trance, I forget that I haven't really been talking to Gram lately, that we've hardly been alone like this in weeks.

"Len." This is definitely her Gramouncement tone, but I don't think it's going to be about Bailey. About expressing my feelings. About packing up Bailey's things. About going to the city for lunch. About resuming my lessons. About all the things I haven't wanted to do.

"Yeah?"

"We talked about birth control, diseases and all that . . ." Phew. This one's harmless.

"Yeah, like a million times."

"Okay, just as long as you haven't suddenly forgotten it all."

"Nope."

"Good." She's patting my hand again.

"Gram, there's no need yet, okay?" I feel the requisite blush from revealing this, but better to not have her freaking out about it and constantly questioning me.

"Even better, even better," she says, the relief evident in her voice, and it makes me think. Things with Joe last night were intense, but they were paced to savor. Not so with Toby. I worry what might've happened if we weren't interrupted. Would I have had the sense to stop us? Would he have? All I know is that everything was happening really quickly, I was totally out of control, and condoms were the furthest thing from my mind. God. How did that happen? How did Toby Shaw's hands ever end up on my breasts? *Toby's!* And only hours before Joe's. I want to dive under the bed, make it my permanent residence. How did I go from bookworm and band geek to two-guys-in-the-same-day hussy?

Gram smiles, oblivious of the sudden bile rising in my throat, the twisting in my guts. She ruffles my hair again. "In the middle of all this tragedy, you're growing up, sweet pea, and that is such a wonderful thing."

Groan.

chapter 20

"Lennie! Lennie! Lennnnnnnnnnie! God, I've missed you!" I
pull the cell phone away from my ear. Sarah hadn't texted me
back, so I assumed she was really pissed. I cut in to say so, and
she responds, "I *am* furious! And I'm *not* speaking to you!" then
she launches into all the summer gossip I've missed. I soak it
up but can tell there was some true vitriol in her words. I'm
lying on my bed, wiped after practicing Cavallini's Adagio and
Tarantella for two straight hours—it was incredible, like turning the air into colors. It made me think of the Charlie Parker
quote Mr. James liked to repeat: *If you don't live it, it can't come
out of your horn.* It also made me think I might go to summer
band practice after all.

Sarah and I make a plan to meet at Flying Man's. I'm dying
to tell her about Joe. Not about Toby. I'm thinking if I don't
talk about it, I can just pretend it didn't happen.

She's lying on a rock in the sun reading Simone de Beau-
voir's *The Second Sex*—in preparation, I'm sure, for her very
promising guy-poaching expedition to State's Women's Stud-

ies Department feminism symposium. She springs to her feet when she sees me, and hugs me like crazy despite the fact that she's completely naked. We have our own secret pool and mini-falls behind Flying Man's that we've been coming to for years. We've declared it clothing optional and we opt not. "God, it's been forever," she says.

"I'm so sorry, Sarah," I say, hugging her back.

"It's okay, really," she says. "I know I need to give you a free pass right now. So that's . . ." She pulls away for a second, studies my face. "Wait a minute? What's wrong with you? You look weird. I mean *really* weird."

I can't stop smiling. I must look like a Fontaine.

"What, Lennie? What happened?"

"I think I'm falling in love." The moment the words are out of my mouth, I feel my face go hot with shame. I'm supposed to be grieving, not falling in love. Not to mention everything else I've been doing.

"Whaaaaaaaaaaaaaaaaaaaaaaat! That is so unfreakingfreaking-freakingfreakingbelieveable! Cows on the moon, Len! Cows. On. The. Moon!" Well, so much for my shame. Sarah is in full-on cheerleader mode, arms flailing, hopping up and down. Then she stops abruptly. "Wait, with whom? NOT Toby, I hope."

"No, no, of course not," I say as a speeding eighteen-wheeler of guilt flattens me.

"Whew," Sarah, says, sweeping her hand off her brow dramatically. "Who then? Who could you be in love with? You haven't gone anywhere, at least that I know of, and this town is beyond Loserville, so where'd you find him?"

"Sarah, it's Joe."

"It's not."

"Yeah, it is."

"No!"

"Yup."

"Not true."

"Is true."

"Nah-uh, nah-uh, nah-uh."

"Uh-huh, uh-huh, uh-huh."

Etc.

Her previous display of enthusiasm was nothing compared to the one that is going on now. She's doing circles around me, saying, "Oh my God. I am soooooooooooooo jealous. Every girl in Clover is after one Fontaine or another. No wonder you've been a shut-in. I would be too, if I could shut in with one of them. God, let me live vicariously through you. Tell me every freaking detail. That beautiful, beautiful boy, those eyes, those *eyelashes*, that unfreakingbelievable smile, that trumpet playing, wow, Lennnnnnnnnnie." She's pacing now, has lit another cigarette, is chain smoking in glee—a naked smokestack maniac. I'm so happy to be hanging out with the marvel that is my best friend Sarah. And I'm so happy to be happy about it.

I tell her every detail. How he came over every morning with croissants, how we played music together, how he made Gram and Big so happy just by being in the house, how we drank wine last night and kissed until I was sure I had walked right into the sky. I told her how I think I can hear his heart beating even when he's not there, how I feel like flowers—Gramgantuan ones—are blooming in my chest, how I'm sure I feel just the way Heathcliff did for Cathy before—

"Okay, stop for a second." She's still smiling but she looks a bit worried and surprised too. "Lennie, you're not in love, you're demented. I've never heard anyone talk about a guy like this."

I shrug. "Then I'm demented."

"Wow, I want to be demented too." She sits down next to me on the rock. "It's like you've hardly kissed three guys in your whole life and now this. Guess you were saving it up or something . . ."

I tell her my Rip Van Lennie theory of having slept my whole life until recently.

"I don't know, Len. You always seemed awake to me."

"Yeah, I don't know either. It was a wine-induced theory."

Sarah picks up a stone, tosses it into the water with a little too much force. "What?" I ask.

She doesn't answer right away, picks up another stone and hurls it too. "I am mad at you, but I'm not allowed to be, you know?"

It's exactly how I feel toward Bailey sometimes lately.

"You've just been keeping so much from me, Lennie. I thought . . . I don't know."

It's as if she were speaking my lines in a play.

"I'm sorry," I say again feebly. I want to say more, give her an explanation, but the truth is I don't know why I've felt so closed off to her since Bailey died.

"It's okay," she says again quietly.

"It'll be different now," I say, hoping it's true. "Promise."

I look out at the sun courting the river's surface, the green leaves, the wet rocks behind the falls. "Want to go swimming?"

140

"Not yet," she says. "I have news too. Not breaking news, but still." It's a clear dig and I deserve it. I didn't even ask how she was.

She's smirking at me, quite dementedly, actually. "I hooked up with Luke Jacobus last night."

"Luke?" I'm surprised. Besides for his recent lapse in judgment, which resulted in his band-kill status, he's been devotedly, unrequitedly in love with Sarah since second grade. King of the Nerdiverse, she used to call him. "Didn't you make out with him in seventh grade and then drop him when that idiot surfer glistened at you?"

"Yeah, it's probably dumb," she says. "I agreed to do lyrics for this incredible music he wrote, and we were hanging out, and it just happened."

"What about the Jean-Paul Sartre rule?"

"Sense of humor trumps literacy, I've decided—and jumping giraffes, Len, growth geyser, the guy's like the Hulk these days."

"He is funny," I agree. "And green."

She laughs, just as my phone signals a text. I rifle through my bag and take it out hoping for a message from Joe.

Sarah's singing, "Lennie got a love note from a Fontaine," as she tries to read over my shoulder. "C'mon let me see it." She grabs the phone from me. I pull it out of her hands, but it's too late. It says: *I need to talk to you. T.*

"As in Toby?" she asks. "But I thought . . . I mean, you just said . . . Lennie, what're you doing?"

"Nothing," I tell her, shoving the phone back in my bag, already breaking my promise. "Really. Nothing."

"Why don't I believe you?" she says, shaking her head. "I have a bad feeling about this."

"Don't," I say, swallowing my own atrocious feeling. "Really. I'm demented, remember?" I touch her arm. "Let's go swimming."

We float on our backs in the pool for over an hour. I make her tell me everything about her night with Luke so I don't have to think about Toby's text, what might be so urgent. Then we climb up to the falls and get under them, screaming FUCK over and over into the roar like we've done since we were little.

I scream bloody murder.

chapter 21

There were once two sisters
who were not afraid of the dark
because the dark was full of the other's voice
across the room,
because even when the night was thick
and starless
they walked home together from the river
seeing who could last the longest
without turning on her flashlight,
not afraid
because sometimes in the pitch of night
they'd lie on their backs
in the middle of the path
and look up until the stars came back
and when they did,
they'd reach their arms up to touch them
and did.

(Found on an envelope stuck
under the tire of a car on Main Street)

By the time I walk home from the river through the woods, I've decided Toby, like me, feels terrible about what happened, hence the urgency of the text. He probably just wants to make sure it will never happen again. Well, agreed. No argument from demented ol' moi.

Clouds have gathered and the air feels thick with the possibility of a rare summer rain. I see a to-go cup on the ground, so I sit down, write a few lines on it, and then bury it under a mound of pine needles. Then I lie down on my back on the spongy forest floor. I love doing this—giving it all up to the enormity of the sky, or to the ceiling if the need arises while I'm indoors. As I reach my hands out and press my fingers into the loamy soil, I start wondering what I'd be doing right now, what I'd be feeling right this minute if Bailey were still alive. I realize something that scares me: I'd be happy, but in a mild kind of way, nothing demented about it. I'd be turtling along, like I always turtled, huddled in my shell, safe and sound.

But what if I'm a shell-less turtle now, demented and devastated in equal measure, an unfreakingbelievable mess of a girl, who wants to turn the air into colors with her clarinet, and what if somewhere inside I prefer this? What if as much as I fear having death as a shadow, I'm beginning to like how it quickens the pulse, not only mine, but the pulse of the whole world. I doubt Joe would even have noticed me if I'd still been in that hard shell of mild happiness. He wrote in his journal that he thinks I'm on full blast, *me,* and maybe I am now, but I never was before. How can the cost of this change in me be so great? It doesn't seem right that anything good should come out of Bailey's death. It doesn't seem right to even have these thoughts.

But then I think about my sister and what a shell-less turtle she was and how she wanted me to be one too. *C'mon, Lennie,* she used to say to me at least ten times a day. *C'mon, Len.* And that makes me feel better, like it's her life rather than her death that is now teaching me how to be, who to be.

I KNOW TOBY'S there even before I go inside, because Lucy and Ethel are camped out on the porch. When I walk into the kitchen, I see him and Gram sitting at the table talking in hushed voices.

"Hi," I say, dumbfounded. Doesn't he realize he can't be here?

"Lucky me," Gram says. "I was walking home with armfuls of groceries and Toby came whizzing by on his skateboard." Gram hasn't driven since the 1900s. She walks everywhere in Clover, which is how she became Garden Guru. She couldn't help herself, started carrying her shears on her trips to town and people would come home and find her pruning their bushes to perfection: ironic yes, because of her hands-off policy with her own garden.

"Lucky," I say to Gram as I take in Toby. Fresh scrapes cover his arms, probably from wiping out on his board. He looks wild-eyed and disheveled, totally unmoored. I know two things in this moment: I was wrong about the text and I don't want to be unmoored with him anymore.

What I really want is to go up to The Sanctum and play my clarinet.

Gram looks at me, smiles. "You swam. Your hair looks like a cyclone. I'd like to paint it." She reaches her hand up and touches my cyclone. "Toby's going to have dinner with us."

I can't believe this. "I'm not hungry," I say. "I'm going upstairs."

Gram gasps at my rudeness, but I don't care. Under no circumstances am I sitting through dinner with Toby, *who touched my breasts,* and Gram and Big. What is he thinking?

I go up to The Sanctum, unpack and assemble my clarinet, then take out the Edith Piaf sheet music that I borrowed from a certain garçon, turn to "La Vie en Rose," and start playing. It's the song we listened to last night while the world exploded. I'm hoping I can just stay lost in a state of Joeliriousness, and I won't hear a knock at my door after they eat, but of course, I do.

Toby, *who touched my breasts and let's not forget put his hand down my pants too,* opens the door, walks tentatively across the room, and sits on Bailey's bed. I stop playing, rest my clarinet on my stand. Go away, I think heartlessly, just go away. Let's pretend it didn't happen, none of it.

Neither of us says a word. He's rubbing his thighs so intently, I bet the friction is generating heat. His gaze is drifting all around the room. It finally locks on a photograph of Bailey and him on her dresser. He takes a breath, looks over at me. His gaze lingers.

"Her shirt . . ."

I look down. I forgot I had it on. "Yeah." I've been wearing Bailey's clothes more and more outside The Sanctum as well as in it. I find myself going through my own drawers and thinking, Who was the girl who wore these things? I'm sure a shrink would love this, all of it, I think, looking over at Toby. She'd probably tell me I was trying to take Bailey's place. Or worse, competing with her in a way I never could when she was alive. But is that it? It doesn't feel like it. When I wear her clothes, I just feel safer, like she's whispering in my ear.

I'm lost in thought, so it startles me when Toby says in an uncharacteristic shaky voice, "Len, I'm sorry. About everything." I glance at him. He looks so vulnerable, frightened. "I got way out of control, feel so bad." Is this what he needed to tell me? Relief tumbles out of my chest.

"Me too," I say, thawing immediately. We're in this together.

"Me more, trust me," he says, rubbing his thighs again. He's so distraught. Does he think it's all his fault or something?

"We both did it, Toby," I say. "Each time. We're both horrible."

He looks at me, his dark eyes warm. "You're not horrible, Lennie." His voice is gentle, intimate. I can tell he wants to reach out to me. I'm glad he's across the room. I wish he were across the equator. Do our bodies now think whenever they're together they get to touch? I tell mine that is most definitely not the case, no matter that I feel it again. No matter.

And then a renegade asteroid breaks through the earth's atmosphere and hurtles into The Sanctum: "It's just that I can't stop thinking about you," he says. "I can't. I just . . ." He's balling up Bailey's bedspread in his fists. "I want—"

"Please don't say more." I cross the room to my dresser, open the middle drawer, reach in and pull out a shirt, my shirt. I have to take Bailey's off. Because I'm suddenly thinking that imaginary shrink is spot on.

"It's not me," I say quietly as I open the closet door and slip inside. "I'm not her."

I stay in the dark quiet getting my breathing under control, my life under control, getting my own shirt on my own body. It's like there's a river under my feet tumbling me toward him, still, even with everything that's happened with Joe, a roaring, passionate, despairing river, but I don't want to go this time. I want to stay on the shore. We can't keep wrapping our arms around a ghost.

When I come out of the closet, he's gone.

"I'm so sorry," I say aloud to the empty orange room.

As if in response, thousands of hands begin tapping on the roof. I walk over to my bed, climb up to the window ledge and stick my hands out. Because we only get one or two storms a summer, rain is an event. I lean far over the ledge, palms to the sky, letting it all slip through my fingers, remembering what Big told Toby and me that afternoon. *No way out of this but through.* Who knew what through would be?

I see someone rushing down the road in the downpour. When the figure gets near the lit-up garden I realize it's Joe and am instantly uplifted. My life raft.

"Hey," I yell out and wave like a maniac.

He looks up at the window, smiles, and I can't get down the stairs, out the front door, into the rain and by his side fast enough.

"I missed you," I say, reaching up and touching his cheek with my fingers. Raindrops drip from his eyelashes, stream in rivulets all down his face.

"God, me too." Then his hands are on my cheeks and we

are kissing and the rain is pouring all over our crazy heads and once again my whole being is aflame with joy.

I didn't know love felt like this, like turning into brightness.

"What are you doing?" I say, when I can finally bring myself to pull away for a moment.

"I saw it was raining—I snuck out, wanted to see you, just like this."

"Why'd you have to sneak out?" The rain's drenching us, my shirt clings to me, and Joe's hands to it, rubbing up and down my sides.

"I'm in prison," he says. "Got busted big-time, that wine we drank was like a four-hundred-dollar bottle. I had no idea. I wanted to impress you so took it from downstairs. My dad went ape-shit when he saw the empty bottle—he's making me sort wood all day and night in the workshop while he talks to his girlfriend on the phone the whole time. I think he forgets I speak French."

I'm not sure whether to address the four-hundred-dollar bottle of wine we drank or the girlfriend, decide on the latter. "His girlfriend?"

"Never mind. I had to see you, but now I have to go back, and I wanted to give you this." He pulls a piece of paper out of his pocket, stuffs it quickly into mine before it can get soaked.

He kisses me again. "Okay, I'm leaving." He doesn't move. "I don't want to leave you."

"I don't want you to," I say. His hair's black and snaky all around his glistening face. It's like being in the shower with him. Wow—to be in the shower with him.

He turns to go for real then and I notice his eyes narrow as he peers over my shoulder. "Why's he always here?"

I turn around. Toby's in the doorframe, *watching us*—he looks like he's been hit by a wrecking ball. God. He must not have left, must have been in the art room with Gram or something. He pushes open the door, grabs his skateboard, and rushes past without a word, huddled against the downpour.

"What's going on?" Joe asks, X-raying me with his stare. His whole body has stiffened.

"Nothing. Really," I answer, just as I did with Sarah. "He's upset about Bailey." What else can I tell him? If I tell him what's going on, what went on even after he kissed me, I'll lose him.

So when he says, "I'm being stupid and paranoid?" I just say, "Yeah." And hear in my head: *Never cross a horn player*.

He smiles wide and open as a meadow. "Okay." Then he kisses me hard one last time and we are again drinking the rain off each other's lips. "Bye, John Lennon."

And he's off.

I hurry inside, worrying about what Toby said to me and what I didn't say to Joe, as the rain washes all those beautiful kisses off of me.

chapter 22

I'M LYING DOWN on my bed, holding in my hands the antidote to worrying about anything. It's a sheet of music, still damp from the rain. At the top, it says in Joe's boxlike weirdo boy handwriting: *For a soulful, beautiful clarinetist, from a homely, boring, talentless though passionate guitarist. Part 1, Part 2 to come.*

I try to hear it in my head, but my facility to hear without playing is terrible. I get up, find my clarinet, and moments later the melody spills into the room. I remember as I play what he said about my tone being so lonely, like a day without birds, but it's as if the melody he wrote is nothing but birds and they are flying out of the end of my clarinet and filling the air of a still summer day, filling the trees and sky—it's exquisite. I play it over and over again, until I know it by heart.

It's two a.m. and if I play the song one more time, my fingers will fall off, but I'm too Joelirious to sleep. I go downstairs to get something to eat, and when I come back into The Sanctum, I'm blindsided by a want so urgent I have to cover my mouth to stifle a shriek. I want Bails to be sprawled out on her bed reading. I want to talk to her about Joe, want to play her this song.

I want my sister.

I want to hurl a building at God.

I take a breath and exhale with enough force to blow the orange paint right off the walls.

It's no longer raining—the scrubbed newness of the night rolls in through the open window. I don't know what to do, so I walk over to Bailey's desk and sit down like usual. I look at the detective's business card again. I thought about calling him but haven't yet, haven't packed up a thing either. I pull over a carton, decide to do one or two drawers. I hate looking at the empty boxes almost more than I hate the idea of packing up her things.

The bottom drawer's full of school notebooks, years of work, now useless. I take one out, glide my fingers over the cover, hold it to my chest, and then put it in the carton. All her knowledge is gone now. Everything she ever learned, or heard, or saw. Her particular way of looking at Hamlet or daisies or thinking about love, all her private intricate thoughts, her inconsequential secret musings—they're gone too. I heard this expression once: Each time someone dies, a library burns. I'm watching it burn right to the ground.

I stack the rest of the notebooks on top of the first, close the drawer, and do the same with the one above it. I close the carton and start a new one. There are more school notebooks in this drawer, some journals, which I will not read. I flip through the stack, putting them, one by one, into the box. At the very bottom of the drawer, there is an open one. It has Bailey's chicken scrawl handwriting all over it; columns of words cover the whole page, with lines crossing out most of them. I take it out, feel a pang of guilt, but then my guilt turns to surprise, then fear, when I see what the words are.

They're all combinations of our mother's name combined with other names and things. There is a whole section of the name Paige combined with people and things related to John Lennon, my namesake, and we assume her favorite musician because of it. We know practically nothing about Mom. It's like when she left, she took all traces of her life with her, leaving only a story behind. Gram rarely talks about anything but her amazing wanderlust, and Big isn't much better.

"At five years old," Gram would tell us over and over again, holding up her fingers for emphasis, "your mother snuck out of her bed one night and I found her halfway to town, with her little blue backpack and a walking stick. She said she was on an adventure—at five years old, girls!"

So that was all we had, except for a box of belongings we kept in The Sanctum. It's full of books we foraged over the years from the shelves downstairs, ones that had her name in them: *Oliver Twist*, *On the Road*, *Siddhartha*, *The Collected Poems of William Blake*, and some Harlequins, which threw us for a loop, book snobs that we are. None of them are dogeared or annotated. We have some yearbooks, but there are no scribbles from friends in them. There's a copy of *The Joy of Cooking* with food spattered all over it. (Gram did once tell us that Mom was magical in the kitchen and that she suspects she makes her living on the road by cooking.)

But mostly, what we have are maps, lots and lots of them: road maps, topographic maps, maps of Clover, of California, of the forty-nine other states, of country after country, continent after continent. There are also several atlases, each of which looks as read and reread as my copy of *Wuthering Heights*. The maps and atlases reveal the most about her: a girl for whom the world beckoned. When we were younger, Bailey and I would spend countless hours poring over the atlases imagining routes and adventures for her.

I start leafing through the notebook. There are pages and pages of these combinations: Paige/Lennon/Walker, Paige/Lennon/Yoko, Paige/Lennon/Imagine, Paige/Dakota/Ono, and on and on. Sometimes there are notes under a name combination. For instance, scribbled under the words *Paige/Dakota* is an address in North Hampton, MA. But then that's crossed out and the words *too young* are scrawled in.

I'm shocked. We'd both put our mother's name into search engines many times to no avail, and we would sometimes try to think of pseudonyms she might have chosen and search them to no avail as well, but never like this, never methodically, never with this kind of thoroughness and persistence. The notebook is practically full. Bailey must have been doing this in every free moment, every moment I wasn't around, because I so rarely saw her at the computer. But now that I'm thinking about it, I did see her in front of The Half Mom an awful lot before she died, studying it intently, almost like she was waiting for it to speak to her.

I turn to the first page of the notebook. It's dated February 27, less than two months before she died. How could she have done all this in that amount of time? No wonder she needed St. Anthony's help. I wish she'd asked for mine.

I put the notebook back in the drawer, walk back over to my bed, take my clarinet out of the case again, and play Joe's song.

I want to be in that summer day again, I want to be there with my sister.

(Found written on the inside cover of Wuthering Heights, Lennie's room)

At night,
when we were little,
we tented Bailey's covers,
crawled underneath with our flashlights
and played cards: Hearts,
Whist, Crazy Eights,
and our favorite: Bloody Knuckles.
The competition was vicious.
All day, every day,
we were the Walker Girls—
two peas in a pod
thick as thieves—
but when Gram closed the door
for the night,
we bared our teeth.
We played for chores,
for slave duty,
for truths and dares and money.
We played to be better, brighter,
to be more beautiful,
more,
just more.
But it was all a ruse—
we played
so we could fall asleep
in the same bed
without having to ask,
so we could wrap together
like a braid,
so while we slept
our dreams could switch bodies.

chapter 23

I used to talk to The Half Mom a lot,
but I'd wait until no one else was home
and then I'd say:
I imagine you
up there
not like a cloud or a bird or a star
but like a mother,
except one who lives in the sky
who doesn't make a fuss
about gravity
who just goes about her business
drifting around with the wind.

*rented is
Aviation Admin
all helicopter and airplane*

*(Found on a piece
of newspaper
under the Walkers'
porch)*

WHEN I COME down to the kitchen the next morning, Gram is at the stove cooking sausages, her shoulders hunched into a broad frown. Big slouches over his coffee at the table. Behind them the morning fog shrouds the window, like the house is hovering inside a cloud. Standing in the doorway I'm filled with the same scared, hollow feeling I get when I see abandoned houses, ones with weeds growing through the front steps, paint cracked and dirty, windows broken and boarded up.

"Where's Joe?" Big asks. I realize then why the despair is so naked this morning: Joe's not here.

"In prison," I say.

Big looks up, smirks. "What'd he do?" Instantly, the mood is lifted. Wow. I guess he's not only my life raft.

"Took a four-hundred-dollar bottle of wine from his father and drank it one night with a girl named John Lennon."

At the same time, Gram and Big gasp, then exclaim, "Four hundred dollars?!"

"He had no idea."

"Lennie, I don't like you drinking." Gram waves her spatula at me. The sausages sizzle and sputter in the pan behind her.

"I don't drink, well hardly. Don't worry."

"Damn, Len. Was it good?" Big's face is a study of wonder.

"I don't know. I've never had red wine before, guess so." I'm pouring a cup of coffee that is thin as tea. I've gotten used to the mud Joe makes.

"Damn," Big repeats, taking a sip of his coffee and making a disgusted face. I guess he now prefers Joe's sludge too. "Don't suppose you will drink it again either, with the bar set that high."

I'm wondering if Joe will be at the first band practice today—I've decided to go—when suddenly he walks through the door with croissants, dead bugs for Big, and a smile as big as God for me.

"Hey!" I say.

"They let you out," says Big. "That's terrific. Is it a conjugal visit or is your sentence over?"

"Big!" Gram chastises. "Please."

Joe laughs. "It's over. My father is a very romantic man, it's his best and worst trait, when I explained to him how I was feeling—" Joe looks at me, proceeds to turn red, which of course makes me go full-on tomato. It surely must be against the rules to feel like this when your sister is dead!

Gram shakes her head. "Who would have thought Lennie such a romantic?"

"Are you kidding?" Joe exclaims. "Her reading *Wuthering Heights* twenty-three times didn't give it away?" I look down. I'm embarrassed at how moved I am by this. *He knows me.* Somehow better than they do.

"Touché, Mr. Fontaine," Gram says, hiding her grin as she goes back to the stove.

Joe comes up behind me, wraps his arms around my waist. I close my eyes, think about his body, naked under his clothes, pressing into me, naked under mine. I turn my head to look up at him. "The melody you wrote is so beautiful. I want to play it for you." Before the last word is out of my mouth, he kisses me. I twist around in his arms so that we are facing each other, then throw my arms around his neck while his find the small of my back, and sweep me into him. Oh God, I don't care if this is wrong of me, if I'm breaking every rule in the Western World, I don't care about freaking anything, because our mouths, which momentarily separated, have met again and anything but that ecstatic fact ceases to matter.

How do people function when they're feeling like this?

How do they tie their shoes?

Or drive cars?

Or operate heavy machinery?

How does civilization continue when this is going on?

A voice, ten decibels quieter than its normal register, stutters out of Uncle Big. "Uh, kids. Might want to, I don't know, mmmm . . ." Everything screeches to a halt in my mind. Is *Big* stammering? Uh, Lennie? Probably not cool to make out like this in the middle of the kitchen in front of your grandmother and uncle. I pull away from Joe; it's like breaking suction. I look at Gram and Big, who are standing there fiddly and sheepish while the sausages burn. Is it possible that we've succeeded in embarrassing the Emperor and Empress of Weird?

I glance back at Joe. He looks totally cartoon-dopey, like he's been bonked on the head with a club. The whole scene strikes me as hysterical, and I collapse into a chair laughing.

Joe smiles an embarrassed half smile at Gram and Big, leans against the counter, his trumpet case now strategically held over his crotch. Thank God I don't have one of those. Who'd want a lust-o-meter sticking out the middle of their body?

"You're going to rehearsal, right?" he asks.

Bat. Bat. Bat.

Yes, if we make it.

WE DO MAKE it, though in my case, in body only. I'm surprised my fingers can find the keys as I glide through the pieces Mr. James has chosen for us to play at the upcoming River Festival. Even with Rachel sending me death-darts about Joe and repeatedly turning the stand so I can't see it, I'm lost in the music, feel like I'm playing with Joe alone, improvising, reveling in not knowing what is going to happen note to note . . . but mid-practice, mid-song, mid-note, a feeling of dread sweeps over me as I start thinking about Toby, how he looked when he left last night. What he said in The Sanctum. He has to know we need to stay away from each other now. He has to. I tuck the panic away but spend the rest of rehearsal painfully alert, following the arrangement without the slightest deviation.

After practice, Joe and I have the whole afternoon together because he's out of prison and I'm off work. We're walking back to my house, the wind whipping us around like leaves.

"I know what we should do," I say.

"Didn't you want to play me the song?"

"I do, but I want to play it for you somewhere else. Remember I dared you in the woods that night to brave the forest with me on a really windy day? Today is it."

We veer off the road and hike in, bushwhacking through thickets of brush until we find the trail I'm looking for. The sun filters sporadically through the trees, casting a dim and shadowy light over the forest floor. Because of the wind, the trees are creaking symphonically—it's a veritable philharmonic of squeaking doors. Perfect.

After a while, he says, "I think I'm holding up remarkably well, considering, don't you?"

"Considering what?"

"Considering we're hiking to the soundtrack of the creepiest horror movie ever made and all the world's tree trolls have gathered above us to open and close their front doors."

"It's broad daylight, you can't be scared."

"I can be, actually, but I'm trying not to be a wuss. I have a very low eerie threshold."

"You're going to love where I'm taking you, I promise."

"I'm going to love it if you take off all your clothes there, I promise, or at least some of them, maybe even just a sock." He comes over to me, drops his horn, and swings me around so we are facing each other.

I say, "You're very repressed, you know? It's maddening."

"Can't help it. I'm half French, *joie de vivre* and all. In all seriousness though, I haven't yet seen you in any state of undress, and it's been three whole days since our first kiss, *quel catastrophe,* you know?" He tries to get my wind-blown hair out of my face, then kisses me until my heart busts out of my chest like a wild horse. "Though I do have a very good imagination . . ."

"Quel dork," I say, pulling him forward.

"You know, I only act like a dork so you'll say *quel dork,"* he replies.

The trail climbs to where the old growth redwoods rocket into the sky and turn the forest into their private cathedral. The wind has died down and the woods have grown unearthly still and peaceful. Leaves flicker all around us like tiny pieces of light.

"So, what about your mom?" Joe asks all of a sudden.

"What?" My head couldn't have been further away from thoughts of my mother.

"The first day I came over, Gram said she'd finish the portrait when your mother comes back. Where is she?"

"I don't know." Usually I leave it at that and don't fill in the spare details, but he hasn't run away yet from all our other family oddities. "I've never met my mother," I say. "Well, I met her, but she left when I was one. She has a restless nature, guess it runs in the family."

He stops walking. "That's it? That's the explanation? For her leaving? And *never coming back*?" Yes, it's nutso, but this Walker nutso has always made sense to me.

"Gram says she'll come back," I say, my stomach knotting up, thinking of her coming back right now. Thinking of Bailey trying so hard to find her. Thinking of slamming the door in her face if she did come back, of screaming, *You're too late.* Thinking of her never coming back. Thinking I'm not sure how to believe all this anymore without Bailey believing it with me. "Gram's aunt Sylvie had it too," I add, feeling imbecilic. "She came back after twenty years away."

"Wow," Joe says. I've never seen his brow so furrowed.

"Look, I don't know my mother, so I don't miss her or anything . . ." I say, but I feel like I'm trying to convince myself more than Joe. "She's this intrepid, free-spirited woman who took off to traipse all around the globe alone. She's mysterious. It's cool." It's *cool*? God, I'm a ninny. But when did everything change? Because it did used to be cool, super-cool, in fact— she was our Magellan, our Marco Polo, one of the wayward Walker women whose restless boundless spirit propels her from place to place, love to love, moment to unpredictable moment.

Joe smiles, looks at me so warmly, I forget everything else. "You're cool," he says. "Forgiving. Unlike dickhead me." Forgiving? I take his hand, wondering from his reaction, and my own, if I'm cool and forgiving or totally delusional. And what about this dickhead him? Who is it? Is it the Joe that never talked to that violinist again? If so, I don't want to meet that guy, ever. We continue in silence, both of us soaring around in the sky of our minds for another mile or so and then we are there, and all thoughts of dickhead him and my mysterious missing mother are gone.

"Okay, close your eyes," I say. "I'll lead you." I reach up from behind him and cover my hands over his eyes and steer him down the path.

"Okay, open them."

There is a bedroom. A whole bedroom in the middle of the forest.

"Wow, where's Sleeping Beauty?" Joe asks.

"That would be me," I say, and take a running leap onto the fluffy bed. It's like jumping into a cloud. He follows me.

"You're too awake to be her, we've already covered this." He stands at the edge of the bed, looking around. "This is unbelievable, how is this here?"

"There's an inn about a mile away on the river. It was a commune in the sixties, and the owner Sam's an old hippie. He set up this forest bedroom for his guests to happen upon if they hike up here, for surprise romance, I guess, but I've never seen a soul pass through and I've been coming forever. Actually, I did see someone here once: Sam, changing the sheets. He throws this tarp over when it rains. I write at that desk, read in that rocker, lie here on this bed and daydream. I've never brought a guy here before though."

He smiles, sits on the bed next to where I'm lying on my back and starts trailing his fingers over my belly.

"What do you daydream about?" he asks.

"This," I say as his hand spreads across my midriff under my shirt. My breathing's getting faster—I want his hands everywhere.

"John Lennon, can I ask you something?"

"Uh-oh, whenever people say that, something scary comes next."

"Are you a virgin?"

"You see—scary question came next," I mumble, mortified—what a mood-killer. I squirm out from under his hand. "Is it that obvious?"

"Sort of." Ugh. I want to crawl under the covers. He tries to backtrack. "No, I mean, I think it's cool that you are."

"It's decidedly uncool."

"For you maybe, but not for me, if . . ."

"If what?" My stomach is suddenly churning. Roiling.

Now he looks embarrassed—good. "Well, if sometime, not now, but sometime, you might not want to be one anymore, and I could be your first, that's where the cool part comes in, you know, for me." His expression is shy and sweet, but what he's saying makes me feel scared and excited and overwhelmed and like I'm going to burst into tears, which I do, and for once, I don't even know why.

"Oh, Lennie, I'm sorry, was that bad to say? Don't cry, there's no pressure at all, kissing you, being with you in any way is amazing—"

"No," I say, now laughing and crying at the same time. "I'm crying because . . . well, I don't know why I'm crying, but I'm happy, not sad . . ."

I reach for his arm, and he lies down on his side next to me, his elbow resting by my head, our bodies touching length to length. He's peering into my eyes in a way that's making me tremble.

"Just looking into your eyes . . ." he whispers. "I've never felt anything like this."

I think about Genevieve. He'd said he was in love with her, does that mean . . .

"Me neither," I say, not able to stop the tears from spilling over again.

"Don't cry." His voice is weightless, mist. He kisses my eyes, gently grazes my lips.

He looks at me then so nakedly, it makes me lightheaded, like I need to lie down even though I'm lying down. "I know it hasn't been that long, Len, but I think . . . I don't know . . . I might be . . ."

He doesn't have to say it, I feel it too; it's not subtle—like every bell for miles and miles is ringing at once, loud, clanging, hungry ones, and tiny, happy, chiming ones, all of them sounding off in this moment. I put my hands around his neck, pull him to me, and then he's kissing me hard and so deep, and I am flying, sailing, soaring . . .

He murmurs into my hair, "Forget what I said earlier, let's stick with this, I might not survive anything more." I laugh. Then he jumps up, finds my wrists, and pins them over my head. "Yeah, right. Totally joking, I want to do *everything* with you, whenever you're ready, I'm the one, promise?" He's above me, batting and grinning like a total hooplehead.

"I promise," I say.

"Good. Glad that's decided." He raises an eyebrow. "I'm going to deflower you, John Lennon."

"Oh my God, so, so embarrassing, *quel, quel major dork.*" I try to cover my face with my hands, but he won't let me. And then we are wrestling and laughing and it's many, many minutes before I remember that my sister has died.

chapter 24

The.
World.
Is.
Not.
A.
Safe.
Place.

*(Found on a candy
wrapper in the woods
behind Clover High)*

I SEE TOBY'S truck out front and a bolt of anger shoots through me. Why can't he just stay away from me for one freaking day even? I just want to hang on to this happiness. *Please.*

I find Gram in the art room, cleaning her brushes. Toby is nowhere in sight.

"Why is he always here?" I hiss at Gram.

She looks at me, surprised. "What's wrong with you, Lennie? I called him to help me fix the trellising around my garden and he said he would stop by after he was done at the ranch."

"Can't you call someone else?" My voice is seething with anger and exasperation, and I'm sure I sound completely bonkers to Gram. I am bonkers—I just want to be in love. I want to feel this joy. I don't want to deal with Toby, with sorrow and grief and guilt and DEATH. I'm so sick of DEATH.

Gram does not look pleased. "God, Len, have a heart, the guy's destroyed. It makes him feel better to be around us. We're the only ones who understand. He said as much last night." She is drying her brushes over the sink, snapping her wrist dramatically with each shake. "I asked you once if everything was all right between you two and you said yes. I believed you."

I take a deep breath and let it out slowly, trying to coerce Mr. Hyde back into my body. "It's okay, it's fine, I'm sorry. I don't know what's wrong with me." Then I pull a Gram and walk right out of the room.

I go up to The Sanctum and put on the most obnoxious head-banging punk music I have, a San Francisco band called Filth. I know Toby hates any kind of punk because it was always a point of contention with Bailey, who loved it. He finally won her over to the alt-country he likes, and to Willie Nelson, Hank Williams, and Johnny Cash, his holy trinity, but he never came around to punk.

The music is not helping. I'm jumping up and down on the blue dance rug, banging around to the incessant beat, but I'm too angry to even bang around BECAUSE I DON'T WANT TO DANCE IN THE INNER PUMPKIN SANCTUM ALONE. In one instant, all the rage that I felt moments before for Toby has transferred to Bailey. I don't understand how she could have done this to me, left me here all alone. Especially because she promised me her whole life that she would never EVER disappear like Mom did, that we would always have each other, always, ALWAYS, ALWAYS. "It's the only pact that mattered, Bailey!" I cry out, taking the pillow and pounding it again and again into the bed, until finally, many songs later, I feel a little bit calmer.

I drop on my back on the bed, panting and sweating. How will I survive this missing? How do others do it? People die all the time. Every day. Every hour. There are families all over the world staring at beds that are no longer slept in, shoes that are no longer worn. Families that no longer have to buy a particular cereal, a kind of shampoo. There are people everywhere standing in line at the movies, buying curtains, walking dogs, while inside, their hearts are ripping to shreds. For years. For their whole lives. I don't believe time heals. I don't want it to. If I heal, doesn't that mean I've accepted the world without her?

I remember the notebook then. I get up, turn off Filth, put on a Chopin Nocturne to see if that'll settle me down, and go over to the desk. I take out the notebook, turn to the last page, where there are a few combinations that haven't yet been crossed out. The whole page is combinations of Mom's name with Dickens characters. Paige/Twist, Paige/Fagan, Walker/Havisham, Walker/Oliver/Paige, Pip/Paige.

I turn on the computer, plug in *Paige Twist* and then search through pages of docs, finding nothing that could relate to our mom, then I put in *Paige Dickens* and find some possibilities, but the documents are mostly from high school athletic teams and college alumni magazines, none that could have anything to do with her. I go through more Dickens combinations but don't find even the remotest possibility.

An hour's passed and I've just done a handful of searches. I look back over the pages and pages that Bailey did, and wonder again when she did it all, and where she did it, maybe at the computer lab at the State, because how could I not have noticed her bleary-eyed at this computer for hours on end? It strikes me again how badly she wanted to find Mom, because why else would she have devoted all this time to it? What could have happened in February to take her down this road? I wonder if that was when Toby asked her to marry him. Maybe she wanted Mom to come to the wedding. But Toby said he had asked her right before she died. I need to talk to him.

I go downstairs, apologize to Gram, tell her I've been emotional all day, which is true every freaking day lately. She looks at me, strokes my hair, says, "It's okay, sweet pea, maybe we could go on a walk together tomorrow, talk some—" When will she *get* it? I don't want to talk to her about Bailey, about anything.

When I come out of the house, Toby's standing on a ladder, working on the trellis in the front of the garden. Streamers of gold and pink peel across the sky. The whole yard is glowing with the setting sun, the roses look lit from within, like lanterns.

He looks over at me, exhales dramatically, then climbs slowly down the ladder, leaning against it with arms crossed in front of his chest. "Wanted to say sorry . . . again." He sighs. "I'm half out of my mind lately." His eyes search mine. "You okay?"

"Yeah, except for the half out of my mind part," I say.

He smiles at that, his whole face alighting with kindness and understanding. I relax a little, feel bad for wanting to behead him an hour before.

"I found this notebook in Bailey's desk," I tell him, eager to find out if he knows anything and very eager not to talk or think about yesterday. "It's like she was looking for Mom, but feverishly, Toby, page after page of possible pseudonyms that she must have been putting in search engines. She'd tried every-thing, must have done it around the clock. I don't know where she did it, don't know why she did it . . ."

"Don't know either," he says, his voice trembling slightly. He looks down. Is he hiding something from me?

"The notebook is dated. She started doing this at the end of February—did anything happen then that you know of?"

Toby's bones unhinge and he slides down the trellis, and drops his head into his hands and starts to cry.

What's going on?

I lower to him, kneel in front of him, put my hands on his arms. "Toby," I say gently. "It's okay." I'm stroking his hair with my hand. Fear prickles my neck and arms.

He shakes his head. "It's not okay." He can barely get the words out. "I wasn't ever going to tell you."

"What? What weren't you going to tell me?" My voice comes out shrill, crazy.

"It makes it worse, Len, and I didn't want it to be any harder for you."

"What?" Every hair on my body is on end. I'm really fright-ened now. What could possibly make Bailey's death any worse?

He reaches for my hand, holds it tight in his. "We were going to have a baby." I hear myself gasp. "She was pregnant when she died." No, I think, this can't be. "Maybe she was looking for your mom because of that. The end of February would have been around the time when we found out."

The idea begins to avalanche inside me, gaining speed and mass. My other hand has landed on his shoulder and although I'm looking at his face, I'm watching my sister hold their baby up in the air, making ferret faces at it, watching as she and Toby each take a hand of their child and walk him to the river. Or her. God. I can see in Toby's eyes all that he has been carrying alone, and for the first time since Bailey's death I feel more sorry for someone else than I do for myself. I close my arms around him and rock him. And then, when our eyes meet and we are again there in that helpless house of grief, a place where Bailey can never be and Joe Fontaine does not exist, a place where it's only Toby and me left behind, I kiss him. I kiss him to comfort him, to tell him how sorry I am, to show him I'm here and that I'm alive and so is he. I kiss him because I'm in way over my head and have been for months. I kiss him and keep kissing and holding and caressing him, because for whatever fucked-up reason, that is what I do.

The moment Toby's body stiffens in my arms, I know.

I know, but I don't know who it is.

At first, I think it's Gram, it must be. But it's not.

It's not Big either.

I turn around and there he is, a few yards away, motionless, a statue.

Our eyes hold, and then, he stumbles backward. I jump out of Toby's grasp, find my legs, and rush toward Joe, but he turns away, starts to run.

"Wait, please," I yell out. "Please."

He freezes, his back to me—a silhouette against a sky now burning up, a wildfire racing out of control toward the horizon. I feel like I'm falling down stairs, hurtling and tumbling with no ability to stop. Still, I force myself forward and go to him. I take his hand to try to turn him around, but he rips it away as if my touch disgusts him. Then he's turning, slowly, like he's moving underwater. I wait, scared out of my mind to look at him, to see what I've done. When he finally faces me, his eyes are lifeless, his face like stone. It's as if his marvelous spirit has evacuated his flesh.

Words fly out of my mouth. "It's not like us, I don't feel—it's something else, my sister . . ." *My sister was pregnant*, I'm about to say in explanation, but how would that explain anything? I'm desperate for him to get it, but I don't get it.

"It's not what you think," I say predictably, pathetically.

I watch the rage and hurt erupt simultaneously in his face. "Yes, it *is*. It's *exactly* what I think, it's exactly what I *thought*." He spits his words at me. "How could you . . . I thought you—"

"I do, I do." I'm crying hard now, tears streaming down my face. "You don't understand."

His face is a riot of disappointment. "You're right, I *don't*. Here."

He pulls a piece of paper out of his pocket. "This is what I came to give you." He crumples it up and throws it at me, then turns around and runs as fast as he can away into the falling night.

I bend over and grab the crumpled piece of paper, smooth it out. At the top it says *Part 2: Duet for aforementioned clarinetist and guitarist*. I fold it carefully, put it in my pocket, then sit down on the grass, a heap of bones. I realize I'm in the same exact spot Joe and I kissed last night in the rain. The sky's lost its fury, just some straggling gold wisps steadily being consumed by darkness. I try to hear the melody he wrote for me in my head, but can't. All I hear is him saying: *How could you?*

How could I?

Someone might as well roll up the whole sky, pack it away for good.

Soon, there's a hand on my shoulder. Toby. I reach up and rest my hand on his. He squats down on one knee next to me.

"I'm sorry," he says quietly, and a moment later, "I'm going to go, Len." Then just the coldness on my shoulder where his hand had been. I hear his truck start and listen to the engine hum as it follows Joe down the road.

Just me. Or so I think until I look up at the house to see Gram silhouetted in the doorway like Toby was last night. I don't know how long she's been there, don't know what she's seen and what she hasn't. She swings open the door, walks to the end of the porch, leans on the railing with both hands.

"Come in, sweet pea."

I don't tell her what happened with Joe, just as I never told her what has been going on with Toby. Yet I can see in her mournful eyes as she looks into mine that she most likely already knows it all.

"One day, you'll talk to me again." She takes my hands. "I miss you, you know. So does Big."

"She was pregnant," I whisper.

Gram nods.

"She told you?"

"The autopsy."

"They were engaged," I say. This, I can tell from her face, she didn't know.

She encloses me in her arms and I stay in her safe and sound embrace and let the tears rise and rise and fall and fall until her dress is soaked with them and night has filled the house.

chapter 25

I DO NOT go to the altar of the desk to talk to Bailey on the mountaintop. I do not even turn on the light. I go straight into bed with all my clothes on and pray for sleep. It doesn't come.

What comes is shame, weeks of it, waves of it, rushing through me in quick hot flashes like nausea, making me groan into my pillow. The lies and half-truths and abbreviations I told and didn't tell Joe tackle and hold me down until I can hardly breathe. How could I have hurt him like this, done to him just what Genevieve did? All the love I have for him clobbers around in my body. My chest aches. All of me aches. He looked like a completely different person. He is a different person. Not the one who loved me.

I see Joe's face, then Bailey's, the two of them looming above me with only three words on their lips: *How could you?*

I have no answer.

I'm sorry, I write with my finger on the sheets over and over until I can't stand it anymore and flip on the light.

But the light brings actual nausea and with it all the moments with my sister that will now remain unlived: holding her baby in my arms. Teaching her child to play the clarinet. Just getting older together day by day. All the future we will not have rips and retches out of me into the garbage pail I am crouched over until there's nothing left inside, nothing but me in this ghastly orange room.

And that's when it hits.

Without the harbor and mayhem of Toby's arms, the sublime distraction of Joe's, there's only me.

Me, like a small seashell with the loneliness of the whole ocean roaring invisibly within.

Me.

Without.

Bailey.

Always.

I throw my head into my pillow and scream into it as if my soul itself is being ripped in half, because it is.

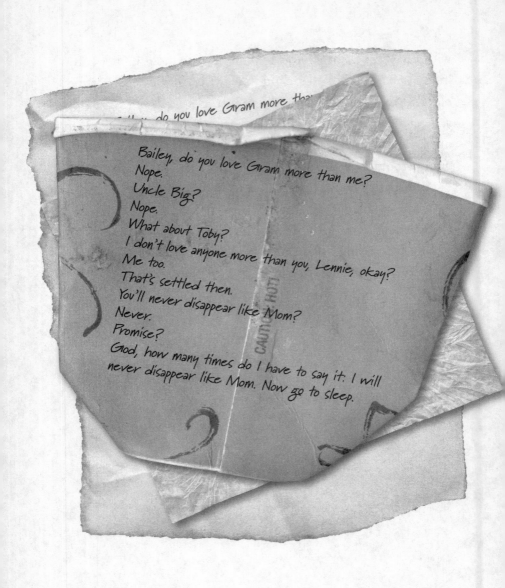

Bailey, do you love Gram more than me?

Nope.

Uncle Big?

Nope.

What about Toby?

I don't love anyone more than you, Lennie, okay?

Me too.

That's settled then.

You'll never disappear like Mom?

Never.

Promise?

God, how many times do I have to say it: I will never disappear like Mom. Now go to sleep.

(Found on a to-go cup, Rain River)
(Found on a lollipop wrapper in the parking lot, Clover High)
(Found on a piece of paper in a trash can, Clover Public Library)

part
two

Len, where is she tonight?

I was sleeping.

C'mon, Len.

Okay, India climbing in the Himalayas.

We did that one last week.

You start then.

All right. She's in Spain. Barcelona. A scarf covering her head, sitting by the water, drinking sangria, with a man named Pablo.

Are they in love?

Yes.

But she will leave him come morning.

Yes.

She'll wake before dawn, sneak her suitcase out from under the bed, put on a red wig, a green scarf, a yellow dress, white pumps. She'll catch the first train out.

Will she leave a note?

No.

She never does.

No.

She'll sit on the train and stare out the window at the sea. A woman will sit next to her and they'll strike up a conversation. The woman will ask her if she has any children, and she'll say, "No."

Wrong, Len. She'll say, "I'm on the way to see my girls right now."

(Found on a piece of paper stuck between two rocks at Flying Man's)

chapter 26

I WAKE UP later with my face mashed into the pillow. I lean up on my elbows and look out the window. The stars have bewitched the sky of darkness. It's a shimmery night. I open the window, and the sound of the river rides the rose-scented breeze right into our room. I'm shocked to realize that I feel a little better, like I've slept my way to a place with a little more air. I push away thoughts of Joe and Toby, take one more deep breath of the flowers, the river, the world, then I get up, take the garbage pail into the bathroom, clean it and myself, and when I return head straight over to Bailey's desk.

I turn on the computer, pull out the notebook from the top desk drawer where I keep it now, and decide to continue from where I left off the other day. I need to do something for my sister and all I can think to do is to find our mother for her.

I start plugging in the remaining combinations in Bailey's notebook. I can understand why becoming a mother herself would have compelled Bailey to search for Mom like this. It makes sense to me somehow. But there is something else I suspect. In a far cramped corner of my mind, there is a dresser, and in that dresser there is a thought crammed into the back of the bottom-most drawer. I know it's there because I put it there where I wouldn't have to look at it. But tonight I open that creaky drawer and face what I've always believed, and that is this: Bailey had it too. Restlessness stampeded through my sister her whole life, informing everything she did from running cross-country to changing personas on stage. I've always thought that was the reason behind why she wanted to find our mother. And I know it was the reason I never wanted her to. I bet this is why she didn't tell me she was looking for Mom like this. She knew I'd try to stop her. I didn't want our mother to reveal to Bailey a way out of our lives.

One explorer is enough for any family.

But I can make up for that now by finding Mom. I put combination after combination into a mix of search engines. After an hour, however, I'm ready to toss the computer out the window. It's futile. I've gotten all the way to the end of Bailey's notebook and have started one of my own using words and symbols from Blake poems. I can see in the notebook that Bailey was working her way through Mom's box for clues to the pseudonym. She'd used references from *Oliver Twist, Siddhartha, On the Road*, but hadn't gotten to William Blake yet. I have his book of poems open and I'm combining words like *Tiger* or *Poison Tree* or *Devil* with *Paige* or *Walker* and the words *chef, cook, restaurant,* thinking as Gram did that that's how she might make money while traveling, but it's useless. After yet another hour of no possible matches, I tell the mountaintop Bailey in the explorer picture, I'm not giving up, I just need a break, and head downstairs to see if anyone is still awake.

Big's on the porch, sitting in the middle of the love seat like it's a throne. I squeeze in beside him.

"Unbelievable," he murmurs, goosing my knee. "Can't remember the last time you joined me for a nighttime chat. I was just thinking that I might play hooky tomorrow, see if a new lady-friend of mine wants to have lunch with me in a restaurant. I'm sick of dining in trees." He twirls his mustache a little too dreamily.

Uh-oh.

"Remember," I warn. "You're not allowed to ask anyone to marry you until you've been with her a whole year. Those were your rules after your last divorce." I reach over and tug on his mustache, add for effect, "Your fifth divorce."

"I know, I know," he says. "But boy do I miss proposing, nothing so romantic. Make sure you try it, at least once, Len— it's skydiving with your feet on the ground." He laughs in a tinkley way that might be called a giggle if he weren't thirty feet tall. He's told Bailey and me this our whole lives. In fact, until Sarah went into a diatribe about the inequities of marriage in sixth grade, I had no idea proposing wasn't always considered an equal-opportunity endeavor.

I look out over the small yard where hours before Joe left me, probably forever. I think for a minute about telling Big that Joe probably won't be around anymore, but I can't face breaking it to him. He's almost as attached to him as I am. And anyway, I want to talk to him about something else.

"Big?"

"Hmmm?"

"Do you really believe in this restless gene stuff?"

He looks at me, surprised, then says, "Sounds like a fine load of crap, doesn't it?"

I think about Joe's incredulous response today in the woods, about my own doubts, about everybody's, always. Even in this town where free-spiritedness is a fundamental family value, the few times I've ever told anyone my mother took off when I was one year old to live a life of freedom and itinerancy, they looked like they wanted to commit me to a nice rubber room somewhere. Even so, to me, this Walker family gospel never seemed all that unlikely. Anyone who's read a novel or walked down the street or stepped through the front door of my house knows that people are all kinds of weird, especially my people, I think, glancing at Big, who does God knows what in trees, marries perennially, tries to resurrect dead bugs, smokes more pot than the whole eleventh grade, and looks like he should reign over some fairy tale kingdom. So why wouldn't his sister be an adventurer, a blithe spirit? Why shouldn't my mother be like the hero in so many stories, the brave one who left? Like Luke Skywalker, Gulliver, Captain Kirk, Don Quixote, Odysseus. Not quite real to me, okay, but mythical and magical, not unlike my favorite saints or the characters in novels I hang on to perhaps a little too tightly.

"I don't know," I answer honestly. "Is it all crap?"

Big doesn't say anything for a long time, just twirls away at his mustache, thinking. "Nah, it's all about classification, know what I mean?" I don't, but won't interrupt. "Lots of things run through families, right? And this tendency, whatever it is, for whatever reason, runs through ours. Could be worse, we could have depression or alcoholism or bitterness. Our afflicted kin just hit the road—"

"I think Bailey had it, Big," I say, the words tumbling out of me before I can catch them, revealing just how much I might actually believe in it after all. "I've always thought so."

"Bailey?" His brow creases. "Nah, don't see it. In fact, I've never seen a girl so relieved as when she got rejected from that school in New York City."

"Relieved?" Now *this* is a fine load of crap! "Are you kidding? She *always* wanted to go to Juilliard. She worked sooooooooo hard. It was her dream!"

Big studies my burning face, then says gently, "Whose dream, Len?" He positions his hands like he's playing an invisible clarinet. "Because the only one I used to see working sooooooooo hard around here was you."

God.

Marguerite's trilling voice fills my head: *Your playing is ravishing. You work on the nerves, Lennie, you go to Juilliard.*

Instead, I quit.

Instead, I shoved and crammed myself into a jack-in-the-box of my own making.

"C'mere." Big opens his arm like a giant wing and closes it over me as I snuggle in beside him and try not to think about how terrified I'd felt each time Marguerite mentioned Juilliard, each time I'd imagine myself—

"Dreams change," Big says. "I think hers did."

Dreams change, yes, that makes sense, but I didn't know dreams could hide inside a person.

He wraps his other arm around me too and I sink into the bear of him, breathing in the thick scent of pot that infuses his clothes. He squeezes me tight, strokes my hair with his enormous hand. I'd forgotten how comforting Big is, a human furnace. I peek up at his face. A tear runs down his cheek.

After a few minutes, he says, "Bails might have had some ants in the pants, like most people do, but I think she was more like me, and you lately, for that matter—*a slave to love*." He smiles at me like he's inducting me into a secret society. "Maybe it's those damn roses, and for the record, those I believe in: hook, line, and sinker. They're deadly on the heart—I swear, we're like lab rats breathing in that aroma all season long . . ." He twirls his mustache, seems to have forgotten what he was saying. I wait, remembering that he's stoned. The rose scent ribbons through the air between us. I breathe it in, thinking of Joe, knowing full well that it's not the roses that have spurred this love in my heart, but the boy, such an amazing boy. *How could I?*

Far away, an owl calls—a hollow, lonesome sound that makes me feel the same.

Big continues talking as if no time has passed. "Nah, it wasn't Bails who had it—"

"What do you mean?" I ask, straightening up.

He stops twirling. His face has grown serious. "Gram was different when we were growing up," he says. "If anyone else had it, she did."

"Gram hardly leaves the neighborhood," I say, not following.

He chuckles. "I know. Guess that's how much I don't believe in the gene though. I always thought my mother had it. I thought she just bottled it up somehow, trapped herself in that art room for weeks on end, and threw it onto those canvases."

"Well, if that's the case, why didn't *my mother* just bottle it up, then?" I try to keep my voice down but I feel suddenly infuriated. "Why'd she have to leave if Gram just had to make some paintings?"

"I don't know, honey, maybe Paige had it worse."

"Had *what* worse?"

"I don't know!" And I can tell he doesn't know, that he's as frustrated and bewildered as I am. "Whatever makes a woman leave two little kids, her brother, and her mother, and not come back for sixteen years. That's what! I mean, we call it wanderlust, other families might not be so kind."

"What would other families call it?" I ask. He's never intimated anything like this before about Mom. Is it all a cover story for crazy? Was she really and truly out of her tree?

"Doesn't matter what anyone else would call it, Len," he says. "This is *our* story to tell."

This is our story to tell. He says it in his Ten Commandments way and it hits me that way: profoundly. You'd think for all the reading I do, I would have thought about this before, but I haven't. I've never once thought about the interpretative, the storytelling aspect of life, of my life. I always felt like I was in a story, yes, but not like I was the author of it, or like I had any say in its telling whatsoever.

You can tell your story any way you damn well please.

It's your solo.

chapter 27

This is the secret I kept from you, Bails,
from myself too:
I think I liked that Mom was gone,
that she could be anybody,
anywhere,
doing anything.
I liked that she was our invention,
a woman living
on the last page of the story
with only what we imagined
spread out before her.
I liked that she was ours, alone.

(Found on a page ripped out of Wuthering Heights, *spiked on a branch, in the woods)*

JOELESSNESS SETTLES OVER the morning like a pall. Gram and I are slumped spineless over the kitchen table, staring off in opposite directions.

When I got back to The Sanctum last night, I put Bailey's notebook into the carton with the others and closed up the box. Then I returned St. Anthony to the mantel in front of The Half Mom. I'm not sure how I'm going to find our mother, but I know it isn't going to be on the Internet. All night, I thought about what Big said. It's possible no one in this family is quite who I believed, especially me. I'm pretty sure he hit the jackpot with me.

And maybe with Bailey too. Maybe he's right and she didn't have it—whatever *it* is. Maybe what my sister wanted was to stay here and get married and have a family.

Maybe that was her color of extraordinary.

"Bailey had all these secrets," I say to Gram.

"Seems to run in the family," she replies with a tired sigh.

I want to ask her what she means, remembering what Big said about her too last night, but can't because he's just stomped in, dressed for work after all, a dead ringer for Paul Bunyan. He takes one look at us and says, "Who died?" Then stops mid-step, shakes his head. "I *cannot* believe I just said that." He knocks on his head nobody-home-style. Then he looks around. "Hey, where's Joe this morning?"

Gram and I both look down.

"What?" he asks.

"I don't think he'll be around anymore," I say.

"Really?" Big shrinks from Gulliver to Lilliputian before my eyes. "Why, honey?"

I feel tears brimming. "I don't know."

Thankfully, he lets it drop and leaves the kitchen to check on the bugs.

The whole way to the deli I think of the crazy French violinist Genevieve with whom Joe was in love and how he never spoke to her again. I think of his assessment of horn players as all-or-nothing types. I think how I had all of him and now I'm going to have none of him unless I can somehow make him understand what happened last night and all the other nights with Toby. But how? I already left two messages on his cell this morning and even called the Fontaine house once. It went like this:

Lennie (shaking in her flip-flops): Is Joe home?

Marcus: Wow, Lennie, shocker . . . brave girl.

Lennie (looks down to see scarlet letter emblazoned on her T-shirt): Is he around?

Marcus: Nope, left early.

Marcus and Lennie: Awkward Silence

Marcus: He's taking it pretty hard. I've never seen him so upset about a girl before, about anything, actually . . .

Lennie (close to tears): Will you tell him I called?

Marcus: Will do.

Marcus and Lennie: Awkward Silence

Marcus (tentative): Lennie, if you like him, well, don't give up.

Dial tone.

And that's the problem, I madly like him. I make an SOS call to Sarah to come down to the deli during my shift.

NORMALLY, I AM The Zen Lasagna Maker. After three and a half summers, four shifts a week, eight lasagnas a shift: 896 lasagnas to date—done the math—I have it down. It's my meditation. I separate noodle after noodle from the glutinous lump that comes out of the refrigerator with the patience and precision of a surgeon. I plunge my hands into the ricotta and spices and fold the mixture until fluffy as a cloud. I slice the cheese into cuts as thin as paper. I spice the sauce until it sings. And then I layer it all together into a mountain of perfection. My lasagnas are sublime. Today, however, my lasagnas are not singing. After nearly chopping off a finger on the slicer, dropping the glutinous lump of noodles onto the floor, overcooking the new batch of pasta, dumping a truck-load of salt into the tomato sauce, Maria has me on moron-detail stuffing cannolis with a blunt object while she makes the lasagnas by my side. I'm cornered. It's too early for customers, so it's just us trapped inside the *National Enquirer*—Maria's the town crier, chatters nonstop about the lewd and lascivious goings-on in Clover, including, of course, the arboreal escapades of the town Romeo: my uncle Big.

"How's he doing?"

"You know."

"Everyone's been asking about him. He used to stop at The Saloon every night after he returned to earth from the tree-tops." Maria's stirring a vat of sauce beside me, a witch at her cauldron, as I try to cover the fact that I've broken yet another pastry shell. I'm a lovesick mess with a dead sister. "The place isn't the same without him. He holding up?" Maria turns to me, brushes a dark curl of hair from her perspiring brow, notes with irritation the growing pile of broken cannoli shells.

"He's just okay, like the rest of us," I say. "He's been coming home after work." I don't add, *And smoking three bowls of weed to numb the pain.* I keep looking up at the door, imagining Joe sailing through it.

"I did hear he had a treetop visitor the other day," Maria singsongs, back to everyone else's business.

"No way," I say, knowing full well that this is most likely the case.

"Yup. Dorothy Rodriguez, you know her, right? She teaches second grade. Last night at the bar, I heard that she rode up with him in the barrel high into the canopy, and *you know* . . ." She winks at me. "They picnicked."

I groan. "Maria, it's my uncle, please."

She laughs, then blathers on about a dozen more Clover trysts until at last Sarah floats in dressed like a fabric shop specializing in paisley. She stands in the doorway, puts her arms up, and makes peace signs with both hands.

"Sarah! If you don't look like the spitting image of me twenty years—sheesh, almost thirty years ago," Maria says, heading into the walk-in cooler. I hear the door thump behind her.

"Why the SOS?" Sarah says to me. The summer day has followed her in. Her hair is still wet from swimming. When I called earlier she and Luke were at Flying Man's "working" on some song. I can smell the river on her as she hugs me over the counter.

"Are you wearing toe rings?" I ask to postpone my confession a little longer.

"Of course." She lifts her kaleidoscopic pantalooned leg into the air to show me.

"Impressive."

She hops on the stool across the counter from where I'm working, throws her book on the counter. It's by a Hélène Cixous. "Lennie, these French feminists are so much cooler than those stupid existentialists. I'm so into this concept of *jouissance*, it means transcendent rapture, which I'm sure you and Joe know all about—" She plays the air with invisible sticks.

"Knew." I take a deep breath. Prepare for the *I told you so* of the century.

Her face is stuck somewhere between disbelief and shock. "What do you mean, *knew*?"

"I mean, *knew*."

"But yesterday . . ." She's shaking her head, trying to catch up to the news. "You guys frolicked off from practice making the rest of us sick on account of the indisputable, irrefutable, unmistakable true love that was seeping out of every pore of your attached-at-the-hip bodies. Rachel nearly exploded. It was so beautiful." And then it dawns on her. "You didn't."

"Please don't have a cow or a horse or an aardvark or any other animal about it. No morality police, okay?"

"Okay, promise. Now tell me you didn't. I told you I had a bad feeling."

"I did." I cover my face with my hands. "Joe saw us kissing last night."

"You've got to be kidding?"

I shake my head.

As if on cue, a gang of miniature Toby skate rats whiz by on their boards, tearing apart the sidewalk, quiet as a 747.

"But why, Len? Why would you do that?" Her voice is surprisingly without judgment. She really wants to know. "You don't love Toby."

"No."

"And you're dementoid over Joe."

"Totally."

"Then why?" This is the million-dollar question.

I stuff two cannolis, deciding how to phrase it. "I think it has to do with how much we both love Bailey, as crazy as that sounds."

Sarah stares at me. "You're right, that does sound crazy. Bailey would *kill* you."

My heart races wild in my chest. "I know. But Bailey is *dead,* Sarah. And Toby and I don't know how to deal with it. And that's what happened. Okay?" I've never yelled at Sarah in my life and that was definitely approaching a yell. But I'm furious at her for saying what I know is true. Bailey *would* kill me, and it just makes me want to yell at Sarah more, which I do. "What should I do? Penance? Should I mortify the flesh, soak my hands in lye, rub pepper into my face like St. Rose? Wear a hair shirt?"

Her eyes bug out. "Yes, that's exactly what I think you should do!" she cries, but then her mouth twitches a little. "That's right, wear a hair shirt! A hair hat! A whole hair ensemble!" Her face is scrunching up. She bleats out, "St. Lennie," and then folds in half in hysterics. Followed by me, all our anger morphing into uncontrollable spectacular laughter—we're both bent over trying to breathe and it feels so great even though I might die from lack of oxygen.

"I'm sorry," I say between gasps.

She manages out, "No, me. I promised I wouldn't get like that. Felt good though to let you have it."

"Likewise," I squeal.

Maria sweeps back in, apron loaded with tomatoes, peppers, and onions, takes one look at us, and says, "You and your crazy cohort get out of here. Take a break."

Sarah and I drop onto our bench in front of the deli. The street's coming to life with sunburned couples from San Francisco stumbling out of B and Bs, swaddled in black, looking for pancakes or inner tubes or weed.

Sarah shakes her head as she lights up. I've confounded her. A hard thing to do. I know she'd still like to holler: *What in flying foxes were you thinking, Lennie?* but she doesn't.

"Okay, the matter at hand is getting that Fontaine boy back," she says calmly.

"Exactly."

"Clearly making him jealous is out of the question."

"Clearly." I sink my chin into my palms, look up at the thousand-year-old redwood across the street—it's peering down at me in consternation. It wants to kick my sorry newbie-to-the-earth ass.

"I know!" Sarah exclaims. "You'll seduce him." She lowers her eyelids, puckers her lips into a pout around her cigarette, inhales deeply, and then exhales a perfect smoke blob. "Seduction always works. I can't even think of one movie where it doesn't work, can you?"

"You can't be serious. He's so hurt and pissed. He's not even speaking to me, I called three times today . . . and it's me, not you, remember? I don't know how to seduce anyone." I'm miserable—I keep seeing Joe's face, stony and lifeless, like it was last night. If ever there was a face impervious to seduction, it's that one.

Sarah twirls her scarf with one hand, smokes with the other. "You don't have to *do* anything, Len, just show up to band practice tomorrow looking F-I-N-E, looking *irresistible*." She says *irresistible* like it has ten syllables. "His raging hormones and wild passion for you will do the rest."

"Isn't that incredibly superficial, Ms. French Feminist?"

"*Au contraire, ma petite.* These feminists are all about celebrating the body, its *langage*." She whips the scarf in the air. "Like I said, they're all after *jouissance*. As a means, of course, of subverting the dominant patriarchal paradigm and the white male literary canon, but we can get into that another time." She flicks her cigarette into the street. "Anyway, it can't hurt, Len. And it'll be fun. For me, that is . . ." A cloud of sadness crosses her face.

We exchange a glance that holds weeks of unsaid words.

"I just didn't think you could understand me anymore," I blurt out. I'd felt like a different person and Sarah had felt like the same old one, and I bet Bailey had felt similarly about me, and she was right to. Sometimes you just have to soldier through in your own private messy way.

"I couldn't understand," Sarah exclaims. "Not really. Felt—*feel* so useless, Lennie. And man, those grief books suck, so formulaic, total hundred percent dreck."

"Thanks," I say. "For reading them."

She looks down at her feet. "I miss her too." Until this

moment, it hadn't occurred to me she might've read those books for herself also. But of course. She revered Bailey. I've left her to grieve all on her own. I don't know what to say, so I reach across the bench and hug her. Hard.

A car honks with a bunch of hooting doofuses from Clover High in it. Way to ruin the moment. We disengage, Sarah waving her feminist book at them like a religious zealot—it makes me laugh.

When they pass, she takes another cigarette out of her pack, then gently touches my knee with it. "This Toby thing, I just don't get it." She lights the smoke, keeps shaking the match after it's out, like a metronome. "Were you competitive with Bailey? You guys never seemed like those King Lear type of sisters. I never thought so anyway."

"No we weren't. No . . . but . . . I don't know, I ask myself the same thing—"

I've crashed head-on into that something Big said last night, that awfully huge something.

"Remember that time we watched the Kentucky Derby?" I ask Sarah, not sure if this will make sense to anyone but me.

She looks at me like I'm crazy. "Yeah, uh, why?"

"Did you notice the racehorses had these companion ponies that didn't leave their sides?"

"I guess."

"Well, I think that was us, me and Bails."

She pauses a minute, exhales a long plume of smoke, before she says, "You were both racehorses, Len." I can tell she doesn't believe it though, that she's just trying to be nice.

I shake my head. "C'mon, be real, I wasn't. God, no way. I'm not." And it's been no one's doing but my own. Bailey went as crazy as Gram when I quit my lessons.

"Do you want to be?" Sarah asks.

"Maybe," I say, unable to quite manage a yes.

She smiles, then in silence, we both watch car after car creep along, most of them filled with ridiculously bright rubber river gear: giraffe boats, elephant canoes, and the like. Finally she says, "Being a companion pony must suck. Not metaphorically, I mean, you know, if you're a horse. Think about it. Self-sacrifice twenty-four/seven, no glory, no glamour . . . they should start a union, have their own Companion Pony Derby."

"A good new cause for you."

"No. My new cause is turning St. Lennon into a femme fatale." She smirks. "C'mon, Len, say yes."

Her *C'mon, Len* reminds me of Bails, and the next thing I know, I hear myself saying, "Okay, fine."

"It'll be subtle, I promise."

"Your strong suit."

She laughs. "Yeah, you're so screwed."

It's a hopeless idea, but I have no other. I have to do something, and Sarah's right, looking sexy, assuming I *can* look sexy, can't hurt, can it? I mean it is true that seduction hardly ever fails in movies, especially French ones. So I defer to Sarah's expertise, experience, to the concept of *jouissance,* and Operation Seduction is officially under way.

I HAVE CLEAVAGE. Melons. Bazumbas. Bodacious tatas. Handfuls of bosom pouring out of a minuscule black dress that I'm going to wear in broad daylight to band practice. I can't stop looking down. I'm stacked, a buxom babe. My scrawny self is positively zaftig. How can a bra possibly do this? Note to the physicists: Matter can indeed be created. Not to mention that I'm in platforms, so I look nine feet tall, and my lips are red as pomegranates.

Sarah and I have ducked into a classroom next to the music room.

"Are you sure, Sarah?" I don't know how I got myself into this ridiculous *I Love Lucy* episode.

"Never been more sure of anything. No guy will be able to resist you. I'm a little worried Mr. James won't survive it though."

"All right. Let's go," I say.

The way I get down the hallway is to pretend I'm someone else. Someone in a movie, a black-and-white French movie where everyone smokes and is mysterious and alluring. I'm a woman, not a girl, and I'm going to seduce a man. Who am I kidding? I freak out and run back to the classroom. Sarah follows, my bridesmaid.

"Lennie, c'mon." She's exasperated.

There it is again, *Lennie, c'mon.* I try again. This time I think of Bailey, the way she sashayed, making the ground work for her, and I glide effortlessly through the door of the music room.

I notice right away that Joe isn't there, but there's still time until rehearsal starts, like fifteen seconds, and he's always early, but maybe something held him up.

Fourteen seconds: Sarah was right, all the boys are staring at me like I've popped out of a centerfold. Rachel almost drops her clarinet.

Thirteen, twelve, eleven: Mr. James throws his arms up in celebration. "Lennie, you look ravishing!" I make it to my seat.

Ten, nine: I put my clarinet together but don't want to get lipstick all over my mouthpiece. I do anyway.

Eight, seven: Tuning.

Six, five: Tuning still.

Four, three: I turn around. Sarah shakes her head, mouths *unfreakingbelievable*.

Two, one: The announcement I now am expecting. "Let's begin class. Sorry to say we've lost our only trumpet player for the festival. Joe's going to perform with his brothers instead. Take out your pencils, I have changes."

I drop my glamorous head into my hands, hear Rachel say, "I told you he was out of your league, Lennie."

chapter 28

(Found on the back of a flyer on the sidewalk, Main Street)

There once was a girl who found herself dead.
She peered over the ledge of heaven
and saw that back on earth
her sister missed her too much,
was way too sad,
so she crossed some paths
that would not have crossed,
took some moments in her hand
shook them up
and spilled them like dice
over the living world.
It worked.
The boy with the guitar collided
with her sister.
"There you go, Len," she whispered. "The rest is up to you."

"May the force be with you," Sarah says, and sends me on my way, which is up the hill to the Fontaines' in aforementioned black cocktail dress, platforms, and bodacious tatas. The whole way up I repeat a mantra: *I am the author of my story and I can tell it any way I want. I am a solo artist. I am a racehorse.* Yes, this puts me into the major freaker category of human, but it does the trick and gets me up the hill, because fifteen minutes later I am looking up at Maison Fontaine, the dry summer grass crackling all around me, humming with hidden insects, which reminds me: How in the world does Rachel know what happened with Joe?

When I get to the driveway, I see a man dressed all in black with a shock of white hair, waving his arms around like a dervish, shouting in French at a stylish woman in a black dress (hers fits her) who looks equally peeved. She is hissing back at him in English. I definitely do not want to walk past those two panthers, so I sneak around the far side of the property and then duck under the enormous willow tree that reigns like a queen over the yard, the thick drapes of leaves falling like a shimmering green ball gown around the ancient trunk and branches, creating the perfect skulk den.

I need a moment to bolster my nerve, so I pace around in my new glimmery green apartment trying to figure out what I'm going to actually say to Joe, a point both Sarah and I forgot to consider.

That's when I hear it: clarinet music drifting out from the house, the melody Joe wrote for me. My heart does a hopeful flip. I walk over to the side of Maison Fontaine that abuts the tree and, still concealed by a drape of leaves, I stand up on tiptoe and see through the open window a sliver of Joe playing a bass clarinet in the living room.

And thus begins my life as a spy.

I tell myself, after this song, I will ring the doorbell and literally face the music. But then, he plays the melody again and again and the next thing I know I'm lying on my back listening to the amazing music, reaching into Sarah's purse for a pen, which I find as well as a scrap of paper. I jot down a poem, spike it with a stick into the ground. The music is making me rapturous; I slip back into that kiss, again drinking the sweet rain off his lips—

To be rudely interrupted by DougFred's exasperated voice. "Dude, you're driving me berserk—this same song over and over again, for two days now, I can't deal. We're all going to jump off the bridge right after you. Why don't you just talk to her?" I jump up and scurry over to the window: Harriet the Spy in drag. *Please say you'll talk to her*, I mind-beam to Joe.

"No way," he says.

"Joe, it's pathetic . . . c'mon."

Joe's voice is pinched, tight. "I *am so* pathetic. She was lying to me the whole time . . . just like Genevieve, just like Dad to Mom for that matter . . ."

Ugh. Ugh. Ugh. Boy, did I blow it.

"Whatever, already, with all of that—shit's complicated sometimes, man." *Hallelujah, DougFred.*

"Not for me."

"Just get your horn, we need to practice."

Still concealed under the tree, I listen to Joe, Marcus, and DougFred practicing: It goes like this, three notes, then a cell phone rings: Marcus: *Hey Ami*, then five minutes later, another ring: Marcus: *Salut Sophie*, then DougFred: *Hey Chloe*, then fifteen minutes later: *Hi Nicole*. These guys are Clover catnip. I remember how the phone rang pretty much continually the evening I spent here. Finally, Joe says: *Turn off the cell phones or we won't even get through a song*—but just as he finishes the sentence, his own cell goes off and his brothers laugh. I hear him say, *Hey Rachel*. And that's the end of me. *Hey Rachel* in a voice that sounds happy to hear from her, like he was expecting the call, waiting for it even.

I think of St. Wilgefortis, who went to sleep beautiful and woke up with a full beard and mustache, and wish that fate on Rachel. Tonight.

Then I hear: *You were totally right. The Throat Singers of Tuva are awesome.*

Call 911.

Okay, calm down, Lennie. Stop pacing. Don't think about him batting his eyelashes at Rachel Brazile! Grinning at her, kissing her, making her feel like she's part sky . . . *What have I done?* I lie down on my back in the grass under the umbrella of trembling sun-lit leaves. I'm leveled by a phone call. How must it have been for him to actually see me kiss Toby?

I suck, there's no other way to put it.

There's also no other way to put this: I'm so freaking in love—it's just blaring every which way inside me, like some psycho opera.

But back to BITCHZILLA!?

Be rational, I tell myself, systematic, think of all the many innocuous unromantic reasons she could be calling him. I can't think of one, though I'm so consumed with trying I don't even hear the truck pull up, just a door slamming. I get up, peek out through the thick curtain of leaves, and almost pass out to see Toby walking toward the front door. WTF-asaurus? He hesitates before ringing the bell, takes a deep breath, then presses the button, waits, then presses it again. He steps back, looks toward the living room, where the music is now blasting, then knocks hard. The music stops and I hear the pounding of feet, then watch the door open and hear Toby say: "Is Joe here?"

Gulp.

Next, I hear Joe still in the living room: "What's his problem? I didn't want to talk to him yesterday and I don't want to talk to him today."

Marcus is back in the living room. "Just talk to the guy."

"No."

But Joe must have gone to the door, because I hear muffled words and see Toby's mouth moving, although he's quieted down too much for me to make out the words.

I don't plan what happens next. It just happens. I just happen to have that stupid it's-my-story-I'm-a-racehorse mantra back on repeat in my head and so I somehow decide that whatever is going to happen, good or bad, I don't want to be hiding in a tree when it does. I muster all my courage and part the curtain of leaves.

The first thing I notice is the sky, so full of blue and the kind of brilliant white clouds that make you ecstatic to have eyes. Nothing can go wrong under this sky, I think as I make my way across the lawn, trying not to wobble in my platforms. The Fontaine panther-parents are nowhere in sight; probably they took their hissing match into the barn. Toby must hear my footsteps; he turns around.

"Lennie?"

The door swings open and three Fontaines pile out like they've been stuffed in a car.

Marcus speaks first: "Va va va voom."

Joe's mouth drops open.

Toby's too, for that matter.

"Holy shit" comes out of DougFred's perpetually deranged-with-glee face. The four of them are like a row of dumbfounded ducks. I'm acutely aware of how short my dress is, how tight it is across my chest, how wild my hair is, how red my lips are. I might die. I want to wrap my arms around my body. For the rest of my life, I'm going to leave the femme fatale-ing to other femmes. All I want is to flee, but I don't want them to stare at my butt as I fly into the woods in this tiny piece of fabric masquerading as a dress. Wait a second here—one by one, I take in their idiotic faces. Was Sarah right? Might this work? Could guys be this simple-minded?

Marcus is ebullient. "One hot tamale, John Lennon."

Joe glares at him. "Shut the hell up, Marcus." He has regained his composure and rage. Nope, Joe is definitely not this simple-minded. I know immediately this was a bad, bad move.

"What's wrong with you two?" he says to Toby and me, throwing up his arms in a perfect mimicry of his father's dervishness.

He pushes past his brothers and Toby, jumps off the stoop, comes up to me, so close that I can smell his fury. "Don't you get it? What you did? It's done, Lennie, we're done." Joe's beautiful lips, the ones that kissed me and whispered in my hair, they are twisting and contorting around words I hate. The ground beneath me begins to tilt. People don't really faint, do they? "Get it, because I mean it. It's ruined. *Everything* is."

I'm mortified. I'm going to kill Sarah. And what a total companion-pony move on my part. I knew this wouldn't work. There was no way he was going to toss aside this behemoth betrayal because I squeezed myself into this ridiculously small dress. How could I be so stupid?

And it's just dawned on me that I might be the author of my own story, but so is everyone else the author of their own stories, and sometimes, like now, there's no overlap.

He's walking away from me. I don't care that there are six pairs of eyes and ears on us. He can't leave before I have a chance to say something, have a chance to make him understand what happened, how I feel about him. I grab the bottom of his T-shirt. He snaps around, flings my hand away, meets my eyes. I don't know what he sees in them, but he softens a little.

I watch some of the rage slip off of him as he looks at me. Without it, he looks unnerved and vulnerable, like a small disheartened boy. It makes me ache with tenderness. I want to touch his beautiful face. I look at his hands; they are shaking.

As is all of me.

He's waiting for me to speak. But I realize the perfect thing to say must be in another girl's mind, because it's not in mine. Nothing is in mine.

"I'm sorry," I manage out.

"I don't care," he says, his voice cracking a little. He looks down at the ground. I follow his gaze, see his bare feet sticking out of jeans; they are long and thin and monkey-toed. I've never seen his feet out of shoes and socks before. They're perfectly simian—toes so long he could play the piano with them.

"Your feet," I say, before I realize it. "I've never seen them before."

My moronic words drum in the air between us, and for a split second, I know he wants to laugh, wants to reach out and pull me to him, wants to tease me about saying something so ridiculous when he's about to murder me. I can see this in his face as if his thoughts were scribbled across it. But then all that gets wiped away as quickly as it came, and what's left is the unwieldy hurt in his unbatting eyes, his grinless mouth. He will never forgive me.

I took the joy out of the most joyful person on planet Earth.

"I'm so sorry," I say. "I—"

"God, stop saying that." His hands swoop around me like lunatic bats. I've reignited his rage. "It doesn't matter to me that you're sorry. You just don't get it." He whips around and bolts into the house before I can say another word.

Marcus shakes his head and sighs, then follows his brother inside with DougFred in tow.

I stand there with Joe's words still scorching my skin, thinking what a terrible idea it was to come up here, in this tiny dress, these skyscraping heels. I wipe the siren song off my lips. I'm disgusted with myself. I didn't ask for his forgiveness, didn't explain a thing, didn't tell him that he is the most amazing thing that's ever happened to me, that I love him, that he's the only one for me. Instead, I talked about his feet. *His feet.*

Talk about choking under pressure. And then I remember *Hey Rachel,* which explodes a Molotov cocktail of jealousy into my misery, completing the dismal picture.

I want to kick the postcard-perfect sky.

I'm so absorbed in my self-flagellation, I forget Toby's there until he says, "Emotional guy."

I look up. He's sitting on the stoop now, leaning back on his arms, his legs kicked out. He must have come straight from work; he's out of his usual skate rat rags and has on mud-splattered jeans and boots and button-down shirt and is only missing the Stetson to complete the Marlboro Man picture. He looks like he did the day he whisked my sister's heart away: Bailey's Revolutionary.

"He almost attacked me with his guitar yesterday. I think we're making progress," he adds.

"Toby, what're you doing here?"

"What are you doing hiding in trees?" he asks back, nodding at the willow behind me.

"Trying to make amends," I say.

"Me too," he says quickly, jumping to his feet. "But to you. Been trying to tell him what's what." His words surprise me.

"I'll take you home," he says.

We both get into his truck. I can't seem to curb the nausea overwhelming me as a result of the hands-down worst seduction in love's history. Ugh. And on top of it, I'm sure Joe is watching us from a window, all his suspicions seething in his hot head as I drive off with Toby.

"So, what'd you say to him?" I ask when we've cleared Fontaine territory.

"Well, the three words I got to say yesterday and the ten I got in today added up to pretty much telling him he should give you a second chance, that there's nothing going on with us, that we were just wrecked . . ."

"Wow, that was nice. Busybody as all get out, but nice."

He looks over at me for a moment before returning his eyes to the road. "I watched you guys that night in the rain. I saw it, how you feel."

His voice is full of emotion that I can't decipher and probably don't want to. "Thanks," I say quietly, touched that he did this despite everything, because of everything.

He doesn't respond, just looks straight ahead into the sun, which is obliterating everything in our path with unruly splendor. The truck blasts through the trees and I stick my hand out the window, trying to catch the wind in my palm like Bails used to, missing her, missing the girl I used to be around her, missing who we all used to be. We will never be those people again. She took them all with her.

I notice Toby's tapping his fingers nervously on the wheel. He keeps doing it. Tap. Tap. Tap.

"What is it?" I ask.

He grips the wheel tight with both hands.

"I really love her," he says, his voice breaking. "More than anything."

"Oh, Toby, I know that." That's the only thing I do understand about this whole mess: that somehow what happened between us happened because there's too much love for Bailey between us, not too little.

"I know," I repeat.

He nods.

Something occurs to me then: Bailey loved both Toby and me so much—he and I almost make up her whole heart, and maybe that's it, what we were trying to do by being together, maybe we were trying to put her heart back together again.

He stops the truck in front of the house. The sun streams into the cab, bathing us in light. I look out my window, can see Bails rushing out of the house, flying off the porch, to jump into this very truck I am sitting in. It's so strange. I spent forever resenting Toby for taking my sister away from me, and now it seems like I count on him to bring her back.

I open the door, put one of my platforms onto the ground.

"Len?"

I turn around.

"You'll wear him down." His smile is warm and genuine. He rests the side of his head on the steering wheel. "I'm going to leave you alone for a bit, but if you need me . . . for anything, okay?"

"Same," I say, my throat knotting up.

Our conjoined love for Bailey trembles between us; it's like a living thing, as delicate as a small bird, and as breathtaking in its hunger for flight. My heart hurts for both of us.

"Don't do anything stupid on that board," I say.

"Nope."

"Okay." Then I slide out, close the door, and head into the house.

chapter 29

Sometimes, I'd see Sarah and her mom
share a look across a room
and I'd want
to heave my life over like a table.
I'd tell myself not to feel that way,
that I was lucky:
I had Bailey,
I had Gram and Big,
I had my clarinet, books, a river, the sky.
I'd tell myself that I had a mother too,
just not one anyone else could see
but Bailey and me.

(Found scribbled on the want ads in The Clover Gazette
under the bench outside Maria's Deli)

SARAH'S AT STATE, since the symposium is this afternoon, so I have no one on whom to blame the *Hey Rachel* seduction fiasco but myself. I leave her a message telling her I've been totally mortified like a good saint because of her *jouissance* and am now seeking a last-resort miracle.

The house is quiet. Gram must have gone out, which is too bad because for the first time in ages, I'd like nothing more than to sit at the kitchen table with her and drink tea.

I go up to The Sanctum to brood about Joe, but once there, my eyes keep settling on the boxes I packed the other night. I can't stand looking at them, so after I change out of my ridiculous outfit, I take them up to the attic.

I haven't been up here in years. I don't like the tombishness, the burned smell of the trapped heat, the lack of air. It always seems so sad too, full of everything abandoned and forgotten. I look around at the lifeless clutter, feel deflated at the idea of bringing Bailey's things up here. This is what I've been avoiding for months now. I take a deep breath, look around. There's only one window, so I decide, despite the fact that the area around it is packed in with boxes and mountains of bric-a-brac, that Bailey's things should go where the sun will at least seep in each day.

I make my way over there through an obstacle course of broken furniture, boxes, and old canvases. I move a few cartons immediately so I can crack open the window and hear the river. Hints of rose and jasmine blow in on the afternoon breeze. I open it wider, climb up on an old desk so I can lean out. The sky is still spectacular and I hope Joe is gazing up at it. No matter where I look inside myself, I come across more love for him, for everything about him, his anger as much as his tenderness—he's so alive, he makes me feel like I could take a bite out of the whole earth. If only words hadn't eluded me today, if only I yelled back at him: *I do get it! I get that as long as you live no one will ever love you as much as I do—I have a heart so I can give it to you alone!* That's exactly the way I feel—but unfortunately, people don't talk like that outside of Victorian novels.

I take my head out of the sky and bring it back into the stuffy attic. I wait for my eyes to readjust, and when they do, I'm still convinced this is the only possible spot for Bailey's things. I start moving all the junk that's already there to the shelves on the back wall. After many trips back and forth, I finally reach down to pick up the last of it, which is a shoebox, and the top flips open. It's full of letters, all addressed to Big, probably love letters. I peek at one postcard from an Edie. I decide against snooping further; my karma is about as bad as it's ever been right now. I slip the lid back on, place it on one of the lower shelves where there's still some space. Just behind it, I notice an old letter box, its wood polished and shiny. I wonder what an antique like this is doing up here instead of downstairs with all Gram's other treasures. It looks like a showcase piece too. I slide it out; the wood is mahogany and there's a ring of galloping horses engraved into the top. Why isn't it covered in dust like everything else on these shelves? I lift the lid, see that it's full of folded notes on Gram's mint-green stationery, so many of them, and lots of letters as well. I'm about to put it back when I see written on the outside of an envelope in Gram's careful script the name *Paige*. I flip through the other envelopes. Each and every one says *Paige* with the year next to her name. Gram writes letters to Mom? Every year? All the envelopes are sealed. I know that I should put the box back, that this is private, but I can't. Karma be damned. I open one of the folded notes. It says:

> Darling,
>
> The second the lilacs are in full bloom, I have to write you. I know I tell you this every year, but they haven't blossomed the same since you left. They're so stingy now. Maybe it's because no one comes close to loving them like you did how could they? Each spring I wonder if I'm going to find the girls sleeping in the garden, like I'd find you, morning after morning. Did you know how I loved that, walking outside and seeing you asleep with my lilacs and roses all around you I've never even tried to paint the image. I never will. I wouldn't want to ruin it for myself.
>
> Mom

Wow—my mother loves lilacs, *really* loves them. Yes, yes, it's true, most people love lilacs, but my mother is so gaga about them that she used to sleep in Gram's garden, night after night, all spring long, so gaga she couldn't bear to be inside knowing all those flowers were raising hell outside her window. Did she bring her blankets out with her? A sleeping bag? Nothing? Did she sneak out when everyone else was asleep? Did she do this when she was my age? Did she like looking up at the sky as much as I do? I want to know more. I feel jittery and lightheaded, like I'm meeting her for the first time. I sit down on a box, try to calm down. I can't. I pick up another note. It says:

> *Remember that pesto you made with walnuts instead of pine nuts? Well, I tried pecans, and you know what? Even better. The recipe:*
> *2 cups packed fresh basil leaves*
> *2/3 cup olive oil*
> *1/2 cup pecans, toasted*
> *1/3 cup freshly grated Parmesan*
> *2 large garlic cloves, mashed*
> *1/2 teaspoon salt*

My mother makes pesto with walnuts! This is even better than sleeping with lilacs. So normal. So *I think I'll whip up some pasta with pesto for dinner.* My mother bangs around a kitchen. She puts walnuts and basil and olive oil in a food processor, and presses blend. She boils water for pasta! I have to tell Bails. I want to scream out the window at her: *Our mother boils water for pasta!* I'm going to. I'm going to tell Bailey. I make my way over to the window, climb back up on the desk, put my head out, holler up at the sky, and tell my sister everything I've just learned. I feel dizzy, and yes, a bit out of my tree, when I climb back into the attic, now hoping no one heard this girl screaming about pasta and lilacs at the top of her lungs. I take a deep breath. Open another one.

> *Paige,*
> *I've been wearing the fragrance you wore for years. The one you thought smelled like sunshine. I've just found out they've discontinued it. I feel as though I've lost you now completely. I can't bear it.*
> *Mom*

Oh.

But why didn't Gram tell us our mother wore a perfume that smelled like sunshine? That she slept in the garden in the springtime? That she made pesto with walnuts? Why did she keep this real-life mother from us? But as soon as I ask the question, I know the answer, because suddenly there is not blood pumping in my veins, coursing all throughout my body, but longing for a mother who loves lilacs. Longing like I've never had for the Paige Walker who wanders the world. That Paige Walker never made me feel like a daughter, but a mother who boils water for pasta does. Except don't you need to be claimed to be a daughter? Don't you need to be loved?

And now there's something worse than longing flooding me, because how could a mother who boils water for pasta leave two little girls behind?

How could she?

I close the lid, slide the box back on a shelf, quickly stack Bailey's boxes by the window, and go down the stairs into the empty house.

chapter 30

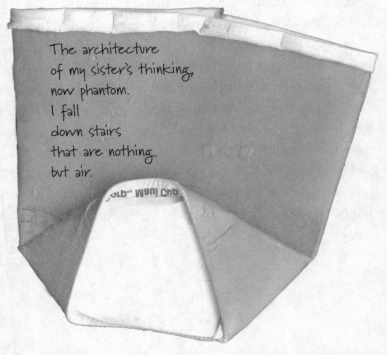

The architecture
of my sister's thinking,
now phantom.
I fall
down stairs
that are nothing
but air.

(Found on a to-go cup by a grove of old growth redwoods)

THE NEXT FEW days inch by miserably. I skip band practice and confine myself to The Sanctum. Joe Fontaine does not stop by, or call, or text, or e-mail, or skywrite, or send Morse code, or telepathically communicate with me. Nothing. I'm quite certain he and *Hey Rachel* have moved to Paris, where they live on chocolate, music, and red wine, while I sit at this window, peering down the road where no one comes bouncing along, guitar in hand, like they used to.

As the days pass, Paige Walker's love of lilacs and ability to boil water have the singular effect of washing sixteen years of myth right off of her. And without it, all that's left is this: Our mother abandoned us. There's no way around it. And what kind of person does that? Rip Van Lennie is right. I've been living in a dream world, totally brainwashed by Gram. My mother's freaking nuts, and I am too, because what kind of ignoramus swallows such a cockamamie story? Those hypothetical families that Big spoke of the other night would've been right not to be kind. My mother is neglectful and irresponsible and probably mentally deficient too. She's not a heroine at all. She's just a selfish woman who couldn't hack it and left two toddlers on her mother's porch and *never came back*. That's who she is. And that's who we are too, two kids, discarded, just left there. I'm glad Bailey never had to see it this way.

I don't go back up to the attic.

It's all right. I'm used to a mother who rides around on a magic carpet. I can get used to this mother too, can't I? But what I can't get used to is that I no longer think Joe, despite my compounding love for him, is ever going to forgive me. How to get used to no one calling you John Lennon? Or making you believe the sky begins at your feet? Or acting like a dork so you'll say *quel dork*? How to get used to being without a boy who turns you into brightness?

I can't.

And what's worse is that with each day that passes, The Sanctum gets quieter, even when I'm blasting the stereo, even when I'm talking to Sarah, who's still apologizing for the seduction fiasco, even when I'm practicing Stravinsky, it just gets quieter and quieter, until it is so quiet that what I hear, again and again, is the cranking sound of the casket lowering into the ground.

With each day that passes, there are longer stretches when I don't think I hear Bailey's heels clunking down the hallway, or glimpse her lying on her bed reading, or catch her in my periphery reciting lines into the mirror. I'm becoming accustomed to The Sanctum without her, and I hate it. Hate that when I stand in her closet fumbling from piece to piece, my face pressed into the fabrics, that I can't find one shirt or dress that still has her scent, and it's my fault. They all smell like me now.

Hate that her cell phone finally has been shut down.

With each day that passes, more traces of my sister vanish, not only from the world, but from my very own mind, and there's nothing I can do about it, but sit in the soundless, scentless sanctum and cry.

On the sixth day of this, Sarah declares me a state of emergency and makes me promise to go to the movies with her that night.

She picks me up in Ennui, wearing a black miniskirt, black minier tank top that shows off a lot of tan midriff, three-foot black heels, all topped off with a black ski hat, which I'm supposing is her attempt at practicality, because a chill blew in and it's arctic cold. I'm wearing a brown suede coat, turtleneck, and jeans. We look like we are spliced together from different weather systems.

"Hi!" she says, taking the cigarette out of her mouth to kiss me as I get in. "This movie really is supposed to be good. Not like that last one I made you go to where the woman sat in a chair with her cat for the first half. I admit that one was problematico." Sarah and I have opposite movie-going philosophies. All I want out of celluloid is to sit in the dark with a huge bucket of popcorn. Give me car chases, girl gets boy, underdogs triumphing, let me swoon and scream and weep. Sarah on the other hand can't tolerate such pedestrian fare and complains the whole time about how we're rotting our minds and soon won't be able to think our own thoughts because our brains will be lost to the dominant paradigm. Sarah's preference is The Guild, where they show bleak foreign films where nothing happens, no one talks, everyone loves the one who will never love them back, and then the movie ends. On the program tonight is some stultifyingly boring black-and-white film from Norway.

Her face drops as she studies mine. "You look miserable."

"Sucky week all around."

"It'll be fun tonight, promise." She takes one hand off the wheel and pulls a brown sack out of a backpack. "For the movie." She hands it to me. "Vodka."

"Hmm, then I'll for sure fall asleep in this action-packed, thrill-a-minute, black-and-white, silent movie from Norway."

She rolls her eyes. "It's not silent, Lennie."

While waiting in line, Sarah jumps around trying to keep warm. She's telling me how Luke held up remarkably well at the symposium despite being the only guy there, even made her ask a question about music, but then mid-sentence and mid-jump, her eyes bulge a little. I catch it, even though she's already resumed talking as if nothing has happened. I turn around and there's Joe across the street with Rachel.

They're so lost in conversation they don't even realize the light has changed.

Cross the street, I want to scream. *Cross the street before you fall in love*. Because that's what appears to be happening. I watch Joe lightly tug at her arm while he tells her something or other I'm sure about Paris. I can see the smile, all that radiance pouring over Rachel and I think I might fall like a tree.

"Let's go."

"Yup." Sarah's already walking toward the Jeep, fumbling in her bag for the keys. I follow her, but take one look back and meet Joe's eyes head on. Sarah disappears. Then Rachel. Then all the people waiting in line. Then the cars, the trees, the buildings, the ground, the sky until it is only Joe and me staring across empty space at each other. He does not smile. He anti-smiles. But I can't look away and he can't seem to either. Time has slowed so much that I wonder if when we stop staring at each other we will be old and our whole lives will be over with just a few measly kisses between us. I'm dizzy with missing him, dizzy with seeing him, dizzy with being just yards from him. I want to run across the street, I'm about to—I can feel my heart surge, pushing me toward him, but then he just shakes his head almost to himself and looks away from me and toward Rachel, who now comes back into focus. High-definition focus. Very deliberately, he puts his arm around her and together they cross the street and get in line for the movie. A searing pain claws through me. He doesn't look back, but Rachel does.

She salutes me, a triumphant smile on her face, then flips an insult of blond hair at me as she swings her arm around his waist and turns away.

My heart feels like it's been kicked into a dark corner of my body. *Okay I get it*, I want to holler at the sky. *This is how it feels.* Lesson learned. Comeuppance accepted. I watch them retreat into the theater arm in arm, wishing I had an eraser so I could wipe her out of this picture. Or a vacuum. A vacuum would be better, just suck her up, gone. Out of his arms. Out of my chair. For good.

"C'mon Len, let's get out of here," a familiar voice says. I guess Sarah still exists and she's talking to me, so I must still exist too. I look down, see my legs, realize I'm still standing. I put one foot in front of the other and make my way to Ennui.

There is no moon, no stars, just a brightless, lightless gray bowl over our heads as we drive home.

"I'm going to challenge her for first chair," I say.

"Finally."

"Not because of this—"

"I know. Because you're a racehorse, not some podunk pony." There's no irony in her voice.

I roll down the window and let the cold air slap me silly.

chapter 31

SARAH AND I are hanging half in, half out my bedroom window, passing the bottle of vodka back and forth.

"We could off her?" Sarah suggests, all her words slurring into one.

"How would we do it?" I ask, swigging a huge gulp of vodka.

"Poison. It's always the best choice, hard to trace."

"Let's poison him too, and all his stupid gorgeous brothers." I can feel the words sticking to the insides of my mouth. "He didn't even wait a week, Sarah."

"That doesn't mean anything. He's hurt."

"God, how can he like her?"

Sarah shakes her head. "I saw the way he looked at you in the street, like a crazy person, really out there, more demented than demented,

(Found on a piece of paper under the big willow)

holy Toledo tigers bonkers. You know what I think? I think he put his arm around her for your benefit."

"What if he has sex with her for my benefit?" Jealousy mad-dogs through me. Yet, that's not the worst part, neither is the remorse; the worst part is I keep thinking of the afternoon on the forest bed, how vulnerable I'd felt, how much I'd liked it, being that open, that *me*, with him. Had I ever felt so close to anyone?

"Can I have a cigarette?" I ask, taking one before she answers.

She cups a hand around the end of her smoke, lights it with the other, then hands it to me, takes mine, then lights it for herself. I drag on it, cough, don't care, take another and manage not to choke, blowing a gray trail of smoke into the night air.

"Bails would know what to do," I say.

"She would," Sarah agrees.

We smoke together quietly in the moonlight and I real-ize something I can never say to Sarah. There might've been another reason, a deeper one, why I didn't want to be around her. It's that she's not Bailey, and that's a bit unbearable for me—but I need to bear it. I concentrate on the music of the river, let myself drift along with it as it rushes steadily away.

After a few moments, I say, "You can revoke my free pass."

She tilts her head, smiles at me in a way that floods me with warmth. "Done deal."

She puts out her cigarette on the windowsill and slips back onto the bed. I put mine out too, but stay outside looking over Gram's lustrous garden, breathing it in and practically swoon-ing from the bouquet that wafts up to me on the cool breeze.

And that's when I get the idea. The *brilliant* idea. I have to talk to Joe. I have to at least try to make him understand. But I could use a little help.

"Sarah," I say when I flop back onto the bed. "The roses, they're aphrodisiacal, remember?"

She gets it immediately. "Yes, Lennie! It's the last-resort miracle! Flying figs, yes!"

"Figs?"

"I couldn't think of an animal, I'm too wasted."

I'M ON A mission. I've left Sarah sound asleep in Bailey's bed and I'm tiptoeing my thumping vodka head down the steps and out into the creeping morning light. The fog is thick and sad, the whole world an X-ray of itself. I have my weapon in hand and am about to begin my task. Gram is going to kill me, but this is the price I must pay.

I start at my favorite bush of all, the Magic Lanterns, roses with a symphony of color jammed into each petal. I snip the heads off the most extraordinary ones I can find. Then go to the Opening Nights and snip, snip, snip, merrily along to the Perfect Moments, the Sweet Surrenders, the Black Magics. My heart kicks around in my chest from both fear and excitement. I go from prize bush to bush, from the red velvet Lasting Loves to the pink Fragrant Clouds to the apricot Marilyn Monroes and end at the most beautiful orange-red rose on the planet, appropriately named: the Trumpeter. There I go for broke until I have at my feet a bundle of roses so ravishing that if God got married, there would be no other possible choice for the bouquet. I've cut so many I can't even fit the stems in one hand but have to carry them in both as I head down the road to find a place to stash them until later. I put them beside one of my favorite oaks, totally hidden from the house. Then I worry they'll wilt, so I run back to the house and prepare a basket with wet towels at the bottom and go back to the side of the road and wrap all the stems.

Later that morning, after Sarah leaves, Big goes off to the trees, and Gram retreats into the art room with her green women, I tiptoe out the door. I've convinced myself, despite all reason perhaps, that this is going to work. I keep thinking that Bails would be proud of this harebrained plan. *Extraordinary,* she'd say. In fact, maybe Bails would like that I fell in love with Joe so soon after she died. Maybe it's just the exact inappropriate way my sister would want to be mourned by me.

The flowers are still behind the oak where I left them. When I see them I am struck again by their extraordinary beauty. I've never seen a bouquet of them like this, never seen the explosive color of one bloom right beside another.

I walk up the hill to the Fontaines' in a cloud of exquisite fragrance. Who knows if it's the power of suggestion, or if the roses are truly charmed, but by the time I get to the house, I'm so in love with Joe, I can barely ring the bell. I have serious doubts if I'll be able to form a coherent sentence. If he answers I might just tackle him to the ground till he gives and be done with it.

But no such luck.

The same stylish woman who was in the yard squabbling the other day opens the door. "Don't tell me, you must be Lennie." It's immediately apparent that Fontaine spawn can't come close in the smile department to Mother Fontaine. I should tell Big—her smile has a better shot at reviving bugs than his pyramids.

"I am," I say. "Nice to meet you, Mrs. Fontaine." She's being so friendly that I can't imagine she knows what's happened between her son and me. He probably talks to her about as much as I talk to Gram.

"And will you just look at those roses! I've never seen anything like them in my life. Where'd you pick them? The Garden of Eden?" Like mother, like son. I remember Joe said the same that first day.

"Something like that," I say. "My grandmother has a way with flowers. They're for Joe. Is he home?" All of a sudden, I'm nervous. Really nervous. My stomach seems to be hosting a symposium of bees.

"And the aroma! My God, what an aroma!" she cries. I think the flowers have hypnotized her. Wow. Maybe they do work. "Lucky Joe, what a gift, but I'm sorry dear, he's not home. He said he'd be back soon though. I can put them in water and leave them for him in his room if you like."

I'm too disappointed to answer. I just nod and hand them over to her. I bet he's at Rachel's feeding her family chocolate croissants. I have a dreadful thought—what if the roses actually are love-inducing and Joe comes back here with Rachel and both of them fall under their spell? This was another disastrous idea, but I can't take the roses back now. Actually, I think it would take an automatic weapon to get them back from Mrs. Fontaine, who is leaning farther into the bouquet with each passing second.

"Thank you," I say. "For giving them to him." Will she be able to separate herself from these flowers?

"It was very nice to meet you, Lennie. I'd been looking forward to it. I'm sure Joe will *really* appreciate these."

"Lennie," an exasperated voice says from behind me. That symposium in my belly just opened its doors to wasps and hornets too. This is it. I turn around and see Joe making his way up the path. There is no bounce in his walk. It's as if gravity has a hand on his shoulder that it never did before.

"Oh, honey!" Mrs. Fontaine exclaims. "Look what Lennie brought you. Have you ever seen such roses? I sure haven't. My word." Mrs. Fontaine is speaking directly to the roses now, taking in deep aromatic breaths. "Well, I'll just bring these in, find a nice place for them. You kids have fun . . ."

I watch her head disappear completely in the bouquet as the door closes behind her. I want to lunge at her, grab the flowers, shriek, *I need those roses more than you do*, *lady*, but I have a more pressing concern: Joe's silent fuming beside me.

As soon as the door clicks closed, he says, "You still don't get it, do you?" His voice is full of menace, not quite if a shark could talk, but close. He points at the door behind which dozens of aphrodisiacal roses are filling the air with promise. "You've got to be kidding. You think it's that easy?" His face is getting flushed, his eyes bulgy and wild. "I don't want tiny dresses or stupid fucking magic flowers!" He flails in place like a marionette. "I'm *already* in love with you, Lennie, don't you get it? But I can't be with you. Every time I close my eyes I see you with *him*."

I stand there dumbstruck—sure, there were some discouraging things just said, but all of them seem to have fallen away. I'm left with six wonderful words: *I'm already in love with you.* Present tense, not past. Rachel Brazile be damned. A skyful of hope knocks into me.

"Let me explain," I say, intent on remembering my lines this time, intent on getting him to understand.

He makes a noise that's part groan, part roar, like *ahhharrrgh,* then says, "Nothing to explain. I *saw* you two. You lied to me over and over again."

"Toby and I were—"

He interrupts. "No way, I don't want to hear it. I told you what happened to me in France and you did this anyway. I can't forgive you. It's just the way I am. You have to leave me alone. I'm sorry."

My legs go weak as it sinks in that his hurt and anger, the sickness of having been deceived and betrayed, has already trumped his love.

He motions down the hill to where Toby and I were that night, and says, "What. Did. You. Expect?" What *did* I expect? One minute he's trying to tell me he loves me and the next he's watching me kiss another guy. Of course he feels this way.

I have to say something, so I say the only thing that makes sense in my mixed-up heart. "I'm so in love with you."

My words knock the wind out of him.

It's as if everything around us stops to see what's going to happen next—the trees lean in, birds hover, flowers hold their petals still. How could he not surrender to this crazy big love we both feel? He couldn't not, right?

I reach my hand out to touch him, but he moves his arm out of my reach.

He shakes his head, looks at the ground. "I can't be with someone who could do that to me." Then he looks right in my eyes, and says, "I can't be with someone who could do that to *her sister.*"

The words have guillotine force. I stagger backward, splintering into pieces. His hand flies to his mouth. Maybe he's wishing his words back inside. Maybe he even thinks he went too far, but it doesn't matter. He wanted me to get it and I do.

I do the only thing I can. I turn around and run from him, hoping my trembling legs will keep me up until I can get away. Like Heathcliff and Cathy, I had the Big Bang, once-in-a-lifetime kind of love, and I destroyed it all.

ALL I WANT is to get up to The Sanctum so I can throw the covers over my head and disappear for several hundred years. Out of breath from racing down the hill, I push through the front door of the house. I blow past the kitchen, but backtrack when I glimpse Gram. She's sitting at the kitchen table, her arms folded in front of her chest, her face hard and stern. In front of her on the table are her garden shears and my copy of *Wuthering Heights.*

Uh-oh.

She jumps right in. "You have no idea how close I came to chopping your precious book to bits, but I have some self-control and respect for other people's things." She stands up. When Gram's mad, she practically doubles in size and all twelve feet of her is bulldozing across the kitchen right at me.

"What were you thinking, Lennie? You come like the Grim Reaper and decimate my garden, my *roses*. How could you? You know how I feel about anyone but me touching my flowers. It's the one and only thing I ask. The one and only thing."

She's looming over me. "Well?"

"They'll grow back." I know this is the wrong thing to say, but holler-at-Lennie-day is taking its toll.

She throws her arms up, completely exasperated with me, and it strikes me how closely her expression and arm flailing resemble Joe's. "That is not the point and you know it." She points at me. "You've become very selfish, Lennie Walker."

This I was not expecting. No one's ever called me selfish in my life, least of all Gram—the never-ending fountain of praise and coddling. Are she and Joe testifying at the same trial?

Could this day get any worse?

Isn't the answer to that question always yes?

Gram's hands are on her hips now, face flushed, eyes blazing, double uh-oh—I lean back against the wall, brace myself for the impending assault. She leans in. "Yes, Lennie. You act like you're the only one in this house who has lost somebody. She was like my daughter, do you know what that's like? Do you? My *daughter*. No, you don't because you haven't once asked. Not once have you asked how I'm doing. Did it ever occur to you that *I* might need to talk?" She is yelling now. "I know you're devastated, but Lennie, you're not the only one."

All the air races out of the room, and I race out with it.

chapter 32

Bailey grabs my hand
and pulls me out of the window
into the sky,
pulls music out of my pockets.
"It's time you learned to fly," she says,
and vanishes.

(Found on a candy wrapper on the trail to the Rain River)

I BOLT DOWN the hallway and out the door and jump all four
porch steps. I want to run into the woods, veer off the path,
find a spot where no one can find me, sit down under an old
craggy oak and cry. I want to cry and cry and cry and cry until
all the dirt in the whole forest floor has turned to mud. And this
is exactly what I'm about to do except that when I hit the path,

I realize I can't. I can't run away from Gram, especially not after everything she just said. Because I know she's right. She and Big have been like background noise to me since Bailey died. I've hardly given any thought to what they're going through. I made Toby my ally in grief, like he and I had an exclusionary right to it, an exclusionary right to Bailey herself. I think of all the times Gram hovered at the door to The Sanctum trying to get me to talk about Bailey, asking me to come down and have a cup of tea, and how I just assumed she wanted to comfort me. It never once occurred to me that she needed to talk herself, that she needed *me*.

How could I have been so careless with her feelings? With Joe's? With everyone's?

I take a deep breath, turn around, and make my way back to the kitchen. I can't make things right with Joe, but at least I can try to make them right with Gram. She's in the same chair at the table. I stand across from her, rest my fingers on the table, wait for her to look up at me. Not one window is open, and the hot stuffy kitchen smells almost rotten.

"I'm sorry," I say. "Really." She nods, looks down at her hands. It occurs to me that I've disappointed or hurt or betrayed everyone I love in the last couple months: Gram, Bailey, Joe, Toby, Sarah, even Big. How did I manage that? Before Bailey died, I don't think I ever really disappointed anyone. Did Bailey just take care of everyone and everything for me? Or did no one expect anything of me before? Or did I just not do anything or want anything before, so I never had to deal with the consequences of my messed-up actions? Or have I become really selfish and self-absorbed? Or all of the above?

I look at the sickly Lennie houseplant on the counter and know that it's not me anymore. It's who I used to be, before, and that's why it's dying. That me is gone.

"I don't know who I am," I say, sitting down. "I can't be who I was, not without her, and who I'm becoming is a total screw-up."

Gram doesn't deny it. She's still mad, not twelve feet of mad, but plenty mad.

"We could go out to lunch in the city next week, spend the whole day together," I add, feeling puny, trying to make up for months of ignoring her with a lunch.

She nods, but that is not what's on her mind. "Just so you know, I don't know who I am without her either."

"Really?"

She shakes her head. "Nope. Every day, after you and Big leave, all I do is stand in front of a blank canvas thinking how much I despise the color green, how every single shade of it disgusts me or disappoints me or breaks my heart." Sadness fills me. I imagine all the green willowy women sliding out of their canvases and slinking their way out the front door.

"I get it," I say quietly.

Gram closes her eyes. Her hands are folded one on top of the other on the table. I reach out and put my hand over hers and she quickly sandwiches it.

"It's horrible," she whispers.

"It is," I say.

The early-afternoon light drains out the windows, zebra-ing the room with long dark shadows. Gram looks old and tired and it makes me feel desolate. Bailey, Uncle Big, and I have been her whole life, except for a few generations of flowers and a lot of green paintings.

"You know what else I hate?" she says. "I hate that everyone keeps telling me that I carry Bailey in my heart. I want to holler at them: *I don't want her there.* I want her in the kitchen with Lennie and me. I want her at the river with Toby and their baby. I want her to be Juliet and Lady Macbeth, you stupid, stupid people. Bailey doesn't want to be trapped in my heart or anyone else's." Gram pounds her fist on the table. I squeeze it with my hands and nod *yes,* and feel *yes,* a giant, pulsing, angry *yes* that passes from her to me. I look down at our hands and catch sight of *Wuthering Heights* lying there silent and helpless and ornery as ever. I think about all the wasted lives, all the wasted love crammed inside it.

"Gram, do it."

"What? Do what?" she asks.

I pick up the book and the shears, hold them out to her. "Just do it, chop it to bits. Here." I slip my fingers and thumb into the handle of the garden shears just like I did this morning, but this time I feel no fear, just that wild, pulsing, pissed-off *yes* coursing through me as I take a cut of a book that I've underlined and annotated, a book that is creased and soiled with years of me, years of river water, and summer sun, and sand from the beach, and sweat from my palms, a book bent to the curves of my waking and sleeping body. I take another cut, slicing through chunks of paper at a time, through all the tiny words, cutting the passionate, hopeless story to pieces, slashing their lives, their impossible love, the whole mess and tragedy of it. I'm attacking it now, enjoying the swish of the blades, the metal scrape after each delicious cut. I cut into Heathcliff, poor, heartsick, embittered Heathcliff and stupid Cathy for her bad choices and unforgivable compromises. And while I'm at it, I take a swipe at Joe's jealousy and anger and judgment, at his *dickhead-him* inability to forgive. I hack away at his ridiculous all-or-nothing-horn-player bullshit, and then I lay into my own duplicity and deceptiveness and confusion and hurt and bad judgment and overwhelming, never-ending grief. I cut and cut and cut at everything I can think of that is keeping Joe and me from having this great big beautiful love while we can.

Gram is wide-eyed, mouth agape. But then I see a faint smile find her lips. She says, "Here, let me have a go." She takes the shears and starts cutting, tentatively at first, but then she gets carried away just as I had, and starts hacking at handfuls and handfuls of pages until words fly all around us like confetti.

Gram's laughing. "Well, that was unexpected." We are both out of breath, spent, and smiling giddily.

"I am related to you, aren't I?" I say.

"Oh, Lennie, I have missed you." She pulls me into her lap like I'm five years old. I think I'm forgiven.

"Sorry I hollered, sweet pea," she says, hugging me into her warmth.

I squeeze her back. "Should I make us some tea?" I ask.

"You better, we have lots of catching up to do. But first things first, you destroyed my whole garden, I have to know if it worked."

I hear again: *I can't be with someone who could do that to her sister,* and my heart squeezes so tight in my chest, I can barely breathe. "Not a chance. It's over."

Gram says quietly, "I saw what happened that night." I tense up even more, slide out of her lap and go over to fill the tea kettle. I suspected Gram saw Toby and me kiss, but the reality of her witnessing it sends shame shifting around within me. I can't look at her. "Lennie?" Her voice isn't incriminating. I relax a little. "Listen to me."

I turn around slowly and face her.

She waves her hand around her head like she's shooing a fly. "I won't say it didn't render me speechless for a minute or two." She smiles. "But crazy things like that happen when people are this shocked and grief-stricken. I'm surprised we're all still standing."

I can't believe how readily Gram is pushing this aside, absolving me. I want to fall to her feet in gratitude. She definitely did not confer with Joe on the matter, but it makes his words sting less, and it gives me the courage to ask, "Do you think she'd ever forgive me?"

"Oh, sweet pea, trust me on this one, she already has."

Gram wags her finger at me. "Now, Joe is another story. He'll need some time . . ."

"Like thirty years," I say.

"Woohoo—poor boy, that was an eyeful, Lennie Walker." Gram looks at me mischievously. She has snapped back into her sassy self. "Yes, Len, when you and Joe Fontaine are forty-seven—" She laughs. "We'll plan a beautiful, beautiful wedding—"

She stops mid-sentence because she must notice my face. I

don't want to kill her cheer, so I'm using every muscle in it to hide my heartbreak, but I've lost the battle.

"Lennie." She comes over to me.

"He hates me," I tell her.

"No," she says warmly. "If ever there was a boy in love, sweet pea, it's Joe Fontaine."

Gram made me go to the doctor
to see if there was something wrong
with my heart.
After a bunch of tests, the doctor said:
Lennie, you lucked out.
I wanted to punch him in the face,
but instead I started to cry
in a drowning kind of way.
I couldn't believe
I had a lucky heart
when what I wanted
was the same kind of heart
as Bailey.
I didn't hear Gram come in,
or come up behind me,
just felt her arms slip around my shaking frame,
then the press of both of her hands hard
against my chest, holding it all in,
holding me together.
Thank God, she whispered,
before the doctor or I
could utter a word.
How could she possibly have known
that I'd gotten good news?

(*Found on the back of an envelope on the trail to the forest bedroom*)

chapter 33

WHEN THE TEA is in the mugs, the window, opened, and Gram and I have relaxed into the waning light, I say quietly, "I want to talk to you about something."

"Anything, sweet pea."

"I want to talk about Mom."

She sighs, leans back in her chair. "I know." She crosses her arms, holding both elbows, cradling herself. "I was up in the attic. You put the box back on a different shelf—"

"I didn't read much . . . sorry."

"No, I'm the one who's sorry. I've wanted to talk to you about Paige these last few months, but . . ."

"I wouldn't let you talk to me about anything."

She nods slightly. Her face is about as serious as I've ever seen it. She says, "Bailey shouldn't have died knowing so little about her mother."

I drop my eyes. It's true—I was wrong to think Bailey wouldn't want to know everything that I do, whether it hurts or not. I rake my fingers around in the remains of *Wuthering Heights*, waiting for Gram to speak.

When she does, her voice is strained, tight. "I thought I was protecting you girls, but now I'm pretty sure I was just protecting myself. It's so hard for me to speak about her. I told myself the better you girls knew her, the more it would hurt." She sweeps some of the book to herself. "I focused on the restlessness, so you girls wouldn't feel so abandoned, wouldn't blame her, or worse, blame yourselves. I wanted you to admire her. That's it."

That's it? Heat rushes up my body. Gram reaches her hand to mine. I slip it away from her.

I say, "You just made up a story so we wouldn't feel abandoned . . ." I raise my eyes to hers, continue despite the pain in her face. "But we *were* abandoned, Gram, and we didn't know why, don't know anything about her except some crazy story." I feel like scooping up a fistful of *Wuthering Heights* and hurling it at her. "Why not just tell us she's crazy if she is? Why not tell the truth, whatever it is? Wouldn't that have been better?"

She grabs my wrist, harder than I think she intended. "But there's not just one truth, Lennie, there never is. What I told you wasn't some story I made up." She's trying to be calm, but I can tell she's moments away from doubling in size. "Yes, it's true that Paige wasn't a stable girl. I mean, who in their proper tree leaves two little girls and doesn't come back?" She lets go of my wrist now that she has my full attention. She looks wildly around the room as if the words she needs might be on the walls. After a moment, she says, "Your mother was an irresponsible tornado of a girl and I'm sure she's an irresponsible tornado of a woman. But it's also true that she's not the first tornado to blast through this family, not the first one who's disappeared like this either. Sylvie swung back into town in that beat-up yellow Cadillac after twenty years drifting around. Twenty years!" She bangs her fist on the table, hard, the piles of *Wuthering Heights* jump with the impact. "Yes, maybe some doctor could give it a name, a diagnosis, but what difference does it make what we call it, it still is what it is, we call it the restless gene, so what? It's as true as anything else."

She takes a sip of her tea, burns her tongue. "Ow," she exclaims uncharacteristically, fanning her mouth.

"Big thinks you have it too," I say. "The restless gene." I'm rearranging words into new sentences on the table. I peek up at her, afraid by her silence that this admission might not have gone over very well.

Her brow's furrowed. "He said that?" Gram's joined me in mixing the words around on the table. I see she's put *under that benign sky* next to *so eternally secluded.*

"He thinks you just bottle it up," I say.

She's stopped shuffling words. There's something very un-Gram in her face, something darting and skittish. She won't meet my eyes, and then I recognize what it is because I've become quite familiar with it myself recently—it's shame.

"What, Gram?"

She's pressing her lips together so tightly, they've gone white; it's like she's trying to seal them, to make sure no words come out.

"What?"

She gets up, walks over to the counter, cradles up against it, looks out the window at a passing kingdom of clouds. I watch her back and wait. "I've been hiding inside that story, Lennie, and I made you girls, and Big, for that matter, hide in it with me."

"But you just said—"

"I know—it's not that it isn't true, but it's also true that blaming things on destiny and genes is a helluva lot easier than blaming them on myself."

"On yourself?"

She nods, doesn't say anything else, just continues to stare out the window.

I feel a chill creep up my spine. "Gram?"

She's turned away from me so I can't see the expression on her face. I don't know why, but I feel afraid of her, like she's slipped into the skin of someone else. Even the way she's holding her body is different, crumpled almost. When she finally speaks, her voice is too deep and calm. "I remember everything about that night . . ." she says, then pauses, and I think about running out of the room, away from this crumpled Gram who talks like she's in a trance. "I remember how cold it was, unseasonably so, how the kitchen was full of lilacs—I'd filled all the vases earlier in the day because she was coming." I can tell by Gram's voice she's smiling now and I relax a little. "She was wearing this long green dress, more like a giant scarf really, totally inappropriate, which was Paige—it's like she had her own weather around her always." I've never heard any of this about my mother, never heard about anything as real as a green dress, a kitchen full of flowers. But then Gram's tone changes again. "She was so upset that night, pacing around the kitchen, no not pacing, billowing back and forth in that scarf. I remember thinking she's like a trapped wind, a wild gale imprisoned in this kitchen with me, like if I opened a window she'd be gone."

Gram turns toward me as if finally remembering I'm in the room. "Your mother was at the end of her rope and she never was someone with a lot of rope on hand. She'd come for the weekend so I could see you girls. At least that's why I'd thought she'd come, until she began asking me what I'd do if she left. 'Left?' I said to her, 'Where? For how long?' which is when I found out she had a plane ticket to God knows where, she wouldn't say, and planned on using it, a one-way ticket. She told me she couldn't do it, that she didn't have it right inside to be a mother. I told her that her insides were right enough, that she couldn't leave, that you girls were her responsibility. I told her that she had to buck up like every other mother on this earth. I told her that you could all live here, that I'd help her, but she couldn't just up and go like those others in this crazy family, I wouldn't have it. 'But if I did leave,' she kept insisting, 'what would you do?' Over and over she asked it. I remember I kept trying to hold her by her arms, to get her to snap out of it, like I'd do when she was young and would get wound up, but she kept slipping out of my grasp like she was made of air." Gram takes a deep breath. "At this point, I was very upset myself, and you know how I get when I blow. I started shouting. I do have my share of the tornado inside, that's for sure, especially when I was younger, Big's right." She sighs. "I lost it, really lost it. 'What do you think I'd do if you left?' I hollered. 'They're my granddaughters, but Paige, if you leave you can never come back. Never. You'll be dead to them, dead in their hearts, and dead to me. Dead. To all of us.' My exact despicable words. Then I locked myself in my art room for the rest of the night. The next morning—she was gone."

I've fallen back into my chair, boneless. Gram stands across the room in a prison of shadows. "I told your mother to never come back."

She'll be back, girls.

A prayer, never a promise.

Her voice is barely above a whisper. "I'm sorry."

Her words have moved through me like fast-moving storm clouds, transforming the landscape. I look around at her framed green ladies, three of them in the kitchen alone, women caught somewhere between here and there—each one Paige, all of them Paige in a billowy green dress, I'm sure of it now. I think about the ways Gram made sure our mother never died in our hearts, made sure Paige Walker never bore any blame for leaving her children. I think about how, unbeknownst to us, Gram culled that blame for herself.

And I remember the ugly thing I'd thought that night at the top of the stairs when I overheard her apologizing to The Half Mom. I'd blamed her too. For things even the almighty Gram can't control.

"It's not your fault," I say, with a certainty in my voice I've never heard before. "It never was, Gram. *She* left. *She* didn't come back—her choice, not yours, no matter what you said to her."

Gram exhales like she's been holding her breath for sixteen years.

"Oh Lennie," she cries. "I think you just opened the window"—she touches her chest—"and let her out."

I rise from my chair and walk over to her, realizing for the first time that she's lost two daughters—I don't know how she bears it. I realize something else too. I don't share this double grief. I have a mother and I'm standing so close to her, I can see the years weighing down her skin, can smell her tea-scented breath. I wonder if Bailey's search for Mom would have led her here too, right back to Gram. I hope so. I gently put my hand on her arm wondering how such a huge love for someone can fit in my tiny body. "Bailey and I are so lucky we got you," I say. "We scored."

She closes her eyes for a moment, and then the next thing I know I'm in her arms and she's squeezing me so as to crush every bone. "I'm the one who lucked out," she says into my hair. "And now I think we need to drink our tea. Enough of this."

As I make my way back to the table, something becomes clear: Life's a freaking mess. In fact, I'm going to tell Sarah we need to start a new philosophical movement: messessentialism instead of existentialism: For those who revel in the essential mess that is life. Because Gram's right, there's not one truth ever, just a whole bunch of stories, all going on at once, in our heads, in our hearts, all getting in the way of each other. It's all a beautiful calamitous mess. It's like the day Mr. James took us into the woods and cried triumphantly, "That's it! That's it!" to the dizzying cacophony of soloing instruments trying to make music together. That is it.

I look down at the piles of words that used to be my favorite book. I want to put the story back together again so Cathy and Heathcliff can make different choices, can stop getting in the way of themselves at every turn, can follow their raging, volcanic hearts right into each other's arms. But I can't. I go to the sink, pull out the trash can, and sweep Cathy and Heathcliff and the rest of their unhappy lot into it.

LATER THAT EVENING, I'm playing Joe's melody over and over on the porch, trying to think of books where love actually triumphs in the end. There's Lizzie Bennet and Mr. Darcy, and Jane Eyre ends up with Mr. Rochester, that's good, but he had that wife locked up for a while, which freaks me out. There's Florentino Aziza in *Love in the Time of Cholera*, but he had to wait over fifty years for Fermina, only for them to end up on a ship going nowhere. Ugh. I'd say there's slim literary pickings on this front, which depresses me; how could true love so infrequently prevail in the classics? And more importantly, how can I make it prevail for Joe and me? If only I could convert him to messessentialism . . . *If only I had wheels on my ass, I'd be a trolley cart.* After all that he said today, I think that about covers my chances.

I'm playing his song for probably the fiftieth time when I realize Gram's in the doorway listening to me. I thought she was locked away in the art room recovering from the emotional tumult of our afternoon. I stop mid-note, suddenly self-conscious. She opens the door, strides out with the mahogany box from the attic in her hands. "What a lovely melody. Bet I could play it myself at this point," she says, rolling her eyes as she puts the box on the table and drops into the love seat. "Though it's very nice to hear you playing again."

I decide to tell her. "I'm going to try for first chair again this fall."

"Oh, sweet pea," she sings. Literally. "Music to my tin ears."

I smile, but inside, my stomach is roiling. I'm planning on telling Rachel next practice. It'd be so much easier if I could just pour a bucket of water on her like the Wicked Witch of the West.

"Come sit down." Gram taps the cushion next to her. I join her, resting my clarinet across my knees. She puts her hand on the box. "Everything in here is yours to read. Open all the envelopes. Read my notes, the letters. Just be prepared, it's not all pretty, especially the earlier letters."

I nod. "Thank you."

"All right." She removes her hand from the box. "I'm going to take a walk to town, meet Big at The Saloon. I need a stiff drink." She ruffles my hair, then leaves the box and me to ourselves.

After putting my clarinet away, I sit with the box on my lap, trailing circles around the ring of galloping horses with my fingers. Around and around. I want to open it, and I also don't want to. It's probably the closest I'll ever get to knowing my mother, whoever she is—adventurer or wack job, heroine or villain, probably just a very troubled, complicated woman. I look out at the gang of oaks across the road, at the Spanish moss hanging over their stooped shoulders like decrepit shawls, the gray, gnarled lot of them like a band of wise old men pondering a verdict—

The door squeaks. I turn to see that Gram has put on a bright pink floral no-clue-what—a coat? A cape? A shower curtain?—over an even brighter purple flowered frock. Her hair is down and wild; it looks like it conducts electricity. She has makeup on, an eggplant-color lipstick, cowboy boots to house her Big Foot feet. She looks beautiful and insane. It's the first time she's gone out at night since Bailey died. She waves at me, winks, then heads down the steps. I watch her stroll across the yard.

Right as she hits the road, she turns back, holds her hair so the breeze doesn't blow it back into her eyes.

"Hey, I give Big one month, you?"

"Are you kidding? Two weeks, tops."

"It's your turn to be best man."

"That's fine," I say, smiling.

She smiles back at me, humor peeking out of her queenly face. Even though we pretend otherwise, nothing quite raises Walker spirits like the thought of another wedding for Uncle Big.

"Be okay, sweet pea," she says. "You know where we are . . ."

"I'll be fine," I say, feeling the weight of the box on my legs.

As soon as she's gone, I open the lid. I'm ready. All these notes, all these letters, sixteen years' worth. I think about Gram jotting down a recipe, a thought, a silly or not-so-pretty something she wanted to share with her daughter, or just remember herself, maybe stuffing it in her pocket all day, and then sneaking up to the attic before bed, to put it in this box, this mailbox with no pickup, year after year, not knowing if her daughter would ever read them, not knowing if anyone would—

I gasp, because isn't that just exactly what I've been doing too: writing poems and scattering them to the winds with the same hope as Gram that someone, someday, somewhere might understand who I am, who my sister was, and what happened to us.

I take out the envelopes, count them—fifteen, all with the name *Paige* and the year. I find the first one, written sixteen years ago by Gram to her daughter. Slipping my finger under the seal, I imagine Bailey sitting beside me. *Okay,* I tell her, taking out the letter, *Let's meet our mother.*

Okay to everything. I'm a messessentialist—okay to it all.

chapter 34

THE SHAW RANCH presides over Clover. Its acreage rolls in green and gold majesty from the ridge all the way down to town. I walk through the iron gate and make my way to the stables, where I find Toby inside talking to a beautiful black mare as he takes her saddle off.

"Don't mean to interrupt," I say, walking over to him.

He turns around. "Wow, Lennie."

We're smiling at each other like idiots. I thought it might be weird to see him, but we both seem to be acting pretty much thrilled. It embarrasses me, so I drop my gaze to the mare between us and stroke her warm moist coat. Heat radiates off her body.

Toby flicks the end of the reins lightly across my hand. "I've missed you."

"Me too, you." But I realize with some relief that my stomach isn't fluttering, even with our eyes locked as they now are. Not even a twitter. Is the spell broken? The horse snorts—perfect: Thanks, Black Beauty—

"Want to go for a ride?" he asks. "We could go up on the ridge. I was just up there. There's a massive herd of elk roaming."

"Actually, Toby . . . I thought maybe we could visit Bailey."

"Okay," he says, without thinking, like I asked him to get an ice cream. Strange.

I told myself I would never go back to the cemetery. No one talks about decaying flesh and maggots and skeletons, but how can you not think of those things? I've done everything in my power to keep those thoughts out of my mind, and staying away from Bailey's grave has been crucial to that end. But last night, I was fingering all the things on her dresser like I always do before I go to sleep, and I realized that she wouldn't want me clinging to the black hair webbed in her hairbrush or the rank laundry I still refuse to wash. She'd think it was totally gross: Lady-Havisham-and-her-wedding-dress gross and dismal. I got an image of her then sitting on the hill at the Clover cemetery with its ancient oaks, firs, and redwoods like a queen holding court, and I knew it was time.

Even though the cemetery is close enough to walk, when Toby's finished, we jump in his truck. He puts the key in the ignition, but doesn't turn it. He stares straight through the windshield at the golden meadows, tapping on the wheel with two fingers in a staccato rhythm. I can tell he's revving up to say something. I rest my head on the passenger window and look out at the fields, imagining his life here, how solitary it must be. A minute or two later, he starts talking in his low lulling bass. "I've always hated being an only child. Used to envy you guys. You were just so tight."

He grips his hands on the wheel, stares straight ahead. "I was so psyched to marry Bails, to have this baby . . . I was psyched to be part of your family. It's going to sound so lame now, but I thought I could help you through this. I wanted to. I know Bailey would've wanted me to." He shakes his head. "Sure screwed it all up. I just . . . I don't know. You understood . . . It's like you were the only one who did. I started to feel so close to you, too close. It got all mixed up in my head—"

"But you did help me," I interrupt. "You were the only one who could even find me. I felt that same closeness even if I didn't understand it. I don't know what I would have done without you."

He turns to me. "Yeah?"

"Yeah, Toby."

He smiles his squintiest, sweetest smile. "Well, I'm pretty sure I can keep my hands off you now. I don't know about your frisky self though . . ." He raises his eyebrows, gives me a look, then laughs an unburdened free laugh. I punch his arm. He goes on, "So, maybe we'll be able to hang out a little—I don't think I can keep saying no to Gram's dinner invitations without her sending out the National Guard."

"I can't believe you just made two jokes in one sentence. Amazing."

"I'm not a total doorknob, you know?"

"Guess not. There must have been some reason my sister wanted to spend the rest of her life with you!" And just like that, it feels right between us, finally.

"Well," he says, starting the truck. "Shall we cheer ourselves up with a trip to the cemetery?"

"Three jokes, unbelievable."

However, that was probably Toby's word allotment for the year, I'm thinking as we drive along now in silence. A silence that is full of jitters. Mine. I'm nervous. I'm not sure what I'm afraid of really. I keep telling myself, it's just a stone, it's just a pretty piece of land with gorgeous stately trees overlooking the falls. It's just a place where my beautiful sister's body is in a box decaying in a sexy black dress and sandals. Ugh. I can't help it. Everything I haven't allowed myself to imagine rushes me: I think about airless empty lungs. Lipstick on her unmoving mouth. The silver bracelet that Toby had given her on her pulseless wrist. Her belly ring. Hair and nails growing in the dark. Her body with no thoughts in it. No time in it. No love in it. Six feet of earth crushing down on her. I think about the phone ringing in the kitchen, the thump of Gram collapsing, then the inhuman sound sirening out of her, through the floorboards, up to our room.

I look over at Toby. He doesn't look nervous at all. Something occurs to me.

"Have you been?" I ask.

"Course," he answers. "Almost every day."

"Really?"

He looks over at me, the realization dawning on him. "You mean you haven't been since?"

"No." I look out the window. I'm a terrible sister. Good sisters visit graves despite gruesome thoughts.

"Gram goes," he says. "She planted a few rosebushes, a bunch of other flowers too. The grounds people told her she had to get rid of them, but every time they pulled out her plants, she just replanted more. They finally gave up." I can't believe everyone's been going to Bailey's grave but me. I can't believe how left out it makes me feel.

"What about Big?" I ask.

"I find roaches from his joints a lot. We hung out there a couple times." He looks over at me, studies my face for what feels like forever. "It'll be okay, Len. Easier than you think. I was really scared the first time I went."

Something occurs to me then. "Toby," I say, tentatively, mustering my nerve. "You must be pretty used to being an only child . . ." My voice starts to shake. "But I'm really new at it." I look out the window. "Maybe we . . ." I feel too shy all of a sudden to finish my thought, but he knows what I'm getting at.

"I've always wanted a sister," he says as he swerves into a spot in the tiny parking lot.

"Good," I say, every inch of me relieved. I lean over and give him the world's most sexless peck on the cheek. "C'mon," I say. "Let's go tell her we're sorry."

There once was a girl who found herself dead.
She spent her days peering
over the ledge of heaven,
her chin in her palm.
She was bored as brick,
hadn't adjusted yet
to the slower pace of heavenly life.
Her sister would look up at her
and wave,
and the dead girl would wave back
but she was too far away
for her sister to see.
The dead girl thought her sister
might be writing her notes,
but it was too long a trip to make
for a few scattered words here and there
so she let them be.
And then, one day, her earthbound sister finally realized
she could hear music up there in heaven,
so after that, everything her sister
needed to tell her
she did through her clarinet
and each time she played, the dead girl
jumped up (no matter what else she was doing),
and danced.

(Found on a piece of paper in the stacks, B section, Clover Public Library)

chapter 35

I HAVE A plan. I'm going to write Joe a poem, but first things first.

When I walk into the music room, I see that Rachel's already there unpacking her instrument. This is it. My hand is so clammy I'm afraid the handle on my case will slip out of it as I cross the room and stand in front of her.

"If it isn't John Lennon," she says without looking up. Could she be so awful as to rub Joe's nickname in my face? Obviously, yes. Well, good, because fury seems to calm my nerves. Race on.

"I'm challenging you for first chair," I say, and wild applause bursts from a spontaneous standing ovation in my brain. Never have words felt so good coming out of my mouth! Hmm. Even if Rachel doesn't appear to have heard them. She's still messing with her reed and ligature like the bell didn't go off, like the starting gate didn't just swing open.

I'm about to repeat myself, when she says, "There's nothing there, Lennie." She spits my name on the floor like it disgusts her. "He's so hung up on you. Who knows why?"

Could this moment get any better? No! I try to keep my cool. "This has nothing to do with him," I say, and nothing could be more true. It has nothing to do with her either, not really, though I don't say that. It's about me and my clarinet.

"Yeah, right," she says. "You're just doing this because you saw me with him."

"No." My voice surprises me again with its certainty. "I want the solos, Rachel." At that she stops fiddling with her clarinet, rests it on the stand, and looks up at me. "And I'm starting up again with Marguerite." This I decided on the way to rehearsal. I have her undivided totally freaked-out attention now. "I'm going to try for All-State too," I tell her. This, however, is news to me.

We stare at each other and for the first time I wonder if she's known all year that I threw the audition. I wonder if that's why she's been so horrible. Maybe she thought she could intimidate me into not challenging her. Maybe she thought that was the only way to keep her chair.

She bites her lip. "How about if I split the solos with you. And you can—"

I shake my head. I almost feel sorry for her. Almost.

"Come September," I say. "May the best clarinetist win."

Not just my ass, but every inch of me is in the wind as I fly out of the music room, away from school, and into the woods to go home and write the poem to Joe. Beside me, step for step, breath for breath, is the unbearable fact that I have a future and Bailey doesn't.

This is when I know it.

My sister will die over and over again for the rest of my life. Grief is forever. It doesn't go away; it becomes part of you, step for step, breath for breath. I will never stop grieving Bailey because I will never stop loving her. That's just how it is. Grief and love are conjoined, you don't get one without the other. All I can do is love her, and love the world, emulate her by living with daring and spirit and joy.

Without thinking, I veer onto the trail to the forest bedroom. All around me, the woods are in an uproar of beauty. Sunlight cascades through the trees, making the fern-covered floor look jeweled and incandescent. Rhododendron bushes sweep past me right and left like women in fabulous dresses. I want to wrap my arms around all of it.

When I get to the forest bedroom, I hop onto the bed and make myself comfortable. I'm going to take my time with this poem, not like all the others I scribbled and scattered. I take the pen out of my pocket, a piece of blank sheet music out of my bag, and start writing.

I tell him everything—everything he means to me, everything I felt with him that I never felt before, everything I hear in his music. I want him to trust me so I bare all. I tell him I belong to him, that my heart is his, and even if he never forgives me it will still be the case.

It's my story, after all, and this is how I choose to tell it.

When I'm done, I scoot off the bed and as I do, I notice a blue guitar pick lying on the white comforter. I must have been sitting on it all afternoon. I lean over and pick it up, and recognize it right away as Joe's. He must've come here to play—a good sign. I decide to leave the poem here for him instead of sneaking it inside the Fontaine mailbox like I had planned. I fold it, write his name on it, and place it on the bed under a rock to secure it from the wind. I tuck his pick under the rock as well.

Walking home, I realize it's the first time since Bailey died that I've written words for someone to read.

chapter 36

I'M TOO MORTIFIED to sleep. What was I thinking? I keep imagining Joe reading my ridiculous poem to his brothers, and worse to Rachel, all of them laughing at poor lovelorn Lennie, who knows nothing about romance except what she learned from Emily Brontë. I told him: *I belong to him.* I told him: *My heart is his.* I told him: *I hear his soul in his music.* I'm going to jump off of a building. Who says things like this in the twenty-first century? No one! How is it possible that something can seem like such a brilliant idea one day and such a bonehead one the next?

As soon as there's enough light, I throw a sweatshirt over my pajamas, put on some sneakers, and run through the dawn to the forest bedroom to retrieve the note, but when I get there, it's gone. I tell myself that the wind blew it away like all the other poems. I mean, how likely is it that Joe showed up yesterday afternoon after I left? Not likely at all.

SARAH IS KEEPING me company, providing humiliation support while I make lasagnas.

She can't stop squealing. "You're going to be first clarinet, Lennie. For sure."

"We'll see."

"It'll really help you get into a conservatory. Juilliard even."

I take a deep breath. How like an imposter I'd felt every time Marguerite mentioned it, how like a traitor, conspiring to steal my sister's dream, just as it got swiped from her. Why didn't it occur to me then I could dream alongside her? Why wasn't I brave enough to have a dream at all?

"I'd love to go to Juilliard," I tell Sarah. There. Finally. "But any good conservatory would be okay." I just want to study music: what life, what living itself sounds like.

"We could go together," Sarah's saying, while shoveling into her mouth each slice of mozzarella as I cut it. I slap her hand. She continues, "Get an apartment together in New York City." I think Sarah might rocket into outer space at the idea—me too, though, I, pathetically, keep thinking: What about Joe? "Or Berklee in Boston," she says, her big blue eyes boinging out of her head. "Don't forget Berklee. Either way, we could drive there in Ennui, zigzag our way across. Hang out at the Grand Canyon, go to New Orleans, maybe—"

"Ughhhhhhhhhhhhhhhhhh," I groan.

"Not the poem again. What could be a better distraction than the divine goddesses Juilliard and Berklee. Sheesh. Unfreakingbelievable . . ."

"You have no idea how dildonic it was."

"*Nice* word, Len." She's flipping through a magazine someone left on the counter.

"*Lame* isn't lame enough of a word for this poem," I mutter. "Sarah, I told a guy that *I belong to him*."

"That's what happens when you read *Wuthering Heights* eighteen times."

"Twenty-three."

I'm layering away: sauce, noodles, *I belong to you*, cheese, sauce, *my heart is yours*, noodles, cheese, *I hear your soul in your music*, cheese, cheese, CHEESE . . .

She's smiling at me. "You know, it might be okay, he seems kind of the same way."

"What way?"

"You know, like you."

Bails?

Yeah.

Can you believe Cathy married Edgar Linton?

No.

I mean would you ever do something so stupid?

No.

I mean what she had with Heathcliff, how could she have just thrown it away?

I don't know. What is it, Len?

What's what?

What's with you and that book already?

I don't know.

Yes you do. Tell me.

It's cornball.

C'mon, Len.

I guess I want it.

What?

To feel that kind of love.

You will.

How do you know?

Just do.

The toes knows?

The toes knows.

But if I find it, I don't want to screw it all up like they did.

You won't. The toes knows that too.

Night, Bails.

Len, I was just thinking something . . .

What?

In the end, Cathy and Heathcliff are together, love is stronger than anything, even death.

Hmm . . .

Night, Len.

(Found on a scrap of staff paper in the parking lot, Clover High)

chapter 37

I TELL MYSELF it's ridiculous to go all the way back to the forest bedroom, that there's no way in the world he's going to be there, that no New Age meets Victorian Age poem is going to make him trust me, that I'm sure he still hates me, and now thinks I'm dildonic on top of it.

But here I am, and of course, here he's not. I flop onto my back on the bed. I look up at the patches of blue sky through the trees, and adhering to the regularly scheduled programming, I think some more about Joe. There's so much I don't know about him. I don't know if he believes in God, or likes macaroni and cheese, or what sign he is, or if he dreams in English or French, or what it would feel like—uh-oh. I'm headed from G to XXX because, oh God, I really wish Joe didn't hate me so much, because I want to do *everything* with him. I'm so fed up with my virginity. It's like the whole world is in on this ecstatic secret but me—

I hear something then: a strange, mournful, decidedly unforest-like sound. I pick my head up and rest on my elbows so I can listen harder and try to isolate the sound from the rustling leaves and the distant river roar and the birds chattering all around me. The sound trickles through the trees, getting louder by the minute, closer. I keep listening, and then I recognize what it is, the notes, clear and perfect now, winding and wending their way to me—the melody from Joe's duet. I close my eyes and hope I'm really hearing a clarinet and it's not just some auditory hallucination inside my lovesick head. It's not, because now I hear steps shuffling through the brush and within a couple minutes the music stops and then the steps.

I'm afraid to open my eyes, but I do, and he's standing at the edge of the bed looking down at me—an army of ninja-cupids who must have all been hiding out in the canopy draw their bows and release—arrows fly at me from every which way.

"I thought you might be here." I can't read his expression. Nervous? Angry? His face seems restless like it doesn't know what to emote. "I got your poem . . ."

I can hear the blood rumbling through my body, drumming in my ears. What's he going to say? I got your poem and I'm sorry, I just can't ever forgive you. I got your poem and I feel the same way—*my heart is yours, John Lennon*. I got your poem and I've already called the psych ward—I have a straitjacket in this backpack. Strange. I've never seen Joe wear a backpack.

He's biting his lip, tapping his clarinet on his leg. Definitely nervous. This can't be good.

"Lennie, I got *all* your poems." What's he talking about? What does he mean *all* my poems? He slides the clarinet between his thighs to hold it and takes off his backpack, unzips it. Then he takes a deep breath, pulls out a box, hands it to me. "Well, probably not all of them, but these."

I open the lid. Inside are scraps of paper, napkins, to-go cups, all with my words on them. The bits and pieces of Bailey and me that I scattered and buried and hid. This is not possible.

"How?" I ask, bewildered, and starting to get uneasy thinking about Joe reading everything in this box. All these private desperate moments. This is worse than having someone read your journal. This is like having someone read the journal that you thought you'd burned. And how did he get them all? Has he been following me around? That would be perfect. I finally fall in love with someone and he's a total freaking maniac.

I look at him. He's smirking a little and I see the faintest: bat. bat. bat. "I know what you're thinking," he says. "That I'm the creepy stalker dude."

Bingo.

He's amused. "I'm not, Len. It just kept happening. At first I kept finding them, and then, well, I started looking. I just couldn't help it. It became like this weird-ass treasure hunt. Remember that first day in the tree?"

I nod. But something even more amazing than Joe being a crazy stalker and finding my poems has just occurred to me— he's not angry anymore. Was it the dildonic poem? Whatever it was I'm caught in such a ferocious uprising of joy I'm not even listening to him as he tries to explain how in the world these poems ended up in this shoebox and not in some trash heap or blowing through Death Valley on a gust of wind.

I try to tune in to what he's saying. "Remember in the tree

I told you that I'd seen you up at The Great Meadow? I told you that I'd watched you writing a note, watched you drop it as you walked away. But I didn't tell you that after you left, I went over and found the piece of paper caught in the fence. It was a poem about Bailey. I guess I shouldn't have kept it. I was going to give it back to you that day in the tree, I had it in my pocket, but then I thought you'd think it was strange that I took it in the first place, so I just kept it." He's biting his lip. I remember him telling me that day he saw me drop something I'd written, but it never occurred to me he would go *find* it and *read* it. He continues, "And then, while we were in the tree, I saw words scrawled on the branches, thought maybe you'd written something else, but I felt weird asking, so I went back another time and wrote it down in a notebook."

I can't believe this. I sit up, fish through the box, looking more closely this time. There are some scraps in his weirdo Unabomber handwriting—probably transcribed from walls or sides of barns or some of the other practical writing surfaces that I found. I'm not sure how to feel. He knows everything—I'm inside out.

His face is caught between worry and excitement, but excitement seems to be winning out. He's pretty much bursting to go on. "That first time I was at your house, I saw one sticking out from under a stone in Gram's garden, and then another one on the sole of your shoe, and then that day when we moved all the stuff, man . . . it's like your words were everywhere I looked. I went a little crazy, found myself looking for them all the time . . ." He shakes his head. "Even kept it up when I was so pissed at you. But the strangest part is that I'd found a couple before I'd even met you, the first was just a few words on the back of a candy wrapper, found it on the trail to the river, had no idea who wrote it, well, until later . . ."

He's staring at me, tapping the clarinet on his leg. He looks nervous again. "Okay, say something. Don't feel weird. They just made me fall more in love with you." And then he smiles, and in all the places around the globe where it's night, day breaks. "Aren't you at least going to say *quel dork?*"

I would say a lot of things right now if I could get any words past the smile that has taken over my face. There it is again, his *I'm in love with you* obliterating all else that comes out of his mouth with it.

He points to the box. "They helped me. I'm kind of an unforgiving doltwad, if you haven't noticed. I'd read them— read them over and over after you came that day with the roses—trying to understand what happened, why you were with him, and I think maybe I do now. I don't know, reading all the poems together, I started to *really* imagine what you've been going through, how horrible it must be . . ." He swallows, looks down, shuffles his foot in the pine needles. "For him too. I guess I can see how it happened."

How can it be I was writing to Joe all these months without knowing it? When he looks up, he's smiling. "And then yesterday . . ." He tosses the clarinet onto the bed. "Found out you belong to me." He points at me. "I own your ass."

I smile. "Making fun of me?"

"Yeah, but it doesn't matter because you own my ass too." He shakes his head and his hair flops into his eyes so that I might die. "Totally."

A flock of hysterically happy birds busts out of my chest and into the world. I'm glad he read the poems. I want him to know all the inside things about me. I want him to know my sister, and now, in some way, he does. Now he knows before as well as after.

He sits down on the edge of the bed, picks up a stick and draws on the ground with it, then tosses it, looks off into the trees. "I'm sorry," he says.

"Don't be. I'm glad—"

He turns around to face me. "No, not about the poems. I'm sorry, what I said that day, about Bailey. From reading all these, I knew how much it would hurt you—"

I put my finger over his lips. "It's okay."

He takes my hand, holds it to his mouth, kisses it. I close my eyes, feel shivers run through me—it's been so long since we've touched. He rests my hand back down. I open my eyes. His are on me, questioning. He smiles, but the vulnerability and hurt still in his face tears into me. "You're not going to do it to me again, are you?" he asks.

"Never," I blurt out. "I want to be with you forever!" Okay, lesson learned twice in as many days: You can chop the Victorian novel to shreds with garden shears but you can't take it out of the girl.

He beams at me. "You're crazier than me."

We stare at each other for a long moment and inside that moment I feel like we are kissing more passionately than we ever have even though we aren't touching.

I reach out and brush my fingers across his arm. "Can't help it. I'm in love."

"First time," he says. "For me."

"I thought in France—"

He shakes his head. "No way, nothing like this." He touches my cheek in that tender way that he does that makes me believe in God and Buddha and Mohammed and Ganesh and Mary, et al. "No one's like you, for me," he whispers.

"Same," I say, right as our lips meet. He lowers me back onto the bed, aligns himself on top of me so we are legs to legs, hips to hips, stomach to stomach. I can feel the weight of him pressing into every inch of me. I rake my fingers through his dark silky curls.

"I missed you," he murmurs into my ears, my neck and hair, and each time he does I say, "Me too," and then we are kissing again and I can't believe there is anything in this uncertain world that can feel this right and real and true.

Later, after we've come up for oxygen, I reach for the box, and start flipping through the scraps. There are a lot of them, but not near as many as I wrote. I'm glad there are some still out there, tucked away between rocks, in trash bins, on walls, in the margins of books, some washed away by rain, erased by the sun, transported by the wind, some never to be found, some to be found in years to come.

"Hey, where's the one from yesterday?" I ask, letting my residual embarrassment get the better of me, thinking I might still be able to accidentally rip it up, now that it's done its job.

"Not in there. That one's mine." Oh well. He's lazily brushing his hand across my neck and down my back. I feel like a tuning fork, my whole body humming.

"You're not going to believe this," he says. "But I think the roses worked. On my parents—I swear, they can't keep their hands off each other. It's disgusting. Marcus and Fred have been going down to your place at night and stealing roses to give to girls so they'll sleep with them." Gram is going to love this. It's a good thing she's so smitten with the Fontaine boys.

I put down the box, scoot around so I'm facing him. "I don't think *any* of you guys need Gram's roses for that."

"John Lennon?"

Bat. Bat. Bat.

I run my finger over his lips, say, "I want to do everything with you too."

"Oh man," he says, pulling me down to him, and then we are kissing so far into the sky I don't think we're ever coming back.

If anyone asks where we are, just tell them to look up.

chapter 38

Bails?

Yeah?

Is it so dull being dead?

It was, not anymore.

What changed?

I stopped peering over the ledge . . .

What do you do now?

It's hard to explain—it's like swimming, but not in water, in light.

Who do you swim with?

Mostly you and Toby, Gram, Big, with Mom too, sometimes.

How come I don't know it?

But you do, don't you?

I guess, like all those days we spent at Flying Man's?

Exactly, only brighter.

(Written in Lennie's journal)

GRAM AND I are baking the day away in preparation for Big's wedding. All the windows and doors are open and we can hear the river and smell the roses and feel the heat of the sun streaming in. We're chirping about the kitchen like sparrows.

We do this every wedding, only this is the first time we're doing it without Bailey. Yet, oddly, I feel her presence more today in the kitchen with Gram than I have since she died. When I roll the dough out, she comes up to me and sticks her hand in the flour and flicks it into my face. When Gram and I lean against the counter and sip our tea, she storms into the kitchen and pours herself a cup. She sits in every chair, blows in and out the doors, whisks in between Gram and me humming under her breath and dipping her finger into our batters. She's in every thought I think, every word I say, and I let her be. I let her enchant me as I roll the dough and think my thoughts and say my words, as we bake and bake—both of us having finally dissuaded Joe of the necessity of an exploding wedding cake—and talk about inanities like what Gram is going to wear for the big party. She is quite concerned with her outfit.

"Maybe I'll wear pants for a change." The earth has just slid off its axis. Gram has a floral frock for every occasion. I've never seen her out of one. "And I might straighten my hair." Okay, the earth has slid off its axis and is now hurtling toward a different galaxy. Imagine Medusa with a blow-dryer. Straight hair is an impossibility for Gram or any Walker, even with thirty hours to go until party time.

"What gives?" I ask.

"I just want to look nice, no crime in that, is there? You know, sweet pea, it's not like I've lost my sex appeal." I can't believe Gram just said sex appeal. "Just a bit of a dry spell is all," she mutters under her breath. I turn to look at her. She's sugaring the raspberries and strawberries and flushing as crimson as they are.

"Oh my God, Gram! You have a crush."

"God no!"

"You're lying. I can see it."

Then she giggles in a wild cackley way. "I am lying! Well, what do you expect? With you so loopy all the time about Joe, and now Big and Dorothy . . . maybe I caught a little of it. Love is contagious, everyone knows that, Lennie."

She grins.

"So, who is it? Did you meet him at The Saloon that night?" That's the only time she's been out socializing in months. Gram is not the Internet dating type. At least I don't think she is.

I put my hands on my hips. "If you don't tell me, I'm just going to ask Maria tomorrow. There's nothing in Clover she doesn't know."

Gram squeals, "Mum's me, sweet pea."

No matter how I prod through hours more of pies, cakes, and even a few batches of berry pudding, her smiling lips remain sealed.

AFTER WE'RE DONE, I get my backpack, which I loaded up earlier, and take off for the cemetery. When I hit the trailhead, I start running. The sun is breaking through the canopy in isolated blocks, so I fly through light and dark and dark and light, through the blazing unapologetic sunlight, into the ghostliest loneliest shade, and back again, back and forth, from one to the next, and through the places where it all blends together into a leafy-lit emerald dream. I run and run and as I do the fabric of death that has clung to me for months begins to loosen and slip away. I run fast and free, suspended in a moment of private raucous happiness, my feet barely touching the ground as I fly forward to the next second, minute, hour, day, week, year of my life.

I break out of the woods on the road to the cemetery. The hot afternoon sunlight is lazing over everything, meandering through the trees, casting long shadows. It's warm and the scent of eucalyptus and pine is thick, overpowering. I walk the footpath that winds through the graves listening to the rush of the falls, remembering how important it was for me, despite all reason, that Bailey's grave be where she could see and hear and even smell the river.

I'm the only person in the small hilltop cemetery and I'm glad. I drop my backpack and sit down beside the gravestone, rest my head against it, wrap my hands and arms around it like I'm playing a cello. The stone is so warm against my body. We chose this one because it had a little cabinet in it, a kind of reliquary, with a metal door that has an engraving of a bird on it. It sits under the chiseled words. I run my fingers across my sister's name, her nineteen years, then across the words I wrote on a piece of paper months ago and handed to Gram in the funeral parlor: *The Color of Extraordinary*.

I reach for my pack, pull a small notebook out of it. I transcribed all the letters Gram wrote to our mom over the last sixteen years. I want Bailey to have those words. I want her to know that there will never be a story that she won't be a part of, that she's everywhere like sky. I open the door and slide the book in the little cabinet, and as I do, I hear something scrape. I reach in and pull out a ring. My stomach drops. It's gorgeous, an orange topaz, big as an acorn. Perfect for Bailey. Toby must have had it made especially for her. I hold it in my palm and the certainty that she never got to see it pierces me. I bet the ring is what they were waiting for to finally tell us about their marriage, the baby. How Bails would've showed it off when they made the grand announcements. I rest it on the edge of the stone where it catches a glint of sun and throws amber prismatic light over all the engraved words.

I try to fend off the oceanic sadness, but I can't. It's such a colossal effort not to be haunted by what's lost, but to be enchanted by what was.

I miss you, I tell her, *I can't stand that you're going to miss so much*.

I don't know how the heart withstands it.

I kiss the ring, put it back into the cabinet next to the notebook, and close the door with the bird on it. Then I reach into my pack and take out the houseplant. It's so decrepit, just a few blackened leaves left. I walk over to the edge of the cliff, so I'm right over the falls. I take the plant out of its pot, shake the dirt off the roots, get a good grip, reach my arm back, take one deep breath before I pitch my arm forward, and let go.

epilogue

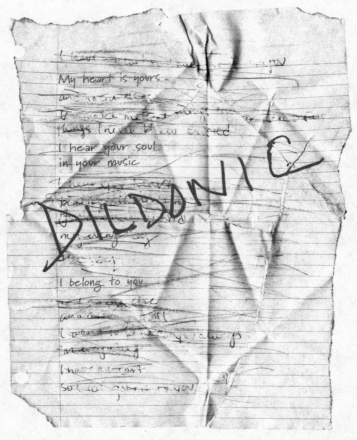

(Found on the bed, in the forest bedroom)
(Found again in the bombroom, in the trash can, ripped into pieces by Lennie)
(Found again on Joe's desk, taped together, with the word dildonic written over it)
(Found framed under glass in Joe's dresser drawer, where it still is)

acknowledgments

In loving memory of Barbie Stein,
who is everywhere like sky

I'D LIKE TO THANK:

First and foremost, my parents, all four of them, for their boundless love and support: my awesome father and Carol, my huge-hearted mother and Ken. My whole family for their rollicking humor and steadfastness: my brothers Bruce, Bobby, and Andy, my sisters-in-law Patricia and Monica, my niece and nephews Adam, Lena, and Jake, my grandparents, particularly the inimitable Cele.

Mark Routhier for so much joy, belief, love.

My amazing friends, my other family, for every day, in every way: Ami Hooker, Anne Rosenthal, Becky MacDonald, Emily Rubin, Jeremy Quittner, Larry Dwyer, Maggie Jones, Sarah Michelson, Julie Regan, Stacy Doris, Maritza Perez, David Booth, Alexander Stadler, Rick Heredia, Patricia Irvine, James

Faerron, Lisa Steindler, and James Assatly, who is so missed, also my extended families: the Routhier, Green, and Block clans...and many others, too many to name.

Patricia Nelson for around the clock laughs and legal expertise, Paul Feuerwerker for glorious eccentricity, revelry, and invaluable insights into the band room, Mark H. for sublime musicality, first love.

The faculty, staff, and student body of Vermont College of Fine Arts, particularly my miracle-working mentors: Deborah Wiles, Brent Hartinger, Julie Larios, Tim Wynne-Jones, Margaret Bechard, and visiting faculty Jane Yolen. And my classmates: the Cliff-hangers, especially Jill Santopolo, Carol Lynch Williams, Erik Talkin, and Mari Jorgensen. Also, the San Francisco VCFA crew. And Marianna Baer—angel at the end of my keyboard.

My other incredible teachers and professors: Regina Wiegand, Bruce Boston, Will Erickson, Archie Ammons, Ken McClane, Phyllis Janowitz, C.D. Wright, among many others.

To those listed above who spirit in and out of this book—a special thank you.

Deepest appreciation and gratitude go to:

My clients at Manus & Associates Literary Agency, as well as my extraordinary colleagues: Stephanie Lee, Dena Fischer, Penny Nelson, Theresa van Eeghen, Janet and Justin Manus, and most especially, Jillian Manus, who doesn't walk, but dances on water.

Alisha Niehaus, my remarkable editor, for her ebullience, profundity, insight, kindness, sense of humor, and for making every part of the process a celebration. Everyone at Dial and

Penguin Books for Young Readers for astounding me each jubilant step of the way.

Emily van Beek of Pippin Properties for being the best literary agent on earth! I am forever mesmerized by her joyfulness, brilliance, ferocity and grace. Holly McGhee for her enthusiasm, humor, savvy and soulfulness. Elena Mechlin for her behind-the-scenes magic and cheer. The Pippin Ladies are without peer. And Jason Dravis at Monteiro Rose Dravis Agency for his vision and dazzling know-how.

And finally, an extra heartfelt double-whammy out-of-the-freaking-park thank you to my brother Bobby: True Believer.

Turn the page for
a discussion guide to

the

sky

is

everywhere

1. A major theme of this book is Lennie's discovery of her sexuality. Do you think this is depicted realistically? Do you think this is tied to her grief or do you think the two are unrelated?

2. Throughout the novel, Lennie writes on anything and everything and leaves these poems scattered around the town. Do you think this is an effective way of showing the reader Lennie and Bailey's relationship? How do these poems ultimately bring Joe and Lennie together? What is the significance of Lennie's scattering these poems?

3. Writing can be a form of therapy for some people. Do you think these poems are Lennie's way of finding an outlet for her grief? If so, what makes you think it works? Doesn't work?

4. When Sarah hears about Lennie and Toby's relationship, she's upset by their actions. Do you agree with Sarah's reaction or should she have reacted differently, knowing Lennie and Toby's situation? What is your opinion on Lennie and Toby's relationship? Do you find it forgivable or heartless?

5. During one of her encounters with Toby, Lennie realizes, "I'm sure a shrink would love this, all of it." (pgs. 146–147) What does she mean by that? Do you agree with this assessment? Discuss whether you believe Lennie's actions in wearing Bailey's clothes and hooking up with her boyfriend are an act to keep Bailey close or to gain the life her sister had.

6. Lennie and Bailey were extremely close sisters. Do you really believe no competition existed between them? Why or why not?

7. Bailey and Lennie's absent mother is a large part of their lives. Ultimately the mystery leads Bailey to search for her. Why do you think she leaves Lennie in the dark about this? Who do you think is a stand-in for Lennie's real mother—Bailey or Gram? Why do you think Lennie decides not to continue with the search? Do you think she'll be content?

8. Lennie's actions hurt Joe very deeply, on account of his relationship history. Do you think his reaction is extreme or understandable? Why do you think he forgives Lennie in the end?

9. Consider the role music plays in the novel. How is this a crucial part of the story? Why does Lennie purposely throw the audition for first chair? How does music help her to heal? Is it just the music that draws Joe to Lennie or something more? How does it shape her relationship with Joe?

10. The novel is saturated with grief. Each person touched by Bailey in the novel—Gram, Big, Lennie, Toby, and Sarah—grieve in distinctly personal ways. Define their grief and how each character learns to move on, if at all. Do you wish any of the characters had worked through his or her grief in a different way? How would you have acted in their situation?

Turn the page
for a Q & A with author

JANDY NELSON

Music plays a large role in Lennie's life. Why did you feel this was an important addition to her character? What made you want to include music in the book in the first place?

Well, the funny thing is I don't feel like I had that much to do with it! Lennie pretty much crashed into my psyche, clarinet in hand. So she was always a musician in my mind and I went from there, believing then that music would be an intrinsic factor in her growth, in the way she coped with her grief, in how she connected in a wordless way with Joe, in how she moved out of Bailey's shadow and into her own light. In the beginning of the story when Lennie's so shut down, she says, to express what she's feeling she'd need "a new alphabet, one made of falling, of tectonic plates shifting, of the deep devouring dark." I think over the course of the story, she realizes that, for her, music is this alphabet. She says, "What if music is what escapes what a heart breaks?" and I think this becomes true for her. More generally, I love music and wanted it to have a curative, aphrodisiacal, celebratory, and transformative role in this story. Like Jack Kerouac said, "The only truth is music." And Shakespeare: "If music be the food of love, play on." I wanted Lennie to play on.

You have an MFA in poetry. Is this why you decided to make Lennie a poet in the novel?

Before writing this book, I'd only written poetry, and *The Sky Is Everywhere* actually started as a novel in verse. I had this image in my mind of a grief-stricken girl scattering her poems all over a town—that was really the inciting image for the whole book and key right from the start to Lennie's character. I kept thinking of her, this bereft girl, who wanted so badly to communicate with someone who was no longer there that she just began writing her words on everything and anything she could, scattering her poems and thoughts and memories to the winds. In my mind, it was a way for Lennie to write her grief on the world, to mark it, to reach out to her sister and at the same time to make sure, in this strange way, that their story was part of everything. So it all began with Lennie's poems, but very early on, like after a couple weeks of writing, it became clear that Lennie's story needed to be told primarily in prose so I dove in and found myself falling in love with writing fiction—it was a total revelation! After that, I wrote both the prose and poems simultaneously, weaving the poems in as I went along.

Why did you want to tell Lennie's story? Did you ever imagine telling Bailey and Lennie's story from another point of view?

No, it was always Lennie's story I wanted to tell and always from her point of view. I wanted the immediacy of first person, to really be able to follow her closely emotionally and psychologically over the course of the story. That image I had of her scattering poems was incredibly persistent; it chased me everywhere until I sat down to write her story. I had lost someone very close to me years earlier and I wanted to write about that kind of catastrophic, transformational life event. I wanted to explore some of the intricacies and complexities of grief, but I wanted to explore them through a love story—or two really. I imagined a story where joy and sorrow cohabitated in really close quarters, where love could be almost as unwieldy as grief. James Baldwin said, "When you're writing you're trying to find out something which you don't know." I think there were things I wanted to explore and discover, and writing Lennie's story helped me do that. She really took me over. What's odd is that despite the subject matter, and even though many days I typed with tears falling onto the keyboard, writing this novel was an incredibly joyful experience, one of the happiest times of my life.

Was setting important to you in writing this story?

Absolutely. I very much wanted the setting to be a "character" in this story interplaying with the other characters. I love California, love writing about it. I'm very inspired by the landscape. The imagined town of Clover, where *The Sky Is Everywhere* takes place, has really dramatic natural elements: roaring rivers, skyscraping redwoods, thick old-growth forests. This landscape is in the DNA of the Walker family, and I wanted it to be instrumental in Lennie's recovery and awakening, as objective correlative, but also as almost a spiritual force in her life.

What do you want readers to take from this story?

It's funny there's a paragraph toward the end of the novel in Chapter 35. Lennie has just told Rachel she's going to challenge her for first chair and she's running through the woods on her way to write the poem for Joe. She's taking steps that will propel her into the future when she's suddenly clobbered (not for the first time) by the realization that she has a future and Bailey doesn't. It's agony for her and it occurs to her that grief is forever, that it will be with her always, step for step, breath for breath, but she also realizes in this moment that this is true because grief and love are conjoined and you can't have one without the other. Grief is always going to be a measure of the love lost. She thinks, "All I can do is love her [Bailey], and love the world, emulate her by living with daring and spirit and joy." Every time I come across this paragraph, I think to myself, Well there it is, the whole book crammed into one paragraph! So for me the ideas in that paragraph kind of ring out, but every reader will take something different from the novel and that's what I want, that's the magic of it all. Reading is such a wonderfully personal and private affair.

What are your favorite parts of the writing process? What were your favorite scenes to write in *The Sky Is Everywhere*?

I have two favorite parts of the whole process. I love the beginning, the first draft, when I'm totally lost inside a story, so immersed that my fictional life overtakes my real one. I love the madness of that, when the story is pouring out and I feel this compulsion to get it down before I lose it. It's fevered, euphoric, like a mad love. And I also adore the later stages of revision, the last draft, when I'm playing with words, fiddling endlessly with this and that. At that point, I kind of just stare zombie-like at my computer screen for days living inside a particular sentence or scene or section trying to make it better, to make it come alive. It's a total blast. I think my favorite scenes to write were the ones where Lennie was falling in love. One of the wonders of writing a love story is you get to swoon right alongside the characters. I love that kind of tumbling rapturous emotion and trying to find language for it. I also loved writing the family scenes with Big and Gram and others around the breakfast table—the two of them were a lot of fun to spend time with, what came out of their mouths always surprised me. And . . . actually I think I have a lot of favorites!

Do you have any tips for aspiring writers?

Yes. Read, read, read. And write, write, write. Also, remember that what makes your voice as a writer unique is the fact that you're you, so don't be afraid to put yourself on the page, to reveal your passions, sorrows, joys, idiosyncrasies, insights, your personal monsters and miracles. Only you can be you and only you can write like you—that's your gift alone. If you have the writing fever, just keep at it—writing takes a ton of practice, patience, and perseverance—make sure to ignore the market and don't let rejection talk you out of your dream. I love this quote by Ray Bradbury: "Yet if I were asked to name the most important items in a writer's make-up, the things that shape his material and rush him along the road to where he wants to go, I could only warn him to look to his zest, see to his gusto."

Have you begun working on your next project? If so, can you give us any hints?

I am currently hard at work on a new YA novel about twins Noah and Jude. It's really two novels in one and it alternates between Noah's story, which takes place when the twins are fourteen, and Jude's, when they're eighteen. It's full of secrets and lies and heartbreak and romance and love and very strong passions. Both narratives revolve around a very charismatic and mysterious sculptor who changes both the twins' lives, and they, his. I'm excited about it—fingers crossed!

For more information, visit
www.theskyiseverywhere.com
or
www.jandynelson.com

Introduction

With the terrorist attacks on the Pentagon and World Trade Center on September 11, 2001, millions of Americans lost their sense of personal and national security. In response, the federal government declared a war on terrorism, involving both military action and the formation of a new cabinet department, the Department of Homeland Security, to assess, prevent, and counter threats within U.S. borders. Laws have been changed giving the FBI, CIA, and other federal agencies sweeping new powers to investigate American citizens and noncitizens. These combined efforts have created a huge new bureaucracy, cost tens of billions of dollars, and focused Americans' fears on terrorism at home and abroad.

The Nuclear Threat

Threats to national security are nothing new, however. During the Cold War, from 1945 to 1990, the United States and the Soviet Union had about fifty thousand launch-ready nuclear missiles aimed at each other. Most of these weapons were hundreds of times more powerful than the atomic bombs dropped on Japan at the end of World War II. During the Cold War years, these weapons were the chief threat to national security, and fears of a nuclear war that could end civilization on earth were central to public debate. Yet Americans worked, prospered, and built the richest nation in the world during this period. Most trusted their government to negotiate with the Soviets to prevent a catastrophic nuclear war.

Since the collapse of the Soviet Union in 1991, many Americans believe that this danger has passed. At the time, President George H.W. Bush announced in an address to Congress "a new era—freer from the threat of terror, stronger in the pursuit of justice, and more secure in the quest for peace, an era in which the nations of the world, East and West, North and South, can prosper and live in harmony."

The end of the Cold War did sharply reduce the threat of nuclear missiles fired as an act of war. To this day, however, the

7

United States and Russia continue to keep about twenty thousand nuclear missiles on hair-trigger alert pointed at one another's cities. The possibility exists that such an arsenal might be launched accidentally, or willfully by fanatical terrorists bent on world destruction. In addition to this significant potential danger, other threats to national security have arisen that were little considered when the first President Bush spoke those words on September 11, 1990—eleven years to the day before the World Trade Center attack.

In the twentieth century, only large nations with great riches were capable of creating nuclear bombs, chemical arsenals, and other weapons of mass destruction. In the twenty-first century, anyone with access to the Internet can find plans for explosives, biological weapons, and even nuclear bombs. While few are interested in building weapons of mass destruction, it is increasingly accepted that one angry loner or a small, well-organized terrorist organization could wreak havoc on modern civilization. Moreover, since 1990 developing nations such as Pakistan, India, Iran, and North Korea have acquired nuclear technology. If long-running hostilities between India and Pakistan, for example, erupt into nuclear war, deadly radioactive fallout could enter the atmosphere and a regional conflict could have global effects.

American politicians also consider Iran and North Korea potential nuclear threats to the United States. Both nations are hostile to America, and fears exist that such a rogue nation might intentionally supply terrorists with small nuclear "suitcase" bombs, smuggled in through U.S. seaports for detonation in an American city. As Clive Cookson and Andrew Ward write in the *Financial Times:* "An astonishingly small amount of plutonium can devastate a city. . . . [Designers] with high technical capabilities could make a bomb with a . . . 20-kiloton yield [equal to the atom bomb dropped on Hiroshima in 1945] with a tennis-ball sized 3 kg [6.6 pounds of plutonium]." Such a scenario could be deadly for millions of Americans and bring the nation's economy to a halt. The same could be true if state-sponsored terrorists were to blow up a nuclear power plant using a hijacked jet or sabotage.

Other Weapons of Mass Destruction

Other weapons of mass destruction pose equally alarming threats. Biochemical weapons are relatively easy to manufac-

ture and use. Anthrax has already been used to terrorize the nation in the weeks following the September 11 attacks. Although only five people died as a result of this still-unsolved crime, biological and chemical agents are produced in dozens of countries, including the United States, and many analysts charge that stockpiled supplies are not secure. Some agents, such as deadly ricin, may be manufactured by anyone with a limited knowledge of chemistry and access to instructions and locations of raw materials available on the Internet. As Loren B. Thompson writes in *Grave New World:* "There was nothing new about biological warfare. . . . What was new in the autumn of 2001 was the widespread realization that modern technology was putting unprecedented destructive power in the hands of ordinary people."

Threats in Cyberspace

Access to technology can threaten national security in other ways. Since the early 1990s, almost every segment of modern society has become dependent on centralized computer networks. These computers keep the electrical grid running; provide for the delivery of freshwater; coordinate the air, rail, and highway networks; and conduct billions of financial transactions among banks, insurance companies, stock markets, and other institutions. While this modern technology allows the United States and other developed nations to prosper, it could potentially be used for destructive purposes. As Dan Verton writes in *Black Ice: The Invisible Threat of Cyber-Terrorism:*

> The next terrorist attack may well be launched—at least partially—in cyberspace. Much of our economy depends on the proper functioning of this digital medium. . . . Without properly functioning computers and the networks that connect them, there would be no ability to generate electricity. . . . Even if electricity can be generated, attacks to computer networks can disable the ability to transmit power if the computers that control the electrical distribution systems are not functioning properly. Cell phones, landline telephones, and other forms of communication (including those used by the military) are computer controlled. . . . Insurance, banking, investment, and financial ser-

vices are all heavily dependent upon both the availability and reliability of information systems. A terrorist attack need not destroy these systems to wreak havoc. Substantially impairing the operation of these systems could undermine consumer confidence, and have a debilitating effect on the economy. Corrupting data or preventing access to data could devastate the financial services sector.

In light of these threats to national security, President George W. Bush stated in September 2002: "Defending our Nation against its enemies is the first and fundamental commitment of the Federal Government. . . . Our enemies have openly declared that they are seeking weapons of mass destruction, and evidence indicates that they are doing so with determination. The United States will not allow these efforts to succeed."

Criticism of U.S. Policy

Despite the president's reassuring words, critics argue that flawed U.S. foreign policy since the end of World War II has provoked hatred toward Americans and itself undermined national security. U.S. support for Israel, for example, including arms sales and $4 billion a year in aid, has outraged Arab countries in the Middle East and made America the target of Palestinian terrorist groups. The United States also has a record of supporting authoritarian regimes in the Middle East and South America. And many, especially in the Arab world, believe that the 2003 invasion of Iraq to topple dictator Saddam Hussein is a pretense for American intervention and occupation of the Muslim world. Militant Islamic extremists who believe in the concept of jihad, or holy war, see the U.S. presence in Iraq as justification for continued terrorist attacks on Americans. As Hani Sibai, director of a London-based jihadist organization, writes on the Al Maqrizi Center for Historical Studies Web site: "Iraq is currently a battlefield and a fertile soil for every Islamic movement that views jihad as a priority. . . . [The] continuation of the anti-occupation resistance will produce several large groups that might merge into one large group." Jessica Stern, author of *Terror in the Name of God: Why Religious Militants Kill*, further explains in the *Los Angeles Times*:

> Holy wars take off when there is a large supply of young men who feel humiliated and deprived;

> when leaders emerge who know how to capitalize
> on those feelings; and when a segment of society is
> willing to fund them. . . . But they are dependent
> first and foremost on a deep pool of humiliation.

Critics such as Stern argue that unless the United States successfully addresses injustice, poverty, and starvation among the billions of the world's poorest people, threats to America's national security will only grow. As Michael Brown writes in *Grave New World:* "Many security problems of the twentieth century will persist in the twenty-first, some will evolve and become deadlier than ever, and new problems will be added to the security agenda. National . . . security will [create] momentous policy problems for the foreseeable future."

Since the September 11 attacks, Americans have become acutely aware of the threats to their homeland. Although most analysts would agree that the nation faces a multitude of security risks, vociferous debate persists about which are the most serious. To be sure, miscalculations in judging which threats demand the greatest attention could have disastrous consequences for homeland security.

1

Nuclear Terrorism Is the Greatest Threat to National Security

Graham Allison

Graham Allison is the professor of government and the director of the Belfer Center for Science and International Affairs at Harvard University's Kennedy School of Government. From 1993 to 1994 he was assistant secretary of defense for policy and plans in the Clinton administration.

The terrorist attacks on the World Trade Center and the Pentagon on September 11, 2001, proved devastating terrorism was possible on American soil. Since that time, the threat of nuclear terrorism has intensified. A group of terrorists armed with a small quantity of nuclear materials could launch a horrific attack on an American city that would kill thousands and leave huge tracts of land uninhabitable for decades due to radioactivity. While members of terrorist groups actively seek to purchase fissile substances such as plutonium to make such weapons, the United States is doing little to control existing stockpiles of nuclear materials in dozens of countries throughout the world, especially in the nations of the former Soviet Union. Unless the United States cooperates with other nuclear nations to secure loosely guarded stockpiles of nuclear weapons and bomb-making materials while strictly preventing new nations such as Iran from producing fissile materials, Americans can expect terrorists to attempt a nuclear attack.

Graham Allison, "How to Stop Nuclear Terror," *Foreign Affairs*, vol. 83, January/February 2004, p. 64. Copyright © 2004 by the Council on Foreign Relations, Inc. Reproduced by permission.

President George W. Bush has singled out terrorist nuclear attacks on the United States as the defining threat the nation will face in the foreseeable future. In addressing this specter [in November 2001] he asserted that Americans' "highest priority is to keep terrorists from acquiring weapons of mass destruction." So far, however, his words have not been matched by deeds. [As of February 2004] the Bush administration has yet to develop a coherent strategy for combating the threat of nuclear terror. Although it has made progress on some fronts, Washington has failed to take scores of specific actions that would measurably reduce the risk to the country. Unless it changes course—and fast—a nuclear terrorist attack on the United States will be more likely than not in the decade ahead.

The administration's inaction is hard to understand. Its behavior demonstrates a failure to grasp a fundamental insight: nuclear terrorism is, in fact, preventable. It is a basic matter of physics: without fissile material [uranium and plutonium], you can't have a nuclear bomb. No nuclear bomb, no nuclear terrorism. Moreover, fissile material can be kept out of the wrong hands. The technology for doing so already exists: Russia does not lose items from the Kremlin Armory, nor does the United States from Fort Knox. Nascent [emerging] nukes should be kept just as secure. If they are, terrorists could still attempt to create new supplies, but doing so would require large facilities, which would be visible and vulnerable to attack.

Denying terrorists access to nuclear weapons and weapons-grade material is thus a challenge to nations' willpower and determination, not to their technical capabilities. Keeping these items safe will be a mammoth undertaking. But the strategy for doing so is clear. The solution would be to apply a new doctrine of "Three No's": no loose nukes, no new nascent nukes, and no new nuclear states.

Getting a Grip

A few numbers starkly illustrate the scale of the problem the United States now faces in trying to control the spread of nuclear weapons materials. Just eight countries—China, France, India, Israel, Pakistan, Russia, the United Kingdom, and the United States—are known to have nuclear weapons. In addition, the CIA estimates that North Korea has enough plutonium for one or two nuclear weapons. And two dozen additional states possess research reactors with enough highly enriched

uranium (heu) to build at least one nuclear bomb on their own. According to best estimates, the global nuclear inventory includes more than 30,000 nuclear weapons, and enough heu and plutonium for 240,000 more.

> *Unless [the Bush administration] changes course—and fast—a nuclear terrorist attack on the United States will be more likely than not in the decade ahead.*

Hundreds of these weapons are currently stored in conditions that leave them vulnerable to theft by determined criminals, who could then sell them to terrorists. Even more "nascent nukes" (the heu and plutonium that are the only critical ingredients for making nuclear bombs) are at risk. Almost every month, someone somewhere is apprehended trying to smuggle or steal nuclear materials or weapons. Last August [2003] for example, Alexander Tyulyakov—the deputy director of Atomflot (the organization that carries out repair work for Russian nuclear icebreakers and nuclear submarines)—was arrested in Murmansk for trying to do just that. The situation is so bad that three years ago, Howard Baker, the current U.S. ambassador to Japan and the former Republican leader of the Senate, testified, "It really boggles my mind that there could be 40,000 nuclear weapons, or maybe 80,000 in the former Soviet Union, poorly controlled and poorly stored, and that the world is not in a near-state of hysteria about the danger."

In making his case against Saddam Hussein [in 2003], President Bush argued, "If the Iraqi regime is able to produce, buy, or steal an amount of uranium a little bigger than a softball, it could have a nuclear weapon in less than a year." What the president failed to mention is that with the same quantity of heu, [terrorist groups such as] al Qaeda, Hezbollah, or Hamas could do the same. Once built, nuclear weapons could be smuggled across U.S. borders with little difficulty. Of the seven million cargo containers that will arrive at U.S. ports this year, for example, only two percent will be opened for inspection. And once on U.S. soil, those weapons would likely be used. Prior to September 11, 2001, many experts argued that terrorists were unlikely to kill large numbers of people, because they

sought not to maximize victims but to win publicity and sympathy for their causes. After the attacks on the Pentagon and the World Trade Center, however, few would disagree with President Bush's warning that if al Qaeda gets nuclear weapons, it will use them against the United States "in a heartbeat." Indeed, [terrorist leader] Osama bin Laden's press spokesman, Sulaiman Abu Ghaith, has announced that the group aspires "to kill 4 million Americans, including 1 million children," in response to casualties supposedly inflicted on Muslims by the United States and Israel.

Steps Taken

If a terrorist nuclear attack did occur in the United States, the first questions asked would be who did it, and where did they get the bomb? Bin Laden would top the list of probable perpetrators. But the supplier would be less certain; it could be Russia, Pakistan, or North Korea, but it could also be Ukraine or Ghana. Russia would probably top the list not because of hostile intent but because of the enormity of its arsenal of nuclear material, much of it still vulnerable to insider theft. Pakistan would likely rank second due to the ongoing links between its security services and al Qaeda, and the uncertain chain of command over its nuclear weaponry. North Korea, the most promiscuous weapon proliferator on earth, has already sold missiles to Iraq, Iran, Pakistan, and Saudi Arabia and so would merit suspicion. As would Ukraine and Ghana, which operate [Russian]-supplied research reactors with enough heu for one or more nuclear weapons. Interestingly, Saddam-era Iraq would not have even made the top ten.

> *It really boggles my mind that there could be 40,000 nuclear weapons . . . in the former Soviet Union, poorly controlled and poorly stored, and that the world is not in a near-state of hysteria.*

To be fair, since September 11, the Bush administration has taken steps to reduce the danger of a nuclear attack by terrorists. It has attacked al Qaeda training bases in Afghanistan and around the globe and enlisted more than 100 nations in a

global effort to share intelligence, enforce antiterrorism legislation, and curtail the flow of terrorists' money. Bush has repeatedly declared that the spread of weapons of mass destruction
(WMD) would be "intolerable," prompting similar declarations
from key allies. [In 2003] he also proposed a UN Security Council resolution that would criminalize WMD proliferation and
promoted the Proliferation Security Initiative, an 11-nation
group that, stretching existing legal frameworks, will search vehicles suspected of transporting WMD cargo on the high seas.
After initial skepticism, the administration has also embraced
the Nunn-Lugar Cooperative Threat Reduction Program to secure and eliminate former Soviet nuclear weapons and has enlisted other members of . . . leading industrialized countries to
match Washington's $1 billion annual commitment to the pro-
gram over the next decade. And the United States has cooper-
ated with Russia to extract three potential nuclear weapons
from Serbia and one from Romania.

Not a Priority

But the list of actions not taken by the administration remains
lengthy and worrisome. Bush has not made nuclear terrorism a
personal priority for himself or those who report directly to
him. And he has resisted proposals by Senator Richard Lugar (R-
Ind.), former Senator Sam Nunn (D-Ga.), and others to assign
responsibility for the issue to a single individual, who could
then be held accountable. As a result, were the president today
to ask his cabinet who is responsible for preventing nuclear terrorism, either a dozen people would raise their hands, or no one
would. Bush has also not communicated his sense of urgency
about nuclear terrorism to the presidents of Russia or Pakistan.
Nor has Bush increased the pace of U.S. cooperation with Russia in securing former Soviet nuclear weapons and materials. As
a result, after a decade of effort, half of the Soviet arsenal remains inadequately secured. More generally, the Bush administration has not acted to change the prevailing practice that allows states to decide for themselves how secure weapons and
materials on their territories will be. More than 100 potential
weapons, such as those extracted from Serbia, still sit in a dozen
countries in circumstances that leave them vulnerable to theft.

In this context, it is impossible to avoid mentioning Iraq.
The Bush administration used the danger that Saddam might
supply WMD to terrorists as its decisive argument for war. The

subsequent failure to find evidence of these weapons has compromised the administration's credibility on the general subject of WMD, as well as the perceived competence of the U.S. intelligence community. Moreover, during the year and a half in which the United States sought to get other countries to support its Iraq policy, North Korea and Iran were able to accelerate their own programs. Mounting a serious campaign now to prevent nuclear terrorism will thus be more challenging than it would have been before the Iraq war.

No, No, No

Preventing nuclear terrorism will require a comprehensive strategy: one that denies access to weapons and materials at their source, detects them at borders, defends every route by which a weapon could be delivered, and addresses motives as well as means. Aggressive offense to disrupt and destroy organizations and individuals that could attack the United States must be matched by robust defenses at home. Washington may still sometimes have to act unilaterally. But the United States will not be able to bully other nations into taking all the necessary steps. Successful counterterrorism requires multinational intelligence and local police enforcement. For example, [the 2003] capture of al Qaeda's Southeast Asia mastermind resulted from a tip from suspicious neighbors, who informed Thai authorities who, in turn, called the CIA. If properly encouraged, foreign nationals and governments can play a huge role in tracking down terrorists. If not, they become a sympathetic sea in which terrorists can swim and hide.

> *During the year and a half in which the United States sought to get other countries to support [the war in] Iraq . . . North Korea and Iran were able to accelerate their own programs.*

The centerpiece of a serious campaign to prevent nuclear terrorism—a strategy based on the three no's (no loose nukes, no new nascent nukes, and no new nuclear weapons states)—should be denying terrorists access to weapons and their components. After all, no nuclear weapons or material means no

nuclear terrorism; it's that simple.

The first part of the strategy—no loose nukes—would require rapidly securing all nuclear weapons or weapons-usable material under a new "International Security Standard" that would ensure that terrorists could not acquire weapons or their components. The United States and Russia should develop such a standard together and act quickly to secure their own weapons and materials in a manner sufficiently transparent to give each other assurance that their stockpiles could not be used by terrorists. Moscow and Washington should then go quickly to other nuclear-weapons states and demand that they too meet this new benchmark for nuclear security and be certified by another member of the club as having done so. If necessary, technical assistance in meeting these standards should be offered. But the United States and Russia should also make clear that this is not a negotiable demand.

> **" Pyongyang, already the world's leading supplier of missiles, could become a sort of Nukes'R'Us, supplying weapons to whoever could pay—including terrorists. "**

Simultaneously, a "Global Cleanout Campaign" should extract all nascent nukes from all other countries within the next 12 months. Since all research reactors in non-nuclear weapons states contain fissile material that came from either the United States or Russia, each has a sufficient legal claim to demand its return. Compensation and wrangling may be required. But the United States and Russia must not take no for an answer.

A "no new nascent nukes" approach will require ensuring that all nuclear aspirants, especially Iran and North Korea, stop producing heu and plutonium. This effort should begin under the auspices of inspections mandated by the Nonproliferation Treaty (NPT) and the International Atomic Energy Agency (IAEA), including the NPT's Additional Protocol that allows more intrusive inspections of suspected nuclear sites. But two other elements must also be added to the current system: a prohibition on the production of fissile material, and actual enforcement mechanisms. Enforcement should begin with political and economic sanctions for recalcitrant states but should

also include threats and the use of military force if necessary, whether covert or overt. Enhanced export controls and greatly strengthened intelligence capabilities (especially human agents) should focus on preventing the work of nuclear aspirants and stopping sales from potential suppliers. Ratification of the Comprehensive Test Ban Treaty (which the Bush administration has rejected, despite support from four former chairmen of the Joint Chiefs of Staff, including Secretary of State Colin Powell) and the negotiation of a cutoff in production of fissile material in current nuclear-weapon states would reinforce this principle. . . .

Beyond the Point of No Return

The test case for a "no new nuclear weapons states" policy will be North Korea. That country remains, as former Secretary of Defense William Perry called it, "the most dangerous spot on earth." If it follows its current course, North Korea will soon be able to produce dozens of such weapons annually. Should it achieve this, South Korea and Japan will likely also go nuclear before the end of the decade. Taiwan could follow suit, risking war with China. And Pyongyang [Capital of North Korea], already the world's leading supplier of missiles, could become a sort of Nukes"R"Us, supplying weapons to whoever could pay—including terrorists. Should that happen, future historians will justifiably condemn today's leaders for their negligence.

Already, the challenge from Pyongyang has become less manageable and much more dangerous than it was when President Bush took office [in 2001]. Indeed, some members of his administration have reportedly concluded that the problem is beyond the point of no return and have started focusing on how to accommodate North Korea and avoid blame. The proposed strategy, by contrast, would begin with an unambiguous stance on this question: no nuclear North Korea. It would focus solely on this objective and subordinate all others, especially regime change. However despicable North Korea's regime, the United States has higher priorities than getting rid of it. The administration should start to recognize the urgency of this threat. Its mantra of "no crisis," evidently chosen to avoid distraction from Iraq, has served U.S. interests poorly. Bush must also get [Russian leader Vladimir] Putin and President Hu Jintao of China to contemplate the consequences of a nuclear North Korea for their own countries. Active cooperation in stopping Pyongyang should be a major test of their security relationships

with Washington. That said, the administration should drop its objections and immediately accept North Korea's proposal for bilateral negotiations. North Korea is correct when it claims that only the United States can address its security concerns.

> **❝** *Horrific as . . . a preemptive attack on North Korean nuclear facilities would be, the prospect of a nuclear North Korea willing to sell its weapons to al Qaeda . . . would be worse.* **❞**

Direct talks will allow Washington to test its presumption that, above all else, [North Korean leader] Kim Jong Il is committed to his own survival. The United States should offer him a deal: survival in exchange for nuclear disarmament. This deal would offer big carrots and threaten a big stick. If North Korea is prepared to visibly and verifiably forgo nuclear weapons and dismantle its nuclear weapons production facilities, the United States should publicly pledge to abandon any attempt to change North Korea's regime by force. It should also arrange for generous economic assistance from South Korea and Japan, which they stand ready to provide if North Korea forgoes its nukes. If, however, North Korea refuses to verifiably relinquish nuclear weapons and persists in its current efforts, the United States should threaten to use all means, including military force, to stop it. Horrific as the consequences of a preemptive attack on North Korean nuclear facilities would be, the prospect of a nuclear North Korea willing to sell its weapons to al Qaeda and other terrorists would be worse.

A Grand Alliance

As the preceding discussion suggests, the United States cannot undertake or sustain its war on nuclear terrorism unilaterally. Fortunately, it need not try. All of today's great powers share an interest in the proposed campaign. Each has sufficient reasons to fear nuclear weapons in terrorists' hands, whether they are al Qaeda, Chechens, or Chinese separatists. All great powers can therefore be mobilized in a new global alliance against nuclear terrorism, aimed at minimizing this risk by taking every action that is physically, technically, and diplomatically possi-

ble to prevent nuclear weapons or materials from being acquired by terrorists.

Construction of this alliance should begin with Russia, where the close personal relationship between Presidents Bush and Putin will be a major asset. Russia will be flattered by the prospect of standing shoulder to shoulder with the United States—especially on the one issue on which it can still claim to be a superpower. Americans and Russians should also recognize that they have a special obligation to address this problem, since they created it—and since they still own 95 percent of all nuclear weapons and material. If they demonstrate a new seriousness about reducing this threat, the United States and Russia will also be able to credibly demand that China likewise secure its weapons and materials. China could sign up Pakistan. And the rest of the nuclear club would quickly follow.

Objections will surely be raised about the unfairness of a world in which some states are allowed to possess nuclear weapons while others are not. But that distinction is already embedded in the NPT, to which all non-nuclear weapons states except North Korea are signatories. Although the treaty also nominally commits nuclear weapons states to eventually eliminate their own weapons, it never set a timetable, and no one realistically expects that to happen in the foreseeable future.

The United States and its allies already have the power to define and enforce new global constraints on nuclear weapons. To make this order acceptable, however, they should undertake a concerted effort to eliminate nuclear weapons and nuclear threats from international affairs. The United States and Russia should accelerate current programs to reduce their arsenals. Moreover, the Bush administration should drop its current plans to conduct research for the production of new "mini-nukes" [small nuclear weapons for use on a battlefield].

Is the course of action outlined above conceivable? For perspective, consider the leap beyond the conventional box that the American president took in enunciating the "Bush Doctrine." With that strategy, the administration unilaterally revoked the sovereignty of states that provide sanctuary to terrorists. Declaring that "those who harbor terrorists are as guilty as the terrorists themselves," the president ordered American military forces to topple the Taliban regime in Afghanistan. Of course, this new principle has yet to be enshrined in international law. It has, nonetheless, already become a de facto rule

of international relations. Any government that knowingly hosts al Qaeda or its equivalent knows that it is inviting attack. True, the move beyond the current war on terrorism to a serious war on nuclear terrorism based on the three no's would be ambitious. But the leap involved would be no greater than the distance already traveled since September 11.

2

Bioterrorists with Chemical Weapons Could Kill Millions in the United States

James Jay Carafano

James Jay Carafano is senior research fellow for national and homeland security at the Heritage Foundation, a think tank whose mission is to formulate and promote conservative public policies.

Terrorists are well aware that deadly bioweapons made from bacteria, fungi, and viruses can create widespread horror and hysteria. Some of these biopoisons are relatively easy to make with basic laboratory skills. If terrorists were to launch an attack in a large city with anthrax, smallpox, or other bioweapons, government agencies, emergency responders, and hospitals would be quickly overwhelmed. With hundreds of nations producing these toxins, often in labs with little security, Americans should prepare for the worst in case bioweapons are used in an attack.

The proliferation of biotoxin threats, in all likelihood, will only grow with time. Of all the areas of emergency response, the federal government is least prepared to deal with catastrophic bioterrorism.

Before the creation of the Department of Homeland Security (DHS) in January 2002, numerous federal departments and

agencies bore responsibility for assisting state and local governments in bioterrorism preparedness and response. There was little coordination. Today, despite organizational changes, much expertise and capacity remains beyond the department. While the Secretary of Homeland Security is mandated to coordinate the federal response, planning and coordination are still inadequate, lines of operational control are unclear, and there is no coherent national preparedness program.

To address these shortfalls, further reforms are needed that cut across a range of federal departments and initiatives.

Why Worry?

There is one simple reason why bioterrorist strikes will be attempted against the United States in the future: They can kill Americans on an unprecedented scale and spread unimaginable fear, panic, and economic disruption. A gram or less of many biotoxin weapons can kill or sicken tens of thousands. Weight for weight, they can be hundreds to thousands of times more lethal than the most deadly chemical agents and can, in some cases, be produced at much less cost.

Some biotoxin weapons are communicable [spread from person to person] and can be spread easily beyond the initial target. They are less difficult to obtain than nuclear arms and potentially more deadly than conventional explosives or radiological and chemical weapons. A terrorist could use a virulent, infectious biological agent to inflict catastrophic damage.

The technical procedures for biotoxin weapons production are available in open-source, scientific literature. Over 100 states have the capacity to manufacture biological weapons on a large scale. A basic facility can be constructed and operated for less than $10 million.

Biotoxin weapons programs, however, are not limited to state threats. Any non-state group might be capable of performing some form of biological or toxin warfare. A terrorist group, given a competent team of graduate students and a facility no larger than a few hundred square feet, could field a small-scale program for a few hundred thousand dollars or less. Individuals with some graduate-level science education or medical training could produce biotoxin weapons. In some cases, biological attacks can be mounted without any scientific skills or medical knowledge.

Moreover, the proliferation of biological and toxin threats

will only grow with time. Biotechnology is one of the fastest growing commercial sectors in the world. The number of biotechnology companies in the United Sates alone has tripled since 1992.

> ❝ *[Bioterrorists] can kill Americans on an unprecedented scale and spread unimaginable fear, panic, and economic disruption.* ❞

These firms are also research-intensive, bringing new methods and products to the marketplace every day, and many of the benefits of this effort are dual-use, increasing the possibility that knowledge, skills, and equipment could be adapted to a biological agent program. The pharmaceutical industry, for example, has invested enormous effort in making drugs more stable for oral or aerosol delivery and thus, unintentionally, is developing the tools for producing the next generation of easily deliverable biological weapons. As the global biotechnology industry expands, nonproliferation efforts will have a difficult time keeping pace with the opportunities available to field a bioweapon.

Easily Spread

Equally troubling, the difficulties in effectively delivering biotoxins can be overcome with some forethought and ingenuity. For example, cruise missiles, unmanned aerial vehicles, or aircraft could perform sprayer attacks, but only if specialized spraying equipment was employed that ensured proper dispersal and prevented particle clumping. Clumping of agents can degrade the effectiveness of an attack. Large particles quickly drop to the ground or, if inhaled, do not easily pass into lung tissue, significantly lessening the potential for infection.

Mechanical stresses in the spraying system might also kill or inactivate a large percentage of particles—by some estimates up to 99 percent. However, if an enemy had a large supply (e.g., 50 kilograms of a virulent bioweapon) or was not terribly concerned about achieving maximum effects, crude dispensers might be adequate.

In creating bioweapons, terrorists might be limited only by

their imagination. For example, a low-tech version of a bio–cruise missile attack could be attempted with a system like the Autonomous Helicopter, a 14-foot-long, pilotless, remote-controlled helicopter built by Yamaha for crop dusting in Japan. The $100,000 aircraft uses a GPS system and video camera to allow its flight route to be preprogrammed and monitored.

Intentional contamination of food and water is another possible form of biological attack. Product tampering or contaminating food supplies is an ever-present danger. For instance, in 1984, the Rajneeshee cult contaminated local salad bars in an Oregon town with salmonella, demonstrating the ease of conducting small-scale, indiscriminate terrorist attacks.

Another means of bioattack is to spread infectious diseases through humans, animals, or insects. Infectious diseases are already the third leading cause of death in the United States, and battling them is an ongoing health issue. Foreign animal diseases also present a serious risk. Many diseases can infect multiple hosts. Three-quarters of emerging human pathogens are zoonotic—in other words, readily transmitted back and forth among humans, domesticated animals, and wildlife. . . .

Why the Current System Is Inadequate

The current federal response system is predicated on the thoughtful and systematic application of resources. Local communities are expected to deal with disasters and emergencies using their own resources. When they lack adequate capacity, they call on the assets from the state and neighboring jurisdictions. Federal resources are brought to bear only after state and local governments find they lack adequate capacity and request assistance from the federal government. In turn, FEMA [Federal Emergency Management Agency] then has to determine the level of required assistance and then coordinate the delivery of support with HHS [Health and Human Services], the DOD [Department of Defense], the VA [Veterans Administration], and other federal agencies.

The current approach could well prove totally inadequate in the event of a virulent biotoxin attack. Effectively negating threats in many cases requires a rapid response capability, and operating on compressed timelines leaves little room for delayed delivery of support or miscues in coordination.

One significant requirement, for example, is quickly emplacing an incident response structure that can detect and as-

sess threats and mobilize appropriate resources. In particular, for a chemical or biological attack, actions taken in the first hours to identify, contain, and treat victims may significantly reduce the scope of casualties and reduce the prospects for the outbreak of an epidemic.

> *In the case of bioterrorist attack, responders could also become victims and unwittingly spread the contagion.*

Complicating any medical response is the plethora of federal, state, and local agencies that would play a role in consequence management. Orchestrating their efforts could be a major challenge. Some organizational chains of command are maximized for responding to infectious diseases, some for natural disasters, others for weapons of mass destruction incidents or investigating crime scenes, and still others for chronic health care issues or emergency or mass casualty treatment. A communicable biotoxin attack, however, could resemble elements of all these problems, requiring perhaps a more sophisticated and integrated response than any other form of terrorist weapon.

Virtually every large-scale exercise or response experiences problems in agency notification, mobilization, information management, communication systems, and administrative and logistical support. Emergency response operations are also frequently plagued by a lack of information sharing and confusion over responsibilities among policymakers, law enforcement, emergency managers, first responders, public health workers, physicians, nonprofit organizations, and federal agencies. The necessity for speed can exacerbate the coordination challenge.

Responders will also have to deal with the demanding conditions and requirements of any terrorist strike. One major command and control challenge is the problem of convergence, a phenomenon that occurs when people, goods, and services are spontaneously mobilized and sent into a disaster-stricken area. Although convergence may have beneficial effects, like rushing resources to the scene of a crisis, it can also lead to congestion, create confusion, hinder the delivery of aid, compromise security, and waste scarce resources. In the case of

bioterrorist attack, responders could also become victims and unwittingly spread the contagion.

The expense of further improving the response capabilities of state and local governments and the private sector that might negate the need for a robust federal response is also a significant issue. The cost of general improvements in the state of health care systems, maintaining infrastructure, trained personnel, and expanding hospitals' surge capacity for acute care would be substantial. For example, the Association of American Hospitals estimates that preparing the nation's hospital facilities for biotoxin attacks will cost over $11 billion. Enhancing the capacity to deal with infectious diseases might require even more investment, since the epidemiology of biotoxin (noncontagious) weapon strikes and infectious disease attacks can be different and require different clinical response and treatment strategies.

Preparing the federal government to deal more effectively with catastrophic bioterrorism requires developing a national system that can quickly move the right kind and level of assistance to local communities. The Administration and Congress need to take . . . actions to streamline the current system, reduce bottlenecks, ensure adequate national surge capacity to respond to a catastrophic threat, and integrate and harmonize operational capabilities *before* a crisis ensues.

3

Terrorism Against Seaports in Large Cities Is a Significant Threat to National Security

Council on Foreign Relations

Founded in 1921, the Council on Foreign Relations is a national organization for scholars dedicated to producing and disseminating information about foreign and national policy choices facing the United States.

Billions of consumer items sold in the United States are produced in foreign countries. Modern free trade policies demand that Americans maintain large seaports where millions of containers filled with computers, foodstuffs, clothing, oil, and other items can be unloaded every day. Unfortunately, the same seaports that stimulate the free flow of goods allow terrorists to smuggle weapons—or even themselves—unnoticed into the United States. Seaports and terminals, where huge repositories of explosive natural gas and petroleum are stored, are usually centralized near large cities where millions work and live. Securing these facilities and inspecting the nearly 8 million containers that arrive on U.S. shores every year is a nearly impossible task. Unless the government allocates billions of dollars to seaport security efforts, these huge facilities will remain a tempting target for terrorists.

Experts warn that U.S. seaports could be tempting targets for terrorists bent on killing large numbers of people, grabbing media attention, and disrupting the U.S. economy. Port, ferry, and cruise-ship terminals are often located in highly congested areas where large numbers of people live and work. Refineries that produce highly volatile petrochemicals and convert crude oil into gasoline and heating oil are also often nearby. Given the importance of foreign trade to the U.S. economy, an attack that shut down a major American port for even a few days could devastate the regional economy that it serves. . . .

Vulnerable to Terrorist Attacks

At current staffing and funding levels, U.S. Coast Guard personnel and Customs agents can thoroughly inspect only a fraction of the arriving ships and shipping containers. Though the Customs Service is using increasingly sophisticated risk-assessment technology to choose which shipments to inspect, many outside experts are unsure about the system's effectiveness.

> ❝ *In May 2002, there were reports about 25 Islamist extremists who may have entered the United States by hiding in shipping containers.* ❞

Some 7,500 ships with foreign flags make 51,000 calls on U.S. ports each year. They carry the bulk of the approximately 890 million tons of goods that come into the country, including 7.8 million containers, 175 billion gallons of oil and other fuels, and hundreds of thousands of cruise-ship passengers and crew members. The volume of traffic gives terrorists opportunities to smuggle themselves or their weapons into the United States with little risk of detection; in May 2002, there were reports about 25 Islamist extremists who may have entered the United States by hiding in shipping containers. . . .

Ports Are Hard to Protect

[Ports are] often large and busy, offering multiple opportunities for terrorists to get in and attack. The port of Houston, for example, is 26 miles long, and thousands of trucks enter and exit

its major terminals every day. Moreover, ships often traverse narrow channels; a sunken ship in such a channel could close the port for weeks or months and cause economic chaos.

There are more than 100 major ports in the United States and many other harbors, piers, and ferry landings.

> **❝** *On average, it takes three hours for a team of five to do a complete physical inspection of a single container.* **❞**

They're mostly guarded by a state's port authority, which often leases pier and terminal space to private companies. These firms generally rely on low-paid contract guards to patrol the facilities and staff the entrances and exits. The captain of the port—an officer in the U.S. Coast Guard—is responsible for inspecting and regulating ships coming in and out. The Bureau of Customs and Border Protection—which has absorbed the personnel and the border inspection functions of both the Immigration and Naturalization Service and Customs—is responsible for inspecting foreign vessels' cargoes and clearing crews and passengers. . . .

Before the attacks [of September 11, 2001], the Coast Guard devoted not more than 2 percent of its operations to port security. In the months immediately following September 11, it spent 50 percent to 60 percent of its time and effort defending U.S. ports. Since then, that figure has fallen to between 20 percent to 30 percent because of other commitments and mounting costs.

Inadequate Measures

To prevent hijackings, sea marshals board ships when they enter U.S. ports. Customs agents screen more cargo and use more high-tech tools, such as X-ray and gamma-ray scanners. Ships must provide electronic information about cargoes 24 hours before they embark for U.S. ports so U.S. agents can target ships and shipments that might be dangerous. . . .

A 2000 federal commission ranked U.S. seaports as "poor to fair" at stopping drug trafficking, cargo theft, fraud, and vandalism. Defending ports from determined terrorists is an even

more daunting challenge, and most experts agree that U.S. ports still have a long way to go. Part of the problem, some experts say, is that in the 1990s facilitating global trade took priority over security. Agencies' funding failed to keep pace with the increase in port traffic. But more resources alone will not reduce the threat significantly. Rethinking the way port security is managed is critical, Coast Guard and Customs officials increasingly argue, as do many outside experts. . . .

Weapons of Mass Destruction

It is extremely difficult to detect suspicious cargoes among the huge volume that enters the United States daily, though Customs is field-testing radiation-detection devices in several ports to help spot primitive nuclear weapons. Experts increasingly agree that more must be done to improve intelligence cooperation and that the private sector must do more to pre-screen cargo. Better use of technology—such as tamper-proof seals and global-positioning systems to track a container—could provide more security while a container is in transit.

But better searching means time, which means money. The Department of Homeland Security and its new Bureau of Customs and Border Protection are looking for ways to find out more about a container's contents without having to open it up; on average, it takes three hours for a team of five to do a complete physical inspection of a single container.

Better Protection

A top priority is better information-sharing among the agencies that work at the ports, as well as with the FBI and CIA. Experts also urge closer cooperation between a port's public agencies and private firms; for instance, transit security would improve if U.S. Customs had stronger relationships with ship operators, freight forwarders, and other links in the global supply chain.

That's the idea behind the Customs Trade Partnership Against Terrorism, known as CT-PAT. Under its terms, companies provide more information to Customs and take on more security-related roles; in return, they receive preferential treatment in the government inspection process.

Another major step forward is the Container Security Initiative, which places U.S. Customs officers at foreign seaports to target and pre-screen "high risk" U.S.-bound cargo contain-

ers. So far, most of the world's 20 largest ports have agreed to participate in the program, as have a number of smaller ports in Europe and Canada.

Finally, programs like Operation Safe Commerce and Smart and Secure Trade Lanes will outfit containers with sensors and Global Positioning System or radio transponders to guarantee that shipments that have been verified as legitimate are not tampered with en route.

4

The Greatest Threat to National Security Is from American and Russian Missiles on Hair-Trigger Alert

Bruce G. Blair

Bruce G. Blair is a former U.S. Air Force nuclear launch officer and president of the Center for Defense Information (CDI). He writes a regular column on nuclear issues for the CDI, a progressive organization that believes national security can be made stronger through international cooperation, reduced reliance on nuclear weapons, and oversight of defense programs.

Before the fall of communism in 1989, the United States and the Soviet Union had thousands of missiles aimed at one another's cities. A nation could launch a missile at a moment's notice and leaders on the other side had only several minutes to decide whether to retaliate. The resulting nuclear war would have killed almost everyone on Earth. After the collapse of the Soviet Union, Russia and the United States became friends with mutual geopolitical interests across the globe. Incredibly, the nuclear missiles were never taken off of hair-trigger alert. While Americans worry about terrorist attacks that might kill thousands, a terrorist penetrating missile defense facilities in either country could

Bruce G. Blair, "Hair-Trigger Missiles Risk Catastrophic Terrorism," www.cdi.org, April 29, 2003. Copyright © 2003 by the Center for Defense Information. Reproduced by permission.

launch a devastating nuclear attack. Even without this possibility, there are dozens of false alarms every year. Until the United States and Russia stand down their launch-ready nuclear missiles, this inexplicable situation remains the biggest threat to national—and global—security.

While the efforts of the U.S. government to assist Russia in preventing the theft of nuclear materials from storage sites and research institutes have been inadequate, the opportunities for nuclear terrorism presented by U.S. and Russian nuclear weapons on hair-trigger alert represent an even greater peril that receives even less attention and effort. In an era of potential nuclear terrorism, the theft of a nuclear weapon from a storage site could spell an eventual disaster for an American city, but the seizure of a strategic missile or group of missiles ready for immediate firing could be apocalyptic for entire nations.

> *War planners in both countries remain, believe it or not, preoccupied with preparing to fight a large-scale nuclear war with each other on short notice.*

Our two governments have not yet overcome the mutual suspicion that is severely impeding their cooperation in preventing nuclear materials theft. They had better leap this hurdle soon, because even greater cooperation is necessary to protect their populations against the multitude of potential terrorist threats to launch-ready nuclear forces.

The distrust stems partially from disputes such as the Iraq war, but it persists in large part because the United States and Russia remain in each other's nuclear cross-hairs. War planners in both countries remain, believe it or not, preoccupied with preparing to fight a large-scale nuclear war with each other on short notice. Both sides keep thousands of weapons aimed at each other and poised for immediate launch. U.S. spy planes still routinely lurk off the Russian border looking for holes in the air defense network through which U.S. heavy bombers and cruise missiles could fly to drop nuclear bombs on Russia in wartime.

Russian missile submarines still find themselves trailed by U.S. submarines as soon as they leave port on patrol. Two massive leadership posts inside mountains in the Urals built to withstand a U.S. nuclear strike are just coming online. Russia is equipping the one at Kozvinsky Mountain with an underground antenna for radioing a launch order to a "dead hand" communications rocket designed to ensure quasi-automatic Russian missile retaliation in the event of a U.S. strike that decapitates the nuclear chain of command.

Nuclear Terrorism Is the Enemy

It behooves the former enemies to kick these old habits and stand down their obsolete confrontation. Nuclear terrorism is the real enemy, and fostering cooperation in tackling it requires that both countries move away from their nuclear confrontation. Taking U.S. and Russian missiles off of hair-trigger alert, moreover, would itself automatically reduce if not remove many of the biggest terrorist threats—which stem largely from the extremely high launch-readiness of strategic missiles. Both U.S. and Russian intercontinental ballistic missiles remain fueled, targeted, and waiting for a couple of computer signals to fire. They fly the instant they receive these signals, which can be sent with a few keystrokes on a launch console.

> *Could sophisticated terrorists generate false indications of an enemy attack that results in a mistaken launch of nuclear rockets in 'retaliation'?*

What kind of terrorist threats? The most obvious is the loss of physical control over such missiles. If scores of armed Chechen rebels could slip into the heart of Moscow and hold a packed theater hostage for days [as happened in October 2002], could terrorists infiltrate missile fields in rural Russia, seize control over a nuclear-armed mobile rocket roaming the countryside, and launch it at Europe or America? It's an open question that warrants candid bilateral discussion of the prospects of terrorists capturing rockets and circumventing the safeguards designed to foil their illicit firing.

Another specter concerns terrorists spoofing radar or satellite sensors, or cyber-terrorists hacking into early warning networks. Could sophisticated terrorists generate false indications of an enemy attack that results in a mistaken launch of nuclear rockets in 'retaliation'? False alarms have been frequent enough on both sides under the best of conditions. False warning poses an acute danger as long as Russian and U.S. nuclear commanders are allowed, as they still are today, only several pressure-packed minutes to determine whether an enemy attack is underway and decide whether to retaliate. Russia's deteriorating early warning network coupled to terrorist plotting against it only heightens the risks.

Russia is not the only crucible of risk. The early warning and control problems plaguing Pakistan, India, and other nuclear proliferators are even more acute. As these nations move toward hair-trigger stances for their nuclear missiles, the terrorist threat to them will grow in parallel.

In addition, U.S. nuclear control is also far from fool-proof. For example, a Pentagon investigation of nuclear safeguards conducted several years ago made a startling discovery—terrorist hackers might be able to gain back-door electronic access to the U.S. naval communications network, seize control electronically over radio towers such as the one in Cutler, Maine, and illicitly transmit a launch order to U.S. Trident ballistic missile submarines armed with 200 nuclear warheads apiece. This exposure was deemed so serious that Trident launch crews had to be given elaborate new instructions for confirming the validity of any launch order they receive. They would now reject a firing order that previously would have been immediately carried out.

If Russian and U.S. experts could instill trust in each other, then they could identify the real deficiencies in the system of early warning and control over nuclear forces on high combat alert. They could also allay unwarranted fears. The value of trust was illustrated [in 2001] when Russian scientists at the renowned Kurchatov Institute alerted their American counterparts in the Department of Energy to software flaws they feared had compromised the U.S. computer system used to keep track of the U.S. inventory of nuclear materials.

The stakes today are too high to let old habits of mind and obsolete practices of nuclear confrontation stand in the way of protecting ourselves against the biggest threat faced by both the United States and Russia. Washington and Moscow need to

stop playing Cold War–like games and confront nuclear terrorism instead. Both need ironclad safeguards against the terrorist exploitation of their hair-trigger arsenals. They should each stand down, and work together not only to protect their own arsenals but also to keep other nations off of high alert, before it's too late.

5

Millions of Lives Are at Risk Because of Loose Security at Nuclear Power Plants

Daniel Hirsch, David Lochbaum, and Edwin Lyman

Daniel Hirsch is president of the Committee to Bridge the Gap. David Lochbaum is a nuclear safety engineer with the Union of Concerned Scientists. Edwin Lyman is president of the Nuclear Control Institute. All three organizations monitor nuclear activities worldwide and pursue strategies to halt the spread and reverse the growth of nuclear arms.

If a terrorist flew a hijacked jumbo jet into a nuclear power plant, the resulting explosion would give thousands of people cancer and make an area the size of Pennsylvania uninhabitable for generations. Despite this looming possibility, the Nuclear Regulatory Commission (NRC) and the nuclear power industry refuse to take steps to lessen the risk. And there are other, more immediate security threats to nuclear power plants. While the NRC and the power plant owners resist improving security in order to save money, terrorists with even a marginal amount of training could easily overrun the lax security at most nuclear power plants. If this ominous scenario came to pass, the terrorists could

blow the plant up and create a nuclear meltdown that would be impossible to contain.

For a quarter of a century, the Nuclear Regulatory Commission (NRC) kept its dirty little secret: Despite the fact that a successful attack on a U.S. nuclear plant could cause thousands of illnesses and deaths in the surrounding area, and despite the clear increase in terrorist threats over that same period, the commission continued to require the country's nuclear power plant operators to maintain only a minimal security capability.

The NRC has not required nuclear facilities to guard against an assault by more than three attackers—and never with the help of more than a single insider. In addition, for purposes of planning security, the NRC assumed that the three attackers would act as a single team, armed with nothing more sophisticated than hand-held automatic rifles.

More troubling, the commission has not required plant operators to be able to withstand a possible attack by boat or plane—nor to have the capacity to defend in any way against an attack by anyone defined as "enemies of the United States"—nations or sub-national groups.

After September 11, 2001, when 19 Al Qaeda recruits acting in four coordinated teams used commercial airliners to attack the World Trade Center and the Pentagon, a great deal of concern was expressed about U.S. nuclear plants' vulnerability to terrorist attack, and questions were raised about increasing security at nuclear facilities. In early 2002, it was widely believed that the NRC would finally upgrade its 25-year-old "design basis threat"—the maximum threat that nuclear plant security systems are required to protect against—and that considerably higher standards would be established.

Failing to Upgrade Security

Although the commission has never advertised the limitations of its design basis threat (DBT), the guidelines are no secret to terrorists. The NRC has long published its security requirements in the Code of Federal Regulations, available at any library or on the Internet, and supplemental information can be found in other publicly available NRC documents. And critics have been pointing out the inadequacy of those security requirements for decades.

Although the nuclear power plants' required security

arrangements are minimal, even a modest attacking force—one that fits the NRC's definition—can easily overwhelm the security guards at many U.S. nuclear plants, as demonstrated by the NRC's own force-on-force testing program, known as the Operational Safeguards Response Evaluation (OSRE). At nearly half the nuclear plants where security has been OSRE-tested, mock attackers have been able to enter quickly and simulate the destruction of enough safety equipment to cause a meltdown [destruction of the reactor that releases massive amounts of deadly radiation]—even though the reactor operators typically have been given six months' advance notice of the day of the test.

In response to these dismal test results, the NRC attempted to quietly kill off the test program.

> **❝** *Defensive tests were discontinued after September 11, and are only now being revived with a few 'volunteer' plants whose owners presumably are confident they can pass.* **❞**

Since the massive terrorist attacks of September 11, the NRC's inaction has been even more troubling. Despite the obvious attractiveness of U.S. reactors as terrorist targets, the NRC and the nuclear industry have done little to upgrade security. . . .

The NRC is considering some sort of modest upgrade that could be issued soon, but it appears to postulate a far smaller assault than that which occurred on September 11. Meanwhile, the NRC and the nuclear industry strenuously lobbied Congress to prevent it from passing legislation that would have forced the NRC to raise the DBT to match the level of attack on September 11.

Additionally, the OSRE defensive tests were discontinued after September 11, and are only now being revived with a few "volunteer" plants whose owners presumably are confident they can pass.

On January 17, 2002, then-NRC Chairman Richard Meserve gave a speech at the National Press Club, titled "Nuclear Security in the Post-September Environment," arguing that little was needed to improve what he characterized as "very strong" reactor security. "First, and most important," he said, "since

September 11 there have been no specific credible threats of a terrorist attack on nuclear power plants." Just 12 days later, however, President George W. Bush said in his State of the Union address that diagrams of American nuclear power plants had been found in Al Qaeda camps in Afghanistan.

One must ask why the NRC is so reluctant to require greater security efforts. There are two obvious answers: Improving security at reactors will cost money; and it may remind the public of the risks associated with nuclear power, making expansion of the nuclear sector, as proposed by the industry and urged by the [vice president Dick] Cheney energy task force, more difficult. But should political factors be permitted to interfere with protecting the population?

Ongoing Review

In March 2002 NRC Commissioner Jeffrey Merrifield defended the commission's apparent lack of progress by quoting [author Ernest] Hemingway's admonition to "never mistake motion for action." It seems instead as if the NRC is hoping that the public will mistake paralysis for action.

Soon after September 11, the NRC announced that it was undertaking a "top-to-bottom" review of its security programs. But the review had no timelines or specific goals. Instead, it has become a graveyard for fundamental policy issues the commission is loathe to address. In the meantime, U.S. nuclear power plants remain dangerously vulnerable to terrorist attack.

The NRC continues to "study" three issues concerning potential damage—the effects of large commercial aircraft attacks on nuclear plants; the impacts of attacks with explosives on spent fuel pools; and the health and environmental consequences of terrorist attacks on nuclear plants.

Another set of issues concerns the nature of defense—the appropriate design basis threat after September 11; the appropriate role of civilian law enforcement and the military in protecting privately owned nuclear plants; and the appropriate qualifications, training, and work schedule of plant security guards.

Even if the review is completed, most results are unlikely to see the light of day because the commission will deem them too sensitive to release. Yet when members of the public, the media, and elected officials demand to know what the NRC has done to increase security, it says little and simply points to the ongoing review.

In the meantime, after more than five months of resisting the call to require security upgrades at nuclear power plants, in February 2002 the commission finally issued a set of mandatory "interim compensatory measures," or ICMs. Although the details of these measures are secret, the NRC has characterized them as providing "additional protection against vehicle bombs, as well as water- and land-based assaults . . . requirements for increased security patrols, augmented security forces, additional security posts, increased vehicle standoff distances," and "tightened facility access controls."

Nuclear plants were given six months to implement the interim measures, which were to be in place by August 31 [2002]. It may take as long as two years, though, for NRC inspectors to verify that they have been correctly implemented. Although the upgrades sound impressive, the actual level of protection is hard to gauge because the security testing program, the OSRE, was suspended after September 11 and is only now resuming on a pilot scale.

The NRC has also failed to approve a new DBT that reflects the current terrorist threats. Without significantly tougher requirements, plant operators will continue to lack a clear, consistent, and legally enforceable security performance standard. For instance, the minimum number of armed responders required per shift is believed to have been increased from five to 10, but security managers still do not know how many attackers they are supposed to be defending against.

Until testing has been completed at all nuclear plants, preferably based on a tough new DBT, no one will know how effective the new measures actually are. Tests are important: Security plans that look good on paper are worthless in practice unless the armed responders at nuclear plants are capable of successfully carrying them out in the event of a commando attack. Mock attacks cannot possibly recreate the conditions of real ones, but they can reveal gross deficiencies in guard response.

The Human Element

For a successful defense, guards must be well-qualified, physically fit, highly trained, and able to react quickly to contingencies in a combat environment. Boredom, stress, fatigue, and low morale are critical performance factors that must be taken into account.

But the commission has been giving short shrift to the hu-

man element. While it has mandated more guards per shift and increased the number of security patrols and posts, it has failed to require plant owners to hire more guards to take up the increased workload. Plant security managers find it more profitable to push the existing security force to the limit than to hire new guards. A recent NRC survey found that 60-hour work weeks were "not infrequent" for security guards at 31 percent of nuclear plant sites. At 11 percent of the sites, 60-hour weeks were "common or routine," and 72-hour work weeks were "not infrequent."

> **//** *Most alarming was the sentiment . . . that guards would not be willing to put their lives on the line, given the pay and treatment they receive from management.* **//**

Since September 11, our organizations and others have received numerous complaints from security guards around the country about poor morale, inadequate training, exhaustion from excessive overtime, and poor compensation (below that of the janitorial staff). Most alarming was the sentiment, heard more than once, that guards would not be willing to put their lives on the line, given the pay and treatment they receive from management.

The disturbing picture painted by these guards stands in stark contrast to full-page ads that ran in 2002 in the Washington Post and other major newspapers sponsored by the Nuclear Energy Institute (NEI) praising nuclear plant security guards as highly trained paramilitary forces. Resentment about the inaccuracy of NEI's ads was also a recurring theme among the guards who contacted us.

Last September, the Washington, D.C.-based Project on Government Oversight compiled guard complaints from more than 20 percent of U.S. nuclear plants, issuing a highly publicized report that was impossible for the NRC to ignore. As a result, the commission began collecting data from nuclear plants on security guard work weeks—something it had never done before. It even proposed limiting overtime and strengthening training requirements. However, the industry bitterly opposes these initiatives, arguing that guards like working six 12-hour shifts in a row. It appears likely that these proposals will get lost

in the endless "top-to-bottom" review.

In addition to the threat of commando attack, the NRC has taken no action to protect against the ultimate September 11–type threat, a jet aircraft attack, other than to initiate long-term technical studies to evaluate the consequences of air attacks and to require plant operators to plan for events that could "result in damage to large areas of their plants from impacts, explosions, or fires." The commission refuses to consider adding structural features to reactor sites that might prevent a successful aircraft attack.

The NRC has also rejected calls by the public and policy-makers to consider the feasibility of directly protecting nuclear plants from air attack by imposing no-fly zones or deploying portable anti-aircraft systems, citing the command-and-control problems inherent in such an approach, the impact on the commercial airline industry, and the risk of accident or collateral damage. These considerations are important, but they must be weighed against the catastrophic consequences of a meltdown and large radiological release, especially at the many nuclear plants in densely populated urban areas—like the controversial Indian Point plant, near New York City. (None of the objections to these defensive measures appear to have prevented them from being taken to protect other buildings; the Pentagon ordered the deployment of heat-seeking anti-aircraft missiles around Washington, D.C. during the recent "code orange" terror alerts.)

Wishful Thinking

Why can't the NRC deal decisively with urgent threats? The major share of the blame lies with the NRC commissioners, who do not seem to fully appreciate the gravity of the terrorist threat or the devastating consequences that could result from an attack on the facilities they regulate. In a speech in March 2002, [NRC] Commissioner Edward McGaffigan called nuclear power plants "hard targets by any conceivable definition" and ridiculed those who dared to suggest otherwise.

In June 2002, Commissioner Nils Diaz warned a meeting of the American Nuclear Society that technical progress toward the revival of the nuclear energy option "could be in jeopardy unless unjustified fears of policymakers and the public with regard to . . . the security of these [nuclear power] plants can be addressed."

Diaz, who succeeded Meserve as NRC chairman on April 1 [2003], also expressed his belief that there would be no signifi-

cant consequence for the public if a 747 loaded with fuel breached the containment of a nuclear plant—because "America will deliver the necessary responses to protect public health and safety."

Given this sort of wishful thinking, it is little wonder that the commission has let the question of strengthening the DBT languish for well over a year and refuses to impose emergency measures to bolster plant defenses against massive, military-style assaults or aircraft attacks.

> *One should not forget to blame Congress for ... creating a department of homeland security that had no authority over nuclear plants.*

Surprisingly, the blame must also be shared by the . . . Office of Homeland Security, the Defense Department, and the FBI, all of which have failed to step into the security vacuum created by the NRC's inaction. After September 11, these agencies asked the NRC for its assessment of the consequences of a jet plane attack on a nuclear power plant. While the response is classified, it doesn't take a security clearance to surmise that the commission provided only reassurance.

And one should not forget to blame Congress for failing to enact legislation that could have fixed the most serious nuclear security vulnerabilities, and for creating a department of homeland security that had no authority over nuclear plants.

Nuclear Industry Resists Changes

The other major player is of course the nuclear industry, which has worked to block upgrades of security requirements. The nuclear utilities have always resented having to spend money to prepare for an attack they believe will never occur. Through the NEI, their lobbying arm in Washington, D.C., they have waged a systematic campaign to weaken security regulations.

Before September 11, public observation of meetings between the commission and the industry helped put the brakes on the worst of their proposals, such as their plan to replace the security testing program with an industry-run "self-assessment" program.

But now the public is no longer welcome at the meetings, even when details of plant security ("safeguards information") are not discussed. All the meetings are now covered under a sweeping but poorly defined new category of restricted information, "sensitive unclassified homeland security information," or "sushi."

The industry is using the new secrecy shield to increase its influence over the regulatory processes. For instance, the interim compensatory measures, although issued by the commission, were the product of multiple closed-door negotiating sessions between the commission and the industry lobby; the NEI actually wrote the document that defined what constituted compliance.

Right now the industry is lobbying hard to significantly weaken any revised DBT. Little wonder that a recent report by the NRC's inspector general found that commission staff believed "that NRC is becoming influenced by private industry and its power to regulate is diminishing."

The NEI has also waged a campaign to convince the public that it has nothing to fear, even if a nuclear plant were attacked by a jet plane fully loaded with fuel. It recently released a summary of a report it commissioned from the Electric Power Research Institute (EPRI), claiming to show that "structures housing reactor fuel at U.S. nuclear power plants would protect against a release of radiation even if struck by a large commercial jetliner."

NEI refused to release the entire report, citing "security considerations," but it was clear from the summary that it had chosen certain assumptions to produce the results it wanted, including a presumed containment wall thickness of four feet—thicker than typical reactor containment walls and domes. EPRI arbitrarily chose an impact speed of 350 miles per hour—well below the nearly 600 miles per hour at which the 767 struck the World Trade Center South Tower. And EPRI ignored the damage that an aircraft could cause to targets outside the containment, like the auxiliary feedwater pumps and the diesel generators.

The Insider Threat

An individual drives to a nuclear power plant in the United States, obtains an access badge at the security gate, and walks freely through the facility. He takes a rubber hose from an equipment locker and cross-connects the hydrogen gas supply

system to the air system. He opens a valve allowing hydrogen gas to flow inside the air system throughout the plant, and within a few minutes, produces combustible levels of hydrogen within the containment building, the auxiliary building, and the turbine building. Using matches, he ignites the explosions and fires that disable the emergency systems needed to cool the reactor core and the systems needed to limit radioactivity releases from the damaged core to the environment.

Sound impossible? Perhaps. But it nearly happened on January 7, 1989, at the H.B. Robinson nuclear plant in South Carolina. An individual made a mistake conducting a test. Luckily, his error was discovered and the buildings were vented of the flammable gas mixture before disaster struck. But what prevents workers from accomplishing by intent that which nearly happened by mistake—sabotage from the inside?

Three conditions are supposed to be met for an individual to have unescorted access at a nuclear power plant:

• A background investigation—to verify identity, employment history, education history, credit history, criminal history, military service, and character and reputation;

• A psychological assessment, to identify any characteristics with potential bearing on the individual's trustworthiness and reliability; and

• Continuing behavioral observation, to detect any changes that might indicate a propensity for sabotage.

Outgoing NRC Chairman Richard Meserve conceded that although these requirements are important, they are not always met. As Meserve wrote to Homeland Security Director Tom Ridge, "enhancing access control may be one of the most effective means of preventing a successful attack."

Background investigations are spotty. Criminal history checks are performed by the submission of fingerprint cards to the FBI's National Crime Information Center, but results are not timely. The NRC has accelerated the turnaround time for the checks since September 11, but individuals continue to gain access by lying about their criminal records. Workers at the Fermi, Perry, and Oconee nuclear plants have recently lost their unescorted access privileges after FBI checks revealed criminal histories.

In addition to being slow, background checks fail to delve deeply enough. According to Meserve:

"U.S. citizens are currently accounted for better than foreign applicants due to lack of information (e.g., credit history

and criminal history) or unwillingness of the [foreign] country to provide such information. Licensees determine access to the facilities regarding foreign applicants on a 'best effort' basis."

In other words, despite fears that foreign terrorist cells may be operating within the United States, background checks for nuclear workers essentially stop at the border. Terrorists could probably get unescorted access to U.S. nuclear plants if they have no traffic arrests or shoplifting convictions.

The questionable value of the psychological assessment screening tool is reflected in the Carl Drega case. Drega was killed in a police shootout in August 1997 after a series of shootings in New England that left four others dead. Police later found bomb-making materials in his home. Drega had had unescorted access when he worked at the Vermont Yankee, Pilgrim, and Indian Point 3 nuclear plants between 1992 and 1997. He had applied for unescorted access to the Seabrook nuclear plant, too, but the plant owner denied his request. The NRC determined that Seabrook's owner would have granted him unescorted access if he had not parked his mobile home on Seabrook property and attempted to live there.

> *" Terrorists could probably get unescorted access to U.S. nuclear plants if they have no traffic arrests or shoplifting convictions. "*

The final protection against insider sabotage is continuing observation. Supervisors are trained to detect changes in behavior patterns that might be symptoms of mental stress caused by problems on the job or at home. Upon detection of any such changes, supervisors are instructed to interact with the worker and suggest counseling. It seems doubtful that if a supervisor identified a saboteur midplot, a suggestion to seek counseling would make much difference. . . .

To turn Meserve's wish for enhanced access control into reality, the NRC should expeditiously:

• Require criminal history checks to be completed before individuals gain unescorted access.

• Require foreign nationals to have background checks comparable to those required of U.S. citizens before gaining unescorted access to nuclear facilities.

• Require the two-person rule for entry into infrequently accessed vital areas and require security camera monitoring of all other vital areas.

The nuclear industry should be expected to resist these security upgrades. In June 2000, Exelon, which owns 17 nuclear plants, proposed that the NRC "eliminate the requirement to protect against the insider threat."

Public Awareness

Better security at sensitive facilities is needed more than ever, but the NRC and the nuclear industry have spent most of their time arguing against improvements. Some of those arguments have been extraordinary—for example, that [the catastrophic explosion at the Russian] Chernobyl [Power Plant] wasn't so bad. Recent commentaries by a group of prominent nuclear industry figures made that assertion and even went so far as to claim that the release of radiation would be good for the public: "Data show detrimental health effects and biological functions when organisms are 'protected' from . . . radiation."

But imagine if the public were told that more than 100 massive radiological weapons—"dirty bombs" on an incomprehensible scale—had been pre-emplaced in the United States, each capable of rendering an area the size of Pennsylvania uninhabitable for decades. Imagine further that the public learned that despite all the hype about homeland security, a powerful industry and its captured regulatory agency had succeeded in blocking security measures that would prevent those weapons from being used against the U.S. population. But one needn't imagine—it's the NRC's latest dirty little secret.

6

Global Warming Poses a Looming Threat to the Security of the United States

Peter Schwartz and Doug Randall

Peter Schwartz is an aerospace engineer, a researcher on climate change at Stanford Research Institute, and cofounder of futurist think tank Global Business Network (GBN) in Emoryville, California. Doug Randall is a senior associate at GBN with over ten years of scenario planning meant to address complex business, social, and environmental challenges.

While environmentalists, politicians, and industry officials debate the seriousness of global warming, military planners in the Pentagon are making plans to defend against the negative consequences of such an event. Many believe the threat is real. Since 1980, nineteen of the twenty hottest years on record have occurred, with 2003 registering as the hottest ever. This warming is melting the polar ice caps and mountain glaciers and is changing weather patterns and ocean currents. By the end of this century, the warming may change the political, social, and economic conditions of the world, plunging Europe into a deep freeze while creating megadroughts and famines across the globe. This, in turn, will cause governmental collapse, mass immigration, and global warfare, most likely against the United States and other nations that are better prepared to deal with the changes. While such a set of circumstances is specu-

Peter Schwartz and Doug Randall, "An Abrupt Climate Change Scenario and Its Implications for the United States National Security," www.gbn.org, October 2003.

51

lative, the Department of Defense must plan for this scenario. Massive changes in weather and ocean current
patterns caused by global warming will make the horrors of terrorist attacks, and even the world wars of the
twentieth century pale in comparison.

W hen most people think about climate change, they imagine gradual increases in temperature and only marginal
changes in other climatic conditions, continuing indefinitely
or even leveling off at some time in the future. The conventional wisdom is that modern civilization will either adapt to
whatever weather conditions we face and that the pace of climate change will not overwhelm the adaptive capacity of society, or that our efforts such as those embodied in the Kyoto
protocol [to reduce man-made gases that contribute to global
warming] will be sufficient to mitigate the impacts. The IPCC
[Intergovernmental Panel on Climate Change] documents the
threat of gradual climate change and its impact to food supplies and other resources of importance to humans will not be
so severe as to create security threats. Optimists assert that the
benefits from technological innovation will be able to outpace
the negative effects of climate change.

Climatically, the gradual change view of the future assumes
that agriculture will continue to thrive and growing seasons
will lengthen. Northern Europe, Russia, and North America
will prosper agriculturally while southern Europe, Africa, and
Central and South America will suffer from increased dryness,
heat, water shortages, and reduced production. Overall, global
food production under many typical climate scenarios increases. This view of climate change may be a dangerous act of
self-deception, as increasingly we are facing weather-related
disasters—more hurricanes, monsoons, floods, and dry-spells—
in regions around the world.

Weather-related events have an enormous impact on society, as they influence food supply, conditions in cities and
communities, as well as access to clean water and energy. For
example, a recent report by the Climate Action Network of
Australia projects that climate change is likely to reduce rainfall
in the rangelands, which could lead to a 15% drop in grass productivity. This, in turn, could lead to reductions in the average
weight of cattle by 12%, significantly reducing beef supply. Under such conditions, dairy cows are projected to produce 30%
less milk, and new pests are likely to spread in fruit-growing ar-

eas. Additionally, such conditions are projected to lead to 10% less water for drinking. Based on model projections of coming change conditions such as these could occur in several food producing regions around the world at the same time within the next 15–30 years, challenging the notion that society's ability to adapt will make climate change manageable.

With over 400 million people living in drier, subtropical, often over-populated and economically poor regions today, climate change and its follow-on effects pose a severe risk to political, economic, and social stability. In less prosperous regions, where countries lack the resources and capabilities required to adapt quickly to more severe conditions, the problem is very likely to be exacerbated. For some countries, climate change could become such a challenge that mass emigration results as the desperate peoples seek better lives in regions such as the United States that have the resources to adaptation. . . .

Rather than decades or even centuries of gradual warming, recent evidence suggests the possibility that a more dire climate scenario may actually be unfolding. This is why GBN [Global Business Network] is working with OSD [Office of the Secretary of Defense] to develop a plausible scenario for abrupt climate change that can be used to explore implications for food supply, health and disease, commerce and trade, and their consequences for national security.

While future weather patterns and the specific details of abrupt climate change cannot be predicted accurately or with great assurance, the actual history of climate change provides some useful guides. Our goal is merely to portray a plausible scenario, similar to one which has already occurred in human experience, for which there is reasonable evidence so that we may further explore potential implications for United States national security. . . .

Warming Up to 2010

[In this scenario] following the most rapid century of warming experienced by modern civilization, the first ten years of the 21st century see an acceleration of atmospheric warming, as average temperatures worldwide rise by .5 degrees Fahrenheit per decade and by as much as 2 degrees Fahrenheit per decade in the harder hit regions. Such temperature changes would vary both by region and by season over the globe, with these finer scale variations being larger or smaller than the average

change. What would be very clear is that the planet is continuing the warming trend of the late 20th century.

Most of North America, Europe, and parts of South America experience 30% more days with peak temperatures over 90 degrees Fahrenheit than they did a century ago, with far fewer days below freezing. In addition to the warming, there are erratic weather patterns: more floods, particularly in mountainous regions, and prolonged droughts in grain-producing and coastal-agricultural areas. In general, the climate shift is an economic nuisance, generally affecting local areas as storms, droughts, and hot spells impact agriculture and other climate-dependent activities. . . . The weather pattern, though, is not yet severe enough or widespread enough to threaten the interconnected global society or United States national security.

> *Climate change could become such a challenge that mass emigration results as the desperate peoples seek better lives in regions such as the United States.*

As temperatures rise throughout the 20th century and into the early 2000s potent positive feedback loops kick-in, accelerating the warming from .2 degrees Fahrenheit, to .4 and eventually .5 degrees Fahrenheit per year in some locations. As the surface warms, the hydrologic cycle (evaporation, precipitation, and runoff) accelerates causing temperatures to rise even higher. Water vapor, the most powerful natural greenhouse gas, traps additional heat and brings average surface air temperatures up. As evaporation increases, higher surface air temperatures cause drying in forests and grasslands, where animals graze and farmers grow grain. As trees die and burn, forests absorb less carbon dioxide, again leading to higher surface air temperatures as well as fierce and uncontrollable forest fires. Further, warmer temperatures melt snow cover in mountains, open fields, high-latitude tundra areas, and permafrost throughout forests in cold-weather areas. With the ground absorbing more and reflecting less of the sun's rays, temperatures increase even higher.

By 2005 the climatic impact of the shift is felt more intensely in certain regions around the world. More severe storms and typhoons bring about higher storm surges and floods in

low-lying islands such as Tarawa and Tuvalu (near New Zealand). In 2007, a particularly severe storm causes the ocean to break through levees in the Netherlands making a few key coastal cities such as The Hague unlivable. Failures of the delta island levees in the Sacramento River region in the Central Valley of California create an inland sea and disrupts the aqueduct system transporting water from northern to southern California because salt water can no longer be kept out of the area during the dry season. Melting along the Himalayan glaciers accelerates, causing some Tibetan people to relocate. Floating ice in the northern polar seas, which had already lost 40% of its mass from 1970 to 2003, is mostly gone during summer by 2010. As glacial ice melts, sea levels rise and as wintertime sea extent decreases, ocean waves increase in intensity, damaging coastal cities. Additionally millions of people are put at risk of flooding around the globe (roughly 4 times 2003 levels), and fisheries are disrupted as water temperature changes cause fish to migrate to new locations and habitats, increasing tensions over fishing rights.

Each of these local disasters caused by severe weather impacts surrounding areas whose natural, human, and economic resources are tapped to aid in recovery. The positive feedback loops and acceleration of the warming pattern begin to trigger responses that weren't previously imagined, as natural disasters and stormy weather occur in both developed and lesser-developed nations. Their impacts are greatest in less-resilient developing nations, which do not have the capacity built into their social, economic, and agricultural systems to absorb change.

As melting of the Greenland ice sheet exceeds the annual snowfall, and there is increasing fresh water runoff from high latitude precipitation, the freshening of waters in the North Atlantic Ocean and the seas between Greenland and Europe increases. The lower densities of these freshened waters in turn pave the way for a sharp slowing of the [deep ocean currents called the] thermohaline circulation system.

The Period from 2010 to 2020

After roughly 60 years of slow freshening, the thermohaline collapse begins in 2010, disrupting the temperate climate of Europe, which is made possible by the warm flows of the Gulf Stream (the North Atlantic arm of the global thermohaline conveyor). Ocean circulation patterns change, bringing less warm water

north and causing an immediate shift in the weather in Northern Europe and eastern North America. The North Atlantic Ocean continues to be affected by fresh water coming from melting glaciers, Greenland's ice sheet, and perhaps most importantly increased rainfall and runoff. Decades of high-latitude warming cause increased precipitation and bring additional fresh water to the salty, dense water in the north, which is normally affected mainly by warmer and saltier water from the Gulf Stream. That massive current of warm water no longer reaches far into the North Atlantic. The immediate climatic effect is cooler temperatures in Europe and throughout much of the Northern Hemisphere and a dramatic drop in rainfall in many key agricultural and populated areas. However, the effects of the collapse will be felt in fits and starts, as the traditional weather patterns re-emerge only to be disrupted again—for a full decade.

> *Most of North America, Europe, and parts of South America experience 30% more days with peak temperatures over 90 degrees Fahrenheit than they did a century ago.*

The dramatic slowing of the thermohaline circulation is anticipated by some ocean researchers, but the United States is not sufficiently prepared for its effects, timing, or intensity. Computer models of the climate and ocean systems, though improved, were unable to produce sufficiently consistent and accurate information for policy makers. As weather patterns shift in the years following the collapse, it is not clear what type of weather future years will bring. While some forecasters believe the cooling and dryness is about to end, others predict a new ice age or a global drought, leaving policy makers and the public highly uncertain about the future climate and what to do, if anything. Is this merely a "blip" of little importance or a fundamental change in the Earth's climate, requiring an urgent massive human response?

Abrupt Climate Change

Each of the years from 2010 to 2020 sees average temperature drops throughout Northern Europe, leading to as much as a 6

degree Fahrenheit drop in ten years. Average annual rainfall in this region decreases by nearly 30%; and winds are up to 15% stronger on average. The climatic conditions are more severe in the continental interior regions of northern Asia and North America.

> *By the end of the decade, Europe's climate is more like Siberia's.*

The effects of the drought are more devastating than the unpleasantness of temperature decreases in the agricultural and populated areas. With the persistent reduction of precipitation in these areas, lakes dry-up, river flow decreases, and fresh water supply is squeezed, overwhelming available conservation options and depleting fresh water reserves. The Mega-droughts begin in key regions in Southern China and Northern Europe around 2010 and last throughout the full decade. At the same time, areas that were relatively dry over the past few decades receive persistent years of torrential rainfall, flooding rivers, and regions that traditionally relied on dryland agriculture.

In the North Atlantic region and across northern Asia, cooling is most pronounced in the heart of winter—December, January, and February—although its effects linger through the seasons, the cooling becomes increasingly intense and less predictable. As snow accumulates in mountain regions, the cooling spreads to summertime. In addition to cooling and summertime dryness, wind pattern velocity strengthens as the atmospheric circulation becomes more zonal.

While weather patterns are disrupted during the onset of the climatic change around the globe, the effects are far more pronounced in Northern Europe for the first five years after the thermohaline circulation collapse. By the second half of this decade, the chill and harsher conditions spread deeper into Southern Europe, North America, and beyond. Northern Europe cools as a pattern of colder weather lengthens the time that sea ice is present over the northern North Atlantic Ocean, creating a further cooling influence and extending the period of wintertime surface air temperatures. Winds pick up as the atmosphere tries to deal with the stronger pole-to-equator temperature gradient. Cold air blowing across the European conti-

nent causes especially harsh conditions for agriculture. The combination of wind and dryness causes widespread dust storms and soil loss.

Signs of incremental warming appear in the southernmost areas along the Atlantic Ocean, but the dryness doesn't let up. By the end of the decade, Europe's climate is more like Siberia's. . . .

Widespread Chaos

Europe. Hit hardest by the climatic change, average annual temperatures drop by 6 degrees Fahrenheit in under a decade, with more dramatic shifts along the Northwest coast. The climate in northwestern Europe is colder, drier, and windier, making it more like Siberia. Southern Europe experiences less of a change but still suffers from sharp intermittent cooling and rapid temperature shifts. Reduced precipitation causes soil loss to become a problem throughout Europe, contributing to food supply shortages. Europe struggles to stem emigration out of Scandinavian and northern European nations in search of warmth as well as immigration from hard-hit countries in Africa and elsewhere.

> *Envision Pakistan, India, and China—all armed with nuclear weapons—skirmishing at their borders over refugees, access to shared rivers, and arable land.*

United States. Colder, windier, and drier weather makes growing seasons shorter and less productive throughout the northeastern United States, and longer and drier in the southwest. Desert areas face increasing windstorms, while agricultural areas suffer from soil loss due to higher wind-speeds and reduced soil moisture. The change toward a drier climate is especially pronounced in the southern states. Coastal areas that were at risk during the warming period remain at risk, as rising ocean levels continue along the shores. The United States turns inward, committing its resources to feeding its own population, shoring-up its borders, and managing the increasing global tension.

China. China, with its high need for food supply given its vast population, is hit hard by a decreased reliability of the

monsoon rains. Occasional monsoons during the summer season are welcomed for their precipitation, but have devastating
effects as they flood generally denuded land. Longer, colder
winters and hotter summers caused by decreased evaporative
cooling because of reduced precipitation stress already tight energy and water supplies. Widespread famine causes chaos and
internal struggles as a cold and hungry China peers jealously
across the Russian and western borders at energy resources.

Bangladesh. Persistent typhoons and a higher sea level create storm surges that cause significant coastal erosion, making
much of Bangladesh nearly uninhabitable. Further, the rising
sea level contaminates fresh water supplies inland, creating a
drinking water and humanitarian crisis. Massive emigration occurs, causing tension in China and India, which are struggling
to manage the crisis inside their own boundaries. . . .

With only five or six key grain-growing regions in the world
(U.S., Australia, Argentina, Russia, China, and India), there is in-
sufficient surplus in global food supplies to offset severe weather
conditions in a few regions at the same time—let alone four or
five. The world's economic interdependence makes the United
States increasingly vulnerable to the economic disruption created by local weather shifts in key agricultural and high population areas around the world. Catastrophic shortages of water
and energy supply—both which are stressed around the globe
today—cannot be quickly overcome. . . .

Impact on National Security

Modern civilization has never experienced weather conditions
as persistently disruptive as the ones outlined in this scenario.
As a result, the implications for national security outlined in
this report are only hypothetical. The actual impacts would vary
greatly depending on the nuances of the weather conditions,
the adaptability of humanity, and decisions by policy makers.

Violence and disruption stemming from the stresses created
by abrupt changes in the climate pose a different type of threat
to national security than we are accustomed to today. Military
confrontation may be triggered by a desperate need for natural
resources such as energy, food, and water rather than by conflicts
over ideology, religion, or national honor. The shifting motivation for confrontation would alter which countries are most
vulnerable and the existing warning signs for security threats.

There is a long-standing academic debate over the extent to

which resource constraints and environmental challenges lead to inter-state conflict. . . . Regardless, it seems undeniable that severe environmental problems are likely to escalate the degree of global conflict.

Co-founder and President of the Pacific Institute for Studies in Development, Environment, and Security, Peter Gleick outlines the three most fundamental challenges abrupt climate change poses for national security:

1. Food shortages due to decreases in agricultural production
2. Decreased availability and quality of fresh water due to flooding and droughts
3. Disrupted access to strategic minerals due to ice and storms

In the event of abrupt climate change, it's likely that food, water, and energy resource constraints will first be managed through economic, political, and diplomatic means such as treaties and trade embargoes. Over time though, conflicts over land and water use are likely to become more severe—and more violent. As states become increasingly desperate, the pressure for action will grow. . . .

When you look at carrying capacity on a regional or state level it is apparent that those nations with a high carrying capacity, such as the United States and Western Europe, are likely to adapt most effectively to abrupt changes in climate, because, relative to their population size, they have more resources to call on. This may give rise to a more severe have, have-not mentality, causing resentment toward those nations with a higher carrying capacity. It may lead to finger-pointing and blame, as the wealthier nations tend to use more energy and emit more greenhouse gases such as CO_2 into the atmosphere. Less important than the scientifically proven relationship between CO_2 emissions and climate change is the perception that impacted nations have—and the actions they take.

Carrying Capacity and Warfare

Steven LeBlanc, Harvard archaelogist and author of a new book called *Carrying Capacity*, describes the relationship between carrying capacity [the ability of the environment to provide food for the population] and warfare. . . . Humans fight when they outstrip the carrying capacity of their natural environment. Every time there is a choice between starving and raiding, humans raid. . . .

However in the last three centuries . . . [states have used] their own bureaucracies, advanced technology, and international rules of behavior to raise carrying capacity and bear a more careful relationship to it.

All of that progressive behavior could collapse if carrying capacities everywhere were suddenly lowered drastically by abrupt climate change. Humanity would revert to its norm of constant battles for diminishing resources, which the battles themselves would further reduce even beyond the climatic effects. Once again warfare would define human life. . . .

A Sense of Desperation

The two most likely reactions to a sudden drop in carrying capacity due to climate change are defensive and offensive.

The United States and Australia are likely to build defensive fortresses around their countries because they have the resources and reserves to achieve self-sufficiency. With diverse growing climates, wealth, technology, and abundant resources, the United States could likely survive shortened growing cycles and harsh weather conditions without catastrophic losses. Borders will be strengthened around the country to hold back unwanted starving immigrants from the Caribbean Islands (an especially severe problem), Mexico, and South America. Energy supply will be shored up through expensive (economically, politically, and morally) alternatives such as nuclear, renewables, hydrogen, and Middle Eastern contracts. Pesky skirmishes over fishing rights, agricultural support, and disaster relief will be commonplace. Tension between the U.S. and Mexico rise as the U.S. reneges on the 1944 treaty that guarantees water flow from the Colorado River. Relief workers will be commissioned to respond to flooding along the southern part of the east coast and much drier conditions inland. Yet, even in this continuous state of emergency the U.S. will be positioned well compared to others. The intractable problem facing the nation will be calming the mounting military tension around the world.

As famine, disease, and weather-related disasters strike due to the abrupt climate change, many countries' needs will exceed their carrying capacity. This will create a sense of desperation, which is likely to lead to offensive aggression in order to reclaim balance. Imagine eastern European countries, struggling to feed their populations with a falling supply of food, water, and energy, eyeing Russia, whose population is already

in decline, for access to its grain, minerals, and energy supply. Or, picture Japan, suffering from flooding along its coastal cities and contamination of its fresh water supply, eying Russia's Sakhalin Island oil and gas reserves as an energy source to power desalination plants and energy-intensive agricultural processes. Envision Pakistan, India, and China—all armed with nuclear weapons—skirmishing at their borders over refugees, access to shared rivers, and arable land. Spanish and Portuguese fishermen might fight over fishing rights—leading to conflicts at sea. And, countries including the United States would be likely to better secure their borders. With over 200 river basins touching multiple nations, we can expect conflict over access to water for drinking, irrigation, and transportation. The Danube touches twelve nations, the Nile runs though nine, and the Amazon runs through seven.

In this scenario, we can expect alliances of convenience. The United States and Canada may become one, simplifying border controls. Or, Canada might keep its hydropower—causing energy problems in the U.S. North and South Korea may align to create one technically savvy and nuclear-armed entity. Europe may act as a unified block—curbing immigration problems between European nations—and allowing for protection against aggressors. Russia, with its abundant minerals, oil, and natural gas may join Europe.

In this world of warring states, nuclear arms proliferation is inevitable. As cooling drives up demand, existing hydrocarbon supplies are stretched thin. With a scarcity of energy supply— and a growing need for access—nuclear energy will become a critical source of power, and this will accelerate nuclear proliferation as countries develop enrichment and reprocessing capabilities to ensure their national security. China, India, Pakistan, Japan, South Korea, Great Britain, France, and Germany will all have nuclear weapons capability, as will Israel, Iran, Egypt, and North Korea.

Managing the military and political tension, occasional skirmishes, and threat of war will be a challenge. Countries such as Japan, that have a great deal of social cohesion (meaning the government is able to effectively engage its population in changing behavior) are most likely to fair well. Countries whose diversity already produces conflict, such as India, South Africa, and Indonesia, will have trouble maintaining order. Adaptability and access to resources will be key. Perhaps the most frustrating challenge abrupt climate change will pose is

that we'll never know how far we are into the climate change scenario and how many more years—10, 100, 1000—remain before some kind of return to warmer conditions as the thermohaline circulation starts up again. When carrying capacity drops suddenly, civilization is faced with new challenges that today seem unimaginable. . . .

Conclusion

It is quite plausible that within a decade the evidence of an imminent abrupt climate shift may become clear and reliable. It is also possible that our models will better enable us to predict the consequences. In that event the United States will need to take urgent action to prevent and mitigate some of the most significant impacts. Diplomatic action will be needed to minimize the likelihood of conflict in the most impacted areas, especially in the Caribbean and Asia. However, large population movements in this scenario are inevitable. Learning how to manage those populations, border tensions that arise and the resulting refugees will be critical. New forms of security agreements dealing specifically with energy, food, and water will also be needed. In short, while the U.S. itself will be relatively better off and with more adaptive capacity, it will find itself in a world where Europe will be struggling internally, large numbers of refugees washing up on its shores and Asia in serious crisis over food and water. Disruption and conflict will be endemic features of life.

7

Terrorists Have Limited Capabilities to Threaten National Security

Luke Mitchell

Luke Mitchell is a senior editor at Harper's *magazine and the coauthor of* Country of My Skull *about the end of apartheid in South Africa.*

Since the terrorist attacks on September 11, 2001, many Americans have become obsessed with terrorism. While the attacks that killed almost three thousand people were horrific, five times more people die every year from preventable food poisoning while nearly ten times more perish in automobile accidents. And none have died on American soil from terrorist attacks since September 11. Despite the low number of comparative fatalities, the George W. Bush administration has declared an unending war on terrorism that will cost more than $50 billion a year for the foreseeable future. His administration has also waged an assault on the Constitution, curtailing freedoms in the name of antiterrorism. All of these actions are unnecessary. While Americans will never be a hundred percent safe from terrorists, there is little that these groups of malcontents can do to hurt the country at large. Even if they were to obtain weapons of mass destruction, the harm would be localized and the country would move on. Americans should be very careful about what policies they accept in the name of fighting terrorism when the personal risk to themselves and their families is very low.

In 2001, terrorists killed 2,978 people in the United States, including the five killed by anthrax. In that same year, according to the Centers for Disease Control, heart disease killed 700,142 Americans and cancer 553,768; various accidents claimed 101,537 lives, suicide 30,622, and homicide, not including the attacks, another 17,330. As President Bush pointed out in January [2004], no one has been killed by terrorists on American soil since then. Neither, according to the FBI, was anyone killed here by terrorists in 2000. In 1999, the number was one. In 1998, it was three. In 1997, zero. Even using 2001 as a baseline, the actuarial tables would suggest that our concern about terror mortality ought to be on the order of our concern about fatal workplace injuries (5,431 deaths) or drowning (3,247). To recognize this is not to dishonor the loss to the families of those people killed by terrorists, but neither should their anguish eclipse that of the families of children who died in their infancy that year (27,801). Every death has its horrors. Anti-terrorism nevertheless has become the animating principle of nearly every aspect of American public policy. We have launched two major military engagements in its name. It informs how we fund scientific research, whose steel or textiles we buy, who may enter or leave the country, and how we sort our mail. It has shaped the structure of the Justice Department and the fates of 180,000 government employees now in the service of the Department of Homeland Security. Nearly every presidential speech touches on terrorism, and, according to the White House, we can look forward to spending at least $50 billion per year on "homeland defense" until the end of time.

It Is Hard to Kill Thousands

Is all this necessary? One of the remarkable things about September 11 is that there was no follow-up—no shopping malls were firebombed, no bridges destroyed, no power plants assaulted. This is, no doubt, partly the result of our post-2001 obsession with preventing just such disasters. We must at least consider the possibility, however, that this also represents a lack of wherewithal on the part of would-be terrorists. Although there may be no shortage of those angry enough to commit an act of violence against the United States, few among them possess the training, the financing, or the sheer ambition necessary to execute an operation as elaborate as that of September 11. The nineteen who have already done so are

dead, and in the two and a half years that they have enjoyed their martyrdom and their virgins, few have stepped forward to join them. In the United States, none have.

> *A successful nuclear attack would not destroy America. It would not even come close.*

This may be because it is very hard to kill thousands of people at once. It turns out, for example, that the radioactive "dirty bombs" of [alleged American terrorist] Jose Padilla's fantasies are in fact "not very effective as a means of causing fatalities," according to Richard Meserve, who is the chairman of the federal Nuclear Regulatory Commission. Smallpox was eradicated from nature in 1978, is impossible to manufacture, and—if terrorists did somehow get hold of what little of the virus remains in Russian and U.S. hands—is exceedingly difficult to spread. It is safe to assume that many aspiring terrorists have killed only themselves, with prematurely dispersed sarin or perhaps an all-too-successful anthrax experiment. And contrary to their designation as "weapons of mass destruction," anthrax and sarin, as well as mustard gas, VX, tabun, and a host of other high-tech horrors, are more accurately called simply "weapons." Aum Shinrikyo [a Japanese cult] which had 65,000 members worldwide, $1.4 billion in assets, and a secret weapons lab run by scientists recruited from Japan's best universities, and spent years underground during which no investigative body knew of them, much less was seeking them—managed to kill sixteen people in a Tokyo subway station. A boy with a machine gun could have done worse.

Real nuclear weapons, of course, are a different matter, but they also are incredibly hard to make. Libya recently gave up on the project. North Korea has been at it since the late sixties and may now have as many as two. As for the much-feared loose Russian nukes, Aum Shinrikyo, with all its money, tried just after the Berlin Wall fell to buy one and failed. This is why Al Qaeda, despite all its well-financed malice, used planes. It was the best they could do.

In the unlikely event that a terrorist organization did manage to steal or, more likely, build a nuclear weapon, smuggle it into the United States, and detonate it near a major population

center, the predicted casualty rate starts at 10,000 and climbs, in some estimates, to as high as 250,000. This would be a singular crime. But it would be a horror not unlike many that this nation has faced before and many that this nation will face again, terrorists or no terrorists. The country would go on, just as it did after the influenza epidemic of 1918 (600,000 deaths) or during the current AIDS epidemic (500,000 deaths and counting). Attorney General John Ashcroft has called terrorists "those who would destroy America," but a successful nuclear attack would not destroy America. It would not even come close.

In this coming election, as in every other, genuine differences of opinion will inform much of the political debate. A tax cut in a time of recession might make sense to you, or it might not. Perhaps we should build a moon colony instead of funding public schools. Reasonable people may differ. Terror, though, will not be argued on logic or ideology or even self-interest. It will be argued on the basis of emotion. It *is* an emotion.

> *The color-coded 'Homeland Security Advisory System'. . . works to terrify Americans without the grisly work of actual terrorism.*

Moreover, it is a seductive emotion. Our current obsession with terrorism is premised on the fiction of an unlimited downside, which speaks darkly to the American psyche just as did the unlimited upside imagined during the Internet bubble. Indeed, this hysteria can be seen as a mirror image of the bubble, a run on terror. Whereas before we believed without basis that we could all be illimitably wealthy with no work, we now believe without basis that we will die in incalculable numbers with no warning or determinable motivation. Both views are childish, but the Internet bubble at least did not require calling out the National Guard.

Contrary to the administration's claims, the War on Terror is not "a challenge as formidable as any ever faced by our nation." It is not the Cold War, in which our enemy [the Soviet Union] did in fact have the ability to destroy the Earth. Nor is it the Second World War (405,399 dead Americans), nor the First (116,516). It certainly is not the Civil War, still the deadliest conflict in American history (364,511 dead on the Union

side, and an estimated 258,000 dead in the South) and one that specifically threatened to end the American experiment. It is not even a war in the "moral equivalent of war" sense of [President] Lyndon Johnson's [1965] War on Poverty. Fighting it does not make us a better people. It is much closer to the War on Drugs—a comic-book name for a fantasy crusade. We can no more rid the world of terror than we can rid it of alienation. This may sound like a splitting of linguistic hairs, but we made a similar category error in Vietnam by calling an invasion a "civil war." That misidentification cost 58,200 American lives.

As opposed to terror, murder, at the hands of Al Qaeda or anyone else, is a very real threat. But it is not a supreme threat, and by calling it what it is we can recognize that it does not require the wholesale reorganization of the American way of life. The prevention of murder does not require the suspension of habeas corpus, nor does it call for the distribution of national identity cards, nor does it require the fingerprinting of . . . tourists. Preventing murder certainly does not require war, which of course is quite murderous in and of itself. What preventing murder requires is patient police work.

In New York City we have a program called Comstat, in which police carefully track various crime statistics, detect anomalies, and marshal their forces appropriately. It works. There were 596 murders here in 2003, down from 2,245 in 1990. This sort of effort lacks election-year grandeur, however, which may partially explain why the Department of Homeland Security does not bother to track the number of Americans killed by terrorists. (The FBI tracks terror fatalities within the United States and the State Department tracks the same abroad, but each uses a different definition of terrorism and neither has domestic numbers beyond 2001.) Similarly, there is no comprehensive watch list of likely terror operatives. What we have instead is a sophisticated public-relations system, the color-coded "Homeland Security Advisory System," that works to terrify Americans without the grisly work of actual terrorism.

Many desired activities, from shopping to watching television, have been cited as examples of what we must do, or else "the terrorists will have won." This is debatable. What is not debatable is that if the American people are terrified the terrorists have won. And, in this regard, they will have been working with the full cooperation of the current administration.

8

Islamic Fundamentalists Are a Threat to the American Way of Life

Alan Caruba

Alan Caruba is a veteran business and science writer, communications director of the American Policy Center, and founder of the National Anxiety Center, a clearinghouse for information about media-driven scare campaigns. Caruba writes a weekly column, "Warning Signs," for the National Anxiety Center.

Millions of fundamentalist Muslims have sworn to kill Americans and their allies and topple their institutions. While political correctness dictates that the war on terrorism is not a war on Islam, followers of Osama bin Laden and other terrorist leaders adhere to no such niceties. They will use any tool from hijacked jet airliners to weapons of mass destruction in order to create terror, panic, and economic havoc in the United States. By blending religious fundamentalism with vicious political ideology, some followers of Islam believe that the way to heaven is through a suicidal terrorist act, and Americans ignore this fact at their own peril.

I think a lot of Americans—especially those favoring withdrawal from Iraq and efforts to negotiate with al-Qa'ida and with nation-states supporting the worldwide Islamic terror war, or "holy war"—have not yet figured out that the Islamic fundamentalists who beheaded Daniel Pearl [in 2002] and Nicholas

Evan Berg [in 2004], who attacked this nation on September 11, 2001, and who represent the insurgents in Iraq are vicious barbarians who behave much more like mad dogs than civilized and sane human beings and who are determined, unyielding, and fanatical enemies of America and the Judeo-Christian West, enemies who want us dead, unless, of course, we convert to Islam and submit to tyrannical rule by the Islamists.

> *The ruling to kill the Americans and their allies—civilians and military—is an individual duty for every Muslim who can do it in any country in which is possible to do it.*

Another thing most Americans don't know is that we are in the midst of the Third Great Jihad [or holy war]. The first was the early spread of Islam after Muhammad invented it [in the Seventh Century], the second was the rise of the Ottoman Turks [in the Fourteenth Century], and this third one began with the toppling of the [secular] Shah of Iran in the late 1970s. We are in Iraq—though the President fails to tell us this—because the only way you kill a snake is to cut off its head. The Third Great Jihad intends to replace all the secular heads of government in the Middle East to insure that Islam remains as it was in the Seventh Century.

We are in Iraq and Afghanistan for a purpose greater than just U.S. national security. We are there because the Middle East is a region seeking to distance itself from a world in which most nations, their economies, their security, their future and ours, is dependent on globalization, our being connected to one another. The United States of America is the only nation that can end the domination of some two billion people worldwide by the petty despots that prosper by not joining their future to ours. That is the overarching reason we are . . . in Iraq.

The Greatest Threat

Having said this, it would be useful if the February 23, 1998, "World Islamic Front" statement issued by Osama bin Laden, along with Ayman al-Zawahiri, Amir of the Jihad Group in Egypt, and three others, were mandatory reading for every

American—indeed, for everyone who enjoys the benefits of a connected world, a modern world of export, import, prosperity, and freedom. Bin Laden spelled out why his movement is the greatest threat we face and why it must be defeated.

The statement issues a "fatwa," a ruling based in Islamic faith and teachings.

> The ruling to kill the Americans and their allies— civilians and military—is an individual duty for every Muslim who can do it in any country in which is possible to do it, in order to liberate the al-Aqsa Mosque (Jerusalem) and the holy mosque (Mecca) from their grip, and in order for their armies to move out of all the lands of Islam, defeated and unable to threaten any Muslim. This is in accordance with the words of Almighty Allah "and fight the pagans all together as they fight you all together," and "fight them until there is no more tumult or oppression, and there prevail justice and faith in Allah."

There is no clearer or more specific explanation of why we are involved in Afghanistan and Iraq, fighting a bloody war to protect our lives. Bin Laden made it abundantly clear that he believes it is—

> Allah's order to kill the Americans and plunder their money wherever and whenever they find it. We also call on Muslim ulema (the worldwide community), leaders, youths, and soldiers to launch the raid on Satan's US troops and the devil's supporters allying with them, and to displace those who are behind them so that they may learn a lesson.

To dismiss such a statement as the insane babbling of some self-deluded religious fanatic is to ignore, at our peril, the fact that it is widely believed among a large portion of the Middle East's Arab population. It also ignores the enormous wealth that bin Laden and al-Qa'ida is able to bring to this holy war.

Struggle for the Soul of Islam

There is a struggle going on for the soul of Islam—a struggle between the fanatics and the moderates of a faith that is estimated to include some 1.2 billion people stretched across the

map of the world. They represent twenty percent of the world's population. Not all, of course, support the declared holy war, but surely enough do to require that we must expend our wealth and the lives of our military servicemen and servicewomen to insure our victory.

> *Islam was and is at war with all other religions—Judaism, Christianity, Hinduism, Buddhism, and any other non-Muslim religion.*

The ignorance of Islam still leaves many Americans wondering why we have witnessed a long history of attack on our military and, on 9-11, our homeland. Few have wanted to publicly cast this war as one between religions, but Islam was and is at war with all other religions—Judaism, Christianity, Hinduism, Buddhism, and any other non-Muslim religion. Muslims divide the world between "world of Islam" and "the world of war."

In an excellent essay on the subject, "Islam and Violence," posted on an Internet website—www.Answering-Islam.org.uk— one can find a brief history of the role of violence in both the rise of Islam and in its philosophical/theological outlook, as found in the Qur'an and its other holy books.

> The point that we'd like to make is quite simple. Muslims who commit acts of violence and terror in the name of God, can find ample justification for their actions, based on the teachings of the Qur'an and the sayings and examples from prophet Muhammad himself!

Unlike Christianity, which teaches that one should love his enemy, Islam offers no quarter for any unbeliever, unless they convert. There are many verses of the Qur'an that invoke Muslims to fight against their enemies, the non-believers. The essay cites just twenty out of 149 easily found in reading of the Qur'an.

Despite the constant repetition of the view that Islam is a religion of peace, only the most naïve and foolish could possibly look at events around the world and conclude there is any truth to this. Time and again, the many biographies of Muhammad reveal that he employed murder and war repeatedly to advance Islam. He was particularly obsessed with killing Jews.

As to the terrible instances of beheadings, such as those of *Wall Street Journal* reporter Daniel Pearl and telecommunications work contractor Nicholas Berg, both American Jews, this practice has its roots in Islamic history.

Muhammad clashed with many tribes in Arabia, among which was a Jewish tribe from the city of Medina. When they were conquered, he ordered the execution of all of the adult males. Muslim sources put the number at 600, and all were beheaded.

The prophet left a trail of assassinations and other bloody acts behind him until his own death, all of which are recorded by Muslim historians. This would become a tradition among Muslims in the early centuries of its development. As the essay notes, these are not just isolated incidents or aberrations. "Such violence, in fact, goes to the very roots of Islam, as found in the Qur'an and in actions and teachings of the prophet of Islam himself."

The holy war that has been declared against us leaves us no choice but to fight for our lives.

9

Criticism of "Islamic Fundamentalism" Is Illegitimate

Abid Ullah Jan

Abid Ullah Jan is a member of the Independent Centre for Strategic Studies and Analysis in Canada and the author of A War on Islam? *and* The End of Democracy.

In recent years, scholars and intellectuals have insisted that Islam is a religion that has been taken over by fundamentalist extremists, who pose a threat to American security. There is no such thing as Islamic "fundamentalism," however, because the teachings of the Koran are infallible and cannot be bent and shaped to fit modern times or fads. People of the Islamic faith have the right and duty to practice their beliefs as they have for more than thirteen hundred years. While Islam may seem fundamentalist to Westerners who sanction all forms of decadent sexual and social behavior, the teaching of Muhammad cannot be changed to please those of other faiths who would rather that Muslims behaved and believed as they do. It is unacceptable to smear the religious beliefs of Muslims with the negative term "fundamentalism" because the tenets of the faith must remain as Muhammad dictated them in the seventh century.

If [Western democracies] do not have enough Nazis, Japanese warlords and Soviet [dictators] to depict as an "evil" and "global enemy," how are they going to justify the existence and functions of American and European global warfare? Ever since

the end of the Cold War the question has plagued Western supermen and the world mastering demi-gods. Now in the past few years, they think they have found an answer. The new enemy is Islam, degraded with the label of "fundamentalism."

The ominous headlines from around the Western world are at first seemingly disconnected: "Islam on the march," "religious extremism threatens the West," "Islamic fundamentalism poses a threat to American national security." Then we realize that these are not disconnected developments at all. Instead, what we observe is the frightening speed at which the West is spreading its propaganda war against Islam. The most disappointing aspect of this grand conspiracy, however, is the fact that our real enemies are from within, while we helplessly try to chase them outside.

Reinterpreting Islam

To our dismay, like the so-called intellectuals of other religions and faiths, some of our Muslim "scholars" tend to interpret and rationalize the salient features of our faith in the terms to what is rising, fashionable system in the industrialized West. They are busy in defining the term "Islamic fundamentalism," propagated by the West, so that we should accept it as a legitimate expression, and start living with a classified Islam, according to their shallow knowledge.

Whereas the fact is that the connotation of the term "Islamic fundamentalism" is basically negative, in the sense that it brands Islamic belief as "outdated," "obsolete" and "impractical," unless tampered with "secularization" (called "moderation" by some), in line with the Western Capitalistic democracies and their value system.

It was not long ago, when some of these "scholars" took pains to show how Islamic economic thought conformed to the contemporary "isms," like socialism, and communism. And now that Western powers are celebrating the temporary "triumph of capitalism," renamed as "free-market economic system" for greater palatability, we notice attempts by the same Muslim "intellectuals," to reinterpret not only the economic principle of Islam, but even the very ideological substance of Islam in terms of the present prevalent Western or economic, social and political thought and practice.

Peter Waldman of the *Wall Street Journal* reported that Islamic thought is on the move, as Muslim intellectuals are "rein-

terpreting the ancient dictates of Islam to fit them to the modern age." Mostly the scholars, who cross the limits under the banner of "reformation" and "modernisation" have superficial knowledge of the Quran and Sunnah [the basic source of Islamic law that explains the Quran] and the relevant Islamic law, or they have been swept off their feet by their desire to please conform with those who are perceived as "Masters" of the modern society.

Before falling prey to Western propaganda and the absurd justification for that by some of our own "scholars," we must contemplate the reality and truth of Islam, which is far from emulating or imitating the man-made system, all imperfect and subject to transitional influences or expediency. Why should we seek to "modernize" Islam by following [the] Western system, that is primarily motivated by self-interest, rather than a comprehensive understanding of human nature and behaviour, and the discipline it needs for a healthy evolution, progress and prosperity of human race?

While defining the Western notion of "Islamic fundamentalism" some of our analysts have described that it has emerged as a religio-political phenomenon, with the revolutionary reform, and negative reactionary response of the Muslim societies against different repressive forces. What is ignored, in fact, is the Truth of the Quran, that Islam is one, universal, perpetual, absolute. It is a ridiculously incorrect perception that Islam was revealed as some kind of response to the prevailing social and moral ills, or it needs to be updated to conform to the "historical process of secularization." Just as God Is, Islam Is—in all conditions, at all times. It has only one substance, one theme, one form—not the artificially devised forms of "fundamental," "reactionary," or "revolutionary" Islam, to suit political expediencies, or serve vested interests of any particular time.

Amoral Materialism, Soul-Less Secularism

We need not be on the defensive or sound apologetic in the wake of anti-Islam propaganda of the West, by trying to explain away the current movements in Muslim societies as a "reaction" to the avalanche of materialism, secularism etc. The truth is that the powers of Western societies find Islam and its universal spiritual appeal as an obstacle and hindrance in their pursuit of unbridled "amoral" materialism and "soul-less" secularism, and irrespective of any movement in Muslim societies,

have openly declared a propaganda and intimidation war to destabilise the Muslim belief by sowing the seeds of doubt and fragmentation.

With a little wise observation, we can easily find out that none of the phenomenon, negative or positive, that is attributed to "Islamic fundamentalism," is limited to Muslim societies alone. In the United States, Rep Vic Fazio, California democrat, chairman of the Congressional Campaign Committee for the Democrats, recently launched a fear mongering attack on Republicans that focussed on something called the "radical right." The president and the vice president echoed the theme, but no one is labelling it as "fundamentalism."

Mona Charen of the *Washington Times* recently wrote, "65% of voters said they would be more likely to vote for a candidate who addressed moral decline than for any other." This is a reaction to the materialistic secularisation, but it is not considered as a "negative response of Christian fundamentalism."

> *Why should we seek to 'modernize' Islam by following [the] Western system, that is primarily motivated by self-interest, rather than a comprehensive understanding of human nature and behaviour?*

An essay, "A long way from Rome" by William D'Antonio was published in *Washington Post* at the eve of Easter 1995, in which the writer bitterly criticised the Pope and the Catholic Church. He wrote the Church is "undemocratic" and the "autocratic style" of Pope's message "reflects a continuing effort to restore the Church absolutist 19th century hierarchic structure."

Instead of describing him as a "Philosopher of Christianity" and a "moderate reformer," Joseph Sobran of the *Washington Times* bitterly criticized him. But he, too, accepted the fact that: "The Catholic Church is not a democracy. It claims the authority Jesus Christ bestowed on his 12 apostles. Christ enjoined them to teach not to take polls, and certainly not to adapt his teaching to the contemporary world."

Islam is not anti-democracy. But Western opinioned leaders' ventriloquial enthusiasm for democracy and reformation in Islam is qualified by the term "educated reformers"—as if

the opinions of these provocative thinkers should carry more weight for the Muslims than the Word of God. It is not less than making fun of Islam in the name of "fundamentalism," as a strong resistance to "adapt" teaching of the Christ to the contemporary world is not Christian fundamentalism, but a reluctance to save the original teachings of the Quran from being polluted by pro-Western reformers is Islamic fundamentalism.

The Failure of Secularism

It is important to realize that Islam is essentially a religion which began from the times of Prophet Adam, and culminated in completion with the revelations through Prophet Muhammad. To give it the historical context of the conditions prevailing in the 7th century A.D. and to imply that its role should be "redefined" in this modern industrial economy, which has become universal amid an "inexorable process of secularism," amounts to giving precedence to man-made institutions and systems over God's chosen religion, which is for all times and all conditions.

If anything, we should change our acquired and borrowed perceptions and concepts in order to conform to the dictates of Islam. At the same time we must not lose sight of the ills of the Western society, which are admittedly the result of losing touch with spirituality, a direct consequence of secularism, where the political power is deprived of moral authority.

> *We must not lose sight of the ills of the Western society, which are admittedly the result of losing touch with spirituality, a direct consequence of secularism.*

Somewhere on the road from "word-of-God" to the new "secular" and "free society" America—leader of Western society—has lost something. David Blankenhorn, founder of the Institute for American Values, thinks he knows what it is. Fatherhood. In his new book *Fatherless America: Confronting Our Most Urgent Social Problem*, Blankenhorn blames fatherhood's decline for many ills "from crime to adolescent pregnancy to child sexual abuse to domestic violence against women."

Are the advocates of secularism in Muslim societies prepared to inherit all these social and moral ills from the West at the cost of modernising Islam? Are we prepared to spend $30 billion a year, like the great civilized America, on social services for teens and their illegitimate babies? Are our reformers and reinterpreters of the Islamic beliefs ready to enter a period where we will no longer be able to reverse the social trend of fragmenting families and growing social disorder? Of course, Not.

> *It does not need too much wisdom to conclude that there are no shades of 'soft,' 'moderate,' or 'fundamental' Islam.*

Western society is the best example of a victim of its own belief in individual freedom, which, taken to its logical extension, relieves individuals of all group responsibilities. These ills are symbolic manifestations of the failure of secularism to uphold universal moral values. Some Muslim countries, to please their Western patrons, have started calling themselves "secular." Will such so-called secular governments permit the society to be ridden by such ills? . . . Being secular, what moral authority have they to enforce Islamic code in respect of such moral degradation? How can they, then, stop this happening with the help of so-called reformers and advocates of these reformers, as it is bound to follow their increasing commitment to secularism?

Western analysts, like Georgie Anne Geyer, who let no opportunity slip their hands to demonize Islam under the label of "fundamentalism," call Ayatollah Khomeini [the former leader] of Iran as "evil leader," but in the same breath accept that they are unable to "reverse the downward trends of a serious moral and social decline" in the West. Georgie Anne Geyer admitted that America cannot turn itself around, as "we know of no civilization that has been able to reverse its decline and to redeem its people." Still, Ayatollah Khomeini was "evil" because he struggled to save his society from such moral bankruptcy.

Despite these admissions of failure every practicing Muslim is a "fundamentalist," without any purpose or mission, and totally irrelevant and disharmonious to the spirit of modern times. We must try to understand what we mean by "modern times"—do we mean advancement of technology? Islam has

never restrained acquisition of knowledge, technology or otherwise. Or we mean moral and ethical values to be imported from the Western society?

On what basis do some of our "scholars" determine that, irrespective of the historical process through which they have been reached, Western values are the "true values" and worth adjusting to. The obvious vices like growing homosexuality and a big part of births taking place out of wedlock are not exceptional to the entire Western model and social fabric—they are a result of it, and cannot be justified by any kind of historical process.

Moreover, not everything "medieval" requires "modernisation." In a way all religions and scriptures are "medieval"; but the perfect Divine action and its manifestation does not fall in category of "medieval"—it falls under the category of "perpetual" and does not require a change by man, with all his imperfections. . . .

Instead of taking cognisance of the Western attack and taking measure to respond suitably and effectively, some of our scholars come up with new ideas about "Islamic fundamentalism." But without a comprehensive understanding of the meaning of IMAN (faith) in Islam, its scope and its applications, both in spiritual and material fields, we shall remain vulnerable and prone to the amoral materialistic and secularistic forces of the West.

It does not need too much wisdom to conclude that there are no shades of "soft," "moderate," or "fundamental" Islam. And those who are willing to accept moral authority of the West, or "the modern world," [rather] than the word of God, have no credibility, whatsoever, to tell us their own preferences; as we know that those who reject Divine teachings of Islam may be guided less by critical intelligence than by their own self-centred impulse.

10

Lax Immigration Controls Are a Breach in National Security

Mark Krikorian

Mark Krikorian is executive director of the Center for Immigration Studies.

The best way to prevent terrorist attacks on American soil is to keep terrorists from entering the United States. The government agencies regulating foreign immigration, however, remain seemingly oblivious to this plain logic. Lax immigration enforcement allowed the September 11 hijackers easy entry into the country and a host of problems remain today. There is a limited budget to find suspects who overstay their visas or come into the country illegally. Political correctness dictates that racial profiling and other screening techniques be ignored. Meanwhile, thousands of illegal immigrants are entering the United States every day. Whether they are here to get jobs—or hatch deadly plots against U.S. citizens—is unknown by the immigration agencies assigned to protect America. The government needs to strengthen immigration enforcement now with money and manpower or suffer the consequences in the coming years.

Supporters of open immigration have tried to de-link [the terrorist attacks on the World Trade Center and the Pentagon on September 11, 2001] from security concerns. "There's no relationship between immigration and terrorism," said a spokeswoman for the National Council of the advocacy group La Raza.

Mark Krikorian, "Keeping Terror Out: Immigration Policy and Asymmetric Warfare," *The National Interest*, Spring 2004. Copyright © 2004 by *The National Interest*, Washington, DC. Reproduced by permission.

"I don't think [9/11] can be attributed to the failure of our immigration laws," claimed the head of the immigration lawyers' guild a week after the attacks.

President Bush has not gone that far, but in his January 7 [2004] speech proposing an illegal alien amnesty and guest worker program, he claimed the federal government is now fulfilling its responsibility to control immigration, thus justifying a vast increase in the flow of newcomers to America. Exploring the role of immigration control in promoting American security can help provide the context to judge the president's claim that his proposal is consistent with our security imperatives, and can help to sketch the outlines of a secure immigration system.

Home Front

The phrase "Home Front" is a metaphor that gained currency during World War [II], with the intention of motivating a civilian population involved in total war. The image served to increase economic output and the purchase of war bonds, promote conservation and the recycling of resources and reconcile the citizenry to privation and rationing.

But in the wake of 9/11, "Home Front" is no longer a metaphor. As Deputy Secretary of Defense Paul Wolfowitz said in October 2002,

"Fifty years ago, when we said, 'home front,' we were referring to citizens back home doing their part to support the war front. Since last September, however, the home front has become a battlefront every bit as real as any we've known before."

> *Analysis of the . . . 48 foreign-born Al-Qaeda operatives who committed crimes in the United States . . . found that nearly every element of the immigration system has been penetrated by the enemy.*

Nor is this an aberration, unique to Al-Qaeda or to Islamists generally. No enemy has any hope of defeating our armies in the field and must therefore resort to asymmetric [terrorist warfare]. And though there are many facets to asymmetric or "Fourth-Generation" warfare—as we saw in Al-Qaeda's pre-9/11

assaults on our interests in the Middle East and East Africa and as we are seeing today in Iraq. The Holy Grail of such a strategy is mass-casualty attacks on America.

The military has responded to this new threat with the Northern Command, just as Israel instituted its own "Home Front Command" in 1992, after the Gulf War. But our objective on the Home Front is different, for this front is different from other fronts; the goal is defensive, blocking and disrupting the enemy's ability to carry out attacks on our territory. This will then allow offensive forces to find, pin, and kill the enemy overseas.

Exploiting Weakness in the Immigration System

Because of the asymmetric nature of the threat, the burden of homeland defense is not borne mainly by our armed forces but by agencies formerly seen as civilian entities—mainly the Department of Homeland Security (DHS). And of DHS's expansive portfolio, immigration control is central. The reason is elementary: no matter the weapon or delivery system—hijacked airliners, shipping containers, suitcase nukes, anthrax spores—operatives are required to carry out the attacks. Those operatives have to enter and work in the United States. In a very real sense, the primary weapons of our enemies are not inanimate objects at all, but rather the terrorists themselves—especially in the case of suicide attackers. Thus keeping the terrorists out or apprehending them after they get in is indispensable to victory. As President Bush said recently, "Our country is a battlefield in the first war of the 21st century."

In the words of the July 2002 National Strategy for Homeland Security:

"Our great power leaves these enemies with few conventional options for doing us harm. One such option is to take advantage of our freedom and openness by secretly inserting terrorists into our country to attack our homeland. Homeland security seeks to deny this avenue of attack to our enemies and thus to provide a secure foundation for America's ongoing global engagement."

Our enemies have repeatedly exercised this option of inserting terrorists by exploiting weaknesses in our immigration system. A Center for Immigration Studies analysis of the immigration histories of the 48 foreign-born Al-Qaeda operatives who committed crimes in the United States from 1993 to 2001 (including the 9/11 hijackers) found that nearly every element

of the immigration system has been penetrated by the enemy. Of the 48, one-third were here on various temporary visas, another third were legal residents or naturalized citizens, one-fourth were illegal aliens, and the remainder had pending asylum applications. Nearly half of the total had, at some point or another, violated existing immigration laws.

Supporters of loose borders deny that inadequate immigration control is a problem, usually pointing to flawed intelligence as the most important shortcoming that needs to be addressed. Mary Ryan, for example, former head of the State Department's Bureau of Consular Affairs (which issues visas), testified in January 2004 before the 9/11 Commission that

"Even under the best immigration controls, most of the September 11 terrorists would still be admitted to the United States today . . . because they had no criminal records, or known terrorist connections, and had not been identified by intelligence methods for special scrutiny."

But this turns out to be untrue, both for the hijackers and for earlier Al-Qaeda operatives in the United States. A normal level of visa scrutiny, for instance, would have excluded almost all the hijackers. Investigative reporter Joel Mowbray acquired copies of 15 of the 19 hijackers' visa applications (the other four were destroyed—yes, destroyed—by the State Department), and every one of the half-dozen current and former consular officers he consulted said every application should have been rejected on its face. Every application was incomplete or contained patently inadequate or absurd answers.

Slipping Through the Cracks

Even if the applications had been properly prepared, many of the hijackers, including [9/11 leader] Mohammed Atta and several others, were young, single, and had little income—precisely the kind of person likely to overstay his visa and become an illegal alien, and thus the kind of applicant who should be rejected. And, conveniently, those *least* likely to overstay their visas—older people with close family, property, and other commitments in their home countries—are also the very people least likely to commit suicide attacks.

9/11 was not the only terrorist plot to benefit from lax enforcement of ordinary immigration controls—every major Al-Qaeda attack or conspiracy in the United States has involved at least one terrorist who violated immigration law. Gazi Ibrahim

Abu Mezer, for example, who was part of the plot to bomb the Brooklyn subway, was actually caught three times by the Border Patrol trying to sneak in from Canada. The third time the Canadians would not take him back. What did we do? Because of a lack of detention space, he was simply released into the country and told to show up for his deportation hearing. After all, with so many millions of illegal aliens here already, how much harm could one more do?

> **❝** *In the end, the lack of effective immigration control leaves us naked in the face of the enemy.* **❞**

Another example is Mohammed Salameh, who rented the truck in the first World Trade Center bombing. He should never have been granted a visa in the first place. When he applied for a tourist visa he was young, single, and had no income and, in the event, did indeed end up remaining illegally. And when his application for a green card [to allow him to legally work in the United States] under the 1986 illegal-alien amnesty was rejected, there was (and remains today) no way to detain and remove rejected green-card applicants, so he simply remained living and working in the United States, none the worse for wear. The same was true of Hesham Mohamed Hadayet, who murdered two people at the El Al counter at Los Angeles International Airport on July 4, 2002—he was a visa overstayer whose asylum claim was rejected. Yet with no mechanism to remove him, he remained and, with his wife, continued to apply for the visa lottery until she won and procured green cards for both of them.

Ordinary immigration enforcement actually *has* kept out several terrorists that we know of. A vigilant inspector in Washington State stopped Ahmed Ressam because of nervous behavior, and a search of his car uncovered a trunk full of explosives, apparently intended for an attack on Los Angeles International Airport. Ramzi Binalshibh, one of the candidates for the label of "20th [9/11] hijacker," was rejected four times for a visa, not because of concerns about terrorism but rather, according to a U.S. embassy source, "for the most ordinary of reasons, the same reasons most people are refused." That is, he

was thought likely to overstay his visa and become an illegal alien. And Mohamed Al-Qahtani, another one of the "20th hijacker" candidates, was turned away by an airport inspector in Orlando because he had no return ticket and no hotel reservations, and he refused to identify the friend who was supposed to help him on his trip.

Prior to the growth of militant Islam, the only foreign threat to our population and territory in recent history has been the specter of nuclear attack by the Soviet Union. To continue that analogy, since the terrorists are themselves the weapons, immigration control is to asymmetric warfare what missile defense is to strategic warfare. There are other weapons we must use against an enemy employing asymmetric means—more effective international coordination, improved intelligence gathering and distribution, special military operations—but in the end, the lack of effective immigration control leaves us naked in the face of the enemy. This lack of defensive capability may have made sense with regard to the strategic nuclear threat under the doctrine of Mutually Assured Destruction, but it makes no sense with regard to the asymmetric threats we face today and in the future.

Unfortunately, our immigration response to the wake-up call delivered by the 9/11 attacks has been piecemeal and poorly coordinated. Specific initiatives that should have been set in motion years ago have finally begun to be enacted, but there is an *ad hoc* feel to our response, a sense that bureaucrats in the Justice and Homeland Security departments are searching for ways to tighten up immigration controls that will not alienate one or another of a bevy of special interest groups.

Rather than having federal employees cast about for whatever enforcement measures they feel they can get away with politically, we need a strategic assessment of what an effective immigration-control system would look like.

Homeland Security Begins Abroad

To extend the missile defense analogy, there are three layers of immigration control, comparable to the three phases of a ballistic missile's flight: boost, midcourse, and terminal. In immigration the layers are overseas, at the borders, and inside the country. But unlike existing missile defense systems, the redundancy built into our immigration control system permits us repeated opportunities to exclude or apprehend enemy operatives.

Entry to America by foreigners is not a right but a privilege, granted exclusively at the discretion of the American people. The first agency that exercises that discretion is the State Department's Bureau of Consular Affairs, whose officers make the all-important decisions about who gets a visa. Consular Affairs is, in effect, America's other Border Patrol. In September 2003, DHS Under Secretary Asa Hutchinson described the visa process as "forward-based defense" against terrorists and criminals.

> *Before 9/11 hijacker Khalid Al-Midhar's second trip to the United States, the CIA learned that he had been involved in the bombing of the U.S.S. Cole.*

The visa filter is especially important because the closer an alien comes to the United States the more difficult it is to exclude him. There is relatively little problem, practically or politically, in rejecting a foreign visa applicant living abroad. Once a person presents himself at a port of entry, it becomes more difficult to turn him back, although the immigration inspector theoretically has a free hand to do so. Most difficult of all is finding and removing people who have actually been admitted; not only is there no specific chokepoint in which aliens can be controlled, but even the most superficial connections with American citizens or institutions can lead to vocal protests against enforcement of the law. . . .

Order at the Border

The next layer of immigration security is the border, which has two elements: "ports of entry," which are the points where people traveling by land, sea, or air enter the United States; and the stretches between those entry points. The first are staffed by inspectors working for DHS's Bureau of Customs and Border Protection, the second monitored by the Border Patrol and the Coast Guard, both now also part of DHS.

This is another important chokepoint, as almost all of the 48 Al-Qaeda operatives who committed terrorist acts through 2001 had had contact with immigration inspectors. But here, too, the system failed to do its job. For instance, Mohammed Atta was

permitted to re-enter the country in January 2001 even though he had overstayed his visa the last time. Also, before 9/11 hijacker Khalid Al-Midhar's second trip to the United States, the CIA learned that he had been involved in the bombing of the U.S.S. *Cole*—but it took months for his name to be placed on the watch list used by airport inspectors, and by then he had already entered the country. And in any case, there still are 12 separate watch lists, maintained by nine different government agencies.

Political considerations fostered a dangerous culture of permissiveness in airport inspections. Bowing to complaints from airlines and the travel industry, Congress in 1990 required that incoming planes be cleared within 45 minutes, reinforcing the notion that the border was a nuisance to be evaded rather than a vital security tool. And the Orlando immigration inspector who turned back a Saudi national—Al-Qahtani, now believed to have been a part of the 9/11 plot—was well aware that he was taking a career risk, since Saudis were supposed to be treated even more permissively than other foreign nationals seeking entry. . . .

And finally, perhaps the biggest defect in this layer of security is the lack of effective tracking of departures. Without exit controls, there is no way to know who has overstayed his visa. This is especially important because most illegal alien terrorists have been overstayers. The opportunities for failure are numerous and the system is so dysfunctional that the INS's own statistics division declared that it was no longer possible to estimate the number of people who have overstayed their visas. . . .

Also, there is continued resistance to using the military to back up the Border Patrol—resistance that predates the concern for overstretch caused by the occupation of Iraq. But controlling the Mexican border, apart from the other benefits it would produce, is an important security objective; at least two major rings have been uncovered which smuggled Middle Easterners into the United States via Mexico, with help from corrupt Mexican government employees. At least one terrorist has entered this way: Mahmoud Kourani, brother of Hizbollah's chief of military security in southern Lebanon, described in a federal indictment as "a member, fighter, recruiter and fundraiser for Hizballah."

Safety Through Redundancy

The third layer of immigration security—the terminal phase, in missile defense jargon—is interior enforcement. Here, again, ordinary immigration control can be a powerful security tool.

Of the 48 Al-Qaeda operatives, nearly half were either illegal aliens at the time of their crimes or had violated immigration laws at some point prior to their terrorist acts.

Many of these terrorists lived, worked, opened bank accounts, and received driver's licenses with little or no difficulty. Because such a large percentage of terrorists violated immigration laws, enforcing the law would be extremely helpful in disrupting and preventing terrorist attacks.

> **❞** *If our immigration system is so lax that it can be penetrated by a Mexican busboy, it can sure be penetrated by an Al-Qaeda terrorist.* **❞**

But interior enforcement is also the most politically difficult part of immigration control. While there is at least nominal agreement on the need for improvements to the mechanics of visas and border monitoring, there is no elite consensus regarding interior enforcement. This is especially dangerous given that interior enforcement is the last fallback for immigration control, the final link in a chain of redundancy that starts with the visa application overseas.

There are two elements to interior enforcement: first, conventional measures such as arrest, detention, and deportation; and second, verification of legal status when conducting important activities. The latter element is important because its goal is to disrupt the lives of illegal aliens so that many will return home on their own (and, in a security context, to disrupt the planning and execution of terrorist attacks).

Inadequacies in the first element of interior enforcement have clearly helped terrorists in the past. Because there is no way of determining which visitors have overstayed their visas, much less a mechanism for apprehending them, this has been a common means of remaining in the United States—of the 12 (out of 48) Al-Qaeda operatives who were illegal aliens when they took part in terrorism, seven were visa overstayers.

Among terrorists who were actually detained for one reason or another, several were released to go about their business inside America because of inadequate detention space. This lack of space means that most aliens in deportation proceedings are not detained, so that when ordered deported, they receive what

is commonly known as a "run letter" instructing them to appear for deportation—and 94 percent of aliens from terrorist-sponsoring states disappear instead. . . .

Create "Virtual Chokepoints"

The second element of interior enforcement has been, if anything, even more neglected. The creation of "virtual chokepoints," where an alien's legal status would be verified, is an important tool of immigration control, making it difficult for illegals to engage in the activities necessary for modern life.

The most important chokepoint is employment. Unfortunately, enforcement of the prohibition against hiring illegal aliens, passed in 1986, has all but stopped. This might seem to be of little importance to security, but in fact holding a job can be important to terrorists for a number of reasons. By giving them a means of support, it helps them blend into society. Neighbors might well become suspicious of young men who do not work, but seem able to pay their bills. Moreover, supporting themselves by working would enable terrorists to avoid the scrutiny that might attend the transfer of money from abroad. Of course, terrorists who do not work can still arrive with large sums of cash, but this too creates risks of detection. . . .

Other chokepoints include obtaining a driver's license and opening a bank account, two things that most of the 9/11 hijackers had done. It is distressing to note that, while Virginia, Florida, and New Jersey tightened their driver's license rules after learning that the hijackers had used licenses from those states, other states have not. Indeed, California's then-Governor Gray Davis signed a bill last year intended specifically to provide licenses to illegal aliens (which was repealed after his recall).

As for bank accounts, the trend is toward making it easier for illegal aliens to open them. The governments of Mexico and several other countries have joined with several major banks to promote the use of consular identification cards (for illegals who can't get other ID) as a valid form of identification, something the U.S. Department of the Treasury explicitly sanctioned in an October 2002 report. . . .

Upholding the Law

Such ambivalence about immigration enforcement, at whatever stage in the process, compromises our security. It is im-

portant to understand that the security function of immigration control is not merely opportunistic. . . . The FBI's use of immigration charges to detain hundreds of Middle Easterners in the immediate aftermath of 9/11 was undoubtedly necessary, but it cannot be a model for the role of immigration law in homeland security. If our immigration system is so lax that it can be penetrated by a Mexican busboy, it can sure be penetrated by an Al-Qaeda terrorist.

Since there is no way to let in "good" illegal aliens but keep out "bad" ones, countering the asymmetric threats to our people and territory requires sustained, across-the-board immigration law enforcement. Anything less exposes us to grave dangers. Whatever the arguments for the president's amnesty and guest worker plan, no such proposal can plausibly be entertained until we have a robust, functioning immigration-control system. And we are nowhere close to that day.

11

Overzealous Immigration Policies Leave America Susceptible to Attack

Joe Feuerherd

Joe Feuerherd is the National Catholic Reporter's *Washington correspondent.*

In the wake of the September 11 attacks in New York City and Washington, D.C., the federal government jailed thousands of immigrants of Middle Eastern descent and held them without charges—in some cases for months. While some were deported for visa violations, none were charged with crimes relating to terrorism. Since that time, federal agencies have continued to harass Middle Eastern immigrants in communities across the country. Instead of making America safer, this harsh policy has created great resentment toward the government in immigrant communities. In this atmosphere of hostility and fear terrorists might be able to recruit disgruntled immigrants or hide in their midst. A policy of cooperation with immigrant leaders would lead to a safer America.

Heavy-handed enforcement of immigration laws designed to unearth terrorist cells within U.S. Muslim communities is backfiring and makes Americans more susceptible to attack, according to some immigration and national security experts.

That critique of the ongoing crackdown on Middle East-erners who overstay visas or who otherwise violate U.S. immi-gration laws is widely shared by civil libertarians and advocates for the undocumented, who argue that the Justice Department and the Immigration and Naturalization Service's [INS] ap-proach to apprehending terrorists within U.S. borders is wrong-headed. (In March [2003], the functions of the Immigration and Naturalization Service were subsumed into the Depart-ment of Homeland Security under two new bureaus: the Bor-der and Transportation Security Directorate and the Bureau of Citizenship and Immigration Services.)

But another voice in the debate is being increasingly heard: Security experts who warn that the government is missing the terrorist forest for the immigration trees.

Tactics Hinder Law Enforcement

Secret detentions, deportations and registration requirements targeted to citizens of 25 mostly Muslim countries have "alien-ated a lot of these communities, caused a great deal of fear and reinforced the tendency of immigrant communities to huddle together and not trust authorities, which works against intelli-gence gathering by law enforcement, particularly the FBI," said Vincent Cannistraro, former director of Counterterrorism Op-erations and Analysis at the Central Intelligence Agency.

"The idea that you stigmatize whole classes of people and profile them because you think this is going to prevent the next terrorist attack is exactly the wrong way [to go about it]," Cannistraro told *NCR [National Catholic Reporter]*. "There may very well be another clandestine al-Qaeda cell in North Amer-ica, but none of these methodologies has contributed to iden-tifying them," Cannistraro said.

Critics of the [George W. Bush] administration's approach point to more than 60 administrative actions taken by the Jus-tice Department and the INS over the past 19 months, includ-ing expanded detention without charges, closed immigration hearings, coordinated arrests of illegal aliens working at air-ports and other sensitive security sites, and a gag order that pre-vents state authorities from releasing information on detainees.

As a recent part of the government's effort, foreign-born, non-citizen males age 16 or over from countries considered high-risk terrorist exporters must register at "a designated im-migration office." The deadline for Pakistani and Saudi Arabian

males was March 21, while citizens of Bangladesh, Egypt, Indonesia, Jordan and Kuwait have until April 25. Those registering will be photographed, fingerprinted and interviewed under oath, according to the immigration officials.

> *“ The idea that you stigmatize whole classes of people and profile them because you think this is going to prevent the next terrorist attack is exactly the wrong way. ”*

Rather than face deportation, hundreds of non-residents who have overstayed their visas—most of them natives of Pakistan—have applied to Canada for refugee status. They are being assisted and housed by the Salvation Army in Vermont.

The rationale for the crackdown was stated by Attorney General John Ashcroft soon after Sept. 11: “Aggressive detention of lawbreakers and material witnesses is vital to preventing, disrupting or delaying new attacks. It is difficult for a person in jail or under detention to murder innocent people or to aid or abet in terrorism.”

And there are those who say the Ashcroft approach hasn’t gone far enough. “The immigration measures taken since 9/11 are small steps in the right direction, for the most part, but remain woefully inadequate,” said Mark Krikorian, executive director of the Center for Immigration Studies. “Immigration enforcement is one of the best tools for tripping up terrorists because if you are coming here to commit an act of terrorism and your visa expires, you’re not going to say, ‘Oh, my visa expired and I have to go back to my home country and give up my dreams of terrorism.’ You’re going to do whatever it takes, even if it includes violating immigration law.”

Arrest, Detention, Deportation

To Don Kerwin, executive director of the Catholic Legal Immigration Network, aggressive immigration enforcement as an antiterror tool is unproductive overkill. “A lot of the security measures have targeted undocumented people and that’s not a very efficient way to go about it because the lion’s share of the undocumented come from Mexico, Central America and South

America—and they're not your al-Qaeda producing countries."
The administration's approach, said Kerwin, "doesn't catch the
right people and it drives the people you ought to be befriending underground or pushes them to Canada, and that is coun-
terproductive as a long-term strategy."

The registration effort, said Kerwin, is particularly punitive.
"It's not just registration. It's arrest and detention and deportation. It would be a little bit different if it was in a different climate, where the FBI was trying to befriend immigrant communities, where it was asking people to come voluntarily forward,
and if there was a firewall between immigration enforcement
and this particular program, but that's not what's happening."

> *It's ironic that the one flow of immigrants that
> was substantially reduced after 9/11 is the only
> immigrant flow that has never contributed a
> terrorist to the U.S.*

Meanwhile, the crackdown has negatively affected one
group of potential immigrants most everyone agrees are unlikely to engage in terrorism: displaced people fleeing political
or religious persecution in their home countries. The number
of refugees entering the United States has dropped from 72,000
in 2000 to 26,000 last year, and will fall far short of the ceiling
of 50,000 approved by the president for this year.

"Terrorists have used every other component of the immigration system, whether it's temporary visas, permanent visas,
the asylum system, sneaking across the border, coming through
airports or land crossing," Krikorian said. "The only thing terrorists seem never to have done is come here as resettled refugees.
It's ironic that the one flow of immigrants that was substantially
reduced after 9/11 is the only immigrant flow that has never
contributed a terrorist to the U.S."

Following Sept. 11, the government suspended its refugee
resettlement program, explained Mark Franken, director of mi-
gration and refugee services for the U.S. bishops' conference.
But even with the moratorium lifted, concerns about security
(combined with a generally understaffed process) have stymied
refugee resettlement, he said.

Now, said Franken, the cumbersome process of checking

refugee backgrounds against government security databases has slowed resettlement to a crawl. "Until there is a response from that [security] process, no refugee can move," said Franken. And in many cases, he continued, "there's just no response"—requests between government agencies frequently "go unanswered."

Franken, too, sees irony. "We are talking about . . . the very people who are fleeing the terrorists and the regimes we are at war against."

From his perspective, former CIA anti-terror chief Cannistraro says the focus on undocumented aliens as terrorists will get worse before it gets better. The policy, said Cannistraro, is driven by Ashcroft, not Homeland Security Secretary Tom Ridge or others likely "to have a more balanced approach."

Said Cannistraro: "The issue is extremism and John Ashcroft, in this policy of trying to put in place legal barriers to terrorism in the United States, is an extremist."

Meanwhile, says Krikorian, asserting control over U.S. borders is "like quitting smoking or ripping off your Band-Aid: It's not without a certain amount of pain. And the people who are going to suffer that pain are the illegal aliens and the businesses that have been employing them. And that's just the way it is."

12

U.S. Political and Economic Policies Threaten National Security

Amory B. Lovins

Amory B. Lovins is an energy consultant who has received both a MacArthur Fellowship and a Right Livelihood ("alternative Nobel") award. He has authored or coauthored twenty-seven books, and he consults for industries and governments worldwide.

Over the next decade the United States will spend trillions of dollars on military equipment ranging from high-tech computerized bombs to jet fighters, naval destroyers, and nuclear weapons. None of these weapons will make American citizens any safer when more than half the world's population lives in dire poverty without fundamental necessities such as food, clean water, shelter, and sanitation. This mass of humanity also lacks the cornerstones of human dignity such as freedom, justice, and access to education. The seething resentment toward the United States among the earth's 3 billion poorest citizens creates a rich breeding ground for terrorists who can and will attempt to destroy the American way of life. Unless the U.S. government spends a great deal more time and money promoting peace, justice, and equality in the world, Americans will always be vulnerable to terrorists.

Amory B. Lovins, "How to Get Real Security: $11,000 Per Second Can't Keep Us Safe," *Whole Earth*, Fall 2002, p. 8. Copyright © 2002 by the Point Foundation. Reproduced by permission of the Rocky Mountain Institute.

On September 11, 2001, the Revolution in Military Affairs shifted into fast forward. The asymmetric warfare [war involving parties of unequal power] we had been worried about for decades became a reality. A poorly financed and technologically impoverished antagonist proved it could mount devastating attacks on the United States.

Asymmetric warfare's first major US episode gave over a million-fold economic leverage to the attackers, doing trillions of dollars of direct and indirect damage with about a half-million dollar budget. What's perhaps most surprising (but understandable, given the historically sheltered nature of our society from such events), is how psychologically effective it was, even though the survival rates were quite high—around 90 percent in the World Trade Center, which is quite astonishing, and roughly 99.5 percent in the Pentagon attack.

Not a Pretty Picture

It's also now very clear that you can't effectively guard an open society, especially one that has inflicted itself with alarming vulnerabilities, built up over decades. Vulnerabilities include water, wastewater, telecoms, financial transfers, and transportation. If you destroy some critical bits of infrastructure, you can make a large city uninhabitable pretty quickly. This threat becomes more worrisome as weapons of mass destruction gain more customers.

Telecoms and financial transfer by electronics are particularly vulnerable. *The Los Angeles Times*, *The Washington Post*, and *The Wall Street Journal* recently reported a greatly increased incidence in recent months of probing cyberattacks from the Middle East on electric grids and other critical infrastructure by computer crackers.

As you look over the list of other issues that erode security—the effect of climate change and conflict on increasing flows of refugees; the risks of famine and war; water problems; disease outbreaks . . . ; the spread of exotic species and invasive pathogens and genetically modified organisms—it's not a pretty picture for a peaceful world.

A Tripolar World

Traditional thinking about all these issues has been influenced by the supposition that governments are the axis of power and

the locus of action, so that we need to focus on governmental and international institutions and instruments. That's the wrong mindset, dangerously incomplete and obsolete, in a world that is now clearly tripolar, with power and action centered not just within governments, but also in the private sector and an Internet-empowered civil society. There are complex interactions among these three actors. Increasingly, government is the least effective, most frustrating, and slowest to deal with, so one ought to focus attention on the other two. Also, each of these three has a kind of antiparticle, as in particle physics. You can have rogue governments like the Taliban, rogue businesses like [bankrupt energy company] Enron, and rogue nongovernmental organizations, like Al Qa'eda.

In a tripolar society, power is enlarged and diffused, and everything can happen a lot faster, because there are a lot more ways and channels for it to happen. In the model that we grew up with, governments rule physical territory in which national economies function, and strong economies support hegemonic military power. In the new model, already emerging under our noses, economic decisions don't pay much attention to national sovereignty in a world where more than half of the one hundred or two hundred largest economic entities are not countries but companies. Governments can no longer control their economies or look after their people. With trillions of dollars of capital sloshing around instantaneously at a whim, you might have more economic growth, but you also have extreme local volatility.

Globalization Has Led to Instability

You might suppose that the rise of the private sector enhances the prospect for peace, because war is bad for most businesses, and business could therefore be expected to take steps to reduce conflict. But so far, taking into account all of the ingredients of stability, globalization is clearly making stability deteriorate. This is mainly because the trends of the past decade or two have made losers greatly outnumber winners. The gap between rich and poor has grown, and is apparently accelerating. According to the World Bank, of the six billion people on Earth, three billion live on less than $2 a day, and 1.2 billion live on less than $1 a day, which defines the absolute poverty standard. Access to clean water is denied to 1.5 million people. Meanwhile, the world's richest 200 people are worth an aver-

age of $5 billion each. This naturally increases envy and anger. Typically, Western and especially American firms get blamed.

The instability of economies and polities erodes a sense of national or other identity, and therefore decreases stability and makes conditions ripe for nationalism and fundamentalism of all stripes. When nations can't take care of their people, people lose confidence in them and often tend not to vote, because they're not pleased with any of the candidates. Then you get movements backing candidates such as Jean-Marie Le Pen in France, with eerie parallels to the rise of Hitler. The growing influence of extreme right-wing parties, now in or tilting governments in at least eight Western European countries, certainly indicates that the problem is not just limited to poor countries.

> *If you destroy some critical bits of infrastructure, you can make a large city uninhabitable pretty quickly.*

Hierarchical government is in quite a few respects losing effectiveness and credence. What needs to emerge, and may be starting to emerge, is networked governance. But that only works if it's really tripolar, engaging all three poles—the public and private sectors, plus nongovernmental organizations (NGOs) or civil society.

While that networked governance—the tripolar world—gels, shifting ad hoc coalitions are seeking topical solutions between pairs or occasionally triplets of those three poles. This is a very sharp contrast to our old mental model of negotiations and treaties between sovereign nations. For example, business and civil society are increasingly joining forces to do what government can't or won't do. Civil society can either grant or withhold the legitimacy that gives business its franchise to operate, and by shifting purchasing and investment patterns, can profoundly accelerate the revolution already visible in business leadership.

Americans Are Thoroughly Disliked

Also, of course, evil globalizes, whether through the spread of weapons of mass destruction (by two or sometimes all three of

the poles in interaction) or through globalized crime and drugs. Homogenization, culturally driven, largely by the media, fosters the Jihad v. McWorld polarity. None of this is welcome, but all of it is being either encouraged or tolerated by US policy—often strongly encouraged, in a way that causes resentment.

In hindsight, it's clearly an error to think of 9/11 as evil in a vacuum. There has been much debate about root causes, trying to figure out why people are so angry with us. A lot has been said about perceptions of humiliation and deculturization, unfairness, bullying, the hypocrisy that weights non-American lives and freedoms as less than our own, and so on.

This is not surprising to readers of such works as Jonathan Kwitny's 1986 book, *Endless Enemies: The Making of an Unfriendly World* (out of print). A *Wall Street Journal* reporter who lived in dozens of countries, particularly in Africa, Kwitny painted an appalling picture of how thoroughly the US government had destroyed what should have been good commercial and cultural relationships—by messing in other people's affairs, backing the wrong people, not understanding whom we were dealing with, and just being disagreeable. His basic conclusion was that if we want other peoples to think well of us, we should be the kind of folks they'd like to do business with, and should ensure that whoever comes to power there should never have been shot at by an American gun. It seems a very pragmatic and principled approach.

> *Of the six billion people on Earth, three billion live on less than $2 a day, and 1.2 billion live on less than $1 a day.*

Working in about fifty countries, I've been endlessly impressed with how stupidly our country can behave, even through its diplomatic apparatus (as we saw this spring in Venezuela). We Americans are thoroughly disliked, to a degree much greater than our political leaders seem to realize. That's going to be very hard to turn around even if we start now. In fact, we're going hard in the opposite direction, eroding or undercutting practically every peace-promoting, risk-reducing effort put forward by the international community, appearing hypocritical and unilateral, imposing mass-media culture, and

showing little understanding of the values of diversity and tolerance, or even, all too often, of the rule of law for which we supposedly stand.

The new American doctrine of exceptionalism (what used to be called "isolationism") is uniting the rest of the world, even our closest allies, against us. I think we will look back on the rapid destruction of treaty regimes that have taken decades to build up, and the credibility we were trying to build, and ask "what on earth possessed us to do that?"

Strategies for Security

In a remarkable speech, almost Churchillian, on October 2, 2001 [British prime minister] Tony Blair said, "We need, above all, justice and prosperity for the poor and dispossessed." Martin Luther King, Jr. reminded us that "Peace is not the absence of war, it is the presence of justice." We also, I think, need to remember [U.S. diplomat] George Kennan's prescient warning, at the start of the Cold War, that the biggest danger was that we'd become like our enemies. Many elements of the Patriot Act passed by Congress after 9/11—abrogating civil liberties, ignoring the Freedom of Information Act, generally constricting the flow of public information—move us in that direction.

> *The new American doctrine of exceptionalism . . . is uniting the rest of the world, even our closest allies, against us.*

Military superiority won't be enough to win the "war on terrorism." It is said that the kind of leadership we need in Afghanistan has five dimensions:

- a political one, in which we enhance stability and marginalize the bad actors, so we don't create more monsters like the Taliban and Al Qa'eda;
- a diplomatic dimension where we try to move potential belligerents into a more sympathetic or at least more tolerant stance;
- an informational dimension in which we show the region, Islam, and the whole world that we're not blaming, but rather trying to help the people;

- a humanitarian and economic dimension, in which we improve people's lives so the seeds of conflict don't flourish;
- and a military dimension, in which we bring bad guys to justice, maybe use covert operations and encourage the overthrow of the bad guys, or as a last resort, defeat them in battle.

Attacks Cannot Be Prevented

But it seems to me that what's missing from this five-sided approach is a strategic context. So I'd like to talk a little about what security is, where it comes from, and who's responsible for it, because it's clearer every day that the world's best armed forces, costing $11,000 a second, are not making us secure. That's because—as military professionals have understood for a long time, but not always articulated—there is no significant military threat to the United States that can be defended against.

That is, it is not technically possible to defend effectively against ballistic missiles. It is certainly not possible to defend against, say, nuclear warheads or other weapons of mass destruction that are smuggled in without leaving a radar track or other return address. Someone could wrap a warhead in bales of marijuana, put it in a shipping container, bring it aboard a ship to any of our harbors, and nobody would notice.

The point is that anonymous, asymmetric attacks can be quite devastating, but are undeterrable in principle, because you don't know who is responsible for them. That can be especially true with suicidal adversaries. We have already learned that interdiction by prior intelligence can't be relied upon. So the only lastingly effective defense is prevention, not so much at the level of intelligence foresight, which doesn't work reliably, but at the level of root causes, of eliminating the social conditions that feed and motivate the pathology of hatred.

Bottom Up Security

This requires a comprehensive (though not indiscriminate) engagement in a geopolitical and ideological sense that goes far beyond traditional military means and digs down to the foundation of what our society aims to become.

Security has two main elements. The dictionary defines "security" as "freedom from fear of privation or attack." Freedom

from fear of privation and freedom from fear of attack are not independent, but are both vital to being and feeling safe.

Can we be and feel safe in ways that work better and cost less than present arrangements? Is there a path to security that is achieved from the bottom up, not from the top down; that is the province of every citizen, not the monopoly of national government; that doesn't rely on the threat or use of violence; that makes others more, not less, secure, whether on the scale of the village or the globe? Can a new approach to building real security also advance other overarching goals, and, ideally, save enough money to pay for other things we need?

I think we can do that.

Freedom from Fear of Privation

Let's start with freedom from fear of privation, which has many obvious elements: reliable and affordable energy, food, water, shelter, sanitation, health; a sustainable and flexible system of production, transportation, communication, and commerce; universal education, strong innovation, vibrant diversity; a healthful environment; free expression, debate, and spirituality; a legitimate and accountable system of self-government at all levels. I would suggest that preserving our security requires all these things for others, too. As Dick Bell of the Worldwatch Institute remarks, weapons and warriors cannot keep us safe "in a world of extreme inequality, injustice, and deprivation for billions of our fellow human beings."

> *It's clearer every day that the world's best armed forces, costing $11,000 a second, are not making us secure.*

Helping others live decent lives is a worthy mission that our nation has undertaken before. General George Marshall said in 1947 that "there can be no political stability and no assured peace without economic security." He said that US policy must therefore "be directed not against any country or doctrine, but against hunger, poverty, desperation, and chaos." That was right then and it's right now.

You can argue about numbers, and certainly there's plenty

of room for innovation in how services are delivered, honestly and effectively. But, for what it's worth, the UN Development Programme says that, today, every poor person on Earth could have clean water, sanitation, basic health, nutrition, education, and reproductive health care for about $40 billion a year. That's a good deal less than we're spending on our antiterrorist program in the United States. It's less than a quarter of the tax cut that the president and Congress bestowed on us [in 2001].

Commitment Is Lacking

But where is the determination to build a muscular global coalition to create a safer world in those fundamental ways? Wealthy nations have reduced their foreign aid contributions in recent years. The $11 billion the United States now allots annually to foreign aid amounts to 0.11 percent of the nation's gross domestic product. (Canada and major European countries spend about three times as much of their GDP on aid.) The Bush Administration has announced a major and long-overdue increase in foreign aid. That could be a very good thing. But it's a small part of what's required, and it's not being framed in the sense or with the vision that General Marshall did half a century ago.

Aid from rich countries is often leveraged to elicit certain behaviors from recipient nations. Treasury Secretary O'Neill said in Ghana that American aid will be directed only to those African nations that exhibit good governance and also "encourage economic freedom"—in other words, those that privatize their industries, reduce subsidies, and open their markets to goods from the United States. But in fact the United States, along with other rich nations, continues to move away from a policy of open markets, slapping tariffs on foreign steel and lumber and instituting an additional $35 billion in annual farm subsidies. This appears to our friends abroad, particularly in Europe, to be pure electoral opportunism, rejecting the very principles of free trade that we have been urging them to adopt, as well as stifling poor countries' exports to the US.

Beyond the simple application of more cash and making trade authentically fair, other routes to economic security in the developing world are available. We wouldn't normally think of a light bulb as an instrument for security, but building real security can be as simple and as grassroots-based as a compact fluorescent lamp (CFL), costing about $3–12, in competitive markets. There are many more techniques like that.

Freedom from Fear of Attack

The other side of security is freedom from fear of attack. In [the] . . . book, *Security Without War*, published in 1993, but written several years earlier, Hal Harvey and Mike Shuman nicely lay out a new security triad: (1) conflict avoidance and/or prevention, (2) conflict resolution, and (3) non-provocative defense.

Conflict avoidance/prevention, which might be called "presponse," has historically been a low priority, but it ought to be the highest priority. It's by far the most cost-effective way not to be attacked. It comprises elements like justice, hope, transparency, tolerance, and honest government. Many governments are still run by crooks or thugs, but I'm encouraged by the movement within the Organization for Economic Cooperation and Development and by such groups as Transparency International to expose and stop corruption.

Conflict prevention also includes what Harvey and Shuman call "leader control." They note that it's almost impossible to find instances of wars between two democracies, or between two societies that, whatever their outward form of government, have effective ways to find out what their government is up to and tangibly express their displeasure if they don't like it.

Effective leader control tends to discourage adventures by leaders who are either crazy or wanting to divert attention from domestic difficulties. It's enhanced by speeding up the information revolution, so citizens can communicate with each other and with the outside world by a diversity of means that will be hard to block. In the earliest days of perestroika [liberal reform in the Soviet Union in the mid-1980s], someone asked [Soviet leader Mikhail] Gorbachev's senior advisor on science, energy, education, and arms control—Academician Yevgeny Pavlovich Velikhov—how the then-Soviet government intended to keep control once citizens got access to modems, faxes, copiers, and the like. His prescient reply was: "You don't understand. The information revolution is our secret weapon to ensure that the reforms of perestroika are irreversible."

Advanced Resource Productivity

Another critical tool for preventing conflict is advanced resource productivity—getting lots more work out of each unit of energy materials, water, topsoil, and so on. As Paul Hawken, Hunter Lovins, and I describe in our book *Natural Capitalism*, advanced resource productivity can actually prevent conflict in four ways.

First, it can make aspirations to a decent life realistic and attainable, for all, forever. It takes a while, but it's definitely going in the right direction. It removes apparent conflicts between economic advancement and environmental sustainability. You can implement it by any mixture of market and administrative practices you want. It scales fractally from the household to the world. It's adaptable to very diverse conditions and cultures.

Second, resource productivity avoids resource conflicts over things like oil and water. As a result, military professionals can have negamissions. Military intervention in the Gulf becomes Mission Unnecessary because the oil will become irrelevant. Just moving to Hypercars will ultimately save as much oil in the world as OPEC now sells.

Third, resource productivity can make infrastructure invulnerable by design. That's the argument set out in our Pentagon study from twenty years ago, *Brittle Power. Energy Strategy for National Security* (now reposted at www.rmi.org).

And finally, an argument that's a little more complex. Resource productivity can unmask and penalize proliferators of weapons of mass destruction. Along with the late Lenny Ross, we made that argument in detail with respect to nuclear proliferation, in *Foreign Affairs* in summer 1980, in an article entitled "Nuclear Power, Nuclear Bombs." It's enlarged in a book, now out of print, called *Energy and War: Breaking the Nuclear Link.*

Making Weapons Harder to Make

The basic argument is that if we use energy in a way that saves money, that is enormously cheaper than building or just running nuclear plants, so any country that takes economics seriously won't want or have nuclear plants. They're simply a way to waste money. In such a world, the ingredients—the technologies, materials, skills, and equipment—needed to make bombs by any of the twenty or so known methods would no longer be items of commerce. They wouldn't be impossible to get, but they'd be a lot harder to get, more conspicuous to try to get, and more politically costly for both the recipient and the supplier to be caught trying to get, because for the first time, the reason for wanting them would be unambiguously military. You could no longer claim a peaceful electricity-making venture. It would be clear that you were really out to make bombs. The burden would be on you to show that that's not what you had in mind—to do something so economically irrational.

Interestingly, there is a parallel argument, which hasn't been fully fleshed out yet, for certain chemical weapons. In particular, adopting organic agriculture, which tends to work better and cost less and be better for health and nutrition, and can at least equally well feed the world, means that you don't have organophosphate pesticide plants, which means that you just removed the main "cover story" for nerve gas plants. And there's even a weaker, but not trivial, form of the argument: if you're not using transgenic crops, which you shouldn't be if you understand biology and economics, that will remove an innocent-looking cover for making genetically modified pathogens.

Reducing Our Vulnerability

Getting back to the roots of conflict in resource rivalries: The broader case I'm making is that resource conflicts are unnecessary and uneconomic—a problem we don't need to have, and it's cheaper not to. For example, 13 percent of US oil now comes from the Persian Gulf, which is clearly risky. Proposed domestic substitutes, such as drilling in the Arctic National Wildlife Refuge, are at least as risky, and probably more so, because the Trans-Alaska Pipeline is about the fattest energy-related terrorist target there is. And therefore, in promoting expanded drilling in Alaska, the Department of Energy has been undercutting the Department of Defense's mission.

Both these kinds of vulnerability, both oil imports and vulnerable domestic infrastructure, are unnecessary and a waste of money. To displace Persian Gulf imports would (at historic refinery yields of gasoline) only take a 2.7 miles-per-gallon increase in the light vehicle fleet. We used to do that every three years, when we were paying attention. Most, if not all, United States oil use could be profitably displaced within a few decades, with current technology. This can happen surprisingly quickly. For example, from 1979 to 1985, GDP increased 16 percent, oil use fell 15 percent, and Gulf imports fell 87 percent. We could do that again in spades. The Department of Defense itself owns many billions of dollars a year of oil-saving potential, as laid out recently through a Defense Science Board on which I served. Everything you could do to achieve that also improves war-fighting capability.

I would call your attention particularly to the second of the October 2001 Shell planning scenarios, Exploring the Future: Energy Needs, Possibilities and Scenarios. It lays out a technological discontinuity that leapfrogs to a hydrogen economy led

by China. This causes global oil use to be stagnant until 2020 and then go down. I think that's perfectly plausible, and in fact, my colleagues and I are helping it to happen.

Conflict resolution is the next layer of defense if conflict avoidance or prevention fails. That's the realm of better international laws, norms, and institutions. Given space constraints, I won't elaborate on it here. There's a huge body of literature and practice on those things. Hal Harvey's and Mike Shuman's book *Security Without War* is especially good.

Non-Provocative Defense

Then, if the previous two layers of protection both fail, and conflict occurs, the last layer of defense, and a very powerful one, is "non-provocative defense," which reliably defeats aggression, but without threatening others. The concept was developed in Denmark and Holland, by the children of World War II resistance leaders, who wanted to apply the lessons from their parents' experience defending their homelands against a powerful invader.

To date, Sweden has executed the most sophisticated design of military forces for non-provocative defense. Its coastal guns cannot be elevated to fire beyond Swedish coastal waters. It has a capable and effective air force, but with short-range aircraft that can't get very far beyond Sweden. The radio frequencies used by the Swedish military are deliberately incompatible with both NATO and the Warsaw Pact, so Sweden will stay neutral.

> *US policy must . . . 'be directed not against any country or doctrine, but against hunger, poverty, desperation, and chaos.'*

In every way, by technical and institutional design, they've sought to make Sweden a country you don't want to attack, but one that is clearly in a defensive posture. This approach can ultimately create a stable mutual defensive superiority—each side's defense is stronger than the other side's offense. Each has, by design, at most a limited capacity to export offense.

The basic point of non-provocative defense is to structure and deploy your forces so your adversaries must consider them

mainly defensive. That is, you minimize your capability for preemptive, deep strikes, or strategic mobility, and you maximize homeland defense. This means four technical attributes: low vulnerability, low concentration of value, short range, and dependence on local support.

Non-provocative defense means layered deployment in non-provocative postures. That's a theory that was well developed, much criticized, and ably defended in Europe in the 1980s. It had to be, because the towns there are only a few kilotons apart. It depends on forces that are at least as robust as the attacker's forces, but with a decentralized architecture that increases their resilience. It doesn't exclude cross-border counterattack, but that would be limited in scope and range. The defensive superiority should reduce the risk and the attraction of adversaries building and using offensive arms. Of course, non-provocative defense doesn't stop terrorism, any more than National Missile Defense would. But the resilient design helps to disincentivize terrorism, by reducing its rewards, just as the full spectrum of nonmilitary engagement undercuts terrorism's ideological and political base.

Avoid the World Cop Role

There seems, however, to be a worrisome contradiction in current strategic doctrine. To combat current threats, the US undoubtedly needs light, agile, deployable, sustainable forces. But those forces don't fit the definition of non-provocative; indeed, their global reach makes them look like just the opposite. In our short-term need, therefore, lie the seeds of long-term danger. We're shifting toward a "global cop" role—and not so much the neighborhood-policing cop who's on the street befriending everyone and heading off trouble, but the SWAT team that forays out of its fortress only to smite perpetrators. Such force structures and deployments will encourage us to act in ways that use those forces. Worse, they are likely to induce in others the attitudes and behaviors that elicit precisely the asymmetric threats to which the US is most vulnerable.

Since what's viewed by others as provocative depends on observed military facts, not on declared political intentions, there is no obvious solution to this paradox. The nearest I can see is to strive mightily to prevent conflict, merit trust, and try to make the global-cop role temporary and brief by making the world safer.

It's a lot better to prevent conflict from scratch than to combat a broadly based terrorist movement. There are some strong stars we can steer by. Our interests in the Third World would be much better advanced by democratization, anti-corruption, sustainable development, resource efficiency, fair trade, demand, side drug policies, pluralism, tolerance, and humility, than by most of what we're doing now. Third World security would be better advanced by those elements plus transparency and collective tripolar security arrangements—possibly even including an idea some people have had, of some countries' giving up their armed forces and buying a credible kind of insurance from, say, the UN, paying fees for sharing in protective forces. And of course, the non-provocative new triad approach that I outlined can enhance everyone's security, but never at the expense of anyone else's security.

Rebuilding Credibility

To start rebuilding America's lately tarnished credibility as a partner in that sort of world, we're going to need renewed US leadership in multilateral tasks, whether it's the Non-Proliferation Treaty, plutonium reduction, Chemical and Biological Warfare treaties and enforcement, climate protection, or anti-landmine efforts. It's a very long list, and right now our government is on the wrong side of every one of those issues.

And, of course, there's America's deepest potential strength: the primacy of underlying moral values and civics, which is much referred to rhetorically, but less honored in practice. This will require us to transform more than the military. Military transformation is only part of the challenge to American idealism and ingenuity to building real security. The foundation, which is a very sound notion from about 1787, is the shared and lived belief that security rests on economic justice, political freedom, respect for laws, and a common defense. To make that work, we're going to have to bridge the widening gulf in our society between its civil and military elements. We'll also need to address the problem that military hardware and service vendors in the private sector have an unlimited self-reinforcing feedback loop where they co-produce weapons and fear, and there is no equilibration—no negative feedback to limit the self-reinforcing cycle of supply and demand.

Until now, the weapons vendors have had a radical monopoly, as [radical social theorist] Ivan Illich describes it, on

providing "security services." If the only way we can imagine to get security is by buying more weapons, then the demand for weapons appears to be inelastic, especially if reinforced by the sometimes-corrupt political process of buying them. Instead, if we have other ways of providing security, of which weapons are just one, and must compete with other modalities, fairly and at honest prices, then we will gain much cheaper ways to provide the security services we want.

In the Cold War, security was viewed as a predominantly military matter. Appended and subordinated to military security were economic, energy, and resource security (consisting, for example, of our Naval fleets in and around the Persian Gulf). Environmental security wasn't even on the agenda. In fact, it was officially viewed as harmful to security and prosperity. But in the post–Cold War view, we need to add back the missing links between these four elements, and to turn the wasted resources into prosperity and peace. You can imagine these four elements as vertices of a tetrahedron, an immensely strong structure, especially if it surrounds a kernel of justice, whose presence, as Dr. King said, is peace.

Organizations to Contact

The editors have compiled the following list of organizations concerned with the issues debated in this book. The descriptions are derived from materials provided by the organizations. All have publications or information available for interested readers. The list was compiled on the date of publication of the present volume; the information provided here may change. Be aware that many organizations take several weeks or longer to respond to inquiries, so allow as much time as possible.

Cato Institute
1000 Massachusetts Ave. NW, Washington, DC 20001-5403
(202) 842-0200 • fax: (202) 842-3490
e-mail: jblock@cato.org • Web site: www.cato.org/index.html

The Cato Institute is a nonprofit libertarian public policy research foundation headquartered in Washington, D.C. The institute seeks to broaden the parameters of public policy debate to allow consideration of the traditional American principles of limited government, individual liberty, free markets, and peace. The institute researches issues in the media and provides commentary for magazine, newspaper, and news show editorials.

Center for American Progress
805 Fifteenth St. NW, Suite 400, Washington, DC 20005
(202) 682-1611
e-mail: kcooper@amprog.org
Web site: www.centerforamericanprogress.org

The Center for American Progress is a research and educational institute dedicated to promoting progressive viewpoints on issues such as media bias, national security, the economy, and the environment. Its daily publication "Progress Report," available by e-mail, analyzes the media and questions viewpoints expressed in the news that are perceived to be biased toward conservative policies.

Center for Defense Information (CDI)
1779 Massachusetts Ave. NW, Washington, DC 20036
(202) 332-0600 • fax: (202) 462-4559
e-mail: info@cdi.org • Web site: www.cdi.org

Founded in 1972 by recently retired senior U.S. military officers, the Center for Defense Information is a progressive organization that believes national security can be made stronger through international cooperation, reduced reliance on unilateral military power, reduced reliance on nuclear weapons, transforming the military establishment, and oversight of defense programs. The center contributes alternative views on security through its bimonthly magazine *CDI Defense Monitor*.

Center for Immigration Studies
1522 K St. NW, Suite 820, Washington, DC 20005-1202
(202) 466-8185 • fax: (202) 466-8076
e-mail: center@cis.org • Web site: www.cis.org

The Center for Immigration Studies is a nonprofit research organization, founded in 1985, devoted exclusively to research and policy analysis of the economic, social, demographic, fiscal, and other impacts of immigration on the United States. The center has a pro-immigrant, low-immigration vision that seeks fewer immigrants but a warmer welcome for those admitted. The organization publishes *Backgrounders*, a monthly magazine about immigration issues.

Centre for Research on Globalisation (CRG)
RR #2, Shanty Bay, ON LOL-2LO Canada
(888) 713-8500 (United States and Canada)
e-mail: editor@globalresearch.ca • Web site: www.globalresearch.ca

The Centre for Research on Globalisation is a Canadian-based group of progressive writers, scholars, and activists committed to curbing the tide of globalization. The CRG Web site and the CRG quarterly magazine *Global Watch* publish news articles, commentary, background research, and analysis on a broad range of issues, focusing on the interrelationship between social, economic, strategic, geopolitical, and environmental processes.

Conservative Communications Center (CCC)
325 S. Patrick St., Alexandria, VA 22314
(703) 683-9733 • fax: (703) 683-9736
e-mail: shogenson@cnsnews.com • Web site: www.therightvoice.org

The mission of the CCC is to provide the conservative movement with the communications skills and vehicles to deliver their ideas to the American people. The group's Applied Public Relations Schools offer communications professionals training in advances and current trends in communications. The organization's Web site offers links to the conservative viewpoint on current affairs.

Council on Foreign Relations
1779 Massachusetts Ave. NW, Washington, DC 20036
(202) 518-3400 • fax: (202) 986-2984
e-mail: communications@cfr.org • Web site: www.cfr.org

Founded in 1921, the Council on Foreign Relations is an independent national organization of scholars dedicated to producing and disseminating foreign policy analysis for policy makers, journalists, corporate clients, students, and interested citizens in the United States and other countries. The council publishes *Foreign Affairs*, the preeminent journal covering international affairs and U.S. foreign policy.

Federal Emergency Management Agency (FEMA)
500 C St. SW, Washington, DC 20472
(202) 566-1600
e-mail: FEMAopa@dhs.gov • Web site: www.fema.gov

The Federal Emergency Management Agency is a formerly independent government agency that became part of the new Department of Homeland Security in March 2003. FEMA is tasked with responding to, planning for, recovering from, and mitigating disasters.

The Heritage Foundation
214 Massachusetts Ave. NE, Washington, DC 20002
(800) 544-4843 • fax: (202) 544-2260
e-mail: pubs@heritage.org • Web site: www.heritage.org

Founded in 1973, the Heritage Foundation is a research and educational think tank whose mission is to formulate and promote conservative public policies based on the principles of free enterprise, limited government, individual freedom, traditional American values, and a strong national defense.

International Action Center (IAC)
39 W. Fourteenth St., #206, New York, NY 10011
(212) 633-6646 • fax: (212) 633-2889
e-mail: iacenter@action-mail.org • Web site: www.iacenter.org

Founded in 1992 by former U.S. attorney general Ramsey Clark, the International Action Center supports policies that aim to end war, racism, unemployment, and sexism. The center has led campaigns against the Pentagon wars and sanctions against Iraq, Cuba, and Yugoslavia. Through the People's Video Network the center produces and distributes educational videos on many topics, including the movement to abolish the death penalty.

Nuclear Threat Initiative (NTI)
1747 Pennsylvania Ave. NW, Seventh Floor, Washington DC 20006
(202) 296-4810 • fax: (202) 296-4811
e-mail: contact@nti.org • Web site: www.nti.org

The Nuclear Threat Initiative was formed in 2000 by CNN founder Ted Turner and former senator Sam Nunn out of concern that the threat of nuclear weapons had taken on less importance after the end of the Cold War. NTI's mission is to strengthen global security by reducing the risk of use and preventing the spread of nuclear, biological, and chemical weapons.

Terrorism Research Center (TRC)
(877) 635-0816
e-mail: TRC@terrorism.com • Web site: www.terrorism.com

Founded in 1996 in northern Virginia, the Terrorism Research Center is an independent institute dedicated to the research of terrorism, information warfare and security, critical infrastructure protection, and other issues of low-intensity political violence.

TomPaine.com
PO Box 53303, Washington, DC 20009
e-mail: editor@tompaine.com • Web site: www.tompaine.com

TomPaine.com is a public-interest journal inspired by the eighteenth-century patriot Thomas Paine, author of *Common Sense* and *The Rights of Man*. TomPaine.com seeks to enrich the national debate on contro-

versial public issues by featuring ideas, opinions, and analyses possibly overlooked by the mainstream media.

U.S. Department of Homeland Security (DHS)
Washington, DC 20528
e-mail: See www.dhs.gov/dhspublic/contactus
Web site: www.dhs.gov

The Department of Homeland Security was created by the federal government in 2002 to secure the homeland from terrorist attacks. The mission of the DHS is to identify and understand threats, assess vulnerabilities, determine potential impacts, and disseminate timely information to security personnel and the American public. The DHS also is charged with leading national, state, local, and private-sector efforts to restore services and rebuild communities after acts of terrorism, natural disasters, or other emergencies.

Bibliography

Books

Michael Barletta, ed. *After 9/11: Preventing Mass-Destruction Terrorism and Weapons Proliferation.* Monterey, CA: Monterey Institute of International Studies, Center for Nonproliferation Studies, 2002.

Michael E. Brown, ed. *Grave New World: Security Challenges in the 21st Century.* Washington, DC: Georgetown University Press, 2003.

Glenn C. Buchan *Future Roles of U.S. Nuclear Forces: Implications for U.S. Strategy.* Santa Monica, CA: Rand Project Air Force, 2003.

Robert J. Bunker, ed. *Non-State Threats and Future Wars.* Portland, OR: F. Cass, 2003.

Ashton B. Carter and John P. White, eds. *Keeping the Edge: Managing Defense for the Future.* Cambridge, MA: MIT Press, 2001.

Raymond J. Decker *Combating Terrorism: Observations on National Strategies Related to Terrorism.* Washington, DC: U.S. General Accounting Office, 2003.

Sidney D. Drell *The Gravest Danger: Nuclear Weapons.* Stanford, CA: Hoover Institution, 2003.

Johan Eriksson, ed. *Threat Politics: New Perspectives on Security, Risk, and Crisis Management.* Burlington, VT: Ashgate, 2001.

Richard C. Leone and Greg Anrig Jr. *The War on Our Freedoms: Civil Liberties in an Age of Terrorism.* New York: BBS PublicAffairs, 2003.

Barry S. Levy and Victor W. Sidel, eds. *Terrorism and Public Health: A Balanced Approach to Strengthening Systems and Protecting People.* New York: Oxford University Press, 2003.

James M. Lindsay and Michael E. O'Hanlon *Defending America: The Case for Limited National Missile Defense.* Washington, DC: Brookings Institution, 2001.

Mahmood Mamdani *Good Muslim, Bad Muslim: America, the Cold War, and the Roots of Terror.* New York: Pantheon, 2004.

Michael Moore *Dude, Where's My Country?* Waterville, ME: Thorndike, 2004.

William R. Schilling *Nontraditional Warfare: Twenty-First-Century Threats and Responses.* Washington, DC: Brassey's, 2002.

Barry R. Schneider and Jim A. Davis *The Gathering Biological Warfare Storm.* Westport, CT: Praeger, 2004.

117

Martin Schram	*Avoiding Armageddon: Our Future, Our Choice: Companion to the PBS Series from Ted Turner Documentaries.* New York: Basic Books, 2003.
Norris Smith and Lynn M. Messina	*Homeland Security.* NY: H.W. Wilson, 2004.
Jessica Stern	*Terror in the Name of God: Why Religious Militants Kill.* New York: Ecco, 2003.
William C. Triplett	*Rogue State: How a Nuclear North Korea Threatens America.* Washington, DC: Regnery, 2004.
Dan Verton	*Black Ice: The Invisible Threat of Cyber-Terrorism.* New York: McGraw-Hill/Osborn, 2003.
Cynthia Ann Watson	*U.S. National Security: A Reference Handbook.* Santa Barbara: ABC-CLIO, 2002.

Periodicals

Edward Alden	"Companies Must Give U.S. Notice of Food Imports," *Financial Times*, October 10, 2003.
Elizabeth G. Book	"Nuke Explosion Would Make 'Nasty Cleanup,'" *National Defense*, June 2002.
Douglas Burton and Jessica Davis	"Identity Theft Has Become a New Threat to National Security," *Insight on the News*, July 22, 2002.
Ashton Carter and Richard Lugar	"A New Era, a New Threat: The U.S. and Russia Should Form a Coalition to Stop Terrorists Obtaining Nuclear Weapons," *Financial Times*, May 23, 2002.
Michael Champness	"The Role of the U.S. Air Force in Fighting Terrorism at Home," *Aerospace Power Journal*, Spring 2002.
Guy Dinmore and Andrew Ward	"N. Korea Nuclear Freeze Rejected by U.S.," *Financial Times*, February 25, 2004.
Neil Ford	"U.S. Concern over 'Nuclear Threat': As Tension Rises over the Potential Nuclear Capabilities of Iraq and North Korea, U.S. Worries over Nuclear Developments in Iran Have Been Less Publicised," *Middle East*, April 2003.
Duncan Graham-Rowe	"Electricity Grids Left Wide Open to Hackers," *New Scientist*, August 30, 2003.
Christine Gray	"The U.S. National Security Strategy and the New 'Bush Doctrine' on Preemptive Self-Defense," *Chinese Journal of International Law*, Fall 2002.
Victoria Griffith	"Why It's Time to Worry About the Bomb: The September 11 Attacks Have Raised the Spectre of Nuclear Terrorism—and Questions over the U.S. Government's Response," *Financial Times*, November 24, 2001.

Peter J. Howe "U.S. Transportation Sector to Step Up Terrorism Watch," *America's Intelligence Wire*, March 23, 2004.

Jonathan Krim "Help Fix Cyber-Security or Else, U.S. Tells Industry; 'We Want to See Results,' Official Says at Summit," *Washington Post*, December 4, 2003.

Michael McCarthy "Attacks Heighten U.S. Concern About Threat of Bioterrorism," *Lancet*, September 29, 2001.

Douglas Pasternak "Assessing Threats," *U.S. News & World Report*, April 28, 2003.

Michael Reinemer "Blue-Ribbon Panel Says Nation Is 'Dangerously Unprepared,'" *Nation's Cities Weekly*, November 11, 2002.

Andrew Roberts "Bring Back 007," *Spectator*, October 6, 2001.

Gwyneth K. Shaw "Fear Factor of Dirty Bomb Would Overshadow the Blast, Experts Say," Knight Ridder/Tribune News Service, June 10, 2002.

Porter Stansberry "Smallpox: Most Lethal Biological Threat," *Officer*, December 2001.

Jim Wallis "Crossing the Nuclear Threshhold: Just Exactly How Are Nuclear Weapons Supposed to Help Us Wipe Out Terrorism?" *Sojourners*, May/June 2002.

Christopher Ytuarte "Chemical Reaction: In These Times of Heightened Security, Safely Transporting Chemicals Is of Paramount Importance to Railcar Designers and Railroads," *Railway Age*, December 2001.

Peter D. Zimmerman "The 'Dirty Bomb' Scenario," *Atlantic Monthly*, April 2004.

John C. Zink "Revealing the Secrets of the Dirty Bomb," *Power Engineering*, March 2003.

Internet Sources

William J. Bicknell and Kenneth D. Bloem "Smallpox and Bioterrorism: Why the Plan to Protect the Nation Is Stalled and What to Do," CATO Institute, September 5, 2003. www.cato.org/pubs/briefs/bp-085es.html.

Michel Chossudovsky "Fabricating an Enemy," Global Research, January 28, 2003. www.globalresearch.ca.

Federal Emergency Management Agency "Are You Ready? A Guide to Citizen Preparedness," May 4, 2004. www.fema.gov/areyouready.

Joshua Green "Weapons of Mass Confusion: There's Anthrax in the Subway. Who You Gonna Call?" Institute for America's Future, September 20, 2001. www.tompaine.com/scontent/4546.html.

Stephen Murdoch "Preemptive War: Is It Legal?" DCBar, January 2003. www.dcbar.org/for_lawyers/washington_lawyer/january_2003/war.cfm.

Nuclear Control Institute — "Nuclear Terrorism: How to Prevent It," September 2002. www.nci.org/nuketerror.htm.

James A. Phillips — "National Security Isn't Just About Terrorism," Heritage Foundation, April 9, 2004. www.heritage.org/Research/NationalSecurity/wm472.cfm.

William Pitt — "Bush, Enron, and Bin Laden: Connections Within Connections," Loompanics, Spring 2002. www.loompanics.com/cgi-local/SoftCart.exe/Articles/BushEnronandBinLaden.html?E+scstore.

Mark M. Pollitt — "Cyberterrorism—Fact or Fancy?" Georgtown University Department of Computer Science. www.cosc.georgetown.edu/~denning/infosec/pollitt.html.

Project on Government Oversight — "Nuclear Power Plant Security: Voices from Inside the Fences," September 12, 2002. www.pogo.org/p/environment/eo-020901-nukepower.html.

Robert Scheer — "Bush's Faustian Deal with the Taliban," Robertscheer.com, May 22, 2001. www.rememberjohn.com/faustian.html.

R. Jeffrey Smith — "Nuclear Security Decisions Are Shrouded in Secrecy: Agency Withholds Unclassified Information," Washingtonpost.com, March 29, 2004. www.washingtonpost.com/wp-dyn/articles/A31788-2004Mar28.html.

Terrorism Research Center — "Terrorism: How Vulnerable Is the United States?" May 1995. www.terrorism.com/modules.php?op=modload&name=News&file=article&sid=5665&mode=thread&order=0&thold=0.

United States 107th Congress — "Dirty Bombs and Basement Nukes: The Terrorist Nuclear Threat: Hearing Before the Committee on Foreign Relations, United States Senate," U.S. Government Printing Office, March 6, 2002. http://frwebgate.access.gpo.gov/cgi-bin/getdoc.cgi?dbname=107_senate_hearings&docid=f:80848.wais.

United States 108th Congress — "Emerging Threats: Assessing Public Safety and Security Measures at Nuclear Power Facilities: Subcommittee on National Security, Emerging Threats, and International Relations, House Of Representatives," U.S. Government Printing Office, March 10, 2003. http://frwebgate.access.gpo.gov/cgi-bin/getdoc.cgi?dbname=108_house_hearings&docid=f:89075.wais.

Index

Contents

LIBRARY OF CONGRESS CATALOGING-IN-PUBLICATION DATA
What are the most serious threats to national security? / Stuart A. Kallen, book editor.
p. cm. — (At issue)
Includes bibliographical references and index.
ISBN 0-7377-2753-5 (lib. bdg. : alk. paper) —
ISBN 0-7377-2754-3 (pbk. : alk. paper)
1. National security—United States. 2. United States—Defenses. I. Kallen, Stuart A., 1955– . II. At issue (San Diego, Calif.)
UA23.W38 2005
355'.033'033073—dc22   2004059679

Printed in the United States of America

What Are the Most Serious Threats to National Security?

Stuart A. Kallen, *Book Editor*

Bruce Glassman, *Vice President*
Bonnie Szumski, *Publisher*
Helen Cothran, *Managing Editor*

GREENHAVEN PRESS

An imprint of Thomson Gale, a part of The Thomson Corporation

Detroit • New York • San Francisco • San Diego • New Haven, Conn.
Waterville, Maine • London • Munich

Other books in the At Issue series:

What Are the Most Serious Threats to National Security?

CONTENTS

FOREWORD

ANN RICHARDS
Former Governor of Texas

HERE IS WHAT you need to know about Louise Raggio:

When there was a fight for women's rights, she was there first. When everyone else had given up and run home to Mama, she was still there. And God help anyone—male or female—who refused to see the strength of her reasoning.

Saying that Louise is a pioneer and a trailblazer does not begin to do her justice. Louise practiced law before women served on juries in Texas. As a full partner with her husband in their marriage and their law firm, Louise has been a role model for young women. As an activist she has changed our lives. Because of Louise's unflagging devotion to passing the Marital Property Act of 1967, Texas women have the right to own property, borrow money, and conduct their financial affairs without dragging their husbands down to the bank or the courthouse to vouch for them.

Louise has played a role in everything good that has happened to Texas women for the last fifty years.

Louise's leadership has extended far beyond the Texas borders. In the 1970s, she led a task force that created the first completed Family Code in the world. This code has been studied and used as a pattern in other states. She has written and spoken nationally on legal and feminist issues.

For many years Louise has been named on multiple lists as one of the best family lawyers in America—long before it was acceptable for women to be professional leaders. Born a poor kid of immigrant parents on a small Texas cotton farm, Louise has made lemonade out of the lemons life handed her. Her clients credit her with giving them hope and strength while walking with them through their darkest days of separation and divorce. Her devotion to the welfare and best interests of the children involved is legend in Texas.

Louise has received national lifetime awards from the American Bar Association, National Association of Women Lawyers, and National Women's Business Owners Organization, as well as many state and local awards.

What is truly important about Louise is that she was always there for other women. At a time when there were far too many victims of the "Queen Bee Syndrome," Louise was a stalwart— always eager to encourage, to provoke, to convince you that you really could do it.

As a young mother living in Dallas in the 1950s, I thought of Louise as a beacon in a storm. Dallas was not notably hospitable to women or minorities in positions of influence back then, but Louise never let that slow her down.

Over the years, Louise has inspired many women to be more and do more. I count myself among those women.

And I count myself among those who are proud to share her friendship.

I know her book will give you a sense of where we've been and I hope it inspires you to reach for your highest potential in the new century.

TEXAS TORNADO

How I Got Here

PRIOR TO 1967, married women in Texas existed under the most restrictive laws in the country. It is almost impossible to remember how bad they were. By the time I was elected chairman of the Family Law Section, State Bar of Texas, I knew that things were bad, but I still hadn't realized how bad. (Later on in these pages I'll detail just exactly *how* bad.) Every time I looked, I found additional legal roadblocks. Texas is unique from any other state in the Union in that it has been ruled by six separate entities—France, Spain, Mexico, the Republic of Texas, the United States, the Confederate States of America, and again the United States. It is also unique because once, for a few years, it was an independent country before it joined the Union. From each of these it inherited bits and pieces, making it a hodgepodge of legalities. Sometimes, it seemed to me, we had snipped the worst possible laws from each of our former "parents" and tacked them onto our books.

Things were so bad that the marriage ceremony might well have said, "From this day forward as long as you are married, only one legal entity exists in this family and that one is the male." Women could not buy or sell their own property, could not sign contracts, could not make decisions for their own children, could not control their own paychecks, or open their own bank accounts except with the permission of their husbands. When she entered into marriage, a woman automatically consigned every legal decision to her husband.

Even property she had inherited from her own family became his to do with as he pleased.

Legally, married women were equated with children, prisoners, and the insane. None of the four groups could sign a legally binding contract of any kind. I was a lawyer who was, in fact, practicing law without the legal right to do so, and I was not alone. Most women, in good marital relationships, behaved as if they were entitled to make legal decisions and got by with it. But, woe unto the individual whose deeds were questioned.

State legislators were not evil men, just unenlighened individuals. In their private stag parties men joked about keeping the little woman barefoot and pregnant. Smart legislators knew that the laws were bad and should be changed, but were not eager to tamper with a system that would make everybody have to learn an entirely new way of operating. Some legislators, especially from the rural areas, did not understand why women should think there was any problem. They were, after all, only protecting the "little woman," their own private property.

In Texas, as a result of the collision of Spanish law with English common law, we were in the legal dark ages. Our land laws, attached while Texas belonged to Spain, include abstracts that go back to the Spanish king. Spain was occupied by the Moors before Columbus ever came to America, and Spanish law, with a Moorish influence, prevailed when Anglos first came to settle Texas. They brought with them English common law from the Eastern seaboard and added their own brand of "frontier justice." What a mess! When these laws—Spanish with Moorish overtones and English common law—were amalgamated, property rights for married women in Texas were not even considered. It was a man's world. Men made the laws and enacted them for men and to "protect" their womenfolk.

It had been a long, difficult journey, but now I had arrived at a position from which I could effect change that would better the lives of women—and men, too, in Texas. The "ripple effect" was sure to improve lives outside of my home state, as well. I have spent the better part of my life correcting some of the flaws, limitations, and omissions that govern the treatment of family members.

It hasn't been easy. And I did not do it all by myself. Some of the best legal minds in the country supported the cause. But there have also been vocal and vociferous opponents. Many men and some women have opposed revision every step of the way. To these I was a mutineer. How did this come to be so?

Well, I guess one way of looking at this question is to answer it by saying I'm good at coping with seemingly insurmountable problems. I often think that almost everything I've ever done has been in response to a disaster.

If I had been the surviving child of my parents' early marriage instead of the third pregnancy in their more mature years after Mother had lost two babies, I wouldn't have had her undivided attention with its stress on education.

If I had been pretty and popular, as I so longed to be, rather than a fat, ugly girl, I would have frittered my time away rather than devote it to academic pursuits.

If I had not married a charismatic man who was often difficult, I would not have mastered negotiation and diplomacy.

If I had not suffered from financial crises and emotional depression, I would not have escaped by entering law school.

If I had not been forced to consider how to support the family when my husband was accused of being a Communist and lost his job, I probably would not have completed law school.

If I had not had a traumatic pregnancy and struggled about a therapeutic abortion, I might not have become a dedicated feminist.

If the male establishment had welcomed me into its fold during my early career, I might never have been named one of the country's outstanding family lawyers.

I am a determined—some would say stubborn—person, so these obstacles and countless others challenged my determination to make it safe for women to live and work in Texas.

I practiced law in Texas before I could legally do so.

I didn't start out as a rebel. As a child I wanted nothing so much as to please, my parents—especially my mother—my teachers, my extended family, and my friends. As a young woman, I wanted to be happily married and the mother of two perfect children, a boy and a girl.

Now, in the eighth decade of my life, I am known by my friends as "mentor" and "sage," and by my enemies, in one of their kinder terms, as "one tough broad." I am, in the most basic of terms, a survivor. Who I am, what I've done, where I've been, and why I have felt compelled to keep opening doors is a matter of record, both public and private.

I have also accumulated an embarrassment of accolades and so many awards that the walls of my office will no longer hold them. In my reflective moments, I wonder if I would have done anything special if the road had been smooth.

Most amazing of all to me is that people now seem to want to hear about my journey when, for most of my life, many have wanted nothing so much as to shut me up.

Of one thing I'm certain: If I—a poor, unattractive, unpopular girl from the mud farms of Central Texas—the offspring of immigrants, could make it, anybody can.

And I'm not finished yet.

1

Down on the Farm

I DIDN'T START OUT very well. Tiny, scrawny and feisty, I entered the word on June 15, 1919, at the home of my maternal grand-mother at 103 Rose Street in Austin where Mother had gone for my birth from her farm home seventeen miles away, in the farming com-munity between Elgin and Manor in Central Texas. Fittingly enough, I made my debut about noon on a Sunday so that my father could be present for the great occasion. If it had been any other day of the week, he probably would have been busy on the farm and not around.

Weighing in at only a fraction more than four pounds, I was the third baby of my parents' eleven-year marriage. Mother had lost a daughter in 1909, the year after she married, and had miscarried a second baby. Mother, my grandmother, Bengta Bodelson Lindgren, and Mother's sister, my Aunt Hulda, were all bent on my survival, but weeks went by before my parents considered it safe to take me home to the big tan-colored house in cotton country.

Along with the bank, my parents owned the farm, one hundred acres of stubborn black land that was attached to another hundred acres owned by my paternal grandparents and farmed as a unit. Dad had bought the farm two years before I was born for $18,000. He did not make the final payment until twenty-three years later, two years after I married.

I grew up lying awake in a cold sweat many nights sharing my parents' concern that a series of failed crops would result in fore-closure on the farm and we would have no place to go. The rich soil would produce almost anything when weather conditions were right, but ideal weather in the heart of Texas seldom happened. Sometimes—almost every July and August, it seemed to me—there would be no rain, and the land turned into black concrete with cav-ernous cracks. When I was a child, I was certain that I could drop a stick into one of those chasms and it would fall straight through to China. Or, sometimes, the rains started and wouldn't stop, and the black land turned into a gummy wax that drowned tender seeds and adhered relentlessly to shoes or boots, making the care of chickens and livestock at the distant barn a constant chore. During the rainy season, no cars could traverse the ruts, and wagon wheels collected globs of black tarlike mud that slowed transportation to a stand-still. The only way off the farm during those rains was by horse-back or by foot. When we had to have supplies and couldn't get out any other way, Daddy would wade across the farm to a distant rail-road and walk the rails to the gravel road and into town.

Our house was one of the finest in the countryside, a mile removed from our nearest neighbor. Mother designed it, and Daddy, with the help of his father and brothers, built it. Mother had drawn the plans for her dream house and it boasted amenities that few farm houses had. Made of wood, its rooms were large and spacious, its ceilings lofty, and its windows almost to the floor. Its heart was a vast sun room with all-around windows opening onto the kitchen, a separate dining room, and the parlor. My bedroom was big and served as my sanctuary. There was a pantry—and closets at a time when farm families hung their clothes on nails hammered into the corner of the bedroom, or at best, behind cloth curtains. There was a front porch that lent grace to the house and two back porches, one of which was converted into a playhouse for me. The house also had a bathroom; when I was ten, Dad put in a bathtub. We had no running hot water, however, so we heated water on the stove and poured it into the tub for bathing. An outhouse served as our toilet.

In the winter, Mother prepared our meals on a wood-burning stove in the kitchen. She also had a kerosene stove that she used during the hot summer months. Ours was the only house in that part of the country with two stoves, and there's no doubt Mother was known for "putting on airs." Like all other farm families, we used kerosene lamps for lighting. Mother saved enough money to buy an Aladdin lamp, which had a meshlike mantle that was so fragile the least little knock would turn it into ashes.

The house was warmed in the winter with wood-burning stoves and cooled in the summertime by natural breezes. No breeze, no cooling. There was no electricity, hence no refrigeration and no way to preserve food except to use it up quickly, can it, or in the case of pork, smoke the meat over extremely low, smoldering heat.

I had a love-hate relationship with the farm. I loved to lie outside in the early warm evenings and count the stars as they appeared in the sky. I loved the soft spring mornings when the calves were new and the piglets squealed their way through a meal at the sow's belly. I hated it when harvest time came and those same animals were slaughtered for food—even when I awoke to the aroma of bacon or ham or sausage coming from the kitchen and relished the taste of those hearty farm breakfasts.

I hated hog-killing, which was one of the busiest days of the year. On the first very cold day of late fall or early winter the adults were up before dawn. Dad and whatever other male relatives were handy slaughtered the hog, which had been especially fed to fatten him up. The carcass was hoisted on pulleys for the blood to drain, then laid out on a large flat surface where boiling waster loosened the hair so that it could be scraped away. We wasted nothing; only the gall bladder, spleen, lungs, and pancreas were tossed to the dogs. The rest became food for us.

The blood became blood sausage, a rare Swedish delicacy made with cornmeal, dried apples, and prunes. The fat was tossed into a huge black wash pot and a roaring fire built under it to render lard, which was then strained and stored in clean tin buckets. This was our supply of fat for the entire year. We never bought oils of any kind. The head of the pig was boiled and made into a Swedish recipe called head cheese, which was sliced and kept in the coolest spot because it was perishable. Hams and shoulders were put into salt brine for a few days and then smoked very slowly in the smokehouse. It was imperative to keep the fire under the meat very low and at an even temperature. Too much heat cooked the meat and too little allowed it to spoil. There was great art to smoking meat, and my father had mastered it to perfection.

All other bits and pieces of the meat were ground into sausage, which we seasoned only with salt and pepper because Daddy did not like sage, hot pepper, or any kind of exotic seasoning. The sausage would then be stuffed into the intestines, which had been thoroughly cleaned inside and out, leaving a thin clear tube similar to today's Saran wrap. We would have yards and yards of sausage, which we cut into eighteen-inch lengths, then tied together and hung over an old broomstick or a pole and smoked in the same manner we'd used for the bacons and hams. These sausages would last all year from one hog-killing time to the next, but along about August they'd be pretty tough and dry.

Beef was different. It spoiled more quickly than pork and was much more difficult to preserve. Usually when we butchered a calf, it would be divided among all the relatives and friends. When one of them did the butchering, we'd share in the resulting bounty. When we could not eat all of the beef in a short time, Mother ground it into meatballs and stored these in a jar covered with hot grease. That way, we could preserve it for several months. Fish had to be eaten almost immediately after it was caught. Whoever brought home a "catch" from the river divided it at once among relatives and neighbors or threw an outdoor fish fry and invited everybody in the surrounding area to a feast.

Chicken and eggs were our staple protein supply. We had eggs the year round, though the supply was scarce in the spring when the hens were molting and in the winter when the hens just stopped laying. Before this happened, Mother rubbed olive oil into a few dozen choice eggs and stored them in the coolest place so that she would have eggs for Christmas baking. We ate an abundance of chicken—fried, made into dumplings, baked, stewed, and roasted—during the late spring and summer. Later in the year, when we'd used up our supply of the year's hatched broods, something else had to suffice because we didn't dare eat the layers lest we wind up with no fresh protein at all. We made our own cheese and churned our butter from the rich cream skimmed from the milk.

Mother was a fabulous cook and a fantastic manager. Our menus might have been monotonous, but we were never hungry and there was always food to share with relatives and neighbors. We grew and preserved almost everything we ate. On the rare occasions when we went into town for supplies, we'd buy coffee, sugar, and flour that would last for up to six months.

Our day began with a hearty breakfast, which was usually hot oatmeal, eggs, and bacon, or ham or sausage and toast, a glass of milk, and coffee. My folks drank a lot of coffee, for breakfast, at midmorning, and in the middle of the afternoon. We'd have iced tea at the midday meal when there was ice—which was delivered to our house by the ice man, wrapped securely in burlap bags to help keep it from melting, and stored in an icebox. Dinner was served at midday and was always the biggest meal of the day. Supper was served for the evening meal and usually consisted of leftovers from the noon meal. Daddy loved homemade soup, and we had some kind of soup almost every day. Mother made it from whatever she had on hand—broth and scraps of chicken or beef, a variety of vegetables such as potatoes, onions, tomatoes, okra, peas, carrots, or beans—and thickened with rice or macaroni. Mother made our own bread—rolls and loaves with yeast—or hot biscuits. We almost always had tea cakes, cookies, gingerbread, pie, or cake on hand. She was the champion angel food cake baker of the entire community, and I spent many a Saturday slowly sifting flour and sugar by tablespoonsful into a bowl of beaten egg whites while she mixed angel food by hand until it looked like pure white satin. It took almost an hour to mix a cake properly. I still marvel that she could create such culinary art by baking it in a wood-burning stove. I could never match her ability even with a modern restaurant oven and its precise gauges.

I loved helping Mother sow the garden seeds, watching for the first tender sprouts and tasting the green beans and yellow corn and crook-necked squash that came from those vines and stalks. I hated canning season when we processed bushels of peas, beans, okra, tomatoes, squash, cabbage, and corn to fill countless cans and jars that would be our winter food supply. It seemed an endless chore— the snapping of beans, shelling of peas, washing greens in water after water after water until every grain of sand was gone, scraping ears of corn into mounds of starchy mass, scraping and cutting carrots into small pieces, blanching tomatoes to remove the skins and then dicing them into pieces, scalding beets and ridding them of the outside skins. It took what seemed to me endless time, but all of it was necessary and I learned to share Mother's pride in the array of jars and cans lined up on the shelves in our storage room. We canned every vegetable from the garden that we did not eat immediately after picking or pulling it. Potatoes we dug and stored for winter use in bins under the house, being careful to keep the bins suspended so that rats and other varmints could not help themselves. We tied the onions into bunches and stored them on rods in the smokehouse to dry.

In the bottom land, Daddy planted watermelons and cantaloupes. We always tried to have a watermelon ripe to enjoy on the Fourth of July, and cantaloupe from early spring until midsummer. We also raised fruit trees, everything the soil and climate would allow—pears, plums, peaches, figs, some small forms of apples and grapes. With different kinds of peach trees, the peach-producing season lasted from May until September and provided all kinds of delicious desserts. Mother either canned or made preserves and jellies from all of the fruit we did not eat while it was fresh. We had oranges only at Christmas and bananas seldom.

From my heritage—Mother's, Swedish, and Daddy's, German— we "inherited" foods, tastes, and smells that have remained with me and nurtured me throughout my life.

Our weeks were ordered almost as rigidly as our days. Monday was wash day, and the laundry was a major undertaking. Our house, like that of every other farm in the countryside, had a large black wash pot in the backyard. Early on Monday morning, Daddy would fill it with water, stack wood under and around the pot, and set the wood ablaze. While we ate breakfast the water came to a boil. Mother sorted the clothes into stacks—whites, towels and wash rags, coloreds, and work clothes. Men's white shirts, fine white linens, and underwear went into the pot first, along with shaved lye soap, and were boiled. After fifteen to thirty minutes, we dipped them out of the boiling water with a broomstick, held them over the pot until most of the sudsy water had dripped back into the pot, and then soused them in the first of several tubs of rinse water, the last of which contained bluing to make them as white as possible. In the first tub of rinse water, each piece was carefully examined for possible spots which were then hand rubbed on a rubbing board until they disappeared. While this was going on, the second pile of clothes—sheets and pillowcases and towels and wash rags—went into the boiling wash pot. This continued until each stack of laundry went through wash water and two or sometimes three rinses if needed to remove the soap suds. Pieces were wrung out by hand, placed in a clean basket, and very carefully stretched on a clothesline to discourage all wrinkles. Every woman in the country prided herself on the whiteness of her line of laundry, and if you saw dingy clothes hanging on somebody's clothesline, you knew the woman was not a good housekeeper!

On a windy day, the sheets would wrap around the clothesline and we'd have to fight to get them stretched tight and pinned with wooden pegs before they got away from us. If it started to rain, we'd dash out to remove the clothes before they got wet. On the coldest days, the clothes would freeze if we left them out, so we'd have to bring them into the house and dry them on makeshift lines around the kitchen. Monday night, whatever else we did, we sprinkled the clothes and wrapped them in clean towels to be ironed.

Tuesday was ironing day. Mother always had a gasoline iron which required air to be pumped into it. I've spent many an hour over an ironing board with a gasoline iron in hand and I'm still amazed, when I think of the amount of gasoline and kerosene we used, that we didn't burn the house down. In the winter, we also used flat irons which were heated on the cookstove. We'd put three or four at a time on the stove. When we first took them off, they were so hot they would scorch the fabric, but they would soon cool off and have to be replaced by a second iron. Irons had to be cleaned to remove any debris and sometimes rubbed over beeswax to keep them smooth. Shirts were starched and very difficult to iron. When

I'd get one almost finished, I'd often get a speck on it and have to toss it back into the laundry for next time. I hated ironing day.

We recycled before there was such a word! Part of my core understanding is that you "make do" or "do without." Nothing points this up so much as my attitude toward water. I cannot bear to see a drop wasted. On the farm, our water supply came from zinc cisterns that caught and stored rainwater from the roof of the house, and we conserved every drop. Our bath water was saved for the flowers and our laundry water to scrub floors and wash windows. Again, we were more fortunate than many of our neighbors because Daddy had dug a well at the back of our pasture, making our farm the only place within several miles with well water. When the cisterns ran low, Daddy would make a trip to the far pasture to haul water to the house for drinking and cooking. Once when a drought lasted for months, farmers lined up to fill barrels with our precious water for themselves and their livestock. They would wait in line for the well to refill before drawing up another bucket. Even then, after sharing all of the water supply available, many cows perished from thirst.

The "make do" philosophy spilled over into the clothes we wore. I was one of the neatest and best-dressed kids in my class, even though I did not have a "store bought" dress until I was grown. Mother took my aunts' outgrown or discarded clothes, laundered them, ripped them up, then pressed them and fashioned beautiful dresses and coats for me. Her grandfather, Jens Bodelson, had been a tailor in Sweden and supported himself with his trade after he came to the United States. He would take his tools from one house to another for a week at a time and make clothing for the affluent who could afford his services. Mother was his assistant, and grew up knowing how to sew the finest seam and turn out the most professional tailoring. Patterns were not available and we couldn't have afforded them if they had been. Mother did not need a pattern. She could look at a garment in a store window, outline it in her mind, and go home and make its duplicate for me. The smaller scraps went into quilts.

We spent money only on thread and needles—two to five cents a spool for thread, no more than a nickel for embroidery thread, a penny apiece for needles. We saved string, which we crocheted into scarves and doilies. Mother had a special box in which she stored "stuff," such as buttons, tiny scraps, bits of yarn, feathers, artificial flowers, anything that might be useful for one of her later creative projects, even the silver foil from chewing gum wrappers, which would become decorations for the Christmas tree. Sometimes when I was sick and had to stay in bed, I would be allowed to entertain myself by going through Mother's box of treasures.

My parents and their relatives did everything on the farm. Daddy was a wonderful carpenter, and his brother, Ernest, could repair anything that went wrong with the mechanical equipment. Together they kept the farm tools honed to perfection and the cars running at peak performance. Mother and Aunt Hulda were the family wallpapering team. In those days wallpaper had edges on both sides that had to be trimmed, and I remember, even before I started to school, using a pair of little blunt scissors and very carefully cutting the edges from the paper. My hands would be numb before I finished because the paper had to be trimmed in a perfectly straight line. Many years later I astounded the neighbors when I papered every room in the house Grier and I bought. I didn't think it was a big deal. I thought everybody grew up knowing how to hang wallpaper.

I also learned to cook and sew, mend, embroider, crochet, and tat. Those were things that every farm girl was expected to master. I started cooking when I was still so small I had to stand on a chair to help stir the batter. Again, years later when I moved to Washington, I couldn't believe that girls didn't know how to cook. I wondered how they had survived all that time without learning the basics of survival.

Mother and Aunt Hulda also were the family nurses, on call for every sickness in the entire community. From the time I was a tiny tot, I would be taken to my grandmother's when she was sick or to a neighbor's house where there was illness, plunked down in a corner and admonished to be a very good girl while Mother tended the sick person.

By the time I was twelve, I was driving the farm truck and tractor. Mother was very protective of me and never allowed me to do any of the heavy farm work, but it was all right for me to operate the tractor. I drove the truck in the hayfields when I was so short I had to stand up to see over the hood. Hay spoiled if it got wet, so when it began to look like rain, the men hurried to gather their crop. Daddy set the gauge on the truck at about two miles per hour and I would steer it while he walked alongside and tossed on the hay bales.

Two of my cousins and I drove the car to school for the same reason I drove the truck, to free an adult for more important things. We were all twelve and thirteen years old. We'd start out from our homes and pick up cousins along the way. By the time we got to school, there would be seven of us in the car. I started driving before I was tall enough to see the road over the hood. I'd look between the steering wheel and front of the hood to keep us on the road. If anybody had seen me—and very few people ever did because these were very remote country lanes—they would have wondered how the car was getting up the road all by itself because they couldn't see the driver even though the car was crammed full of kids. We weren't allowed to go more than twenty miles an hour, and none of us ever had a wreck. We thought nothing of driving ourselves to and from school; everybody's kids did it. Driver's licenses weren't required in Texas until about 1937. By that time, I'd been driving for eight or nine years.

Religion was very important in our farm community and served a social as well as spiritual purpose. My mother's folks were Swedish Lutheran, and I became active in the church from the time of my birth. I went to Swedish Lutheran Sunday school and to confirmation classes. I memorized the catechism and had read the Bible word for word by the time I was thirteen. I could recite the commandments, the catechism, numerous Bible verses, and the creed by heart. The minister, called a presten in Swedish, was the most revered person in the Swedish Lutheran community. When the presten was coming we cleaned the house extra special and prepared the finest meal. Daddy had a deck of cards in the house which we hid before the presten came because my grandmother believed that card-playing was the work of the devil. Alcohol of all kinds was strictly forbidden, though there were a number of alcoholics in the community. I remember the preacher roaring from the pulpit about the sins of alcohol and regularly condemning to hell everybody who didn't obey every letter of the Bible.

My Grandmother Ballerstedt and all of her daughters belonged to the Roman Catholic Church, which was also very strict—but in a different way from the Swedish Lutheran. My Catholic relatives were not allowed to enter our church, not even for nonreligious services, and I was not permitted to go to Catholic mass, but when my Catholic relatives died we all attended the services the night before the funeral. I remember how strange the reading of the rosary seemed to me. Uncle Ernest, Dad's brother, married a Baptist. Everybody in both families thought they were doomed, but I was allowed to attend when their daughters, Doris and Marion, my first cousins, were baptized.

In the summertime there were all kinds of tent revivals where visiting preachers of every denomination ranted about hell and damnation. It was really a marvelous show; the singing was wonderful, and everybody except the Catholics went. Services were held every night, beginning about dark and lasting for a least a couple of hours. As I recall, these events were more recreational than religious—at least for me.

I accepted everything I was taught as gospel truth, not only about religion, but about the status of different individuals who lived in our community. We were a rigidly segregated society, and it never occurred to me to question racial segregation. Black and Hispanic people helped work the fields, but they were not included as guests in our homes or at any of the social events in our Swedish-German community.

Farm life demanded a sunup-to-sundown day, as many as twelve to fourteen hours in the summertime, so there was very little time or incentive for recreation. Farmers and their wives who worked many eighty-hour weeks fell into bed exhausted as soon as supper was over and got up before dawn the next morning to do it all over again. Even so, we found the time for recreation. Television hadn't been invented yet, but Daddy managed to buy a secondhand battery-operated radio when I was six. It had a horn on it about two feet high, and in the summertime, Dad would put the horn up to the window and turn the radio on full-blast so that the neighbors could enjoy the music. Sometimes Daddy could get stations as far away as St. Louis and Chicago and he'd get so excited that he'd call up relatives to listen. I stayed glued to it as much as Mother would allow. I remember *Amos 'n' Andy*, the *Billy Jones* and *Ernie Hare* shows, the Interwoven Pair, and especially George Burns and Gracie Allen. There were soap operas around noon every day, continuing "sob sister" sagas that I seldom heard because Daddy tuned in to the farm news when he came in for dinner. Radio delivered mostly comedy shows and music; there were no educational shows.

We had our own telephone line just for the family. Grandpa Ballerstedt put it in and had it connected to the switchboard in Manor. It was always breaking down, especially in a heavy rain, and Dad would take bailing wire and go patch it. The phone worked on batteries and had a crank you turned to make it ring. One ring was for the operator in Manor; two rings was my grandparents' house; two and a half rings was ours; and so on. We paid ninety-five cents a month for telephone service. We could call as far away as Austin, but that was long distance and cost twenty cents, so we almost never used it. When the phone rang, no matter who it was for, you could hear the receivers being picked up on the entire party line. When Mother talked to her sisters, she always spoke Swedish so that our German family couldn't understand.

Every fall we had fairs. Every little town had its own fair and prizes were awarded for the biggest and best produce, livestock, canned foods, cakes, pies, breads, arts and crafts, and other things. Everybody attended. The Travis County Fair was the really big deal. Almost all farm children were members of the 4-H Club (Head, Heart, Hand, and Health); I joined as soon as I was old enough. Each of us had a project for the year. The year I was ten, my project was Ancona chickens, and I won the blue ribbon at the county fair for showing the best chickens. I highly treasured that ribbon, one of the best prizes I ever won in my life, and I kept it for years. Few farm families in our part of the state ever got to the State Fair of Texas held every October in Dallas. It was too far for us to travel, about two hundred miles.

We had no organized athletics. There was no stadium, no equipment, and no incentive. When families got together on Sunday afternoons, the boys scrambled around in the dirt playing baseball. Athletics for girls was unheard of.

I don't remember much about the band that Daddy and his brothers formed in the early 1900s, though I heard them talk about it many times. All of them played by ear; none had music lessons. Daddy played the banjo and the accordion. His brother Dick played the violin and his brother Willie was the caller for square dances, which at that time was the major entertainment in the farming community. This band hired itself out for community dances up to fifteen and twenty miles away. They traveled by buggy, played until midnight, earned a dollar apiece, and got home around sunup to milk, slop the hogs, and look after any other livestock. Square dances were inevitably on Saturday nights, so three tired young men mostly dozed through Sunday worship services. Obviously, after the brothers were married and had children, the band was disbanded.

I have no musical talent at all. For a couple of years I had piano lessons but no "ear" for music and played only because I practiced. My gift to the community public meetings lay in my ability to speak.

I had no idea, as a little girl, where this talent would lead.

2

Child of Ambivalence

My EARLIEST AND LIFELONG IMPRESSIONS of myself are based in two diametric realities. I am the offspring of poor immigrants who were not welcomed into the United States and especially in our farm neighborhood. But, equally significant, I am the child of parents who desperately wanted me and loved me unconditionally. These mixed messages of rejection and acceptance formed my earliest set of values and the framework for the way I view myself and others.

Mother was the most important person in my early life, both my proponent and my opponent, my protagonist and my antagonist. She made all my decisions and I didn't question them—until much, much later. She moved mountains of opposition from my path. Without her pushing and prodding, I never would have achieved the educational advantages that were not available in our part of the state and were denied to most farm children. Mother was domineering and dominating, one of the most determined people I have ever known, and she was also my first and most significant mentor. With her as my primary model, it is not surprising that I have let nothing stand in the way of what I needed to achieve.

Daddy was totally different, a very gentle soul. He was a man of the soil, in sync with the universe more than anybody I have ever known. He took time to enjoy the sunsets. He loved planting time in the spring and exulted over the tiny green plants as they came out of the earth. He cared for the new animals. His word was his bond. He was first to volunteer when anybody needed help. He went along with Mother's ambition for me, but he would have been just as pleased if I'd taken a secretarial course, lived on the farm next door, and remained in Travis County for the rest of my life. He could never quite understand Mother's driving ambition for me to get a good education or my need to do so. Even after I was at the University of Texas, Dad drilled it into me that I must get a teaching certificate. Being a country schoolteacher was the limit of his ambition for me.

Daddy would go along with Mother until she started to pressure him too much and then he would disappear to the barn. For years after I grew up, when I went to see my parents, Dad and I would go down to the barn and the two of us would sit on bales of hay and talk. These are some of the fondest memories of my life. He was a wise man and a surrogate father to many kids, very important to my three sons. They called him Beepaw; he taught them to hunt and fish.

Dad was a lifelong Democrat and precinct chairman of the Littig Precinct, which had a total of about one hundred voters, many of whom were blacks. He was relentless in persuading registered voters to cast their ballots. Often newspapers reported that the highest voter turnout in the state was the Littig Precinct in Travis County. Almost always 90 percent or more of the voters would turn up at the polls; once 97 percent voted. Dad was very proud of this record. He did it by calling everybody ahead of time and reminding them to go to the polls. Beginning around 2 P.M. on election day, he would again call everybody who had not voted. He "inherited" his dedication to the right to vote from his father. Grandpa Ballerstedt had lived under a Prussian dictator in Germany and felt that voting was his sacred duty. Because he could not read, somebody would have to read the ballot to him, but he always voted.

My thoughts about participating in a democracy by casting a ballot came from both my parents, and is so ingrained in me that I've crawled out of bed when I had a high fever to go to the polls. Mother worked tirelessly to help pass the Nineteenth Amendment giving women the right to vote. Before I was born she and Aunt

Hulda toured the entire countryside talking to all of the farmers and encouraging them to vote for suffrage. Aunt Hulda's daughter, Jeannette, was seven years older than I, and next to my mother was my closest female relative. Jeannette told me many times about being plunked into the backseat of the Model T Ford that my mother and her mother drove around our entire rural area in 1916, '17, and '18, encouraging the women to support the amendment and the men to vote for it. Mother was very proud that Texas was one of the first states to approve the Nineteenth Amendment. Women got the right to vote in 1920 when I was a year old. Mother always voted and she would have been brokenhearted if I had not done so.

Both of my parents loved me unconditionally, but had very different ways of showing it.

As an adult, I've come more and more to understand them and to see that I have inherited traits from both. They were first-generation Americans, Mother from Swedish ancestry and Dad from German. Neither learned to speak English until they went to school, and both had very little formal education. They both dropped out in the sixth grade, which was when immigrant children traditionally quit school. In the fall during harvest season and in the spring during planting season, farm kids worked in the fields instead of going to class. For Dad, that existence was good enough. For Mother, it never was.

Both of my parents came from very large families. Mother was the fifth of the ten children born to Nils and Bengta Bodelson Lindgren. Nils arrived in America in 1880 believing that riches awaited him in Texas. He left Bengta and their two little girls, Alma I and Minnie I, in Sweden. Bengta was pregnant with their third child but neither knew it when he left. The oldest child died and Alma II was born eight months after Nils left for America. When the infant was six weeks old, Grandma, with her two babies and her sister, Ingrid, left their home in Sweden to join Nils in Texas. They endured a horrible sea voyage and land trek from Galveston to Manor where Grandma found, not a promised land, but a hovel in the middle of mud as her new home. It was a raw, wild, untamed agricultural area about fifteen miles east of Austin, thickly overrun with mesquite bushes and highly populated with rattlesnakes.

I never knew Grandpa Lindgren. He died in 1910, nine years before I was born, but according to family stories he was very smart. He came to the United States with no money, but by 1900 he had paid for a 200-acre farm and the large house in Austin in which I was born. He not only supported the family, but made sufficient investments to take care of my grandmother, who outlived him by twenty-one years and died in 1931. Mother learned sewing and finishing as the apprentice to her grandfather, Jens Bodelson, the Swedish tailor.

We were taught to adore Grandma Lindgren and I would happily sit at her side talking to her as she taught me to embroider, crochet, and tat. But when the male grandchildren came, I was shoved aside. After I grew up I better understood the European preference for male heirs, but as a child I felt rejected.

Grandma had a hard life in America. She had a new baby every two years until she was forty-four. Minnie, the two-year-old she brought to America, died as a little girl, so when my mother was born, Grandma had two children, Aunt Alma (the second Alma) and Uncle Enoch. Her next baby after Mother was my Aunt Hulda, born when my mother was two years old. The two were not only sisters, but best friends. They did everything together. Even after they were married, they lived on connecting farms and continued to be very close. Grandma's last child, my uncle Edgar, was born in 1898. He was only twelve when his father died, so she had eight surviving children, and most of them were still at home.

I don't remember Grandma on the farm; my Lindgren grandparents had moved into Austin around 1900 and bought the house on Rose Street where I was born. Going to Austin was a great treat. My grandmother had asthma and was sick a lot, and my mother and Aunt Hulda nursed her. The house was a gray two-story on a very large lot that ran back to the railroad tracks close to the Colorado River. It had a fenced yard with lots of flowers where I loved to play. At the back was a place for horses because everything was horse-drawn. I was especially impressed with three things about that house—electricity, gas, and an indoor bathroom. Electric lights were a marvel. They hung from the ceiling in the center of the rooms and held bare bulbs. The gas stove downstairs operated by feeding quarters into a slot. When the gas went off, we'd have to find quarters to feed into it so that the gas came on again. The one bathroom downstairs was quite small, but it was wonderful to have indoor plumbing.

When a foundry went in next door and took most of the yard, Grandma sold the house and moved in with Aunt Minnie and Uncle Henry Kron about a block away. My most impressive memory of Aunt Minnie was formed when her daughter, Helen, was an infant. Aunt Minnie had been married for several years before she got pregnant and she spent a lot of time with us on the farm, where she talked endlessly to me about this wonderful baby coming to our family. She said it would be my baby to love and care for. I had always wanted a little sister or brother and I was so excited. Then the baby was born and brought home and they wouldn't let me hold her or even get very close. I was five years old, but I remember vividly how upset I was about being kept away from my baby. One day when Helen was a few weeks old, I went into the back bedroom where she was sleeping in her crib and locked the door. Then I got the baby out of her bed and sat down on the floor with her. Mother and Aunt Minnie were hysterical trying to get me to open the door, but I wouldn't. I said, "This is my baby and I am taking care of her." Finally they bribed me into opening the door. Aunt Minnie never again told me that Helen was my baby, but the story was told and retold and probably embellished for the rest of their lives.

The Ballerstedts, my paternal grandparents, lived and died on their family farm adjacent to the Lindgren farm. My paternal grandfather, Herman, was a teenager about to be conscripted into the Prussian Army when he ran away to the docks of Hamburg in Germany, and stowed away in a sack of potatoes. Weeks later, when the ship landed at Galveston, he had no idea where he was. He spoke no English but made it known that he needed to find German-speaking associates, and was pointed toward Brenham. He walked the railroad track for some hundred miles to reach the German settlement in Brenham where he hired out as a farm laborer for four dollars a month. When he heard about a better opportunity, he again walked the railroad tracks to Manor and again hired out as a laborer. His food and housing was paid, so he saved every cent; eventually, with a grant plus the money he'd saved, made a down payment on a 200-acre farm of his own. John and Teresa Schneider came to the United States from Coswick, Austria, with their daughter, Frances. At seventeen, Frances Schneider married Herman Ballerstedt.

My father was the fifth of Frances and Herman's sixteen children. There were nine girls—Annie, Dora, Frances, Laney, Minnie, Mary, Hattie, Alice, and Blanche—and seven boys—John, Willie, Richard, Louis (my father), Ernest, Edwin, and Frank. The last two died in infancy.

My grandfather died when I was seven. I would have liked to have known Grandpa Ballerstedt better, but I probably would not have liked him and his domineering ways too much. My father and his brothers were closer to their grandfather, John Schneider, than they were to their own father. Grandpa Schneider lived with Frances and Herman after Grandma Teresa died in the 1890s and was very close to his grandson. Dad often talked about his grandfather, what a great person he was, and how much fun the boys had with him.

I'm told that Grandpa Ballerstedt was a hard-drinking, hard-working old German. I'm sure he had to be tough to feed, house, and clothe sixteen kids. He probably could read German, and although he never learned to read and write English, he was a smart old codger. I often heard how good he was at math. Once he took five bales of cotton to sell. They were different weights and different qualities, so the price of each varied. Grandpa went off by himself, and in a few minutes came back with the total amount he was due for his cotton. He'd figured it out in his head faster than the buyer who was using pencil and paper.

Grandpa arrived in Texas right after the Civil War. He never got over his hatred of carpetbaggers and Republicans. His daughters knew they might get by with a suitor who was a ne'er-do-well, a drunkard, or even a criminal, but they'd better not bring home a Republican because Papa would take his shotgun and run him off the farm.

Grandpa was a Protestant and all his sons were Protestant. Grandma and all her daughters were Catholic. That was the usual arrangement in those days. Grandpa tolerated priests and his wife's

Catholic rituals, but he said his sainted mother was a Lutheran and he'd promised her he would always be a Lutheran.

I adored Grandma Ballerstedt. She lived until shortly after I married in 1941. She was a tiny little thing, just about my size. She lived on a farm near us. Her house had a cellar where she stored huge crocks of sauerkraut. The family's staple diet was pork, sauerkraut, and potatoes. I get nostalgic to this day when I smell sauerkraut and sausage.

All of her kids were very loyal to Grandma, and on Sunday afternoons everybody went to her house. She was usually a very gentle person, but when she got riled up we all got out of her way. Grandma read everything about what was happening in the world, especially in Germany. She was upset about Hitler when nobody else around us knew who Hitler was. Grandma would go around muttering, "Dat Hitler! Dat Hitler!" She died in April, before we got into the war when the Japanese bombed Pearl Harbor on December 7, 1941, but the Germans were overrunning Austria, Czechoslovakia, and Poland, and Grandma was terribly upset about it.

Mother was self-educated and very smart. I can almost hear some of my early teachers groaning when they saw her coming, because she was always showing up at school to see how I was doing and to offer suggestions. She was well organized and could speak and write beautifully. She was president of the PTA at Kimbro shortly after I started to school. She was determined that I should have the education and advantages that she had never had. I was a pliable and willing learner.

One of my earliest memories is standing on a chair in the kitchen reciting poems. Mother coached me while she cooked. Communities had their home talent shows and plays, and there was always a need for somebody who could give a declamation. Mother insisted that I stand straight, look the audience in the eye, and project my voice to the back of the room. I remember going over and over and over pieces until she was pleased. She would take me to the Fireman's Hall in Manor. When I was a kid I thought it was a huge place, but later I saw it was a pretty small building. Mother would put me on the stage and stand at the back of the hall, and I would repeat a poem over and over with her saying, "Get your voice back to this row!" and I'd try again. She was constantly on the lookout for poems and short essays that she thought I should learn to recite. She'd clip or copy them and I'd learn them for the next performance.

Not many farm women had the inclination, the time, or the drive with their kids that my mother had. Most of the time when my classmates had to recite, they would mumble and nobody could hear, so I got the lead in the church plays and was the speaker for most of the community meetings. Often I was the "keynote speaker" at Manor, New Sweden, Lund, Carlson, and all the little farming communities around us when there was a talent show or play of any kind.

When the weather made it impossible for me to go to school, Mother taught me at home. I remember her drilling me on addition, subtraction, spelling, and the multiplication tables. I think I won every spelling bee ever held in Kimbo. Mother just never let up.

I learned to read when I was four. The extent of our home library was the Bible, the Sears and Roebuck catalog, the Montgomery Ward catalog, and the local daily newspaper. I devoured all of them. I longed for books. I remember being curious about the funny squiggles in the paper. I would lie on the floor and pick out things that looked alike, pleased when I found two things that matched. Mother not only noticed what I was doing, but encouraged it. I would circle two words that looked alike and she would hover over me and say "the" or whatever the word happened to be. She taught me the letters of the alphabet, how to spell my name, and how to count. The school that the Negro children attended was across the road from our house, and Mother borrowed books from them when I was five and let me read them. I learned all about Baby Ray and his adventures. It was marvelous!

I was six and a half before I started school, a two-teacher school at Kimbro. My teacher was Miss Bertha, who later married a local farmer. I don't think Mother was ever too impressed with any of my teachers. There was no library at Kimbro, only a few books in an old bookcase, and I read all of them in the first few weeks after I entered school. I was desperate for reading material. I devoured the *Austin American* that came to our house daily except on the weekends, reading about everything that kids probably shouldn't—

murder, violence, everything. When Gertrude Ederle was the first woman to swim across the English Channel in 1926, I was entranced; I was only seven. I was almost eight when Charles Lindbergh flew solo across the Atlantic and landed the *Spirit of St. Louis* in Paris. I was captivated with the story and followed every detail of the Lindbergh baby kidnapping almost five years later. In 1932, Amelia Earhart was the first woman to fly across the Atlantic. It was also in 1932 that Babe Didriksen (who would later change the spelling of her name to Didrikson) became the first woman in history to win two gold medals in the Olympics. At the end of the century, she would be termed the greatest female athlete of the twentieth century. The front-page stories of my childhood and youth are now pages in American history books. They were subjects of my daily school reports, but my knowledge of them did not endear me to my classmates.

At the end of my first year in school, even though I had been able to attend school only thirty-seven days during the spring semester, I was promoted to the third grade. This was terrible for some of my classmates. Some of the farm boys were twice as big as I was and some quit school rather than go to class with me. I was a tiny thing, and it must have been traumatic for these big farm boys, who'd never had a chance and didn't have parents who valued education, to have a little shrimp like me in class. I wasn't trying to show off, but I knew all the answers because Mother had drilled me on everything at home the night before.

Uncle Milton, my Aunt Alma's husband, was superintendent of the streetcar company in Austin. He had been born in England and had lived in Australia and was one of the few people in our family who loved to read. He subscribed to *National Geographic* and I thought that magazine was the most wonderful thing I'd ever seen. When we went to their house in Austin, I would take copies and disappear into a corner and read for the entire time I was there.

When I reached the seventh grade, life suddenly changed—and all because of another negative experience. My teacher wasn't teaching me anything. After several conferences to try to improve the situation, Mother pulled me out of Kimbro and sent me to complete the seventh grade at Manor. I stayed there only a year and a half, completing the seventh and the eighth grades. I was excelling in every course, always brought home straight A report cards, but Mother knew I wasn't learning very much.

The country was in the depths of the Great Depression that officially began in October 1929 when the banks failed. If we had been poor before, we were now destitute. There was absolutely no money. Cotton brought five cents a pound—when you could sell it at all. In the summer of 1933 we moved into Austin. All three of us—Mother, Daddy, and I—were crowded together in one little room in Aunt Minnie and Uncle Henry Kron's home at 1006 West Fifth Street. Daddy got a job as a laborer on the county roads for eighty dollars a month. His income supported the entire family. On weekends we went back to the farm, where Daddy tried to do the work that had previously taken him all week to accomplish.

For Mother, there was a hidden agenda to our move into Austin. I could go to school there! She insisted that I repeat the second half of the eighth grade. Even though I still had straight A's, I'd been sick and missed part of the eighth-grade year at Manor. Too, Mother knew I would be taking harder courses with greater expectations in Austin, and she wanted me to continue to excel. I was still a very young eighth grader.

To me Austin High School was immense—and magnificent! It had a library! How I loved those books. I did honors reading and got a Golden R that was given to students who read a certain number—I've forgotten how many—of the classics. I had a wonderful algebra teacher whose name was Mr. Taylor. He was working on his Ph.D. and his thesis was on helping students improve their reading. I volunteered to be one of his guinea pigs. Using a mechanical device called a Tatchiscope, he measured and took pictures of the movement of our eyes as we began the exercises, again as we progressed, and again when we finished. I went to these exercises regularly for one full semester and quadrupled my reading speed and comprehension. I had the fastest reading speed of anybody he tested and became Exhibit A for his thesis. He worked very hard with me to see just how much I could improve. Because I had been such a good subject for his reading project, Mr. Taylor took a special interest in me and I became a whiz at math and took every math course he taught, including trigonometry and advanced algebra. Learning to speed-read has helped me immeasurably, both in college and my career.

A bonus of my speed-reading was learning that I did not need glasses, which I'd been wearing for several years. Doubtless I'd strained my eyes in the poor lighting we had at the farm, but there was nothing really wrong with them, so I got to toss the glasses aside. It's one of the few physical assets of my high school years. I hated the way I looked. When I was eleven, I was at my full adult height, five feet two inches. At thirteen I began to gain weight and no matter what I did, I was a fat, pudgy little thing instead of the tiny person I'd been as a kid. I was almost as wide as I was tall. At one time I weighed 145 pounds. I couldn't wear the cute dresses that other girls wore. Mother still made all my clothes and she had a terrible time fitting me. Once, after I'd graduated from high school, I wrote to a friend, "Mom is so disgusted with my spare tire at the waist and fanny that she is all but putting me on a bread and water diet—without the bread. She says I look like a blimp with mumps." I tried to diet and exercise, but nothing helped until I was about twenty-two years old, when the weight started going away— and I've never had a weight problem since.

I longed to be cute and popular like my good friend Mary Love Armacost. She was the most popular girl in school—high school queen, high school sweetheart, drum major of the band. Mary Love's mother encouraged her friendship with me, I think because I insisted that Mary Love study. She was smart and could have made excellent grades, but she was satisfied with her B's, which gave her time for her social life. I was a poor nobody from the country, not socially acceptable. I never belonged to the classy clubs in high school because they were by invitation only, and I was never extended an invitation. My best friends were boys, but only as buddies. I certainly wasn't the date bait that I longed to be. In retrospect, I know how fortunate I was, because the popular girls dated all the time and spent so much time socializing that they didn't have time to study. Mother expected me to make top grades and I had lots of time for studying!

Life wasn't entirely a grind. I had two and a half years of Spanish in high school and joined the Spanish club. When I was a junior, we put on a play and I was the duena, the Spanish grandmother. It was a comedy role, and I must have been pretty good at it because we presented the play several nights, mostly to audiences of Mexican Americans, and it went over well. I joined the Red Jackets, the drill team for football games, and enjoyed that.

I took all of the required academic courses—chemistry, biology—and some that were not required, but my favorite course was journalism. We had a wonderful unmarried male teacher, Jimmy Markham. He was the sponsor of our high school paper, *The Austin Maroon*. I was associate editor and wrote a column during my senior year. I was also one of the chief proofreaders, and spent nights that the paper came out at the print shop until around nine o'clock proofreading the dummies—which you had to read backward. I got very good at it, which was fortunate because Mr. Markham, who usually was a very jovial person, really lost his temper when he found an error in the paper. The guys I worked with on the paper—Kenneth Clark, Mac Roy Rasor, and Bo Byers, among them—were my buddies and have remained close friends. There was much joking and laughter as we worked together. I still see and hear from them and we still laugh a lot when we are together. My first high school date was with Bo Byers. We went dancing when I was thirteen; he and I are friends still.

In Austin High School, the girls had a Big Sister–Little Sister Club, its purpose for junior and senior girls to serve as mentors and helpmates to incoming freshmen and sophomores. My Little Sister was a girl from Salado whose name was Elizabeth Sutherland. Today she is known as Liz Carpenter.

James V. Allred was governor of Texas when I was in high school, and Mrs. Allred became very special to me. When they entertained, she asked high school girls to be unofficial hostesses. It was an honor to be asked to these state occasions, and I was often included. Mother made me several evening dresses from gauze, which we bought for fifteen to twenty cents a yard, so that I could be appropriately dressed. We'd help to greet and serve guests, pick up dirty dishes, and be the ears and eyes for Mrs. Allred to make her guests all feel welcome. This was during the Great Depression, and we high school girls saved the state a lot of money by performing duties that would have required hired help. For us it was marvelous, and we all vied for an invitation to help entertain at the Governor's Mansion. It taught us social graces and diplomacy and allowed us to meet the most important people in the state. We loved it!

I graduated from Austin High School at midterm, in January 1936, as valedictorian. I guess this was pretty good for a kid who had come in green from the country with no advantages, no family of power, no money, not much of anything except the ability to work hard, set goals, and stick with them . . .

And a mother who never let me forget what those goals were!

3

The World Beyond
the Cotton Fields

My WHOLE WORLD BEGAN TO CHANGE when I entered the University of Texas in Austin. I enrolled at midterm in 1936 just after graduating from high school. My parents had moved back to the farm, so I had to have a place to live. Mrs. Armacost, Mary Love's mother, offered me room, board, and transportation to school if I would tutor her daughter, Jane, especially in math. Jane was four years younger than Mary Love. She'd had a kidney ailment and missed a lot of school. I also slept with Jane because she was afraid to sleep alone.

Mary Love, who was very popular, had a little Buick convertible and we went together every day to the university. We both went through rush and she pledged Chi Omega. I did not have the money or the clothes for sorority membership, so I did not join anything. It was only later when my grades were all A's that sororities began to rush me, and by that time I didn't have time for them.

When the winter term ended, Mother thought it would be a good idea for me to go to summer school, and I agreed, so I enrolled for two courses and moved into a co-op house, where my room cost eighteen dollars a month. We did our own cooking, housekeeping, and laundry. I was seventeen that summer.

In September, when the fall semester started, I moved into Littlefield dormitory. I had always wanted to live in a girls' dorm, but it was expensive and the country was still deep in the Depression. Money was very, very scarce. I got a job waiting tables in the dorm that paid half of my board and I went to work in the ex-students' office, where I earned fifteen cents an hour.

Tuition was twenty-five dollars a semester. Gym and laboratory fees were extra and I had to buy my books. They cost an average of four dollars each. In all, tuition and fees ran around forty dollars a semester.

Mother still made all my clothes. She came to Austin about once a week throughout my college years to see that my clothes were laundered, mended, and pressed, which saved me a lot of work. Mother loved to come to the university. She was so proud to have a daughter in college, but she took a lot of criticism. Some of the relatives told her that it was throwing money away to educate me because I'd just get married and all that money would be wasted. It was a scandal in our community for a poor girl from the farm to be going to college!

I very much wanted to major in journalism in college; I'd had more pleasure from my high school journalism course than anything else, but there were two strikes against my going into journalism. First, there were absolutely no jobs open for women journalists and, second, reporters were considered a bit radical and the career inappropriate for women. A woman had a choice of becoming a nurse, a teacher, a secretary, or a librarian. Nothing else was acceptable. I took all the courses to become a public school teacher and did my practice teaching. This meant that I had to take extra courses to get a permanent teacher's certificate along with my degree, so I had to do two semesters of summer school to work it all in.

Geology was the most significant course I've ever taken. It shook up the world that had existed for me. It made me ask questions about the order of the universe and my place in it. For a time it almost destroyed my faith. I'd been taught that the world was created in 4004 B.C. I had taken my religion extremely seriously and believed every word of the catechism, dogmas, creeds, and the history of the human race as it was presented in my fundamentalist church. I believed in the literal Bible. Then, in the fall of my freshman year, I got into a big geology lecture class—there were some 1,500 of us in an auditorium—which included labs.

Because of the Balcones Fault, the rock layers west of Austin were 1,500 feet higher than the layers east of Austin. In lab, we were given little hammers and told to go out into the hills and find out about the different layers. I remember finding *Kingena wacoencis*, a strata named because the first specimen had been found in Waco, and *Exigiro texana*, the first that had been found in Texas. By figuring the time of sediments and the numbers of layers of rocks on top of other rocks, I tried to figure out how the world could have been created in 4004 B.C. if these specimens had been laid into the sediment hundreds of millions of years ago. I was absolutely fascinated by all of this new information, but I was also in conflict. I went to see my minister and asked him to explain how these layers of rock got into the world if it wasn't created until 4004 B.C. He stormed around and stomped off saying, "I told your parents to send you to a church school. The University of Texas is a training ground for hell!"

In retrospect, I feel sorry for the preacher. He had no answers to my questions and he felt threatened. I was very confused. There was a basic conflict between my religious training and my scientific discoveries. The next few years were painful. Gradually my whole fundamentalist faith collapsed. I was not yet mature enough to see that there was a lot of truth to what I'd been taught. At that time, when some of it went, everything came tumbling down. In my mind there was a clear division between what my religion had taught and the scientific realities I was learning from books and professors. It took me many years to work through the conflicts. I could talk to nobody. I couldn't ask my mother or any of her relatives because they already thought I was going to hell. I couldn't talk to my dad about it because he was such a sweet man and smart in so many ways, but religious puzzles would have been over his head; he was happy accepting what he had been taught all his life. I couldn't ask the minister because he had already made his opinions clear. I couldn't ask my teachers because I perceived them to be totally on the scientific side of the conflict. So, I learned to keep my mouth shut.

Dr. Harry Ransom taught me English in my freshman year at the university. He was a new teacher, a beginning instructor, and he was wonderful. All of us who were fortunate enough to have him as a teacher knew that he was headed for great things. His passion was libraries and books. When he became president and then chancellor of the university system, he was very influential in getting some rare books and making the University of Texas a research library.

How I loved the magnificent UT libraries! I would go to the library to study, and I'd sit there just enjoying looking at the vaulted ceilings with the artwork and the carvings. To me it was a fairy tale come true. And all those books! There was a book that would help you learn everything in the world you wanted to know if you just knew how to ask for it and read it! To this day, I rejoice that a *public* education was provided so inexpensively for someone like me.

A lot of funny, amusing things happened in my life during this time, too. I was only seventeen, away from home for the first time, living in a dormitory without my mother around to tell me what I should do at every minute. Miss Martha Lockett took the place of my mother and, if anything, she was more exacting than Mother. She was the housemother in Littlefield dorm, an old maid, and a dormitory mother right out of Central Casting. She had a great pile of meticulously coiffed white hair. Her clothes were as prim as her manner. She made it clear that we were to act like ladies at all times. Once, one of the residents was caught in a rainstorm. Rather than ruin the pair of new shoes she was wearing, the girl very sensibly took off her shoes and carried them under her arm into Littlefield. Miss Lockett caught her coming in barefoot and chastised her severely. No Littlefield lady must ever be caught barefoot!

Once, Miss Lockett's idea of proper behavior caught me. It was the fall of 1936, not long after I'd moved into the dorm. Kenneth Clark asked me to go with him and some of his friends into a wooded area west of Austin to gather berries and leaves. Kenneth's father was a very distinguished English professor at the university. His mother was in charge of decorating the faculty club for a party. She asked her son to take some of his friends and go out into the country to select autumn leaves and berries for her to use as decorations. It was a bright, clear, wonderful fall Saturday morning. Kenneth and two of his friends pulled up to the dorm with a trailer attached to his car and came in to collect me. They were dressed in jeans and boots. I came down in boots, a pair of old riding pants, and a long-sleeved shirt, ready to go out into the bushes. Miss Lockett spotted me. She saw the three guys waiting and said, "Miss Ballerstedt, come into my office."

I was puzzled, but of course I followed her and closed the door. "Where are you going?" she asked, and I said, "Oh, we're going out into the hills west of Austin." She said, "And what other girls are going with you?" I said, "No other girls . . . just me and the boys." She was aghast. "Miss Ballerstedt," she said, drawing herself up to her full height, "you simply cannot go out into the hills west of Austin with *three* men!" I thought she was out of her mind. I had no idea what she was thinking. I said, "But we're just going out there to gather leaves and berries." Then she asked who the driver was. I told her Kenneth Clark, so she called him into her office. I don't know what she said to him or he said to her, but she learned that he was the son of a very outstanding professor and that we were running an errand for his mother, so she let me go. We went off and got our leaves and berries for Mrs. Clark's party, and all the way there and back talked about what on earth had got into Miss Lockett. She was really acting strange.

When we left the dormitory in the evening or for anything off campus during the daytime, we had to sign out. College regulations were strict and housemothers served as our surrogate parents. Curfew on weeknights was 11 P.M. and it was a serious offense if you came in after curfew. The doors were locked at 11 P.M., and always there'd be a frantic rush of girls pushing into the dorm at deadline. If you were late, the housemother was waiting up with a key to let you in. You'd always get a lecture, and sometimes, depending on how late you were and the excuse you had, the withdrawal of certain privileges. You were always reminded that it must never happen again. On the second infraction, you were "grounded." This meant that you were not allowed to leave the dormitory except for class for a period of time. Smoking and drinking in any amount—even a glass of wine—would get you expelled.

I enrolled for summer school again in 1937, to begin the extra classes necessary for a teacher's certificate. That summer I moved into Caruthers dormitory with Rose Munves as my roommate. She was very popular. She often insisted that I go along with her on a double date, and for the first time in my life I began to really relax and have fun. Older women—mostly teachers who came to the university to fulfill requirements for their permanent teachers' certificates—filled the dorm that summer. They'd come to school to study and learn, and here were these two frivolous kids more interested in dating than in studying. No rooms had telephones; they were located only at the end of the halls. Rose and I would yell back and forth, planning our dates. "Can you double date with me on Saturday?" "No, I already have a date. What about Sunday afternoon?" I'm sure our older dorm mates wished that something would happen to make us drop out of school.

In the fall of 1937, I found a room at the Women's Building, which had very small single rooms and was the second oldest building on campus. I loved having a single room because I could study more efficiently and on my own schedule. I'd go to bed early, set my alarm for 4 A.M., and study from four until eight before my first class. I always worked at least two jobs, so time had to be planned carefully. Daddy made me a board with a cutout to fit around me on the one rocking chair in the room. It served as my desk and worked very well. I'd sit in that rocking chair with my books and papers spread over the board, and really concentrate so that I'd go to class prepared. I continued to make straight A's.

One of my extra jobs was tutoring in trigonometry and college algebra. It paid fifty cents an hour, a gold mine in those days. I dropped each fifty cents into a fruit jar on my windowsill and saved them until I filled the jar. I remember taking the fruit jar over to the registrar's office and paying for my registration with the fifty-cent pieces. I tutored in math through the rest of college. I must have done a good job, because some students who had already flunked math twice passed the course with my tutoring. I remember doing all sorts of interesting things to illustrate solutions to problems. One of my favorites was cutting apples into pieces to show how problems worked. When one of my "students" finally passed a math course, I'd be so excited!

Pearl Chadwick was the housemother at the Women's Building. Behind her back, we called her "Chatty." She ran a tight ship but was not nearly so rigid as Miss Lockett. An enclosed circular fire escape on one side of the building served as the entryway for numerous girls who came in after curfew. They usually had slipped out of the dorm without signing out, so they didn't have to sign back in—sometimes they'd get a roommate or friend to sign them in—and they'd take off their shoes and silently climb up the fire escape to the second floor. My room was at the top of the stairs near the fire escape. I never did have to use it, but I opened the second-story window for many girls after hearing a tapping outside.

During my sophomore year, I met Florence Eastman Myers in the Women's Building; she and I became the closest of friends and remained so until her death in January 2002. She was one of the few people in whom I could confide. She got her teacher's certificate and taught in Conroe, and later in Dallas for many years. Our families and careers kept us from seeing much of each other, but when we were together, it always took me back to that special time we shared as girls. I spoke at her memorial service.

During my junior year, I got a job as student assistant to Dr. Leigh Peck, who taught educational psychology and had written a number of books. Dr. Peck was a brilliant woman, warm-hearted and dear, but she couldn't have cared less what she looked like. She was very obese. Her hair was iron gray and straight. I think she cut it herself. She seemed to plan her numerous illnesses around projects I could conduct for her. She'd call and say she was ill and I'd "teach" the class, take the roll, direct whatever questionnaires she had planned, and report back to her. I graded all the true-false and multiple choice questions on tests. I loved the job. It paid fifty cents an hour!

A special passion of Dr. Peck's, eidetic imagery, kept her busy testing and writing. Eidetic imagery is an educational theory based on knowledge from form and shape. It is especially experienced in childhood. The more perceptive people are to eidetic imagery, the

better able they are to look at something and later be able to see and
know clearly what they observed. By testing college students, I
assisted Dr. Peck with her research. The test was simple. I'd take a
picture and show it for a few seconds, then take the picture away
and ask questions. How many pickets in the fence? What color were
the flowers? How many people wore hats? Where was the picture
located on the wall? Specific things like that. I have no eidetic
imagery whatsoever. My freshman roommate, Etta McDonald, did.
She studied chemistry and all the heavy science courses, with almost
immediate recall of very complicated tables. She became a doctor.
Another girl I tested said when she heard music, she played it over
in her head and heard every note, a problem because sometimes she
could not turn the music off. Her eidetic imagery was in hearing.

One especially interesting experiment involved a dormitory
friend, Rebecca Brisenio, a Mexican-American girl from the Rio
Grande Valley. She made a perfect score on the test. She questioned
me about eidetic imagery and then she started to cry. She said she
had been repeatedly punished in school because she could do things
perfectly. When she saw a mathematical table in a book, she
absorbed it, and when the test was given, she could mentally project
it onto the wall. Her teachers could not understand her perfect
answers and thought she was cheating. She was so relieved to learn
there was a name for her ability, and that it was a sense she had
that most people didn't. She considered it a blessing and a great gift,
but had repressed it because she had been punished for using it.
Interestingly, she was surprised that not everybody had her gift.

I haven't heard of eidetic imagery in years and wonder what has
happened to the theory. Dr. Peck believed that our schools repress
children's innate ability to absorb knowledge through their senses
and that most of us lose the gift by the time we are twelve.

I was student assistant for Dr. Peck all through my junior and
senior years. When I was a senior, I was also a student assistant in
the government department.

Even though I was carrying a full load of courses and working
two or three jobs, I still found time for fun. I became very active in
the Y. It sponsored a lot of stimulating programs and many weekend

camp-outs. If I could afford the time at all, I always went. All the Y activities were free, and I suppose the best times I had at the University of Texas came through the Campus YM/YWCA. The C stands for Christian, but it was okay if we asked questions. In fact, questioning was encouraged and I found this so refreshing! A Y camping experience at Branson, Missouri, provided my first opportunity for associating with international students and young people of different ethnicities.

An incident with Dr. Peck illustrates another aspect of life in Texas in the 1930s. At camp, I danced with a young black man, a first-time experience for me. I was excited to share it with my mentor, but when I told Dr. Peck I had danced with a Negro boy during my stay in Missouri, she was so upset at my being willing to cross racial lines, even on that small scale, that she almost fired me. She was brilliant in many ways, but not ready for racial equality. I also became active in the Wesley Foundation at the Methodist Church, where the minister, Dr. Edward Heinsohn, preached provocative and challenging sermons. I found them so much more intelligent than the sermons I'd heard at my fundamentalist church. With every experience, my world continued to open up. But I didn't tell my mother.

I continued to date a lot, too. I loved to dance and once won a Big Apple dance contest. I dated William Bandy for two years at the university. We'd been in high school together, and, in fact, we started going out together soon after I graduated from high school. Dating was so innocent! We never kissed or petted. Having sex never entered our minds. I mean, literally! We didn't go steady, either. I remember going out on a double date with Bill as my date and Bo Byers as my friend's date, and maybe the next time we went out, we'd switch partners. Bill lived in Austin with his parents and had an old used car that was a great luxury! Sometimes he'd even get to drive his dad's car.

The Depression had not let up and money was still very scarce. Sometimes a group would get together and ride the streetcar to the end of the line and back. If the guy had a dime, we'd each have a Coke and that would be our date. Movies cost fifteen cents, sometimes as much as a quarter. It was a really big deal if we had a movie date. Nobody had money for luxuries like going out to dinner or to fancy dances, but we had lots of fun.

I loved to dance, and every social event included dancing. The Student Union Building held a big dance very Saturday night. It was the era of ballroom dancing and a big band always played. It cost sixty cents a couple to attend, and we'd all hoard our nickels and dimes to get into a Student Union dance.

I dated a lot of guys at the university. I remember Bill and Bo, Kenneth, Harley, Hugh, Jimmy, Johnny, Jack, another John, and an older guy whose last name was Rosenblatt. There were others whose names I don't remember. Harley was killed in a traffic accident. Jimmy and Johnny were brothers, but that didn't make any difference. Rosenblatt—I've forgotten his first name—was an older student doing research on fruit flies and working on his Ph.D. We thought he was something else!

A girl never ever bragged about making good grades. If she wanted to be popular—and how I longed to be—she said nothing or lied when she made A's. I started dating this one dumb guy because he was such a wonderful dancer. We'd go to the Student Union dances and I'd have a marvelous time. I acted like I didn't have a brain cell working, and he invited me to go to the library with him and he'd help me study. So, I'd go and he'd explain something in detail, and I'd bat my blue eyes and exult, "Oh, you've explained that so clearly!" It was worth listening to him stumble over the lessons because he'd invite me to the Saturday night dance on our way back to the dormitory. I don't think I ever outright lied to him about my grades, but he had the distinct impression that I was just barely passing. It worked very well until the Sunday morning the *Daily Texan* came out listing students who had been elected to Phi Beta Kappa. I was one of the four juniors whose name was on the list. Around 8:30 A.M. I got a telephone call from my dancing boyfriend. His voice was ice. "Could there be more than one Louise Hilma Ballerstedt attending this university?" I didn't have the grace to say, "Look, I like you and I like dancing with you, but I figured you wouldn't ask me if you knew I was making good grades." Instead,

I said, "I don't think so." He said, "That's what I assumed," and hung up. He never asked me for another date.

During the summer of 1938, I signed up with American Friends Service Committee to do peace and service work for two months in Illinois. This was a Quaker-sponsored program and the Quakers were always responsible for wonderful projects. They placed students in various communities to teach children or provide other needed services. We took a Greyhound bus to Naperville, Illinois, where we had two weeks' training at the Institute for International Relations. Three other girls and I were then sent to Galena, Illinois. Galena was a very interesting place, very old, at one time a booming town and the biggest city in Illinois. The Fever River ran through it, wide enough for steamboats from the Mississippi to reach it. The four of us who wound up in Galena were Edith Allen, a Quake from Colorado; Myra, whose last name I don't remember, a Jewish girl whose family had escaped from Russia because of persecution of the Jews in 1927; and Nettie, a red-haired girl from Kansas. We lived in the home of a Presbyterian minister who was away for the summer, and we did our own housework, cooking, and laundry.

The Quakers sent out information to all the surrounding communities that we were there and available for community services. Many of the churches took this to mean that we could fill their pulpits on Sunday so that the minister could have a brief vacation. I spoke in churches practically every Sunday. I don't think any of us ever "preached" the pure Quaker pacifist line, but the experience gave me a lot to think about.

I believed what the Bible said about "Thou shalt not kill," and "Love your neighbor," but I'd never tested my own reaction to it. Deep down, I knew that violence never solved anything, and yet I was not ready to lie down in front of Hitler's tanks to prevent him from overrunning the smaller countries around Germany. We really didn't know at that time about Hitler's persecution of the Jews. Germany later invaded Poland and Czechoslovakia, but we were hearing only the official news our country wanted us to know, and in Congress bitter debates erupted about how we should handle the Nazis. Everybody assumed Russia and Germany would band together to overrun Europe. Having Russia as an ally was one of the strangest things that came out of World War II. We heard all about "Good Old Uncle Joe" Stalin for years until the war ended, when we gradually found out he was a despicable creature, a real tyrant.

The Galena experience enhanced my education remarkably. I went into work with the Quakers very naively thinking I would have a summer of fun away from the farm. I've never worked harder in my life. Besides the Sunday sermons, there were radio talks, speeches to all kinds of organizations, newspaper interviews, stories to read to children, classes to teach. The four of us fanned out all over the area. Soon I saw that the work was exhausting but fun. We were in constant demand and we woke people up. Everybody seemed happy to see us. They picked us up, fed us, and returned us to where we lived. But we had to be very careful about our behavior. We had to watch our grammar when we spoke, be careful of the way we dressed—no red nail polish in Galena! No flirting, no late hours. I learned enough self-control to last a lifetime and enough patience to rival a saint.

All of the young men seemed intrigued at having college students from so far away in their midst, and I had one fairly intense summer romance. At least it was intense for him. His name was LeRoy. He hung around while I was making presentations and took me on one fabulous date, a steamboat ride to Dubuque, Iowa. We shared a few chaste kisses, but nothing more involved. LeRoy, as I recall, had no ambition to go to college and was perfectly content to remain in Galena for the rest of his life, but he was fascinated to have a college girl pay attention to him. Before I left at the end of the summer, he professed undying love for me, proposed, and gave me an engagement ring, which I am embarrassed to say I accepted. I didn't know what else to do. I kept his ring and actually wore it from time to time during my senior year in college. When I got the chance to go to Washington for graduate work with the Rockefeller Foundation, I wrote to him and he had a fit. He thought we were going to get married. I sent his ring back with a perfectly charming "Dear John" letter. He acknowledged receipt of the ring, wished me good luck, and I never heard from him again. He was an excellent mechanic, could fix anything with his hands. Through mutual friends I heard that he had moved to Florida and opened an auto repair shop. I wonder what happened to LeRoy. I wonder what kind of girl accepted the ring. I'll bet, if he survived the war, he was a great success in his chosen profession.

My senior year in college was hectic. I enrolled for six courses, worked three jobs, and did my practice teaching. The nearer the time came to graduation, the more I dreaded becoming a country schoolteacher, but I dutifully applied for teaching jobs. And then I saw a notice on the bulletin board about the Rockefeller Foundation offering graduate work in public administration to qualified college seniors. I copied the notice and took it home to my folks. Daddy was less than thrilled and Mother was torn. It would be a real coup for her to have a daughter awarded a cherished internship in Washington, D.C. It might even prove to the relatives that "sending" me to college had not been such a bad idea, after all. But it also meant that we'd have to find the money to pay my way to Washington, which was just about as far removed from Central Texas as Venus is from us today. My parents agreed that I should apply, and we borrowed a car to drive to Houston for the personal interview.

I was one of ten girls and forty boys from all over the United States chosen for an internship. A graduate student, an older guy in one of my classes, learned about my good fortune. He lived in New Orleans and invited me to stop off on my way to Washington and he would show me the city. I rode the train all night from Elgin, Texas, to New Orleans, where he and two friends met me. What a day we had! Except for my summer in Galena and the Y camp in Missouri, I'd never been anywhere before. The sight of the Mississippi River is a thrill I'll never forget. My eyes were as big as saucers when we went to the French Quarter where I had my first mixed drink in a bar!

But first there was college graduation. I was second in my class; I'd made a C in administrative law. The rest of my grades were solid A's. Grandmother Ballerstedt came with my parents to graduation exercises, and I basked in the reflected glory of their pride. I was the first of my extended family to graduate from a university.

Mother and I were thrown into a panic that summer getting me ready for Washington. She sewed a new wardrobe for me, being careful to select slimming styles because I still had a weight problem.

We got together the twenty-eight dollars for my train ticket from Elgin to Washington. A huge crowd—many members of my family and many friends from Austin—gathered at the depot to see me off. It compared to today's launching of a space shuttle! I wrote a friend: "It's a far piece from Central Texas to the nation's capital and it will be a long time before I can get home. The natives think Washington is next door to the North Pole and across the fence from Siam, and they're sure I'll never be the same after being contaminated by foreign ideas."

Daddy, who had been so protective of me, said he guessed it was all right if I went to Washington. Lyndon Johnson and Lady Bird would look after me. He had great faith in the congressman from our district. After all, he'd supported him in every election.

I smiled and waved as the train pulled out. Then I found a seat and cried. I was really scared.

4

Capital Insights

EXPLOSIVE! Incredible! Mind-expanding! Enriching!

Superlatives are the only way to describe my year in the nation's capital as a White House intern. The University of Texas had been invigorating, but Washington was intoxicating! I did more, explored more, sought more, learned more, cared more, enjoyed more in that one year than any other of my life.

The year was 1939–1940; I became an adult, both literally and figuratively.

The fat, tacky farm girl from the cotton fields of Central Texas formed close associations and some lifelong friendships with other Rockefeller interns; took graduate courses at American University; visited congressional offices; attended conferences and briefing sessions with the nation's leaders; and was an invited guest at Texas dances, foreign embassies, and the White House. I met some of the most powerful people in the country—Secretary of State Cordell Hull; Secretary of Agriculture Henry Wallace, Secretary of the Treasury Henry Morgenthau, and First Lady Eleanor Roosevelt among them. I dated John Connally two or three times. We attended the gala Texas parties in Washington where I danced with Lyndon Johnson. I'd called Congressman and Mrs. Johnson as soon as I got to Washington because my father insisted. Lady Bird was especially lovely to me. She was a pretty, shy, almost timid woman, but warm and gracious in a face-to-face meeting, and concerned that I was safe, experiencing a quality education, and having a good time.

People—who they were, not as public figures, but as individuals—delighted me, but I was equally enthralled with the place. I spent a lot of time on my three-day train journey from Texas to Washington making a list of the places I must see. It included the White House, Washington Monument, Lincoln Memorial, Smithsonian Institution, and many, many more. I methodically visited the places on my list and countless others I did not even know to list. Feelings of awe and wonder surfaced as I viewed the Lincoln Memorial in the moonlight, and I'd sometimes find myself in tears in the presence of giants of the past immortalized in marble and brick and granite.

I was a part of the excitement that pervaded the great city in one of the most unsettling years in our nation's history—1939–1940. In Europe, World War II started. Hitler, on a rampage of conquest, invaded Poland and annexed Danzig, then invaded Norway and Denmark, Holland, Belgium, and Luxembourg. The Japanese occupied Hainan and blockaded British shipments; in Italy, Mussolini invaded Albania. Russia invaded Poland. On September 3, 1939, Britain and France declared war on Germany. Winston Churchill became British Prime Minister, and a few months later made his famous "blood, toil, tears, and sweat" speech. Japan, Germany, and Italy signed a military and economic pact. In the United States, Franklin Roosevelt asked Congress for $552 million for defense, demanded and got assurances from Hitler and Mussolini that they would not attack thirty-one named states, declared the U.S. still neutral, and announced he would run for an unprecedented third term.

In 1939, the first women and children were evacuated from London to safer, neutral countries, including many to the United States; Richard Llewellyn's book, *How Green Was My Valley*, was published, and John Steinbeck won the Pulitzer Prize for *The Grapes of Wrath*. Only one picture stood a chance at the Academy Awards: *Gone With the Wind* starring Clark Gable and Vivien Leigh, which had earlier premiered in Atlanta in a glittering first night fit for royalty. Anna M. Robertson, better known as Grandma Moses, found fame with her art. Pan-American Airways began the first regularly scheduled commercial flights between the United States and Europe.

And the U.S., still pulling itself out of the Great Depression, began to flourish as European countries ordered arms and war equipment. In a more mundane, but overwhelmingly important development for women, nylon stockings were introduced.

Washington seethed with unrest; the nation's leaders debated foreign policy far into the nights; the Rockefeller interns were aware of and on the periphery of the unrest and attended several of the sessions. One of our government professors told us how lucky we were that an ocean on either side of our country protected us from the bombs falling on European cities.

As exciting as all this was, daily living had to go on. I required food and shelter in a city where I could ill afford them. The National Institute of Public Affairs rented rooms for us at Wesley Hall, 1703 K Street NW, for forty-five dollars a month. We ate out. Meals cost me about three dollars a day. I knew I had to find less expensive accommodations.

I arrived in the nation's capital on September 14, 1939, and the next day went to a get-acquainted reception for the fifty Washington interns. I had previously written to all of the girls and had received replies from most. They were all from influential, affluent families from the east and west, all graduates of the Seven Sisters colleges. All, that is, except one girl from Perth Amboy, New Jersey, who had graduated from New Jersey College for Women, a branch of Rutgers University. Her name was Arista Sarkus, she was Greek, and, if anything, poorer than I! About my size with flashing black eyes and the world's most winning smile, I immediately liked her and she liked me. Arista, brilliant, aggressive, and with boundless energy, was the perfect foil for my quieter manner. I learned so much from her.

Within days we were talking about sharing an apartment. Arista left nothing to chance. She went out right away and found one—a basement affair at 1923 I Street, and as soon as our first month's rent ran out, we moved in together.

What an apartment! It provided the best and the worst, the best that it was cheap and convenient to American University, near the White House, and near the center of Washington; its worst a string of negatives too long to enumerate. It was tiny—a living room, a bedroom, a kitchenette, and a bath. The furnace, between the bath and the kitchen, burned coal and was extremely temperamental. The door often blew open and we'd come home to find a film of soot over everything.

Our landlady was Jessie Brantley, a textbook stereotype of a frustrated old maid—tall and prim, hair in a bun, long skirts, and a face with a perpetual scowl. She worked in a menial government job. Her chief interest in life was the Eastern Star, a Masonic organization. When I told her I had been a Rainbow Girl, a member of a Masonic organization for teenage girls, she decided I must be all right, after all, and she insisted that Arista and I go to Eastern Star meetings with her. We couldn't have been less interested, but one or the other of us would go. We'd flip a coin. The winner got to do the dirtiest job in the house—clean the oven, scrub the bathroom, clear the furnace. The loser got to go to Eastern Star with Miss Brantley.

I was amazed to discover that I was the only one of the interns who knew how to cook. Most of the other girls came from homes where their mothers planned the menus and cooks prepared them. None of the guys cooked; it would have shattered their masculine image. Arista didn't cook, because she'd worked in a store since she was eight years old while her mother took care of the housekeeping and cooking.

Our arrangement was that I'd cook the first six months; she'd observe and learn, as well as do the dishwashing and cleaning—and the next six months we would reverse roles. I made lots of soup; a pound of ground meat at forty-nine cents served for two meals—a meat loaf one night, meatballs and spaghetti the next; a baked chicken, seventy-nine cents to a dollar, provided three or four meals. Arista kept meticulous books on our household expenses. Our discussions about balancing our budget demanded all the weighty attention of a White House conference.

When it was Arista's turn to cook, we had some colossal disasters. She had to learn the basics—how to break eggs, mash potatoes, fry bacon, make coffee, chop vegetables—everything. I instructed and laughed! The first roast she cooked was a lovely brown on the outside and raw inside. She tried to copy the recipe my mother had given me for soup, and put so much salt in it that we couldn't eat it. Her first cake resembled a huge pancake, its frosting drooling off onto the plate.

Our lack of money didn't stop us from entertaining; in fact, it challenged us to save a few pennies on our meals so that we could invite a couple of friends to dinner and serve pork chops! During the year we had every one of the interns to supper at least once. And how they loved to come! A home-cooked meal was manna to people who ate out all the time.

Friends came to our house, not only for meals, but to spend the night. Arista had lots of friends; her New Jersey home was close enough to Washington that the "kids" would hitchhike or take a bus and crash with us. They'd throw their sleeping bags on our floor, shower in our bathroom, and use our apartment as a launching pad for their capital expeditions. The distance from Texas made it impossible for most of my friends to visit, but in a quirk of fate, a visit from my friends was the straw that broke the camel's back with Miss Brantley.

Early in January 1940, there was a youth convention in Washington and kids from all over the country flocked in. When letters came from my friends in Texas, saying they'd like to come to the conference but had no place to stay, I promptly wrote back, "You are welcome to stay in our apartment." Arista's friends didn't really need an invitation; they'd always been welcome to drop in.

On the day the conference opened, fourteen people showed up! The boys from Texas slept in the National Guard armory, but they came over and used our shower and ate at our house. The girls all stayed; they slept on makeshift beds in every square inch of the living room. Everybody chipped in for groceries. I cooked huge pots of oatmeal, toasted two loaves of bread, and made gallons of coffee for breakfast, created a monstrous pot of soup, a giant meat loaf, and a couple of gallons of scalloped potatoes. It was a cold, rainy weekend. People arrived "home" wet and freezing and we'd take care of them, see that they were dry and warm, had a hot shower, ate something, drank something hot.

For some reason, Miss Brantley was unhappy with us. I am certain she was on the verge of asking us to move, but something wonderful happened that saved her the trouble and gave us a new lease on life.

Arista exploded into the house one afternoon shouting, "Tex, we're going to move!" and I said, "How? How can we move? Where can we find a place as cheap as this?" She said, "Trust me," and then she explained. Mildred Burns, the mother of James Mac-Gregor Burns, one of the interns, weary of the winters in cold, ice-bound Lexington, Massachusetts, had come to Washington for its social life—to attend theaters, symphony, operas. Mrs. Burns, who we soon called Thea, Greek for "aunt," also wanted better living accommodations for her son. She'd rented an apartment, the top floor of an old building that was the French Embassy when the British stormed and burned Washington in 1814. At 1713 H Street, a couple of blocks from the White House, it was a lovely, spacious apartment with a wood-burning fireplace in the living room. Steeped in history and with an ambiance of real class, the apartment also sported modern conveniences. Thea offered to rent a room to Arista and me. We moved! Our room had windows and light, twin beds, and even a closet. We had only a small kitchen, a dining area, and one bath, which never seemed to be a problem. A stairway leading to the third floor had a lock, but it never worked. If you hit your left knee sharply against the staircase, the door would fly open. All of our friends knew how to get into the house, but Washington was so safe that we never thought of being frightened.

Thea cooked for herself and her son when she was at home; Arista and I fed Jim when she was away. Because her son was a part of our crowd and because she was often out in the evenings at one or another social event, Thea did not mind our entertaining. And entertain we did! We had "dinner parties" at least once a week. All our friends cherished an invitation to join us for a home-cooked meal.

In late March, Thea and her friends went on a garden tour, the Azalea Trail, and to see the spring flowers in Alabama and Mississippi. She was to be gone for two weeks. I don't think she was out of the city limits before Jim came down with a sore throat that turned out to be strep and the flu. We put him to bed. The next day Arista got sick. Their temperatures soared to 104 degrees. A flu epidemic raged; doctors were overworked and the hospitals were full. Arista didn't have the money to go to the hospital even if one had been available.

I became their nurse. I called the National Youth Administration to which I'd been assigned as a part of my government training and told them I had two very sick people on my hands. I stayed at home for a week nursing my friends. I'd never been so grateful that I'd been stashed in a corner while Mother and Aunt Hulda nursed my grandmother. I'd learned by osmosis. The weather was frigid, so I wrapped myself in my warmest clothes, put on my snow boots, and sloshed out to drug and grocery stores. I bought rubbing alcohol, a thermometer, aspirin, chicken, vegetables, and fruit juices. I knew I had to get a lot of liquids into them. Both were moaning and groaning in their misery. Jim's bedroom was across the landing from the stairway, a hall, past the bathroom, and through the kitchen and dining room, so far off that I couldn't wait on both patients at once. When both were throwing up at the same time, I had to race from one side of the house to the other trying to help. I had to think of something more practical. So I moved Jim into my twin bed and left Arista in hers; I slept in Mrs. Burns's bed, near enough that I could hear if they called at night. I took them glasses of orange juice and water and other liquids, tried to feed them chicken soup, gave them alcohol rubs, bathed their faces and arms in cool water, kept damp cool rags on their foreheads. Jim would say, "Let me alone. Let me die," and Arista would turn her face to the wall and beg, "Go away. Go away." I couldn't go away. I knew if their temperatures got too high, they would go into convulsions and then I'd be in real trouble.

I didn't think it at all unusual to be nursing my friends. A lot of the other interns also got the flu. I kept a pot of chicken soup on the stove. The guys would come over, have a bowl of soup, and lie down on Jim's bed for a while until they gathered enough strength to go back to their rooms. This was before we had sulfa and antibiotics. A lot of people got pneumonia and many died, but all of us pulled through.

Mrs. Burns was having such a good time that she delayed her return and was away for three weeks. By the time she got back, Jim was recovering. Arista was up and I was exhausted, but I didn't even get a sore throat!

A few weeks after we arrived in Washington, each of us was assigned to a department to work and learn about the federal government. I went to the National Youth Administration, one of President Roosevelt's government programs created by Congress to train young boys and girls for work. I was Thelma McKelvey's special charge. A bright, aggressive, politically active woman, she was a friend of Anna Boettinger, the only daughter of President and Mrs. Roosevelt. She had a nice disposition—and very little time for me because she was so busy promoting herself. She was also a misfit in her job. She was—or thought she was—socially elite; the NYA sought and trained kids from the poverty pockets of the country, individuals to whom she could not possibly relate. I could, and made great friends in the department. I especially liked Mary McLeod Bethune. She was an astute, articulate, lovely woman, an educator from the south who had a college named for her. She was large, obese, and black, and for me a new and lasting lesson on the imperative to racially integrate our country. If I had experienced nothing more than her presence, she would have taught me much; I've always been grateful that she also helped me to learn the NYA ropes.

The highlight of the year came when Mrs. Roosevelt invited all fifty of the interns for supper at the White House. Alexander Heard and Jim Burns asked Arista and me to go with them. When they arrived at our apartment, Alex hailed a cab. We couldn't believe it! The White House was all of three blocks away. It was a pleasant late afternoon. I said, "Alex, are you out of your mind? It's just three blocks. Why are you hailing a cab? Cabs are expensive! It'll be at least twenty cents plus a nickel tip for us to go just three blocks," and Alex said, "All of my life I've wanted to get into a cab and say, 'Cabbie, to the White House.'" All four of us crowded into the backseat of a cab and there was absolute silence. Then Alex said, "Cabbie, to the White House, please." We arrived at the North Entrance in great style. Alex later became chancellor of Vanderbilt University and a renowned educator, political historian, writer, and lecturer. I saw him a number of times in Washington and we always laughed about our evening together at the White House.

We trekked upstairs to the family quarters where Mrs. Roosevelt received us. She was one of the most gracious people I have ever met. She served the supper herself, being especially attentive to each one of us, offering seconds. The plates were stacked buffet style with doilies between each to keep them from chipping. One of our interns, a guy from California, was so nervous that he put his food on top of the doily. Mrs. Roosevelt noticed and very adroitly took the plate, handing him another with the doily removed. We sat around in chairs and on the floor and she talked with us, answered our questions, made each of us feel welcome and special.

This was at a time when attacks on Mrs. Roosevelt were vicious. Terrible cartoons and jokes appeared every day in the nation's newspapers and horrible stories were passed around. She ignored the criticism and went right on being kind and gracious and doing the things she thought were important. We know now that Eleanor was actually a strong force along with Franklin, but she was a woman of her times, and everything she did had to be funneled through him.

Arista and I both adored Eleanor Roosevelt. She was my role model—not a mentor, because a mentor is a guide, teacher, or educator; Mrs. Roosevelt was my example of how a woman ought to run her life. Things were informal in Washington at that time. It was not at all unusual to see the nation's First Lady taking a walk alone or out shopping by herself. I ran into her several times walking alone on the sidewalk near the White House; she would nod and speak. I never engaged her in conversation because I could tell by her manner that she was in deep thought, working through some special project or speech. I also ran into her a couple of times while shopping at the department store Woodward and Lothrop. To me she represented the epitome of grace and class, a very wealthy person who never looked down on anyone but did everything she could to lift them up.

My social life in Washington was very, very busy. Guys outnumbered girls in Washington about three to one, so I dated a lot— I could have gone out every night—and almost did! This girl from Texas began to feel worthy. I didn't date a lot of the interns, but a number of Texans and others asked me out. Bob Anthony and J. Ford Johnson called me when they wanted to talk about home.

John Connally, who was already dating Nellie and very much in love with her, asked me to a couple of Texas dances. A Marine stationed at Quantico in Virginia, whose name was Bill something-or-other, thought he was in love with me, and showed up every weekend. I had other things to do, so I finally had to write him a "Dear John" letter. Lois Burton, one of the other interns, dated a guy from West Point, and she invited Arista and me to New York for a West Point dance at the Waldorf Astoria. My date was a cadet from Texas who could talk about nothing but himself and the military. I was bored stiff, but a dance at the Waldorf Astoria in New York City was really something else for this kid from the country. I dated a man named Mack White, who loved music and took me to the concerts and symphonies at Constitution Hall. I went with Manny DeAngelis, an Italian about my height, a little older than I, with a terrific personality. Boy, could he dance! He also had a full-time job and an automobile. I never hear the popular songs of those days—"You Are My Sunshine," "How High the Moon," "The Last Time I Saw Paris," "Oh Johnny," "When You Wish Upon a Star," "Roll Out the Barrel," "Lili Marlene," "Three Little Fishes," "Over the Rainbow," "I'll Never Smile Again"—that I don't think of Manny and those days when we'd dance until the wee hours of the morning. It was the year that Kate Smith introduced "God Bless America," and we heard it everywhere.

I went on an official NYA trip to some of the projects in Appalachia where I saw poverty that made me ashamed I'd ever thought I was deprived. I visited a number of NYA training centers in the hills of West Virginia and spent ten days traveling through Kentucky, West Virginia, and Tennessee seeing firsthand how the training projects worked. Once I went over into Ohio on an NYA fact-finding trip. Everywhere people were kind to me, eager to share what they were doing. I was only twenty, but they took me seriously and I had a wonderful time.

Arista often dragged me to New York. We always took the bus because it was the cheapest way to get there and neither of us had any money. Once we got there we'd travel by subway to see all the glorious sights of the city. We visited Arista's family in Perth Amboy a number of times, usually on our way to New York. The Sarkuses were a very large family, parents, three girls and two boys, the oldest daughter married and out of the house when I knew them. The parents spoke Greek, and never learned to speak English. They were all scrunched up together in a tiny crowded apartment in the tenement section of town, and the one time Arista and I stayed overnight, we slept on cots in the living room. They were so proud of Arista, and welcomed me as a part of the family. When we visited, Arista whisked me from apartment to apartment introducing me to all her aunts, uncles, and cousins. Everyone was very hospitable, and we had to eat something in each apartment. It would have been unspeakably rude not to. By the time we completed the round of visits, I was so stuffed that I waddled.

Once, Arista's mother and two of her sisters, Antoinette and Pitsy, visited us in Washington. Antoinette was married, but Pitsy was an eighteen-year-old beauty. Arista told me that her parents did not allow Pitsy to date and she hoped we could show her a good time while she was in Washington, so that weekend I pretended to have an enormous amount of library work to do. I invited Pitsy to go with me; she could read while I worked. Arista and I had arranged dates for the three of us to go dancing. I shall always remember what a marvelous time Pitsy had dancing at the Maryland Club Gardens. Mrs. Sarkus commented to Arista later that she was so impressed that I spent Saturday night at the library studying.

On Sunday morning, we almost had a fiasco when Johnny Crone, a friend from Texas, showed up. We were all sitting around in our housecoats drinking coffee and talking about our evening at the library when I heard someone come stomping up the stairs. I met Johnny on the stairway and whispered, "Arista's parents are here. You're my cousin! If you ever want to come back to this house, play along." I introduced them, and Mrs. Sarkus immediately saw the family resemblance between Johnny and me.

In that magic place, at that wonderful time of my life, with my social life exploding, it was inevitable that I fall in love. When it happened, I went off the deep end—moved around in a daze, starry-eyed, impatient for the phone to ring, and nearly rude when it wasn't Reggie Thomas. Whoever it was, I wanted him to hang up because Reggie might call. Our apartment was always full of people dropping in, but when Reggie showed up, I got all trembly, couldn't focus on anything but him, daydreamed about him when we were apart, and tried out the name Mrs. Reggie Thomas on all of my papers. I thought he was the most wonderful man God ever created—very tall, blond, blue-eyed, handsome. He'd been an intern four years before so he understood my excitement about being in Washington. He had an excellent job and a new Dodge automobile. Most wonderful of all, he seemed to feel the same way about me. He showed me rather than told me. When I was with him, everything was more beautiful. One of his friends had a boat, and Reggie would take me sailing on the Chesapeake Bay. He made me both very happy and miserable because he never spoke the words I so longed to hear.

Outside Arista, Jim Burns was my dearest friend. I could confide in him things I didn't even tell my roommate. Ours is a relationship— it continues to this day—that proves men and women can be friends without romantic involvement. There wasn't ever the faintest hint of any sexual liaison. I knew very well if anything was going on with Jim, Arista and I would find ourselves looking for a new apartment. His mother cared about us, but she was a true New England matron and she expected her son to marry a girl from their own "class." I knew this without anything ever being said. I had no brothers, Jim had no sisters, so we developed a sibling relationship. We'd often go together to the library, and to the Capitol and to intern meetings. We were so comfortable with each other. On evenings when Mrs. Burns and Arista were out, Jim would build a fire in the fireplace and we'd sit and talk, endlessly sharing thoughts. He thought he was in love with Katherine, a girl from New York, and I *knew* I was in love with Reggie, so we'd sit around and cry on each other's shoulder about our unfulfilled passions.

This wonderful relationship continued after I returned to Texas. Jim wrote me long letters telling me about all our friends and all the political doings in Washington. I wrote back equally long letters. After I left, his friendship with Arista deepened, but he went away to Harvard in September 1940 to begin work on his Ph.D.

Years later, Jim sent me a copy of his first book, *Roosevelt: The Lion and the Fox*, and later an autographed copy of his Pulitzer prize–winning, *Roosevelt: The Soldier of Freedom*. Once, in the early sixties when I was in New York, I drove to his home in Williamstown, where he was a professor of history, and had a very short visit, about twenty minutes, before I had to leave to meet friends. Our correspondence diminished after I married; Grier was a jealous husband, and I heard about Jim only through the press for many years. In the last few years, we have renewed our acquaintance and we visit often by telephone, sometimes sharing our thoughts, asking each other for advice, and renewing one of the most precious friendships of my lifetime.

The spring semester continued to be as busy and exciting as ever. I finished fifteen hours of graduate work with the thought that I would return to American University for summer sessions until I completed my master's degree. I never did. As the day drew near for my departure, I was torn. I was still madly in love with Reggie and I wanted desperately to remain in Washington, but I had promised my folks that I would go home to Texas when the year was out. With an NYA job in Austin promised, I sadly packed my bags.

Jim, Reggie, and Arista went with me to the train station. I've never known such wrenching misery. We all kissed and hugged. Arista and I were crying and the boys blinked back tears, too. I stood on the platform and waved to my friends as far as I could see them. Then I went in and found a seat and cried and cried and cried.

I was kidded to pieces by the conductors, porters, and some of the passengers about my promiscuous display of affection at the station, and my weeping after the train pulled out. I cried all the way to Alexandria, then dropped off and slept to Charlottesville. When I woke up, the porter said, "Which of those gentlemen was your man?" I was embarrassed, but I said, "The one I kissed first." He shook his head. "You sure gave that last one a plenty powerful kiss. Looks like he was your man." I said, "No, he belongs to my friend," and he informed me that if he'd been in my friend's place, he'd have allowed no such goings-on. Then he consoled me by declaring that *both* the young men would be married before I got to New Orleans!

5

A Gift from Grief

WITHOUT BEING AWARE OF IT, because she died at the age of thirty-four, Arista gave me one of the loveliest gifts I've ever had. She saved the letters I wrote to her from June 7, 1940, through June 11, 1941, the year I returned to Texas and began a new career. Her daughter, Phyllis Ann (Anna) Richmond Gold found them in the attic of her parents' home after her father's death, forty-one years after Arista died. She read them and then sent them to me. I read them at first with a sense of great sadness for the loss of a friend so young, and with reluctance lest I discover myself foolish in my youth. It was with relief, a letting go of long-buried mourning and appreciation to Arista and her daughter, that I completed them—for in rereading my words of that year, at first so painful and at the end so joyful, that I better understood myself as a young woman. No matter how vivid one's memory, years and experiences alter past perceptions. Some memories are enlarged, almost to the point of fiction; others that once seemed so vivid are buried in the minutiae of daily life. The letters not only gave me total recall of the past, helped me see clearly who I was with all of my fears, insecurities, and lack of self-worth, but gave me a greater compassion and understanding of young people.

When the train bringing me from Washington pulled into the station at Elgin shortly after noon on June 7, 1940, I was met by my parents and other family members, some of whom had long since given me up for lost! I had come by way of Atlanta, where I stayed with a friend, took a 350-mile sojourn into northern Georgia to visit NYA projects, was entertained royally, and offered a job by the state NYA administrator, Bouiffelet Jones. I almost stayed! Everything around Atlanta was, to me, similar to the wonderful Washington I had left behind. Only the promise I had made to my parents compelled me to continue my journey. Then I stopped to visit friends in New Orleans where, again, I was welcomed and royally entertained. We celebrated with cocktails at the Court of the Two Sisters on my last night there. Then, I took the 11 P.M. train for Houston where I changed trains for Elgin.

Home was a giant step. I made every effort to belong again— and shed tears only at night after Mother and Daddy were in bed. I wrote to Arista, "Home is wonderful! The peace, quiet, tranquility, ah, there is nothing like it. I didn't know how much I missed a stroll through the pasture . . . and the broad expanses of cotton misting the hills to the south . . . We have a new calf, lots of chickens. How much you'd enjoy . . . being here. You could even turn the separator and see the cream run out in a pan and the milk pour out in buckets."

Mother was so glad to see me home! She gave dinner parties so that all my relatives could see that I hadn't become too Yankeefied. . . . A bunch of my old buddies led by Bo Byers, Mac Roy Rasor, and Kenneth Clark came out to welcome me. I wrote to Arista, "A whole gang of people came out yesterday. I'm honor guest at two dinners tomorrow. Next Sunday there will be a terrific blowout celebrating my arrival at the age of discretion. . . . Everybody is anxious to see if I have a Yankee accent, smoke, drink, swear violently, am expecting a baby, or am a Communist, atheist, or Nazi."

Mother, I wrote to Arista ". . . is a peach . . . unpacked my trunk and had all my clothes in apple pie order when I got here. She has dropped everything to get me ready for work next Monday . . . isn't even shocked at my wild stories of Washington. I even told her about the beer party you gave . . . and she said she hoped I had the beer cans gathered up before Arista's old maid friends arrived. This woman is a wonder. We could probably teach her to jitterbug."

Even though I'd had a brief fling in Atlanta with a great guy who begged me to stay to check out, as he termed it, our potential for the future, and even though I loved seeing old friends from high school and college, I longed to hear from Reggie—and didn't. I appreciated all the attention my relatives and friends lavished on me, and I think I did a fairly good job of being gracious, but even in the welcoming whirlwind, I longed for the life I had left behind.

Mother had written me that they were, at last, getting electricity and I was delighted, but I was unprepared for the mess that greeted me. We couldn't see the farm for the REA (Rural Electric Administration) power lines traveling through it. Double lines went the length of the place, and the private line to our house crisscrossed the other way. Another line ran in the other direction to the Negro schoolhouse at our front gate. Our telephone poles were lost in the jumble. Limbs were gone from the trees, some trees cut down. I wrote Arista, "The place looks like the Argonne Forest. . . . I'm watching men stretch wires. They tie the wire on a truck and drive the truck away from the pole until the line is taut . . . quite interesting. . . . But last week the REA men drove a truck all over our front lawn when it was muddy and left ruts a foot deep . . . I filled them, hauling bucket after bucket of dirt. I then swore at the REA with all my might! . . . We will have the power turned on in two weeks."

Through the festivities, I was preparing to go to work on the following Monday morning at my new NYA job in Austin. Because the roads were still mud trails when it rained, there was no way I could live on the farm and drive back and forth to Austin. Even so, I knew I had to have a car because my job included scouring the countryside for potential NYA trainees. I made arrangements to use my dad's 1936 Chevrolet, leaving them for a time with only an old pickup truck for transportation. No way could I afford a new car on my $110 per month salary.

Austin was still a small town, around 70,000 people, but it was "home" because I'd been born there and had gone to college there. It was small enough that you could walk down Congress Avenue and know about every third person you met. Even so, it was more cosmopolitan than any other part of the state because of the university. And it was headquarters for state government and all of the state agencies. I loved Austin, always have, still do, but the city I knew is gone. It's now a metropolis with big-city problems.

I rented a bedroom from my cousin, Jeannette Swahn Johnson, and her husband, Harry. Seven years older than I, Jeanette had served as my big sister when I was a kid. Their tiny home on 44th Street was barely big enough for them, but Jeanette and Harry generously gave me the front bedroom.

On Monday morning I took a bus to a brown building on Lavaca near 8th Street in Austin, and arrived for my first day at work. The state administrator and the deputy interviewed me and seemed impressed that I had worked in the national office, had visited projects while in Washington, and had even looked over some projects in Atlanta on my way home. I was assigned to the state office as a research clerk at a salary of $115 a month, five dollars more than I had been promised. I thought it very puny until I was told I was on the administrative level and making more than anybody else in the office except for the head of the division.

At first my work was almost clerical, but I did go to San Antonio and other NYA projects around Austin to get an idea of what was going on in Texas. Lyndon Johnson had been the first Texas NYA administrator, and it was very much his baby. Jessie Kellum was named administrator after LBJ was elected to Congress, but it was clear to me from the very first that the key employees were Johnson people and there was a direct grapevine from Austin to Washington to report on everything we did.

Lyndon's pipeline to the people of his district was also through our offices. We understood that we reported anything of significance in our areas to our superiors, who transmitted it immediately to Lyndon. If a farmer's pig won a blue ribbon at the local fair, Johnson wanted to know and would write a congratulatory letter to the farmer. I have been in terrible little shacks where people brought out their dearest possession, a letter from Lyndon Johnson congratulating them on something or other. I have seen him walk down the street in a little town, and shake hands with every man and call him by name and ask about his family. The farmers and small town residents ate this up. Lyndon could have been elected emperor or pope if the election depended on Texas's Tenth Congressional District. It's no surprise that he became president of the United States.

The first question everyone asked of a female job candidate was "Can you type?" I was a whiz at typing. I could knock out seventy-five words a minute on a manual typewriter, had even won a couple of speed tests, but I knew if I said yes I would be stuck behind a keyboard most of the time, so I lied. I said, "I can sort of hunt and peck, but no, I am not a typist." They put me on the payroll anyway. They must have thought, because I was just out of Washington, that I had a direct pipeline to Congressman Johnson.

A few weeks later my lie could have finished me off. It was after hours; everybody had gone home, so I went into the back supply room where there was an old typewriter and started to write letters to a host of friends in Washington. I could write four or five letters by typing them in the time it took me to write one by hand. My fingers were going like mad and I was deep in concentration when I became aware that I was being watched. I turned around and there stood my boss, hands on his hips, just looking at me. Neither of us said a word. He turned and walked away. I think he got the message that I did not intend to get stuck in a clerical job.

At first my days were routine and monotonous. I wrote to Arista: "This is my schedule: Rise at 6:15, get dressed, eat breakfast; 7:00, leave for work; 7:40, get to work; 12 noon to 1 p.m., home for lunch; 4 p.m., off work, come home, go swimming; 5 p.m., eat dinner and play in the sandpile with Baby Jeannene until 8 p.m.; come inside and play with Jeannene until 9 p.m.; get ready for bed and am sound asleep by 10:15. The next morning, I get up at 6:15— and on to another day."

I brought a lot of the monotony on myself because I had let only a few of my friends know I was living in Austin. I gave all the fellows my Elgin address and they thought I was out in the sticks. I wasn't in the mood to go out with any of them. I did go to dinner with Mary Love, who was, I wrote to Arista, "as big as a blimp. She got married December 24 and the baby is due in October . . . see, I've been in Texas only a week and I'm already getting ultra-conservative."

Arista was admonished to deliver a message to Reggie. "Tell him," I wrote, "what a sensible life I am leading. Tell him I'm taking my job so seriously that I get nine and a half hours sleep every night so as to perform efficiently. I haven't smoked, taken a swig, sworn, petted or anything! I sit in the amen corner in church and sing 'Hallelujah.' "

After being in the state office for a little while, I was assigned to the area office headed by Jake Pickle. He advanced my title to Area Counselor. My work consisted of going out into the cedar brakes and the forks of the creeks to recruit kids for NYA work training. We'd take kids who'd barely been off the farm in their entire lives and teach them a trade—carpentry, sheet metalwork, plumbing, auto mechanics, welding, and a lot of other stuff. We had a girls' project, too, and taught them sewing, cooking, personal hygiene, and home-making skills. The girls lived in houses and the boys in camps. It was exhausting work with a lot of travel, but it was exhilarating, too, and when I had a chance to take a different, better paying job, I turned it down.

I covered ten counties all the way from San Saba and Blanco and Burnet down to LaGrange and Schulenberg, and over to San Marcus and New Braunfels. It was a huge territory. I had a regular run every two weeks. I'd go to Lampasas, Llano, Burnett, and Lamesa one day, to Georgetown and Taylor another, and to Gittings and LaGrange another. I'd spend one or two nights out each time I went on a recruiting drive.

The first thing I did when I went into a different community was to find out who was in charge there. Somebody always was! In Bas-trop, a judge, named C. B. Maynard, ran the town. He was eager to help his community and would round up a bunch of kids for me to interview every time I went there. In Schulenberg, there was this big, jovial Catholic priest, Father Geortz. He literally ran the community and was concerned about poverty and the lack of opportunity for the young folks. He knew my grandmother was Catholic and every time I went to his area, he'd see that I had lots of applicants.

Fayette County was a part of my territory. Settled by Czechs, Poles, Germans, and Slavs (each group maintained its own customs) and very Republican, the people there did not welcome outsiders. All government projects were suspect, ours especially because we were perceived as putting foreign ideas into their kids' heads. The NYA had been trying to recruit there for years with almost no results. So I went in, slung around the few German words I knew, and they started opening up. I wrote to Arista, "Ten kids go to NYA projects this week and a gang went last week. Our area director is absolutely speechless—he can't see what I have that he hasn't." There was nothing magic about what I was doing; it was that I belonged! My name was Ballerstedt and his was Crider, and folks in the community knew either my dad's or my mother's families or both, so I had to be all right.

Often I'd go places that weren't on any map. I'd get directions like "It's over yonder, thataway." Fortunately, I had a good sense of direction and could go down mud roads and find people. Not long after I finally got a new car and returned Dad's, much more worn, I had a blowout. I was way out in the sticks and there was nobody to help me, so I changed the tire and completed my rounds.

I had known Jake Pickle back at the University of Texas, where he was the president of the student body, the first non-fraternity man to hold that office. He'd worked up a political organization that later elected both John Connally and Sidney Reagan as student body presidents. He would later be elected to Congress from the same district as Lyndon Johnson, his mentor, and serve with distinction for thirty-one years. At the time he was my boss, he was only twenty-six years old, very attractive, and all the women were chasing him. Jake and I were immediately attracted to each other and expressed our admiration by continually fighting. "You're too goddamn smart," he'd yell, and call me "Phi Beta Ballerstedt" and slam the door as he left my office. I thought up all kinds of tricks to play on him. This continued to be our relationship until I quit my job in October 1941. One time his secretary went on vacation and he made arrangements for me to take her place. I wrote to Arista, "He's the meanest guy who ever wore trousers . . . he pulled every string in sight to get me as steno for the week. He knows that I can't take shorthand and am ignorant of the million forms that go out of this office. He wore the cat-that-ate-the-canary look as he swaggered about. He dug up every old letter in the recesses of his desk that had to be answered . . . right now!

"The other morning when I opened the door of my office, there was standing right in the door a lifelike dummy of a Texas Ranger— six feet tall and so realistic with its two guns that I couldn't tell whether it was breathing. I jumped about four feet and gasped. Pickle thought it was hilarious. He'd put the dummy there because, he said, he had heard old maids always like to find men in their rooms. . . . I was his date at a Lion's Club banquet. None of the Lions had ever seen Pickle with a skirt before and they insisted he introduce me. He did. He said my name was Larruping Lou . . . They wouldn't let him dance with me all evening. When we would get together, they did everything but play the wedding march. Their paper carries a full account of the Pickle-Lou affair. . . . He has the paper buried somewhere in his desk. He knows I'm dying of curiosity to see it, but. . . ."

In October, Madeleine Lewis, Jake's secretary and I rented an apartment on Oldham Street with a living room, bedroom, kitchen, dinette, bathroom, and hall. We'd hardly unpacked when we gave a party for all the women who worked with us at NYA.

I LOVED LIVING WITH MADELEINE. She grew up on a ranch riding horses and branding cattle, and didn't wear a dress until the night she graduated from high school. There was no money for college, so she took a business course and at age eighteen was court reporter for Burleson County. Nobody was better at shorthand, and she could transcribe at a typing speed of 100 words a minute. She had a rambunctious sense of humor that made living with her such fun.

When young men were being drafted for military duty, Jake, typical of the reaction of most young men, was petrified. On his birthday in October, Madeleine Lewis and I decided to play a trick on him and got the entire office to go along. Jake was out of the office all day and we knew he wouldn't be back until after dark, so Amos hauled in a male mannequin. We put it in a casket and fixed up a funeral bier. I bought a white lily at the dime store. We folded the dummy's hands around the lily and rigged up the electricity so that when he pushed the switch, a spotlight fell on a sign, REST IN PEACE, JAKE PICKLE, beside the catafalque. We were all hiding in different places in the office when he came whistling in and turned on the light. He stood there absolutely stunned and we erupted into gales of laughter.

It didn't take but a few days for Jake to respond. Madeleine and I had rented a garage apartment from friends of my parents who lived in the house just in front of our apartment. Our decorum was pristine. It was after midnight and we were in bed sound asleep when bedlam broke loose. A car came careening up the street, its horn blasting as it pulled into our driveway. Two men staggered to our front door and began hammering on it, yelling that they were too drunk to drive and needed us to make coffee and sober them up. We did everything we could to shush them and persuade them to go away, to no avail. Finally, we put on our housecoats, let Jake and Amos in, and made bacon, scrambled eggs, toast, and coffee.

I held more jobs in a short time than I can remember—everything from a researcher in the state office to traveling aide in the district office to stenographer in the area office—but my principal responsibility was to keep the training classes full. I decided a traveling exhibit, which could be transported from one place to the next and displayed at county fairs, would be an ideal way to reach people. Jake thought it was a terrible idea, but I went ahead and got it ready. The first fair was at Manor. It was only seventeen miles away, and I needed an NYA truck to transport the stuff. I asked Jake if I could borrow one. He was mad at me for continuing with the exhibit when he'd all but told me not to, and he yelled, "Get your goddamn stuff to Manor the best way you can," and went out and slammed the door.

I spied a big government truck on the parking lot and conned some of my coworkers into loading everything on it. I found the keys, got behind the wheel, and went careening down the highway. I did not have permission to drive a government truck and I had no commercial driver's license. I just knew I was right and would prove it. I needed three sheets of plywood to set up the exhibit, so when I got to Manor, I pulled into the lumberyard, planning to pay for it out of my own pocket. The truck was so big that I couldn't step out, so I had to jump down. This scared the owner so badly that he gave me the lumber. I drove everything out to the fair, located on the school yard, and set up my booth. Then I drove the truck back to Austin, where I found Jake almost having a heart attack. We had another fight.

We won the blue ribbon for best exhibit. I took it back and waved it under Jake's nose and said, "See there! I was right."

I took the exhibit to several fairs and won other awards. When people stopped by, I'd explain about the youth projects, the training we offered kids. Many parents were won over when they learned we not only trained their kids, but paid them while they learned. Many we trained found excellent jobs during World War II.

My job included a lot of things other than teaching mechanical skills. Some of the kids couldn't read and write; we'd try to teach them the basics. Some had never used a toothbrush; most had never been to a dentist. None had inoculations. I'd con dentists and doctors into donating their time to take care of the kids.

We also had socials for the girls and boys. We'd truck the boys to the parties; the kids were shy. The boys would stand on one side and the girls on the other. Jake and I chaperoned, and it was our job to see that they mixed and had a good time.

I was younger than some of the kids I recruited for the NYA programs, but the word got around that I was twenty-six, had spent three years in Washington, and held a Ph.D. They were awed, and I had to smile more than once when one came to me for advice. I very soon began to feel proprietary about them. I knew if I didn't round them up and get them to a place where they could learn something, they'd probably spend the rest of their lives back in the sticks and never know there was a wider world. "I feel like a mother," I wrote to Arista, "when I see about fifteen or twenty kids I have picked out really learning things in a project and becoming more confident."

I was sexually harassed at work and didn't even know what to call it! One of the bosses insisted that I be transferred to the office directly under his supervision, and I was flattered because it amounted to a promotion. It didn't take me long to see that he had an ulterior motive. He was married and had a family but he constantly made lewd remarks, touched women inappropriately, and bragged about his sexual liaisons. Unfortunately some of the other girls giggled and smiled, encouraging him. He began to eye me. My skin crawled every time he came near. When I could no longer ignore him, I told him off. I was afraid I'd be fired; I knew for certain I'd never be able to climb the career ladder as long as he was in charge, and I wouldn't go along with his little affairs. It never dawned on me to register a complaint higher up. I thought it was a part of the job.

Jake was a born politician and encouraged my political inclinations. I wrote to Arista, "My life has been just as hectic as it was in Washington. Bob Eckhardt needs plenty of assistance if he shows up at all against the insurance trust he is bucking, so we . . . spend time we're supposed to be sleeping thinking up political schemes. . . . My life down here is just one qualm after the other on account of the Hatch Acts." The Hatch Acts consisted of two laws, the first passed by Congress in 1939 and the second in 1940, restricting political activities for federal service employees. The second extended the ban to include the political actions of all state and local governments that received federal money.

One Sunday night Jake came out to the house when I was at home visiting my parents and they fell in love with him. Mother served coffee and cake; I noticed he got the biggest piece. With a straight face, he entertained them with wild tales about me—said I'd almost ruined his new Chevy taking some boys to San Antonio for a project, getting lost and having to drive on goat trails for twenty miles or so. He also said I'd driven his car up a mountain on another project. My parents believed every word and fussed at me later for "being so mean to that nice young man." Little did they know!

I worked an average of fourteen hours a day five days a week, counting the public relations events and socializing that went with the job. "Last night," I wrote to Arista, "I went to a real country dance here at the fair. These Germans and Czechs are the world's best dancers. People from three to 103 dance all night. I love the Paul Joneses. Grandpas who sit at home all week complaining with rheumatism do these polkas and waltzes all over the floor. I'm not exactly creaky in the joints, but it's all I can do to keep up with them. . . . Mother says you won't have time to read my long letters, but I know better. If I intersperse them with a few nice things to say about Jim, you'll read it if it takes all night. You are right: Jim is wonderful, stupendous, colossal, superb, magnificent, unexcelled, intelligent, clever, witty, good-natured, and exotic . . . oh well, he'll pass. . . . Reggie is quite definitely a memory now. If we met, I don't know what my reaction would be."

When I visited my parents, I was eager to help them find and install the best electrical supplies, lighting, and appliances possible. We planned all of the fixtures and floor plugs. I wanted a chandelier for the living room; I knew Dad would not go for the extra ten dollars one cost, so I bought it myself and didn't tell them. I also bought their first electric refrigerator. The salesman tried to convince them to buy the one that Consumer's Union rated as the worst on the market, but I prevailed and we ordered a General Electric. It cost $125. I thought Daddy would die.

The country still turned into a mud puddle when it rained, and in the middle of the summer, unpredictably, it poured and a long-awaited letter from Reggie almost went astray. The letter wound up in the middle of the creek along with the mail carrier, who almost drowned. His horse turned a flip in a raging stream about a mile from our house and he had to swim out, rescuing the mail as he went. My letter lost its envelope, so had no identity except the salutation "Dear Tex." After reading it carefully, swear words and all, the postman decided it had to belong to me and delivered it to the farm mailbox.

I was deeply in debt, and owed $900. My salary remained at $115 a month, but I got an extra $75 travel allotment. In November Arista asked how I'd spent my money. At that time I'd been working for NYA five months and had made a total of $675 in salary, plus the travel stipend. I wrote back that I had paid $150 on my debt, $100 on wiring and fixtures for the farm, $40 for life insurance, $40 for new tires, $31.75 for car repairs, $80 for health expenses (doctor, dentist, and medicines), $30 on old debts, and $26 for an electric churn for Mother for Christmas. In addition I'd paid for rent, utilities, and food and had bought six pairs of shoes, several dresses, three hats, and accessories. When I traveled, I never spent more than $1.50 a day for food and $3 for a hotel room when I had to spend the night out of town. In December I bought a new 1941 Master DeLuxe Chevrolet Town Sedan for $750 cash. My aunt Mary was the teller at the local bank, and got the loan at 6 percent interest, with Dad co-signing. It was such a joy to be driving a dependable car; I've never had another one that meant so much to me.

Shortly before Christmas Reggie came to see me and I was right back in the same romantic swoon I'd experienced in Washington. I wrote to Arista, ". . . the nice speech I made to you about not giving two hoots for him is hooey. He's the only fellow I've ever cared for—though I'm not romantic enough to say he's the only one I could ever care for. . . . I wonder how a particular individual can have such an effect on one? . . . As for Reggie, I gather he thinks a lot of me, but he won't ask me to marry him or even tell me he loves me. . . . I had lunch with him, his mother, his father, and his kid brother. I was treated like one of the family. . . . I was supremely happy when he was here . . . wouldn't it be wonderful if both of us were married and living in Washington next year?"

Little did I know that I would be married to someone else in only three months.

"I met [Grier Raggio] just three months ago today," I wrote to Arista on April 14. "I walked into his office in Georgetown where he was organizing the Food Stamp Plan . . . I was doing my usual politicking trying to find out about the county. Grier suggested we have coffee. Two hours later we were still talking. We had lunch. I had to move on . . . so he took the afternoon off and went with me. Freddie, his coworker, tagged along . . . Both came to Austin with me that night, and Grier matched Freddie up with Madeleine. He didn't try any fast stuff. Merely asked me to marry him. I thought it was a big joke and naturally I said yes. I knew it wasn't liquor talking because Grier doesn't drink.

"The next day I went to Burnet and Llano. Grier called me at the Llano Hotel. Said he was lonesome . . . next day I passed through Georgetown on the way to Austin and called him and he came on to Austin with me . . . we went out to dinner . . . then danc-ing. Next night he called me long distance and confirmed our date for Saturday night." He fixed Freddie up with Madeleine again.

On Saturday night, Grier and Freddie arrived and all of us went out to dinner and dancing again. Freddie drank like a sponge. We finally got him to our apartment, where he passed out cold and was too big to move. We couldn't budge him, so Madeleine and I went to a motel for the night. It was scary because both of us were well known in Austin and we didn't dare register under our own names at 3 A.M. on a Sunday. When we got back to the apartment on Sunday morning, Grier was playing nursemaid to Freddie while making bacon and eggs.

We drove back to Georgetown where we had lunch and then went hiking. The next week, Grier was in Austin every night. He assumed we were going to get married as soon as possible. After all, I had accepted his proposal! He told me he had long ago determined exactly what he wanted in a wife, had dated a lot of girls, and had given up ever finding his ideal until I walked into his office.

I had no intention of "going off the deep end" for Grier, I told Arista, "because I know of the impending draft and I learned a bitter lesson when I had to return a ring to LeRoy." But Grier had other ideas. On January 31, seventeen days after we met, Grier gave me a beautiful diamond engagement ring, "one of the loveliest I've ever seen," I told Arista. "Large diamond with four smaller ones around it. Platinum and yellow gold."

Grier had "staked his claim" before his job took him off to Mis-sissippi, where he worked for a month and I had time to think things over. Well, hardly. He wrote every day. He sent flowers. He sent gifts. He called. He got back to Texas on March 7 and I joined him for four days in Dallas. "He was a perfect gentleman," I wrote to Arista, "no sex until after we are married."

The next weekend, we went to Beaumont and Port Arthur to visit his sisters and brother. I was delighted with the family and was "Aunt Louise" to his nephews. On the last week of March, Mother went with Grier and me for a trip into Mexico. We drove through the Rio Grande Valley, Corpus Christi, Monterrey, Saltillo, and Reynosa, had a marvelous time. My mother was delightful. She had two cocktails in a nightclub and danced with Grier and a Mexican man! Grier bought me a beautiful hand-carved coffee table and some towels. He said the table would be our living room, dining room, breakfast nook, and utility table, and the towels our linens. Neither of us gave much thought to how we would pay rent, buy food or clothing, and pay other necessary living expenses.

Grier was strikingly handsome, outgoing, and personable. He charmed everybody he met. I described him to Arista: "He's tall and thin, black hair, steel blue eyes, and a black beard that grows back fifteen minutes after he shaves. He has one of the most pleasing per-sonalities—people like him instantly . . . He has a marvelous sense of humor . . . is too restless for his own good . . . has marvelous speech, well controlled and an excellent flow of words, great ana-lytical ability. . . ."

I also told Arista about Grier's background—the little I knew and understood. He was born in Louisiana; his mother died when he was four, his father soon afterward. His mother came from an old southern family and left property; his father had been a highway engineer. He had two sisters and two brothers, all much older than he. Grier had graduated from high school in 1929. The Depression kept him out of college, so he left home and bummed around for two years. At first he and three friends drove an old Model T Ford, hiring themselves out during harvest season in different parts of the country. He picked strawberries and oranges, harvested wheat and corn, picked cotton, bailed hay. When the other guys went home, he became a hobo, lived in hobo jungles, rode the rails, stowed away on boats. It sounded very romantic.

I would learn later that at that time his father was dead only to Grier (he was already grown when his dad died in 1937). His step-mother, a spinster when she and his dad married, had abused Grier. All during his school years, as a child and adolescent, he had moved often, living for a few weeks or months with whatever relative or friend would provide food and shelter in order to escape his penu-rious stepmother.

In the fall of 1932, tired of bumming around and knowing that he must plan for his future, Grier hopped a freight train and wound up in Washington. He didn't know a soul, but found a job as a day laborer at twenty cents an hour. When he got another job paying a few cents more, he enrolled in night school at George Washington University, completed his undergraduate work there and at American University, and, while working numerous jobs, received his law degree, a master's in law, and a master's in patent law. His field was labor economics.

The international situation worsened. Great Britain was in crisis as the German army rolled over everything in sight, including invading Russia, where it took over Minsk, Smolensk, Tallinn, Leningrad, Kiev, Orel, and Odessa, and marched on toward Moscow. In the United States, German and Italian assets were frozen. An Office of Price Administration froze steel prices, rationed rubber products, and soon would ration sugar and gasoline and establish rent controls. In the summer of 1940, Congress had enacted a Selective Service program to train men for military duty. On October 16, sixteen and a half million men registered and a national lottery determined the order they would be called.

From our area, Grier was number five. On April 14, I wrote to Arista, "Grier spent the remaining five days before he was drafted with me. We stayed out in the country with Mom and Pop . . . he adjusted perfectly to farm life, left by plane to be inducted into the Army in Dallas on April 7. He is in Fort Sill, Oklahoma . . . now locked up in a barrack because one of the group had measles and the whole bunch is quarantined. Anyone else would be bewailing Fate, but he's having the time of his life . . . has been in the Army only a week, holds Kangaroo Court regularly, probably has the barrack organized into an affiliate of the CIO [a labor union federation]. You can't feel sorry for him—nothing daunts him. If I saw a steamroller flatten him out, I'd say, 'Oh, he'll be up in a moment!' Nope, no wedding for another year."

My intentions were good, but again I had not counted on Grier.

Oh, what a difference a week can make in one's life. On April 21, exactly a week after I claimed I had no intention of getting married for another year, I wrote Arista another letter . . .

6

Married Lady

GRIER AND I WERE MARRIED on Saturday, April 19, 1941, in Dallas.

It was not, I insisted in a letter to Arista on April 21, a marriage in haste. "Grier decided on it a long time ago—the day he met me—and I've mulled over the pros and cons until they were pretty straight in my mind."

We had known each other for three months and five days. I had worn his engagement ring for two and a half months.

He had a weekend pass from Fort Sill. We met in Dallas. I flew up from Austin, my first flight, and it was almost as momentous as my wedding! I wrote to Arista, ". . . more fun! The trip up there takes about an hour and twenty minutes. It's a good five hours in my car. I'm sold on flying, but it's a little expensive for an NYA counselor.

"I told Grier of my decision to get married at 3 o'clock on Saturday afternoon and . . . at 5:30 we were married."

In an hour and a half, we had medical examinations, got the license, bought the wedding ring and a corsage. Grier called the Y and asked for names of ministers. We went out to the home of a Reverend Rogers—I think he was a Baptist minister—and he performed the ceremony.

My wedding dress was an outfit I worked in—a dress I bought in Atlanta—a blue coat to another outfit, my usual conglomeration.

Grier wore the only shirt he had with him. It was borrowed and water-soaked around the collar.

Grier didn't drop the ring and neither of us stammered. I wrote to Arista, "I'm so happy . . . Grier . . . is more than I had ever hoped for in a husband . . . so understanding, and that's so important in the man you promise to take 'for better, for worse, for richer for poorer, until death do ye part.'"

On Sunday night Grier went back to Fort Sill and I flew back to Austin. We did not intend to tell a soul about being married. "It would be too annoying," I wrote to Arista, "to have to explain to every Dick, Tom, and the neighbor's cat *where* my husband is, what he is doing, and *when* he is coming back. . . . I don't want to explain to anybody that I am a groomless bride. . . . I'm telling you and Madeleine and nobody else."

I put a P.S. on my letter: "I don't know what to tell Reggie . . . guess I'll write that I'm engaged and let it go at that."

The secret lasted all of five days. It was a rainy day that Thursday, and we were all lazing around the office, catching up on paperwork and trying to keep busy when a coworker, Tom Brashear, let out a war whoop. We all made a beeline to see what was going on; he had *The Dallas Morning News* spread out in front of him, and was pointing to the listing of the week's marriage licenses. There was no mistaking it. No other couple could possibly have had our unusual names: Louise Hilma Ballerstedt was Mrs. Grier H. Raggio. I knew I had to tell Jake, so when he came in I headed him off and said there was something I must talk to him about. We went out on the upper porch and I told Jake I was married. I've never seen a person look more stunned. He was speechless, and finally said, "Son of a gun! Son of a gun."

I don't think anybody immediately congratulated me or wished me well. They were all too shocked, but they soon got used to it and started addressing me as "Mrs." Then it was my turn to be shocked! I took my wedding ring, a beautiful yellow gold band with seven diamonds, out of my purse and put it on.

Mother had a fit when she found out that her only baby was now a wife. On the last day of April I wrote to Arista, "Mom . . . is used to the idea now. She'll probably wind up liking Grier better than she does me."

Two weeks after the wedding, Grier managed another weekend pass and went with me to Mom and Dad's. He didn't get in until 6 A.M. on Saturday and had to leave at nine on Monday morning. We spent most of the weekend introducing him to relatives he hadn't previously met and he charmed my parents into thinking he was the best possible son-in-law.

Between working, writing to Grier, and planning trips to visit him in Oklahoma or to meet him in Dallas or Fort Worth, there were a few tag-end details I had to finish. I wrote to Reggie, spending a lot of time trying to find the proper words to tell him that I was married. I dreaded like crazy seeing his family, because they had let it be known that they were delighted at the prospect of having me in the family. At work, one of the guys I'd dated a few times tried to tell me how devastated he was. He said he had intended to propose to me very soon and had been looking at rings. I wouldn't let him divulge any further confidences because it was sinful after a girl got married even to give a single thought to the idea that there could have been anyone else. My time going out with the old crowd, even in groups, was over.

Madeleine and I continued to live together. I kept my job and continued to travel my territory.

In June, Arista dropped her bombshell. She married Emil Richmond. I don't remember when or where she met him. Tragically, their marriage alienated them from both of their families. Arista's Greek family could not accept that their daughter had married a Jew, and Emil's Jewish family disowned him for marrying out of the faith.

"Marriage," I wrote in my congratulatory letter to Arista, "is both a wonderful and a terrible thing. When you put your whole heart, soul, and spirit into a contract, you let yourself in for living hell if the other partner isn't the person you judged him to be. Only last Sunday I visited a dear friend who was married last October and divorced in April. She found that her bridegroom had not one, but three other women on the string with no notion of reforming." I assured Arista that my marriage was made in heaven. ". . . just received a special letter from Grier . . . that he will be in Dallas Friday afternoon and I'm dashing around the office getting annual leave . . . It's so hard being separated, but it would be even harder if we weren't married."

My letters to Arista ended in June, though I know we continued to correspond. I ended the June letter on a bittersweet note:

"We are strange women. Last year at this time, both of us were so totally in love that we weren't conscious of outside events. We were breaking up the remnants of a lovely and unreal year in our nation's capital to take our places in the maze of government work. Both of us were in love with men who were not our types, but who we thought we could not live without. Now both of us are married, I on April 19, you on June 7. Both very suddenly. I knew Grier only three months and five days before I promised to be faithful to him for the rest of my life. You had known Emil only six weeks. Both of us married quietly and quickly without friends present. Both of us daring Fate. I feel that I'm tasting the parts of life that most people miss. It's harder than blazes at times, but the happy times are oh! so! wonderful!"

I look back in amazement that both our marriages worked. Arista and Emil moved to California where they had two children, Anna and Lewis. She visited me at the farm when Anna was a baby; Anna and my Grier Jr. are almost the same age. She continued to be active in intellectual and humanitarian causes and was planning to enter law school when she died so very young. Her children were eight and four. Her obituary requested that memorials be sent to the Intercultural Club Scholarship Fund, which she supported. When Emil remarried, all remnants of Arista disappeared from the home only to surface in my letters to her after Emil died and Anna was an adult. I still miss Arista.

IN SEPTEMBER 1941, the international crisis eased and all the "old men" in uniform were sent home. This included Grier, who was past the twenty-eight-year limit. As soon as he was released, he returned to his job with the government and a month later, I quit my job with the NYA to make a home for my husband and to travel with him. We piled everything we owned into my '41 Chevrolet and headed to Dallas, where he was headquartered. Our entire possessions consisted of a few dishes, sheets and towels, and the wonderful table he had bought for me in Mexico. Everything we owned went easily into the backseat of the car. We rented an apartment on Corsicana Street. We were enthralled with the very affordable rent for such a spacious furnished apartment in a nice brick building— until we later learned that we were living in the red light district and our neighbors in surrounding apartments were prostitutes.

Grier's work with the U.S. Agriculture Department was undercover, very hush-hush. The entire country was under a program that issued stamps for the purchase of essential food items. Some stores bent the rules, allowing their customers to use food stamps for the purchase of beer and other illegal commodities. Grier's job was to ferret out the offenders and report them to headquarters. I became his unauthorized typist and confidante on the numerous files he had to maintain and report. He did the legwork, I did the office work. This multiplied our time together, allowed us to really get to know each other and to explore our new world together.

I also had more personal time. Like the pattern that had worked for me so well in Washington, I made lists of the places I wanted to see and the things I wanted to do, being careful that I spent no money. We were on a tight budget. Our apartment was only a few blocks from Titche-Goettinger, one of the leading downtown Dallas department stores; I explored every floor of it from the basement up. I did the same at Neiman-Marcus, A. Harris, Kahns, Wolf Brothers, and Sangers. I had a wonderful time spending an entire day exploring and maybe spending a quarter for a newspaper and a cup of coffee.

Our social life was severely limited. We could not afford to make close friends or get involved in community activities lest our "cover" be blown. Acquaintances asked questions and we could not give them details.

After a "decent" interval of time to keep all the old biddies from counting on their fingers, it was appropriate and accepted for a young couple to announce they were going to have a baby. Grier and I were only too happy to comply. It didn't take long. Soon after

I dispensed with the diaphragm, I made an appointment with a gynecologist and counted the days until he confirmed my pregnancy on December 3, 1941. The day the doctor made it official, Grier and I celebrated by packing our car and heading for the farm on the way south.

Grier had been ordered to the lower Rio Grande Valley. He was being transferred; we would be headquartered in Edinburg.

We spent Friday and Saturday night with Mother and Daddy at the farm. When I told them I was pregnant, they reacted as if I'd announced a funeral. Daddy cleared his throat, got quiet, and went off to the barn. Mother congratulated me through tears.

Early Sunday morning we left the farm, headed to South Texas. We were bouncing along, bubbling in good health, congratulating ourselves on our good fortune, singing now and then with the radio, when suddenly the programming was interrupted.

The Japanese had bombed Pearl Harbor. In one instant our world came apart. Trepidation supplanted jubilation. Grier turned the volume up. I felt tears behind my eyelids. We dared not look at each other. We were numb by the time we pulled into a roadside motel for the night—I don't remember where. Neither of us could eat. There were moments of stunned silence, until we would start to say something and stop to hear the other, who also paused, both of us choking back emotions that we dared not express. Neither of us slept. On Monday, when President Roosevelt delivered his speech about "the day that will live in infamy" and asked Congress to declare a war that was already under way, we drove into Edinburg, Texas, too physically and emotionally frazzled to care where we were. I knew that the father of my unborn child would be recalled to service and that I, pregnant, with no job and no money, would have to go back to the farm to live.

Grier applied to the war board and got a deferment until September so that we could be together until the baby's birth. We found a tiny duplex in Edinburg and went through the motions of normal living even as the world we had known dissolved around us. Grier's "secret service" work still circumscribed our activities. My natural social tendencies had to be kept in check. I couldn't go out and meet people because they always asked what my husband did, and I couldn't tell them. I did meet the two young women who lived next door and gave them some wild tale about Grier's work. They started telling me about the new man in town, a "dreamboat," they said; they were dying to meet him. I plotted a way to introduce them, and there came Grier, driving up. "That's him," one whispered in a stage voice. "That's the man!" I said, "Oh, goodness. That's my husband." They were crestfallen.

Grier and I had a good laugh. It was one of our few moments of mirth in those cloudy days. We attended the Methodist Church. Everybody was so friendly, made a big splash over us and wanted us to join. We thought up some sort of lame excuse and didn't go back.

Even though Grier's work still entailed countless reports, he could not hire a local secretary who might leak his cover, so I continued as his in-house unpaid assistant. I didn't resent it because it gave us more free hours together and we spent the time going from one end of the Rio Grande Valley to the other. I don't think we missed anything from Padre Island to Laredo. We went across the border to Reynosa in Mexico and explored all the little Mexican towns. We crossed the Rio Grande on a barge that had to be hand-pulled with ropes.

As the days passed, we relaxed. We were told that Grier would be indefinitely deferred and permanently located in Edinburg, so in the spring we rented a two-bedroom brick house with orange trees in the yard. The owners were transferred for several months; they agreed to rent us the house only if we would keep their maid. Her salary was two dollars a week. There I was in a town where I didn't know anybody, where I wasn't allowed to meet people, and with a maid to do all the housework. I settled in, found a doctor, and planned to have my baby in Edinburg.

Then the government transferred us to Corsicana. We found a tiny little apartment. I knew I must not keep changing doctors, so I made arrangements to stay with Jeannette and Harry and have my baby in Austin. The summer was sweltering. I was as big as a tub. And the baby was two weeks late.

Grier Henry Raggio, Jr. arrived on August 6, 1942, at Austin's St. David's Hospital; both Mother and Grier were at the hospital. Anesthetics erased all memory of the actual event, and I was so weary afterward that even in the heat of that summer, I dropped into a deep slumber. My first conscious memory is waking up the next morning and seeing Grier dressed in a white suit with a flower in his lapel sitting beside my bed. As soon as he saw my eyelids flutter, he was beside me. "Honey"—he beamed—"we've got a boy!" Euphoric at having a son, he could not say enough, do enough, promise enough about our future as a family. Unaware of all the fuss he had created, Grier Jr., eight pounds, eight ounces, slept peacefully in the nursery.

The hard part lay ahead. I was in the hospital for a week and in bed another week at Jeannette and Harry's house. Mother came to see that the baby was properly launched. The house was small, the summer sizzling, the baby fretful. In those days women stayed in bed for two full weeks after childbirth, so I was not allowed to do anything for my son. Jeannette and Harry had to be saints to have given us sanctuary.

After a week, we took Grier Jr. to the farm. This would be our home for the next three years.

They were my "lost years."

I was grateful for electricity—at least I could read—and our precious refrigerator made ice. But we still had no hard-surfaced roads, no indoor toilet, no hot water heater, and no washing machine. I hand-washed all of the baby's clothes including the diapers, hung them out on the clothesline in good weather, and dried them in the house during damp weather and when winter and freezing weather arrived. The scrub board became both familiar and despised. I wrote long and loving letters every day to my husband.

Because Grier was back in the army. When Grier Jr. was six weeks old, his father's deferment ended and he was back in uniform, supposedly headed for Officers Training School and for a future in military intelligence. He qualified for fifteen of the seventeen officer candidate groups. In midwinter—January or February—he was ordered to New Orleans and jauntily sallied forth, driving the car packed with all our worldly possessions. He would complete OCS, be assigned to the secret service, and stationed somewhere in the United States. Then the baby and I would join him and we'd be a family with wonderful new adventures ahead.

It didn't happen.

I didn't hear and didn't hear and didn't hear. I did not know whether he had safely arrived in New Orleans or had been hijacked on the highway. Nothing. I wrote daily but did not know where to send the letters. I was afraid to leave the house lest the telephone rang and I missed a call. Days dragged into weeks. When I finally did get a message, there was even greater cause for worry. I was to go to New Orleans to pick up the car.

My husband was being shipped overseas.

Madeleine, my Austin roommate, had married and was living in Orange, Texas. She invited Mother, me, and the baby to come to her house, where Mother and Grier Jr. stayed while I took a train to New Orleans to retrieve the car before driving back to Orange to pick them up on our way home. I had three days in New Orleans with Grier. They were dark, foreboding days. We had no idea where he was going. We had no idea why he had so suddenly been pulled out of consideration for officers training and designated to go into the thick of the fighting as a buck private.

It would be years and years before we had answers, and to this day the answers make no sense.

I drove back to Orange, sometimes through tears that all but obliterated the highway, picked up my mother and my child, and headed back to the farm. I hope I remembered to thank Madeleine for her hospitality. All the accumulation of things, which we had crammed into the car when Grier left, now were taken out and replaced in the farmhouse, many stored in the boxes we had so hopefully packed only months before.

Again I was in a waiting game, waking up every morning in a gray haze, lying awake nights hoping, praying, spending my waking hours on a seesaw of emotions, willing myself not to worry, crying until I was limp, coercing myself not to shed the tears that froze me, finally falling into a nightmare-disturbed sleep and awakening again and again until another gray dawn arrived.

The baby and I had my old bedroom. Mother and Dad had installed butane gas on the farm. When winter came it was a great luxury to have our room heated with a butane stove. We also had butane heaters in other parts of the house.

Mother took over the care of my baby. She saw me as inexperi-enced, disturbed, and incapable of making sane decisions. I should have exercised my responsibility and my right to fill the role of my child's mother; I doubtless would have been a healthier person had I done so, but in my mid-twenties, with circumstances compelling me to fill the role of daughter I thought I had left behind, it was easier to acquiesce. I felt I was already imposing just by being there. As she had done for me in my early childhood, Mother made every decision about the care, feeding, and well-being of my son.

Both Mother and Daddy adored Grier Jr. With them he could do no wrong. She, who had disapproved of my marriage, was unhappy over my choice of a husband, and had been crushed by my preg-nancy, suddenly found nothing but abundance and joy in the child who was a product of that union.

Grier had warned me that I might not hear from him for some time. Both of us knew he would not be allowed to tell me where he was, so we contrived a simple scheme using a code to tell me, at least, which direction he was headed. When the first letter came sev-eral weeks later I knew he was on the West Coast. I also knew, from news reports, that he was headed into the dangerous zones of the war, into the treacherous waters of the Pacific, packed on a troop ship with hundreds of other soldiers and sent across the ocean with other ships in large convoys, no gun cover, no air cover, no defense mechanism at all, a flotilla of sitting ducks for Japanese aircraft and submarines.

Returning to life on the farm was the hardest thing I have ever done. Just getting by was an everyday challenge. Almost everything was rationed. We paid for supplies not only with money, but with stamps. We had stamps to buy gasoline, tires, and farm equipment, stamps for sugar and meat and clothes. Shoes were extremely diffi-cult to find, even if we had stamps to buy them, and it seemed to me that Grier Jr.'s feet grew a full size every two months. Aunt Minnie Kron helped keep me supplied with stamps so that I could buy shoes for my child.

Everybody was encouraged to maintain a Victory garden. In the cities, even the tiniest plots of land were planted with vegetables. We had always had a large garden in the country, but we added to it and during the growing season I took great buckets of okra, cream peas, green beans, tomatoes, onions, potatoes, and everything else as it ripened, into Austin where it was shared with the relatives and the remainder sold for cash.

The monthly pittance I received from the government as the wife of an enlisted man did not cover basic essentials. My parents had a separator, a contrivance that daily separated gallons of milk from cream. We turned the cream into butter, another rationed food item, and very valuable. We made as many as twenty pounds of butter at a time, which I took into town and sold at government-approved places. Relatives and friends were also supplied with butter. Grier treasured pictures of us; in almost every letter he requested pictures of me and "the kid." I traded a pound of butter every month at a photography studio for a roll of film. This was the only way that Grier could watch his son grow. Sometimes I sent Grier the roll of film so that we could have pictures of him. He said my letters and the pictures kept him sane.

"War is hell." Those three words, first spoken by William Tecumseh Sherman in a speech to the graduating class of Michigan Military Academy in 1914, has echoed down through time and is as true today as it was when it was first uttered. Grier and I lived its truth. Even though World War II has gone down in the history books as "The Good War," there was very little good in the anguish, uncertainty, and constant fear that pervaded our days—both together and apart. In the fighting zones, no man knew which bullet might have his name on it. At home, nobody was safe from fear that we might be invaded, bombed, or gassed.

War was hell for Grier. He hated the military and everything connected with it. Nothing in his past experience had prepared him for the regimentation and, too often, the stupidity of the armed forces. A brilliant man who read voraciously and thought deeply, he always met and often exceeded my intellectual curiosity, but in service he was a misfit from the start. He tried. Oh, how he tried! In letter after letter after letter, he promised me, "Don't worry; I am not going to do anything stupid." Then in the next paragraph he divulged stupid things that made me quiver for his safety.

I suffered my own hell. I was in almost constant grief for friends, classmates, and neighbors who were killed in service, people like Eddie Cravens and Dudley Rugley and Curtis Popham and Clayton Moden. The young men of my generation were the very first to go to war; many, many of them never returned. I did my grieving back on the farm, a place that continued to hold a love-hate relationship for me. I was the "little girl" my parents adored, but who had grown up and been places and moved beyond the daily confines of the farm. I was a woman married to a man I had sworn to "love and honor" for the rest of my days, but who in truth I barely knew. I was a mother to a son I adored, but whose daily care had been usurped. I was a bright woman, who had graduated from college summa cum laude, who had a year of graduate work in the nation's capital, who had launched a successful career, and who again had been relegated to a regime controlled by outside forces. Most fearful of all was the thought that each letter I received from my husband might be his last.

I wrote to Grier every day, and every day that he possibly could he wrote to me, even when I could tell that the danger he was in or his weariness—often his boredom—was overwhelming. Sometimes we wrote two letters a day. I spent hour after hour searching for and clipping stories that I thought he would enjoy or might challenge his intellectual curiosity, and I mailed packet after packet to him in the years we were apart. I subscribed to magazines I knew he would like and mailed them to him as soon as I devoured them so that we would have ideas to exchange. If he suggested a book he had read, I got it and read it so that I could respond to his questions. If he saw a movie at the Post Exchange and liked it—which was rare because he often wrote that he left a film after ten minutes because he was bored—I made it a point to see the movie and give him my ideas.

The mail was so undependable. Sometimes I would not get his letters for days, and then receive a week's mail at the same time. The mail service from Elgin, Texas, to his post in the South Pacific was even more undependable. In April 1945, after weeks of not hearing from me, he wrote, "Got your letters of February 23, 25, 26, 27, 28, and March 2, 4, 5, 7, 8, 9, 11, 12, 13, 14, 29, and April

4 and 6 today." What a bonanza! Even more annoying was the censorship. Almost all of us, if we were reasonably bright, knew—from both daily news reports and from letters—where our loved ones were stationed, but government-controlled military censors felt it imperative to cut tiny holes in our letters. How Grier railed at the censorship! Once, when I mentioned that a neat razor-blade hole had been cut in one of his letters to me, he responded, "You had received my letter which the goddam censor had opened. It infuriates me to think that some SOB has read my letters to you."

I had to be so careful what I wrote to Grier. The folks at home were trained and conditioned to write only the good news to their men in uniform. We were not to tell them anything that might make them worry or be concerned about us. We were to be cheerful, positive, loving, and happy at all times. How can one be eternally optimistic every moment of every day for a period of years? I tried so hard—as I was conditioned—to be that wonderful, sweet, joyous person when I wrote to my husband.

But all of us read between the lines. Many things I shared so lovingly with him came home to haunt me. Both his letters, many of which I refer to here, and mine, which he was unable to keep, created rifts in our relationship that took us years to bridge.

The insecurities of his childhood and adolescence haunted both of us. I was too inexperienced to understand how Grier's rearing, his past history, and his legal training impinged on our personal relationship. I knew that I loved him and I had no choice but to make our marriage work because when I said "'til death us do part," I took my vows seriously. It would have helped immeasurably if I had also had some insight into the countless past conditions that triggered his negative reactions to some of the most innocent experiences I shared with him in letters. Increasingly, I walked on eggs—measuring every word for his potential reaction. Early, after he was overseas, he wrote "I don't know why I have to be so childish, but you have said things that tend to make me unhappy." Later, in a rare moment, after he had learned both through me and the Red Cross—which he contacted when he did not fully trust me—that I had an ovarian cyst, he wrote, "I am better now that I know you are feeling better and are reasonably happy. I always get headaches and all kinds of ailments of a problem child when you are not well." The truth, which I was not able to divulge, was that doctors said my physical condition might require immediate surgery that would make me sterile. I was petrified, but when I tried to share it with my husband, he wrote back, "I am wondering if a part of your present illness is more mental than physical." And later, "The last report I had from the Red Cross indicated that your condition was not serious . . . an operation might be necessary in the future. I hate to think of the possibility of you being sterile, but you have always been more important to me than our children will ever be. I love children. We can always adopt."

My behavior was squeaky clean. I would not have dared to go to a party or out to dinner or even to lunch with any male friends who had been in my life prior to Grier. But that was not good enough for him. He was jealous of everything I did that appeared to him to expand my life without him. When the superintendent of Manor schools asked me to teach because good teachers were so few, I thought it could well be a springboard to a richer future for both of us. Grier didn't see it that way. He thought any job that removed me from my primary responsibility—him and our son— diminished his control over my life. "It is only logical for me to assume that if you told me about teaching, it was because you thought I might dislike it. Well, I do . . . all I can say is that it's your game and your rules. I hope I'm not making a mountain out of a molehill. My reaction is motivated by my loving you so much.

"It is only natural that I should want you to wait for me . . . as you would want me to wait for you . . . you might be doing some interesting things which are incompatible with a proper marital relationship, particularly when I [am] your husband. If you . . . decide to do a lot of things that I would disapprove, my disapproval would not be rational; it would be severe."

Desperate for crumbs of intellectual challenge, I joined the League of Women Voters in Austin. I loved it! Because older, more experienced women were serving on war boards and doing volunteer or paid work for the war effort, organizations like the League were left to us "kids." My high school and college friends were running the Austin League, and I moved up very fast in the organization.

The state convention was held in Dallas that year, and our projects and accomplishments astounded state leaders. We were young, energetic, enthusiastic; nobody told us what we couldn't do, so we apparently performed miracles! We were in and out of the offices of our elected state officials almost daily. I remember being in the office of the lieutenant governor when we got the message of President Roosevelt's death. We were lobbying for the secret ballot, which Texas did not have at that time. Our votes were an "open secret" and curtailed our independence; if an election judge knew you'd voted against his people, the recriminations could be devastating.

I was enthralled with the women I met through my work in LWV—women like Jane Y. McCallum who later became secretary of state in Texas, and grand ladies like Minnie Fisher Cunningham, who told us about her work with the suffragists. When the Nineteenth Amendment giving women the right to vote was up for approval by the states, Texas legislators sneaked out, planning to take the train out of Austin so there would not be a quorum for voting. The women learned about it, boarded the train, and marched them back to the capital for their "aye" vote.

The League of Women Voters saved my sanity, and with great joy I shared my enthusiasm with my husband. His response stunned me. "It would be erroneous to assume that your activity in the League . . . would constitute . . . any wrong. However, it would be presumptuous to assume that things that follow such activity would not be wrong. . . . We are going to have several adjustment problems when we start to live normally again," he wrote. "[Even though] I favor many of the political things that you are scrapping for and realize that what you are doing is to our mutual benefit . . . I feel that without your original attributes (with which I fell in love), you could and would mean little to me other than a wife by law . . . and that worries me. I know myself and what I want. I do not object to your making the most of a truly abnormal situation by taking part in any activity that you desire. What I emphasize is that you should, as an intelligent woman, a wife, and a mother, know what things you should do and should not do and it is needless for me to say what I expect."

It did not occur to me that his legal work in the South Pacific exacerbated problems we might later have in our personal lives. Assigned to handle the legal work of troubled marital and family relationships among his buddies, he was entangled with marriages that had gone sour, with "Dear John" letters from wives and sweethearts, children born to women whose husbands had not been home in years. Grier tortured himself with the notion that I, too, might stray. "I am handling some legal and personal affairs," he wrote in April 1945, "most of it divorce actions or related problems. Several women have decided that one or more good men back in the States is worth more than one good man in the Pacific. I take considerable personal and professional pride in making it as difficult as legally possible . . . some are nothing more than goddam whores, and unprincipled ones at that." Later he wrote, "The chaplain came over to talk about a legal point with me. If ever there was a Christian in the true sense, it is our chaplain. His philosophical views are quite different from my legal and personal views, but he is rational. We agree on one thing: 99 out of every 100 women can be *had* under the proper circumstances. We also agree that the same is true of men."

With that opinion, Grier was convinced that I had only one chance out of one hundred to be faithful to him!

In July 1945 one letter should have self-ignited from the flame of his anger. "I haven't written in the last few days because I violently and unalterably disagree with you in many respects for the last two years. You have given me some double talk. . . . Until recently I felt I owed it to you and the kid to be around to soothe your bruises when you got your pins knocked out from under you. I don't feel that way now and I seriously [believe] you have a chronic case of juvenile exhibitionism." Four days later, only a trifle contrite, he wrote ". . . received your sweet letters . . . don't forget that it isn't one thing that makes a fellow blow his top. It is one thing on top of nine or ten other things, each in and of themselves of no damned importance, but taken as a whole give a picture out of proportion. You are the integral around which everything else evolves."

Every letter I wrote to Grier was filled with information about our son. I told him about every inch, every pound, every advance that Grier Jr. made, but even though I knew in my heart that he wanted to be a part of his son's life, it was difficult for him. On the farm, where my little boy had the undivided attention of two adoring grandparents, there were no wishes unfulfilled in his young life. He was safe. He was unconditionally loved. An adult responded to his every desire. When he did not talk as the experts indicated he should, I was concerned. My parents passed it off as negligible. I did not dare mention my growing anxiety to his father. I took him to see my old mentor, Dr. Leigh Peck, an eminent child psychologist, who went through her routine testing for an almost three-year-old. Grier Jr. was pleasant—and reticent. The testing entailed showing him pictures of ordinary things to which most children of his age recognize and respond. When Dr. Peck showed him an airplane, he sat there quietly studying it. I all but came apart! My son could not even recognize an airplane! And then he spoke—for the first time during the session. "I fink it's a B-29," he said. So much for the intelligence of my son! I wrote to his father in jubilation. Grier's response: "Surely was glad to hear that the kid is developing nicely. I would have thought that he would not have inherited any speech impediment or backwardness."

Grier almost always referred to our son as "the kid," and never in all of his letters by the child's name. In retrospect, I think he may not have known how to express the depth of emotion he felt for our child. Occasionally feelings crept through. "I showed you and the kid off to the fellows by showing them all of the pictures I have. I . . . try to remember that other people are only courteously interested. You will never know how much those pictures and other things concerning you and the kid really mean to me." Repeatedly, through his letters, he made it clear that I was first in his life and he expected to be first in mine. Our children would be an addition to our love, but never in first place.

In March 1945, after days of not getting any mail, Grier wrote, "This is an island of volcanic origin, considerably north of [censored by a hole cut in the letter]. It will be interesting to read the accepted history of the battle for this island and compare it with . . . our real experiences. I suspect there will be quite a variance. . . . We have been living in dugouts in an area that was until comparatively recently occupied by Jap troops. Each man has been doing his own cooking . . . we couldn't get our rations off the boat for a few days after we arrived. I am surprised at the chances Americans take to get souvenirs . . . many lives have been lost . . . you may be sure I have not and will not take foolish chances." I would learn later that Grier landed on Iwo Jima on day five of the American conquest of that tiny Volcanic Island 750 miles south and east of Tokyo with little vegetation. It was a worthless scrap of territory except that the Americans needed it as a base for fighter planes to attack the Japanese mainland. The Japanese were completely entrenched there, and our troops were picked off like flies. The Japanese came out of caves at night, slashed open tents, and threw in grenades. Hundreds of GIs, along with the grenade throwers, were killed. The next morning, a military detail dug a trench, tossed in the arms, legs, heads, and other body parts of their buddies killed the night before, covered the trench, and went about their daily routines. Iwo Jima was one of the bloodiest prolonged battles of World War II.

I had long since understood that Grier was on Iwo, but not until August 1945, days before the war ended, could he tell me. "We finally have permission to say that which probably everyone already knows—we are on Iwo Jima . . . we are still not allowed to be specific; this is amusing inasmuch as the island is only about seven square miles." In a second letter on the evening of the same day, he wrote, "I took off about three hours and rode over the north end of the Island and went up to the top of Mount Suribachi" (the site of the famed photograph of Marines raising the American flag on enemy territory).

Throughout our correspondence, I continued to be awed by Grier's intelligence and his interest in world events and politics, the books he read, the movies he left after a few minutes because they bored him, the "bull sessions" he instigated with any and all military associates—enlisted men or officers—who challenged his thinking. On November 9, 1944, he was so pleased that "our man [Roosevelt] won. Wonder how many years will pass before an American governmental chief will serve for a period of twelve to sixteen years again and what kind of government we will have at that time?" He thought Churchill was "pompous." On July 27, 1945, he wrote, "I

was glad to hear that Churchill was the loser in the recent elections."
He was ambivalent about Truman. On August 20, 1945, he wished
"I could share some of Truman's optimism. As . . . obnoxious and
repulsive as [MacArthur's] supreme egotism is to me, I feel he is by
far the best man for allied commander of the Occupation Forces."
Even though Grier strongly questioned victory at any cost, he would
have "liked to attend the Grand Review to be held in Tokyo within
the next few days [August 23, 1945]. MacArthur is in his glory when
he can have a big show. . . . I like him . . . I feel that Truman is less
an international statesman than I hoped. Nepotism is bad enough
but he seemingly has a chronic case of Missouritis. I hope he hits his
stride soon—or I will consider voting Republican! . . . You haven't
said anything recently about Lyndon Johnson. Is he going to run for
the Senate?"

Grier always saw every experience from the viewpoint of "the
natives," and sought opportunities to learn the customs and the
languages of others. "The Natives [in New Caledonia] and I are sitting around the campfire and they are telling me some interesting
things. . . . They are much more human than most of us so-called
cultured people."

Grier should have been in the diplomatic corps, so willing was
he to see the views of every individual; he sanctioned human rights,
always asked "what if?" and posed questions about accepted
"truths." He was never willing to "go along in order to get along."
It often got him into trouble, especially in the Army, but also as a
civilian, both in his professional and his personal relationships. As
the war wound down, "We had a lecture today on . . . what to do
with Germany after the war. I disagree with most of the views . . .
most are opposed to my 'forgive and forget' attitude. . . . Most
Germans have no more knowledge of why they are fighting than
we do."

Grier's dislike of the military never diminished. On this one area
there was no compromise. "I just hate, loathe, and despise anything
that is built on the unprincipled and stupid foundations that . . . is
the U.S. Army's."

On August 7, 1945, the day after the first atom bomb was
dropped on Hiroshima, Grier asked, "What do you think of the

atom bomb? I hate to think of the additional thousands who will be killed if the bomb reaches any stage of perfection that reports indicate," and on August 8, the day before the second bomb dropped on Nagasaki, ". . . the predominant reaction [here] is that if it permits them to go home, well and good. Very, very few give consideration to the humanitarian aspects."

On August 15, 1945, Grier's letter began, "The war is over. I am happy. . . ."

It was an anticlimax, such a quiet phrase . . . so loaded with foreboding of what lay ahead for us.

7

Celebration and Cessation

OUR REUNION WAS FRAUGHT with impending doom.

Both of us had looked forward to this occasion from the moment we parted in New Orleans in March 1942. When the day finally came, more than three years later in September 1945, I would not have recognized my husband except that he had told me exactly where to meet him. There had been so many written words between us—more than one thousand letters from me to him, at least five hundred from him to me. And in those letters were multitudes of misunderstandings that had to be resolved, bushels of innuendos that needed addressing, mountains of bridges that required crossing before we could go on with our lives. What he had said in those letters to me and what I had not said in my letters to him weighted us down.

I knew I should go on pretending, but I couldn't. An ovarian cyst had kept me in increasing pain for more than a year. I was sick, scared, and uncertain. I had lost weight. I wanted to look my best for Grier's homecoming, but I felt like a scarecrow.

He was far, far worse. The 165-pound, six-foot-two-inch, clean-cut man I had kissed good-bye, and who held out his arms to me in that Abilene, Texas, hotel was a gaunt 128 pounds with a thick black beard and moustache. His eyes were haunted—mirroring the death and devastation he had witnessed since we parted.

I knew him only because Grier had sent me specific instructions about the time and place I was to meet him in Abilene. My physical condition had precipitated release for him a few weeks earlier than might have been expected. When I learned that the doctors were determined to perform an operation that would remove an ovary and limit my chances of conceiving another child, I could not make such a decision alone, and through Red Cross intervention both from Grier in the South Pacific and me in Central Texas, his homecoming was hastened by a few weeks.

We spent the night in the hotel. We were strangers to each other, saying and trying to do the things expected of us, but each frightened and scarred. I did not understand until much later how sick he was. Whatever reservations and criticisms he had about me in his letters, he had always assured me that he was as physically safe as possible and I was not to worry. He'd written that he'd lost weight, but never told me how thin he actually was. We had never heard of post–traumatic stress syndrome. No matter how much carnage a soldier experienced in war, he was expected to go home, pull up his socks, and proceed with his life as if nothing had happened.

In our lives and in the lives of countless millions, something devastating had happened and our "going on" had rough sledding.

After our first night together, we headed home to the farm so that this father could see "the kid." The reunion could not have been more disappointing.

Grier had never been around children, had no concept of child psychology, no clue of how to relate to his little boy. He expected his son to run into his open arms, hug him tight, call him "Daddy," and we should all live happily as a family ever after. As hard as I'd tried to prepare our son for his father's homecoming, the results were devastating. In simple terms, Grier Jr. hated his father. He could not understand why this tall, bearded individual was disturbing his safe world. He could not comprehend why this stranger was usurping his mother's time. He could not fathom this stranger intruding into his life. He was a little boy, just three years old.

In response, most of the time, his father reacted like another three-year-old.

I had two babies on my hands—and no idea what to do.

Grier had carried with him another scar. He had missed going to officer's candidate school because he was considered a security risk. He had no comprehension what charges had been filed against him, who had filed the bogus accusations, or how to clear his name. He was determined to find out. The first thing he wanted to do was go to Washington, clear up the misunderstanding, and begin civilian life with a clean slate. And I would go with him. He had been away from me as long as he intended; our place was with each other. He did not mention taking our son, and when I mentioned it he was not willing even to consider it. Grier Jr. was happy at the farm; my parents were happy to have him; we would be on a lengthy automobile trip; nobody knew what might happen in Washington; it was better for everybody that Grier Jr. remain on the farm.

Even though such an arrangement made good sense, I was torn. The three of us being separated from each other for another period of time was no way to reunite our family.

I insisted, before we left, on going back to the doctor because he had told me that the cyst on my ovary was the size of a grapefruit and that surgery was imperative—the sooner, the better. The surgery would entail removing the ovary. When he examined me, lo, the cyst had completely disappeared. I was relieved to the point of tears. Grier was happy, too, but the diagnosis confirmed, in his mind, that my health problems were more mental than physical. He was, doubtless, partially correct. Stress, as we have come increasingly to understand, triggers amazing physical reactions that usually erupt in the most vulnerable parts of the body.

The last impediment to Grier's planned trip had now been resolved and he could not wait to be on the road. He managed to get new tires for the car and enough gas coupons for the trip, and we set out.

It was an absolutely horrible experience. All access to information was sealed off. Everywhere we turned, a door was closed to us, sometimes gently and sometimes slammed. Friends from Grier's Washington days were sorry but couldn't do anything to help him. His sister, who was the administrative assistant to Perry Brown,

CEO of a major company and a leader of the American Legion, had access to inside information, but was afraid for her own job and declined to help. Everybody was scared of being tainted by the un-American stigma that had somehow been attached to this man, who should have been hailed as a hero because he had spent three years serving his country in some of the worst of the Pacific battles. Every avenue we tried reached a dead end. Grier was crushed to be rejected by everybody, both family and friends. I wanted to take our problem to Lyndon Johnson—and I still think I should have done so—but Grier would not let me. Even with door after door after door slamming in our faces, Grier still thought he could clear his name without Congressional intervention.

We left Washington knowing no more than we'd known when we arrived in the nation's capital. We came home by a long and exhausting route—first to Florida to visit his aunt in Orlando, on to Jacksonville to visit people he'd known when he worked there before the war, including an old girlfriend, back through Louisiana for a visit with his brother Earl and Earl's wife Aurora and their kids in Lafayette, to see his brother Jimmy and Jimmy's wife Bee in Natchez. In all we made about a dozen stops through Florida, Louisiana, and Mississippi, and then back to Texas to Beaumont and Port Arthur to visit his sister Rita and her husband Andre Breaux, and his sister Winnie and her husband Leon Breaux.

By the time we reached the farm, both of us were exhausted, frazzled, and angry. Neither of us was in the mood for a festive homecoming. There were no parties. Dad did not understand the gravity of Grier's situation. Mother probably understood how serious the charges were but was not happy about it and might even have had her own doubts. Grier was an outsider. One aunt told the neighbors that it was too bad Louise hadn't married a white man instead of an Eye-talian who spoke French!

Grier did not want to go back to work for the government, but with charges of un-American activities hanging over his head, his options were severely limited, if not completely curtailed. Finally, in November 1945, after he had been home for two months, he went to Dallas and reclaimed his old job, which meant that he would be doing a lot of traveling. He had been away from home and from me for almost four years, Grier said, and he could not bear to continue to be separated from his family. He arranged to transfer to the Veterans Administration to do legal work. The job sounded promising. It didn't turn out that way. It was the most routine, dulling, brain-numbing, paper-shuffling desk job imaginable, and Grier hated every minute of it.

I was on the farm with Grier Jr., struggling with the thousands of small pieces of my fragmented life, puzzling over the dark cloud of un-American charges attached to my husband's name—and by marriage, to mine, as well—burdened by the emotional anguish that haunted Grier. Sometimes, in the midst of the most innocent remarks, a cloud over his face obscured every vestige of the man I loved. Occasionally, he hugged himself with both arms and started to shiver, but the worst nightmares came at night, when his sleep was interrupted with flailing arms and legs, a thrashing torso and, sometimes with screams. My strongest disquietude involved our child. Though no words were spoken, I knew my mother would have been happy if I had divorced Grier, gone to work, and left our son on the farm for her to rear. An "I told you so" attitude pervaded our home. I couldn't pose my dilemma to Grier because I feared that he would also be happy to have our child remain with my parents so that he could have me all to himself. Although he spoke the proper words about wanting us to be a family, he was, at best, uncomfortable with his son.

Grier was in Dallas working at a job he despised, living in a rented room, eating in the least expensive restaurants he could find, trying to gain back some of the weight he had lost in the South Pacific—and spending every spare moment seeking a place for us to live.

There were no places to rent. From the first days of the war, very early in 1942 through its ending in the waning days of 1945, a period of four years, absolutely no residential construction took place—and Dallas was bursting at its seams with people. In 1940 Dallas had been a small town with a population of 360,212; by war's end it was approaching half a million with no end in sight.

Eleven thousand veterans and their families in Dallas County, by official records, were homeless.

City officials responded to the housing crisis with numerous appeals and threats; every newspaper was filled with pleas from one city leader or another to citizens, imploring them to share their living space with returning veterans. Classified advertising was a lucrative business with column after column of requests for housing. Charlatans often took advantage of couples and families desperate for a home. If an individual or a couple could not find an apartment, the situation was doubly difficult for those of us with children.

Grier finally rented a cracker-box-size one-bedroom apartment for us in Eden Place of Mustang Village. An Eden it was not; a more appropriate name would have been Hell's Headquarters. A virtual shanty town that had been thrown up overnight to house war workers, its shoddy construction revealed peeling paint on cardboard walls so thin that we could hear everything that went on from two or three apartments away. Our southwest complex in the mud flats of Southwest Dallas at Hampton Road and the Fort Worth Pike consisted of a combination living-dining room, a minute kitchen, a nine-by-ten bedroom, and a tiny bath/shower.

We moved to Eden Place in January 1946. The complex housed a motley collection of people—some wonderful, many reprobates. For every marvelous older couple named Sippel, and returning veterans including Ned and Genie Fritz, there were dozens of disturbed, miserable masses.

An assortment of undisciplined and unruly children roamed the neighborhood, bullied the younger children and stole their toys. I knew that many were hungry and many were locked outside on days that were either too cold or too hot. The lack of parenting skills among our neighbors appalled me. I longed to rescue their children, but I couldn't. The Raggios were existing on a budget that barely covered our own expenses. Nor was I physically capable of taking care of anybody else's problems; I could barely cope with our own. The cold, wet, muddy winter eased into a stormy spring. My intellectually curious three-and-a-half-year-old became a moody, morose little boy. The wonderful world to which he was accustomed—the wide open spaces of the farm, his chickens, his calves, his dogs and other animals—had disappeared. He could not run and play outside without my constant supervision even when the days were sunny and the weather warm because the big kids harassed him.

The water hose, for which I'd spent almost a dollar of our precious budget, saved our home when Grier Jr. accidentally set fire to our apartment. We'd packed a box of fruits and jellies in newspapers at the farm, brought them home, and stored them in a corner of the kitchen. Grier Jr. found a box of matches, lighted one, and when it burned his fingers he dropped it into the box of jars. The newspapers ignited. I was in the shower when I smelled smoke, grabbed a towel and housecoat, and dashed out to find my kitchen in flames. I raced for the hose and put out the fire, which had reached the kitchen closet where I'd stored our linens. The sheets afterward bore burn scars and some of them had tiny holes on every fold.

I spent endless hours reading stories and playing games with my son, but I knew I could not compensate for the life he missed. I was his only constant playmate and I wasn't a very good one.

Grier drove our only car to and from work because no city transportation was available. This left Grier Jr. and me stranded with no way to the grocery store, a city park, or a public library. I could clean our tiny apartment in less than an hour, make and remake menus and grocery lists, read everything available, write letters, and have time left over. Desperate for adult conversation and companionship, I eagerly awaited my husband's homecoming only to find him utterly incapable of response. He dragged himself out to work every morning, arrived home absolutely exhausted, ate, and fell into bed, where nightmares disturbed his sleep. We could not sleep together because Grier feared he might injure me with his uncontrollable thrashing. Between nightmare interruptions he slept on our one full-size bed in the bedroom and I shared a cot with Grier Jr. in the kitchen. More often than not during his waking moments, Grier was so irritable and critical, especially to our son, that our lives were mired in misery. I know now he was in a deep, deep depression, but at that time I knew only that the bright dreams we had for our future were dissipating. . . .

And I was pregnant.

Grier and I both knew we wanted a second child—and then a third and fourth if all went well—and a new baby was sometimes the only bright promise of that first year we lived in Dallas. But nothing for us was as simple as it seemed. Tests showed that I was Rh negative. This negative blood factor, only recently discovered in 1946, predicated grave results. My blood and that of the fetus might be incompatible. My life could be at risk. More likely, our baby might not survive or could be deformed. Because of my voracious reading, I knew far too much to make me comfortable with my pregnancy. One magazine article spelled out the dire consequences of an Rh negative birth, showing pictures of an infant with a deformed head. Babies born from a mother with Rh negative blood were likely to be born jaundiced. They came too early. They were stillborn or died at birth. The mother might not survive childbirth.

I called Alice Smith, a friend from my University of Texas days and a resident physician at Southwestern Medical School, and asked her to help me find the very best obstetrician/gynecologist. She advised me to come to the medical school where the ob/gyn department was headed by Dr. William Mengert, whose special interest was in the newly discovered Rh negative factor. Dr. Mengert became my doctor.

With a new baby coming, we were desperate for space, and Grier doggedly went to the complex office every day, insisting on a two-bedroom apartment. He was told over and over that there was nothing, but finally, near summer's end, the administrator was so tired of Grier going up there every day that he said he had a three-bedroom becoming available and we could have it temporarily until a two-bedroom opened up. In August 1946, we moved across the way into Trainer Circle. Except for the wonderful additional space, conditions surrounding us did not improve.

One of our neighbors was an absolute lunatic. A returned veteran, he had been certified with mental problems. The family had six kids about a year apart and they were like little wild animals. We'd hear screaming and pleading when their father beat them. Sometimes he'd turn loose on his wife and all six kids would be screaming at once. There would have been no use in calling the police; in those days family violence was called "domestic disturbance," and nobody intervened.

Another crazy person lived next door to us on the other side; this time it was the woman who was nuts. She was the neighborhood gossip. I felt so sorry for her husband; he was a nice man, but she was a shrew. I've never heard a woman berate her husband like she did. Every morning she'd scream at him as he left the house that she wouldn't be there when he got home because she was going to kill herself. On the night she almost made good her suicide threat, she fired off a shotgun. We heard this terrible blast in the middle of the night and raced out, very shook up. She was bleeding like crazy and carted off to the hospital. The shotgun blast penetrated our flimsy walls and missed a sleeping Grier Jr. by a little less than a foot. Fortunately the shot had gone high and hit our ceiling, otherwise our child would have been murdered in his bed. She had only superficial wounds and was home the next day.

Across the way, another neighbor sweetly waved good-bye to her husband as he left for work in the morning, then locked her two children out of the house and entertained an endless parade of male visitors until shortly before his return in the afternoon.

THROUGHOUT MY PREGNANCY, I was carefully monitored. Toward the end, I had a blood test weekly to determine if my blood and that of the infant remained compatible. I was so fortunate that it did! As my due date approached, we sent Grier Jr. to the farm to be with Mother and Daddy. He was overjoyed and I was relieved that he would be safe and happy. On the night of September 10, 1946, as Grier and I sat on the back porch of our apartment, my water broke, but I was in no pain and not sufficiently aware that the time had really come! I insisted that all was well and I would let him know when I needed to go to the hospital. Fortunately, Grier said absolutely not. As he nervously walked the floor of our apartment, he declared that we would not stay out there on the Fort Worth Pike many miles from the hospital and have me go into hard labor in the middle of the night. Always in charge in a crisis, he bundled me up and delivered me to the hospital. I was admitted. Dr. Smith, my old friend, was taking care of me. She examined me and said the baby would not arrive until the next day. Grier insisted that I remain in the hospital and the authorities relented. There were only two private rooms in the hospital and I lucked out to get one of them.

Around 11 P.M. we were sitting in the room talking when the chief resident came by to check me. He practically fainted! The baby was in the birth position and the head was crowning. There were frantic calls to my doctor, who was nowhere to be found. I recall the rolling cart being pushed, none too gently, down the hall, the doctors and nurses running alongside, pushing the cart to get me to the delivery room before the baby arrived. I remember looking up in all the confusion and seeing Dr. Mengert's face as he pulled on his scrub coat and gloves. I delivered Tom Raggio without the aid of even an aspirin! I was fully awake, fully alert. I heard his first cry! And the reassuring voices of doctors and attendants that this baby was fine. I felt a sense of great triumph. He arrived in this world shortly after midnight on September 11, 1946; had my delivery not been postponed, he would have had a September 10 birthday. His ears were as flat as a cookie sheet. He had ten fingers, ten toes; his cries were normal. He had no wrinkles, no disfigurations. He seemed whole and healthy! So I fell asleep.

Dr. Mengert warned us never, never, never to have another child.

I was in Parkland Hospital for a full week. Even then it was a city/county hospital. Thomas Louis Raggio's nursery roommates included one other Anglo baby (ours of French/Italian/German/Swedish ancestry!), forty-nine other black and Chicano, and one Eskimo baby. What a great beginning to life, this child of mine! It is no wonder that he has turned out to be so wonderful!

In the four years since Grier Jr.'s birth, there had been some advances. With Tommy, I was up the day of his birth and walking up and down the halls the afternoon of September 11. Sore and a bit weary, I leaned on Grier's arm as together we peered into the nursery at the miracle of our love. Some time in that week of awakening, I began to believe that things were going to be better for us.

It didn't happen overnight.

We brought a very, very unhappy four-year-old Grier Jr. home. Now that he had a room of his own, a place for his toys, and a baby brother, his life should have been better, but it wasn't. He begged to go back the farm. My mother didn't help, because she did everything to encourage him to stay and that made Grier furious.

Tommy was not an easy baby. He cried constantly. He never napped in the daytime. He'd fall asleep around 10 P.M. and sleep through the night, but he demanded constant attention every waking moment. I was utterly exhausted. I knew the baby was absorbing all of me and I was neglecting my little boy, and that made me feel guilty.

Before Tommy's birth, Dr. Mengert had taken little Grier to the nursery and told him to pick out the baby that he wanted. Grier Jr. thought and thought and finally chose one. After we were home for a few days, with Tommy crying all the time, Grier Jr. solemnly said, "Mother, I sure made a bad choice when I picked out this baby!" I think this was the beginning of my oldest son feeling responsible for others. He carried the weight of the world on his shoulders for a long time.

The weather turned raw and wet. We had no washing machine and couldn't afford diaper service, so I washed diapers and all of our other laundry by hand. We did not have a bathtub either in Eden Place or Trainer Circle, but there was a deep sink next to the regular sink in each unit and that's where I did the family laundry. It rained so much that I couldn't hang anything outside, so I strung clotheslines all over the house and had a constant crop of drying diapers, which made the house all the more damp and miserable. On the rare occasions when the sun came out, I'd wade through mud to stretch sheets and diapers on the clothesline so that they could get a little sun.

Sometimes I used that deep sink for a bathtub! I longed for a good hot bath to ease my sore muscles, so when Grier was at home and in charge of the two boys, I'd run a tub of hot water and immerse my body in it. Never mind that my head, legs, arms, and hands stuck out in all directions!

We had no telephone. When I had to make an emergency call, like calling for doctor's appointments, I would leave Grier Jr. sitting by Tommy's crib, admonish him not to move, and run all the way down to the corner pay phone, make my call, and run all the way back. We put our names on a waiting list to get a telephone. Months later, when Tommy was about six months old, we finally got a phone. Its mere ringing was music to my ears! Little did I know.

We had no refrigerator and the most cantankerous icebox ever created! Food and milk were stored in the bottom of the box and blocks of ice in a top compartment. I had to be careful how and where I placed the ice because at the slightest pressure or jar, the bottom collapsed and the block of ice crashed down onto fruits and vegetables stored below. Sometimes things broke. I was constantly humoring that icebox!

Very few refrigerators were being produced; everybody put their names on a list and had to wait until their name reached the top before they could buy any appliance. We'd put our names on every list, but were so far down the scale that I thought the boys would be grown before we had electric refrigeration. One of our neighbors, a Mr. Haynes, had also put his name on every list in town. After a long wait, his name reached the top of a list and he bought his refrigerator. Then Sears called and told him that his name had reached the top of their list and he was now eligible for a refrigerator. He bought the refrigerator; we paid for it. It was delivered to his house. He and Grier and some of the other neighbors moved the refrigerator up the sidewalk and into our apartment. It was bare bones—had two ice trays and one shelf, but it was the most wonderful purchase of our lives. I was so glad not to put up with that miserable icebox and all the spoiled food.

Grier's health was still precarious and his temperament erratic. We lived on a very, very limited budget, often with only a few pennies left by the time the next paycheck arrived. Even if we had known how and where to seek medical help for Grier, we could not have paid for it. He had begun to gain a little weight. I am a good cook, and even on our meager food budget I planned and prepared good, wholesome meals. But, if anything, the nightmares were worse. Grier now had his own room, Grier Jr. another room, and Tommy and I shared the third bedroom. I'd hear a noise in the middle of the night and find Grier sitting up in his bed, his arms wrapped around his body, literally holding himself together and shaking until his teeth rattled.

I suffered my own depression, only we didn't know what to call it then and wouldn't have admitted it if we had. I had no friends, lived in isolation from all social and intellectual challenge, had the full-time care of two children, one a frail, crying infant and the other a miserable four-year-old. We had no money for a baby-sitter, so we couldn't escape to a movie. Television hadn't come along yet.

And I was constantly concerned about my children. They begged to play outside, but I dared not leave them alone. Once when I tried it for a few minuts, I heard Grier Jr. screaming and raced outside to find Tommy's mouth literally stuffed with sand. One of the big kids had force fed him. I scooped out the sand with my fingers, grabbed the hose, and washed his mouth. None of us felt safe on Trainer Circle.

My whole life had narrowed to a small apartment in a mud hole in a poverty pocket. Even though centered with a husband I loved and didn't know how to help and two little boys I adored, my day began and ended in what seemed to me an interminable dead end with no way out.

I didn't know what to do.

But my husband did. . . .

8

Escape

THE DAY THAT GRIER CAME HOME and said, "Louise, you're going to law school," I thought he was kidding. I said, "Oh, sure," and when I saw he wasn't joking, I thought he'd lost his mind, had gone completely off into fantasy land. True, there'd been a time in Washington when many of my friends were going on to law school that I had toyed with such an idea, but it hadn't once crossed my mind in the past six years.

Married women with children did not go to graduate school. Married women with children did not have careers. Married women with children stayed at home, supported their husband's careers, and reared children. If they were fortunate to have enough time and money, they did unpaid work in worthwhile community programs as volunteers.

The limit of my expectations in those Mustang Village days was to get back into the League of Women Voters.

I had no idea that, beneath his depression, beneath his exhaustion, beneath his nightmares, beneath his outbursts of temper, Grier was gravely concerned about me and spending long hours, as he drove to and from work and sometimes even at work, trying to figure out a way to get me out of the house, into something that would salvage my intelligence and my self-esteem. I did not know that he missed the girl who once sparred with him on history and politics and current events as much as I missed the man who could make all my troubles disappear just by holding me in his arms and loving me!

When I recognized that he was absolutely serious, I was stunned and all the "what if's" and "how to's" began to surface.

As usual in times of critical decision-making, Grier passed everything off with humor. "Law school is the cheapest way to get you out of the house," he declared. He'd already done "our" homework and he'd already met and crossed off almost every objection I could raise.

I would enroll in night law school at Southern Methodist University. Tuition was eight dollars per course per hour. I would enroll for five hours. That would be forty dollars. We'd find the money somewhere. He would continue to work. I would continue to look after the kids, the housework, and the cooking in the daytime. He would get home from work, we'd have dinner, and he would take over. He'd do the kitchen, look after the children, and see that they were safely in bed. I would take the car and drive across town to SMU. On weekends, we'd share the household chores, grocery shopping, laundry, and child care and he'd not only see that I had time to study but would help me if I needed it.

I continue to this day to be amazed at how clearly Grier had thought everything out. I know that his physical condition had something to do with sending me to law school, because the uncertainty of his health and the cloud of un-Americanism could well have limited his future ability to support us. I am also amazed, as I have observed our situation and others similar through the years, how individuals in depression react in a crisis. Almost without exception, they may be living in a deep cobwebby haze unable to respond to daily trivialities, but let a crisis occur and they inevitably take over and make almost perfect decisions.

Grier literally pushed me through the door to enroll in law. All the way to the campus, I balked. I thought of thousands more "what if's." What if I didn't qualify? That would lower my self-esteem to the breaking point. What if I got in and we couldn't manage the tuition money? What if I did enroll and pay the fee and he got sick or fired and couldn't take care of the kids? What if I did get in and couldn't hack it? What if one of the kids got sick and we couldn't take care of them? To every "what if," Grier had a simple answer. "If that happens, we'll meet it when it comes. Now, you go get yourself enrolled."

I finally said I would talk to the admissions people and apply. I did it because I thought if Grier's emotional health completely collapsed, legal training might qualify me to teach business law or simple consumer law courses in high school. My permanent Texas teacher's certificate only qualified me to teach through the junior high years, and I'd already learned I was not suited to handle a classroom of adolescents. If I had a law degree, or even some solid law course, I could qualify for a high school, or maybe even a junior college, teaching post.

But I had another problem. My mother. I held off as long as I could in telling her that I planned to go to law school. She thought I had completely lost it. She said it was too bad that I hadn't married a man who was able to support me and the children.

Qualifying for law school was no problem. After all, I was a summa cum laude graduate of the University of Texas, second in my class with a year of graduate work at American University in Washington, D.C. Staying there was the problem.

If ever there was a persona non grata, in Southern Methodist University's night law classes, I was it!

A lovely old gentleman by the name of Charles Potts was dean of the law school, and he was, indeed, of the old school. His bearing, behavior, and ideas were those of a male of the Civil War era. His standards for females were a throwback from the 1870s instead of the 1940s. Professor Arthur "Bull" Harding was in charge of admissions. He did not believe there was a place for *any* woman in law school, and he almost choked when I presented myself as a likely candidate. Everybody in a position of authority at SMU discouraged me. I was reminded that law was a male profession, that the rough-and-tumble charges and countercharges of the courtroom was no suitable contest for a lady, that if I *were* admitted (and my qualifications were better than any other candidate) I would only be taking up space that could be occupied by a man who would *do something* with his degree. They tried to play on my patriotic sympathies. There were only a limited number of slots, they told me, and returning veterans under the GI Bill deserved all of them.

I could have easily given up, because they were right! Most female attorneys—and there were precious few—were not practicing law simply because no firms would hire them.

Typical of Grier Raggio, every obstacle they threw in my way was a challenge for us to overcome. I had to be the front person, the one pushing and prodding, making myself available at the whim of their professional timing, but Grier was behind me all the way— shoring up, feeding me answers to their negative input, determined that I should and would enroll in law school. To every reservation I presented, he had a positive refutation.

I enrolled in night law school at SMU in February 1947. I was really scared. I felt like paying the forty-dollar tuition fee was taking milk from the mouths of my babies. I had to learn to study all over again. I had to manage all of my responsibilities at home to make it as easy as possible for Grier to take over at night. Talk about a supermom. I was it! I cooked and baked with a law book instead of a recipe book open in front of me. I wonder what kind of concoctions I fed the Raggio males.

Grier was as good as his word. He stopped complaining. He became more lenient with our children. He drove our one car home from his hated job at the Veterans Administration at his Love Field office. When he walked in, I'd have dinner on the table. Sometimes we had time to eat together. Often, if he were in the slightest delayed, I'd give him a hasty kiss as I walked out the door to a car that was still warm from his trip across Dallas.

I never enjoyed law school—I can't say I enjoyed a single class— but I thoroughly enjoyed my classmates. They were all men, mostly older men, many returning from service in World War II. The day students were kids, but the night classes were comprised of people like me who had finished undergraduate degrees five to fifteen years back. Their experiences made them lenient and supportive. If a woman wanted to be "one of the guys," no sweat. My professors were puzzled, but my classmates counted me as one of them. Slowly my mind began to expand again, to grasp and wrestle with ideas, to be challenged. In the best of all possible worlds, I would have been perfectly satisfied to be at home with my children, to be a volunteer in the community, and to make my mark as the "better half" of a traditional family, but my husband gave me no choice.

Gradually, I began to understand that we were a team—Grier and I. He held things together at home while I was away. When I got home around 10:30 P.M., he and I took time to talk a bit. There was absolutely no time for either of us to air grievances—even if we had them! All we had time to do was share information critical to the care of our sons before we both fell into bed exhausted. I don't know when I studied—or even if I studied—but my grades were good and Grier remained my number-one cheering section.

When summer came, I enrolled in an evidence course. I didn't know what I was doing—and I still don't. I never knew what the teacher was talking about and I never did grasp that course, but my grades held strong. In the fall I enrolled for two courses, six hours. My grades remained passing to high even when the kids were sick, my housekeeping chores were overwhelming, and my mom still thought I had lost my mind.

Very honestly, I never thought I would graduate from law school. Grier thought I would. To me, becoming a full-fledged attorney seemed beyond my capabilities. I just knew I had to get enough credits to help secure a good job in the event I had to support our family.

The boys remained my greatest challenge. I did not want anything to interfere with their health, well-being, and educational promise. Tommy was still such a frail child. He looked like he would blow away if anybody breathed on him, so I spent a lot of time preparing foods I thought a baby would like and tried my best to get him to eat and gain weight. At night I cuddled with him, encouraging him to sleep and rest, but try as I would Tommy planned his own course and basically did what Tommy wanted to do! Grier Jr. was so much help. I never could have made it without that little boy. He took Tommy outside and watched him while I did housework. When the neighborhood hoodlums interfered, he sounded the alarm and I'd go rescue my children.

The Dallas Independent School District put a first grade in one of the buildings at Mustang Village—they had to do something with all our kids—and we enrolled Grier Jr. His intellectual curiosity was honed, and for the first time since his days on the farm he began to be a happier child.

As my world opened, the neighborhood also expanded. Genie and Ned Fritz remained our friends and Tom and Khaki Green joined our circle of special acquaintances. But Trainer Circle continued to harbor more than its share of riffraff.

In the midst of all these challenges Grier and I found the Unitarian Church. As I recall, Elizabeth Brownscombe, who had been president of the State League of Women Voters when I was president of the Austin League, first invited us. Grier's religious heritage was Methodist and he had no collapse of faith, but I did. I'd left the conservative church of my childhood and had no intention of seeking another of a similar denomination. But increasingly I had a longing for a spiritual connection and I knew that I wanted our sons reared in a church.

We visited the Unitarian Church located in a tiny building on Maple Avenue, and it was a revelation. I had been taught that humanity is sinful and unclean. I had grown up with a long list of negatives, of "thou shalt nots," and I was desperate for a spiritual journey based on a positive approach to living. Very early I had wondered why, if I were made in the image of God, I was so unworthy. When I first began to ask for an explanation about the tenets of my faith at about age fifteen, everybody reacted as if my very questioning was sinful.

Grier and I started going to church regularly with our boys. We had no money for baby-sitters, and we looked forward to Sunday morning when we could put our kids in the nursery and in kindergarten class, where they were safe and happy, and we could be with adults! Until then people who knew both of us had no idea we were married because one of us always was home baby-sitting. Robert Raible was the minister, one of a whole flock of marvelous people who encouraged us to use our minds, ask questions, to use our creativity, and be aware of the unfolding wonders of the universe.

The Reverend Raible's sermons were so wonderful. I'd get a lift every Sunday; he'd give me nuggets of wisdom that challenged my thinking all week. It was wonderful to go to church and hear him talk about all kinds of things. It was spiritually comforting. I knew I'd found my place.

We attended groundbreaking ceremonies for the new church on Preston Road at Normandy in 1949. One of the pictures is of our little Tommy in the background standing on tiptoes and looking around to see what was going on. I attended the first services held in the new sanctuary.

We did not officially join the church until 1949. I held back because of my mother. She said Unitarianism was not a religion, was in fact anti-Christ and extremely evil. People who had never been in a Unitarian Church, had never studied anything about it but thought they knew everything, fed my mother a lot of horrible lies. I didn't want to do anything to disturb Mother and Dad, who were happy in their faith.

Mother never reconciled to my being a Unitarian; my religious beliefs became another of the many things I could never share with her. She fought it to her dying breath. When the boys went down to the farm in the summer, she paid them to learn the Apostle's Creed and the Ten Commandments and to go to Bible study, because she thought Grier and I were leading them straight to hell. Grier and I agreed that the boys be christened in my parent's faith. If it meant so much to Mother, it was okay with us. Grier Jr. was christened in church, Tommy and later Kenny in home ceremonies. When I was home, I always went to church with her and took Holy Communion. It meant so much to her. I found that I could be two people. At Mother's church in the country, with relatives and old friends, I'd go with the women and talk about recipes and gardening and children. At my church in Dallas, couples together had deep and meaningful discussions about every topic under the sun.

Had it not been for the Unitarian Church, I don't know what would have happened to me when the charges that Grier was a Communist sympathizer finally came to a head. It was the bleakest period of my life.

Grier was more and more unhappy in his job, but we had to have his paycheck, so he kept working and I kept going to law school.

Then the unthinkable happened. Grier was fired.

We were charged with the ultimate crime: un-Americanism. We did not know exactly what we were accused of doing. We did not know who our accusers were. I say "we" because I was just as involved as Grier. We knew that our telephones were tapped. We knew we were under constant surveillance, but for what we did not know. Our livelihood was gone. Most people under such charges collapsed and a number committed suicide, but Grier always had the ability to fight back when cornered.

Eight charges were filed against him. The letter of his dismissal from his job is dated November 3, 1948, and was sent to Grier at his offices at the Veterans Administration at Love Field in Dallas. It reads in part:

I.   That you are a member of the Communist Party.

II. That you are a member of the American Spanish Aid Committee . . . a Communist Front organization.

III. That during 1940–41 you associated with members of the Communist Party and attended meetings of the Ayuda a la Renovacion de Espana, a Communist Front organization in Tampa, Florida.

IV. That you made statements to fellow workers during 1930–40 that you were a member of the American Civil Rights Union . . .

V.   That . . . [while living] in Washington, D.C., you . . . consistently expressed yourself in favor of Communism as opposed to a democratic form of government.

VI. That during 1945 you advocated and praised the Russian system of government to your fellow workers.

VII. That you made a statement to a fellow worker that "there is no difference between Stalin forcing Communism on the countries of Europe and the United States forcing democracy upon them."

VIII. You expressed in 1946 to your neighbors . . . the overthrow of our form of government by force.

These were horrible charges. There was not a word of truth to any of them. The letter was signed by Fred R. Carpenter, Director of Personnel, Branch Office 10, Veterans Administration, and by Eric

Eades, chairman of the VA Loyalty Board. Removal from his job would be effective thirty days from receipt of the letter. Until that time, he would carry on his regular work and his pay status would be unaffected. He would be permitted to respond to the charges in writing within ten calendar days from the date of the receipt of the notice, had the right to an administrative hearing on the charges, and could appear personally before the Veterans Administration Loyalty Board.

I helped Grier with his response. We polished every phrase, every word. His response is dated November 15, 1948, and reads in part:

I. I have never been and am not now a member of the Communist Party.

II. I have never been a member of the United American Spanish Aid Committee.

III. I have no recollection of ever having seen or heard of the Ayuda a la Renovacion de Espana and am unable to pronounce or translate into English its name.

IV. I have no recollection of having made such statements . . . I am not a member of the American Civil Rights Union.

V. I have no recollection of having made this statement. . . . The most cherished right [of Americans] is the right to make up [their] own minds on social, economic, religious, and political matters. I am diametrically opposed to living under any kind of dictatorship.

VI. During the first nine months of 1945, I was serving my third year overseas in the Pacific Theater from New Caledonia to Iwo Jima. . . . I emphatically deny saying that the economy of Russia in 1945 was superior to our own.

VII. This statement was lifted out of context. I believe that . . . people should, so far as possible, be permitted to choose their own form of government. . . .

VIII. I categorically deny having made this statement. . . . I have always believed and now believe that any evil in our government should be corrected by constitutional means.

Grier was cleared of all charges.

"The Board has determined that on all the evidence, reasonable grounds do not exist for the belief that you are disloyal to the Government of the United States."

But the damage had been done. My husband got his hated job back, but from then on he never got a promotion, never got a raise except those routinely ordered by Congress for all government employees. He never made more the $500 a month throughout his career with the government until he left to open his own law practice in 1955.

Grier was a marked man. We lived through this period of time in silence. Grier told his sister and a few people in Washington he thought were his closest friends because he needed their assistance. Nobody came to his aid. Our friends disappeared. The few Grier told deserted us because they were afraid of being tainted with the term "fellow traveler." After Grier died, his sister Rita told me that one of the great regrets of her life was that she did not come to the defense of her brother.

I could never talk about the un-American charges against my husband to anybody. I certainly couldn't tell my folks or any other of my other relatives. Mother disliked Grier so much that I could never tell her anything or get any consolation from her. I did not even discuss it at church or with my minister, but I knew from the Reverend Raible's sermons that we were accepted. The church was the only place where I found people who had any understanding of the witch-hunt that was going on in our country.

My reaction to the trauma was to redouble my efforts to get through law school. I think it was the first time that I knew I must graduate and pass the bar because I very well could wind up being the sole provider for our family. If he had been convicted of the charges, Grier could not have gotten any kind of job—not even that of a window washer—and if other charges were filed, well, his very fragile mental health might not hold up.

Christmas of 1948 and January 1949 were especially bad. All four members of our family were sick. Both Grier and I had the flu; both Grier Jr. and Tommy had colds and earaches. The weather was rainy and cold. We were restricted to our tiny apartment.

I'd get out of bed, take care of the boys, and drag myself to class—I think I only missed one night during all that terrible time. Grier had a little more leniency because of "sick days" he'd accumulated on his job, and he did his best to help with everything. We didn't want food and we weren't interested in sex. For that entire period of time we were almost totally abstinent.

And in February I missed a period. My first thought was that the cyst had come back. I was sure I couldn't be pregnant. As an SMU student I had free medical care, so I went to see Dr. Minnie Lee Maffett at the health service. A very bored receptionist, a student assistant filing her nails, finally condescended to acknowledge my presence. "What's the matter with you?" she asked. When I said, "I think I may be pregnant," I got her attention. "Are you married?" she asked, and when I said, yes, she then courteously asked me to have a seat. The doctor would see me! I have always wondered what would have happened if I'd said no. Would I have been banished? Would the doctor have made an appointment after hours and after dark? Were there two different sets of rules for the medical care of married and unmarried mothers-to-be? Dr. Maffett saw me and said yes, I was pregnant. It was the last straw. Our circumstances were deplorable. Our finances were zilch. Dr. Mengert had cautioned me never to get pregnant again.

When life was its blackest, I could always count on Grier. When I told him Dr. Maffett said I was pregnant, he got this twinkle in his eye. "Well, you should have gone to law school that night," he said, and then demonstrated that touch of humor, "Maybe you did go to law school!"

I made an appointment with Dr. Mengert immediately. He confirmed that I was, indeed, pregnant and talked to me very seriously about the possible complications of a third pregnancy when I was Rh negative and both of my previous children had been positive. He considered my pregnancy so critical that he offered me a therapeutic abortion. Grier and I discussed it very seriously. Grier was not averse to my having a termination because he was so afraid that something would happen to me. He left the final decision totally up to me.

I don't think I ever honestly considered giving up the pregnancy, but the experience taught me to be an adamant freedom-of-choice advocate. I chose to have my baby. Other women for other reasons could make a different choice, and I would be completely support-ive. Until you go through the mental trauma of making a decision like that, you have no idea how serious and wrenching it is. The issue of pregnancy termination is almost never a clear black-and-white decision; almost never do women easily choose abortion; almost always there are serious consequences for either choice. I have no right to make that choice for anyone except myself and nobody else has the right, certainly no man and no woman unless she has walked in the same shoes, to offer their unsolicited opinion to anyone else. Grier's health was so fragile that the possibility of my dying and leaving him with the sole responsibility of raising two or three babies was horrible. On the other hand, both of us had planned for and wanted another child. Even though we could not figure out how we would manage either the health or the financial issues, I decided to continue the pregnancy.

I also decided to continue to go to school for as long as I could. All kinds of weird things happened to me—especially to my circula-tory system. I developed such terrible varicose veins in my right leg that I could not walk across the floor without a rubber stocking. If I tried, it felt like hot lead shooting through my leg and into my body. My heart raced all the time, sometimes doubling its normal rate. I was so tired I hurt.

Dr. Mengert monitored me every step of the way. He warned me that going to school together with caring for a six-year-old and a two-year old, continuing to do all of the cooking and most of the housework, was more than a healthy person should undertake. Grier helped as much as he could, but the primary responsibility was up to me. And I couldn't give up.

One night around 10:30 P.M. as I drove back to Mustang Village from law school, my 1941 Chevrolet suddenly went dead. The motor died; the lights disappeared; the car stalled. All by myself in the middle of a weed patch surrounded by trees and brush in the Trinity River bottoms, five months pregnant, bone tired, with no other traffic anywhere in sight, I was stranded without a flashlight. It was pitch black. I remembered that earlier that day we had installed a new battery, so I felt my way out of the car, lifted the hood, and felt around for the battery. Sure enough, the battery connection had jumped off. Feeling my way, I reconnected the cable. The lights went on, the motor started, and I drove the rest of the way home—only about twenty minutes later than I normally would have arrived.

Grier was frantic. He said we must do something. I must not continue to drive through the rugged terrain alone at night in an undependable car. I was too tired to respond, so again it was Grier who came up with an impossible solution—that worked! He said we should move closer to law school. I couldn't believe my ears. We were already stretched beyond our financial limit and now my husband wanted us to move to University Park!

The next day we started looking for housing in Park Cities. I no more believed we'd find something than I thought I would be able to sprout wings and fly to and from SMU. But Grier said anything was possible, and we kept looking.

The house we finally found at 3211 Amherst was old and in the most awful condition you can imagine. I said it should be burned or torn down; it was a disgrace to the neighborhood. Grier said it had great possibilities. We bought it! The down payment was $3,000. Grier had GI benefits, but the house would not pass government inspection. We cashed in his life insurance policy and borrowed money from my dad and somehow scraped together the down payment.

In order to meet our living expenses we had to have additional income. The upstairs of the house had two bedrooms and a bath, so Grier built an outside stairway and opened a private entry at the back of the house. We rented these bedrooms for thirty-five dollars per room to two men. During the time we lived there, we had some special men in the upstairs bedrooms of our home and became friends especially with a man named Eddie Seid. This seventy dollars a month made it possible to meet our expenses.

I desperately wanted an automatic washing machine, and when I had seen there was one sitting in a corner of the kitchen, I was ecstatic. Grier and I went right out to Sears and bought our own Kenmore washing machine to be delivered the day after we moved into the house. It cost $37.50 and we put it on time payment; with interest, the payments came to $3.25 a month for a year. The sellers moved out, taking their machine and leaving behind a blank wall. There were no hook-ups! Whoever would have thought to check behind a washing machine for connections, or would have dreamed that a washing machine was mere window dressing! It took an extra thirty-five dollars to hire a plumber to install the connections. I could not imagine where we'd find the money, but we somehow did. Together with the purchase of my Chevrolet, it was the best money I ever spent. The machine was a joy to operate and I laundered thousands of pieces of clothing and linens in the next decade. It worked well for the entire ten years we lived on Amherst.

We moved from Mustang Village into our "new" home on Amherst in September 1949. Neither Grier nor I had any idea what adventures lay ahead.

9

Life Among the Elite

IF YOU'D DONE A SURVEY of the residents living in the Park Cities area of Dallas in 1949, I'm absolutely certain you'd have found that the Raggios were the poorest family there—financially, that is. We were literally living from payday to payday, supporting a family of four with a new baby soon to arrive on $500 a month!

Park Cities, made up of two different cities within a city—Highland Park and University Park—is an elite enclave centered by Southern Methodist University. Its residents are educated, professional, and financially secure. Boy, were we out of place! Only we weren't. We had everything except money.

And money was so tight I'd regularly borrow the thirty-five dollars Grier Jr. had in his saving account at Hillcrest Bank, money that he'd earned selling tomato plants and through various similar projects. With those borrowed dollars, I'd tide us over until Grier's next paycheck came. That few dollars toward the end of many months meant that we could continue to eat! I still have that little passbook and it shows that every few months I'd borrow thirty-five dollars from my son and ten or twelve days later return the money, always with interest.

The Park Cities house on Amherst was both our salvation and our nemesis. With no insulation, it was sweltering in the summer and frigid in the winter. We had neither central heat nor air conditioning. The windows were all so loose that when the cold winds started, they blew right through, as if there were no deterrent at all. Slowly, as time and money became available, we caulked every one of them. Grier slept in the bedroom in the northeast corner of the house where he felt as if we'd opened the door onto the Arctic. Even in the warmest underwear and pajamas he could find, he'd shiver with cold in addition to his recurrent nightmares. The kids and I huddled together in the back bedroom where there was one small space heater. Both inside and out, the place literally was falling apart. I papered the back bedroom, the bathroom, and the kitchen. I learned later that some of my neighbors were amazed at that woman who dared do her own wallpapering—and in Highland Park yet! To me, it was nothing at all. I had learned both the necessity and the art as a kid from my mother and aunt.

Mother was an indispensable addition to our family during those first early days in Park Cities. She came to help us move. She cooked for us and looked after Grier Jr. and Tommy while I, eight months pregnant, supervised the packing, moving, and placement of furniture in our new abode with Grier. The most talented and efficient seamstress I have ever known, Mother made curtains for our living, dining, and bedrooms. She helped to unpack everything and put it away, insisting that I must not do any climbing or high reaching.

We enrolled Grier Jr. in the second grade at University Park School and Mother stayed to see that his first day went well. The school was only two blocks from our house; Mother walked him to school on his first day, carefully pointing out landmarks so that he would know his way home when the day ended. The time came for him to be at home and no little boy arrived. He didn't come home and he didn't come home. I was so worried, but had no idea how to go about looking for him. Suddenly, a police car drove up in front of our house and Grier Jr. got out. It was our first experience with the University Park police and the beginning of a deep and lasting appreciation of the way they operate. Police officers, it turned out, always drove around the schools when the kids were released from class and made it their business to rescue any child who needed attention. Grier Jr. had turned the wrong way when he started home, got lost, and wound up in the middle of the street, where he was rescued by the officer. The policeman was so nice, so kind, both to Grier Jr. and to us, and we were eternally grateful. I cannot praise too highly the police department at that time in our lives—or any police personnel who go the extra miles to check up on children.

A month after we moved to Amherst, on October 18, 1949, Kenneth Gaylord Raggio was born. For the last several weeks before his birth, Dr. Mengert had me come in every week for a blood test. When I went into labor, he asked if medical students could observe the birth and I said yes. He used a saddle block to alleviate the pain. The medication went up instead of down, paralyzed my upper body and stopped the labor. I was on the delivery table for almost five hours, awake all of the time and aware of the frenzy that went on around me. Nurses and medical students in addition to the doctor worked on my body. A young resident from the Middle East was in charge of rubbing my neck. Nurses massaged my legs and arms, all of it to keep the blood flowing because my bodily functions had almost closed down. All the time they kept talking to me and checking my eyes to see how dilated they were. I heard someone said, "She's going out," and another time, "Give her more ephedrine," and the answer, "We can't give her more ephedrine; she's higher than a kite now." The response to that was, "She's got to have more ephedrine; her blood pressure's going out the bottom of the tube."

With the use of forceps, my baby finally arrived. I heard Dr. Mengert say, "Good god! What a big baby!" My infant did not breathe. I lay on the delivery table while they pounded and shook him until I finally heard his first cry. My own tears of relief blended with a simultaneous intake of breath from everybody in the room— and it seemed to me a small convention was present.

We were not yet home free. The length of my labor and the forceps delivery caused Kenneth to be born with a hematoma on the top of his head. With his pointed head, he looked like a clown. Weighing nine pounds and three ounces, he was most definitely a ten-month baby, just as I had tried to tell my doctors. When there's no sex, there can be no pregnancy—at least not at that time! I knew I had become pregnant in December, not in January as all the experts said.

We did not know until Kenny was eighteen months old whether he was normal. We knew he was very bright because he was at the top of the scale for measuring development for infants of his age, but we also knew that something was amiss with his coordination. He never learned to crawl. At the stage when most babies begin to crawl, I'd put him on the floor on his hands and knees and show him how to navigate. He'd flatten himself out and snake along. His sequence of motor coordination was completely off schedule. He did not sit up, creep, then crawl, then walk as the experts said babies should. He just slithered along on the floor until he was almost two—and then he stood up and walked!

My recovery was long and slow. On the day after Kenny was born, my body swelled until I thought I would explode. A nurse examining me assured me, "Honey, you'll soon have your baby and things will be all right." When I told her I had the baby yesterday, she said, "Oh, my god!" and ran out of the room to page the doctor. The medication had stopped all normal bodily functions and it took some time to get them back in rhythm.

I was in the hospital for a week. Mother came to care for me and the three boys. With Grier Jr. in second grade, Tommy running all over the place, an infant that we worried about, and my own fragile health, her work was very difficult and our appreciation of her contributions boundless. We could not have paid for the care Mother gave us even if we'd had money for it.

For the first three months of their lives, I nursed all three boys, but crises—Grier's leaving for the South Pacific when Grier Jr. was an infant, the trauma of Mustang Village and law school when we had Tommy, and a severe cold when Kenny was three months old—dried up my milk and the boys were bottle-fed thereafter. We knew nothing about trying to save breast milk in those days.

Kenny was only a month old when winter arrived. Now there were four of us in the back bedroom. I slept with a still fragile Tommy in a double bed. Grier Jr. slept on a cot pushed against the wall. Kenny had a crib at the foot of my bed. We had no furniture, not even a chest of drawers. We were so scrunched together that there was only a little trail to walk through.

And then the spring of 1950 came and for the first time in several years—a time that seemed an eternity while I was going through it—life looked good! Grier and I had decided that I would stay out of law school for a few months to look after my own health and that of the family.

One of the greatest things about the Amherst house was its large backyard, where our children had a place to play without being harassed. When we moved in, an older couple named the Claytons, who had no children, lived next door. Effie Davis Clayton was very kind to us and welcomed the boys to play in her yard. The Rudy Biesele family lived down the street. I had known the Biesele family in Austin when I was in high school, and Rudy's father, Dr. Biesele, taught me history at the University of Texas. It was wonderful to make this reconnection and to learn that the Biesele children were about the same age as our boys.

Children turned our entire neighborhood, with its numerous trees and wide open spaces, into their playground. They spilled in and out of yards and houses, roamed the blocks, and were welcome everywhere. Every adult assumed responsibility for everybody's kids. Police officers cruised now and then, keeping an eye on our children. As I look back, it was a virtual paradise, both for parents and kids. We'd never heard of child molestation. No homes were unsafe for children. The streets in front of our houses were our only hazard. Cars whizzed down Amherst, and we were all afraid that some child darting across the street might be hit by an automobile. We trained our kids not to play in the streets and to look both ways before crossing. Even so, we knew that little children forget. I did not believe in corporal punishment—and still don't—but I remember spanking Tom once when I saw him dart across the street, hoping it would remind him to stop and check for traffic, no matter how enticing play on the other side looked.

Finally we scraped together enough money to have a chain-link fence installed, and planted roses along the north and west sides of the fence, the prettiest roses I've ever seen. How Grier and I loved them! I have pictures of my boys when they were little with the flowers.

When we got the fence, Tom begged to keep the animals he constantly rescued. He had a way with animals. Once, I looked on, petrified, as Tom approached a dog bigger than he was, which could have inhaled him in one breath, and almost instantly he was petting it, had it tamed and following him home! He'd come into the house holding a pitiful-looking kitten and beg, "Mommy, please, can I keep him?" I could never resist my child's pleas and was so grateful to have the space to house his menageries. At one time or another we had chickens, ducks, geese, rabbits, gerbils, parakeets, goldfish, a motley collection of cats, and more dogs than I can remember to count—sometimes several at once.

I tried hard to grow grass in our backyard on Amherst. I planted and sodded and tended and watered, pulled weeds, hoed, and raked—and finally gave up. We grew kids instead of grass. As the neighborhood expanded, it continued to be a safe harbor for our children. At one time and another, with spillover kids from adjacent streets, we'd look out our windows and see as many as twenty kids of similar ages playing together.

The little kids walked to almost all of their activities. When they were older, they rode bicycles. We were two blocks from school, two blocks from the swimming pool, within a short distance to the Park Cities Y. By the time they were old enough to go to the Y, our boys had bicycles and got themselves there and back. Our sons also biked to middle school and to junior high several blocks away.

During the summer and fall of 1949 and the spring of 1950, I was a law school dropout. I threw myself into becoming a supermom. From the moment of their births, I was determined to open every door of educational opportunity for the children. I exposed them to every free adventure that our new neighborhood provided. I haunted the library, read every storybook in it, became room mother at Grier Jr.'s school and Sunday School teacher for Tommy's class. I provided a haven for all my sons' friends, kept all the household accounts, budgeted, paid the bills, made menus for weeks ahead so that I could watch every penny, grocery shopped, cooked and cleaned, scrubbed, mopped, dusted, and polished, redecorated every niche in the house to the limit of its possibilities, and was available for every extracurricular activity and every sport in which the boys showed an interest. I also began to look after my own interests again. I joined the League of Women Voters, which had been so important to me as a young woman in Austin, and I became active in the Women's Alliance at the Unitarian Church.

By the time I re-entered law school in the fall of 1950, our lives had begun to shape up and I could even laugh a little about the last semester I'd gone to school before Kenny was born.

Another woman student now shared the fallout from professors who were so threatened at having females in their classes. Barbara Culver had enrolled. Her husband, John, who had been blinded in World War II, entered law school on the GI Bill, and she was paid as his reader and note-keeper. She had graduated from journalism school while he was overseas and, quite wisely, decided to study law along with her husband. They, of course, took the same courses. They had no children, and Barbara had been told it was doubtful that she would ever conceive. *Voila!* She got pregnant about the same time I got pregnant with Kenneth, so there were two women expecting babies who, by our very presence, upset the status quo. Several of our classmates were also soon-to-be fathers, so we staked out a row in the classroom where we sat together and called it Pregnant Row. When one of the guys was absent from class, we'd know another baby had arrived.

Barbara continued her studies through January because she had to go to class to read to her husband. Her son, Larry, was born in January two days after she took her finals. She had to enroll one week late for the next semester because of her infant and was penalized for it. Barbara later became a justice of the Supreme Court of Texas and has an outstanding record as a distinguished judge and trial lawyer. Together, she and I have accumulated more awards than the rest of the law class put together! We continue to be friends and often chuckle over the old days, when professors would have done almost anything to keep the two of us in such delicate conditions out of law school because each of us was taking the place of a man.

I remember taking the criminal law course taught by a very nice professor named Moss Wimbish. I almost gave him heart failure. The course entailed recitation of some pretty grisly crimes. When it was my turn to relate some of the gory details, Professor Wimbish suffered far more than I did. If I even put my hand to my head, he would say, "Mrs. Raggio! Mrs. Raggio! Are you all right?!" Doubtless it got around that I was in precarious health.

I think all of the professors would have gladly given me an A in their courses if I'd promised never to attend another one of their classes while pregnant.

Everybody who was in law school with me has one tale or another, most of them true, about the days when three tow-headed little boys tagged along while I studied. If I went to the library during the day, I'd often borrow Grier Jr.'s bicycle, put Kenneth in the basket, and pedal over to SMU. Hibernia Turbeville was the librarian. She was very tolerant and allowed Kenny to play on the floor in her office while I studied.

One of my favorite courses was Legal Aid Clinic. The law school arranged with the Dallas Bar Association and a number of judges for law students to try cases in their courts. A member of the Dallas Junior Bar was assigned to accompany us. I thoroughly enjoyed the course because it took me into a real courtroom in direct contact with practicing lawyers and day school law students, most of whom were younger men, and with my own classmates, most of whom were older serious students who had returned from service. While the professors were mostly "mossbacks" from another era, the men in my classes were buddies, but we were all so busy with our studies and our families that we didn't have time to get to know each other outside the classroom. Legal Aid Clinic gave us a chance to work together on real cases.

I shall never forget my first experience in the courtroom. I had a real live client who wanted a divorce. I had all the papers ready, and with Bill Fogelman, who was chief counsel, appeared before the judge. The Junior Bar member did not show up, so Bill and I were before this quite elderly, very deaf judge. Either I did not articulate very well or he could not hear, but something went wrong and the judge got the idea that Bill and I were divorcing. He undertook to give us marriage counseling. He told us we were such a nice young couple and he knew we could work out our problems if we would only try hard enough. As soon as I understood what was happening, I shouted, "Judge, I'm married to somebody else." This really upset the nice old fellow, who thought that Bill was the cause of my marriage problems. Finally, an older, more experienced lawyer accustomed to dealing with the judge stepped in to rescue us both, explaining that we were law students representing a client who wanted a divorce. Eventually the judge got the message, checked the papers, interviewed the client, signed the decree, and everybody breathed a sigh of relief.

By the fall of 1951, I'd accumulated a hodgepodge of law credits, but lacked several courses required for graduation because those I needed were not offered every semester. Both Grier and I were weary of our schedules, so we decided that I should attend law school both day and night during 1951–52.

Talk about pressure!

Finally, somehow, I got enough credits together to graduate in the class of June 1952. In the class of one hundred, I was the only woman; I finished right in the middle, fiftieth, at the very bottom of the top of my class and the very top of the bottom! I prefer the latter designation. Mother, who'd opposed my going to law school every step of the way, came for all the festivities and had a marvelous time. You'd have thought she was the one graduating! My personal cheering section—my mother, my husband, nine-year-old Grier Jr., five-year-old Tommy, and two-year-old Kenny—made my walk down the aisle in cap and gown to receive my diploma a defining moment in my life.

Time to enjoy the Hilltop experience was fleeting. I had to pass the bar. No cram courses existed at that time, but a few SMU law professors donated their time to tutor and counsel us. We met in the mornings at SMU Law School. Law students not only from SMU, but from other schools in the state, came to learn. Professor Clyde Emery was especially wonderful. He had long been my favorite professor, because he was genuinely interested in pulling out the talents of individuals and having his students excel when it seemed that most other professors were far more interested in us failing. Also, his wife Lorinne was an attorney and he was comfortable with women as students. He carefully went over everything we could expect, and as I took the examinations later, I could close my eyes and picture him calmly explaining details.

Even so, the Texas State Bar examination was one of the most horrible experiences of my life. Bar exams were given in only one place, the House of Representatives in the State Capitol in Austin. It was July 1952, during one of the hottest summers on record in Texas. The official temperature was in excess of 100 degrees. Those of us who opted to take our typewriters were placed in a tiny corridor behind a wall behind the speaker's stand so that the clatter of our keys would not disturb the rest of those taking the exam in the chambers. Along with six others, I had a little niche in that narrow space without a breath of outside breeze, even had there been any. I know the temperature hovered around 115 degrees. No air conditioning, of course. There I was, dressed in a girdle, hose, and high heels—no woman would have dared to present herself in informal attire in those days—with a copy of the exam. I pored over questions even as I poured perspiration. I sweated so badly that puddles of water stood under my feet when I kicked off my shoes.

By the third and final day of the exams, everything was a blur. I was functioning on automatic. My brain was numb. I wanted to run away—and might have if Grier hadn't been with me every moment that I was outside the examination room. He'd taken time off from work and was in Austin with me. We had an old quilt we spread on the lawn of the capital. Grier brought food and made me eat. Then he'd give me a rubdown and make me stretch out on the quilt until it was time for me to return to yet another grueling examination. Together we gutted it through. I'll never know how I passed the bar; 75 was the passing grade and I made 75! Grier and all three of our sons made higher grades on their bar exams, but that 75 was the most wonderful grade I've ever received.

After bar exams, I crammed one of the most exhausting experiences of my life into late July and early August of that year. Grier had been faithful to support and sustain me as he'd promised, but without Grier Jr. I never could have made it. That little boy had been so much help with his younger brothers, I'd promised him a special treat as soon as school was out. I had no idea what it would be or how we could afford anything special.

The Women's Alliance of the Unitarian Church selected me as a delegate to a weeklong conference at Asilamar on the Monterey

Grandparents: Lindgren family (1890), Nils and Bengta Lindgren, with children *(left to right)*, Enoch, Alma, Hulda, Nora, Minnie and Hilma, Louise's mother, here at age 5

Louise's parents, Louis and Hilma Ballerstedt, on their fiftieth wedding anniversary, 1958

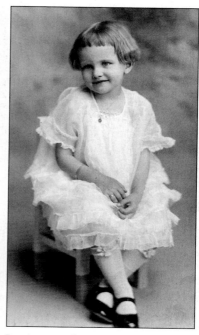

Louise, age three

Louise with boys, Grier Jr., Tom, and Ken, June 1952 (*courtesy Dallas Public Library*)

Louise in 1956 (*courtesy Vivian Castleberry*)

WOMAN ASSISTANT Sun., 3-21-54.

DA's Staff Adds

Dallas Morning News

Feminine Touch

wife of Grie
lawyer. She i
e Ballersted
Ballerstedt,
er. At the Ur
where she w
she was a F

up law at nig
t took her fe
he had to ta
nother baby

Signing the Marital Property Act on May 30, 1967, at the Texas State Capitol in Austin: Governor John Connally is seated at right; standing behind him are Dean Angus McSwain (Baylor), Prof. William Huie (Texas), Louise Raggio, and Rep. Gene Fondren (Taylor) (*courtesy Texas Bar*)

The family homestead in Manor, Texas, where Louise Raggio grew up

Louise in the library, 1970
(courtesy Vivian Castleberry)

Louise and Grier Raggio in 1971

Lady Bird Johnson, Louise, and
James MacGregor Burns visit
LBJ State Park in May 1993

With James MacGregor
Burns on Sanibel
Island, off the Florida
coast, in 1992

LOUISE RAGGIO

LEGAL LEGACY

Texas women
endured some
of the most
discriminatory
laws in the

Houston Chronicle Magazine

TEXAS

March 31, 199

The small, pretty woman pictured above is the first wor
criminal courts. She is Mrs. Brier H. Raggio. Judge Joe E.
torney Henry Wade on the right.

Mrs. Grier Raggio, First V

The energetic, blue-eyed woman, who studied at Southern
Methodist University for her law
degrees "between children," has
been handling juvenile delinquen-
cy and child support cases for

Now her authority ex
other types of cases.

Born on a farm in Tra
ty, Mrs. Raggio gradua
the University of Tex
she worked on the coll

Granddaughter Julie Raggio,
Louise, and Governor Ann
Richards at the Texas Women's
Hall of Fame in Austin, 1993
(photo: Karen Dickey)

Louise and First Lady Hillary Clinton
after a speech to the Southern Methodist
University Law School in 1997

Louise after receiving an
honorary doctorate of law
at SMU in 1996

ng attorney in the Dallas
he center with District At-

n Prosecutor

Fourteen years ago she mar-
d Grier H. Raggio ,an attorney
civil practice in Dallas and
came interested in law. She
ined her license three years
ro.
The 5-foot, 114-pound lawyer

Louise speaking
with a Women's
Studies class at
SMU in 1997

Longtime legal assistant Alice Hernandez, Louise, and Gloria Steinem at SMU in 1998. Steinem was the first speaker at the Louise B. Raggio Endowed Lecture Series.

With Patricia Schroeder and daughter-in-law Janice Raggio at SMU in 1999. Schroeder was the second speaker in the lecture series.

The small, pretty woman pictured above is the first woman prosecuting att criminal courts. She is Mrs. Brier H. Raggio. Judge Joe E. Brown is in the cel torney Henry Wade on the right.

Mrs. Grier Raggio, First Woman P

With longtime friend Vivian Castleberry in 2000

Gwen Ifil, Louise, and Matrice Kirk after a Raggio lecture at SMU in 2001

Left to right: (front) Thomas Raggio, Janice Raggio, Louise, Gwen Ifil, and Patricia Raggio; *(back)* Grier Raggio, Jr., Lorraine Raggio, and Kenneth Raggio, at SMU Louise Raggio Lecture Series in 2001

With David McCullough, receiving the Planned Parenthood of North Texas Humanitarian Award in 2002
(photo: Steve Foxall)

With Geraldine Laybourne, Raggio Lecturer in 2002 *(photo: Kenneth Raggio)*

I fought the law, and the law lost

Texan leaps over barriers for women

By Laura Duncan

Louise Raggio, a 76-year-old Dallas lawyer who has long fought for women's equal rights, first realized that Texas laws needed an overhaul when she couldn't sign her own contracts for clients.

It was in the early 1960s, and the state's laws were considered the most discriminatory in the nation because they did not allow married women to have any property rights or independence. Even though Raggio was a licensed lawyer in Texas, she and other women had no control over the money or property they brought into a marriage. By state law, no woman could get a bank loan or start a business without her husband's consent.

"I was really tired of that, having to run and get...

Surrounded by friends and admirers at the American Bar Association Family Law luncheon in Washington, D.C., after receiving the Lifetime Achievement Award in August 2002
(courtesy M.H. Photography)

Peninsula in California and gave me expense money for enrollment, lodging, food, and transportation. I sat down with pencil and paper and started figuring. If I used the expense money for two cut-rate bus tickets instead of a plane ticket, if we stayed with friends along the way and back rather than get a hotel room, if we ate only two meals a day and that as frugally as possible, Grier Jr. and I could both go to California. It would be a special treat for me as well as my son, because I'd never been to California. I had, in fact, never been west of Abilene, Texas!

I planned our bus trip so that we could spend a night or so with different friends along the way. One college friend, Murtice Easley, lived in El Paso. She'd been trying to get me to come out for a visit for several years, so I wrote to her and she wrote back, "Wonderful! Glad to have you!" In no way could I have imagined the vastness of the West! We got on that bus and we rode and we rode and we rode. There is a sameness about West Texas that is mind-numbing. Grier Jr. was the most excited little boy, but when he grew tired of looking at the prairie stretching interminably ahead of us, he'd curl up and go to sleep. I couldn't. This continued throughout our journey. We finally arrived in El Paso, where Murtice's mother had planned a whirlwind tour of the West and we were on the go from the moment we arrived until the moment we left. We went to Carlsbad Cavern, to the Guadalupe Pass, climbed the mountains in West Texas, and went across the border to Tijuana, Mexico. We spent two nights in El Paso and were exhausted when we got back on the bus to travel west. Both of us enjoyed going through the Painted Desert. I found an inexpensive motel near the Grand Canyon and we took in the sights there. I had never seen anything to compare with the Grand Canyon and other wonders of the West and I was as wide-eyed as my son. He collected rocks everywhere we went and our luggage became almost too heavy for the two of us to manage.

While we were at the Grand Canyon, an earthquake hit California, causing major detours. We continued through Arizona and into California in very inferior buses, in sweltering heat, and with no air conditioning. When we arrived in Los Angeles, I was a zombie, and again lay awake all night because of the merciless noise that continued unabated around the cheap motel where I rented a room near the bus station. Early the next day we were up and on another rickety bus that took us through the valley into Fresno and Bakersfield, where we saw souvenirs of the recent earthquake. The earth had been rearranged, cracked open in places, accordion-pleated in others. Railroad cars were scattered around like toy trains that a kid had kicked off the tracks.

We detoured here and there all the way to San Francisco, where I arrived so sick that I thought I was having a heart attack. Food nauseated me, but I thought if I could just get a glass of buttermilk to settle my stomach I might survive. I couldn't possibly have dragged myself out of bed, so Grier Jr. went in search of buttermilk, found some, and brought it back to me. I spent a night in agony, physically ill and worried sick that I would die and leave my little boy alone so far from home. Early the next morning I got in touch with a Unitarian doctor who examined me and diagnosed my condition as sheer exhaustion. He would not let me pay him and I was grateful, because my frugal budget could not tolerate even one extra expense.

Everything thrilled Grier Jr. He kept a journal, and every new experience, every scene was an unfolding wonder. Since that day, he's become a very sophisticated attorney who has traveled all over the world, but insists that cheap bus trip was the most exciting experience of his young life.

Our week at the Unitarian encampment gave me a chance to relax a bit with the kindest and most loving people imaginable. I attended every session so that I could report to my Unitarian sisters back in Dallas. Our idyl was interrupted when Grier Jr. fell off a borrowed bicycle. I panicked when I saw him all bruised, scraped, and bloody and with a chipped front tooth, but his injuries proved superficial. Our dentist back home was even able to smooth out the jagged edge of his tooth without major repairs.

We didn't do much sightseeing on our return trip. We couldn't afford it. We existed almost entirely on hamburgers at fifteen cents each and milk at a nickel a glass. The highlight was celebrating Grier Jr.'s tenth birthday in three different states. On August 6, we boarded the bus in California, made our way through Nevada, and slept overnight in Salt Lake City, where we saw the Mormon

Temple. We traveled through Wyoming and the breathtakingly beautiful Rocky Mountains into Denver, where we stopped again for a night. Then we rode straight through from Denver back to Dallas.

Mother and Dad kept Ken and Tom while we were away. No way can I give enough credit to my parents for their love and attention to my children. Tommy especially loved to stay at the farm. He was such a live wire. Grier Jr. and Kenny were easy to handle. Tommy arrived in this world trying to change it! At home in Dallas I knew I had to be constantly on the alert for his safety and welfare. Being on the farm around the animals with acres and acres to explore calmed him. To this day, the farm is his favorite place. Increasingly as he grew up, he'd spend summers with my parents. When he was older, my father bought him a .22 rifle and taught him how to use it. He'd spend all day hunting up and down the creek bed and roaming around on the acreage. He liked to be there without his brothers, so that he got 100 percent of the attention from his grandparents.

Mother made almost all of my boys' clothes when they were little. She could still take almost any old discarded rag and whip up a good-looking shirt. As they got older and into jeans, we bought them, but they continued to wear shirts she made until they were almost grown. She continued to make my clothes, too.

It was September before I got word that I'd passed the bar exams. Along with all the other law students who'd passed the bar, I went back to Austin, was sworn in, and given my certificate.

I was, at last, a full-fledged lawyer. Without a job.

10

A Lawyer with No Place
to Practice

BACK HOME, after the trip to California, I did not look for work for a number of reasons. I planned to "coast" for awhile, to look at options, to care for my family, and get some much-needed rest. We had no dining-room furniture at the Amherst house, so Grier had turned it into an office-bedroom with a typewriter on a makeshift desk and a big cot where Grier Jr. slept in the summertime. I "practiced" law from there, doing a few wills and one personal injury case. These were "dropped in my lap" from friends we'd met through church, and occasionally from people Grier knew from his government practice. I charged fifteen dollars to write a will!

I had absolutely no idea how difficult it would be for a female lawyer to find work. The employment bureau at SMU would not schedule me for interviews because it said, quite correctly, that no jobs existed for women and it would depress me always to be turned down. One job offer came from Joe Stephens, with the firm of Carrington Stephens and Johnson (later Carrington Coleman). He was a church acquaintance. He wanted me to head his firm's typing pool. It was clear to me that the firm thought that I, as a woman, could train and handle the secretaries better than they could.

For the latter part of 1952 and through 1953, my time was devoted almost exclusively to my family and volunteer activities. I took an active role in the League of Women Voters, joined Kappa Beta Pi, a legal sorority for women (which we later disbanded when the men's legal fraternity finally had to accept women), participated in the Women's Alliance of the Unitarian Church, and in helping to give birth to a Dallas Chapter of the United Nations. Sarah T. Hughes, our spirit, sparkplug, and fire, was instrumental in getting it started. I met Judge Hughes the first time at a Veterans Administration picnic at Flagpole Hill on a hot summer day in 1946 when she was running around in shorts and sneakers, passing out cards and asking for our votes for her congressional campaign. At that time I had a little boy and was quite pregnant with another. Her husband George worked with Grier at the Veterans Administration, and they were friends. Grier introduced her as "George's wife." At the time she was probably the only female district court judge in the state. She'd been appointed by Gov. James V. Allred in 1935, and then had run regularly for the 14th district court judgeship and won. I was singularly unimpressed. What did I know? I could not comprehend that she was the area's strongest advocate for women's rights and that she would later be so influential in my life.

By 1952, I knew who Sarah Hughes was! She was Judge Hughes—and she recognized a "fellow traveler" when she saw one. Me! I was her sidekick, at times gladly her errand girl.

George Hughes was as unassuming as Sarah was powerful. He always seemed perfectly content to operate in the shadows while she held the center of attention. He supported everything she did. The Hugheses were a perfect example of role reversal. George did most of their shopping, put on an apron, and did most of the cooking. Sarah greeted the guests and presided at the meetings.

It was in Sarah and George's house that I once more met former First Lady Eleanor Rooesvelt. Grier and I were invited there on many occasions for supper while we were getting the new chapter of DUNA launched, and Mrs. Roosevelt, a strong supporter, came several times. She had been a United States UN delegate. I was so privileged to be included in these small, intimate parties and to renew acquaintance with a great lady who I'd first met when I was a White House Fellow.

In Dallas, a strong right-wing element created a backlash against the United Nations Association that would have staggered or defeated a less determined person than Sarah T. Hughes. She went right on expanding our organization even when telephone threats were made, when the press was less than supportive, and when GET THE U.S. OUT OF THE U.N. bumper stickers appeared on countless cars running up and down our city streets. Sarah Hughes, all five feet, two inches and a hundred pounds, was a formidable match for oilman H. L. Hunt and his followers, who financed and spearheaded the opposition. They charged the United Nations with being a Communist front and everybody who dared speak up for it with being a Communist.

Grier, who had already been charged with communist leanings, who successfully had weathered a personal attack and who had always championed the disenfranchised, was only too happy to work for the UN. He and I participated in many programs, several radio debates, and early television debates against the far right-wingers who were following the Richard Nixon/Joseph McCarthy line.

McCarthy, then a little-known senator from Wisconsin, had convinced President Harry Truman that Communist agents had infiltrated the State Department, and grabbed the spotlight as leader of a national witch-hunt looking for Communists under every cabbage leaf. He had no proof of any charges, his tactics were innuendo and intimidation, but for a period of four years he swept the nation into hysteria and ruined the lives of countless innocent citizens—including ours. McCarthy's mad tirade, aided by his own "fellow travelers" in the government, including Sen. Richard Nixon of California, continued with few voices of dissent. Margaret Chase Smith, Senator of Maine, delivered the first Declaration of Conscience in opposition to her fellow Republican. Speaking to the Senate, she denounced the tactics of McCarthy, saying ". . . those who shout the loudest about Americanism . . . are all too frequently those who, by their own words and acts, ignore some of the basic principles of Americanism. The right to criticize, the right to hold unpopular beliefs, the right to protest, the right of independent thought" is guaranteed by the Constitution of the United States. Finally, on June 9, 1954, McCarthy's stranglehold on the American public was broken in nationally televised hearings when Joseph Welch, special counsel for the United States Army, in defense of employee Fred Fisher, ended his testimony with these words: "Let us not assassinate this lad further, Senator. You've done enough. Have you no sense of decency, sir? At long last, have you left no sense of decency?" The committee room burst into spontaneous applause. Soon afterward McCarthy was censured by the Senate.

Nobody had spoken up when Grier faced similar charges back in the 1940s. We were, I guess, naive, because we were shocked when Communist charges resurfaced because of our involvement with the United Nations. We learned that we were again being scrutinized when neighbors on Amherst told us that a couple of well-dressed men in dark suits were ringing their doorbells and asking questions that could only be interpreted as questioning our loyalty to the United States. Grier was furious. He telephoned the local offices of the FBI and told them he was available at any time to answer any questions they might have—and warned them to lay off asking our neighbors about us. We would not know until much later that the FBI was monitoring our every public utterance, that moles watched, heard, and reported back to the FBI everything we said when we spoke about the United Nations at Stonewall Jackson School, when we defended the UN on radio talk shows, and even when we spoke to neighbors and friends in informal gatherings. I would learn about the scope and depth of the probe into our personal lives only after Grier's death, when almost a year after I requested the records from the FBI under the Freedom of Information Act, I received pages of government files.

Grier and I were also passionate about our commitment to our sons and our role as a family in the community. Both of us were very involved with our boys in the activities they chose. All three joined the Boy Scouts as soon as they were eligible, first becoming Cub Scouts, and for Grier Jr. and Ken continuing on to become Eagles. Tommy was resistant to doing anything that his older brother had done and did not want to join the Scouts. We made a deal with him that if he got his Tenderfoot badge and still wanted to drop out, it would be fine with us. He received his Tenderfoot badge and never went to another Scout meeting. We were a little sad, but we did not believe in trying to make the boys carbon copies of each other. From the first, we recognized their individuality and did our best to provide a structure in which each could excel to the limit of his own ability.

We had a family membership in the YMCA where Grier Jr. was very active in its sports programs. During the summer, we all swam together. As soon as Grier got home from work—and later after I'd gone to work and returned home—all five of us took swimsuits and headed for the University Park pool. Grier taught all three boys to be good swimmers.

Grier Jr. joined the University Park School orchestra, where he first played the cello using an instrument that belonged to the school and then the clarinet, which he continued to play all through grade school and junior high. He dropped out of orchestra in high school to devote more time to sports and other activities. When Tommy was in the third grade, we pushed him to get into music and ran into the same resistance that we'd had with Scouting. He simply rebelled at following in the footsteps of his older brother. We pushed him to try it and bought him an ocarina. He dutifully took it to school several times and then solemnly said he was sorry, he had lost it. We searched everywhere for that ocarina and never could find it. By that time, it was too late for him to catch up with the other children in music, so he dropped out. Years later, he confessed that he had thrown the instrument in the park pond. He did it because the leader had said, "Oh, Tom, I'm so glad to have you! You'll be such a good student, just like your brother, Grier." Kenny was musically talented. He inherited Grier Jr.'s clarinet, joined the school orchestra, and later took up the saxophone. Later, when we could afford it, we bought a small Kahn organ. Kenny sat at the organ for hours at a time and played by ear until he, too, became enamored with sports and dropped out of music.

The pittance I made from my law practice became the financial edge we needed to reclaim our house. We let our renters know that we were expanding into their space, and moving day was exciting for all five of us. Grier Jr. took the west bedroom upstairs and

Tommy the east room. They had their own bath. Kenny remained downstairs, but we were no longer all scrunched together. As soon as Tom got his own room, he began to invite his friends for sleepovers. Grier Jr. did not often have friends stay overnight, but Tom was prone to have a party every weekend, and I remember all the raucous noise from upstairs while I was trying to sleep beneath them.

LIFE NEVER SLOWS DOWN while we're doing other things. And it was during this period I lost two close friends. I wonder why, for most of my life, my best friends have been male? Doubtless it would take a specialist in human relations more experienced than I to discover why, but I have some insights, however questionable they may be.

As a child, a second generation American, growing up in an insulated community with first generation German and Swedish heritage, my closest associates near my own age were male. In high school, desperately longing to be petite and pretty, I thought I was fat and homely. I was no threat to the girls and not date bait for the boys, who considered me their buddy. In college, I'd have given anything to be pretty and popular, but my scholastic excellence and dedication to my studies set me apart. I was no competition for the popular girls, and the boys sought me out as a friend and advisor. And the subjects that most interested me were male-dominated. This trend followed me to Washington, where the male fellows often sought me out as confidante. At that time it didn't occur to me that I was competition for any of the other women. When Grier Raggio paid court, he was the most handsome, daring, overpowering person I had ever met, and it was inevitable that I would fall in love with him and live up to my promise of lifelong fidelity. And then we had sons! Three of them!

Because I never felt comfortable confiding my innermost thoughts and feelings to my mother or any other female relative, I unconsciously held the opinion that women were not to be trusted. There was bare opportunity or incentive for me to think otherwise. My male parent was the one who understood and was closest to me.

In my early life I did not miss having a close girlfriend because I'd never had one. I could not abide what I perceived as idle chit-chat, in which my female classmates indulged, and I was genuinely puzzled over their preoccupation with their appearance. There were casual female friends and classmates, through grade school and high school but no bosom, secret-sharing friends, no all-night whispering during sleepovers, no lingering sighs over high school heroes in lengthy telephone conversations. I didn't miss these things because I didn't know they existed!

After high school, in college, then in Washington and back in Austin, three women became important in my life. And I lost two of them, which along with my law school experiences and professional practice, further alienated me from close female friendships.

Florence Eastman Myers was my first and most long-lasting female friend until her death in 2002. We were in and out of each other's lives for more than half a century, in touch at all of the most critical times, whether good or bad. Our friendship always enriched me. Florence, the oldest of six girls, grew up in a farm family in Bellville, Texas. She, too, worked her way through college and then helped to support each of her sisters, in turn, through college as they grew up. She became a teacher, working first in the school system in Conroe, Texas, and later in Dallas, transferring then to Highland Park, where she retired. Florence married late and had one son, Brooks Myers. We've visited when we could, talked on the telephone frequently, and developed the kind of friendship that is always close, but has never been smothering. She visited me on the farm during World War II and we watched, from a distance, as her son and my three boys grew up.

Florence and I went to the fiftieth reunion of our graduating class at the University of Texas in 1989. It was a disaster. Many of the liveliest, most perky people I remembered as UT students were old, crippled, and decrepit, and some were senile. Florence and I looked at each other and suggested that we'd been caught in a time warp. These people were not our people! All of our classmates were so much older than we were! Girls we envied as the gorgeous prom queens were often the saddest specimens of human beings. Their eternal seeking after youth—many facelifts, surgeries, lifelong diets—

had prolonged their years but delivered them to their fiftieth reunion as skeletons of their former selves. And the men: Many were paunchy. Bald. Mottled. Crass! To stay mentally and physically alert, people have to keep busy doing things that are significant. Florence and I noted that many of our classmates retire, then lose their mental alertness, sense of humor, lean on canes, talk about their aches and pains—and by the next reunion are in their graves.

Arista, my Washington roommate, died so very young, in her thirties. We were together for only one year, but that year was a turning point in my life and her contribution to my persona both intense and imperative. Even though we had gone our separate ways, I to marriage, motherhood, and a law degree in Texas, and she to marriage, motherhood, and volunteer work in California, I was enraged at her death. It felt like a part of me was gone.

Then I lost another friend, Marian Storm. She and I were young women together in Austin in the League of Women Voters. We were soul mates, thought alike, brought out the best in each other. We shared visions, dreams, and were well on our way to becoming the proverbial "best friends" women tell their kids about when they are older. On her way to Dallas to an LWV meeting, Marian was killed when her car was hit broadside by another car out of control, which crossed the median and slammed into her. Unconsciously, I think, I "closed down" at the idea of having a close female friend.

Grier's reaction to my male friends has always been a puzzle. He was so jealous of the male friends I had before he met me that if I mentioned one with whom I'd had an intellectual or friendly bonding, he would get very quiet and soon make a cutting remark about that person. I learned very early to avoid the subject. If I saw the name of an old friend in the paper, I read the story in silence and filed it away among my most personal souvenirs. It was hard not to read about those guys because many of them—Jake Pickle, John Connally, Lyndon Johnson, Bo Byers, Mac Roy Rasor, James MacGregor Burns, and others—went on to become figures of national prominence. I hid from Grier some of the books written by my old friends because I dreaded his reaction to the glowing autographed notes in them.

What puzzles me most is that the male friends I made after Grier and I married never seemed to bother my husband. When I worked so hard and such long hours to help change and shape our country's laws dealing with family issues, I would often be in late-night conferences with many lawyers, almost all of whom were men. Grier's attitude toward those meetings was "Way to go, girl!" Everybody with whom I worked knew that I was an early riser, at my best in the morning's wee hours, but when the sun went down I slowly began to fade. Nobody could expect me to come up with clear, sharp ideas after dark. We'd often meet for evening sessions in the hotel room of one of our members and I'd nod off in the midst of a discussion. The guys kidded each other with the titillating jibe: "You haven't lived until Louise has slept in your room." One slightly tipsy cohort threw his arm around Grier at a party and said, "I appreciate it that you let your wife come to my room and sleep!" Grier never mentioned it.

IN THE WANING DAYS OF 1953, I made finding a job as a lawyer a priority. I didn't want to waste all the training I'd had, and the Raggios needed an additional income. The boys were growing up. Grier Jr. had reached the teenage years. College for all three loomed ahead. Through my associations in Kappa Beta Pi, I sent out feelers. I also let it be known in church circles and the League of Women Voters that I was ready to go to work seriously.

Older women attorneys shrugged me off. All of them were either single or married with no children. They had bought into the prevailing assumption that a married woman with children had no place in the professional world. Some joined their stay-at-home sisters, pulling their shrouds of smugness about them, the attitude being that their own life choices not only were the norm but were the ideal for all females. Some were "queen bees." Jill Ruckelhaus defined a queen bee as a woman "who, having made it to the top, pulls up the ladder after her so that no one else can make the climb." Queen bees were into protecting their turf.

Though I opted to combine marriage and family with a career, I am empathetic with those women who went before me. Historically, only widows, childless women, or those with a bevy of servants gained any degree of power. Without birth control—and there was no reliable method until recent years—if a woman is married and not sterile, she will produce a child every two years. One of my grandmothers had sixteen children; the other had ten. No matter how much talent they may have had, they were tied to long, grueling hours of housework and child care. Imagine the thousands of diapers that my grandmothers laundered, hung to dry, and folded. It staggers my imagination.

Judge Sarah Hughes was, in many ways, typical of the women of that time. She was married but had opted not to have children, explaining that "it doesn't matter to George, and children would short-circuit what I need to do with my life." But Sarah Hughes was a feminist to the core and determined that doors of opportunity must be opened to women. By the time she made that remark, I'd worked with Judge Hughes many different times, had been a guest in her home, and she'd had occasion to scrutinize me.

It wasn't, I am certain, that she wanted to promote me personally that led her to call me in February 1954. Any bona fide female lawyer would have done. "Louise," she said, in her brusque, businesslike, no-nonsense way, "there are two jobs open for women in this community, and I want you to apply for them." If Sarah Hughes had asked me to stick my head in the oven with the gas turned on, I'd have done it, so I got myself gussied up to the height of my ability—I was still wearing a wardrobe Mother made—and went out to face the world.

My first interview was with Hexter Title Company. They'd concluded that a woman would work for far less money than would a male attorney, and likely would do just as good a job. The work was legal, all right, but consisted exclusively of doing title work, and to me would have been brain-numbing. Even so, I was overjoyed that I was offered the job and asked for time to think it over. What I really wanted was to apply for the second job and see how it went.

At ten o'clock the next morning, dressed in my best polyester suit, with butterflies in my stomach, I arrived at the offices of the Dallas County District Attorney, Henry Wade. His reputation preceded him. One of eleven children of a country lawyer, Mr. Wade was your stereotypical Texas male. Big! Gruff! Cigar chomping!

And—this is a cliché that fits—smart as a whip. He'd graduated from the University of Texas Law School in 1938 second in his class, joined the FBI after college, quit after his brother was taken prisoner in the European theater during World War II, and joined the Navy. He served in the invasions of Okinawa and the Philippines as a night controller for fighter planes, returned to Texas, and started law practice. He made no secret of hiring the smartest lawyers right out of law school, training them, and firing them if they didn't measure up. In one year, I learned later, he lost thirty-eight assistants—fired half of them and the other half quit to go into practice elsewhere.

I'd also heard a little about him at the University of Texas. Wade was one of the guys who'd broken the Greek monopoly on student elections. Members of a group called Delta Theta Phi Socio-Legal Fraternity, all of them law or pre-law students—he, Jake Pickle, John Connally, Sid Reagan, Joe Kilgore, and about twenty-five other guys—decided to take over politics at UT, which had always been controlled by social sorority and fraternity members. They enlisted the aid of independents, ran Jake Pickle for student body president, and he won. The next year they ran John Connally and he won. Then they ran Wade for law president and he won. Then they ran Sidney Reagan for student body president and he won.

Henry Wade could easily have chewed me to pieces in the interview. But he didn't. He asked a few sharp questions, seemed genuinely interested in my answers. He knew enough to know he didn't know enough! Few men, I've learned, have that ability. I was scared of Mr. Wade, but I liked him from the moment of our meeting.

The interview was brief. Mr. Wade introduced me to Dan Ann Morgan. She was not an attorney, but by default was in charge of all the crying women who came to the DA's office. Then he offered me a job and showed me where I would be working. He told me much later that he thought I'd probably fall flat on my face, but at least he would have Sarah Hughes off his neck! In all honesty, I think he would have hired anybody with a law degree because the stacks of papers in the corner of what would be my cubbyhole office consisted of cases that were pending . . . and pending . . . and pending.

My title would be Assistant District Attorney, in charge of child support, juvenile cases, delinquent dads—everything dealing with families—at the phenomenal starting salary of $350 a month. I said "When do I start?" and walked out feeling like I was about to make a million dollars a month. It was a dream job with unlimited potential for a beginning attorney.

Then I had to go home and prepare my family for an entirely different kind of life.

Grier was an immediate convert. He growled, lightly, that I was worth more money. Grier Jr. was reluctant and Kenny too young to care; he'd entered the world with a mother who always looked after him even when she was involved in many other activities, and so long as he felt loved and secure he didn't care what I did with the rest of my time. Tommy felt abandoned. He wailed that he would be the *only* kid in the Park Cities whose mother *worked!* He was right. I was assuredly an abnormality. Ours was not a neighborhood where it was acceptable for a mother to have a job. I called a family meeting and made it clear that life "as usual" would not be usual any more. The boys' always available mother would not be always available. I would have to have their support and their cooperation. We'd have to realign our expectations of each other.

We were three against two, but the adults had the final say! I accepted the job and we set down guidelines for an entirely new way of living. I continued to do the family meal planning, cooking, and shopping. Each of the boys had regular chores. They took turns doing the dishes at night; on Sundays after church their father was the dishwasher. We shared the housecleaning on weekends. The trash went out daily, the chore delegated to each son in turn. We hired a maid for the first six months because Kenny was still a preschooler and needed care. Summer came and she moved away. We enrolled Kenny in preschool at the Lutheran Church on Lovers Lane and hired someone to come in half a day, pick him up at noon, and stay until one of us arrived home around five. In a couple of years this helper also moved out of town and we never hired anyone else.

My boys' wives should be grateful that they had a working mother—and I think they are! All three Raggio men can keep house and look after children as well as their wives. In this respect, Grier Raggio set a good example for his sons. Grier Jr. and Kenny both learned to cook. Tommy didn't. He still walked to the beat of his own drummer. The boys might not prepare gourmet dishes—but then, they might. Food preparation is wonderful therapy for those who like it—and most people do not know whether or not they like it until they try it.

I did all the ironing—and the chore was formidable because we did not yet have wash-and-wear fabrics and Grier wore starched white shirts to work every day. On weekends I'd iron a full week's supply of shirts. When Kenneth got old enough, he took over and became the best ironer in the family. We paid him ten cents a shirt— and he made his spending money that way. When he was a teenager, I remember walking in the house from work one afternoon and hearing laughter coming from the dinette where Ken was ironing. At that time, he was captain of the track team and his classmates cheering him on included the captain of the football team and the captain of the baseball team. I found the captain of the basketball team out in the kitchen preparing a milk-and-cookies snack. We may have raised the consciousness of a whole group of young men, even though I'll wager none of them did those chores at home. Ours were the only boys in the Park Cities who could put a meal on the table, sew on buttons, iron shirts, vacuum rugs, dust furniture, make beds, and clean toilets!

On weekends, I cooked in large quantities It takes very little more time to turn four pounds of ground chuck into a meat loaf that will feed five hungry people two complete meals—with slices left over for sandwiches—than it takes to turn a pound and a half into one meal for five. I prepared as many as four meat loaves at one time, cooked one and crammed the others into the the freezing compartment of the refrigerator. I planned wonderful, nutritious meals— a main dish, two vegetables, a salad, bread, and dessert—and could have everything on the table in thirty minutes after I walked through the door in the afternoon.

It was a matter of planning ahead. If I hadn't, we'd have gone hungry. There was no fast food, no place to drive in on the way home and pick up a ready-made dinner. We couldn't have afforded it if there had been. Nor had microwaves been invented, so thawing out a chunk of meat at the last minute was out of the question. I tried to plan for up to a month ahead so that I could take advantage of sales on food, and I always had menus for at least a week ahead. If I wanted to vary anything or plan a whole new menu at the last minute, I was free to do so, but having something in mind gave me a lot of freedom. We never ate out.

We didn't have an actual budget. There's not much need for one if you've been frugal all your life and the money is so limited it must be stretched each month to cover bare essentials. We knew what we had to spend, and if we couldn't afford something, we didn't buy it. We used credit cards very, very sparingly and only when we knew we could pay up at the first of the month. We didn't dare accumulate interest payments.

Conferring with Grier and the boys, I spent only a few days shoring up the home front and then I went out to begin my law career. Grier dropped me off downtown on his way to work.

I hope I looked more confident than I felt.

11

Almost Paradise!

MY CUBBYHOLE OFFICE, all six by eight feet of it in the Records Building, furnished with a desk, two chairs, a typewriter, and a telephone, was identical to the "offices" occupied by the other twenty-five male assistant district attorneys. The sixth floor of the building had been partitioned into "spaces" for us. Minuscule aisles allowed each of us to reach our own "office" and to communicate quickly and easily with our coworker attorneys only a few steps removed. Communication was no problem since the "walls" were only six feet high, reaching about a third of the way to the high ceilings. The decibel level when several of us were in our offices at the same time was deafening.

I thought I had arrived in paradise!

Legal files at least three feet high greeted me on my first day of work. Between 400 and 500 reciprocal cases—I soon lost count—languished there, some as much as two years old. Marital "squabbles" and child support cases, on the very lowest level of the male attorney's priorities, had arrived in the DA's office from almost every state in the union and were stacked one on top of the other collecting dust.

I took off my hat and went to work, plowing through as many as twenty-five a day, reading and making notes. It soon occurred to me that almost all of them were alike, or sufficiently similar that the same laws applied. I devised a form that I could fill out hurriedly—name, address, telephone, state, and county from which the case had been forwarded, with a blank space to note any unique or unusual legal angles. That way, I could work through dozens of cases in the time it would normally take to study two or three. I don't know how good the form was, but it remained in use for many years after I left the DA's office. Some of the cases were moot, the solution having already been resolved, but the majority were pending. In many, the culprit had already moved from the area where the case had been filed and left no forwarding address.

While I was plowing my way through the stack of cases that awaited me from other states, I was also initiating cases for parents in Dallas County who were trying to collect back child support payments from former spouses who had moved to other states.

The Uniform Reciprocal Enforcement of Support Act was relatively new on the law books at that time. It made legal the enforcement of nonpayment of child support across state lines. Deadbeat parents who moved from one state to another continued to be liable at their new addresses. Other states agreed to enforce delinquent child support and we in Texas agreed to enforce delinquent child support sent to us from other states. The idea was great and the law a good one, but the logjam of cases made it extremely difficult to enforce the law. I sent out hundreds and hundreds of cases, and I prosecuted hundreds that came to us from other states. It took an act of faith for me to spend the time required working up a case and sending it to appropriate authorities in other states, because I knew that most would end up filed the same way I'd found my work stacked the first time I entered the office. I had the distinct impression that all my effort was dropping reams of legal papers into a black hole.

While this sounds formidable, two other realities handicapped my commitment to resolve reciprocity cases: Child payment reciprocity cases occupied the lowest possible level in the legal system, and even more frustrating, we had no family district courts or juvenile courts. Since each document had to be signed by a judge and since there were no family court judges, I begged, cajoled, and charmed civil district judges throughout the building to please give me a scrap of time from their documents to hear my cases. With the assistance of Chief Deputy District Clerk Jelly Isom, I fine-tuned this so that no judge would need to spend more than a few minutes to clear as many as twenty cases. I'd have all the papers ready, all the people in the courtroom—in those days they were always women filing suits—all sworn in, and ask the group the necessary legal questions. Then I'd line the papers up on the judge's desk and he could affix his signature in a matter of five minutes or less. It may not have been entirely legal, but it worked so that I could ship out those cases by the hundreds. We devised a real assembly line.

In especially bad situations, District Attorney Wade gave me permission to go to the grand jury with an indictment against the culprit, who could then be extradited. I used this cautiously because tracking down the offender and bringing him (or her) to justice was extremely costly, and the county soon would have balked at the expense involved if I had not been so careful. Even though I used it only in the worst cases, I was before the grand jury many times and never had a turn-down.

It was much harder to get the cases heard that arrived from other states. I would beg a judge to give me some time, any time, and then I would have as many as ten cases set at the same time. Most of my clients were women, and when their husbands or former husbands would not appear, we'd get default judgments, but when a man appeared and had excuses or a sob story, it took up precious time that a judge with a crowded docket was reluctant to give.

I am certain that this was one time being a woman helped me, because the judges were really nice. I appeared at one time or another before every district judge in Dallas County and not one of them was ever rude. They knew I was trying to collect support for little children and they wanted to help.

Judge Bill McCraw was especially wonderful. He had been Attorney General of the State of Texas. Everybody thought he was a shoo-in for the next governor until W. Lee O'Daniel—Pappy O'Daniel who campaigned with a bunch of singing country music stars—decided to run and swept the state. Pappy O'Daniel was elected twice and then was elected senator. So far as I can tell, he never did a single good thing for Texas, but he sure had a good time doing it, and from time to time turned the governor's mansion into an open house that welcomed the masses—including the time his daughter, Molly, married and he invited the entire State of Texas to come to the wedding. From the reports, I think about half of the invitees showed up. Having lost the governor's race, Judge McCraw ran for and was elected district judge in Dallas. When I had a particularly difficult case or needed something signed, I could always count on Judge McCraw to take the time to listen to me. Not once did he refuse anything. He would not accept praise, saying he was just doing his duty. When I tried to thank him, he changed the subject or turned it off with a joke. Judge McCraw had a heart attack and died suddenly. I attended his funeral in the Oak Cliff Baptist Church, and regretted that I never got to tell him how much he had helped me and how much he meant to me. The tears flowed so freely that those around me surely thought I must be the other woman!

This taught me something: When I appreciate what someone does for me, I offer my thanks *now*. I don't want to wait until it's too late to let that person know.

Disposing of Uniform Reciprocal Enforcement Support cases still would have been relatively easy if that's all I had to do. It wasn't. It amounted to only about a tenth of what I was expected to accomplish.

My job description included a lot of unpleasant things, some spelled out and others I acquired because nobody else wanted to do them. As the low "man" on the totem pole and the only female, I got all of the "crying women" who arrived in the office. Male attorneys ran from them. When we had an alleged rape charge, the guys asked me to talk to the complainant. I got all juvenile cases from arson to incest to murder.

It was a good thing I was so inundated with work that I did not know how unpopular I was at the beginning of my legal career.

When I first arrived, my male colleagues were extremely hostile. It wasn't anything they said, but how they acted. Very polite. Distant. Noncommunicative. Wary. They were certain I would wreck their Good Old Boys Network. Later, when they began to tell me how they felt when Mr. Wade hired me, we all had a good laugh. One admitted that he expected to see lace curtains hanging at the windows when he learned Mr. Wade had hired a *female!* I said, "What windows?" Our cubicles were singularly without windows!

Within six months, when the guys saw that I was professional, doing my job competently, working hard, and not bothering anybody, they began to change their attitude. Many became lifelong friends, my strongest supporters, and best buddies. One by one, all dropped by my cubbyhole to say hello, and soon began asking my advice on cases where they thought my perspective would be helpful.

Bill Alexander appointed himself as my protector. He was as hardened a prosecutor as I've ever seen. He loved to prosecute and won a great many death penalties, after which he would celebrate raucously. He was a great big guy and had a permit to carry a gun. If someone came to my office and became loud or abusive, Bill would appear at the door and pull back his coat to show this big .38 pistol. This had an immediate calming effect on the visitor. When I had a client who might be dangerous, Bill always managed to walk through the courtroom at the same time and walk alongside me. He never said anything about protecting me, but he was always there when he thought I was in danger.

All of us in the DA's office were in danger, though we never mentioned it to each other. Our offices were not off-limits to drop-ins, and there were a lot of crazies in some of the families whose members we were prosecuting.

R. J. Luther was another very special friend. He had been a police officer for many years and he came to the DA's office as an investigator. My wife and child section did not fall under his list of duties, but when I needed someone located, R.J. would come up with the person in a few days. I could tell him that I needed to find "Horseshoe" or "Curly Top," no last names and no addresses. That's all he needed. He never failed to find someone I really wanted to prosecute. R.J. was one of several on Wade's team of investigators. I'd put that team up against anybody in the country at any time (even *with* a powerful computer) in their ability to find the people and ferret out the facts for a case.

Jim Bowie was another of my favorites. He was one of the most talented and funny lawyers I've ever known. Always cracking a joke and doing ridiculous things around the office, he relieved stress by making us laugh until we were practically ill. When Jim wasn't pulling a fast one on somebody, Homer Montgomery was. Both were very professional, hard-working attorneys dedicated to their jobs, accomplishing everything required of them and more, but also understanding that we needed the relief of jokes and laughter. Jim got cancer and died soon after his appointment as a criminal district judge. He was a brilliant lawyer who died too young

That group of district attorneys and staff became an extended family. We knew one another's spouses and children and were together often outside the cubbyholes and courtrooms where we worked. Grier and I didn't have much money, but we had many, many of my coworkers to spaghetti suppers on Saturday or Sunday nights. I learned to make a great spaghetti sauce with meat and wine, and served spaghetti, a vegetable salad, garlic bread, and cookies for a very excellent but inexpensive meal. The bachelors and single people especially enjoyed a home-cooked meal.

Henry Wade kept his hand firmly on the tiller as the captain of this group of mavericks. He ran a tight ship, hired the best young attorneys right out of law school, became our mentor/teacher, delegated responsibility, expected results, and got out of our way. He was available to his staff but didn't look over our shoulders.

Wade came to my office no more than four times during the two years I worked for him. He never asked that I go easy or let up on anyone. On the contrary, he always requested that I really go after those who had broken the law. Once he eased his large frame into my minuscule office, sat down, and asked me to go after a gang member. During World War II gangs had begun to flourish in Dallas, and Wade was hot to have them arrested and locked up. The problem: All the gang members had moved to Nevada, which refused to extradite them on criminal charges. One especially crafty gang member had adopted three children during World War II in order to get a deferment and avoid military service. After the war he abandoned his wife and the children and was not paying any child support. Wade asked me to go before the grand jury, and try to get an indictment. I talked to the man's former wife, worked up the case, went before the grand jury, and got the indictment. Nevada honored our indictment for nonpayment of child support. The man was sent back to Texas. The moment he crossed the state line, Wade had him arrested for his criminal offenses. He was tried, sentenced, and spent several years in prison. It was an office joke that nobody could get the man back to Texas for attempted murder, embezzlement, and gaming, but we could nab him for nonpayment of child support.

Wade would have asked for an indictment against his own grandmother if he thought she had done something wrong. While I was there he prosecuted and convicted a very popular county official for driving while intoxicated. He prosecuted and convicted his own brother for the same offense. He demanded honesty and integrity from his employees and I never saw him try to cut a corner or give anybody an advantage just because of who he was.

In the courtroom, Wade's manner and his record of convictions were legendary. Shortly after being elected district attorney, he tried his first capital punishment case, the murder of a Dallas police officer. The jury was out for eight minutes when it returned with a conviction and sentenced the man to death. When President Kennedy was assassinated in Dallas in November 1963, Lee Harvey Oswald was arrested and charged with murder. The next morning, while being transferred from the city to the county jail, he was shot and killed. Jack Ruby, arrested for the murder, hired Melvin Belli, one of the country's most flamboyant lawyers, to defend him. Wade went one-on-one with Belli and got the death penalty from the jury in less than two hours of deliberation.

In his last courtroom case, he prosecuted Franklin and Woodrow Ransonette, kidnappers of Amanda Mayhew Dealey, a popular young socialite. Mandy's parents, Audrey and Charles Mayhew, were friends of the Wades, but it wouldn't have made any difference to Henry if they had been his worst enemies. He was out for justice and he got it. The jury came back with the longest prison sentence ever handed down in this country, 5,005 years.

Henry is also the Wade of the *Roe v. Wade* abortion ruling by the U.S. Supreme Court. His name is attached to the case because it was his responsibility to uphold the law and prosecute the case, which was filed in Dallas by Linda Coffey, who later asked Sarah Weddington to assist. In an odd twist of reality, Wade personally favored a woman's right to control her own reproductive system.

One of my jobs was to talk to the men in jail for nonpayment of child support. I'd go to the jail several times a week, sometimes several times in a single day. The jailers teased me unmercifully. I had no trouble getting in, but when I started to leave they'd banter back and forth, pretending I was a prisoner trying to coerce them into letting me out. They would solemnly call each other and say, "This woman says she's supposed to get out of jail. Have you ever heard of her?" The other would say, "Never heard of her. Send her back to her cell." They had a great time with me in that jail, but they were also very good to me. I never had a problem. The cook would let me eat with the prisoners sometimes.

All this was happening at a time when there was no emphasis on people's civil rights. The laws protecting a prisoner's civil liberties were not yet in place, so without being aware of it, I violated some civil rights. I especially remember one case. I had a man jailed for nonpayment of child support. He was a professional man in the community with a good income, but absolutely refused to pay child support. He was arrested and jailed. Normally a contempt is for twenty to thirty days, but at that time there were no limits. Usually after a very few days in jail, a man would see the light, come up with the money and pay the child support. Then the charges would be dropped and he would be released. Not this man! He didn't pay. And I forgot about him.

Eight or nine months went by. One day a DA investigator dropped by my office and said, "Mrs. Raggio, there's a man you had arrested and jailed, and he's sure been there a long time." I nearly fainted. I dropped what I was doing and went over to the jail to see him. He had lost all of his suntan and was real pasty-looking. We worked out something pronto, and he was released. You can imagine the lawsuit the DA's office would be faced with if anything like that happened today.

Every day at the DA's office was another soap opera.

Incest was one of the terrible issues I dealt with. I remember one little blue-eyed blonde girl, eleven years old, pregnant by her father.

We had the father in jail, and the mother came to my office ranting and raving because I'd had her husband arrested. She wanted to know how I expected the children to be fed when I was holding their father in jail. I explained to her that her husband had been having sex with his eleven-year-old daughter. The mother totally dismissed the accusation and said, "So what?" She had been initiated into sex by her father and her brothers when she was just a kid and it hadn't hurt her; she saw nothing unusual about her husband having sex with their daughter.

There were some bad rape cases, but there were also cases in which the woman yelled rape when sex had actually been consensual. When one of the attorneys had a rape case, he'd ask me to talk with the complainant. Every now and then a young woman would tell me she hadn't really been raped. She and her partner had been caught and she knew her father would kill her if he thought she'd consented, so she'd said she was raped.

I tried not to follow these cases. Bill Alexander told me very soon after I went to the DA's office that I should never follow what happened to the children in cases of incest, adoption, or termination of parental rights. This advice worked to my advantage when I was subpoenaed as a witness in a case when a mother whose children were taken away from her sued to have them returned. The children had been adopted, but I had no idea by whom or where any of them lived. I could go before the court and very honestly say I had no knowledge of them.

One case I did follow for a time, because I was required to do so, involved an infant born to a thirteen-year-old girl who had been impregnated by her fourteen-year-old brother. She gave birth with the assistance of the brother. The child was stabbed some twenty times and thrown into a neighbor's garbage can. Somebody came along, heard a sound like a kitten, found the baby, and turned it over to the police. The child was a beautiful little girl, such a sweet, bright child. It was my job to report her condition to the court while she was in foster care. I'd go out and carry her around and cuddle her. I prosecuted the case to take the child away from the mother. The grandmother and other relatives demanded the child back. They said it was all a mistake. The baby had not been killed, had not really been harmed. We got the termination, and the baby was adopted by a family far away from Dallas. She had a number of scars on her abdomen that could very easily have identified her until she later had plastic surgery.

We were all a cheering section for each other in the district attorney's office. Everybody supported everybody else and rejoiced in our victories when we got convictions. The guys were especially nice to me, and it was all right with Wade if I watched the guys try criminal cases. When my work allowed it, I visited and sat second or third chair with my coworkers, learning how a trial worked, absorbing information and techniques that served me well all of my life. Nothing is so important as being prepared for a case, knowing the law, and digging and digging so that there are no surprises, but it also helps to have the experience of watching how other lawyers handle cases.

A year and a half after I went to work for Henry Wade, he offered me an assignment to the county criminal court of Judge Joe B. Brown, Sr. This would be in addition to keeping my wife and child section running, and meant I would now be handling all the juvenile cases, all the reciprocity enforcement cases and all domestic cases plus criminal prosecutions. I was delighted. I was photographed with Judge Brown and District Attorney Wade and the picture appeared on the front page of *The Dallas Times Herald*. It was front-page news when a woman was assigned to do criminal prosecution. Any fool *knew* that women could not handle criminal cases. With the new assignment my salary climbed to $400 a month. I felt rich.

About the time of my promotion, by constitutional amendment in Texas, women received the right to serve on juries. The day the law went into effect, I was on Judge Brown's court on an aggravated assault case. The jury panel brought into the county criminal court consisted of ten women and two men. Naturally, I struck the two men and we tried the case with the first all-woman jury ever to sit in a Texas courtroom. There had been so much nonsense, so many stories, and so much ballyhoo about women serving on juries. It was charged that women had such soft hearts that they'd turn every criminal in the country loose. The women on that jury sat there with fixed jaws and steely eyes, listened to the testimony, and came in with a conviction in a matter of minutes. The man was guilty, but I'm not sure he got an altogether fair trial because that all-woman jury was determined to convict *somebody*. If they hadn't had a legitimate individual, they'd have convicted the bailiff or me or even the judge.

Women could now serve on grand juries, too, and it was Henry Wade's custom to take each grand jury group to Huntsville to the penitentiary so that they could see the penal system in the state. When two women were appointed to the grand jury, my boss asked me to go along with them. I was only too happy to comply. A Dallas oil man offered his private plane for the trip. On a beautiful May morning we all boarded the plane. Immediately the capricious Texas weather turned nasty. Black clouds, thunder, lightning, wind, and rain whipped that little plane all over the sky. We'd toss around like a feather in the wind and suddenly drop one hundred feet. It was the worst flight I have ever had. We made it and spent a full day visiting the male prison in Huntsville and the nearby women's prison in Goree, with authorities explaining everything to us. The trip was interesting, but I couldn't put my mind entirely on it because I so dreaded the flight back to Dallas. Here I was on a trip I didn't have to take and what would happen to Grier and the boys if I crashed? If there had been any other way to get back to Dallas, I would not have reboarded that plane.

I BEGAN TO BE well-known around town. Henry Wade was inundated with invitations to speak to all kinds of clubs—civic, social, auxiliaries, schools. He'd send me out to fill the speaking engagements when he hadn't the time or the interest to do so. He also understood that I was a good representative for the office with the press. I'd worked for the campus newspaper in college, and had enough journalism background to understand reporter's needs, the information they required, and the need for immediate response so that they could meet their deadlines. I was comfortable with the press. Reporters soon knew that they could talk to me. I would not lie to them or try to mislead them, feed them false information, or try to stonewall them. If I could not answer their questions, I'd tell them so, not beat around the bush. I also talked to them promptly because news is very fragile and a reporter has to meet deadlines, so I'd get back to a questioner in a timely fashion. I was quoted frequently. There were many stories about me because at the time it was "weird" for a married woman with children to be a criminal prosecutor. I clipped all those stories and put them in my scrapbook. My first name was never used. Stories quoted Mrs. Grier H. Raggio and almost always referred to my physical characteristics—height, weight, color of my eyes, all of the sexist stuff that would never be used to describe a male. One story began, "A little blonde, weighing no more than a small stack of law books . . ."

When I started to work for Henry Wade, Sarah Hughes told me to join the Business and Professional Women's Club, as well as the Quota Club, a women's business organization. I joined Town North B&PW and Quota, continued to be active in the United Nations, and was as involved as time allowed in church groups because we had kids in Sunday school. I had to drop out of several things, including my beloved League of Women Voters, because there was simply no time for them all. By the time I received the Zonta Award for public service in 1970, I'd made around 1,000 speeches throughout the Metroplex. I loved my job at the DA's office. I had more fun and made more friends there than any job I've ever had.

In April 1955, Grier quit his hated government job and opened a private practice with Ennis Walden. They rented a small suite, two offices plus a reception room, in the Rio Grande Building on Pacific Avenue in downtown Dallas. Immediately Grier began to pester me to quit my job, join him in a private law firm, and we'd be partners.

I held out for a year. Finally, in April 1956 I resigned and joined my husband. We became Raggio and Raggio.

12

Raggio and Raggio,
Attorneys at Law

I'D KEPT A FILE of all the people I helped while I was in the DA's office and all the groups to whom I'd spoken. When I went into private practice with my husband, we sent announcements to all these people telling them that I was no longer an assistant district attorney, but was now in private practice. We listed our address and phone number. From this list I got our first clients after Grier and I opened our law practice together.

Grier and Ennis, who moved out of the offices when I joined the firm, had signed a contract with Tupperware to collect from their creditors. It brought in almost nothing, but every penny mattered. We did credit collection work, misdemeanors, criminal work, wills, anything that came through the door.

Our goal was to gross $1,000 a month. That would cover the office rent of $200, our house payment of $75, utilities, and have enough to run the law office and support the kids. I was scared stiff. We had no savings, no cushion of any kind. I never would have had the guts to jump out into the world with no safety net, but Grier always had so much more courage than I did. I guess when you've bummed around in hobo jungles as a teenager and experienced the worst of fighting in a war, nothing can faze you.

Grier's and my style of practicing law couldn't have been more different. If I'd set out to find a partner whose manner and behavior was the opposite pole, I could have looked no farther than my husband. He was the darter, I the plodder. He relied on charisma, I on slow, hard, intense effort. He absorbed the persona of his clients by osmosis. I was the listener and the hand holder. Charles Robertson, one of the area's excellent attorneys, once described Grier as the best street fighter any client could have. Grier would go into court with nothing and pull himself up by his own boot straps. I, on the other hand, spent hours interviewing and poring over every detail, and would not go to court unless I was over-prepared. Grier questioned everything. I was far more trusting. A well-known man in the community was arrested for driving while intoxicated, hired me as his attorney, and convinced me that he was innocent. He'd had a bad cold, he said, and was literally guzzling cough medicine. When arrested, he tested above the legal limit for intoxication, but everything he'd ingested was for a health condition. I believed him absolutely, went to court, and lost the case. He was convicted and sent to jail. I was devastated. Here was my poor client wrongly locked up because I'd done such a poor job defending him. I learned later that not only was he as guilty as hell, but an alcoholic, and it wasn't the first time he'd been in trouble for drinking.

Grier could not tolerate injustice and spent a great deal of time doing pro bono work. Anyone whose civil liberties were violated found a defendant in my husband. The American Civil Liberties Union sent him a steady stream of clients. Day after day our office was filled with society's misfits and oddballs, almost all of them men, often men who hadn't bathed in several days—if then—whose clothes were disheveled, whose long hair and beards were filthy. They made me uneasy, but Grier was eternally pleasant and helpful.

Not long after we opened our private practice, I was elected president of Town North Business and Professional Women. The club always sent its president to the national convention and included a small expense account, enough to fly the person there and back and provide for lodging and food. The meeting was to be held in Seattle. Grier and I had gone into debt and bought a Ford station wagon. Through all the years preceding this, we'd not been able to travel at all, or to take any vacation together with our children. Grier thought it would be great fun to take a camping trip with our boys. All agreed.

My four guys loaded up the station wagon and took off. Grier Jr. was fourteen; Tommy, ten, and Kenny, seven. They took the southern route through New Mexico, Arizona, California, and up the coast through Oregon to Seattle. They camped in parks, along roadsides, in remote terrain, and on paved parking lots all the way to Seattle, where Grier found a motel room with cooking facilities. They were out of touch and I didn't hear from them, wouldn't have had time to "visit" on the phone if they had called, because I was at home running the office and the house all by myself.

Ten days later, on a Saturday, I bought a round-trip ticket to Seattle and flew out to meet them. Never have I been so welcomed! All the way from the airport to the motel, the boys and their father regaled me with hilarious tales about their adventures. All claimed they were half starved because they'd had to "make do" with food from the day they left home. On a tight budget they'd been able to afford only the most basic "grub," and the boys claimed their dad was an absolutely horrible cook. As soon as I put my luggage in the motel room, I checked the cooking equipment and then went to the grocery store, where I bought a four-pound roast, potatoes, onions, carrots, salad greens, and rolls. Back at the motel, I prepared the first home-cooked meal they'd had in almost two weeks. All four were ecstatic. They ate every scrap and literally licked their plates.

Early on Sunday morning, Grier got on the plane, using the second half of our two-way ticket, and flew home to Dallas. After all, we couldn't afford to close our law offices even for a day. I hope he felt guilty as he smilingly made his way up the runway to the plane. The marvelous adventure he had planned and talked me into was now left to me to conclude.

On Sunday afternoon I signed the roster as the official Town North B&PW delegate.

Meetings were held every day from early in the morning until late in the afternoon, and I could not miss a single one. I must earn the money that the club had given me for expenses. But what to do with the boys? Boys cannot be left in a strange city on their own. At least, not in threes!

I knew that I could not take both Tom and Ken with me. I knew that Grier Jr. was absolutely responsible and I could depend on him to do whatever was needed. A park and play areas near the motel provided my answer. I left Grier Jr. with Kenny in the park, took Tommy with me . . . and worried until I could get back to check on them. One day I tried leaving Tom with Grier Jr. and taking Ken with me, and it was a disaster. My oldest son was a total wreck by the time I got back; Tommy was a handful at that time. I should have known better! As soon as the meetings were over, I collected all three of my sons and tried to make it up to them for being out of their lives all day. We drove all around Seattle. We watched salmon being smoked on outdoor fires. We took in the scenery so special to that West Coast city. I would get up every morning and make a wonderful breakfast, then prepare a lunch of sandwiches, chips, and cookies for all of us, drop Grier Jr. and Kenny at the park with specific instructions for their behavior all day and an emergency telephone number where I could be reached, take Tommy with me, and head out for the next B&PW meetings. In the afternoon, I'd collect all three, take them back to the motel, and prepare the best dinner our facilities and our budget allowed. I had learned that I could call on all kinds of creative resources within myself to make my children involved and happy while I was doing what had to be done to provide as good a life for them as possible. It's a trick every mother with two careers—one at home and one in the workplace—soon learns. It may not be the best of all possible solutions and it most certainly will be frowned on by those who subscribe, without exception, to the traditional family's way of doing things. But it works. The point is: A mother who neglects her children will always do it—whether she is a professional woman with a career both at home and outside the home, or whether she is a stay-at-home mom who overinvolves herself with volunteer commitments. Good moms find a way to work it out, no matter what path they choose.

For the week of the convention, I attended every meeting and made copious notes to report to my club back home. Then I took off with the boys across the mountains, headed home. I was surprised to see trees, trees, and more trees. Finally we were on the other side of the mountains and through Spokane, where we spent the night sleeping in our car in a park. Grier Jr. insisted on sleeping outside, but soon crowded in with us because there were all kinds of animals roaming around. Noises and scratches kept me awake all night. I was worried that some wild animal, a cougar or a lion or some such beast, might tear into the car. I headed out to Idaho, so exhausted that I could hardly think straight. We felt safer in Idaho and spent two nights there where I rested.

Our itinerary included a trip to a national park on the Canadian border with Montana, but by the time we arrived, an extreme cold spell had closed the park—even in July! So we dropped down to Yellowstone and spent three night there in a primitive cabin. The boys were excited to see bears, but I was less so—especially at night, when the bears came and ravaged our garbage cans until they were chased away by the park rangers. We drove all over Yellowstone, saw Old Faithful and the other geysers, the mud pots, the wild animals, all the flora and fauna. After our marvelous stay there, we headed home—and did not stop! I was exhausted when we pulled into Tucumcari, New Mexico, where I had one good night of rest before getting up the next day and heading home to Dallas. We had put thousands of miles on our new Ford. Even though they complained about many less-than-perfect experiences while they were going through it, the boys talked about that trip for years.

I took my barber tools along when I went to Seattle. I had become the family barber shortly after Grier came back from World War II and swore he would never stand in another line as long as he lived. There was only one barbershop in the entire area when we lived in Mustang Village. Grier would go to get a haircut and come home swearing. His hair grew longer and longer because he refused to stand in line and wait. One day he came home with a set of barber tools and told me that from now on I would cut his hair. It didn't faze me. Mother had always cut my dad's hair. Most of the farm women cut their husband's hair, but I'd never cut hair in my life and was not eager to learn. Grier said he'd teach me! After all, what was so difficult about snipping off a few hanks of hair? So, I learned. And as the boys came along, I cut their hair, too. I never had a lesson, never read a set of instructions. But when there are four males in the family, hair cutting is not an insignificant part of the family budget. I cut all my boys' hair through high school and got up early to barber Grier Jr's. hair the day he got married. My being the family barber saved us hundreds of dollars.

I've always done my own hair, too. In the early days of our marriage, I did it because I couldn't afford to go to the beauty shop. Once I could afford a professional hairdresser, my time was too precious to waste waiting for somebody else to shampoo and set my hair. I shampooed and set it late at night after everybody else was in bed. The only time I have my hair done is for very special occasions. Even then, I sometimes go home and redo an expensive professional hairdo.

OUR LAW PRACTICE gradually grew.

My first really big case involved a divorce suit brought by a top executive of one of the country's leading corporations. I think he came to see me by mistake. He had heard of a woman lawyer in Dallas who could perform miracles, and he needed a miracle. He was a married man with children, but for several years had been having an affair with a woman he hoped to marry as soon as his wife gave him a divorce. After I got to know him well, I was convinced that the marital rift had been a long time coming because his wife was very jealous, selfish, and vindictive. He took out his frustration in work, quickly rose to the top of his profession, and almost never was at home. The lives of both husband and wife were miserable, but she would not consent to a divorce.

Adultery was a bar to divorce in those days, and if his wife had learned about his extramarital affair she could have barred their legal parting indefinitely.

Henry Strasburger, one of the most honorable lawyers Dallas ever produced, represented the wife.

The ramifications were extremely complicated. That year graduates of Highland Park High School in Dallas were the top seniors in both major military academies, West Point and Annapolis. Pictures of the young men were featured together on the cover of one of the top news magazines in America. One of the young men was the son of the "other woman" in my client's life, and he wanted to go with her to the graduation exercises. The woman, still his legal wife and the mother of his children, would have barred the divorce indefinitely if such a thing had happened. My client wanted to make his decisions freely. It was a mess.

I'd never heard of contractual alimony at the time, but Mr. Strasburger had. Together we worked out a compromise to please both of our clients. My client was in the top tax bracket. Working with Mr. Strasburger and a number of other top-notch lawyers, we arrived at a settlement that would give the wife $75,000 a year until her youngest child was eighteen. With tax breaks, the $75,000 would actually cost my client $15,000 a year. The wife was happy; my client was ecstatic. Internal Revenue chewed over this contract for about three years. It would have been a total disaster if it had not passed muster, but it did—and my client was convinced I could walk on water! He went off to the graduation exercises with his true love, married her, and they lived together for the rest of his life. The ex-wife had enough money to live the good life she had always desired.

Until his death, this client consulted me every time he had a knotty legal problem. He went on to head the company for which he worked, which had all kinds of top lawyers in the world's leading firms. He'd fly me to New York or anywhere else in the country to be on the consulting team for his legal problems. I probated his will and to this day continue as the lawyer for his widow. He told me once, "During all these years, you have never given me any bad advice." He was a good man and I worked hard to justify his faith. His was the most significant case I've had in my entire career, and proved to me that I can handle the most complex issues. If, indeed, he came into my life while seeking out some other female lawyer who could perform miracles, I am eternally grateful that he made that mistake and even more pleased that he lived to know it wasn't a mistake.

My sons were growing up and I was determined that they not leave home without knowing how valuable each was to our family, how much I loved them, and that I would go to any honest lengths to see that each had the best opportunity to become his own best self. I made it a point to talk individually with each son every day. It wasn't easy, but it was imperative. I needed to know what they were thinking, who their friends were, what they envisioned for their future, how I could best help, and when I needed to back off.

Backing off was the most difficult.

Grier and I learned how difficult this was when Tommy was the victim of a terrible accident and lost an eye. He was eleven, in the fifth grade, and still the smallest kid in his class, but he played in every sport that came along. He and some friends were on the University Park playground tossing balls around when one kid picked up a piece of tile and sailed it, lacerating Tommy's right eye. He was rushed to Children's Hospital. We were called. A medical team began immediately trying to save the eye. Days went by. There were countless medical procedures and several surgeries. Blindness in both eyes threatened, so we had to make the painful decision to give up on the right eye and save the left. Tommy was in total darkness, both eyes bandaged, lying in what can best be described as a large baby bed, and he was terribly frightened. I spent every night with him, curled around him so that I could ease his terror when he woke at night. Every morning Grier got Grier Jr. and Kenny off to school and then came to the hospital. Either his father or I were with Tom around the clock.

This continued for thirty days. Tommy handled it better than we did. Grier and I determined that we would encourage Tom to have as normal a life as possible and supported his every effort to be like his peers. We went through untold agony when Tom was playing sports, especially baseball in junior high school.

The accident changed our family, made us more conscious of each other and of the fragility of life. One moment everything is fine, everybody healthy, and in a split second it can all change.

As OUR PRACTICE EXPANDED, we slowly added other lawyers and staff personnel and I began quietly to work on my own, separate from Grier. From the day we went into practice together, I made more money than he did, which is not at all unusual when you consider that he was doing so much pro bono work. His wit and special charm camouflaged a very fragile ego, and I was constantly on the alert to protect him. In the early days of our practice together, I was the office gofer. I did almost all the housekeeping chores and all the secretarial work—typing, copying, and bill paying. I kept the books and paid the taxes until the day we were audited by the Internal Revenue Service. They spent three days in our office going over every minute detail. It was a terrible experience. After that I handed Grier the checkbook and told him he could either be the business manager or hire somebody to do that job. It didn't take long for us to get a business manager. Because I had kept the records, I knew that the disparity between my income and Grier's had continued to widen, but neither of us talked about it. Later, when I began to accumulate honors, I always had Grier in the front row and gave him the credit he deserved. I was something of his creation because I never would have become a lawyer if he hadn't prodded me. I walked on eggs in our relationship because Grier could be very demeaning and extremely critical. I think he was proud of me, but he and my mother were alike in this one way. Neither could tell me that.

I wasn't the easiest woman to live with, either. I could be hardnosed and stubborn, and often was. Once, at a party when the guys were all drinking, one threw his arm around me and said, "I don't see how Grier stays married to you; no way would I stay married to you." I lifted my water glass and toasted him. "That makes us even. I wouldn't stay married to you either!"

Money may not be the root of all evil, but it plays a central role in a marriage. Women who are the chief wage earners or who make more money than their husbands often have a difficult time keeping their career and their home life on an even keel. Recently a woman walked into my office requesting that I handle her divorce. I always interview potential clients thoroughly, and when I listened to her story I learned that she and her husband had gone into business together. It started on a shoestring, but became more and more profitable and now was worth about $5 million. They were still working together, but she was fed up. In the beginning her husband sought her advice, applauded her efforts, and appreciated her help. Now he saw her as a challenge, a threat to his ego, and he criticized her all the time. She admitted she still loved him and wished she could save her marriage, but she could no longer live with him both at home and at work. I told her she would have to make some choices, that I was not a psychologist, and could not help remedy the human relations segment of her life, but before she filed for divorce, she should try counseling. I sent her to an excellent therapist as well as an industrial business psychologist whose specialty was family-owned businesses. We salvaged the marriage.

Grier Jr. graduated from Highland Park High School in 1960 with high honors. He was president of the student body and had spent the summer after his junior year as an exchange student in Indonesia. He earned the Blanket Award, given to the most outstanding boy in the senior class. He applied to a number of colleges and was admitted to every one, including Harvard and Stanford. He qualified for Plan 2 for exceptional honor students at the University of Texas and I very much wanted him to go there, but he chose Harvard and entered as a freshman in September 1960. He attended both his freshman and sophomore years on a financial scholarship, but by the time he reached his third year we were making enough money to afford to send him and felt he should not apply for financial aid.

Grier and I seldom had a vacation together because we needed to keep the office open at all times, so if he wanted to take a break, I'd stay at home and run the office, and if I took a break, he'd keep the office open.

After World War II, there were many new and almost-new propeller airplanes suddenly obsolete when the airlines bought jets. The propeller planes were for sale at very low prices. People got together, formed clubs, and purchased flying rights. That way they could take trips at a bargain. Through one of the clubs, Grier, one other man, and twenty-nine women, most of them widows, took advantage of this chance. They took short weekend jaunts and sometimes longer trips across country. Grier loved the excitement of traveling with small groups. I mostly stayed at home and worked. Or, when I traveled, it was on law business. Grier once took a cruise alone and had a lovely surprise. After he'd boarded the ship, the first person he ran into was Rita, his sister. Neither one knew the other was on the cruise. They had a wonderful time together.

Except for very infrequent road trips with my intrepid traveling son, Kenny, most of my time away from the office was devoted to bar work. In 1960, just as Grier Jr. was leaving for college, I began to acquire leadership bar roles. I had joined the Junior Bar as soon as I was admitted to practice and was almost immediately elected secretary, then advanced to vice president, and was scheduled to become president when time ran out. At age thirty-six, attorneys dropped out of the Junior Bar to become more involved in the Dallas Bar. Some members urged me to fudge a little and assume the presidency, but I did not think it would be right to cut age corners, and declined. Later the rules changed to allow Junior Bar members to stay active for a longer period.

Grier and I always made it a practice to attend the State Bar conventions and it was through this exposure that I began to assume leadership in bar work. The year was 1960, the convention was in Houston, and Paul Carrington was president. He asked Gordon Carpenter to chair a group and select a committee to work on the newly organized Family Law Section of the State Bar. Gordon stopped me in the hall and asked if I would serve on the committee. I immediately accepted. Also named were Hawthorne Phillips, later on the Supreme Court of Texas; Sproesser Wynn of Fort Worth, the state's leading expert on adoptions; Judge Paul Martineau of Corpus Christi; Judge Charles Betts of Austin; Scott Red of Houston; and Judge Beth Wright of Dallas.

We held our first meeting at the Rice Hotel in Houston that summer. All of us paid our own expenses and none of us had any idea what we were supposed to do, so much of that original "work" consisted of good old boys exchanging war stories. Naively we thought we could accomplish everything that needed to be done in family law with half-day meetings three or four times a year, and at the outset we wasted several good years.

In 1964, I was elected vice chairman of the Family Law Section, and the following year, when the convention was held in Fort Worth, I was asked to remain as vice chair. Traditionally, unless there were extenuating circumstances, the vice chairman of a bar committee automatically advanced to chairperson. I confided to a committee member—can't remember who—that I would not be skipped over. A woman chairing a bar committee? There was no precedent for such a thing! By that time I knew what needed to be accomplished in the Family Law Section as well as anyone in the bar, and much better than most, because I had lived the legal restrictions of a married woman, both professionally and personally. As a lawyer, I required the signature of my husband before I could file some documents. As an only child, the inheritance I would receive from my parents would be legally controlled by my husband. Unless I was elected chairperson, I would resign and use my time and talents elsewhere. Since I was doing a great deal of the work, they overlooked my gender and elected me to lead the section.

This marked the beginning of a series of amazing advances for women and families in Texas law.

13

Woe to the Wedded Woman

ONE OF ONLY SEVEN community property states in the nation, Texas laws hold that property acquired or earned during marriage belongs equally to the husband and wife, but in order to control her property, a woman must die. What a drastic way to gain control of what is yours! As long as she was married, her husband was in control of everything. Only in death could she give her half of the property to her children or anyone else of her choosing. If a couple sold their community property, she had to sign the deed, but she had to swear before a notary, with her husband not present, that she had voluntarily affixed her signature. In many cases, women were far better educated than their husbands. In the early days, many could read and write while their husbands could not, but they still had to be examined privately when entering into a legal contract to sell property.

A single woman's bank accounts came under the control of her husband when she married. If he told the bank not to allow her access to her own money, the bank had to obey. If she owned real estate, say a fourplex completely free of debt, once she said "I do" any transfer of the property had to have the signature of her husband. She could not borrow money in her own name. She could not make bond without her husband's signature. If she wanted to start a business, she had to go before the court and file a lawsuit asking to have her disabilities removed. And if her husband refused to join in the suit, she was out of luck. Disabilities of coverture were removed only for mercantile and trading purposes; professionals could not have their disabilities removed. All of us who were married and professional women prior to 1967 were practicing illegally because the existing laws made our husbands accountable for everything we did.

Women lawyers knew this and talked in secret with each other about challenging the law, but we would have been killing our own livelihood and we didn't dare.

A woman could legally run her own affairs if she were single, widowed, or divorced, but if she were married, she could control her own life only with the approval and consent of her husband. The husband, on the other hand, could sell his property without even telling his wife.

It is easy to understand that these archaic laws held Texas back from developing as an industrial state because no married woman could legally function in business. Once married, the assumption was that she no longer had the sense to function as an independent person.

These antiquated laws often were as restrictive to men as to women. Our courts were filled with cases where a husband and wife connived to have the woman not be questioned separately from her husband—or used some other legal loophole—and the couple sold the property and were perfectly happy with the sale—until oil was discovered there. They could then go to court declaring the deed defective.

Our law firm once represented an automobile company that had sold several cars to a divorced woman. She had always faithfully paid her debts. Then she remarried, and the company did not think to have her new husband come in and sign with her for a new car. She failed to take out insurance, and when her teenaged son wrecked the car, she called the automobile company to come and get their car. The dealership had no legal recourse.

The Business and Professional Women's Clubs, recognizing the legal restrictions of married women, had begun a campaign in the late 1950s to persuade the male-dominated State Legislature to enact an Equal Legal Rights Amendment. At every new session, they found a legislator to introduce the bill and the women would try everything in their power to get it passed. Each year the legislature played a game of charades, with representatives claiming to favor its passage. But each year it died in committee, or if introduced, by political maneuvering failed to come to a vote. By pre-arrangement, legislators who were under the most pressure could vote for the bill, go home to their districts, and say, "See, I favored your bill." But, year after year, the bill got nowhere.

The truth was that legislators were extremely hostile to giving married women equal legal rights, and a great deal of the animosity was a personal vendetta against its sponsors. B&PW's purposes may have been pure, but its diplomacy defeated every possibility of getting an amendment passed.

In the meantime, back in the Dallas office, Raggio and Raggio was gaining a reputation as a reputable, trustworthy law firm, seemingly in spite of Grier's pro bono clients, some referred by the ACLU, some with questionable reputations.

Then came November 22, 1963, and the long-anticipated visit of President and Mrs. John F. Kennedy to Dallas. The threatening clouds on that fateful day had dissipated by the time the President, First Lady Jacqueline Kennedy, Texas Governor John Connally, and First Lady Nellie Connally rode in a slow-moving parade toward the Dallas Trade Mart, where they were to be honored at a luncheon. Grier and I were in the audience. The guests of honor were late arriving. And later. And later. By the time Dallas Mayor Erik Jonsson announced that there had been an accident and the president would not be arriving, most of us had a sixth sense that something terrible had happened. Before we made our way back to our office, we knew, along with the hundreds of others, that the president had been assassinated and that Vice President Lyndon Johnson was being given the oath of office on Air Force One.

The assassination, at the Triple Underpass in downtown Dallas, occurred not three blocks from our Raggio and Raggio offices. Later that day, following the arrest of Lee Harvey Oswald as the suspect, Grier got a call from the Washington office of the ACLU imploring him to be at the arraignment later that evening. Rumors were rampant that Oswald had been abused by his captors. Believing in the guarantee of the Constitution that all people are innocent until proven guilty, Grier agreed. I persuaded him to be cautious, to take another ACLU member with him.

At the arraignment, which took place around ten that night, Oswald said an attorney would step forward and answer for him. Grier never agreed to represent Oswald, only to be present for the hearing to be sure that Oswald was read his constitutional rights.

On the following Sunday morning, when Oswald was shot and killed while being transferred at the jail, the question of anyone serving as his attorney became moot. But the situation was clouded further in a complication that nobody could have foreseen. On the week before November 22, Ruth Payne had filed for divorce with me as her attorney. Oswald had spent the night of November 21 in Ruth Payne's home. The gun from which the fatal shot was fired had spent the night in Mrs. Payne's garage.

Talk about "evidence" for conspiracy theorists! The Raggios had innocently provided several!

All of the country, and especially Dallas, grieved for its lost president. But in the midst of mourning, life went on. My personal life, both at home and at the office, was going well, but women's legal rights were at an impasse when Joyce Cox, a male, became president of the State Bar in 1964. By this time, the clamor of women for equality had mounted to the point that he felt compelled to do *something*. That something was to name a committee to draft a bill to take away some of the disabilities of coverture of property rights for married women. Professors Joseph McKnight and Eugene Smith of Southern Methodist University drafted the bill, and I was on the committee that met several times to work on it. We found a sponsor; the bill was introduced. The legislature took no action and the committee was disbanded. Even its drafters and those of us who worked on it knew that it was entirely inadequate.

But, for me, it revealed just how bad Texas laws were. We found forty-four different laws that discriminated against married women in Texas, twenty-seven legal disabilities of coverture. At that time, I thought it would be rather simple to write a bill to remove these legal restrictions. I thought that a few of us who were "legal experts" could get together over a weekend and draft a bill that would include everything we wanted.

During the next two years I learned how complicated a project we had undertaken. Every law had an impact on at least one other one. If we removed legal restrictions on community property, we impinged on legalities on real estate. If we tampered with probate law, we could well hamper workings in corporate law. I soon became convinced that an Equal Legal Rights Amendment, if passed, under the laws that existed in Texas would have been disastrous. It would have thrown everything into chaos because there were no statutes in place to carry out equal legal rights. I am confident that an Equal Legal Rights constitutional amendment at that time would have been rescinded because, like Prohibition, which was passed and then rescinded, it was much too complex a subject to be handled with a single unstudied stroke of the pen.

Because I opposed equal legal rights as a constitutional amendment before statutes were put into place to enact the laws, I was accused of being a traitor to women. Both Hermine Tobolowsky and I were active members of B&PW. I had served as president of the Town North B&PW Chapter and she had advanced to state B&PW president. But when I was nominated for a major civic award, she made an impassioned speech opposing me, accusing me of being an "Aunt Tom." Women who carried banners and made speeches demanding "ERA Now" clearly did not understand that we would have created an absolute mess if we had an equal rights amendment without the "teeth" to enforce the laws.

This was the framework of legal rights for married women in Texas when I became chairperson of the Family Law Section. By serving on committees and by watching what happened to the B&PW-sponsored legislation, I had learned a lot. I knew we would get absolutely nowhere by pushing and threatening. I knew we had to use other tactics to gain the legal rights we so richly deserved. I spent a great deal of time considering how best to go about achieving this goal.

I am not above maneuvering and manipulating when nothing else works. There's truth in the old axiom that when the fox is in charge of the henhouse, we must first find a way to get rid of the fox before we can rescue the hens. I wanted the Marital Property bill assigned to the Family Law Section. So, I pondered and waited for a successful lure that would remove the fox from his vigil.

It came at a party. With liquor flowing freely, the State Bar climaxed its meeting in San Antonio with its usual convivial event where old animosities faded away and every lawyer loved every other lawyer! Standing next to Clint Small, newly elected State Bar president, I had my chance. Clint was a big, jovial, happy-go-lucky kind of guy, everybody's pal. I liked him, but I took advantage of him in a party setting. Since neither Grier nor I drank, my head was clear and my intentions pure when I laid my hand on Clint's arm and said, "Clint, I've been elected chairman of the Family Law Section. Would you assign the Marital Property bill to our section instead of putting it into a special committee? Please?" He threw his arm around me and declared, "Honey, you can have anything you want!" I said, "Oh, thank you so much," and wandered off.

But I wasted no time. On Monday morning, back at the office, I immediately fired off a letter to Clint thanking him for assigning the bill to the Family Law Section, and promising that we would take our work seriously and do everything in our power to write a good bill that would pass the legislature. I knew that most members of the Family Law Section were not especially interested in changing laws dealing with women's rights, so I wrote an enthusiastic letter to each committee member, exulting over our good fortune in having such an important bill assigned to our section. I gave them a deadline to respond with their disapproval. I was fairly certain that the letter would languish on their desks until the deadline had passed, and that is exactly what happened. I received only one response, a negative vote, but it came after the deadline and didn't count! I wrote them again thanking them for their approval and announcing that it was now our responsibility to produce an honorable bill that the legislature would pass.

My next move was to create a task force to write the bill. I still thought we could write a bill in a matter of hours that would take away all of the legal disabilities under which married women in Texas lived.

It took two years and seven separate drafts!

And men, with some of the best legal minds in the state who I asked to serve on the task force, took their work seriously. Assisting in the study, writing, and editing were Hank Hudspeath and Charles Saunders, who headed the State Bar's Real Estate/Probate Section; Angus McSwain, dean of Baylor Law School; Eugene Smith and Joseph McKnight of the SMU School of Law; Dewey Lawrence, a distinguished lawyer from Tyler; William Huie, a legal scholar from the University of Texas/Austin; and Bob Johnson, a former legislator and head of the legislative services for the State Bar. They all gave their time and talents freely. All of us paid our own expenses for countless weekend meetings. At first, Raggio and Raggio, our law offices, paid for most of the secretarial help and postage. Eventually, the Hoblitzelle Foundation, and later the Moody Foundation, provided some funding.

When the bill was as complete and thorough as our task force could make it, the next hassle was to get it through committees and to a vote by both houses of the legislature. Its first hurdle was to clear the legislative committee of the State Bar. What a tension-filled day that was! Davis Grant, State Bar of Texas Chief Counsel, was adamantly opposed to change and confident that the bill would not be approved. When it was, he was furious. On the way out of the meeting, he said, "You got your bill approved. Now see if you can get it passed." I was just as flippant. I said, "I will."

Next, we had to find legislators to sponsor it, then get it approved by the legislative committee—always a slow, agonizing process. At every step I was warned that it stood no chance of getting to a vote. There was no Southwest Airlines at that time flying frequently between Dallas and Austin, so the task force members made countless automobile trips to Austin and back, leaving around 4 A.M. to testify at a legislative meeting at 9 A.M. Sometimes we'd arrive only to find that our hearing had been postponed until another day. Our task force members pulled every political favor owed to them. I worked my own charm and shenanigans.

Four women from the B&PW, including Hermine, testified against it. They had not been able to get their ERA amendment passed, and their tactics had made many enemies among legislators, all of whom were male and in total control of the vote. The chairman of the Senate Judiciary Committee asked me only one significant question. "Little lady, are you one of those women?" I knew exactly who he was referring to. Even though the question startled me, I knew what I had to do. "No, Senator," I said, "they testified *against* my bill." "That's all I wanted to know," he responded, and promptly voiced his approval.

Both committees approved our bill in toto. The legislative session was winding down when the bill became law, unanimously approved by the House of Representatives and approved with only two negative votes by the Senate.

The impossible had happened. In one fell swoop, married women in Texas could now legally conduct their own affairs and be responsible for their own legal omissions. I called Judge Hughes in Dallas to tell her about our good fortune. She responded, "Oh, no, Louise. That bill could not possibly have passed. It will take twenty years to make all those changes in Texas law!"

I went to Austin in June 1967 to watch Gov. John Connally sign the bill into law.

We may be the only proponents of legal change in the state, maybe even in the nation, who requested postponement for the work we had done to become the law of the land. So all-inclusive and sweeping were the changes that we knew we had a giant task ahead of us.

We had secured legal equality for married women. Now to make it work! Texas lawyers did not know what had hit them. Some 99 percent hadn't any idea how many changes they would now be required to make. Many of the laws under which we practiced were null and void. Most of the forms were obsolete—and this at a time before automation, when changes can be made by hitting a few keys on the computer. It meant reprinting masses of forms on everything from deeds to contracts to stock certificates. We had to give lawyers time to learn the new laws and revise every office procedure. We asked for a postponement of the law's effective date until January 1, 1968, and began the almost insurmountable task of explaining to lawyers the implications of the new law.

I chaired a series of sixteen seminars, arranging for four to six legal experts, most of whom had served on the task force which wrote the bill, to speak and answer questions at each seminar. I didn't do much legal work in my own office for the last five months of 1967, but we did blanket the state of Texas. From August until January, when the new laws took effect, I traveled constantly. I went to Amarillo in a sleet storm, to Midland in a dust storm, to Houston in a monsoon, and to Tyler in a heat wave.

I was not welcomed. You can't imagine how much grumbling and complaining I heard. We'd practiced law for more than a hundred years in the good old-fashioned way, and now many things lawyers had been taught in law school no longer applied. I was the most unpopular lawyer in Texas. I couldn't have been elected dog catcher!

But it paid off—not only for every citizen in the state, but for me personally.

Accolades began to accumulate from legal experts throughout the country, who almost immediately used our bill as a model for revising their own laws. Even as our task force began its work, news of our efforts had reached beyond the Texas borders. As early as 1966, Father Robert Drinan, dean of Boston College School of Law, invited me to speak at the annual American Bar Association which met in Montreal, Canada. At that meeting, Father Drinan discussed with me his concerns about legal conflicts in the various states dealing with family law, and asked me to chair an ABA Committee on Family Law in the 50 States. I accepted, began to collect material, and soon learned that each state was reinventing the wheel. There was absolutely no communication among them. When a new do-nothing group took control of the ABA Family Law Section, I was so frustrated that I didn't attend the national convention that met in Philadelphia in 1968. After the inspired leadership of Father Drinan, the group that took over was so lethargic, nothing got done. Imagine my surprise when a letter arrived telling me that I had been elected to the Council of the ABA Family Law Section. What we had done in Texas was paying off bigtime across the nation. The ABA Committee on Family Law in the 50 States eventually grew into the most successful committee in the ABA Family Law Section.

I had my special moment in the spotlight when in 1967 the Texas State Bar gave me one of its three most prestigious awards, the Citation of Merit in 1967 for the Marital Property Act. It came as a complete surprise. I clearly had not done it alone, and I accepted by thanking the bar leaders for being so perceptive and advanced in their thinking.

The award, as special as it was, pales beside a far more significant accomplishment: Not one single part of the Marital Property Act has ever been declared unconstitutional. With the careful drafting and redrafting by legal scholars and practicing lawyers, we wrote a marital property act that has stood the test of time and an onslaught of challenges.

I continued as chair of the Family Law Section through 1967 and remained on its board for two years following that. Family law had always been something of a stepchild of the State Bar. In a world where value is measured by the amount of money one accumulates, family lawyers were near the bottom of the pecking order. But in a world that gives lip service to the value of human relationships, especially to children, family law should be at the very top of the order. As chairperson of what I considered to be the most important section of the State Bar, I was determined to upgrade the section's personnel, its function, and its clout. I had persuaded Harris Morgan of Greenville to redo the bylaws and to chair the nominating committee for the 1966–1967 election. With our new bylaws, we selected new members and officers who represented a microcosm of the state's lawyers. We not only sought racial diversity, but got religious diversity, age diversity, representatives from small law firms as well as large ones, men and women. We secured council members who were both hard-working and enthusiastic. Our meetings were excellent, well-attended, and highly productive. The Family Law Section developed into one of the best of the State Bar.

It was in this state of euphoria that I got a call from the president of the State Bar, who said we had done such a good job with the Marital Property Act that he felt it imperative we take on a new assignment. Would the Family Law Section undertake a complete revision of all family laws in the State of Texas?

Of course, I said yes.

14

Family Law Matters

THE FAMILY LAW SECTION of the Texas State Bar created the first complete Family Code of laws in the world.

That sentence, which required only a few seconds to type, took us a decade to realize. And we're not finished yet!

A code is a set of laws, and when the Marital Property Act of 1967 was put into code language, it became the first section of the Family Code.

With a strong new working committee and the continuing expertise and assistance of law professors and other outstanding attorneys, we chipped away at outmoded statutes and eventually brought Texas, which in the 1960s was at the lowest possible level in family law reform, to number one in the nation.

I appointed qualified members of the Section to different task forces. Once the new laws were written and checked by members of each task force, they were brought to the entire council, which again reviewed them, asked questions, fine-tuned, and prepared them to the best of our ability before they were introduced to the legislature for a vote.

Angus McSwain, arguably the most outstanding authority on the legal manifestations of marriage and divorce, chaired that task force. Our purpose was not only to clarify legal fine points, but to write documents that anybody could understand. Until that time, lawyers wrote laws for other lawyers—just as academicians write for other academics—and it took yet another lawyer to explain to the average person what each meant. We revised everything from laws pertaining to securing a marriage license to clearing up conflicts of residency. We added no-fault divorce to our statutes and eliminated adultery as grounds for divorce.

Marriage and Divorce became a part of the new Family Code when it was passed by the legislature in 1969. After the Marital Property Act, it was added to the Family Code.

Our prior success with the Marital Property Act had generated so much acceptance and good will that working on the Family Code was much easier. Joe McKnight established a Family Code Project at Southern Methodist University, where he was a professor, that continued for almost a full decade. Its work helped us immensely. Our success had also generated money. We were funded by several foundation grants.

In 1967, McSwain succeeded me as chairman of the Family Law Section and we were on a roll—or thought we were.

Two years later OrbaLee Malone from El Paso took over as Family Law Section chairman. A wonderful lawyer and a great guy, he was very trusting and completely blindsided by the legislature. No important pieces of our work were passed during the 1971 session.

We used every honorable tool at our disposal—public relations, timing, and supporters—to educate the constituency.

Public relations was a large block. My good friend, attorney Reba Rasor, a former newspaperwoman, knew that the week between Christmas and the New Year is usually "dead" for breaking news, so she wrote countless articles about the Family Code, and we sent them during that holiday season to every newspaper and radio and television station in Texas. It surprised us how many of the stories were published. I wrote articles for the *Bar Journal*. We literally plastered the state with stories. We also made ourselves available for public speaking, and invitations came from throughout the state. This time, I was not only welcomed in the large and small towns of Texas, but was often honored when I was introduced.

Almost always, while introducing me, the person would say that I was responsible for the Marital Property Act and I had to keep reminding people that I did not create the Marital Property Act all by myself. It took the concerted effort of a very wonderful committee, the backing of the State Bar, and the cooperation of their elected legislators.

All of us had also learned to lobby. We talked about the Family Code at business meetings, parties, and in informal conversations—wherever it was appropriate to do so, and probably on occasions when it was not! We learned how, by staying focused on our goal, to secure the support of individuals and groups who usually might be at opposite political poles. We learned that politics do, indeed, breed strange bedfellows.

Nothing pointed this out so clearly as our strongest supporters for Marriage and Divorce, a coalition of Baptists, Catholics, and Jews, groups which seldom shared similar political views. We had the enthusiastic support of the Baptists through Phil Strickland, and the backing of the Catholics through Archbishop Robert Lucey of San Antonio, a very forward-thinking individual who knew that the Marital Property Act and the Family Code were greatly needed in Texas. We told the Catholics that we would stay clear of abortion, which was an easy promise, because it had never been a part of the Family Code.

But it was the Jewish women who cinched a victory for us. At one time when it looked as if the bill were stuck and would die in the legislative session, Jewish women turned up en masse from all over the state to testify. Anita Marcus and Jeanne Fagadau of the Dallas Section, National Council of Jewish Women, sent out the alarm, and at their own expense, from Amarillo to Beaumont, from El Paso to Tyler, from Dallas to Brownsville, from San Antonio to Clarksville, Jewish women turned up in Austin on the appointed day. When these well-turned-out, intelligent, prepared, persistent, and articulate mothers descended on the Texas legislature, nobody would have dared tell them no. They buttonholed legislators in offices, hallways, on their way to lunch and back. It was said that on that day the only safe place for a legislator to escape was the men's room, and it was standing room only there.

The day after the group stormed Austin, I called my contact and asked if the legislators would like to have another group come and lobby. He said, "God, no, Louise! Keep those women away! We'll pass your bill!"

In 1971, Eugene Smith succeeded OrbaLee Malone as chair of the Family Law Section. He agreed to take the position only if I returned to the board, so in 1971 I became a retread and remained active until 1976. Again, we made trips back and forth to Austin. Usually Joe McKnight, Gene Smith, and I traveled together, but sometimes I made the trip alone, dead tired after a long day of dealing with legislators, and arriving back home in the wee hours of the next day.

Once when we had to make a trip to Austin, Joe's car was in the shop and mine had bad tires. My son Tom, a student at the University of Texas, had driven home for the annual Texas–University of Oklahoma football game and the partying afterward. I made arrangements to borrow my son's car for the trip to Austin and back. At 4 A.M. I sashayed out of the house to go pick up Joe, and there was no car in the driveway. I raced back to Tom's room, shook my very inarticulate son and demanded to know what he had done with the car. He mumbled something about following his dad's instructions to park the car if he'd had too much to drink. He said I'd find it "at the convention center." By that time, I was running late, so I got in my car, picked up Joe, and we drove all over several parking lots searching for the car, weaving like we'd also had too much to drink. We could not find it! Finally, we had to get on the road, so we had no choice but to drive my car, with its bad tires, to Austin and back. Fortunately, we made it.

Nobody was happier than I when Southwest Airlines started flying to Austin and back several times a day. From Love Field in Dallas to Austin, we could fly in thirty-five to forty minutes the distance that took us four hours to drive.

In 1973, we got the Parent and Child section of the Family Code passed by the legislature.

Other committees worked on the Juvenile section and on adoption. We never could get a paternity bill nor an alimony bill passed. We easily could have cleared the halls of the entire legislature by yelling "Paternity!" or "Alimony!" because our "enlightened" law-makers were scared spitless about both. I suppose they felt guilty that paternity and alimony might come home to haunt some of them personally.

We did not get a paternity bill until the Supreme Court of the United States ruled that Texas would not get federal funding for child support unless all children were treated equally. Until then we had bastardized our children born out of wedlock in Texas. Until the Supreme Court made it clear that we'd better shape up if we wanted to continue to get federal dollars, a man could acknowledge that a child born out of wedlock was his; the child could even be named Junior, and yet the father was not responsible for support or under any legal obligation to the child. When money became the issue, the Texas legislature very reluctantly passed a paternity bill.

Ken Kramer of Wichita Falls succeeded Eugene Smith as chairman of the Family Law Section. Under his leadership, we made great headway operating as a section should, concerned with the welfare of families in our state rather than the selfish needs of section members. Serving with him was a joy.

Two very significant family events had happened back in 1966 when I was in Montreal to make my speech on the Marital Property Act at the American Bar Association convention. First, I took Tom with me, one of the first times my second son had been included in one of our professional projects. He was still at UT at the time and had never shown any interest in going into law. He was, in fact, our party boy, but it turned out he'd always wanted to go to New York and this was a great time for him to do so. I was as excited as my son because I had not been to New York for years and stopping off there would give me an opportunity to renew a longtime friendship with Carla and Ray Trapp and to meet their infant daughter, Laura Louise, who was named for me.

As Tom and I were getting on the plane, we heard an announcement that there was shooting from the top of the tower at the University of Texas. Students and faculty were being killed. We had no way of knowing whether any of our friends or relatives, many of whom were on campus at that time, had been killed or injured by the sniper. We had to get to our friend's home in New York before calling back to learn that no one we knew had been hurt in the shooting spree that killed sixteen people and closed the tower for years.

From New York City we took a train to Albany where we rented a car and spent several days sightseeing in Vermont and the Finger Lakes area. Then we drove on to Montreal. Tom's plans were to spend the night in Montreal with me and the next day drive back to New York, where he had friends to visit. It didn't turn out that way. Tom went out that evening and discovered the French girls! Young people there went out in groups instead of one-on-one dates. Tom made a marvelous addition to these groups and had such a good time that first night that he said he'd like to stay for another. And then another. And then another. This continued all week! I had to call the rental agency in Albany and tell them we were keeping the car much longer.

Neither of us knew many of the people at the ABA convention, but I was invited to some of the parties and crashed others! Tommy was my escort and loved it. The convention was huge, so nobody had the faintest idea who had been invited to which event. Everyone was cordial. Both of us had a great time. Sharing a room with my son worked out well because Tom was out almost every night, almost all night, and I was out all day almost every day. I attended all of the meetings of the Family Law Section of the ABA and spent additional time sightseeing. I had never been to Canada before and I so enjoyed Montreal, especially the subway system and the clean, well-lighted shops in the underground tunnels.

It was on that trip that Tom decided to go to law school, probably convinced that the life of a lawyer was one long entertainment. He had a lot to learn.

My second wonderful family bonus at that convention came in a call from Grier Jr. He had graduated from Harvard in 1964. His father and I insisted that he return to Texas, so he enrolled in the University of Texas Law School that fall. In November he married Susan Fahl in a small family ceremony we arranged in our home. The 1960s were very troubling years for young people in the United States. The Civil Rights movement was in full swing, Kennedy was assassinated in Dallas, and the Vietnam War was heating up. Grier Jr.

was caught up in these turbulent times. Mother and Dad often heard from him, but Grier and I very little. He completed his first year of law school, then he and Susan moved to New Orleans. He called us once in June, when they lost their first child, Marie, who lived only a short time after birth. Later, two other healthy daughters, Julie and Bridget, were born to them.

Then he called me in Montreal and said he wanted to return to law school. He did not want to go back to the University of Texas, and Harvard Law School would not accept his year at UT. He wanted me to talk to Dean Drinan to see if he would be allowed to enter Boston College Law School with credit for his year in Texas. I was overjoyed because I had been extremely worried about what he was doing in New Orleans. I knew that my son was deeply involved in the Civil Rights movement in Mississippi and Alabama, where young people disappeared and some were killed as violence escalated.

So I talked to Dean Drinan, who graciously agreed to let Grier Jr. enroll as a mid-law student at Boston College. I called Grier back and he and Susan almost immediately moved from New Orleans to Massachusetts.

IT SOON DAWNED ON ME that there was method in their madness in inviting me back into the ABA inner circle. The 1969 national convention was scheduled to be held in Dallas. Its Family Law Section and its Association of Women Lawyers needed a liaison in order to arrange for meetings and plan social events. It would take a local person to make those arrangements, and I was the one local person they knew! Leave it to me to accept the responsibility of planning all of the events for women lawyers from throughout the United States and become the liaison for events for the Family Law Section of ABA.

I yelled for help. I called twelve of my good friends who were also women lawyers, and we started meeting informally once a month at the Dallas Bar headquarters then located in the Adolphus Hotel. Dallas was still cringing from the stigma of the Kennedy assassination and every woman on our committee was determined to show our visitors a positive side of our city. I've never had better cooperation from any group and the events we planned were hugely successful.

We women got to know each other so well, to work together on a common goal so successfully, and to have such a good time, that we continued our monthly meetings after the convention ended. We were a group without a constitution, officers, dues, bylaws, or any other form of official organization because we did not want to give the Dallas Bar Association any reason to exclude us from participation and leadership in the Big Bar. We knew if we had a women's organization, it would give men a perfect excuse to say, "Well, you've got your own organization, so you don't need us." So we were very low key. But we did have fun, and so spooked the male attorneys that sometimes some of the guys would sit in on our meetings to see what we were up to. We were covert and undercover, bringing the attention of the community to the endless list of discriminatory practices against women. We got the credit or the blame for lots of things, some of which we did and some of which never occurred to us.

We were just a group of "know-nothings," female attorneys having a good time together.

Or that's the way we came across, and it was the truth, only not the whole truth. There were still few jobs for women lawyers, so we served as a network to help women get jobs. When any one of us heard of the possibility of a job, we would immediately set off the alarm, calling each other by telephone to spread the word, and especially reaching younger women who were looking for work. We celebrated each woman's victory. When there was a breakthrough of any kind, it was an occasion for joy. Every victory, no matter how small it seemed initially, was a breakthrough to something more significant.

We also started using the country's new laws to change life "as usual."

What a tool we had in the Equal Employment Opportunity Commission (EEOC) passed by Congress in 1964! Slow on the uptake, it took us about four years to comprehend our good fortune. That we had this tool for major change in our hands came as the result of a fluke. When the bill to outlaw discrimination in employment came before Congress, it was meant to assure that minorities were legally entitled to the same job opportunities as Anglos, and it was bitterly opposed by some representatives, especially "mossbacks" from the

South. An aging, conservative senator, Howard Worth Smith of Virginia, added the word *sex* to the bill because he thought that his fellow legislators just might pass a law making it illegal to discriminate against African-Americans, but they would certainly have enough sense not to allow women full employment opportunity. Surprise!

The bill passed. Now, along with prohibiting discrimination in equal employment because of color, the law also prohibited discrimination because of gender.

Women were underrepresented in every business and profession. They were the last hired and the first fired. They were woefully underpaid. Males were hired for better starting salaries and received promotions much faster. Even on assembly lines where men and women were doing identical jobs, men earned more per hour than their female counterparts. In many professions, the top jobs were reserved for men only. No woman need apply. No matter how badly she needed a job and a good paycheck, no matter if she were a single mother responsible for the rearing of children, it was assumed that the male was the "breadwinner" in the family and women's salaries were supplementary. Business found it highly profitable to promote this myth.

Our small group of women lawyers began to make big waves. Using the EEOC ruling, we sued an airline, a shoe store, a bank, and an accounting firm. Airlines were notorious for hiring young, pretty, lithe women and dismissing them when they gained weight or began to age. The very few banks that had women officers either were family-owned, the woman in question enjoyed an intimate relationship with a director, or the bank did a lot of business outside the United States, required a person in a responsible position to translate and communicate in another language, and could not find a qualified male to do the job.

We almost never went to court because the in-house attorneys for these large organizations read the same law we did and advised their employers to shape up or be out big sums of money in lawsuits. The accounting firm, for instance, hastened to brings its organization into compliance with the law, and every other accounting firm in town adjusted its pay scales so that their male and female employees were paid equal wages for equal work.

Then we turned our attention to our own profession. Not a single large law firm in the city had a female attorney on its staff. Women law graduates were still encountering the same restrictions I had faced when I graduated from law school back in the 1950s.

In 1975 five young women students, all at the very top of their class at the SMU Law School, filed suit against some of the leading Dallas law firms after their applications for summer clerkships were turned down and many of their male classmates with lesser grades were hired.

Only one of the cases ever reached court, and it was lost on a technicality. The other four firms settled, and shortly women's names began to appear on law-firm letterheads. It is astonishing how fast organizations can find qualified women and/or qualified minorities to hire when the law requires them to do so. Some of the women who filed the suit paid dearly for their pioneering roles. Known as "troublemakers," none of the five was hired by the law firm she sued. Some had to leave Texas and secure licenses to practice in other states in order the fulfill their potential as attorneys. Women lawyers who have followed owe an eternal debt of gratitude to those five brave students who jeopardized their own careers to open doors for others.

The women's law nonorganization supported its efforts by passing the hat when we needed money, and everybody was generous. The backbone of our group was made up of older women, like me, all of whom had suffered the sting of exclusion, including Adelfa Callejo, Margaret Brand Smith, Norma Beasley, Lillian Edwards, and others, including Linda Coffey, who filed the landmark case of *Roe v. Wade*, which wound up in the Supreme Court and gave women the right to reproductive freedom. We were all determined that another generation of women should not be categorically denied a chance at employment and advancement in legal annals.

Sarah T. Hughes, who by that time was a federal judge and beholden to nobody, was one of the strongest supporters of our group. She called me up one day and said, "Louise, I want you to buy twenty-five shares of stock in Republic National Bank." I said "Okay, but why?" and she told me. She had been to a party the night before where the chairman of the bank had bragged that *his* bank had no female vice presidents, and as long as he had anything to do with it, there never would be a female vice president. "We are each going to buy stock in that bank, and we're going to that stock-holders' meeting and raise hell," she said.

We bought the stock and tried to keep it very quiet, but I guess you didn't have to be a rocket scientist to figure out that if Sarah Hughes and Louise Raggio have bought stock, trouble might be brewing. About two weeks before the stockholders' meeting, that bank promoted not one, but two women as vice presidents. Judge Hughes was furious, but she said, "We're going anyway, and you're going to speak first."

On the appointed day, I got myself all gussied up in my finest clothes and wore my new fur stole and up we went. There were about twelve million shares, and there sat all the financial and polit-ical powers in the city of Dallas. And there we were, both tiny little women, each a little more than five feet tall and weighing about 110 pounds each soaking wet. We took our places. When it came time for the stockholders to talk, I got up and complimented the bank for its enlightened position by appointing the two women to vice pres-idents, and said that I knew they would be the first of many women who would become bank officers. All those powerful men were preening. Then Sarah Hughes got up and gave them holy ned for not having women directors. Practically overnight that bank found a woman to name as a director. To be sure, there were only token women as bank officers for years, but each small advance was a beginning, and within a short time every bank in town got on the bandwagon.

We also ran one of our members each year for office in the Dallas Bar Association. Most of the time we'd be defeated. A woman could easily be elected secretary, but if she ran for director, she lost. I ran twice for secretary. The second time, Judge Hughes nominated me; Justice Harold Bateman from the Court of Appeals seconded the nomination, then Gordon Simpson, a Texas Supreme Court Justice, spoke in my behalf, and somebody moved that the nominations cease. So, I was elected by acclamation and served for a year. The next year when I ran for director, I was defeated. Finally, Harriet Miers broke the mold. She was elected a director and started her long climb in the bar to become, at last, the first female president of the Dallas Bar and later the first female president of the State Bar of Texas. Harriet had come to our women's law group right out of SMU Law school and we found it a great joy to support her every step of the way.

The EEOC was the greatest tool women ever had to demand and receive the right for employment opportunities and advancement. Our organization was able to use it effectively to prove, again, as Margaret Mead put it: "Never doubt that a small group of thoughtful, committed citizens can change the world; indeed, it's the only thing that ever has."

15

Beyond the Borders

WHAT WE HAD BEGUN TO ACCOMPLISH in the State of Texas with the Marital Property Act and the beginning of a code of laws dealing with family issues created a ripple effect throughout the nation. Every couple of years or so we'd get another segment of the Family Code through the legislature. Sometimes it was like taking two steps forward and one step back because our laws are eternally tampered with, altered, changed, tossed out, reenacted. Law is a living body of principles that create the structure under which we all live, and as such must respond to the needs of changing times, but sometimes we tamper with laws just for the sake of change. Every two years when the legislature gets through with its work, Texas lawyers practice under different statutes. Sometimes it's maddening.

But by far the most far-reaching crisis has been in creating a body of laws that spans boundaries. Laws created and applied in the separate states during an era when people often lived their entire lives without going far from where they were born served the populace well. But in a day when travel from one part of the world to another is not only easy but commonplace, laws that apply across state boundaries are increasingly imperative. Farsighted leaders in the American Bar Association understood this, and I was tapped to create the first committee to study and report on family law in the fifty states. The enthusiasm with which I began the work quickly evaporated. In the climate that prevailed in the 1960s, there was simply no place to begin. No common ground, no communication, and no desire to create any. Each state held tightly to its own autonomy. Support for "States' Rights" was pervasive, and there was little understanding that the shrinking world demanded reciprocal laws.

But while I was it, I had some good times that opened avenues for service in other directions.

The American Bar Association was as reluctant as the Texas Bar to elect women to positions of leadership. Neva Talley had been secretary of ABA's Family Law Section for seven years. She wanted to advance to vice chairman and then chairman, but was always skipped over. In 1969, I determined to see that she got elected. The ABA Family Law business meetings were run by a small group of hand-picked lawyers, and the nominees for office were not announced until the chairman read the slate at the meeting. Many delegates did not even bother to attend the business meetings. So, I alerted every woman lawyer that she must show up to vote for Neva. Quietly, they filed in and took their places: so many women turned up that we could have elected Minnie Mouse to office had we so desired, but we lost our chance to be rebels. The nominating committee had learned about our plot and put Neva on its slate! She was elected without opposition, the first woman to be named chairperson of ABA's Family Law Section. Later, I would follow.

In 1971, the American Bar met in both New York and London. Grier and I bought three tickets for the London leg of the trip. Tom had married Janice Savage and was graduating from law school, and we wanted to give our son and his bride a trip to Europe as a wedding present. I suggested that Grier, Tom, and Janice take our three tickets because I would be attending meetings in New York and was not even sure I would be able to make the European meetings because of health problems. We concluded our sessions in New York four days before the charter flight with my husband, son, and daughter-in-law on board was to leave from Houston. By that time, I knew I wanted to go on to London, so I checked around and found a fabulous price on round-trip tickets on Icelandic Airlines.

My flight landed in Glasgow, Scotland, and I took a train from there
to Edinburgh.

My trip was absolutely delightful. I found a travelers' aid bureau
at the railway station. I know they looked at this little old lady in
tennis shoes out traveling all alone without the slightest idea how to
take care of herself and came to my rescue. I found a bed and breakfast on the third floor near Princess Street, right in the middle of
downtown Edinburgh, and had three glorious days in Scotland for
only $3 per day, which included room and breakfast. The best bar-
gain of my life.

Then I caught the train that took me to London, where hotel
rates reserved by the ABA were prohibitive for our budget. I found
another hotel right in the middle of London with two big rooms. As
an official delegate, I got to go to Westminster Abbey for the opening ceremonies of the ABA with all the pomp of the lords in their
curly wigs. Grier and I both got to go to the queen's tea.

After the convention ended, Grier and I flew to Scandinavia, to
Copenhagen, and on to Norway. For me, the most wonderful part of
the trip was going into Sweden, where we stopped at Malmo, my
maternal grandmother's native village, and to the church where she
was baptized. It was a pilgrimage that allowed me for the first time
to understand my Swedish grandmother, who never got over her
longing to go home.

Grier and I parted in Hamburg and he went to Amsterdam to
reunite with the Texas charter. I went to Luxembourg, where I found
a special flight that allowed me to stop over in Reykjavik and tour
the city before returning to the States.

On the flight back to New York a businessman was sitting across
from me and we introduced ourselves. I admitted that I was not
accustomed to flying overseas and was a bit leery of going through
customs. He told me to find a line with the oldest people in it and
stand in that line. He said customs agents traditionally looked very
quickly through the luggage of older people, but often took apart the
luggage of youngsters. That seemed very reasonable to me and I
thanked him. Later, I was counting my money to see if I could afford
a night in a New York hotel, in case I could not get a connecting

flight to Dallas. My new friend noticed and asked if I was short on money, and I said, "Well, if I have to find a hotel in New York, I surely will be." He handed me a hundred-dollar bill and his card, and said, "Send me a check when you get back to Dallas. You don't need to be short on cash in New York City."

I had never seen that man before and have not seen him since, but it was another lesson in human generosity. As it turned out, I got through customs in a few minutes and found out I could get a flight back to Dallas that night. I didn't need the hundred dollars, but what a comfort it was to have it! The first thing I did when I got to my office was write a check and a thank-you letter to my "savior."

I'M ESPECIALLY PROUD of the people I involved in the Family Law Section of the American Bar, many of whom later became the leaders of the entire bar, people like Leonard Loeb, who would become chairman of the section of the American Academy of Matrimonial Lawyers and a governor of ABA; Mike Albano and Sam Schoonmaker, both of whom later became chairmen of the Section; and Tom Cochran, my favorite parliamentarian. Sometimes, working in that section was like a shoot-out at the O.K. Corral, with the old guard resisting everything. I was often beaten and bloody, but I also succeeded. New people were elected and the Section headed off into a fine new direction. Along the way, a couple of the old guard charged that I had bankrupted the Section and ripped apart my spring program. The truth was that we had $35,000 left in the account at the end of the year but ABA finances were so screwed up that nobody knew this. From one day to the next, I considered resigning, but could never bring myself to do it because if I left office, it would look like I had done something wrong, and I knew I hadn't. Henry Foster, a very distinguished family law authority from New York University, criticized everything I did, but when he followed me as chairperson of the Family Law Section, he made not a single change in the committee structure I had set up. Professor Foster, along with my good friend Doris Jonas Freed, authored many volumes of family law books and treatises and both were widely recognized as outstanding authorities on family law in the United States. Foster got the credit, but it was Doris who did most of the work on those books.

I continued to be active in the Family Law Section of ABA because my youngest son, Kenneth, had become interested and was on the council as the law student representative from the University of Texas. Following graduation from law school, he was the young lawyer representative, and following that was elected to the council for two terms. There followed such a jockeying for leadership that Ken dropped out. When finances got so bad that the ABA was threatening to take over the Family Law Section business, Harvey Golden, the chairman, asked Ken to take over as financial officer. Ken mastered the ABA way of accounting, unraveled the financial mess, and whipped the Section back into financial shape. He was then elected secretary of the Section, then vice chair, and finally became chair in 1991–1992. So far, we are the only mother-son leaders of the Section.

During all this time I remained active in order to support my son, but when his term ended in 1992, I was ready to do other things.

I never dropped my responsibilities to the Texas Bar, where I felt I could make the most enduring impact. In 1978, I ran for bar director and was defeated. The man who defeated me did such a miserable job that the next year the Dallas hierarchy supported me and I won with no opposition. So it was that in 1979 I became the first woman ever to be elected a director of the State Bar of Texas.

My election precipitated several amusing incidents.

The staff and directors were not accustomed to having a woman on board, so when Grier and I went to our first meeting, they had made no plans to have a woman as director and her husband as the spouse, since until that time it had always been the other way around. As was customary, we first enjoyed a social hour together and then adjourned for the board meeting. The spouses traditionally went off to socialize in another area. Everybody kept trying to get me to join the wives until it finally dawned on them that I was the director and my handsome husband was the spouse. It was both embarrassing and amusing as they pushed and prodded us into our separate directions. Grier, bless his heart, found it very funny and, I have no doubt, charmed every "spouse" in the room in his new role as the "significant other."

It was also the custom that when new board members met for the first time with old members, the new members were presented with a token gift from the outgoing members. I duly got my present—a set of gold cufflinks with the seal of the State Bar on them. It was clear that nobody had thought of an appropriate token for a woman board member. I graciously accepted the cufflinks with no mention of the fact that I had no shirt on which to wear them. At the party ending the board meeting, I wore a low-cut gown. My jewelry was a thin gold chain prominently displaying my new gold cufflinks. This drew a lot of attention and comment, but I played it innocent all the way, batting my eyes and explaining that I wore the cufflinks as a necklace because they were my first present as a director of the State Bar of Texas. Within a couple of months a new present arrived, a gold pendant with the State Bar insignia. I loved it, I kept it, but I did not give back my gold cufflinks. They were my badge of acceptance. My key to the future for all women.

Directors of the State Bar in all official business settings were addressed as "Gentlemen." The speaker would say, "Gentlemen," and then look around and add, "And Mrs. Raggio." That obviously gave me too much clout! To be singled out as one among many was not what anybody had in mind. The guys, my fellow board members, finally handled this awkward situation by officially proclaiming me a "gentleman." I did not protest. It was by far better than most things they may have called me.

I thoroughly enjoyed my tenure as a director of the State Bar of Texas. I worked very hard at it and all the jobs assigned to me. Grier was a great sport. He never acted as if he resented being the "other" spouse in a roomful of women. The wives were wonderful, too; they'd never before had a husband as a member of their auxiliary and they made Grier feel very special. What they thought in private they kept to themselves as my tall, good-looking, charming husband went off to style shows, luncheons, cosmetics shows, and antique shopping. The women loved him; how could they have not! They thought he was the greatest thing that ever came down the pike. He even helped them to plan their parties. They would meet me and say, "Do you know what a wonderful husband you have?"

I would think, if you only knew the rest of the story. But, of course, I never said that.

Along with my bar activities, both State and National, I never forgot that I was first and foremost a wife, a mother, and now a grandmother, as well as a community citizen obligated to respond to the best of my ability as a concerned, committed individual in my own arena. As a result, I was often asked to make speeches.

In 1972 I was a speaker for a major women's event in Fayetteville, Arkansas, at which Martha Griffiths was the keynoter. A Congresswoman from Michigan, she had resurrected the national Equal Rights Amendment from obscurity and reintroduced it in Congress. I was honored to appear on the same stage with her. Even though the national ERA did not pass Congress, Martha and the women in Congress whittled away at the inequalities facing women, just as we had with our separate statutes in Texas, until almost all of them became illegal.

Because I had not stood up and waved the banner for the Texas Equal Legal Rights Amendment, I have been accused by some ERA opponents of "selling out," of being opposed to equality of human rights. Nothing could be further from the truth. There are ways of doing things, and ways of doing things. And, in my long association with human and political rights issues, I have learned that sure defeat is certain when things are not done appropriately.

My way of being sure that equal rights would work was to put the statutes in place first. Ben Barnes, who then was Speaker of the House, and I worked out a deal. I would speak against the Equal Rights Amendment, which was doomed for defeat by the legislature, calling it "premature," and he would do everything in his power to see that the statutes were enacted. He was as good as his word. Once those statutes were made into law, the Equal Rights Amendment breezed through the legislature in 1971. I was one of its strongest supporters, and it became a part of the Texas constitution in 1972. I am grateful that we now have the Equal Rights Amendment because it helps to guarantee that the framework for which we worked so long and hard is stable and will hold.

In the 1970s, the governor of Texas created a Texas Commission on the Status of Women and named me, along with dozens of other women, to the commission. From Dallas, Sarah Hughes and Mary Kay Ash and Vivian Castleberry were members. We had an executive secretary in Austin, but very little funding. I was elected secretary of the group. In those days, it was politically appropriate for officials to *appear* to favor equality for women. The men thought they could throw us a carrot and we'd go away satisfied that we'd had a whole meal, but we thought different. Even though most of us understood the Commission was only window dressing, we worked hard, captured some headlines, and served as another opening wedge for women's rights.

At the end of my middle year on the state board of directors, Wayne Fisher, then president of the State Bar, asked me if I would serve as liaison from the board of trustees to the Texas Bar Foundation. Had I ever declined a challenge? Of course, I would.

As a State Bar director, I had worked for a couple of years with Evelyn Avant, executive secretary of the board, to create a procedures manual for the State Bar of Texas, which was adopted at the end of my second year on the Bar board. When I walked into the meeting of the trustees of the Bar Foundation, as the liaison from the Bar board, Frank Baker, then chairman of the board of trustees of the Bar Foundation, stopped me to ask if I would create a procedures manual for the Texas Bar Foundation. I went to work. We (meaning mostly "I") put together a loose-leaf booklet so that changes could easily be made, new pages added or deleted, new sections slipped in without having to reprint the entire manual.

At the end of my term as liaison between the State Board of Directors and the Bar Foundation, I was elected a trustee of the Bar Foundation, its first female member, and began what has been my most enjoyable legal work. In this role, I have contributed my best work to the Bar. At the time I became a trustee, the Foundation corpus stood at $750,000 and quarterly meetings lasted for four hours, from 10 A.M until 2 P.M., and consisted mostly of lawyers exchanging wild and woolly tales of their latest legal escapades. We almost never got down to any real business until it was almost time to adjourn. I was appalled. With so many things to be done, I considered this a colossal waste of time. None of the trustees seemed to have any concept of the potential of our organization. I started to make notes and plant ideas and gently presented them to my associates. Together we began to talk about what the Bar Foundation could accomplish.

Small ideas reaped great benefits. We put together a think tank at Columbia Lakes near Houston, where for three days the board of trustees and some former members of the board exchanged ideas. We broke up on a Sunday morning pledging to make the Foundation a potent arm of the Bar. Our first objective was to conduct a fund drive to raise money to carry out other plans.

In the spring of 1984, I was elected chairman of the Bar Foundation in a contested election. Some of the men were still not willing to entrust leadership to a woman. My election gave me the clout to carry out further progressive ideas.

I could do a lot of things without asking permission from the board. Most significant was communication. It was not surprising that we had wasted a lot of time in meetings because we'd never had a planned agenda. I started communicating with the men. An informal, personal letter or note works wonders. I remembered to tell them how much I appreciated their time and effort. I sent out newsletters. We asked for time on the program at the black-tie dinner that opened the State Bar meeting each year to give a report on the Foundation and request feedback.

I got the consent of the board to invite all the Fellows to a meeting in Austin so that each could tell what the Bar Foundation meant and what it should be doing. I argued that if only twenty-five showed up to dialogue and exchange ideas, it would help us chart the direction for the future of the Foundation. We arranged for the Bar headquarters, set a date, and sent out invitations.

We planned for twenty-five, fifty at the very most. One hundred and fifty lawyers showed up! They paid their own expenses and came from all over the state, eager to talk, enthusiastic that they had been asked. The small group planning the event, including me, was in a panic. We knew that good results were possible only if the discussion groups were kept small. Where on earth were we to put one hundred fifty lawyers in separate groups of ten or twelve? We put them everywhere—in the basement, in the hallways, throughout the unfinished sixth floor. We met altogether for some talk and direction, and then broke into small groups and came back together at the end of the meeting for reports from all.

I have never chaired such a successful meeting as this one. The men were enthusiastic and full of ideas. They gave us our marching orders, an agenda both full and rich. In that one session, they came up with programs and projects that would have taken us ten years to accomplish. It was a great experience and set an entirely new tone and direction for the Bar Foundation.

LIFE HAS A WAY of delivering the bitter with the sweet, and so it was in my personal life. I had lost my father in 1971—a direct result of his kindness to animals. It is not at all unusual for city folks to take animals they no longer want to the country and turn them loose, so strays often found the farm. One Sunday, a dog with a rope around its neck wandered into the yard. Dad was trying to remove the rope because he knew it might catch on something and trap the poor animal. Doubtless the dog had been badly abused because he was terrified and started to run. The rope got wrapped around Dad's legs and pulled him to the ground; the jolt knocked him out. Two of my sons and a daughter-in-law had driven up for a visit just about the time this happened and called me. Dad was eighty-six and had a history of high blood pressure and heart trouble, so I insisted that he be taken to the hospital in Elgin and kept overnight for observation. Late on the afternoon of September 26, 1971, he had a massive heart attack and died.

Men from the entire countryside came to sit at the funeral home all day. One said, "We just want to be with Louie; he was always there for us."

Now, in 1984, my mother's life was winding down. My mother! The most significant, important, inspiring, challenging individual in my early life, and the most courageous, critical, compelling person in my later years. I could not imagine life without her even as I accepted the inevitable and made plans for her leaving me. She had been her usual most competent and independent self throughout most of her life. She understood when it was time for her to leave the home in which she and Dad had lived together, and where they had reared me, until she was into her early nineties. Then, without "permission" or even counseling with me, she put herself into a Lutheran retirement home in Round Rock where she continued, for some time, to be in charge of her life—and, often, of mine.

When she was ninety-seven, Mother's years began to take their toll. She became more sedentary, had moments of memory lapse. As long as she was interested at all, I kept up the family home and took her often. After she moved into the Lutheran facility, I visited her as often as I could, at least once a month, and more often when I thought I should or when she pressured me to do so, but as her memory faded, she accused me of never coming. When I reminded her that I had been there only a few days before, she swore that I made it up. The home provided wheelchairs for its patients, but in August 1984 the director told me Mother needed a better one than the home could provide, and I immediately saw that she got the best. I wish I hadn't. Mother took one look at that chair, complete with every gadget I could find to make her life easier, and decided that she was now obsolete. She took it as the moment when her life was in decline. From August until December she deliberately tried to die.

Through all the days I was running the conference in Austin, my mother was letting go. She died three weeks after I chaired the Texas Bar Foundation symposium in Austin. I'll never know how I survived through those terrible days while running back and forth between Elgin and Round Rock and Austin and Dallas. On the day before the symposium opened, I went to Elgin and made funeral arrangements, picked out the casket, and the pink dress that would be my mother's burial shroud. I did all of this by rote—as she had trained me, as I had trained myself, the way life had conditioned me to behave.

Mother had lived a long and wonderful life. She died on December 24, 1984, at age ninety-eight, four days before her ninety-ninth birthday.

I survived. I have always been a survivor. My mother would have expected nothing less of me.

I WAS FOLLOWED as chair of the Texas Bar Foundation by a very fine lawyer, David Beck of Houston, who continued to carry out the vision and the work of the Foundation. Increasingly, excellent lawyers responded with appreciation and humility when asked to become a member of the Foundation. Since 1965, the Texas Bar Foundation has returned $4.2 million to the community in grants to support the administration of justice; legal assistance to the needy; education of the public about the law; ethics and the profession; and legal research, publications, and forums. Only earnings from the endowment may be expended for grants and these have grown tremendously through the years. The endowment is now approximately $13 million.

We were followed in leadership by a strange group of men who, to this day, I do not understand. Two leaders in a row did their best to sabotage the progress we had made. This is not my opinion only, but was confirmed by the defeat of one of these Bar "leaders" when he ran for president of the Texas Bar Association. Some people have great difficulty acting on any idea not their own and often do everything possible to see that it fails. So it was with these two guys.

But despite a few missteps, the Bar Foundation moved upward and onward. I remained active, either on a committee or in an advisory capacity. In 1992 I became secretary of the Fellows, then vice chair, and in 1993 and 1994 chairman of the Fellows, and I am still an active member.

16

Out of the Depths

WHEN YOUNG PEOPLE LOOK AT ME and women of my age, they see a finished product and most likely have no idea of the struggles and setbacks that have brought us to this point in our lives.

And, unless we love wallowing in our mishaps or having attention focused on us for overcoming unbelievable odds, or becoming martyrs who try to force our families to lavish more attention on us, we forget, make a joke of, or conveniently overlook impediments to our progress.

I abhor martyrdom. I've had a small taste of it with my own mother and seen enough of it in my law practice that I shun all possibilities of hypochondria. If I have health problems, I try to get the best professional help to overcome them and to live as creatively as possible with the limitations I cannot heal. And if I have problems in my family life or my professional life, I follow the same policy. This attitude is rooted both in my genes and my conditioning. I've always thought there's a lot of truth in the saying "If you make your bed, you have to lie in it," so I've done my best to live comfortably with what happens to my body and with the decisions I make.

Sometimes the journey through life has been lonely.

And so it is that I share these personal glimpses of my life, not to seek or expect sympathy, but in part to let young women know that none of us escapes trouble in our lives.

As a premature baby, I didn't have the healthiest start in the world, and it was only when I had children of my own that I understood my mother's overprotectiveness. My world was populated with dozens of cousins, but I had few friends outside the family, and even in the family, as close as we were, we seldom had sleepovers. At night we went home to our own beds.

I had the usual childhood illnesses—whooping cough, typhoid fever, and pneumonia—all of which were far more serious then than they later became when new medicines and vaccines made them far less life-threatening. Susceptible to colds and sore throats, I had a tonsillectomy when I was three. At that time there was a virtual epidemic of tonsillectomies; they were the "in" thing to have done. Through the years, I have observed with interest children's "fashionable" illnesses and the sometimes drastic solutions. When I was a child, doctors enjoyed something of a godlike image, and it took determined parents to hold off on a procedure when the doctor suggested it as a remedy for their children's illnesses.

I have no idea whether or not I needed to have my tonsils removed, but removed they were, and as small as I was I remember the trauma associated with surgery. The worst part was they didn't stay removed. When I was in high school I had a second tonsillectomy.

When I was in the eighth grade, I had neck surgery. A lymph gland swelled and got infected. When home remedies failed, my parents put me in the hospital. Still the infection could not be controlled, and my entire system was poisoned so badly that my kidneys and other vital organs shut down. I was listed as "critical" when they cut a gash in my neck and inserted tubes to drain the poison. Periodically a nurse came in to wash the wound, a very painful procedure. I remember vividly the whispering that went on between my mother and the relatives who came to visit. I was not expected to recover.

After high school, the sickly child blossomed with good health and I had nothing more troubling than colds or the flu until I had a tubal ligation after Kenneth was born.

Then, as my law practice was taking off and my Bar work increasing, I was battling another illness.

Beginning in the early 1960s, Grier and I, who had always vaca-
tioned separately, finally could spare the time and find the money for
a long weekend together now and then. We always went to Mexico
because we could do it on a financial shoestring. Tom and Kathy
Green, friends from our Mustang Village days, lived in Mexico, first
in Mexico City and later in Puebla. We'd go to their house and then
fan out with them to see all of the local sights. Every time I went to
Mexico, no matter how careful I was, I'd get sick. In January 1966,
we visited Tom and Kathy for a week and I came home with the
most horrible dysentery of my life. The doctor prescribed one medication after another. Nothing helped. I'd seem to be a little better,
then my fever would shoot up and my insides give up. I lost weight,
and was down to a little less than a hundred pounds.

Dr. Jabez Galt could not figure out what was wrong with me.
Three months after my initial bout, in March of '66, I entered Epis-
copal Hospital and was there for a week while every known test
was done. They all came back negative. Nothing was wrong with
me. The doctor ordered that I stay at home and rest, this at a time
when I was chairing the Family Law Section and trying to raise
money for the Family Code project. I did stay home for three
months, but I had to use the telephone and get out my correspondence, and I could not let anyone know that I was ill. I was
absolutely miserable. The pictures taken of me in July at the Bar
convention show a gaunt and drawn individual.

Slowly, with no further medication and no other help, I began to
mend. I went back to work part-time and then full-time and I continued to take on more and more responsibility. I got by with it,
pushing myself all the way, for a little better than a year, and in February 1968 the black despair hit me again. By that time I knew
what was wrong with me. I was suffering from depression, an illness
that nobody had mentioned earlier.

Not only had I read and studied about depression, learning
about symptoms almost identical to my own, but I had probated an
estate for the mother of Dr. Claude Nichols, who was a psychiatrist
on the faculty at Southwestern Medical School. I went to see him.
He took one look at me and confirmed that I was in a depression.
He prescribed medication. I continued to see him once a week for

about three months. He probed into my background, my rearing, my relationship with my mother, with my dad, my eating habits, my potty training, the whole routine that circumscribed psychiatric treatment at the time. I knew I wasn't "cured," but I also knew I couldn't waste any more time wallowing in my past, so after three months, I declared myself well and left treatment.

So little was known then about depression. The public and many doctors confused it with mental illness. Even though I knew better, I also confused my illness with personal weakness, so I told nobody. I swore my husband and sons to secrecy about my condition. My law practice would have suffered immeasurably, maybe even have evaporated entirely if it had gotten out that I was depressed. Today there are volumes of material on depression; it is one of the most common known illnesses, and there are countless treatments for it, but at that time there was very little. Only Grier, Grier Jr., Tom, and Kenneth knew about it. I did not tell my mother or any other member of my family, and I did not have a single friend in whom I could confide.

Every year for the next eight years, from 1969 through 1976, basically the same thing happened to me. I would begin to feel incompetent, helpless, hopeless. Each time I knew what was happening and returned to Dr. Nichols. He would give me medication. I would come out of it and swear that it would never happen again. Each year as I began to get well, I told myself I was stupid, that something was deficient in me, that if I only had enough fortitude, I could pull myself out of it.

I had no clue about what was really happening in my body and how my body and mind connected. Nobody told me that a receptor in my brain was firing incorrectly. We knew nothing then about chemical imbalances as a cause of depression.

In the depths of each episode, I lost interest in everything and felt I didn't have enough sense to push an elevator button. Dr. Nichols was wonderful. He kept telling me I had so much talent, so much ability, and I must not stop. He was insistent that I not sit and rest and do nothing, even when all I wanted was his permission to do the only thing I really wanted to do—go to bed, pull the covers over my head, and die.

But he also told me that there was a strong possibility I would suffer bouts of depression for the rest of my life.

I could not imagine living with this dark cloud hanging over me and I wished I could find a way out of life without it looking like suicide. The pain and anguish my family would suffer kept me from going over the brink. I remember one day walking in the heart of downtown Dallas on my way to a meeting, and praying that a building would collapse and crush me so that my husband and sons wouldn't have to endure the stigma of my committing suicide.

Grier, Tom, and Ken were wonderful; Grier Jr. was not in Dallas at the time. Kenny came home from school to take me on trips. I didn't want to go; I didn't want to do anything, but my family gave me no choice. Ken and I went down the east coast of Florida to Key West and back up the west coast, stopping at every tourist trap on the way, camping out at night in the van we had purchased. Another time, we took the van to West Virginia for an ABA meeting. Ken did everything possible to encourage me, to find things that interested me, to tempt me with food. He was all-caring and all-comforting— and I responded as best I could, but the moment the excitement ended, I was again on the brink of an abyss.

Tom also did more than his share to pull me through that awful time. From the time he graduated from UT until he married in May 1970, he lived at home. When I couldn't sleep, which was most of time, he'd walk me around the block at all hours of the night until I was so tired I'd literally crash and be able to sleep for a few hours.

Grier was just there for me. If I expressed the slightest desire, he rushed to fulfill my wishes. All three of the "boys" coddled and protected me, and together we'd get through another bout of the dreaded torment.

I was desperate. I resented those depressions so much. I was really ill for most of those eight years because the bouts lasted from a few weeks to a few months, and the rest of the year I was trying to recover from the last one and dreading the thought of another one. Even while I was making legal history with the work on the Marital Property Rights law and the Family Law Code, I was sick.

Finally I was able to confide in my long-term dear friend, Florence Eastman Myers. When I learned that her husband had been treated for depression in Veterans Administration hospitals in Waco and Dallas, I ventured to tell her my story. She said her husband had only momentary relief from his depression bouts with traditional treatment, so she had researched alternative treatments. When she heard about a homeopath in Mexico who had wonderful results with treating depression she decided to take her husband to him and insisted that I go there, too. Remembering the bouts of dysentery I suffered every time I went to Mexico, I told her no way.

One day Florence called and said that she had found a homeopath in New York. He was a graduate of the Medical School in Galveston, had studied homeopathy, and decided that was his calling. Since Texas did not license homeopaths, he opened his practice in Brewster, New York. I was resistant. At the time, I was in such a deep depression that I could make no plans at all. Grier Jr. was living in Manhattan and insisted that I come for a visit and try EST training. He thought that would help me. I felt sure nothing would, but since I wasn't in any condition to make decisions for myself, I let Grier Jr. and Florence make them for me. I signed up for the EST training in New York City and made an appointment with Dr. Jack Cooper in Brewster.

This was in July 1976. Ships were sailing up and down the Hudson River, a breathtaking panoramic view, commemorating the two-hundredth anniversary of the Declaration of Independence. I barely noticed.

I was totally negative when I took the train to Brewster. This, I told myself, was the most ridiculous thing I had ever done. But at least I could tell Florence I had tried her remedy and it didn't work.

I got to Dr. Cooper's office and he invited me in for a chat. He did not ask me to disrobe so that he could examine me. He never touched me. He did not take my blood pressure or my temperature. He just sat there looking pleasant and asking me the most stupid questions imaginable. He asked if I were right-handed or left-handed; in a roomful of people was I colder or hotter than most of the others, did I prefer foods that were sour or sweet, did I like a lot of salt or foods that were more bland? All the time he was questioning and listening, he was flipping through a set of cards.

Two hours passed. He finally said, "You're going to be fine. It's one of five remedies. I'm not sure which, but I'll start you on the most likely one. If it doesn't work, I'll give you something else." He gave me some tiny white pills and told me to put them under my tongue, which I dutifully did. He added that I was not to eat or drink anything for two hours and to let him know what happened. My session was over. He charged me thirty-five dollars.

I returned to the depot and got back on the train. The car was empty except for me, because everybody was leaving the city and the trains were returning empty. I put several of the little pills under my tongue and in a few minutes the strangest, most wonderful thing happened. I felt the depression lifting. It was like I was shedding a sweatshirt. I felt better than I'd felt in years! I started to cry and then to sing! I could make a fool of myself if I wanted to; there was nobody but me in the car.

I thought, Well, he's given me some kind of narcotic, and the depression will come back. It didn't. It never has. For a long time I kept looking around corners and over my shoulder dreading its return. A year later, still well and beginning to believe in miracles, I went back for a visit with Dr. Cooper and told him what had happened. He said it wasn't a miracle. We just hit it very lucky. He'd happened to give me the thing that triggered the proper reaction my brain needed to recharge and overcome the depression. He said my depression was likely triggered first by the illnesses I'd had in Mexico, that these bouts of dysentery and fever had depleted a chemical in my brain, and just because a doctor had been unable to find a parasite or an organism in my body did not mean it wasn't lurking there all the time. It just meant he wasn't able to find it. I recalled that the onset of each depression had been preceded by the flu or a cold, and he said that put a new stress on my body that caused my resistance to be so low that the bug or whatever it was caused the reaction in my brain.

I went back to see Dr. Cooper several times when I was in New York. He was mild-mannered and low-keyed and refused to believe he had worked miracles. He reiterated that I was one of the lucky people homeopathy had especially helped. Now deceased, he kept miserable records, so I don't know exactly what he gave me, either the name or the potency. Homeopathy worked wonders for me.

Since then I have read and studied a lot about homeopathy. I later found Dr. Joe Goldstrich in Dallas, who helped me through several problems.

This does not mean I use homeopathy instead of traditional medicine; I use it in addition to regular health checks with my medical doctors. I would much rather take a homeopathic remedy than antibiotics and other medications that are so overly prescribed. I believe in and practice good health measures. I do not smoke, do not use alcohol, and sleep eight hours a night by going to bed early and getting up early. I eat good food, cook for myself when I am not being entertained at some event, and I walk every day and swim when I can.

The quality of my life has never been better. I doubt that I would be alive today if I had not found some way to handle the depression. For the sake of others suffering from depression, and for their families who live in so much fear and anguish over their loved one's condition, I wish I could describe exactly what it's like to live with this evil. The best I can do is describe the symptoms and try to share my feelings. Some symptoms: Everything is exaggerated. The patient either wants to sleep all the time or cannot sleep at all. He or she talks nonstop, sometimes making no sense, or withdraws and does not communicate; has compelling sex drives or cannot tolerate sex; eats all the time or has no appetite; cries or shuns all emotional contacts. The feelings: The world stops. In a deep depression, we have no hope, no self-confidence, no ego, no enthusiasm, no ability to make decisions. The world is entirely dark and not a single good thing that has happened in our past appears to be worthwhile. With depression, we stand on the brink of a bottomless black pit and wish someone would give us a tiny shove.

And we are helpless to correct our malady without help. The good news is, *there is help*. I can tell when someone who walks into my office is suffering from depression, and I've suggested to more than one client or friend, *Get help*. I do not like to accept a client who is depressed because often the depression has created or exacerbated his problem. I want him to get well first. Living with depression is not living; it's existing in a chasm of torment.

I am astounded that I could have carried on my life and my

work during those years of depression, but I did. For being able to do so, I am indebted to the four men in my family who covered my tracks, and to doctors whose medication provided brief respites until I finally came up with something that worked, for it was not only during this period of time that so many good things were happening in Texas laws, but it was also the time that I first began to be my own, independent self.

I had been a dutiful daughter, an achieving student, a loyal employee, a faithful wife, a loving mother, a contributing lawyer, a dependable community volunteer. But I had never been myself.

Now it was my turn. I had passed the half century mark. It was time to explore other roles.

I had always believed in equal rights, but it would have been professional suicide to have appeared to be a "flaming liberal," because men held all the power. I had consistently downplayed feminism because I knew there was so much antagonism toward women and I could accomplish far more if men thought I was just a helpless dumb blonde. Most of the lawyers and the judges assumed that I was a secretary or a legal assistant until we got to court and they found out I was not only a lawyer, but a well-prepared one. This "innocence" was a ploy that worked well with my buddies at the district attorney's office, with state legislators, and with the fellows at the American Bar Association until I could earn my credentials and the respect of my associates.

It was time to "come out of the closet."

My first venture came when Emmie Baine asked me, among many other women in Dallas, to be on her advisory committee to plan a Symposium on the Education of Women for Social and Political Leadership. President Willis Tate of SMU had asked Mrs. Baine, Dean of Women, to "do something special for the women" to celebrate the university's fiftieth anniversary in 1966. She asked a group of us to meet and discuss possibilities. Across the nation women were clamoring for equal rights. There were organized protests in many American cities, but we knew that Dallas was not ready for a women's revolt. How innocent it was! We planned a three-day event run by women students that brought together students, community leaders, and faculty to hear nationally known keynote speakers and then break into small discussion groups and workshops to explore points that had been raised in the plenary sessions. The symposium was so well organized and so productive that it has continued for more than three decades, the longest-running university-sponsored program of its kind in the nation. It was the opening spark for a solid, inclusive, and comprehensive women's movement in our area that has been overwhelmingly successful.

I continued to remain pretty much in the background of the feminist movement, even while knowing that I very much enjoyed working with women and women's groups. The League of Women Voters in Austin and later in Dallas, the Women's Law Group, and the symposium committee proved to me that working with women was both enjoyable and rewarding, but both professionally and personally I lived in a man's world, still had work to do, and was not yet ready to call myself a feminist.

I was an evolutionary, not a revolutionary. I worked within the system to change the system, and I did it for the entire human family. Men, though they were slow to recognize it, had as much to gain from the new equality laws as did women.

Until the Family Code laws were enacted, men almost never were awarded custody of their children in contested cases. Unless there were drastic extenuating circumstances, the mother won the children. In the majority of the cases I believe this is appropriate—and that the mother should also get the financial support she needs to care for them. But in some cases fathers are the better parent of the two—and men need, and now have, the legal right to be granted custody.

Equal justice under the old laws was virtually nonexistent. Take the case of murder. When a woman committed a crime, she almost always received a lesser sentence than a man. "Protective" laws for women handicapped both males and females. We had this stupid law that women could work only so many hours a day. For this reason, jobs that required intense dedication for long periods of time were almost categorically denied to women, which meant that their chances of promotion were curtailed. Especially in two-career households, it also placed an added burden on the husband, who was expected to work whatever hours were required in order to get ahead. In reality, the law was usually ignored. Professional women—business owners and officers, physicians, lawyers, journalists, social workers, academicians, and many others—worked as long as was required to do a job, but should a woman become disgruntled and file suit, she had a good chance of winning against a company which "allowed" her to be at work extra hours.

When I went to work in the district attorney's office, for a lesser starting salary than any man, I was not even aware of the legal handicaps for working women. I was so glad to have a job—any kind of job—that discrimination never crossed my mind, and if it had, I would only have been frustrated because there were no laws to protect me.

My conscience was raised daily as I began working more and more with women and in women's groups. The stories of discrimination and abuse I heard would fill volumes. Every woman had her own story, and bits and pieces of their stories were also mine. I had personally borne the brunt of overt discrimination and sexism for all of my professional life. I became sick and tired of being treated like a fifth-class citizen. Although I never experienced any direct sexual harassment or discrimination in court, outside the courtroom was a different story.

The most flagrant sexual harassment episode I encountered took place in the offices of a highly respected attorney, a past president of the Dallas Bar. I was collecting for the Community Chest (later renamed United Way), and this man, whose offices were in downtown Dallas, was very cordial. He gave me a long spiel about how terrible it was that women were out in the workplace. He put his mother on a pedestal, he said, and was so grateful she didn't have to sully her hands in the workaday world, especially in the furor of a courtroom. He felt so sorry that I did! "I wouldn't let my wife work," he added. "I wouldn't tolerate having her put up with what goes on in the world." I felt worse and worse, didn't know what was coming next, couldn't insult the old duck, needed his donation to the city's leading charity.

Then he grabbed for me, and when I dodged, he started chasing me around the desk. I escaped to the foyer, my heart thudding. Here was a leading citizen of the city, a man whose name was in the papers almost every day, declaring that his mother and his wife were the flowers of womanhood, and not giving a hoot that I was also a wife *and* a mother. That incident firmed up my attitude toward men who said they wouldn't *let* their wives work, when in reality many of them had mistresses and didn't care what they did to women, either their wives or their other women. That man has been dead for many years, but I still shudder every time his name is mentioned. I never could have told Grier about it, or about any of the passes and suggestive remarks that came my way. He would have gone down and beaten the guy up—and that wouldn't have proved anything. There were no laws to protect women like me. I had to handle all of the harassment by myself.

Even as I share these memories, I must make it clear that most men were wonderful. Times were changing. Neither men nor women had the laws, customs, or attitudes to deal with them. They would come. And have come.

I live every day in gratitude that my granddaughters—and grandsons—live in a whole new era.

17

Keeping the Faith

PEOPLE OFTEN ASK what is the most important thing in my life. The answer is *my family*.

I am pleased to have been at a place at a time to change the laws of our state so that women have full legal equality. I am pleased that we were able to encode the first family laws in the United States, and quite possibly in the world, under my chairmanship. These are wonderful accomplishments that I had the privilege of helping to make happen and to share with all those who served on the committees, with whom I spent those long hours, who authored the legislation, and called on their friends to get the laws passed. I feel both highly honored and greatly humbled that these laws are in place.

But everything I did in my professional life would have meant very little to me if I could not, at the same time, point with pride to my family. These people—my husband, Grier; my son, Grier Jr., and his wife Lorraine, Grier's children, Julie, Bridget, and Greer Alicia; Tom and his wife Janice and their children, Stephen and Kristen; Kenneth and his wife Patricia and their children, Jeffrey and Michael—are the crowning achievement.

It is the simple things that give meaning to my life.

My marriage. I am glad I lived up to the commitment I made, was faithful as a wife, that Grier and I reached harmony and pleasure in the latter years of our marriage, and that I was able to take care of him at home in his final days.

My sons are all exceptional men. I have no favorite child, no favorite grandchild. Each moves in and out of my life responding to my needs and theirs. They are distinct individuals and I try always to reflect back to each his own strengths and not impose expectations of one upon the other.

I try never to compare.

Grier Jr. is most like my dad—caring and sensitive. He is a scholar. After an early failed marriage, he met Lorraine Albino, a brilliant banker who is now an attorney, and she became his partner and the love of his life. Their daughter, Greer Alicia, is a junior at Wake Forest. Because she spent so much time with me, his daughter Julie is the daughter I never had; she and her husband, Cameron Cover, are both physicians living in Washington, D.C. Bridget is a brilliant artist in New York.

Tom is Mr. Straight Arrow, the son who is a delightful surprise. In his teenage and young adult years, he walked to the beat of a different drummer and his dad and I despaired of ever getting him through college. Now he is the most conservative of my three sons. The first of the three to join Raggio & Raggio, he is the manager of the law firm. His wife, Janice Savage Raggio, a former merchandising executive, who now holds a real estate license, but has concentrated on rearing their son Stephen and their daughter Kristen. Stephen graduated magna cum laude in finance from Southern Methodist University, where he was a soccer star, and is now working toward his MBA at the University of Texas at Austin. Kristen was also a soccer star, but gave it up to concentrate on her studies and is a registered dietician living in San Diego.

Kenneth can take the most complex issue and simplify it. A computer buff, he lectures on computerizing law firms. He can fix anything. To help work his way through university and law school, he earned a plumber's license and hung that license alongside his law degree. He is married to Patricia Thornbury Raggio, a former teacher; they are parents of my two marvelous teenaged grandsons, Jeffrey and Michael.

We are a very unusual family. We all like each other! My pro-

fessional life has proved to me how unusual this is, for every day I
see riddled family relationships—parents who struggle with problem
kids; siblings who do not speak to each other; husbands and wives
who tear each other to shreds in bitter divorce cases, or at best live
together in bare tolerance of each other; young women who despise
their mothers-in-law, and mothers-in-law who demand priority in
the lives of their married sons and daughters, thus threatening the
relationships of these new, often fragile, families. This experience in
my professional life, together with coping with the animosity that
existed between my husband and my mother, has made it even more
imperative that I create a climate of mutual appreciation for every
member of the family. A warm and accepting place, a center of trust
and love exists in our home. Not that things have been perfect; they
never are. My husband's lifelong problems with his personal demons
often strained our marriage and our professional careers and threatened the bonds he felt but had trouble expressing with our sons.
And, sometimes, for reasons I do not understand, perhaps for their
own growth, a family member removes himself or herself from the
center of this mutuality, but this distance never destroys the center of
caring. The place of warmth and welcome remains and when the
time is right, individuals always return.

And it wasn't always easy to keep the family together. Countless
marriages that began in haste during those turbulent wartime years
in the 1940s came apart, but never—even in our most trying times—
did we consider divorce. Grier's early rearing—the absence of his
mother, neglect by his father, abuse by a stepmother—created a child
distrustful of intimate relationships and possessive with those who
were closest to him. His South Pacific war experiences erupted in
sleeplessness and nightmares for his entire life. Sometimes we would
be sitting quietly, talking or reading, and a word or phrase would
trigger an awful memory; I would see the curtain come down on my
husband's face and he would often get up and walk away in silence.
At those times I could not reach him no matter how hard I tried.
When something or someone threatened him or someone he cared
about, Grier often erupted into anger as if he had no control. I constantly compensated. Keeping the peace between him and my mother
was hard, and teaching the boys to overlook his flare-ups was

harder. At times, it was as if I had four children, and the grown-up one was by far the most difficult to handle.

For me, these bouts of anger and unpredictability in my husband were balanced by his love—and I never for one second doubted that he loved me—his intelligence, charm, charisma, courage, and continuing support.

In the early years of our marriage after we moved back to Dallas, we needed the support of my parents and they gave it willingly. Grier had no family at all that we could turn to for support. In the summertime, the boys spent a lot of time on the farm with Mother and Dad in charge. When I was too sick to care for my family, Mother came to look after us. On holidays and summer vacations, we always went to the farm. Not only did Mother expect it, but we had no money to travel anywhere else. Those occasions that should have been so very special were loaded with friction. When we were at my parents' home, Mother—sometimes in words, but more often by innuendo—let me know that I was not a good and dutiful daughter. She compared me unfavorably with my cousin, Jeannette, whose attention to her mother, my Aunt Hulda, was—at least in my mother's eyes—beyond reproach. Nothing I did or said measured up. She stressed Grier's shortcomings to me, sometimes in the presence of the boys. In our home she was a superlative manager, but she never let me forget that she disapproved of my husband. She thought the boys were being neglected because I worked and predicted that they become juvenile delinquents. It would have been all right, she said, if I'd become a teacher, but a lawyer?! She asked why I wanted to have children if I hadn't intended to stay at home and rear them.

Grier didn't help smooth the troubled waters. He and my father liked each other immensely and became great friends, but he and my mother established, at best, an uneasy truce.

Mother's disapproval of my marriage continued all the days of her life. After Grier was ill and none of us thought he would live to celebrate our fiftieth wedding anniversary, our sons and their wives threw a beautiful celebration for us on our fortieth anniversary. Mother came . . . and confided to some of my friends that the marriage had been a mistake and couldn't last!

Practicing law with Grier was not easy, either. Our styles were totally different. Grier could be trigger-happy in his interaction with other lawyers, and when he had a difficult client or a stressful case, I'd be in a state of nervous exhaustion until it was over. Grier had a brilliant mind, but he could pick a fight with a fencepost, and in his legal practice did many self-destructive things. He got into several fights at the courthouse. Once he was representing a woman in a divorce case. The attorney representing the man insisted on bringing out the most lurid sexual details of the couple's lives. Grier objected and was overruled. The opposing lawyer was shredding Grier's client with the language he used and the questions he asked. Grier got madder and madder. In the jury room the two squared off and Grier beat him up, tore his shirt and his suit. I felt humiliated, but Grier thought the guy had it coming to him and was reluctant even to apologize. The judge served as mediator and no charges were brought.

Grier got into real trouble when he had a fight with an attorney during another case. Major disagreements between the two erupted again in a jury room. The opposing attorney came out swinging. Grier ducked and retaliated with a solid blow to the guy's face, flattening him, breaking his cheekbones and his nose, and landing him in the hospital. We were sued in civil court and the bar grievance committee brought charges to disbar Grier. We fought the bar ruling, appealed it, and won. The civil law suit against us was dropped. Our lawyers' fees cost between $10,000 and $15,000 dollars. Grier's lack of control was far more painful for me than it ever seemed to be for him. I never knew what he might do next.

Partly in reaction, I became an overachiever. I was as methodical and careful in my practice as he was spontaneous in his. I got in as much affirmative community work as I possibly could manage, got appointed to all kinds of boards and committees. I was determined to be known as an ideal citizen in the hope that it might help to counterbalance Grier's erratic behavior. I was equally determined to be a model lawyer. I did not condone Grier's behavior, but I felt that the bar grievance committee had been unfair because there were no canons of ethics preventing a person from defending himself when someone else tried to hit him. It was not against the law to have private confrontations in the jury room in the courthouse. But I did not condone Grier's response. I vowed that I would get positions of bar leadership, partly because I wanted our little law firm to be powerful enough that we could not be kicked around.

Trying lawsuits with Grier was painful, again because our styles were so totally opposite. He was reputed to be "the best street fighter in the bar"; I'm not sure what mine was, and maybe I don't want to know! But I overprepared for my cases, listened to every word and every nuance, researched and briefed. Gradually, we became two separate lawyers accepting and working on different cases. So I went it alone, kept my own counsel, and learned to be a very good lawyer.

Grier was a man of enormous appetites. He loved good food, and, like a child, often indulged in forbidden sweets and fats. Diagnosed with high blood pressure, high cholesterol, and high triglycerides, he was advised by his doctor to eliminate fried foods, most sugar and salt, to eat lots of fresh fruits and vegetables, and to exercise regularly. I constantly struggled to fix things I knew he should eat and to make them as tempting and appetizing as possible. At about age sixty, he also developed diabetes. At that time there were very few guides to good nutrition, almost no recipes, and a limited number of food substitutes, so I experimented and managed to turn out meals that were attractive and tasted great. I learned to cook without salt, without sugar, to use corn oils and skim milk long before it was fashionable to do so. Grier would compliment me on the meal, then push back his chair and wander off to a fast food place for fried chicken or barbecue or a hamburger, and a candy bar or ice cream. He loved sweets and persistently and consistently did not watch his diet. Smoking was no problem. He had not smoked when we married, but took it up while he was in the Army and smoked a lot when he first got home from overseas. Around 1948 he quit cold turkey and never bought or smoked another cigarette.

Grier had always liked sex, and he could always find a good reason for us to have it. He was especially eager when we were away from home in a hotel. We'd be on a bar trip and as soon as we checked into our room, he was ready for us to go to bed. In 1976 we were in Boca Raton at a joint ABA Family Law and American Academy of Matrimonial Lawyers meeting. We'd had sex when we arrived and again after dinner when we went to bed. The next morning, Grier was eager for another session, but he could not get an erection. We laughed about it, joking that we never thought what we'd read about happening to other couples could happen to us! Later, during the same trip, we tried again, with the same results. We still joked about it, but both of us were concerned. Shortly after the trip, when the condition persisted, I insisted that Grier see his doctor. The physician laughed and said this was not at all unusual; it sometimes happened to men when they got older, to forget about it. Grier continued to make jokes, but I knew something was terribly wrong. I made an appointment with his doctor without telling Grier, and went alone to talk to him. I expressed my concerns and my fears. I told the doctor that I knew something was wrong because my husband's erections and ability to have sex had stopped overnight and something had to be blocking his system. The doctor dismissed my concerns. It happened to a lot of guys, he said. Don't worry about it and find other ways to express affection. Clueless about what to do next and determined not to nag Grier, I let it go and worried alone.

Two years later we found out the reason in an emergency that all but ended Grier's life.

It was Palm Sunday, 1978, and we were in church. Toward the end of the services, we were standing to sing when I glanced at Grier, who had turned a gray-green color. He whispered, "I don't feel well; let's get out of here." He leaned on me, and we slipped out. Two friends saw what was happening and followed us out. Grier tried to dismiss them, saying that we had to get home, but I knew something was terribly wrong. We took him to an adjoining room and made him lie down. One of the women called the medics and they were at the church within five minutes. In the meantime I had removed Grier's shoes, belt, and tie and had started to unbutton his shirt. He was protesting mightily. He said this was stupid! He just needed a little rest and he would be fine. The medical team that arrived was wonderful. They had radio contact with our city/county Parkland Hospital. They started blood pressure and other tests for a heart attack, and said they must stabilize him before they moved him. They worked with him for about thirty minutes on the floor of that room in the church and then took him by ambulance to St. Paul Hospital. I followed in the car, and stayed with him while they did tests. Nothing showed up. They said he had not had a heart attack. He said, "See, I told you! Now take me home," but I refused. I told him he must spend the night in the hospital where he could be watched. I took his clothes, his shoes, and his money with me when I left so that he couldn't escape.

When morning came, I was back at the hospital where follow-up tests showed that he had indeed had a heart attack. The doctors said it was slight. All he needed was remain in the hospital for a few days under observation and he would be fine. I was getting ready to bring him home the next day when he called me and said additional tests had discovered a lot more trouble than the doctors originally thought.

Within forty-eight hours he was in surgery. I called our sons. Grier Jr., still in New York, wanted to come down, but I said no. I wouldn't let Tom or Ken come, either. I wanted to be alone with my husband. I went with him as far as I could to the door of the operating room and then back to his room, where I sat alone for about an hour and a half. The nurses were very understanding. They left me in silence, as I insisted, sobbing out my anger and frustration at the doctor who had not done an examination to determine what was going on with Grier. Even the most perfunctory earlier tests should have indicated that something was wrong. When I stopped crying long enough to wash up and groom myself to wait for him to come out of surgery, I called Tom and Ken to come to the hospital. They were there almost before I hung up the phone.

Grier had eight bypasses. The doctor said the surgery had gone well. Eventually, after what seemed like a lifetime to me, he was wheeled down and placed in the intensive care unit. It was one of the most disturbing places I have ever been, for me a really horrible place. Bright lights shine all the time. All the patients are critically ill. There are all sorts of machines beeping all kinds of messages that I did not pretend to understand. Needles and tubes lead from patients to machines that keep them alive. Doctors and nurses are in constant attendance. We were allowed to see Grier for five minutes every two hours, only two at the time, so one or the other of us stood by every minute. I'm not sure I even would have recognized him on that first visit if I had not been coached. He did not know us. He did not respond to anything we said. Those five minutes were among the longest of my life as I stood and touched my husband, lightly rubbed his hand, and told him over and over and over that everything would be fine. On the second day, he opened his eyes briefly and I knew he recognized me, but there were so many tubes and needles attached to him that he couldn't move.

On the fourth day, the first time I had gone home to sleep after they declared him out of danger, I was awakened with a phone call from the hospital. They said it was an emergency. I called Ken and Tom and within minutes was dressed and on my way to the hospital, only seconds ahead of my two sons who had dropped everything and raced to meet me there. All three of us expected the worst. We were certain Grier had died, or at least was dying.

Not so.

I walked onto the floor of the intensive care unit to see my husband pacing down the corridor. He wore his little short hospital gown, and his red fanny, which they'd painted for some part of the surgical procedure, flashed with every step as he stumbled along, all hunched over, two or three nurses trailing behind him holding the intravenous bottles and wheeling the machines to which he was still attached. He was livid. They were distraught. He said he had stayed in that blankety-blank intensive care unit as long as he intended to and he was not going to stay there another minute. Together with the nurses, other medical attendants, and my sons, we got him back to bed. I went in for a conference with the doctor who said for the sake of the other patients in the intensive care unit and the rest of the medical personnel, they were going to transfer Grier to a private room. I suggested around-the-clock nurses. Instead, the doctor recommended that perhaps a family member could stay with him all the time. The nurses were aware of the medical problems. Doctors were on call all of the time. But a family member would recognize any and all emergencies and could call for help if it were needed.

Oh, joy! Now I had a husband, a borderline emergency patient, behaving like a brat—and I was supposed to be the final authority on his condition.

Grier Jr. arrived from New York. From 7 A.M. until 10 P.M. every day, either Grier Jr., Tom, or I kept vigil at Grier's bedside. Around 9 P.M. Grier got medicine to put him to sleep, the idea being that he needed as much rest as possible. Shortly before 10 P.M. Ken arrived to take the night shift, and stayed every night until one of the others of us got to the hospital the next morning. We never left Grier alone. He was not an easy patient!

After a week, I took Grier home where the four of us attended him constantly. As soon as he was sufficiently improved, other family members and friends started dropping by. We allowed him time to rest but not time to fall into a depression, which so often happens after surgery of his kind. For the most part, his temperament smoothed out but he always seemed angry at Kenneth. Finally I asked why and he blurted out, "Do you know, that son of mine *never* once came to see me while I was in the hospital!" I was astounded. Ken had been there every night. Because he arrived after Grier had gone to sleep and left before his father woke up in the morning, Grier did not recall seeing him. It took some convincing, but I finally proved to Grier's satisfaction that all of us had been at his side.

For the next six months, Grier and I faithfully followed the outlined program for his recovery. His blood pressure and heart were rate checked daily, then he would exercise and be rechecked. I was not involved in the medical part of the program, but walked with him every day. As long as I had him captive Grier had no choice but to eat the foods that were prescribed on his diet, and that I carefully prepared, but as soon as he was well enough, he'd sneak out and eat forbidden foods. His doctor and I had many conversations and agreed that we could only do so much; the rest was up to Grier.

Not long after he got out of the hospital, Grier began showing up at the office for brief periods almost daily, but his heart was not in the practice of law anymore. He decided and I concurred that instead of sitting in a rocking chair and being an invalid, he would live as normal a life as possible. Since we knew his time was limited, we decided to travel to some of the places we'd long talked about but had never had the time or the money to enjoy. As we planned yet another trip, he would joke, "If I die while we're on this trip, have me cremated and forget it." I knew it wouldn't be that easy, but his attitude helped to ease over the rough spots even when I knew he was in pain most of the time. When you care about someone, you suffer their misery right along with them.

Grier liked to take cruises, and we took a number of them, meant to be relaxing, but they were the most stressful form of travel for me. Rich foods prevailed at every meal and Grier did not even try to resist and I gave up trying to monitor his eating. Every time we returned home, his cholesterol and blood pressure would be off the charts.

A year after Grier's surgery, he talked to a lawyer from Chicago who had been to Romania for heart treatments, and convinced Grier that he must go to Bucharest to be treated by a world-renowned specialist there, who had perfected a new treatment. Grier's Dallas doctor did not condone the treatment, but knew that Grier would do what he wanted to do, so he gave us all the medical records and medication to thin his blood. We spent the night before our departure for Romania in Grier Jr.'s apartment in New York where Grier had a severe nose bleed. We got it stopped and didn't think much of it. The following day we flew to Athens, Greece, where we waited ten hours in a miserable airport before boarding the worst airplane I've ever been on to fly into Bucharest. Grier's seat was not securely bolted down, and in turbulence it flipped over and dumped him on the floor. We finally arrived at the Bucharest airport shortly before midnight.

The clinic was located in a hotel where we lived and had our meals while Grier was undergoing treatment. About 4 A.M. on the first night we were there, Grier started hemorrhaging from his nose. I called emergency and the doctors were with us in a matter of minutes, but they could not stop the flow and removed Grier to a hospital in downtown Bucharest where they finally got the bleeding under control. Grier was in bed for four days there, during which time the treatments we had gone to Bucharest to receive were started. Many of the patients were repeaters, a lot of them people who were trying to hang on to eternal youth. One extremely wealthy patient from Saudi Arabia tried to bribe Grier and me to go home with him. He thought Grier looked like Anthony Quinn, and he wanted to impress the folks back home that he had a famous friend. He said he was willing to pay any amount if we would only take him up on the invitation.

I had also signed up for health treatments in Bucharest, and I admit that my sessions at the clinic were among the most enjoyable of my life. I would start out in the morning with supervised exercise under a special instructor assigned to me. I had everything from mud baths to facials to the most wonderful massages. It was great. After a few days, Grier was allowed to exercise with the rest of us. Every kind of mechanical equipment imaginable was there for our use.

I am sure the treatment Grier received in Romania extended his life for several years, and I had never felt better than after my three weeks of treatment at the clinic.

When Grier's treatment ended, we left on an extended vacation in Europe, the most important and meaningful trip in our forty-seven years of marriage. Even though Grier was not physically well and had to rest a lot, he enjoyed it every bit as much as I did. For the first time over any prolonged period, the two of us were in harmony. I began to relax and enjoy myself without constant concern that Grier would erupt into frustration and anger. We talked to each other as we had not communicated since the days of our courtship. It was a period of falling in love again—and I'll treasure it all the days of my life.

If this was the best of our travels, our trip to China in 1975 was the worst. Grier had always wanted to go to China, so when the Texas Bar sponsored a trip, ostensibly a meeting between Texas lawyers and Chinese lawyers, we signed up. The trip was ill-planned, ill-directed, and almost altogether unsatisfactory.

As he came less and less to the office, Grier began to do some of the other things he had always longed to do. For several years he had repeatedly mentioned that he'd like to have a cottage or a lake house in the country. One Friday morning, he thought he'd found the answer to his dreams. A log cabin on top of a hill on several acres in East Texas was advertised for sale. He called; I drove—I almost always drove now—and we located the salesman, who took us to this dreamy log cabin. The house *was* on top of a hill surrounded by acreage, but then the bubble burst. It was a dark, dreary, unhappy place that gave me the creeps. The ad had also neglected to mention a sickening stench from a nearby pig farm.

As we left, Grier looked crestfallen, crouching in the seat like a little boy sucking his thumb! The day was still young and I insisted we spend it exploring other possibilities. We stopped in every little town and were shown one miserable place after another. Shortly after midafternoon, Grier said he was tired and wanted to go home. We were nearing Grand Saline and I said, "Let's try here. If nothing works, we will give up for today." We went into a real estate office and Grier described exactly what he wanted. The realtor said, yes, he thought he had the right place. He took us about five miles to a little cottage on a private lake. Grier and I both fell in love with it the minute we saw it. We had previously bought two houses—the one on Amherst and the one on Colgate in Dallas—both within fifteen minutes after we saw them. It was the same with this house. It took us less than fifteen minutes to know it was our place, and we were fortunate to get it for a wonderful price.

Grier really enjoyed the lake place. We added a large glassed-in living room with a big hearth where you could sit and look out at the lake while enjoying the warmth of a fire. We'd get up at daybreak, start a fire, and sit with our tea or coffee while looking out as the dawn came on and the sun peeped up. Awakening birds flying out over the lake made our reverie almost picture-perfect. We also worked very hard on the place. Grier put in a double gravel road, added two tool sheds, and a chain-link fence. We had a boat dock and a boat. Our grandchildren loved to come to the lake and fish. We bought geese and ducks; the ducks hatched several nests of ducklings and the kids really enjoyed them. We landscaped the place with peach, pear, plum, and fig trees, blackberry and dewberry bushes. We had a great vegetable garden, every kind of vegetable that grows in East Texas, including asparagus. We had an abundance of flowers. Grier had always loved red roses, so we started with rose bushes. We added gardenias with their waxy bushes and the most heavenly fragrance when they blossom. A nearby abandoned house was falling into decay, but had lots of flowering bulbs. Grier and I took big boxes and filled them with more than a thousand daffodil and iris bulbs of many varieties, all of which we replanted at our cottage. Everything flourished.

Grier would leave for the lake around Thursday and stay through the weekend. Unless I had bar business, I joined him on Saturday morning and spent the rest of the weekend there. Nothing in his life had ever afforded Grier so much pleasure as puttering, planting, and building on that little farm. He did so many things there he'd missed as a kid growing up without a family. Not long after we bought the place, we discovered that it was overgrown in places with poison ivy, so he bought a tractor and we worked at uprooting the plants until the acreage was clear and our grandchildren could run around in the woods without coming back with pesky rashes. We also shared the place with our family, friends, law associates, and clients. We had lots of family outings and dinners there. Our time at the lake together also afforded a change for the better in Grier's diet because he couldn't quite so easily sneak out for fats and sweets.

Back in Dallas, Grier started buying property, houses to fix up and rent. In all, he acquired twenty-three and spent most of his time in the city taking care of this extensive property.

DURING THE SUMMER OF 1987, Grier and I went to the State Bar meeting in Corpus Christi. After we registered and went to our room, Grier said he was not feeling well and wanted to rest. He thought he'd skip the opening luncheon, so I wandered downstairs alone to the room set up for the luncheon, the first person there. An executive committee meeting was being held in another room of the hotel, so I was alone and began to snoop around. Several plaques rested at the head table and I checked them out. Lo and behold! My name was on one of them—and it was the most prestigious one! I had won the President's Award. Awed and shaking, I hastily replaced the plaques and ran for the telephone. I said, "Grier, get your clothes on! I'm getting the President's Award—and I want you here!" If I had not been a snoop, I would have been given the most outstanding award of my lifetime with not a single family member or friend there to share the pleasure with me. Grier not only rallied to the occasion but was his charming best—and I, of course, have never been so surprised in my life as I was when my name was called!

The summer wore on, one of those hot, miserable Texas summers. Grier complained of arthritis and his doctor altered his medication. We'd enjoyed nine good years since his heart surgery, and then one early morning in August, somewhere between 4 and 5 A.M., I was awakened by a slight noise coming from the bathroom. When I eased the door open, the place looked like there had been an ax murder. Grier was bleeding from his mouth and his nose. There was blood all over the place. I called his doctor and told him I was calling an ambulance. He said not to wait for an ambulance to get Grier in the car and get him to the emergency room at St. Paul's. Somehow I got him in the car, and broke all speed limits getting him to the hospital, where everybody was waiting for us. He was put in intensive care and tests were started. Within a short time they had the verdict: the new medication had eaten a hole in his stomach. They kept him in the hospital until the crisis had passed and he was on his way to recovery.

But Grier never snapped back. We tried everything. I talked to doctors about a possible heart transplant. They shook their heads. With diabetes, which he developed in the late sixties, high blood pressure, and his general deteriorating condition, they said Grier would probably not survive surgery even if a new heart could be found. We tried everything possible, with no noticeable improvement. Slowly, one day at a time, I accepted the truth—that my husband was terminally ill. Our sons thought otherwise. When I tried to tell Ken and Tom—Grier Jr. was still in New York—about the doctor's diagnosis, they would not believe it. They insisted on another opinion, so in January Grier saw a new set of doctors at Medical City Hospital. Their diagnoses were the same: Grier had but a few months to live. He had always been such a fighter. He had beaten so many odds in his life. Intellectually, the boys knew their father was not invincible, but emotionally, they were convinced that he could and would beat this illness, too. We were in a little room together—Tom, Ken, and I—and I shall never forget the meeting with the doctors when our sons realized that their father did not have long to live.

We had a family conference and decided to take Grier home, surround him with our presence and love, and make him as comfortable as possible. He had always so hated hospitals.

Tom and Janice took the responsibility of turning our downstairs office into a bedroom for a very sick man. They bought bedroom furniture, rugs, and the needed hospital paraphernalia—a hospital bed, oxygen equipment, a commode, everything they could think of to make his life as easy as possible. We brought him home from the hospital in January. Grier Jr. arrived from New York. Janice found a service where women came and stayed for a week at a time. Toward the end we had nurses with him twenty-four hours a day. Tom and Janice, Ken and Patty, Grier Jr. and I took turns being at his every beck and call. Our friends and all the neighbors were wonderful. Our granddaughter Bridget, who had always felt especially close to her grandfather, came from New York. She thought that if she came, Grier would get well. She stayed about three weeks until we persuaded her that she must go back home. I told her the greatest gift she could give her grandfather would be to go back to school so that she could graduate in June with her class. There was nothing we could do for Grier except to keep him as free of pain as possible. His attitude was formidable. On Easter Sunday, he gathered his strength and we went to Ken's house to watch the kids hunt Easter eggs.

Grier wanted me to continue to practice law, so to keep my sanity I checked into the office almost every day. When he would not take his medicine or when special attention was required, I was always on call and could do more with Grier than anybody else. We eased into a schedule of sorts. Unless a real emergency developed, I would go to my room and rest, and hopefully sleep, from 10 P.M. until 4 A.M., when I'd get up and go curl around Grier in his bed. He was always quieter when I was next to him and he'd relax and rest.

His humor was resilient. On the day before he died, two nurses and I were on his bed trying to turn him when he got this grin on his face and said, "This is wonderful. All my life I've had this fantasy of being in bed with three women at the same time."

A week after Easter, on April 10, 1988, nine days before our forty-seventh wedding anniversary, Grier smiled, closed his eyes, and stopped breathing.

A life had ended.

Another chapter of my life was about to begin. But it would take time.

18

Future Unlimited

I WAS COMPLETELY WORN OUT after Grier died. For many years my every thought had begun and ended with his welfare. I had been running on automatic for so long that I had to learn how to handle myself in a world where every second was not scheduled.

We had a beautiful, upbeat memorial service for Grier in the sanctuary at the Unitarian Church on the Friday following his death. We honored a life that had been well lived and resilient to the end.

For a while I let myself vegetate. The lake place where we'd had the happiest days of our marriage was the one place I simply couldn't go. I'd cry every time I entered the house, so before long I sold it just as it was—all the furnishings, kitchen equipment, dishes, furniture, pictures, TV, all the farm equipment—everything. I went back twice to pick up a few personal possessions and then just walked out because I could not bear the memories that flooded me there.

A few times I felt as if I were slipping back into the old depression and it scared me so that I made an appointment with my homeopathist. He said it was not depression, but deep grief, and he gave me homeopathic remedies to help me cope. I took no medication to drown out the pain.

Perhaps what he gave me helped, and I found therapy in work. And in travel.

First, there was the hard stuff. I'd sold the lake place we both loved so much. Now, what could I do with his other acquisitions, most of which I knew about only vaguely? What about the real estate? What about the acreage in the Pleasant Grove area of Dallas? The acreage in the outlying counties? What about the partnership he'd made with a guy in Van, Texas, to start a tree nursery that was supposed to make a fortune? Grier had piddled and played and bought. I had been far too busy making a living for us during those last years of his life to keep up with what he was doing.

In closing out the businesses he had started, I made some mistakes. I went to a shelter for the homeless in Dallas and found a man who had been recently released from the penitentiary. We agreed for him and his wife and child to move into one of Grier's houses in exchange for taking care of another one. At a time when citizens were being urged to befriend persons released from prison, I knew Grier would want me to do whatever I could to help. The renter did not have a car, so I gave him the use of my Dodge van. He never lived up to any of his promises, mismanaged the property where he lived, made no effort to care for the other property, and stole all kinds of equipment and tools. Finally, he disappeared in the van, leaving nothing behind. We finally found the car and I hired a service to pick it up. I went through several other renters before I found an honorable couple to help me.

Dealing with renters was not the way I wanted to spend my time, but a considerable amount of our estate was tied up in twenty-three rental houses at a time when real estate property had taken a plunge, so I couldn't let it go without taking a severe economic loss. I had to hang on. I dealt with innumerable properties that Grier had accumulated, some of which I did not even know "we" owned. There was, for instance, the two hundred acres of land in Caddo Mills in East Texas that he had contracted with the government to terrace. For the next five years I dealt with agricultural agents to conclude the contract before I could sell the property.

The worst pain was that nursery deal in Van, Texas. Grier had contracted a block of land to a nurseryman in Van who employed inexperienced and undocumented workers from Mexico to plant trees at Caddo Mills. The nurseryman did not supervise them, so they planted the trees so close together that it was impossible to get a tractor through to cultivate them. Things were a total mess. The nurseryman declared bankruptcy, picked up, and moved off without even letting me know. He left five thousand shrubs and small trees in five-gallon containers sitting at the nursery. They could not live long without being watered, so for the three months following Grier's death, I had to find people to water the trees while I tried to get rid of them. Wholesale nursery people offered me fifty cents each. I knew similar trees and shrubs were selling for an average of twenty dollars each. I declined. I said I would throw everything in a ditch before I would let them have the trees and plants for fifty cents each.

I gave half of them to a black church in South Dallas, which sold them at a garage sale for a profit. I gave most of the others to the Dallas Park Foundation for replanting in Dallas City Parks. I had a friend bring a lot of them to Dallas and paid workers to plant them around our rental houses, but the tenants failed to water and care for them, and they all died. The only plants and shrubs I have from Grier's misguided efforts to open a nursery business are some hollies I replanted at my Colgate home in Dallas. I had the nursery stock I gave away appraised, and the best I could do was earn a tax write-off of some $36,000 for the four thousand trees and plants that Grier had thought would make us at least $100,000.

During those final years of Grier's life when I was stretched to handle my law practice and meet my husband's needs, he'd often tease me. "Don't you dare die and leave me with all the mess you're into," he would say. We'd laugh, but during that terrible first year after Grier's death, I wanted many times to remind him that he had died and left me with a mess I wasn't prepared to handle.

SHORTLY AFTER GRIER'S DEATH, I got a letter from Leonard and Karen Loeb from Milwaukee announcing that they were hosting a people-to-people trip for lawyers to Australia and New Zealand during the latter part of September and the first of October. I had wanted to travel there with Grier, who had been there on leave when he was in the South Pacific, but he had never really wanted to go. I suspect that his memories were too painful. Now I signed up, and I could not have done anything better for a learning/healing experience.

I've never been treated better anywhere in the world than in Australia and New Zealand. Their lawyers not only planned good exchanges with us but entertained us royally. In Sydney we visited the Supreme Court while it was in session. When the justices learned who we were, they took a recess and invited us to tea in their chambers.

We flew from Sydney to Wellington, the capital of New Zealand. On the southernmost tip of the North Island, it has all the bustle of a metropolitan area but all the charm and hospitality of a small town. An independent country with its own government, New Zealand lives up to its motto, "Where paradise was never lost." No artist could capture the overwhelming natural beauties of the countryside.

I HAD NOT BEEN BACK IN DALLAS long from my Australia/New Zealand trip when I learned that the International Women's Forum, a group I'd help to organize in Dallas, was planning a trip to Russia in the spring of 1989. I signed up. I had never been to Russia and hoped this powerful group of American businesswomen would have access to people and places that would be off limits to the average tourist. We flew nonstop from New York to Amsterdam, where we toured a wooden shoe factory, tulip gardens, the canals, and on into the countryside to see the windmills and magnificent flowers blooming everywhere. Late in the afternoon, we took off in a Russian plane for Moscow.

Women's groups in Russia are well organized and the members were eager to show us around. A brilliant female Russian general escorted us around their space control center, similar to our NASA, and we were told that we were the first foreign group to see it. Two Russian women astronauts were our luncheon hosts, and a top minister entertained us in the Kremlin.

The women were so eager to hear how we ran our businesses in the United States and how we organized and ran our women's groups. Most were convinced that women in Russia were totally equal to men, the "party line" they had been taught, and many of us believed it, too, until we were there and discovered the double standard showed up in countless ways. True, a woman can follow any career or profession of her choosing. There are more women doctors than men doctors in Russia. In both the military and the space agency we saw many women. They may own their own businesses and reach high ranks in the military, but there equality ends. Women must run their private lives without assistance of the male members of the household. Russian women are not only expected to work, but must also do all of the housework, the shopping, food preparation, and most of the country's rough work. When a man goes home from his job, his work day is concluded, but when a woman goes home, she begins her second career, that of managing the home.

We had some pleasant surprises in Russia. In Moscow we saw one of the finest fashion shows I've ever attended. High-fashion models paraded in beautiful, well-made clothing. The wives of Russia's elite wear fashions comparable to those in Paris. A second surprise was finding so many people going to church, apparently undisturbed. I'd always been told and believed that Christianity was dead, or at least forbidden, in the vast Communist country, but when I wandered into a Russian Orthodox church near our hotel I was surprised to find it crowded. Most of the worshippers were middle-aged to elderly, but they seemed free enough to be able to worship as they chose.

From Moscow we flew to Kiev, where we were escorted through some of the bloodiest battlefields of World War II and visited a park that the Russians have turned into a shrine honoring thousands of their people who were killed and buried in trenches.

From Kiev, we flew to Odessa on the Black Sea, and then to Leningrad (since the fall of Communism the name is again St. Petersburg), a fascinating city where we spent a full day in the Hermitage, arguably the most magnificent museum in the world. It would take weeks to see and absorb its splendors. Everywhere, my eyes feasted on magnificent treasures—paintings by the world's master artists, jewels of incomparable worth, fine china and crystal, every imaginable treasure.

Despite being so well treated in Russia, when the plane left Leningrad, our group spontaneously broke into a cheer. Freedom is such an overwhelmingly wonderful thing and this trip to Russia, if nothing else, made me remember how grateful I was to be an American citizen.

Almost as soon as we landed in Helsinki, Finland, we made our way to a restaurant where we acted like kids on Christmas morning. Everything imaginable was on the menu, but we most appreciated the lavish fruits and vegetables. We'd had no meal we enjoyed for three weeks since we left Amsterdam, and we gorged ourselves.

We toured Helsinki, and in the evening boarded a ship that belonged to one of the members of the International Women's Forum and was sailing to Stockholm, Sweden. I had the largest stateroom I've ever had, a big, private room, beautifully furnished. The food on shipboard was manna. Very early the next morning, I went out on deck to see the beautiful Swedish islands. Early spring in Sweden, the leaves and flowers were magnificent. The Swedes live mostly in metropolitan areas but have cottages on these lovely islands.

Swedish members of the International Women's Forum met us at the docks, and again we were royally entertained. Some of the members held high offices in the Swedish government and invited us to visit them. We went to City Hall and to the great hall where the Nobel Prizes are presented. We had only one day in Sweden; I could easily have stayed a month and never been bored. From there we went to London for four days. A British lord escorted us to the British Parliament. We were entertained at tea at No. 12 Downing Street by the British equivalent of our Attorney General. Since Margaret Thatcher was out of the country, we did not see No. 10 Downing Street.

What a trip! I would take nothing for having experienced it. And I was glad to get home.

There have been other marvelous trips since Grier's death, to the Virgin Islands, Puerto Rico, Hawaii, and points throughout the United States with the American Bar and the American Academy of Matrimonial Lawyers. Other than these bar-related excursions, my two most interesting trips were with two of my granddaughters.

In the early '90s Bridget and I went to Europe on a back-packing expedition. We had Eurorail passes and toured France, Austria, Switzerland, and Germany. We had a very loose itinerary, going wherever a train was available and our desires dictated. The only reservation we made was a sleeping car from Paris to Vienna. Otherwise, we arrived at a city, found a place to stay, went sightseeing for as long as we wanted, and then moved on. Usually we allowed a couple of days for each place we stopped, long enough to see a few of the sights and launder our very limited wardrobe.

One day we arrived in Heidelberg, Germany, about noon, found a room and, without waiting to clean up, went out to find something to eat and check on possible things to do the next day. Since neither of us had showered or changed clothes, we probably looked like two bag ladies. We topped a hill and looked down on a bridge, half of it cordoned off, filled with people and centered with a long stretch limousine. Kleig lights and cameras everywhere left only a small part of the bridge for crossing. As we made our way downhill, we speculated on what could be going on. Bridget guessed they were filming a movie. I thought maybe government officials were ready to make a speech. In any event, we were determined to find out what was happening. As we started single file across the bridge, the door of the limo opened and an exquisite lady, perfectly coiffed and made up and wearing an elegant purple suit, stepped out. My mouth fell open. "Mary Kay Ash," I shouted, my mouth taking over before my brain reacted. "Louise Raggio," she called back, "what are you doing here?" Both pleased and embarrassed, I succumbed to Mary Kay's hug! She was in Germany to introduce her cosmetics line there. Dirty and bedraggled, I thought later that I should have sneaked quietly away. I was no credit to her world-renowned cosmetics, but it is a credit to Mary Kay that she acknowledged our friendship as if I were groomed in the best of her offerings.

After our European adventures, Bridget and I parted in France, where she went to Blois for the fall semester of college and I returned to Dallas.

I had always wanted to go to Costa Rica and when Julie, Bridget's older sister, expressed an interest in going, we made reservations. For a week we visited the country, studied the ecology, checked out the natural resources, the mountain, the volcanoes, the agriculture. We were so impressed with the way the people partici-pate in their government. and with the literacy rate. Almost all of the adults in Costa Rica vote, putting our record to shame, and around 93 percent of the citizens are literate. Back in the 1940s, the country disbanded its army, and instead of supporting a military, spends its money on education, health, and tourism, the latter a very significant part of its economy.

Julie, with her background in French and Italian, got along with the Spanish language better than I did with my five years of high school and college Spanish. I was never more aware of the injustice we do to our children and youth because we do not teach them to be bilingual.

Learning to live with discretionary time was entirely new and took some adjusting—but, oh, what a wonderful gift! All my life the needs and wishes of others—my mother, my husband, the boys—had defined my possibilities.

Closure to that phase of my life came with the establishment and dedication of the Grier H. Raggio Memorial Garden at the First Unitarian Church. Dedicated in March 1989, a year following his death, it is a beautiful, serene spot where people can go to sit, med-itate, think, pray, or just be quiet. I hope that people of all faiths, from all backgrounds, of all ethnicities will wander into this sanc-tuary and find solace. I dedicated the garden to the memory of a person who, above all else, believed and lived for human rights, a man who stood up at all times for the underdog, who used his talents, his personality, and his wits to befriend those who were without friends.

Because so many women in the history of our city have created art and cultural centers in the names of male members of their fam-ilies and turned the leadership over to men, some of my friends have gently chastised me, questioning why I did not establish the garden in both of our names. I did it this way because I truly believe that Grier Henry Raggio deserves a spot that is his alone. I want people to understand that he was a man passionate about human rights, who demonstrated this by his love of every member of the human family and whose love and devotion to me, our children, and grandchildren was demonstrated every day of his life, especially in those final days as he approached death uncomplainingly.

After spending all of my life responding to the needs of others, I woke one Saturday morning, stretched, checked a mental list for my day's commitments, and for the very first time realized there was absolutely nothing that I *had* to do. The day stretched before me in all its luxurious splendor, with nobody whose demands I had to fulfill, no essential errands I had to run, no schedule I had to meet in thirty-minute increments, no telephone calls I had to make, no case I had to research. . . . I lay in bed and thought about what *I wanted to do*, what kind of legacy *I wanted to leave*.

This was the first of many days of sheer luxury. I still kept a tight schedule because I work best and accomplish more on a schedule, but now it is self-imposed and I am free to alter it if the need arises.

I began to cultivate friendships outside the legal profession and discovered the pleasure of being with women friends. In groups of women I did not have to prove myself before they would accept me. I could speak my truth as I saw it without fear that it would be taken the wrong way or limit my future chances to succeed on more important issues. When I did say something, I was heard! Most of all, the women's groups I was involved with did not waste time! They came to a meeting with an agenda, moved it through the processes, and ended it, almost always in the allotted time. Only then, if they wanted to tarry with special people or talk about personal matters, they sought each other out one-on-one after the meeting or made future appointments.

In 1989, a small group of women—Dr. Suzanne Ahn, Barbara Cottrell, Dr. Catalina Garcia, Maura McNiel, Shirley Miller, Barbara Watkins, and Virginia Whitehill—organized the Dallas Summit "as a force . . . so that women become full participants in all decision-making processes . . ." Women invited to join were not only leaders in their own business, professional, or volunteer fields, but also represented a microcosm of the community, inclusive by ethnicity and by political and religious beliefs. I was surprised that I was asked to chair the nominating committee to select officers and even more surprised when the group insisted that I serve as president. It was exhilarating to lead an organization of leaders and rewarding because it gave us an opportunity to serve as a force for equality for women.

I became more active in the local charter of the International Women's Forum, an organization whose members either own businesses or are important decision-makers within their companies. I've served on the board and as secretary.

I also became more active in the Dallas Women's Foundation. One of the women tapped by Helen Hunt in 1984 when she began to explore creating a local group to collect and disperse money to groups working to increase the potential of females, I had been compelled to bow out after the group was organized because, at that time, I was heading a capital fund drive for the Texas Bar Foundation and could not simultaneously solicit funds for two major groups. My work with the Bar Foundation having been successfully concluded, I was now free to be an active member of the Women's Foundation, agreed to become a board member in 1991, and have been active in the organization since that time.

Working with women has been exciting. For many years I was the sole female in all-male groups where I had to be careful to nurse their often fragile egos, sometimes even giving them credit for things I had done myself. With women I could just be me! I've made more women friends since reaching the age of seventy than I'd made in the entire preceding decades of my life.

And I didn't have to give up anything to create this wonderful new experience. I have continued my law practice, continued with Bar activities, and expanded my friendships with men.

FOR MANY YEARS, in those rare moments I had to consider it, I longed for a friend with whom I could share confidences, someone whose interests and experiences would enhance my own, someone I could trust utterly, and someone whose advice and wisdom would expand my own limitations. As I worked more and more with women, I learned that many of these yearnings could be met with my new women friends, yet I still longed for a male friend with whom I could share confidences.

I found this person fifty-four years after we first became friends in Washington, D.C. I found him in James MacGregor Burns, a brilliant, seasoned, compassionate individual with whom I had sat in front of a fire in his mother's home more than half a century before and shared every confidence of our exciting young lives.

I found him by accident—if accidents ever really occur—while seeking a speaker for the Dirty Thirty, the self-selected group of thirty outstanding family lawyers in the United States who had met annually since 1984 for three-day conferences on topics of current interest, mostly at Troutbeck in Amenia, New York. Volunteers in the group plan the meetings and invite the speakers. This meeting was important both to my professional and my personal sanity, but I had never been able to spare the time to help arrange it. In 1991 I found the time and volunteered. Four of us—Norman Schersky of New York; Burton Young of Miami; Larry Stotter of San Francisco; and I—met to brainstorm what we could do in October 1992 that would be informative, interesting, and educational.

Our meeting would be held in a presidential election year, and at the time it looked as if President George Bush was a shoo-in for re-election. I knew the group would be fascinated by an inside glimpse of the election, the presidency, and Washington, D.C. We talked at length about one individual who could speak on such a topic. In a second of inspiration, I said, "I know. James MacGregor Burns of Williams College!" Three pairs of eyes turned to me and there followed three voices of affirmation. "Yes!"

The "kid" I'd known during the days when both of us were Washington Fellows back in the Franklin Roosevelt era had become an eminent authority on the American presidency. An erudite scholar, careful observer and researcher, teacher and speaker, Jim Burns had written more than a dozen books on leadership and the presidency.

In October 1991, I went back to Texas and sent an invitation to James MacGregor Burns at Williams College, the only address I had. Weeks went by. There was no response. So much for a great idea! This man, too busy and too important, was ignoring me. Then came his reply. He was a visiting professor at the Jefferson School of Leadership in Richmond, Virginia, where he had spent the fall semester and had just received my letter. He was cordial, interested, and wanted to hear more. I followed up with a telephone call. We exchanged several letters, mine outlining our plans, and he agreed to speak at our meeting. Finally, in one letter I mentioned Grier in the past tense, and Jim responded immediately asking if Grier had died.

Jim and I met for the first time in fifty-four years at an old restored hotel near the White House in Washington. Except for a few letters in the months after I returned to Texas and one fleeting visit years before, we had not seen each other since our early twenties. It took us less than ten minutes to build a bridge across that span of time and we were right back into the deep mutual exchange of confidences that had marked our earlier relationship.

We talked about our kids—his four; my three. We talked about our grandchildren. But most of all we talked about our personal interests and commitments, the career successes we both had enjoyed, and the evening dissolved until suddenly it was midnight. I had to be up at a committee meeting breakfast at 7:30 the next morning, but I met Jim afterward and we spent the rest of the day together. We revisited a few old haunts and saw some new ones, but mostly we sat under the cherry trees and talked until our planes departed around 6 P.M.

Our first agreement was that our relationship would not be serious. I did not want to get married again and did not want any serious commitments. I made it clear to him that if he became seriously interested in another woman, I would graciously bow out of his life.

Jim and I have since had some wonderful times. We continued to correspond and talk over the phone about the October program and he invited me to come to see him in Williamstown. I had promised Bridget, who was then at Dartmouth, that I would come to see her, so in September I flew to Albany, where Jim picked me up and I spent the night in his home, a converted barn in Williamstown. That evening we went to a program to hear his daughter Deb, who was conducting a choir and singing in a program. I met his first wife, his daughter and son-in-law, and two of his grandchildren. The following day I visited with Bridget and then returned to Williamstown for another wonderful evening with Jim.

In October we had the Dirty Thirty meeting. Jim did a great job assessing the presidency and the American system of government. I was pleased at how many members had read his books, especially the books on leadership. He had to leave very early the next day to tape a program that later aired on CBS television.

In early December we booked two rooms at the Registry Hotel in Naples, Florida, and spent four days sightseeing, walking on the beach, going to a movie, and talking nonstop. I've never had a more wonderful vacation. In the spring, at my invitation, Jim came to Dallas to speak at several significant meetings. When Lady Bird Johnson learned that Jim was in Texas, she invited Jim and me to the LBJ ranch for lunch on Sunday. Jim had been her host in Williamstown when she received an honorary degree from Williams College. We flew to Austin, rented a car, and drove to the ranch, where we had a leisurely luncheon and then a personal tour of the wildflowers. We were having such a great time that leaving was difficult, and we cut the time so short that I had to speed to get back to the airport in time to make the last plane that night back to Dallas.

Jim and I have continued to see each other during these last few years and frequently converse by telephone. I enjoy a friendship with him unlike any other. Our time together is intellectually exhilarating, but magically personal. We are totally honest with each other. We can disagree—and often do—with no concern that our candor will destroy the friendship.

These last few years have been the richest of my life. Of course I miss Grier. I will always miss Grier. One cannot be married for almost half a century and forget the missing partner. But I have not experienced the prolonged grief that takes over the lives of so many widows. I know how lucky I am. I have a demanding profession, a wonderful family, a home I enjoy, and enough money to meet my needs, but most all a host of new friends, both women and men.

Now I am in charge of me! These are my bonus years.

19

Resolutions and Revelations

THE RUMORS THAT I AM RETIRED are categorically untrue! My step may be a bit slower, but I still walk every morning and run and up and down the stairs in our two-story offices half a dozen or more times daily. My office is at the top of the stairs.

As I reflect on the past, it is clear to me that I have led a life of protective coloration. Like a chameleon whose colors alter to fit into different environments, it was imperative that I presented the facade essential to get where I needed to go. Both my appearance and my manner are deceptive, for I am small in size—five feet two inches, and only about a hundred pounds, retiring in appearance—do not stand out in a crowd, and quiet in manner, raising my voice only when it is appropriate. I am meek until it is time to put the hammer down, but as many an opposing attorney can testify, tough and unrelenting when challenged.

The vicissitudes of my life conditioned me to strategize, and in the end, I almost always got what I wanted. And my abiding, overwhelming wish is that what I wanted is the very best for everybody concerned.

I find it refreshing to have at last found my own voice and to speak my own mind. I agree with Helen Thomas, a White House reporter for more than half a century, who said recently: "It's wonderful to know that I haven't given up being a citizen with personal beliefs even though I am a public figure." I don't know how long it took Helen to express and act on her personal beliefs, but I spent almost eight decades doing it!

My reflections brought me full circle—and in the past several months I have paid attention to some unfinished business. One of the major pieces—probably the most significant piece—of this has been finding out, at last, why Grier was charged with Communist leanings, refused entrance to Officers Training School, and sent as a "buck private" to the South Pacific where he served on Iwo Jima during World War II. Grier was rebuffed many times in his efforts to uncover the details of the Communist charges. He died without ever knowing the truth. I lived all of my married life with unanswered questions. And I had to know.

On October 27, 1999, under the Freedom of Information Act (5 U.S.C.s.552) I wrote a letter to the Federal Bureau of Investigation requesting access to and copies of all documents pertaining to both Grier and me. "I look forward to your reply within twenty business days, as the statute requires," I wrote. I sent it registered mail and received acknowledgment that it had reached its destination, together with a note explaining that because of the backlog of requests, my request would take a little time.

Nine and a half months later the U.S. Department of Justice, Federal Bureau of Investigation, sent me what it said was a 204-page document (actually, there are 214 pages counting everything). The cover form (no personal letter) indicated that the entire file consisted of 387 pages, some of which was being withheld because the investigation "originated with another government agency," or "contained information furnished by another government agency."

Two weeks later, on August 16, 2000, I received an additional 153-page document from the Department of the Army. If the total documentation of the investigation ran to 387 pages, as indicated in the response from the FBI, this means that a few pages of the investigation are still missing. The form that came with the document from the Army indicates that material may be withheld because it "relates solely to the internal personnel rules and practices . . ."; it pertains to "personnel and medical files . . ."; it "could reasonably . . . constitute an unwarranted invasion of personal privacy . . ."; or it "could reasonably be expected to disclose the identity of a confidential source."

The documents I did receive are riddled with blacked-out names.

The investigation began ever so innocently because of a book we left behind among a stack of magazines in a closet of our apartment in Edinburg, Texas, in April 1942. Grier's job with the U.S. Department of Agriculture entailed checking to determine whether or not ration stamp regulations were being violated by merchants. Grier's supervisor, in an interview with an FBI agent on August 27, 1942, reported "Subject's work was necessarily undercover and confidential, and Subject worked alone practically all of the time . . . [his] work entailed a great amount of typing at [his] home, and would also require many reports and much correspondence with [his] superior in Dallas, Texas."

This secretiveness, in a small town, made us highly suspect, and when our landlady, while cleaning the apartment we had vacated, discovered one of Grier's employee instruction books marked RESTRICTED, she turned it over to the local sheriff, who in turn gave it to the FBI, thus setting off a chain of investigations that haunted us for the rest of Grier's life. The investigations—and the charges kept lifting their ugly heads, first in the 1940s, again in the 1950s, and again in the 1960s—were in-depth, often confusing, and continuous for a long period of time. Agents were assigned to track his every move from his birth onward, and once his name was in the system, Grier was suspect everywhere he turned and whatever he did.

In several specific instances, there is a clear case of mistaken identity. For instance, he was charged with being a member of *Ayuda a la Renovacion de Espana*, and of attending meetings of that organization and other Communist front groups in Tampa, Florida, in 1940–1941. Not only had he never heard of such an organization, but he was not *in* Tampa at the time he was accused of attending meetings there. At one time, an agent was tracking someone named *Riggio*, a confusion of spelling that doubtless became a part of our files. Grier had reported on every form requiring a résumé that his mother, Mary Elizabeth Grier Raggio, was deceased, but when an FBI agent found a Letha (or Litha) R. Raggio living in Lafayette,

Louisiana, he concluded that "Subject's unwillingness to have his mother connected in any way with his personal history . . . suggests an opportunity to conduct an investigation." Letha Raggio was Grier's stepmother. Nobody bothered to ascertain the relationship.

The most clarifying point to me is that people who knew Grier well filed positive reports filled with superlatives as to his character, behavior, personality, intelligence, work habits, and ability to work with others, and, conversely, people who did not know him or had only a fleeting acquaintance filed negative reports.

On January 1, 1943, an employer [name blacked out], said of Grier, "He is a young man of fine traits, more than average intelligence and great earnestness . . . he will in every way be a loyal employee." That boss checked "excellent" about Grier's habits and conduct at work, his attendance record, his attitude toward work, his ability to handle his workload, his ability to negotiate with others, and his courtesy and cooperation. A former supervisor in the Department of Agriculture found him "a pleasant individual, good company . . . and of excitable temperament." An associate who worked with him for three years "remembered Subject distinctly, but had never known him very well, that he was very efficient in performing his duties, that his association with fellow workers was pleasant but never close, that she has never known anything derogatory . . . and considers him a loyal, trustworthy American." A former neighbor in Washington, D.C., stated that he "knew Subject for five or six years, that he was frequently associated with him in evenings at home, that Subject was a hard-working and studious young man who worked for the government and went to night school concurrently, that he was an interesting and well-informed conversationalist . . . who gave every indication of trying to improve his position educationally and professionally, that Subject was well-behaved and apparently of good habits, well-liked by his acquaintances, intimate with no one." An Army sergeant, who had bunked across the aisle from Grier during basic training, said, "Subject seemed to be well-educated, was a good conversationalist and was good at reportee (sic) . . . was neat and clean in his personal habits . . . did not go out very much, worked hard and had not objected to the work." He added that he "admired Subject . . . considered Subject to be loyal and never observed anything on the part of Subject that was unfavorable or derogatory."

People who did not know us, or who had only a fleeting acquaintance with Grier, said things and made accusations in interviews with FBI agents that made us suspect. One woman described me as "turning white, acting scared, and changing the subject" when, while trying to be friendly, she asked me what my husband did. Trained to be good citizens and let our legislators know how we felt about critical governmental issues, Grier and I had written letters to Congressman Milton West, who represented the Texas area in which we lived. One of the letters expressed our desire to have the poll tax banned and another opposed repeal of the forty-hour work week. Both of these letters were considered anti-American, and Congressman West, in an interview on December 2, 1942, while admitting that he "did not know the Subject," added "he did not believe Subject should be employed by the government if the letters indicated the attitudes of the Subject." A former supervisor, interviewed in Corpus Christi, Texas, on August 27, said "Subject's work was entirely satisfactory and he turned in an amazing amount of work," but "Subject disagreed with him when he said that the United States should have excluded the Japanese from coming to this country because they had given us nothing but trouble. Subject," the ex-supervisor added darkly, "seemed inclined to defend foreign people . . . is the sort of fellow, although you have no definite reason to suspect as disloyal, yet would not be surprised at anything he did."

One interviewee admitted he did not really know Grier, but added "apparently Raggio is considered a radical . . . he looks like a wop." Another said, darkly, "He has traveled to Canada, Panama, and Cuba." Another wondered "what he was doing when he took those trips to Mexico." Another concluded "Raggio still has enough European characteristics to resent the American way of life. . . ." The desk clerk at William and Mary Hotel in Wichita Falls reported to the FBI that "Subject received a great deal of mail after his departure from the hotel."

One of Grier's ex-sergeants, interviewed at Fort Leonard Wood, Missouri, on January 29, 1943, was especially venomous, to the extent that the Agent qualified the report. The sergeant is reported to have said, "I disliked the man the very first time I saw him. [He] obeyed orders very reluctantly and always created the impression of knowing more than anyone else . . . he talked when he should have been listening . . . had his own ideas as to how things should have been done. . . ." The sergeant called Grier "The Guardhouse lawyer [because] he advised others as to how things should be run in the Army." At the end of his report, the FBI Agent made this note: "Informant is a stern Sergeant, having been in the Army for sixteen years, and apparently disliked the subject because of his superior attitude."

As I read through the pages and pages of innuendos, charges and countercharges, misrepresentations, and outright lies, I became, quite literally, ill.

What a *waste!*

What a waste of taxpayers' money: three hundred and eighty-seven pages, much of it single-spaced, of reports from April 25, 1942, to February 9, 1943, taking the time and travel expenses of countless FBI agents (the exact number not available because agents worked undercover and their signatures are blacked out). This took approximately 233 working days of time with no accounting for how many people were working each day. This investigation alone cost us, the taxpayers, thousands and thousands of dollars. And Grier and I were "small potatoes" compared with the countless loyal citizens whose lives were turned wrong-side-out during the Communist witch-hunts.

Most of all, what a waste of talent: Grier Raggio, directed and supported, could have made brilliant and long-lasting contributions to this country, and when you multiply that by the number of people whose lives were virtually destroyed in the Communist witch-hunts it is a staggering waste of human potential.

And enough to make everybody quite ill.

In times of national crisis there is often a tendency to overreact and abuse freedoms that are guaranteed by the Constitution. It happened again following the terrorists' attacks on the World Trade Center and the Pentagon on September 11, 2001. In their zeal to protect citizens, some officials have condoned, some even encouraged, actions that are constitutionally suspect. Individuals have been locked up for periods of time without having any charges filed against them. Citizens have been encouraged to report suspicious actions of their neighbors, friends, and coworkers to appropriate authorities.

I shudder when I hear these things because I know how devastating it is to have false charges on personal records. Encouraged by the propaganda of her times, our landlady in 1942 set off a chain of events that haunted my husband all the days of his life.

The American Civil Liberties Union and other watchdogs seeking to guard our constitutionally guaranteed freedoms have my undying gratitude for, in the paraphrased words of John Philpot Curran (1750–1817), "eternal vigilance is the price of freedom."

It is exceedingly gratifying to have lived long enough to be honored for some of my actions that once were highly suspect and got me into trouble.

In the days before lawyers were allowed to advertise—when I observe some of the sleazy ads in print and on TV today, I sometimes wish we still had that rule!—I was called before the grievance committee of the Dallas Bar Association. Somebody had accused me of hiring a publicist. The charge was ridiculous, and was, of course, dismissed out of hand. The truth was my name appeared in the paper often, and for three specific reasons: I made myself available to talk to the press; I knew the crunch of their deadlines and immediately returned telephone calls. Second, I was one of the few attorneys sufficiently knowledgeable about and willing to be quoted on family issues, so reporters often called me when they were writing a story on divorce, child custody, family violence, and other family-oriented subjects. Third, it was *news* that a woman held her own in the courtroom, the grueling world where human conflict landed for resolution.

The scars and bruises that brought me to this stage of my life make me appreciate all the more the recognition that has come.

One's most prestigious recognitions are those bestowed by one's own professional associates, and the most revered are the first of

one's career. So it is that when I think of my many blessings, I immediately recall the Citation of Merit awarded by the Texas State Bar
in 1967 and the President's Award from the State Bar in 1987. These
two honors, two decades apart, largely mark the beginning and conclusion of my cutting-edge-of-change efforts within the State Bar.
(With very little humility, I've listed my honors and acccolades in
an appendix.)

National recognition awes me. In September 2000, I received a
letter notifying me that I had been named by my peers for inclusion
in the 2001–2002 edition of *The Best Lawyers in America*. The list
is composed after exhaustive peer reviews that include 15,000 leading attorneys from throughout the country who are asked to "vote"
on the legal abilities of other lawyers. My name has been on the list
since the first "best lawyers" were chosen in 1970.

In 1995 I received from the ABA the Margaret Brent Award, the
country's outstanding accolade for women lawyers, named for
America's first woman lawyer, recognized as the first woman in
America to make a stand for the rights of her sex. I am humbled to
be among the illustrious women who have received the award,
among them Janet Reno, Chief Justice Ruth Bader Ginsburg, Barbara Jordan, Rep. Patricia Schroeder, Chief Justice Sandra Day
O'Connor, and Dovey J. Roundtree.

When I am inclined to think that I endured the world's most
oppressive discrimination because of my gender, I remind myself of
Dovey Roundtree's travails. My own struggles pale into insignifi-
cance when compared to the obstructions she has had to endure and
overcome. Dovey was a leader in efforts to integrate the Women's
Auxiliary Army Corps during World War II. Even after she rose to
the rank of captain, discrimination plagued her because of her color.
Once, while on official Army business, she was removed from a bus
in Miami to give her seat to a white male soldier. Following the
Army, she earned a degree from Howard Law School and opened a
practice in North Carolina. Not only were there no restaurants in
the town that would serve African-Americans, toilets in the county
courthouse were unavailable to people of color. Dovey prevailed,
winning her first major victory as a lawyer when she tried the case

of Sarah Keys, a WAC arrested for failing to give up her bus seat to a white male Marine. That case, *Keys v. Carolina Coach Company*, ended in 1955 and is widely hailed as a major victory that ended segregation of travel across interstate lines.

Of most significance to me personally is the endowed Louise Raggio Lecture Series at Southern Methodist University to advance the causes of women in our country. This event, established in 1998, annually presents outstanding speakers on issues of current concern. This is important, not because it bears my name, but because it reaches out to everybody across age, ethnic, and gender barriers to help affirm the history, advances, and future of women in society. SMU, whose law school deans and advisors did everything possible to discourage me and all other women from enrolling in the late 1940s, presented me with an honorary doctorate of law in 1996. We women have come a long way in my lifetime! We still have a long way to go.

MY COMMITMENT TO MY FAMILY is total and has been discussed in a prior chapter. I add only that I do not "grandmother" in the traditional manner and in the way that many women find satisfying. Instead, I try to be present in the lives of each of my grandchildren according to their individual needs, and to open doors of opportunity for them when I can. I try to be available to stay with the children when their parents are out of town and my home is open to any one of them at any time.

Nor am I a "typical" attorney because I support the emotional needs as well as the legal needs of my clients. I am a good listener—and often that is all a person needs in order to work through her own problems.

As a community volunteer, I make myself available as a speaker, always without remuneration, to countless organizations locally, statewide, and nationally. When an organization presents an honorarium, I donate it to a worthy cause.

I have spent both my personal and my professional life committed to families and believe that there is no substitute for family as the basic and most enduring human structure.

Though I have filed divorce suits far too numerous to recall, I am not *in favor of* divorce because in many ways divorce is worse than death, especially where children are involved.

The only thing worse than divorce is living in a cancerous marriage. In cases of spousal abuse, whether physical or emotional, divorce is imperative.

I have a reputation in the community of always taking the side of the female in a divorce suit, but that is not true. About 50 percent of my clients are men. I have handled divorce cases for several males whose battering—almost always emotional abuse—has left them no alternative but to get out.

In either case, whether it is the wife or the husband seeking a divorce, it is imperative that children of the marriage be safe. Both parents have an obligation to make the lives of their children as normal as possible. I believe that all couples, especially where children are involved, should seek counseling and enter into mediation. The courts should exert their authority to demand this, and many Dallas judges do.

Divorces should be handled as amicably as possible. Vindictive retribution never solves anything. I conduct in-depth interviews with potential clients before I agree to take a case. When there is no alternative—when the lawyer for the other client is determined to battle—I go to court and I usually win, but I consider all cases that wind up in the courtroom to be a loss. This is especially true in custody cases. Men and women who have children together will never be totally separated from each other, no matter what the courts say. They will be at the same place at the same time in many situations—when their children marry, when they become grandparents, when there are funerals—throughout their future lives, and the less rancor there is when going through a divorce, the greater the chances for a peaceful coexistence in the future.

The parsimonious alimony law of Texas should be expanded. It currently allows only $2,500 monthly for a maximum of three years to a divorcing spouse—and not that if there is community property to be divided. (When I chaired the Family Law Section, I did everything in my power to get an improved alimony bill passed. It did not happen.) Making a home should be considered a career. Wives who devote their lives to keeping the house, and caring for their husbands and children, should be financially compensated for the years they have spent in nonsalaried positions.

I have seen countless cases of men with the middle-age crazies shedding the wife who helped them through the rough times for a sexier, younger woman. Their brains fall out when they unzip their pants and they seek or are entrapped by a trophy wife at the very time when they, as a couple, are old enough to retire and enjoy the harvest years of their lives together.

Deserted spouses, both women and men, arrive in my office distraught. Women come without career qualifications, having years ago given up their budding careers to have a family, to care for children, and to cushion the bumpy roads as their husbands advanced in careers. Many haven't the remotest idea of finances. Some have never opened a bank account, have never written a check, never paid a bill. Each sobbing woman, dumped for a prettier, sexier, younger model, has lived in false security that her husband would live up to his promise to take care of her for the rest of her life.

It is not enough, in this community property state, for a woman to get half of what they have accumulated together. Too often, a man liquidates their community assets before filing for divorce, or, in the case of a recent client, inherits a fortune from his family—his separate property—which cannot normally be touched by the courts. A woman winds up with the house, a car, custody of the children, and child support—very often not paid. On the surface, this may look like a good deal, but it never is. At middle age, she is alone and vulnerable, inexperienced in the world of work, unprepared to meet the challenges that lie ahead. In almost every situation of this kind, were you to take a survey three years following a divorce, you would find the man remarried, supporting a second family, and financially better off than the wife he divorced. And you would find the left behind woman struggling to make ends meet, worried about her children's welfare, wondering how to replace a leaky roof or a worn-out car and existing singly in a world for which she is totally unprepared. Spouses who devote the prime money-amassing years of their lives to home and hearth should be cushioned with a monthly income while they restructure their lives.

I do not always file divorce suits for those who come seeking them. In the initial interview, I try to determine what is best for the client and what is most advantageous for the family involved. I send many clients to counseling and, in turn, become the lawyer for many clients referred to me by psychiatrists and psychologists.

Fortunately I have the luxury of advising some potential clients not to file for divorce. Many lawyers do not share my attitude, and individuals determined to end their marriages can easily find an attorney without my scruples.

Financial equations in families have shifted greatly in the past few years. As women gain equality in the workplace and their incomes rise, some have higher incomes than their husbands, and many men feel threatened by this. We also see an increasing number of clients who are in business together. Often they have opened their business on a shoestring, and over the years gained prestige and made money. It is very difficult for two people to live together and work together in harmony. I know! It is not only from my professional expertise but from my personal life that I counsel clients to look at all the options before they dissolve the relationship.

A divorcing person—male or female—even under our current unfair state laws, can come out of the experience relatively unscathed, and a few years later be a much happier person. I have seen it happen repeatedly, and if I sometimes am tough on my clients, badgering them to pull themselves together and get on with their lives, it is precisely because I know that, in most instances, after the struggle to survive, people thrive.

Again, I liken divorce to death because the range of emotions is similar. A woman whose husband leaves her or who is forced into divorce against her will almost always goes through a stage of disbelief. She may hover in this state for some time depending on her personal inclination, the support system she has outside the marriage, and on the pressures brought by her departing spouse. Disbelief is followed by dysfunction, a form of depression during which a woman feels useless and incapable of making the most mundane decision. Finally, compelled by time and circumstances to do *something*, she becomes angry. Too often she lets herself get trapped here and wastes time and effort in retributive thoughts and actions against the departing spouse. Or she can use anger as an incentive to stop feeling sorry for herself and take control of her life. Finally, in healthy situations, there comes acceptance—and with it survival and renewal.

I came, as I have explained, late to declaring myself a feminist, but I have always known—even while finding it expedient to bow to the dictates of my mother, my husband, and the prevailing male climate in which I forged my career—that I could take care of myself. I see the feminist movement as an extension of women's constant attempts to control their own lives. My mother and Aunt Hulda, who toured the countryside in a Model T Ford campaigning for voting rights for women, were feminists; only at the time they and the countless likeminded women of their times were called suffragists. Their primary concern was in gaining the vote for women. Many thought, naively, that everything else would fall into place once women were allowed to cast a ballot.

Capital punishment, the legal right to end a life, is increasingly a subject brought to the fore by the media and discussed by people at both formal meetings and informally among family and friends. Basically I oppose capital punishment, and those who think that *every* person the state of Texas has put to death is guilty doesn't have the brains of a gnat. It is beyond my comprehension that many who vehemently oppose abortion are, at the same time, in favor of capital punishment. I know that we have to protect society, and some crimes are so heinous that the perpetrators should be locked away for all time, but I do not believe that legally taking a life is ever justified. Sister Helen Prejean, the country's most outstanding spokesperson opposing capital punishment, works tirelessly for the day "when the violence of our justice system . . . will be changed." I applaud her.

The world in which I grew up was highly segregated, not only by color but by national origin. To a certain extent I know what it feels like to be "different," because my German/Swedish heritage set me apart in school and social situations from the "pure" American white children and I was ostracized. I was not aware of the discrimination endured by the blacks in our midst, but I understand their frustration and anger at being made to feel like second-class citizens. The dearth of reading material available to me as a child and other limited forms of communication did not expose me to ideas and ideals far beyond the farm on which I grew up. I do not recall a déjà-vu moment when I knew that segregation by color is evil, but I am grateful to live at a time and in a place where segregation barriers are tumbling every day. Exposure and education are the keys to human equality. We fear what we do not know. I long for the day when we no longer label ourselves by color or heritage.

And that day must come, for today all of us live together in a global community. The days of isolationism are over. One of my college professors—around 1938 or 1939—told us how lucky we were to have the Atlantic Ocean on one side and the Pacific on the other, which made us safe. That was before the missiles came. Advanced technology has made us all citizens of the world and responsible for each other. We have no option but to learn how to live with each other, whether we like each other or not.

I believe that we must move toward living under a world governing body—and we have one in place if we would only use it. The United Nations is not perfect, but it is a giant step in the right direction. I get so mad at Congress when it doesn't pay our UN dues and take advantage of the United Nations as a peace-making, peace-keeping instrument.

War on a global scale is not the only immediate danger we face. The gap between the rich and the poor must not widen. We have only to look at history to comprehend that revolutions result when the oppressed rise up to demand their share of the "good life." It makes me furious that the wealthiest people in our country are those most opposed to raising the minimum wage. It is not wise just to *give* people things. The old saying, "If you give a man a fish, he eats a meal, but if you teach him to fish he eats for a lifetime," is so true. What we must give is the opportunity for people to take care of themselves and we cannot do it when we continue to compensate them at slave wages for their contributions to our society.

Of course, I do not know how to solve these problems, and anyone who thinks that he or she has all the answers is abysmally ignorant. I look to my faith for some help. It strengthens me and gives me a foundation and a root system that nurtures me. I believe there is a Supreme Being, and mine is a growing, constantly expanding faith. I don't expect to have the same ideas about religion and my journey of faith tomorrow or next year that I have today—because my ideas have changed at each step of my life.

I don't know what will happen when I die, but whatever happens will be the same for everybody. Everybody has to die sometime, and I hope I have the equanimity to just relax and die when it is my time.

Until then I plan to get up every day and try to make a positive difference in this magical world.

EPILOGUE

At AGE EIGHTY-THREE, what have I learned? What can I say that may be of value to those who pass this way after I can no longer speak or write? How would I summarize my life?

First would be gratitude. Gratitude for being a part of this marvelous planet and witnessing the changes from horse and buggy days to aspirations of living on other members of our solar system. Do we stop to be grateful for the multitude of opportunities we enjoy now as in contrast to those we had in 1919, the year of my birth? What even greater discoveries will crown our future? Do we allow our senses to explore the wonderful world around us?

Along with gratitude, do we realize that we face many hazards—known and unknown—in our fast-changing world? Can we visualize that we must be a part of the solutions, innovations, and different ways of affecting change for the benefit of our cosmos?

All of us have much to do. We do not have to be rocket scientists or Ph.D.'s or wealthy or even gifted. We merely have to look at our little part of the universe and decide how even our little bit can make a difference.

I have so many reasons to be grateful, beginning with my peasant grandparents who braved the perils of coming to America. Theirs was a hard life, full of sorrows and losses, but they had the vision that their children, grandchildren, and great-grandchildren would have opportunities not possible to the poor, uneducated masses in Europe.

I am grateful for my parents, who deprived themselves of so many necessities so that their only child would have opportunities not available to them. They gave me total love and support. How many of us do the same for our children?

I am grateful for the public education system where the poor kids had the same chance afforded to the rich and powerful to learn to be significant contributors to our system. Tuition at the University of Texas was only $25 for an entire semester of classes. I am grateful for the taxpayers of Texas for their support for kids like me.

I am grateful to the brave men who created a new concept for government in the late 1700s, knowing full well that they would be hanged as traitors if their rebellion did not succeed. John Adams, Thomas Jefferson, George Washington, and Ben Franklin risked their lives, their fortunes, and their sacred honor to create the structure that has evolved through the years to give us the right to dissent, criticize, and express our thoughts even though our thoughts may at the time be unpopular. Notice that I said I am grateful to "brave men." Women, slaves, indentured servants, and poor people were not included, although our Constitution has grown to encompass these groups. But how many of us stop to appreciate the world-changing ideas of these men?

Every generation witnesses attacks on our freedoms, from early days to the present time. How many of us realize that keeping our rights of free speech is a never-ending task, and we—all of us—have the duty to protect our precious heritage? Persons under the thumb of dictators daily risk their lives for the right of free elections. How many of us take the time to learn the issues, weigh the choices rather than the rhetoric, and participate in the electoral process? The spirits of the framers of our Constitution and Bill of Rights must be very saddened by the numbers of our citizens who do not even take the time to vote. Remember, your vote counts as much as the vote of the richest person in town.

I am grateful that the framers of our Bill of Rights included freedom of religion. I agree that we are a religious nation, and I certainly am a religious person, but there is no state religion or any authority telling me what I have to believe. This freedom is also being attacked by certain groups who want to impose their "religion" on the rest of us. I am glad we are free to worship as we choose, and that also means that we must respect the right of others to worship in their own way.

I am grateful for the opportunity I have had to change the lives of women in our society. From the dawn of written history, women were the chattels and possessions of men. From pre-history, if the tribe was to survive, women had to produce children and nurse the babies for extended periods if the children were to live. One of my grandmothers gave birth to sixteen children, the other grandmother gave birth to ten. With the many years of pregnancy and breast-feeding, plus cooking for the broods, my grandmothers did not have the energy or time to participate in the political process. I am grateful to Margaret Sanger and contraceptives so that women—and men—can plan their families. But even this right is under attack. What are we doing so that we do not have the reproductive problems of my grandmothers?

I am grateful that I was trained as a lawyer, and had the opportunity to participate in obliterating many laws that were discriminatory to women. Until January 1, 1968, when a woman married in Texas she took on twenty-seven "disabilities of coverture" that she did not have as a single woman or a widow. Translated into simple English, that meant that she had no control over her property or property earned during marriage. Husband and wife were one, and he was the important one. Other states had similar laws, though not as restrictive as the laws in Texas. I am grateful for the ten men (yes, men) who worked without pay with me for two years on the Marital Property Act of 1967. Changing the statutes is a tedious, time-consuming, and frustrating process. These men, and the men who guided the changes through the Texas Legislature, are heroes in my book. No doubt they were thinking of their daughters and grand-daughters and did not want them to be restricted by the antiquated statutes.

I am also grateful for the men and women who worked with me for another ten years to produce the first completed Family Code in the United States. The Code puts all laws affecting the family "under one roof" and later has been reproduced in many other states.

Since 1968, I have been grateful for the invitations from women's groups for me to tell about the changes in the laws and their new rights. This included challenging business organizations who were not obeying the new laws, and on occasion participating in legal actions against certain corporations. I am grateful for the many, many new women friends I have made since 1968 and the wonderful experiences we have had in mentoring younger women who have not had to overcome the obstacles we older women encountered.

I am grateful for the many awards I have received since 1967 for my work in various fields, from the American Civil Liberties Union (ACLU) to the National Association of Business Women Owners Association to the American Bar Association. I often feel that I am "over-appreciated" but I enjoy that groups are aware of the changes in which I have participated.

I am grateful for having had a husband who loved me totally and unequivocally from the day we met on January 14, 1941, until the day he died on April 10, 1988. I am grateful that he had the ego and strength of character to want a wife who also was a professional. In those days, it was rare for a man to want a wife who was his equal. He took a lot of criticism from his male peers for promoting my law studies and being his partner in a law firm.

I am grateful, and unbelievably lucky, for us to have had three sons who not only were athletes, scholars, and house helpers, but who are superior lawyers and my partners in our law firm. It is unique for a family to work together for the many years we have, and still to love and respect each other. I am doubly grateful that their wives are one another's best friends, and that we have a close family relationship. I love my daughters-in-law, and they love me! We have many family gatherings.

My gratitude is even greater for my seven wonderful, beautiful, talented, and exceptional grandchildren—spoken as only a grandmother can speak. The oldest is a Fellow at Georgetown Medical Hospital, together with her husband, Dr. Cameron Cover, she in nephrology and he in infectious diseases. The youngest grandchild is a sophomore at Highland Park High School, and a fierce ice hockey star. Those in between are in various businesses and activities or are in college or high school.

There are many, many more things and occurrences for which I am grateful, but the hour grows late. Let's talk about challenges and the future.

Every generation has had its challenges, but TV, the Internet, instant communication, e-mail, and all the other recent developments have intensified and compressed our time and manner of dealing with the challenges. I remember life before radios, TV, and commercial air flights. We have new crises every day. The whole world seems to land on our shoulders.

The millions of women who had worked for seventy-five years to get the vote meekly went back to their kitchens until they were called during World War II to fly airplanes, weld, and shipbuild like "Rosie the Riveter." Again they meekly went back to their kitchens until the 1960s and the new drive for women's rights. We are not "there" yet and the challenge of the new generations is to honor our foremothers by keeping on keeping on.

Women have been coping with the challenge of the "glass ceiling" for decades, and much progress has been made. The challenge now is how much of ourselves—both men and women—to invest in climbing the corporate ladder to the detriment of our families and private lives. If a woman in leadership chooses to have a child, how much time should she devote to the child from infancy through adolescence? Fortunately, many men now realize the importance of quality time with their children. Co-parenting is a reality for many couples. And men and the children are both beneficiaries.

We have the challenge of the continued attacks on the right of a woman—and man—to make reproductive choices without the interference of the state or federal government. With our planet choking from pollution, natural resources being depleted at a staggering rate, with the specter of a lack of potable water and the fouling of our seas, it is so puzzling why we all are not making contraceptives and family planning available to the entire world. Not forcing the issue—just educating populations about the alternatives.

The challenge to our environment grows greater every year. We put more burdens on the same God-given resources by depleting resources that took billions of years to accumulate. The gap between the lifestyles and use of resources of the very rich and the very poor continues to widen.

A further challenge is to reach the underlying causes of the radical hate that exists in our country, pepetuated by so many who wrap themselves in religious justification.

It is no longer a choice. We have the challenge to live as a part of this very small planet rather than an isolated entity protected by two oceans.

But we have strengths, determination, ingenuity, and ways to effect change. We have the models of the brave men of the late 1700s who built a new way of living and governing and the models of prior generations who safeguarded those rights.

Most of my generation is no longer with us. This is the challenge the remainder of us give to the younger people. We hand you the torch we carried and for which we sacrificed. We implore you to carry the torch onward for an even better, more sustainable, more equitable, and fair society for the future.

AFTERWORD—OTHER VOICES

WRITER'S PRIVILEGE: For the last year and a half I, Vivian Castle-berry, have "been" Louise Raggio and have found it a daily revelation of surprise and delight.

I had no intention of writing this book, had in fact done my best to find for my friend Louise a writer who would understand her, who would have traveled a similar path, who would be both empathetic and objective, who would encourage her to reveal the truth to the limit of her ability, and would help her to share with other women both the profits and the pitfalls of her journey.

Someone not so close to her would be a better writer, I thought, because Louise and I had known each other for almost half a century. We had not been close friends because both she and I were too busy to give the time and effort required to form close relationships, she as a lawyer married to a lawyer and rearing three sons, and I as a journalist married to an educator and rearing five daughters. Each of us had struggled to define ourselves in our separate careers during a period of time that was totally male-dominated.

But my life had been vastly enriched many times because of her presence in it and support of it.

I did not want to do the book because of two very special reasons.

First, I knew that a very close and sometimes abrasive relationship can develop between a subject and her writer—and I did not want anything to threaten our friendship.

Second, I was very deep into researching another book to follow *Daughters of Dallas, a History of Greater Dallas Through the Voices and Deeds of Its Women*, published in 1996, and eager to begin writing it.

When the search for another writer failed, I knew that Louise's story was so important that it must be told, and perhaps I was the one to tackle it. She and I share so many things. We were born in the same time period, were children of the rural South, grew up during the Great Depression, found our solace and inspiration in reading, and were determined to get an education. We both worked our way through college, took very seriously our commitment to our marriages, reared children who all turned out to be responsible, contributing adults, carved and succeeded in careers at a time when it was frowned upon for women to work outside their homes, and look back over our lives with the conviction that it has been a good journey!

The "deal" was cinched at a Christmas party when Louise said: "You've been putting words in my mouth for almost fifty years. Why do you want to quit now?"

The experience of writing this book has been tremendously satisfying. I owe immeasurable gratitude to Louise, who several years ago dictated and taped her life story, and especially to her granddaughter, Julie Raggio, for transcribing the tapes. Without the letters that Grier wrote to Louise during World War II, and that she kept, I could have never created the atmosphere of that time period, even though I, too, lived it. We forget so much—and our memories are altered by later life experiences. I am indebted to Phyllis Ann (Anna) Richmond Gold, the daughter of Arista Sarkus Richmond, who saved Louise's letters to her mother and returned them to Louise following her mother's death. Without those letters, written in 1940–1941, the nuances of Louise's life in Washington, D.C. and as a young career woman in Austin, Texas, would have been far more difficult to capture.

Delightful surprises have surfaced all along the way. The Louise I thought I knew so well has entranced me with facets of herself I had no idea existed. I never knew she was one of the first Washington, D.C., interns, had only an inkling of the Communist conspiracy charges against her and Grier, knew nothing about the years of debilitating depression that she suffered, and was recurrently charmed by her sense of humor. I had known her mostly as a serious lawyer, and serious she can be. What I learned is that she could have just as easily succeeded as a journalist—she writes exceptionally well—or as a stand-up comedian. She is a master of comedic one-liners, as she proved when expressing gratitude to Planned Parenthood. "My grandmother had sixteen children," she said. ". . . they were too poor to have a mistress."

The biggest revelation of all has been the opportunity to see Louise Ballerstedt Raggio through the eyes of others. Because of the personal and almost sacred relationship existing between an attorney and her client, Louise never would have divulged information about the cases she has handled or the countless times she has been able to avoid bitterness in families during divorce proceedings and child custody cases.

But her former clients, numbering in the hundreds, have told me. When people ask what I am doing and I tell them I am writing Louise Raggio's book, the person to whom I am speaking, or someone who overhears, says, "Louise Raggio saved my life." And then they begin to tell me, some with tears in their eyes, their stories. And I have included one here.

Important people in public life have also spoken out and/or written letters of affirmation and support for this project, either to Louise or to me.

What follows are some of the Other Voices:

C. E. (KIM) SEAL II

Attorney and CEO, Allegiance Title Company, who has known Louise since she handled his divorce in the 1970s and has since become a close friend: My divorce, as divorces go, was simple, but I had no idea about the legal and personal ramifications involved and Louise was my counselor and advisor. We'd been separated for years—I'm Catholic and didn't believe in divorce—but when the divorce came Louise got in my face and made me deal with some realities. She's so different from many family lawyers because she never vilifies the other person involved—and she does her best to keep her clients from being vengeful—but she knows every jot and tittle of family law and she leaves nothing to chance. Even when she was being tough with me, she was also gentle.

I call Louise "Mom." I've sent many people—mostly guys—to her through the years, and she becomes "Mom" to many of them, too. She's done more things for more people than any of us will ever know. She did my brother-in-law's divorce pro bono. He was ill, a diabetic, didn't have money. Louise cared for him in the same way she would a paying client.

My wife—I've been very happily married for better than twenty years—adores her. We consider her one of our dearest friends.

There've been times I was so concerned about Louise's safety. She's had many death threats. I remember one time before Grier died that they put a bed in their offices in downtown Dallas because it wasn't safe for them to leave their building. A few lawyers and their irate clients hate the Raggios. She's never let it seem to bother her any longer than it takes to do whatever she needs to do to keep herself and her clients safe.

What does bother her are the innocent victims, especially the kids. One teenager, caught in the crossfire between battling parents, committed suicide. Louise has never gotten over it. She feels responsible—even though the kid was under the care of a psychiatrist at the time, and the professional didn't see it coming. Two or three women whose divorces she was handling have been murdered by controlling, angry spouses. A male client was murdered by his wife's new boyfriend. Those things break her heart—and make her vulnerable.

Louise is an attorney's attorney. She was the driving force of the Family Code, the mother of Texas Family Law. She is honest, practical, down-to-earth—and yes, so compassionate. You don't get the combination often in a lawyer.

Patricia Schroeder

President and chief executive officer, Association of American Publishers, Inc., and former Congresswoman from Colorado: I cochaired the Congressional Caucus for Women's Issues for many years and was constantly involved in issues that got me picketed and booed all over America. As we say out West, "You know a person by their enemies," and I had a great list. Ollie North called me one of the most dangerous people in America. Yahoo!

But I also found a great friend as I foraged around America to build support for military and federal pension-sharing upon divorce and many other women's property issues.

That friend was Louise Raggio, a legal eagle from Dallas, Texas.

I was invited to address a group of Texas lawyers in Austin on family law. There she was. She'd been herding that group and fighting with them to do the right thing for years. Eighty pounds of raw energy that drove them nuts. I loved it. She had her whole family working on family law in Texas and was the driving force behind every major reform in the state.

Well, Louise was instantly a friend for life. She never had "erectile dysfunction" on any cause for fairness or equity. She stood up to be counted first! . . . Louise is a Texas tornado with more energy in her little finger than most have in their whole body.

KAY BAILEY HUTCHISON

United States Senator from Texas: Louise Raggio is a trailblazer. When I graduated from the University of Texas School of Law in 1967, only five women were in my class of five hundred.

Louise Raggio had already been practicing law for fifteen years.

I met her when I was a member of the Texas Legislature in 1973; we were updating the Family Code of Texas. She was known as the most respected expert in the field and became the principal advisor on the project.

Years later, when I moved to Dallas, I found that Louise was one of the very top women in the community, as well as one of the distinguished leaders in the Bar Association. When we established the Dallas Women's Foundation to fund projects for women and girls, Louise was among the small group of founders. When we began to gather support for a National Women's Museum, Louise was in that small group. If anything is done to promote women, Louise is in the leadership. She is always on everyone's list of the five most prominent women in Dallas.

LIZ CARPENTER

Author, lecturer, spokeswoman in the Johnson Administration as press secretary and staff director for Lady Bird Johnson, who has served four presidents (Johnson, Ford, Carter, Clinton), and a friend of Louise Raggio since high school: Louise Raggio knows the history

of the women's movement for liberation first hand. She lived it—
step by step—better than some of the headliners. Louise was always
there for us, making strategy and hammering it out. I have known
her since Austin High School, and admired her for more than half a
century. You can count on her . . . for details which few others
know.

J. J. (JAKE) PICKLE

*Congressman from the 10th Congressional District of Texas for
thirty-two years, who has known Louise Ballerstedt Raggio since
1940:* When I was transferred (from Washington, D.C.) in early
1940 to Austin, Texas, as an Area Director of the National Youth
Administration, my territory consisted of ten Central Texas Counties, an area identical to that then represented by Congressman
Lyndon B. Johnson, [who] in his earlier years had been the NYA
State Director. . . . In those days the NYA, a part of the Works Project Administration established by President Franklin Roosevelt,
trained young people ages eighteen to twenty-four to perform part-
time work and training for a small monthly reimbursement. Our
agency built sidewalks, improved schools, made and put up road
signs, wood and metal boxes, completed city improvements, repaired
public buildings, restored parks, taught wood- and metal-working,
and created residential centers for boys and girls, programs that gave
young people the opportunity to learn work skills and improve their
education. The pay was extremely small, but it put boys and girls to
work, and gave them a bit of cash and a feeling of confidence and
security.

One of our area assistants was Louise Ballerstedt. She added a
new dimension to our work and training projects. . . . She became a
loyal and effective voice on how we should appeal to youths. We
were accustomed to checking the cards, organizing route papers, and
getting on with the work. Louise would protest: "The young people
need personal attention and personal training. We need to inspire
them. We need to hold group meetings to draw them out." She was
aggressive and progressive, always trying new approaches. "It is not

enough to build; we must also train," she would say, hammering her small fists on the table!

We were all young and full of FDR's New Deal programs. We would work all day and into the night. At district meetings we would agree, debate, challenge, and drink a few beers. It was a great democratic pastime: work hard and play hard. After the young people were asleep, we'd get together and talk over our day. Louise would sound off loudest!

She was progressive, energetic, and possessed of high moral characteristics. She was a cut above. Brilliant. Determined to get things done. Very little foolishness. When FDR held his fireside radio chats, we would gather with close friends and drink in every word of "our" president. . . . It was a happy, giddy time. We were part of a group of Americans trying to get our country moving again [because] we were still in the closing days of the Great Depression. I believe we helped give our young people a sense of working, growing, and developing, and gave them a sense of renewed hope. Louise felt the forlorn, empty, listless spirit of the group and helped mold them into a new spirit. . . . We should have known then that Louise would become a lawyer and be one of the most recognized attorneys in the country. She was an early Jeannette Rankin and a modern-day Gloria Steinem and I am proud to say she was and is one of my dearest friends.

SARAH WEDDINGTON

Attorney, who with Linda Coffey successfully argued Roe v. Wade *before the United States Supreme Court:* I first met Louise when I was a member of the Texas Legislature. . . . She was an invaluable source of information. . . . Since those days in the early '70s, Louise has been a constant participant in meetings of women lawyers, in meetings to promote the interests of women, and in important events to help support organizations which provide help and information for women . . . Louise is known internationally, nationally, and in Texas as a wonderful, stalwart, dedicated, and capable advocate for women. I'm proud to know her as a friend.

GLORIA STEINEM

Feminist, author, lecturer, founder of Ms. Magazine: In 1970 I was invited to be the first female speaker at a Harvard Law Review banquet. As a non-lawyer, I said no—until I was contacted by a handful of embattled women Harvard law students who persuaded me with such research as: (a) Harvard's course on regulatory law didn't consider the Equal Employment Opportunity Commission important enough to include (though it did include whaling law and offshore oil law), and (b) Harvard Law School was so sure that a female would never teach there that its Men's Room simply said, "Faculty."

I say this because it not only explains my delight at hearing about Louise Raggio two years later when I was working in Dallas, but it also gives a hint of the barriers she had to overcome as the only woman in her Southern Methodist University Law School class in the 1940s. By 1976, she had not only become a distinguished lawyer, but drafted the Texas Marital Property Act to help the female half of her state out of economic dependency. Yet, I doubt that the women law students I talked to at Harvard knew—at that time—about this role model who could have given them so much strength and inspiration.

That's exactly why I'm grateful to Louise Raggio for taking time out of her professional life, still busy and enormously productive in her eighty-third year, to write about a career that has not only spanned all the major events of the twentieth century, but is now shaping the twenty-first century.

Hers is a story that every law school, every women's studies course, and every aspiring woman should know. It is also a story to inspire both women and men who are looking for models for their energetic use of our extended life expectancy.

As historian Gerda Lerner observed, the most shared characteristic of women's history is that it is lost and discovered, lost again and rediscovered, relost and refound yet again. . . . We need Louise Raggio's personal account so that the history she has observed and made will never be lost again.

JAMES MACGREGOR BURNS

Professor, Department of Political Science, Williams College; Pulitzer prize-winning author, lecturer, and consultant, who has known Louise Ballerstedt Raggio since they were interns in the same "class" in the nation's Capital in 1939–1940: In the more than sixty years I have known Louise Raggio she has never ceased to amaze me. From her stories of growing up in Texas in a farm family; driving herself and schoolmates to school when she was around thirteen; coming east to join a group of impressive government interns in Washington and excelling among them; going back to Texas to take on a job that called for her going singly into remote areas simply to help people; surviving McCarthyism that was waged against her husband; bringing up three sons when conditions were very difficult; and then soaring in the Texas legal firmament to lead a highly successful law firm where she has the pleasure of working with her sons. Through all this she has been a spunky, yet charming woman who in her later years did not forget the students, teachers, and other persons who had once supported her, and who has now become a leader herself in the work on leadership and its practical application through the country.

ROBERT F. DRINAN, S.J.

Professor of Law, Georgetown University Law Center: I first met Louise Raggio when I was the chairman of the Family Law Section of the American Bar Association. She had already had an extensive career in marital counseling and in every aspect of family law. She was a very productive and effective member of the Council of the Section on Family Law.

I have followed the remarkable career of Louise Raggio since the days in the 1960s when we were first associated. Louise has accomplished everything that a good citizen and a fine lawyer can do. I have many times marveled at her energy, her vision, and her dedication. I am happy to know that her memoirs will be forthcoming.

This is a woman, an attorney, and a moral leader of whom we can all be proud.

AWARDS AND HONORS

1967   State Bar of Texas for Marital Property Act—Citation of Merit Award

1967   Y.W.C.A. of Dallas Award

1970   Zonta of Dallas Award for Community Service

1972   Southern Methodist University Outstanding Alumni Award

1974   Business & Professional Women Extra Mile Award, for leadership in law reform

1979   Women's Center of Dallas Award for Service to Women

1980   American Bar Association Award for Family Law Service

1985   Business and Professional Women of Texas, Woman of the Year Award

1985   Texas Women's Hall of Fame inductee (legal category)

1985   Chairman of Board of Trustees Award, Texas Bar Foundation

1987   President's Award for Outstanding Lawyer of the Year, State Bar of Texas

1988   Trustee Emeritus Award, Texas Bar Foundation

1990   Unitarian of the Year Award, Dallas

1990   International Women's Forum Award, "Woman That Has Made a Difference"

1990   Founder of Fellows of the Dallas Bar Foundation Award

1992   Southern Methodist University Outstanding Law Alumni Award

1993   Sarah T. Hughes Outstanding Attorney Award, given by the State Bar of Texas

1993   Dallas Bar First Outstanding Trial Lawyer Award

1994   National Business Women Owners Association Award

1994   American Civil Liberties Union Thomas Jefferson Award

1995   Girls, Inc. "She Knows Where She's Going" Award

1995   North Texas Association of Women Journalists, Courage Award

1995   Margaret Brent Outstanding Woman Lawyer Award, given by American Bar Association

1996   Doctor of Laws Degree *honoris causa*, from Southern Methodist University, Dallas

1996   Texas Trailblazer Award
1997   Women in Executive Leadership Award
1997   Dallas Bar Foundation Award for Distinguished Career and Civic
       Contribution
1997   Texas Bar Foundation Ethics & Professionalism Award
1997   North Texas Legal Services Equal Justice Award
1998   Austin High School Distinguished Alumni Award
1999   Texas Women of the Century Award
1999   Veteran Feminist of America Award
2000   Gillian Rudd Award from National Business Women Owners
       Association
2000   *Fortune Magazine*, one of fifteen Heroes in Hall of Fame
2000   *Fortune Small Business Magazine*, one of fifteen small business
       owners cited as Heroes in Hall of Fame, November 13, 2000
       edition
2001   Individual Rights and Responsibilities Award, State Bar of Texas
2002   Lifetime Humanitarian Award, Planned Parenthood of Dallas
       and North Texas
2002   Lifetime Achievement Award, Family Law Section, American Bar
       Association

PROFESSIONAL RECOGNITIONS AND ASSOCIATIONS

Past Chairman of the Family Law Section of the State Bar of Texas,
    1965–1967, and Drafting Committee for Family Code, 1966–1975.
Governor, American Academy of Matrimonial Lawyers, 1973–1981.
Past Chairman of the Family Law Section of the American Bar Associa-
    tion, 1975–1976.
Editorial Advisory Board of Shepard's, Inc. of Colorado Springs, 1978–
    1980.
Women Lawyers at Work, 1978, Elinor Porter Swiger, Messner, Simon and
    Schuster (devotes one chapter to Louise and her contributions to law).
Director, State Bar of Texas, 1979–1982. First woman ever elected as a
    director in the one hundred year history of the Texas Bar.
Council, American Academy of Matrimonial Lawyers, 1981–1987.
Life Fellow of American Bar Foundation, 1981 to present.
Trustee, Texas Bar Foundation, 1982–1986, and Chairman of the Board,
    1984–1985. First woman trustee.
Trustee, National Conference of Bar Foundations, 1986–1992.

Chair, Fellows of Dallas Bar Foundation, 1991–1992.

Trustee, American Academy of Matrimonial Lawyers Foundation, 1991–1994.

Trustee, Dallas Women's Foundation, 1992–1995.

The Divorce Lawyers, 1992, Emily Couric (devotes one chapter to Raggio firm).

Advisory Board, Academy of Leadership, University of Maryland 1997.

Southern Methodist University establishes an endowed "Louise Ballerstedt Raggio" annual lecture series, 1997.

Wise Women of Texas, 1997, P. J. Pierce (devotes one chapter to Raggio firm).

Texas Lawyer Legal Legends of Century, 2000.

Books, journals, directories, magazines. Listed for many years as one of best family lawyers in America and one of the best specialty firms in family law in the United States.

Dallas Women Lawyers and National Business Women Owners Association each have established "Louise B. Raggio" awards given annually to outstanding women.

INDEX